DATE DUE	
OCT 20 1986	
NOV 2 1986	
DEC 10 1986	

PRINTED IN U.S.A.

Randolph

Randolph

A Study of Churchill's Son

by

Brian Roberts

Hamish Hamilton London

First published in Great Britain 1984
by Hamish Hamilton Ltd
Garden House 57-59 Long Acre London WC2E 9JZ
Copyright © 1984 by Brian Roberts

British Library Cataloguing in Publication Data
Roberts, Brian
Randolph: a study of Churchill's son.
1. Churchill, Randolph
I. Title
941.083′092′4   DA566.9.C/

ISBN 0-241-11109-9
Phototypeset by Wyvern Typesetting Ltd, Bristol
Printed in Great Britain by
St. Edmundsbury Press, Bury St Edmunds, Suffolk

For
R. I. B. Webster

Contents

Illustrations

Acknowledgements

In researching this book I have received valuable help from the friends, colleagues and acquaintances of Randolph Churchill. While the views expressed in the book are entirely my own, I would like, in particular, to record my sincere thanks – for talking to me about Randolph, allowing me to read his letters to them, giving me permission to quote from their published writings and help in a variety of ways – the following:

The Rt Hon. Julian Amery M.P., Sir John Betjeman, the late Sir Robert Birley, Mr André Bothner, Mr James Cameron, Mr Peter Coats, Miss Angela Collingwood, Lady Diana Cooper, Mr Thomas Flintoff, the Rt Hon. Michael Foot M.P., Mr Brocas Harris, Sir Rupert Hart-Davis, Mr Thomas Hartman, Mr J. Keith Killby, Mr James Lees-Milne, the Earl of Longford, Mr Roger Machell, Sir Fitzroy Maclean, Laura, Duchess of Marlborough, Lady Mosley, Mr Christopher Sykes, Mr Hugo Vickers, Mr R. I. B. Webster, Miss Gertrude Wissa and Mrs Rosemary Wolff.

For answering my queries and general assistance in my research, I would also like to thank Mr Peter Charlton, Deputy Editor of the *Lancashire Evening Post*, Mr J. L. Wooding, Secretary of the Preston Conservative Association, Mr W. I. Turner, Chairman of the Devonport Conservative Association, the Librarian and staff of the Liverpool Public Library and Mrs S. Bane and staff of the Frome Public Library.

My final, and undoubtedly my greatest debt, is to Mr Theo Aronson whose unfailing interest, encouragement, expert advice and constructive criticism have aided me every step of the way.

In addition, I gratefully acknowledge permission from the following: Curtis Brown on behalf of C. and T. Publications Ltd. for quotations from the writings and papers of Winston S. Churchill. The Rt Hon. Winston S. Churchill M.P. and the Executors of the late the Hon. Randolph Churchill deceased for quotations from the writings and papers of Randolph Churchill. The Lady Soames D.B.E. for quotations from *Clementine Churchill* by Mary Soames and *Keep on Dancing* and *A Thread from the Tapestry* by Sarah Churchill. Weidenfeld (Publishers) Ltd. for quotations from *The Diaries of Evelyn Waugh* edited by Michael Davie and *The Letters of Evelyn Waugh* edited by Mark Amory. Macmillan, London and Basingstoke, for quotations from *The Diaries of Sir Robert Bruce Lockhart 1915–1938* and *1939–1965*. William Heinemann Ltd. for some quotations from *Winston S. Churchill* by Martin Gilbert and *Randolph S. Churchill: The Young Unpretender* edited by Kay Halle.

CHAPTER ONE

Such A Pretty Boy

British Prime Ministers are not noted for their humour. Some have been entirely lacking in wit, others have found it politic to adopt an air of gravity in the House of Commons. Apart from an occasional quip at the expense of an opponent, or the odd topical allusion, they have done little to enliven proceedings in parliament. Levity is considered unbecoming in a statesman. Even that most flamboyant of leaders, Benjamin Disraeli, was careful to measure his words in debate; his flippancies were kept for the dinner-table or his books. For the most part, the great parliamentary wits have sparkled more effectively on the back benches.

One of the few exceptions to this convention was Winston Churchill. Throughout his career, whether in or out of office, Churchill's sense of fun was irrepressible. The sight of the Honourable Member for Epping, notes in hand, peering mischievously over his spectacles before injecting a witticism into an otherwise weighty speech, was as familiar to his fellow politicans as his bulldog stance was later to become to the world at large.

That many of his 'impromptu' remarks were carefully rehearsed is undeniable, but this does not detract from his reputation as a wit. A.P. Herbert, no mean political joker himself, rated Churchill as the greatest humorist of his day. 'At any time, in any conditions, in any company, on any subject,' he claimed, Churchill could make laughter when he willed. That, according to Herbert, was the true test of a natural humorist. He refused to accept that Churchill's quips lacked spontaneity. Most of his 'good things' came bubbling up, without notice or effort, from an inexhaustible spring,' Herbert insisted. Who else could have dismissed a colleague's pompous speech by saying: 'It must have been good, for it contained, so far as I know, all the platitudes known to the human race, with the possible exception of "Prepare to meet Thy God" and "Please adjust your dress before leaving" '? Or have remarked as the door closed behind a tall, lugubrious visitor, 'Thank God, we have seen the last of that Wuthering Height.'? Churchill's wit was part of his genius.

No one was more aware of this than his wife. Almost from the day he married the beautiful Clementine Hozier in September 1908, Churchill had involved her in his world of whimsy. They had pet names for each other. To him she was always the 'Cat' or 'Kat'; to her he was the 'Pug', 'Pugdog', 'Amber Pug' and later, affectionately, the 'Pig'. Quaint drawings of cats and pugs decorated their letters: fat cats, smiling cats, snoozing cats, cats with curly tails and spiky ears; pugs begging, prancing and playful, aggressive pugs, tranquil pugs, pugs that capered off the edge of the page. Occasionally other animals intruded but usually the cats, the pugs and an assortment of pigs served their purposes splendidly. Family life allowed the Churchills to indulge their love of nonsense to the full.

Even so, they were thrown into a quandary by the expected arrival of their first child. Would it be a little cat or a little pug? They took no chances. The prospective baby was merrily referred to as the 'Puppy Kitten' or the 'PK'. And the 'PK' the baby remained long after being revealed as a daughter; it was some months, following her birth in July 1909, before she was fondly dubbed a 'Kitten'. The fact that she was christened Diana was a mere formality.

A wilder flight of fancy heralded the second child. This time the Churchills gleefully awaited the arrival of the 'Chumbolly'. How or where this bizarre sobriquet originated, or what it meant, nobody could later remember. Worthy of the nonsense world of Edward Lear, it probably sprang from the same source as the Jabberwokky. Warm, friendly and cuddly, the image conjured up by the 'Chumbolly' could have reflected a boy or a girl, but this was not a prime consideration. Clementine Churchill seems to have had no doubts about her next baby's gender. 'I am counting the days till May 15th when the Chumbolly is due,' she wrote to her husband in April 1911. 'I hope he will not have inherited the Pug's unpunctual habits.'

Her confidence in the child's sex was rewarded; her hopes of reliability sadly misplaced. The 'Chumbolly', a boy, was born at 33 Eccleston Square – the Churchills' London home – on 28 May 1911, two weeks late and only just in time to allow his mother to attend the coronation of King George V. Clementine Churchill had, in fact, resigned herself to missing the coronation. It was only by a special arrangement – which permitted her, as a nursing mother, to arrive at Westminster Abbey in time for the crowning and then slip away by a side door – that she was present at the great occasion of 22 June. From the very outset the 'Chumbolly' displayed a talent for keeping his mother on tenterhooks.

Five months were to pass before the baby was christened. In their letters the Churchills continued to call him the 'Chumbolly'. He was a healthy, lively, demanding infant whose assertive nuzzlings delighted his mother. The speed with which he put on weight was a comfort to both his parents. 'At his age', declared the approving Churchill, shortly after his son's birth, 'greediness and even swinishness at table are virtues.'

The baptismal ceremony was eventually conducted, on 26 October 1911, in the crypt of the House of Commons. Of the three godparents – chosen to balance Churchill's personal and political loyalties – only two were present: F. E. Smith (the future Lord Birkenhead) who was Churchill's great friend, and Sir Edward Grey, Churchill's political colleague who was then Foreign Secretary. The third godparent, Churchill's cousin, the Viscountess Ridley, was represented by Clementine Churchill's cousin, Venetia Stanley. In choosing names for their son the Churchills had been equally diplomatic. The child was christened Randolph, after his dead grandfather Lord Randolph Churchill, Frederick, after F. E. Smith, and Edward, after Sir Edward Grey. To these christian names, the family's correct surname of Spencer Churchill was added.

That the ceremony was performed in the crypt of the House of Commons was not unusual. Many a senior politician's child was christened there. In the case of Randolph Frederick Edward Spencer Churchill, however, the choice of the parliamentary building was particularly appropriate. Politics were to play an important role in his life. 'I took [politics] in with my mother's milk,' he was to say. 'I was practically born on a political platform.'

✳   ✳   ✳

Neither Winston Churchill nor his wife had enjoyed carefree childhoods. Churchill's relationship with his parents had been especially unfortunate. As a boy he had seen little of his mother. Beautiful, socially accomplished and much sought after, the former Jennie Jerome was too preoccupied with the demands of fashionable society to pay attention to her sons. 'She shone for me like the Evening Star,' Churchill wrote. 'I loved her dearly – but at a distance.' His father was even more remote. Lord Randolph Churchill, brilliant, erratic and relentless in pursuit of his political ambitions, had no time for family life. The young Winston was more aware of his father as a public figure than as a parent. What contact there was between them tended to result in clashes of temperament, with Lord Randolph forever criticizing his son's apparent lack of ability and Winston trying to defend himself. As a result Winston became resentful and unsure of himself. Deprived of the affection and reassurance which a boy expects from his father, he envied the children of lesser men. 'I would far rather have been apprenticed as a bricklayer's mate,' he was to claim, remembering his schooldays, 'or run errands as a messenger boy, or helped my father dress the front window of a grocer's shop. It would have been real; it would have been more natural; it would have taught me more; and I should have got to know my father, which would have been a joy to me.' Proud as he was of his father, much as he came to revere Lord Randolph's memory, he never fully reconciled himself to this feeling of alienation.

The rifts in Clementine Churchill's family were more obvious. Her parents' marriage was an unhappy one and, when Clementine was six years old, they parted. There were faults on both sides. Henry Hozier, Clementine's father, was a difficult man, much older than his somewhat eccentric wife, Lady Blanche Hozier – the eldest daughter of the 10th Earl of Airlie – and, although ostensibly it was Lady Blanche's infidelity that caused the break up, it is doubtful whether the marriage could have lasted. As it was, the separation ushered in a period of tension and uncertainty for Lady Blanche and her four children. Clementine and her elder sister, Kitty, were first claimed by their father and then grudgingly allowed to rejoin their mother and their little brother and sister, the twins, Bill and Nellie. Most of Clementine's childhood and youth were spent in England and France, living in furnished lodgings with the impoverished Lady Blanche, never certain of her father's intentions. There was very little stability in the Hozier children's lives. For all that, Clementine emerged from these early upheavals a poised and dignified young woman. Whether she completely overcame her feelings of insecurity is another matter.

There can be little doubt that the emotional scars left by their childhood experiences profoundly influenced Churchill and his wife in their attitudes towards their own children.

For his part, Churchill, determined not to repeat his father's mistakes, did his utmost to involve himself in the day-to-day routine of family life. His letters to his wife, when his daughter Diana and his son Randolph were babies, are evidence of this. He rarely wrote without enquiring after 'the Kittens'; or, when in charge of the household during his wife's absence, giving a full report on the children's progress. He kept a jealous watch on the nursery, delighted in the babies' growth, noted their mannerisms and, on one occasion at least, took a hand in bathing the infant Diana. His response to Randolph's precociousness was one of amusement, indulgence and fatherly pride.

Clementine's attitude was not so simple. Reserved by nature, her love for her children, although equal to that of her husband's was not so openly expressed. Hers was an enigmatic personality and her approach to family life was more guarded, more critical and, in many ways, more demanding. There could have been good reasons for this. Experience had taught her the need for a firm family base and she no doubt recognized that only her husband could provide that base. Winston Churchill was the hub around which her life revolved and any threat to his well-being roused her fierce protective instincts. Not only did she view many of her husband's friends and colleagues with ill-concealed suspicion, but she expected total loyalty from her children. Even as babies, the Churchill children were made to realize that their father's career was all-important, that there was a larger world outside the nursery and that disruptive intrusions could not be tolerated. Unfortunately, these were conditions that young Randolph found difficult to accept.

But, like his sister Diana's, Randolph's childhood was decidedly influenced by his father's career. Churchill, for all his good intentions, was unable to see as much of his children as he would have liked. Every bit as ambitious as his father, he was obliged to devote most of his time to politics, snatching the odd holiday when he could. A seaside snapshot of a jubilant Churchill, shouldering his year-old son, was treasured as much for its rarity as for the family record. Holidays at that time were infrequent luxuries.

Just over a year before Randolph's birth, the thirty-five year old Churchill had been appointed Home Secretary in Mr Asquith's struggling Liberal administration. He was the youngest man to become Home Secretary since the appointment, in 1822, of Sir Robert Peel. It was the most important and exacting post he had held and it commanded all his time.

Until then Churchill's political career had been erratic. He had first entered parliament, after returning from his much-publicized adventures as a war-correspondent in South Africa, as the Conservative Member for Oldham in October 1900. His reputation for daring established, and with memories of his brilliant father still fresh, his political future seemed promising. He would surely learn, it was thought, from his father's mistakes. But a self-willed, rebellious streak and a love of controversy – typical of his family and a major cause of Lord Randolph's downfall – soon began to manifest itself. In less than four years his support for Free Trade and social reform led him to break with the Conservative party and join the Liberals. By impetuously crossing the floor of the House, he earned the lasting distrust of many of his former colleagues who, perhaps predictably, were convinced that he was following the same downward path that had led to his father's ruin.

But other gods presided. Far from leading downwards, his path took him to unforseen heights. It so happened that his switch of loyalties coincided, more or less, with a general election which resulted in a landslide victory for the Liberals. In the new Government which took office in January 1906, Churchill was given the post of Under-Secretary for the Colonies. His opponents could not have relished the incidental fact that his much-praised biography, *Lord Randolph Churchill* – vindicating his father's political career – was published during the election campaign. Nor could they have watched his further progress with equanimity. His inclusion in Asquith's Cabinet as President of the Board of Trade, in 1908, and his appointment as Home Secretary two years later were further milestones on his upward path. But it was not an easy climb. Political slopes are notoriously slippery and as he scaled them Churchill made enemies.

The hostility came mostly from the Conservative benches. With a few outstanding exceptions, such as his friend. F. E. Smith, the majority of his former colleagues regarded Churchill as a traitor to his class and his family traditions. They never lost an opportunity to let him know this. Their animosity was particularly apparent during the bitter clashes between the Liberal and Conservative parties which resulted from the rejection of Lloyd George's famous 'People's Budget' by the House of Lords in 1909. Churchill stood firmly behind Lloyd George. He was outspoken in his criticism of the Lords, both in and out of parliament, and fully supported the Liberal threat to create more peers so that the Budget could be accepted. These were the days when he not only outraged the Tories but caused an indignant King Edward VII to dismiss one of his speeches as being full 'of false statements of Socialism in its most insidious form.'

The following year, 1910 – the year before Randolph's birth – the Liberals were obliged to fight two general elections. They emerged from the first contest, in January, with their huge majority sliced to a mere two seats over the Conservatives; after the second round, at the end of the year, their claim to power depended on a single seat. Only with the consent of the Labour and Irish Nationalist members were they able to govern. In both elections, Churchill held on to his seat in Dundee in Scotland but, like the other Liberals, he found himself in a state of political siege. As Home Secretary, he enjoyed very few home comforts.

The Churchills' family life was more seriously threatened when Randolph was five months old. On 24 October 1911 it was officially announced that Winston Churchill had been appointed First Lord of the Admiralty. The appointment was given a mixed reception by the Tory press but this did not spoil the delight of Churchill and his wife. For some weeks they had been kept in suspense about the appointment and were overjoyed when the Prime Minister (Asquith) reached his decision while they were staying with him in Scotland.

If Clementine Churchill had any reservations about the new post, they were entirely domestic. She found the prospect of abandoning her home for the First Lord's London mansion financially daunting. It would mean employing at least six or seven more servants as well as the extra expense of nursemaids for the children. But her pleas for caution were only partly successful. The upheaval was delayed for over a year, until finally, in the spring of 1913, they left their home in Eccleston Square and moved to that most elegant of official residences, Admiralty House.

*　　　*　　　*

In later life, Randolph Churchill had no recollections of the house in Eccleston Square: the house in which he had been born and where he spent the first two years of his life. Indeed he remembered very little of his infancy and marvelled at men like Sir Osbert Sitwell whose childhood memories were so vivid. Randolph's earliest impressions were extremely hazy. They were confined, for the most part, to the years his family lived at Admiralty House and were far removed from Sir Osbert Sitwell's world of cosy nursery teas, pony-cart rides and faithful family retainers. What Randolph best remembered were the long-running battles he fought with his sorely-tried nursery staff.

He must, by his own admission, have been a little horror. No servant ever stayed long enough to tame him. Headstrong, impudent, insufferably precocious and argumentative he was capable of reducing the tightest-lipped nanny to tears. He had no sense of shame. Remembering the time when he hurled a nursery maid's wrist-watch from an upstairs window and smashed it, he showed no remorse. Nursery maids were there to be tormented. On another occasion, when he and his sister Diana had been taken out to tea, they shocked the maid who returned them to Admiralty House by deliberately rolling on the steps in their new white fur coats and, when scolded, added to their sins by pertly explaining that they always behaved like that when their nanny was not with them. Nor did they attempt to hide their delight as, one after another, their nannies admitted defeat and left. Each departure was accompanied by shrieks of joy from the Churchill children as they bumped the vanquished servant's bags down the stairs. But, for all her complicity, Diana was no match for Randolph; she merely followed where he led. 'Diana was more docile that I was,' admitted Randolph: 'I could never brook authority or discipline.'

His memories of these early days were patchy and not always reliable. Sometimes they relied more on hindsight than fact. He was, for instance, to recall a scuffle in Green Park when – or so he claimed – an attempt was made to snatch him from his pram. This incident was apparently part of a militant campaign that a group of suffragettes were waging against his father. Whether things ever reached the stage of baby-snatching is, however, another matter. Certainly the suffragettes had no love for Winston Churchill. Several of his public meetings had been disrupted by women demanding the vote; on more than one occasion missiles had been hurled at him, and, as Home Secretary, he further enraged the militants by sanctioning the forced feeding of political prisoners on hunger strike. His change of office had not lessened the hostility. Letters threatening to kidnap the Churchill children arrived at Admiralty House shortly after the family moved in and, in May 1913, a detective from Scotland Yard was detailed to accompany Randolph and Diana on their daily outings. But, although photographs of two sturdy nurses pushing a large bassinet, shadowed by a bowler-hatted policeman, appeared in the newspapers, no mention was made of the attack that Randolph claimed to remember.

His memories of the outbreak of the first World War were equally muddled. He seemed to think that in the summer of 1914 his parents were enjoying a seaside holiday at a place called Hoe Farm and that their holiday was rudely interrupted when his father was summoned to London. In fact the Churchills did not rent Hoe Farm – which was several miles inland, near Godalming in Surrey – until some months later and, in the tense weeks preceding the declaration of war in August 1914, Clementine Churchill, then pregnant with her third child, was relaxing with Randolph and Diana on the Norfolk coast. With Europe on the verge of war, Winston Churchill's comings and goings were erratic and, although he managed to spend the last week-end in July playing with his children on the beach, his return to London was not unusual or entirely unexpected.

That Randolph could not remember returning with his mother to Admiralty House later that summer – or the birth of his sister Sarah in October – is hardly surprising. He was, after all, only three and a half years old at the time.

But there was no mistaking the impact that the war had on his family. The beginning of the following year, 1915, saw the launching of the disastrous Dardanelles campaign and, in the controversy resulting from the failure of that ill-fated operation, Winston Churchill was forced to resign as First Lord of the Admiralty. Randolph was too young to appreciate the bitterness felt by his parents at this cruel turn of events, but he did dimly recall including 'the Dardanelles' in his nightly prayers. Of more immediate concern to the children was the upheaval caused by their father's resignation. In the middle of June, the Churchills left Admiralty House and, as the house in Eccleston Square was let to Randolph's godfather, Sir Edward Grey, they moved in with Jack Churchill's family at 41 Cromwell Road.

Jack Churchill was Winston's younger brother. In 1908 he had married Lady Gwendoline Bertie – daughter of the Earl of Abingdon, known in the family as 'Goonie' – and they had two sons: John George, then aged six, and Peregrine, aged two. Winston was very fond of his less ambitious brother, their wives had quickly become friends, and the two families were close. They often shared holidays and regularly spent Christmas with their cousin the Duke of Marlborough at Blenheim Palace. The prospect of the Churchill families living together brought a new dimension to their relationship.

For the children, the new arrangement was a particular delight. Randolph and his elder cousin, Johnny, were already good friends – despite the difference of two years in their ages – and now they looked forward to a time of uninhibited fun and games. Unlike the docile Diana, Johnny responded to Randolph's naughtiness with a devilishness of his own. 'My cousin Randolph,' he later admitted, 'brought out the imp in me. We could not be in the same room together without there being a frightful prank. The outcome was usually a frantic chase throughout the house, upstairs and downstairs, with cushions being snatched from chairs and sofas and hurled around as ammunition; how our parents stood for it I do not know.'

For the most part, it was their mothers and an overworked nanny who had to cope with their antics. When Winston Churchill and his family moved to Cromwell Road, Jack Churchill was already serving abroad as a major in the Queen's Own Oxfordshire Hussars. Four months later, the disillusioned Winston Churchill – who was also a major in the same regiment – abandoned politics and left for France. He had, for some time, been nagged by a desire to see active service and, as early as July that year, had prepared the way by writing a letter to be given to his wife in the event of his death. 'I have appointed you my sole literary executor,' he wrote. 'Randolph will carry the lamp. Do not grieve for me too much.' This letter was

9

found among his papers many years later and was probably never delivered to Clementine Churchill.

Such thoughts do not appear to have been uppermost in his mind when he arrived in France. He was only too thankful to be free of the frustrations of politics and was soon sending home enthusiastic reports from the front, with kisses for the children and urgent requests for extra clothes and equipment. His wife did her best to supply his wants, scouring the London shops for rubber waders, khaki trousers, a sheepskin sleeping bag, a leather waistcoat and a periscope. She was ably assisted by the bright-eyed Randolph who, she was delighted to report, had suggested sending his father a spade in case he needed it to dig himself out sideways from a bombed trench. Churchill considered this a splendid idea. 'It is the very thing we have all been doing,' he told his wife.

Major Winston Churchill did not have to rely entirely upon his wife for news of his children. By the beginning of December, the newspapers reaching the trenches carried so many photographs of Diana and Randolph that their father began to fear for their vanity. Randolph, in particular, was much in demand by society photographers. Blonde, blue-eyed and impishly pretty, he featured prominently in two well-publicized weddings. On 30 November 1915, when the Prime Minister's daughter, Violet Asquith, married her father's Private Secretary, Maurice Bonham-Carter, little Randolph was one of the four velvet-suited pageboys. He looked, according to his mother, '*quite* beautiful'. At the Downing Street reception afterwards, he was surrounded by dozens of admiring women who kissed, hugged and flattered him outrageously. A few days later, he, Diana, and their cousin Johnny, all dressed girlishly in white satin, fur-trimmed skirts, acted as train bearers to Clementine Churchill's younger sister, Nellie Hozier, when she married Lieutenant-Colonel Bertram Romilly in the Guards Chapel. Once again the photographers clicked away and once again little Randolph was a focus of attention. His father had good reason to fear for his vanity.

Both in public and in private, Randolph was gushed over, spoiled, praised and petted by a host of doting admirers. 'Clemmie's eldest child [*sic*]' Lady Cynthia Asquith noted in her diary, after a children's fancy dress party, 'is a most beautiful boy – Randolph.'

*   *   *

Shortly before leaving Admiralty House, the Churchills had rented Hoe Farm in Surrey as a week-end retreat. The upheavals which followed had prevented them from spending much time there but rural life had cast a spell. In 1916 they decided to find a more permanent country home. Earlier that year Winston Churchill had returned from France, having attained the rank of Colonel, and had again taken his place in the House of Commons. As luck would have it, the house in Eccleston Square became vacant a few months later and the reunited family were able to move back to their own home. But having a London house was not entirely satisfactory. Clementine Churchill longed for a more peaceful refuge for her children, somewhere away from the pressures of London and the threat of air raids. The place they eventually found was called Lullenden, a charming grey-stone house, near East Grinstead in Sussex. At first Lullenden served as a holiday home. In time, however, a barn adjoining the house was converted for the children's use and Randolph and his sisters were installed there on a more permanent basis. They were soon joined by their cousins Johnny and Peregrine.

For Randolph and Johnny, life at Lullenden was a continuation of their life at Cromwell Road. Their memories of specific incidents tend to differ but they agree that their behaviour was as rumbustious as ever. There was the time, for instance, when they loaded Sarah and Peregrine, who were little more than babies, into a covered cart and, as an experiment, sent them crashing to the bottom of a hill. Randolph does not mention this disaster but Johnny never forgot the rumpus that followed. 'Nurses, parents and relations started running out of the house,' he says, 'shouting and wringing their hands. We had a fearful ticking off as usual, but miraculously Pebin [Peregrine] and Sarah stepped from the wreckage with nothing worse than a shaking.' Neither of them could remember precisely why or when Randolph's nanny forced him to swallow a spoonful of mustard. Randolph thought it was the 'very horrible' nanny's way of silencing his demands to sample the contents of a mustard pot; Johnny claims it was Randolph's punishment for tipping his baby sister, Sarah, out of her cot. But they both remember Randolph's shrieks of rage as the teaspoon was rattled against his teeth. Such incidents were not unusual. This one was memorable because it led to yet another nanny being sacked.

One of Randolph's more vivid recollections of Lullenden is, perhaps, of greater significance. It concerned his attendance at the nearby village school. The elder Churchill children were taken to this school by pony-trap every morning and it was there that they first became acquainted with the local children. For Randolph this was a delightful new experience. Gregarious, if not particularly sociable, by nature, he tried to chum up with one of his class-mates. He was surprised when his overtures were curtly rebuffed. With childish bluntness, the boy told him that he wanted nothing to do with the son of Winston Churchill because Winston Churchill was responsible for his own father's death at the Dardanelles. This completely bewildered the five-year-old Randolph. Until then 'the Dardanelles' had been merely a name he included in his prayers; he could not understand why it should make the boy so hostile. On returning home, he asked his mother for an explanation and was neither distressed nor dismayed by what she told him. On the contrary, he says, he felt immensely proud to learn that his father 'was a boss man who could order other fathers about.' It must also have occurred to him that to be the son of such a man was something special.

Both Johnny and Randolph treasured memories of the important week-end visitors at Lullenden. Johnny recalls spying on Lloyd George and his uncle Winston talking outside his bedroom window and trickling the contents of a chamber-pot on Lloyd George's hat. Randolph's memories were more mercenary. They centred on the crinkly five-pound notes he was given by Sir Ernest Cassel. When his nanny later explained that the white bearded Sir Ernest was a 'millionaire' he was doubly impressed: it was the first time he had heard that magic word. He was to be greatly disappointed, on meeting other millionaire friends of his father's, to find that the magic did not always work and that fivers were not so freely handed out.

The Churchill family's grand connections were also apparent to the children when they again began to spend their Christmasses at Blenheim Palace. Here, amid the monumental splendours of the house which Vanbrugh built to honour John Churchill, 1st Duke of Marlborough, they were surrounded by reminders of their family's heroic past and noble traditions. Not that the boys were unduly impressed, or subdued, by Blenheim's grandeur. For Randolph and Johnny the ducal palace was simply a labyrinth of corridors, passages, staircases, terraces and ornate nooks and crannies in which they could extend the romps they enjoyed at Cromwell Road and Lullenden. 'Randolph and I continued to terrorise Blenheim with ferocious energy . . .' admitted Johnny. 'Randolph kept daring me to do dreadful things. Occasionally I refused; I was too frightened of the wrath that would follow.' No such fear inhibited Randolph. Young as he was, he set the pace for all their games.

At Blenheim he was given greater scope to act as a ringleader. Besides his cousins, Johnny and Peregrine, and his sisters, Diana and Sarah, there were often other children crowded into the nursery wing of the palace. Various members of the Churchill clan arrived during the holidays with their offspring and occasionally Randolph's godfather, the future Lord Birkenhead, would spend

Christmas at Blenheim with his son, Freddie, and his daughters, Eleanor and Pamela Smith. Tobogganing, snow fights, fancy dress parties and charades, all provided Randolph with opportunities for devilment.

Guests, and the staff, at Blenheim were shocked and startled by his wild behaviour. Favourite places for sky-larking were the nursery bathrooms and once, when an unsuspecting maid was bending over one of the huge tubs, Randolph disgraced himself by creeping up behind her and giving her a push which sent her sprawling headlong into the water. Another playground was the Long Library where the boys could slide on the polished floors and stage bear-fights by wrapping themselves in the bear-skin rugs. It was from the Long Library that Randolph was banished to bed one evening after embarrassing the assembled guests by climbing onto the pedestal of a nude female statue and, for a dare, gleefully slapping the lady's marble buttocks. 'Everyone agreed,' says Johnny, who goaded him on, 'that decency had been violated in a way which was quite beyond a joke.'

The joke might have been better appreciated had it been played by one of the other children. What set Randolph apart from his cousins was his intractability. His open defiance of authority, his determination to shock, and his indifference to punishment, invariably made Randolph's high-spirits seem a shade less than innocent.

None of this appears to have bothered his father. The older Randolph grew, the more indulgent Winston Churchill became. Remembering his own childhood, he tended to wink at Randolph's rebelliousness. To him it was nothing more than a predictable family trait, something to be expected from any Churchill worth his salt. 'Randolph,' he boasted to his brother Jack, in a letter written from Blenheim in July 1916, 'promises much. He has a noble air, and shows spirit and originality.'

*　　*　　*

The First World War ended in November 1918. Coming home from the village school near Lullenden on Armistice Day, Randolph saw one of the gardeners hoisting a Union Jack from a chimney of the house and realized that something important had happened. That Christmas, at Blenheim, they had a huge bonfire, roasted an ox, and burnt an effigy of the Kaiser. Randolph was then seven and a half years old.

For almost two years after the war the Churchill family was rootless. The lease of the house in Eccleston Square had expired in 1918 and they were without a permanent London home. When, a few days after the Armistice, Clementine Churchill gave birth to her fourth child – a daughter, Marigold Frances, who was to die before she was three years old – she was staying in a house lent to the family by Winston's aunt, Lady Wimborne. Not until the end of 1919 did they find another suitable London house in Sussex Square, just north of the Bayswater Road. By that time they had also sold Lullenden and, in the intervening period, had been staying with other relations – this time Winston's cousin, Captain Freddie Guest and his family – at a house called Templeton near Roehampton. Randolph was to remember Templeton mainly for its indoor tennis court, its stable of polo ponies, and his struggles to master the political columns of *The Times* under the supervision of his governess, Miss Kinsey.

His lessons were soon to become more purposeful. In 1920, at the age of nine, he was told he was to be sent to boarding school. Unlike most boys, he was tremendously excited at the prospect; he was to treasure the thrill of unpacking his first school suit and discovering it included a pair of long trousers. The thought of wearing such magnificent clothes, he says, completely eclipsed any fear he might otherwise have felt at being sent away to school.

The fashionable preparatory school chosen for him was Sandroyd, near Cobham in Surrey; a school geared to coaching boys for the better-known public schools. Winston Churchill might have been influenced in selecting this school by his friend Lord Beaverbrook who already had a son, Max Aitken, enrolled there. Randolph was instructed to make friends with Max Aitken but the friendship, if it ever started, was short lived. Within a matter of days Randolph had decided that Max Aitken was the most objectionable boy at the school and it was not until many years later that the two of them became friends.

In fact, Randolph appears to have made very few close friends at Sandroyd. He claims that his first weeks at the school were spent in waging a war against a gang of bullies who terrorized the younger boys. Together with four other boys – three of them Spanish princes – he fought back until the bullies were, as he puts it, 'demoralized'. Precisely how this victory was achieved he leaves regrettably vague. All the same, the story is probably true. But, unfortunately, his quest for justice made no lasting impression on those he sought to protect. Randolph was not to be remembered at Sandroyd as the champion of the oppressed.

He was an aggressive, quarrelsome little boy and the battles he fought at the school were not particularly noble. Nor, it seems, did he always emerge from them triumphant. 'My only memory of Randolph at Sandroyd,' said one of his contemporaries, 'is of being sent home from a choir treat for hitting his head against a tree.' Obviously Randolph was not the most popular boy in the school.

The only boy he acknowledged as a friend – in fact he claims he was his greatest friend – was Terence Rattigan. How close this friendship was is another matter. Certainly it did not last beyond their schooldays. So completely did Randolph forget the young Rattigan that, when they met accidentally many years later on board the *Queen Elizabeth*, Randolph had to ask the famous playwright whether he was indeed the boy he knew at Sandroyd. On being assured that they had known each other, Randolph was delighted. From then on he never hesitated to refer to Rattigan as 'my old private school friend.'

Perhaps it was Randolph's lack of intimacy with the other boys that made him unaware of the school gossip. He seems to have been entirely ignorant of the nudges and winks accompanying talk about one of the younger masters, and he was taken completely by surprise by what he calls his 'one disagreeable experience at Sandroyd'. It happened about a year after he arrived at the school. On what must have been the flimsiest of pretexts, Randolph was one day summoned to the master's room and told to sit on the bed. The young man, sitting beside him, then undid his flies and, says Randolph, 'caused me to manipulate his organ.' More startled than shocked by this extraordinary exercise, Randolph did not realize there was anything wrong in what he was doing until a housemaid barged into the room to deliver some laundry. The master, blushing furiously, sprang to his feet and quickly adjusted his trousers. Only then did Randolph decide it would be wise to leave. The next day the master warned him to say nothing about the incident.

That Randolph was comparatively unruffled by this paedophiliac encounter – which he loosely describes as his 'only homosexual experience' – says much for his ten-year-old aplomb. He was naturally puzzled by the master's strange behaviour, but it did not occur to him to tell his parents about it. Nor would they have found out had not the nanny overheard him discussing his experience with his sister Diana when the family were on holiday at Rugby the following summer. Not surprisingly, the nanny told Clementine Churchill who, in turn, told her husband. Randolph was immediately summoned to his father's bedroom and interrogated. On learning what had happened, Winston Churchill was furious; Randolph had never seen him so angry. Leaping out of bed, he ordered his car and drove all the way to Surrey to interview the headmaster. But he was too late. The offending master, he was told, had already been sacked for other reasons. All Churchill could do was warn his son never to allow such a thing to happen again.

15

Academically Randolph showed promise but lacked application. Reports on his progress during the years he was at Sandroyd all told the same story. He had an alert mind, a ready tongue and a lively imagination but his work was slipshod. 'His thoughts,' said his headmaster, when he was twelve and a half, 'appear to fly from one thing to another with an uncontrolled rapidity that spoils his chances of achieving his best.' This judgement was confirmed by other teachers. Throughout his school career, Randolph was urged to make the most of his undoubted talents, to concentrate, to be neater in his written work and to think before he spoke. They were difficult precepts for an impetuous young Churchill to follow. Randolph was always looking for shortcuts on the road to success.

*　　　*　　　*

With his parents now settled in their house in Sussex Square, Randolph thoroughly enjoyed his school holidays. Sussex Square was not far from Hyde Park and Randolph and Diana became regular riders in Rotten Row. They were also able to master the perilous art of roller-skating at a rink in nearby Holland Park. Even more exciting were the seaside holidays at Bournemouth and Frinton-on-Sea. Randolph was to cherish fond memories of digging furrows and damming up streams with his father on Frinton beach; and of the tennis tournaments in which he and Diana competed against a pretty sixteen-year-old girl and her partner. The Churchill children lost the match and their mother had the humiliating task of presenting them with booby prizes – two buckets of toffees – before a large crowd. Randolph remembered the prizes but forgot his mother's embarrassment. But there were compensations. His pretty opponent, he says, was the first girl to excite his romantic interest.

It was during Randolph's holidays in September 1922, shortly after the birth of his sister Mary – the fifth and last of the Churchill children – that his father sprang a surprise on the family. Bundling Diana, Randolph and Sarah into a car, he took them on a drive to the country. They were going, he told them, to see a house he was thinking of buying and wanted to know what they thought of it. The house was Chartwell Manor, near Westerham in Kent. Sarah, then almost eight years old, was never to forget this exciting journey or the thrill of seeing Chartwell for the first time. The house, which stood on a hill, was in a bad state of repair and the grounds were wild and overgrown but this did not bother the children. The views, southward across a valley, were magnificent.

'We did a complete tour . . .' says Sarah, 'my father asking anxiously – it is still clear in my mind – "Do you like it?" Did we like it? We were delirious. "Oh, do buy it! Do buy it!" we exclaimed.

"Well, I'm not sure . . ." He kept us in anxious suspense.'

But not for long. On the way home Churchill told them he had already bought the house: Chartwell was to be their new country home. The children were overjoyed.

Their enchantment was not shared by their mother. Clementine Churchill had inspected Chartwell earlier and, although enthusiastic at first, had come to dislike the house. Her practical eye had quickly detected Chartwell's faults and she realized that, before they could move in, enormous structural alterations would be necessary. She was deeply dismayed when she learned her husband had made an offer for the house. But nothing could deter Churchill. Certain that his wife would eventually be won over, he went ahead and bought Chartwell and its eighty acres for £5,000.

In order to supervise the conversion of Chartwell, Churchill rented a house near Westerham called Hosey Rigge. The family lived there for over a year, but most of the children's spare time was spent playing in the grounds at Chartwell. It was probably during this period – although Randolph dates it later – that a new and mysterious character entered their lives. Randolph, uncertain of the precise date, remembered the arrival of the stranger vividly.

One of Winston Churchill's first contributions to Chartwell was to build a tree house for the children in a huge lime in the front drive. He was busy working on the tree house one day when a tall, bespectacled man, with bright red hair, strolled into the garden. Randolph, who was playing with his sisters, went to meet him. They greeted and the man asked the children to call him 'Peter'. His real name he said was Brendan Bracken but he preferred to be called Peter. Randolph was entranced. Indeed the stranger's friendly manner and engaging frankness captivated all the children. They were even more intrigued when their father came down from the tree and walked back to the house with the charming Mr Bracken's arm round his shoulder. Never before had they seen a new acquaintance behave in such a familiar manner.

Bracken spent the night at Hosey Rigge. Not only did he ingratiate himself with the children but talked the staff into making up a bed for him. When Clementine Churchill returned from the seaside the following day, she found what she called 'this red-haired freak' installed as if he were a member of the family.

This brash intrusion into the Churchill household marked the beginning of an extraordinary friendship. Arriving out of nowhere, unknown and unvouched for, Brendan Bracken latched onto Winston Churchill and remained his trusted companion, on and off, for forty-five years. He was well rewarded. Not only was he accepted as Churchill's protégé but, under Churchill's guidance,

17

went on to achieve high office. During the Second World War he became Minister of Information and then, for a brief period at the end of the war, he was appointed First Lord of the Admiralty. He died a respected member of the British peerage.

For all that, Brendan Bracken remained a man of mystery. Such was the confusion he created about his birth and upbringing that his closest friends could only guess at his origins; often they were wide of the mark. 'Being impish as well as devious,' says one of his biographers, 'he made it a rule politely to ignore or fend off all direct personal questions. Very rarely, if harried by persistent or insensitive interrogators, he would urge them bluntly to mind their own business or, if their status and influence warranted gentler handling, might advise them to consult his friend Churchill, then blithely change the subject.' Had anyone been bold enough to consult Churchill, they would have been disappointed. If Churchill knew his friend's secret – which is unlikely – he kept it to himself. Even the notoriously nosy Randolph had to admit he was completely baffled by Bracken's lies and evasions. Not until several years after Viscount Bracken's death was the mystery finally solved.

The truth, when it emerged, was neither as sinister nor as sensational as the gossips hinted. Brendan Bracken, the son of a stonemason, was born in Templeton, a market town in North Tipperary, Ireland, on 15 February 1901. At the age of fifteen he was sent to Australia, where he lived for three years, returning in 1919, claiming to be an Australian. It is thought that he adopted this new nationality because he feared his Irish birth, if it became known, would hamper his political ambitions. Determined to establish himself in England, he then spent a term at a public school in Yorkshire, Sedbergh, where he paid his own fees. After trying his hand as a preparatory school master, he turned to journalism and it was as a representative of a small monthly magazine, *Empire Review*, that he first met Winston Churchill. They are said to have been formally introduced to each other at a dinner party given by J. L. Garvin, the editor of the *Observer*, in the summer of 1923. A few days later Bracken turned up, uninvited, at Chartwell. From then on there was no getting rid of him.

Randolph's relationship with Bracken was to be greatly influenced by the gossip surrounding Bracken's origins. Inevitably the sudden, seemingly inexplicable, friendship between Winston Churchill and this strange young man caused talk. The most popular rumour had it that Brendan Bracken was Churchill's illegitimate son. There were several versions of this titillating story. One account claimed that Bracken – whose distinctive thick lips and somewhat flat nose gave him a slightly negroid appearance – was the child of a coloured woman whom Churchill had known in South Africa during the Anglo-Boer War. Others said that Churchill had formed a liaison with an Irish girl shortly after the Boer War and that Bracken was their son. Such stories were by no means uncommon where well-known politicians were concerned; it was simply the close relationship which developed between Churchill and Bracken that gave them extra force. Certainly Bracken did nothing to discourage them.

Churchill treated the rumours as a joke. He is said to have been rather flattered and amused by the gossip and when tackled about it by his wife, delighted in 'keeping her guessing'. The fact that Clementine Churchill was known to have taken an instant dislike to Bracken only added spice to speculation.

Randolph's attitude towards his father's friend was ambivalent. He seems to have been torn between treating the tittle-tattle as amusing, and defending his status as Churchill's only son. He loved to rag Bracken about their supposed relationship but there were times when his teasing became slightly hysterical. His constant references to 'my bastard brother' were not as light-hearted as he made them appear. All too often the tenuous link that bound Randolph and Bracken together came very close to snapping.

But that was later. When the red-headed Irishman first appeared on the Churchill scene the children adored him. Bracken was a practised charmer; friendly, attentive, full of fun, indulgent and endearingly generous. 'Brendan,' says Sarah, 'would shower us children with delightful gifts, seeming magically to know what each of us wanted at that particular time.' Only Clementine Churchill remained aloof. The children found her coolness, coupled with the gossip about Bracken's relationship to their father, a huge joke. One of their Mitford relations recalls a typical conversation at Chartwell: 'Diana said: "There's a rumour that Mr Bracken is papa's *son!*" with shrill giggles, and Randolph added: "Mummy won't call him Brendan because she's so afraid he might call her Clemmie." ' It was to take many years for Clementine Churchill to succumb to Brendan Bracken's charm.

The Mitfords were regular visitors to Chartwell. They were the children of Clementine Churchill's cousin, Lady Redesdale, and Randolph and his sister Diana regarded them as very special friends. Of the six remarkable Mitford girls, the third, Diana, was nearest to Randolph in age and she and her brother Tom occasionally stayed with the Churchills during the holidays. Diana Mitford (now Lady Mosley) was to remember these visits with affection. She came to appreciate a side of Randolph that was hidden from his more casual acquaintances. He could be very tiresome, she says, 'but one simply had to be indulgent . . . one of the charming things about him was that he adored and admired his friends and they could do no wrong. I was very fond of Randolph and my brother Tom, a clever and serious person, really loved him.'

It may have been the thought of joining Tom Mitford, when he left Sandroyd, that made Randolph look forward to going to Eton.

CHAPTER TWO

The Youngest Pitt

Winston Churchill was fond of explaining why he sent Randolph to Eton rather than to his own old school, Harrow. It made a good story and has been retold, with embellishments, by a number of his associates. Apparently, sometime before the First World War, Churchill and a friend – some say it was Lord Birkenhead – were driving through Harrow on the Hill and, on an impulse, decided to visit the school. Hardly had they entered the grounds than they were spotted by a group of boys who, recognizing Churchill as a Tory turncoat, began to hiss at him. Not surprisingly Churchill was furious. Turning abruptly, he stormed back to his car, and drove away. Shortly afterwards he put Randolph down for Eton.

There are various accounts of this incident and they differ in detail; but they agree in broad outline. That something of the sort happened seems fairly certain.

But Randolph tells a different story. He says that not only was he asked to choose between Harrow and Eton but, when the time came, was allowed to inspect the two schools before making up his mind. Eton won out because it appeared to have 'fewer rules and much less discipline.'

Again there seems no reason to doubt him. Whatever his faults, Randolph never told unnecessary lies. Respect for the truth had been instilled into him by his parents and it was a lesson he prized. He was often vague, forgetful, and careless of facts but he was rarely dishonest. 'Most people,' he once observed, 'prefer lies to the truth. I consider truth the buckler of all virtues.' In lighter vein he would claim that lies were boring, the truth more amusing. However he put it, he insisted on telling the truth even when it acted to his own discredit. Often it did. Not everyone appreciates being told the truth; Randolph's outspoken, sometimes brutally frank, remarks tended to win him more enemies than admirers. But this, in Randolph's terms, was simply the price an honest man paid for his principles.

As far as his choice of school was concerned, he may have been misled by his father. Winston Churchill could well have decided to send his son to Eton but, not wanting to play the heavy-handed father, he may have gone through the motions of offering Randolph a choice and gently influenced the final decision. Randolph, after all, was very young at the time. However it came about, Eton was chosen.

Randolph was not the first Churchill, or even the first Randolph Churchill, to go to Eton. The Churchill family had favoured Eton for generations; Winston was the odd-man out. Randolph's grandfather, the tempestuous Lord Randolph Churchill, had been educated at Eton and so, for a time, had Lord Randolph's elder brother, Lord Blandford, the future 8th Duke of Marlborough. Neither Lord Randolph nor his brother was a model Etonian. Lord Blandford had been expelled after what Lord Rosebery described as 'some difference with the authorities as to the use of a catapult' and Lord Randolph's wild behaviour had brought him close to a similar fate. The Churchill boys were notoriously difficult to educate.

Randolph started well enough. In October 1924, five months after his thirteenth birthday, he joined Colonel Arthur Sheep-shanks' House at Eton. His father had promised him a pony if he took Middle Fourth in the Common Entrance Examination. Randolph did better than that. He took Upper Fourth and was rewarded with one of Churchill's polo ponies.

His success was partly due to his father's training. During the South African war, Winston Churchill had been forced, when escaping from the Boers, to hide at the bottom of a Transvaal coal mine for three days. Isolated and in the dark, he had whiled away the time by reciting poems he had learned by heart. This experience, it is thought, had taught him the value of memorizing long extracts from books. It could also explain why he insisted on his children following his example. 'Great lashings of poetry were stashed away inside us,' says his daughter Sarah, 'and in the long summer evenings, when we would be sleeping out in the garden, it became fun to see how long we could keep reciting poetry and even famous bits of prose.' Randolph, she adds, 'excelled in this.'

Certainly Randolph benefited from it. Bad as was his memory for detail, he could always produce an apt, often lengthy, quotation to back up his arguments. It was a rare accomplishment. No doubt his examiners were duly impressed.

The same, unfortunately, cannot be said of his school fellows. To them young Randolph Churchill seemed more conceited than clever. He was just as unpopular at Eton as he had been at Sandroyd. He was far too full of himself, too ready to air his opinions, altogether too assertive for a boy of his age. Nor did he help things by his attempts to mix with the senior boys. Most of his early friends at Eton were the friends he had made at home – older boys like Tom Mitford and Freddie Furneaux, the son of Lord Birkenhead – and he saw nothing wrong in trying to continue these friendships at school. That in doing so, he was breaking a revered schoolboy code does not appear to have occurred to him.

James Lees-Milne, one of the older boys, was to remember the unfortunate impression created by Randolph on his arrival at Eton. A typical incident occurred when, during one of Colonel Sheepshanks' lessons, Lees-Milne was asked to translate a passage of English into Latin. Somewhat unsure of himself, Lees-Milne stood up and began to stammer through the opening sentences. He had not gone far before he was interrupted. 'I can do that, I can do that,' piped a voice behind him. Looking round he was astonished to see Randolph standing on a chair, book in hand, reading the passage in Latin with apparent ease. 'Churchill!' bellowed Colonel Sheepshanks, 'sit down at once and let Lees-Milne continue.' More bewildered than abashed, Randolph did as he was told.

The boys were obviously not alone in thinking young Churchill too big for his boots. By the end of his first year, Randolph's exasperated tutors were complaining of his 'obstinacy', his 'constant interruptions in the form of queries and quibbles' and his 'wasteful' remarks, which frayed everyone's patience and were 'very largely cheap, pointless and irrelevant.' Only the mathematics master found him 'hideously ingenious' and 'extremely good fun.' Even so his praise was not unqualified. 'One does not,' he admitted, 'talk much when he wants to.'

*   *   *

Tom Mitford was probably Randolph's closest friend at Eton. Their friendship, which blossomed during their school years, was to last until Tom Mitford's death in Burma at the end of the Second World War. Almost as important to Randolph, during these early years, was his link with the young Viscount Furneaux. Randolph had known Freddie Furneaux as a small child, their fathers were friends, and they were bound together in a special relationship: each was the godson of the other's father. But it was not until they came together at Eton that the two boys got to know each other well.

When Randolph first arrived at Colonel Sheepshanks' House at Eton, he was delighted to find that Freddie Furneaux was one of the 'great swells' of the House. He was even prouder of his friend when Furneaux was made Captain of Games and he, in turn, was appointed Furneaux's fag. This was a stroke of luck for Randolph. Fagging was not something that he took to naturally and he had good reason to be thankful for Freddie Furneaux's indulgence of his bungling efforts. He was later to admit that it was by practising on the long-suffering Furneaux that he acquired what skills he possessed as a fag. Certainly Freddie Furneaux kept a watchful eye on Randolph during his early years at Eton.

Whether Furneaux enjoyed his role as protector is another matter. There were times when his patience was sorely tried. On one occasion he became so exasperated with Randolph's incessant chattering that he tossed him out of a first floor window to silence him. Randolph survived unharmed. On picking himself up in the street, he went on talking as if nothing had happened. In later years, Furneaux's attitude towards Randolph was equally short-tempered. 'Randolph was very fond of Freddie,' says a friend of them both, 'but Freddie could not stand Randolph. He found him a perpetual irritant.' At Eton, however, Furneaux could not allow himself to be provoked too often. He was under orders from his father, Lord Birkenhead, to see that no serious harm came to Randolph. The orders originated, of course, with Winston Churchill and provide an example of Churchill's unobtrusive concern for his son's well being. Randolph was never far from his father's thoughts.

But more than Freddie Furneaux's protection was needed to rescue Randolph from his innumerable scrapes. He was forever in trouble. Only too well was he to remember the fear aroused by a summons to the 'Library' – where a group of older boys, presided over by the Captain of the House, administered punishment. The ritual of Library beatings features prominently in his recollections of Eton. One occasion he was to remember vividly. It happened after Freddie Furneaux had left and concerned a trivial misdemeanour. Indeed Randolph claims he was falsely accused and that it was his attempts to establish his innocence that decided his fate. 'Anyway,' his accuser retorted, after listening to his protests, 'you have been bloody awful all round – bend down, you are going to have six up.' Randolph returned to his room, smiling bravely, but seething with anger.

He received little sympathy. When he later recorded the incident, there were some who thought 'bloody awful all round' was a justified verdict. Many a would-be cane wielder had come to the same conclusion when dealing with Randolph Churchill.

His housemaster at Eton would certainly have agreed. Colonel Sheepshanks was driven to near despair by Randolph's outrageous behaviour. The boy, he complained to Winston Churchill, was headstrong, obstinate, argumentative, conceited and given to the most appalling displays of temper. 'He will never persuade himself that he is wrong,' he wrote, after enduring Randolph's tantrums for two years, 'and becomes quite intolerable for everyone.' Only with the utmost reluctance would Sheepshanks confess to finding Randolph 'very attractive' when he was not angry.

To be fair, the fault may not have been entirely one-sided. Opinions are divided about Colonel Sheepshanks. Some boys considered him to be a hearty, sports-loving, relatively harmless, busybody; others remember him as 'sly, facetious and snobbish.' Randolph was decidedly in the second group. His growing distrust of Sheepshanks he says, was confirmed when he discovered that his housemaster – forbidden to cane boys himself – had connived to have Randolph beaten unfairly by the Captain of the House. Such treachery in Randolph's eyes was unspeakable. The confrontation with Sheepshanks which followed this episode was so stormy that from then on, according to Randolph, the perfidious house-master kept his distance.

With the other masters Randolph maintained a cheeky, sometimes intimidating, relationship which most of them appear to have found more amusing than offensive. His high spirits, combined with a runaway tongue, made him a formidable pupil to discipline. 'At first,' confessed one of his Maths masters, 'I dared to answer him back (in fear and trembling) but, finding I was not completely withered, I persevered and I have managed to keep his effusiveness slightly in check. It has been good fun (but poor Maths).' Mathematics was not one of Randolph's strong points. He was far happier with subjects which stirred his imagination; subjects like English and History, in which he could indulge his rhetorical talents and which allowed him to substitute effect for precision. Robert Birley, his history tutor, summed up his academic attainments in what was, as Randolph later acknowledged, an extremely perceptive report. It is worth quoting at length.

'Let it be said at once,' wrote Birley, 'that his work was not always satisfactory. There was a period when he seemed to be reading the books extremely sketchily, though he certainly improved in this, and he is very careless about showing up his work in time. But he answers fairly well to expostulation. He is not by any means a bad worker, and there is all the difference between a boy who takes a holiday and then does nothing, and one who reads widely and does not waste his time. But he needs discipline and he must not get into the habit of working only when he wants to.

'His real trouble is his facility. He finds it a great deal too easy to do moderately well, and he is developing too early the journalist's ability to "work up" a little information or a solitary idea. I can give a good, though rather unfair, example. The other day, when he was with me we talked for five or ten minutes about Shaftesbury, and I told him one or two points. The next morning one of the questions in the trial paper was on Shaftesbury's career. As he was up to me in trials I happened to look at his paper and saw he had done the question. He served up just the few things I had said, turned into a longish answer. It was extremely well done. There were some excellent allusions and the whole thing was thrown into the form of a good summary of his character.

'The trouble is it was far too well done. There is nothing wrong in his putting down the ideas given him or in his expanding them. But for all the allusions and the good writing there really was hardly any original thought or real thought at all in the whole answer. It was, in fact, a piece of very good journalism.

'There is no need for him merely to do this. He has a first-class brain. But he must be prepared to do some hard thinking for himself and not to take an easy course. His easy course will not be a dull one, in fact it will be an amusing and interesting one. But it will be second-rate for all that. . . .

'I have attacked him pretty often about his style, though I am not really alarmed about it. It is at the moment abominable, extremely rhetorical, windy and involved, full of clichés and pomposity. All these, however, are faults on the right side. They are due partly to his reading a good deal of Macaulay, mostly to an attempt on his side to form a style (which is to be commended). I think he should try to get out of it and write more simply. It makes his answers now very heavy and rather jaded.

'He is trying I think to improve his handwriting, but not very steadily. He must persevere in this. He is quite one of the most interesting pupils I have had, and he is a very pleasant one. His mind is vigorous and his interests are wide.'

Birley's shrewd assessment of Randolph's abilities was, for the most part, to stand the test of time.

*　　　*　　　*

His failure to attract friends of his own age at Eton did not unduly worry Randolph. In fact he was inclined to exaggerate the extent to which he was shunned. He liked to think of himself as a misfit: it singled him out from the common run, it boosted his sense of superiority. The conventional paths to schoolboy popularity, in any case, held no attractions for him. He felt no shame in his lack of success as a sportsman – though he did, almost by accident, get his house colours by being included in a winning rugby side – and positively revelled in his contempt for spectator sports. 'I have never been given to playing games,' he would boast, 'even less to watching them.' Not to be interested in sport was almost a family distinction:

neither his grandfather nor his father had shone of the playing fields of Eton and Harrow. The Churchills were plainly destined for higher things than the mindless pursuit of balls. There was no disgrace in being unclubbable.

All the same it would be a mistake to picture him as a morose and solitary schoolboy, a would-be Napoleon at Brienne. He was by nature too gregarious to isolate himself completely. Always the exhibitionist, he needed an audience whom he could impress, an audience who would appreciate his wit and wisdom. And, for all his disagreeable traits, he was not without the means of attracting such an audience. For one thing there were his dazzling good-looks. The older he grew the more striking his physical appearance became. He had inherited his mother's classical features – the patrician profile, fine bone-structure and intelligent blue-grey eyes – which, added to his forceful personality, inevitably commanded attention. Few people who met him as a youth failed to comment on his noble appearance and – when the mood took him – his bewitching effervescence. 'He has a Greuze face; uncommon good looks for a boy,' noted Hector Bolitho, the writer, who met Randolph and his mother at an Eton tea-party in June 1926. 'I talked with him in the library; at least he talked at me. He is only fifteen, but he does not listen with ease. It was delightful to hear him speak of his father with a sort of hero-worship.'

Nor was it only visiting adults who were captivated. Randolph made friends among his schoolfellows; not always uncritical friends, but friends for all that. Even James Lees-Milne – with whom he had got off to a bad start – came to appreciate Randolph's more likeable qualities, was invited to Chartwell, and remembers him as an 'affectionate boy'. The young Alfred Ayer, who first met Randolph when they were both in the signals section of the Officers Training Corps, became a sympathetic ally. 'Randolph Churchill . . .' he says, 'did not appear to have many friends at Eton. It may have been partly that which drew us together. He was a remarkably good-looking boy, who shared my interests in ideas which were not directly related to our work in school.' This fellow feeling appears to have softened Randolph's belligerence. 'He had a great deal of charm,' Ayer adds, 'and had not then developed the arrogance which made him difficult company in his later years.' Not all Randolph's fellow Etonians would have agreed. But Sir Alfred Ayer retained his fond memories, even after he had experienced the sharper side of Randolph's tongue. 'I never wholly lost my early affection for him,' he later confessed.

Far from being an outcast, Randolph shared many of the usual schoolboy escapades, including breaking bounds with another boy and sneaking to London – dressed in sports clothes and homberg hats – to eat strawberry ice creams at Gunter's restaurant. Like the other boys, also, he mastered the current affectations and peppered his talk with fashionable 1920s slang. Outings were 'too, *too* wonderful', parties 'too, *too* divine' and the prospect of a river trip 'too, *too* marvellous.' So long as he was not opposed or provoked, Randolph could be a charming, witty, endearing and unshakably loyal companion. 'He would always defend his friends,' said one of his masters. 'He would cheat for his friends.'

Unfortunately his friends were not always well chosen. Once Tom Mitford and Freddie Furneaux had left Eton, Randolph began to seek an audience among the younger boys. This gave rise to a number of suspicions. Colonel Sheepshanks, a notorious sniffer out of homosexual liaisons, was immediately put on the alert. Making his round of the boys' rooms one night – as was the custom at Eton – he had the temerity to question Randolph about his friendship with one of the younger boys. He should have known better. Randolph heard him out and then exploded. Was he, he wanted to know, being accused of unnatural vice? If so Sheepshanks had better beware. There were laws that guarded against slander and, if the accusation was repeated in front of others, those laws would be invoked. Then, to add to his housemaster's embarrassment, Randolph blurted out the truth. Yes, he confessed, he was friendly with the boy, and yes, there was romance in the air. But that romance was very different from Sheepshanks imaginings. It so happened that he, Randolph, was in love with the boy's sister. (He appears, in fact, to have been conducting a love-lorn correspondence with the girl and to have used her brother as a go-between.) This revelation brought the interview to an abrupt end. After that, crowed Randolph, 'I never had any more rot from Sheepshanks.'

Robert Birley was more sensible; but he was no less critical of Randolph's ill-advised friendships. 'He seems to find his friends,' Birley observed, 'entirely among people who are either more stupid or much younger than himself. I am really more worried about the former. He really must not search out foils. It is far too easy a way to be clever. This fact is due, of course, to the difficulty he finds to get on with his contemporaries. Here I think he has shown great improvement. Knowing that he was likely to become so unpopular in any division he was in, I was rather uneasy about mine this half. But he behaved really well, without aggressiveness and conceit. This is a very good sign.'

No doubt Birley's strictures were warranted. The same cannot be said for Colonel Sheepshanks' suspicions.

There was not the slightest possibility of Randolph being tempted to homosexual dalliance. He was far too preoccupied with girls. His attraction to the opposite sex was, to anyone other than Colonel Sheepshanks, only too obvious. Almost from the onset of puberty, he had been a relentless pursuer of desirable young women. The romance he confessed to Sheepshanks was only one of many similar infatuations. As it happened that particular romance was shattered (the girl was in love with Tom Mitford) but Randolph was quick to seek consolation. When, in February 1927, the popular actress Sylvia Hawkes married the son of the Earl of Shaftesbury, Randolph, then a precocious sixteen-year-old, was publicly listed as one of the bride's more persistent former admirers. His Eton letters to James Lees-Milne are full of meetings, or proposed meetings, with girls.

The most fervent of these juvenile crushes was his enchantment with the young Diana Mitford. 'Diana M was too *too* wonderful,' he enthused to Lees-Milne, after a chance encounter, 'so sweet and so kind.' His infatuation with the lovely Diana had started when he was fifteen and lasted throughout his schooldays. He was not alone. 'We were both in love with her,' says James Lees-Milne. But, alas, they were both to be disappointed. In January 1929, shortly after Randolph left Eton, the eighteen-year-old Diana Mitford married Bryan Guinness, son of the future Lord Moyne. Randolph had again to seek consolation.

*   *   *

Sir Osbert Sitwell liked to describe himself in *Who's Who* as 'educated in the holidays from Eton.' The same claim might have been made, with a greater semblance of truth, by Randolph Churchill. Certainly his holidays were instructive. There could have been few among his contemporaries, even among the well-connected sons of Eton, who were drawn so intimately into the world of high politics and introduced to so many public figures, as was Randolph during his school vacations. This was no accident. Winston Churchill, anxious not to repeat the mistakes of his own parents, was determined to smooth his son's path, to widen his experience, and to treat him as an equal. From a very early age, Randolph was encouraged to take an active interest in his father's career.

That career underwent a number of significant changes during Randolph's school years. When he first entered Sandroyd, in 1920, his father was Secretary of State for War and Air in Lloyd George's post-war coalition; the following year he became Colonial Secretary. In the general election of 1922, however, the Conserva-

29

tives were victorious and there was a sharp increase in votes for the Labour Party; Churchill was among the Liberal casualties. He was defeated at Dundee and, for the first time in twenty-two years, found himself without a seat in parliament. Failure to be re-elected was a blow and an embarrassment – 'What use is a W.C. without a seat?' giggled Randolph and his sisters – but it gave Churchill the opportunity of reassessing his position in politics.

He spent the next two years completing his war memoirs, writing articles for the newspapers, working on the reconstruction of Chartwell – which he intended to leave to Randolph – and pondering his future. He had become thoroughly disillusioned with the Liberal Party and, in 1923, he began to think seriously of returning to his old loyalties. Adopting his father's old stance, he now described himself as a Tory Democrat. But he could not yet steel himself to break with the Liberals. That same year, when the Conservative leader, Stanley Baldwin, called another general election with the intention of reintroducing Protection, Churchill was persuaded to contest West Leicester as a 'Liberal Free Trader'. Baldwin's majority was slashed, but again Churchill failed to win a parliamentary seat.

It was not until some months later, when Mr Asquith gave his support to the first minority Labour Government, that Churchill made his first open move away from the Liberals. At a by-election in the Abbey Division of Westminster, in March 1924, he stood as an 'Independent anti-Socialist'. He was hoping to attract support from moderate Liberals and Conservatives, but he was only partly successful and was beaten by the official Conservative candidate by a mere 43 votes. A closer step towards full reconciliation with the Conservative Party was taken later that year. First, in May, Churchill launched a passionate, widely reported, attack on the Labour Government at a Conservative mass meeting in Liverpool – his first appearance on a Tory platform in twenty years – and then, in September, after a great deal of backstairs wire pulling, he was adopted as a prospective candidate by the West Essex (Epping) Conservative Association. In yet another general election – the third in three years, this time following the fall of the Labour Government in October 1924 – Winston Churchill, standing as a 'Constitutionalist' with Conservative backing, won the Epping seat with an impressive majority. He was to represent this Essex constituency, later renamed Wanstead and Woodford, for the next forty years.

A few months after the election, Churchill formally rejoined the Conservative Party. The break with the Liberals was complete. It had been a slow and far from easy process. Churchill, after all, had served as a Cabinet Minister in Liberal administrations for the best part of his political career. He had no doubts about the rightness of his actions, but he could not help being aware of the danger of being labelled an opportunist. Nor was his wife particularly happy about the break. A convinced Liberal, Clementine Churchill was deeply suspicious of the Tory leadership – her daughter Mary says that, although her mother never voted Liberal again, she remained an 'old-fashioned radical' at heart – and she urged her husband to move with caution. But, once the move was made, Clementine Churchill brushed aside her political misgivings and followed where her husband led.

Randolph appears to have had fewer hesitations. He was only thirteen when Churchill returned to the Conservative fold, but his youth did not prevent him from holding strong opinions. 'I was born a Liberal,' he recalled, 'but the Liberal Party came to an end. My father and I both decided our duty was to join the Conservative Party in order to maintain Britain's liberal heritage against the onrushing tide of totalitarian Socialism. One of the reasons the Liberal Party came to an end . . . was really that it had achieved all it set out to do . . . Of course, things can be improved. But basically what's important is to preserve our liberal heritage. That is the foundation of my political thinking.' It was not a very firm foundation. Randolph's political thinking, spiked as it often was with personal prejudice, was rarely liberal; nor, for that matter, could it be described as consistent.

Churchill's victory at Epping was part of another swing to the Conservatives. Stanley Baldwin again became Prime Minister and set about forming a Government. There was immediate speculation about the post he was expected to offer Winston Churchill. That the prodigal son would be rewarded, few doubted. Churchill himself half expected to be sent to the Colonial Office; his wife wanted him to become Minister of Health. But, to everyone's surprise, not least his own, Churchill was appointed Chancellor of the Exchequer. His astonishment was equalled only by his delight. Not only was the Chancellorship considered the second most important Cabinet post but, in assuming this exalted office, Churchill was fulfilling a cherished ambition. It was as Chancellor of the Exchequer that his father, Lord Randolph, had dramatically resigned from Lord Salisbury's Government in 1886 and so ended a promising career; now, after almost forty years, a Churchill was again to occupy No. 11 Downing Street. 'I realize the truth,' Churchill observed at a celebratory dinner, 'of the remark of Disraeli that "the vicissitudes of politics are inexhaustible."'

For Randolph, his father's elevation opened new vistas. When

31

Churchill presented his first Budget, in April 1925, Randolph was seated in the Stranger's Gallery of the House of Commons with his mother and sister, Diana, to witness the great event. One of the more important announcements made by Churchill in his two and a half hour Budget speech concerned the Government's decision to return to the Gold Standard. The following month the Gold Standard Bill was debated and Randolph was in the House to hear his father reply to the debate. From then on Randolph took a lively, though superficial, interest in the Budget debates.

Somewhat more to his taste were his father's informal and extra-parliamentary activities. Visitors to Chartwell were often surprised at the way in which Churchill encouraged his son to join in complex political discussions. Self-effacement was not one of Randolph's notable characteristics and, even as a boy, he never hesitated to air his opinions. When, for instance, Thomas Jones – the Deputy Secretary to the Cabinet – dined with the Churchills in August 1926, he found that the fifteen-year-old Randolph was allowed to sit up until after midnight expressing his views on the current coal crisis. Not only did Randolph appear well-informed but, Jones noted in his diary, Churchill frequently deferred to his opinions. 'The boy,' Jones added, 'was extremely intelligent.' Also present at this dinner was Churchill's enigmatic friend Professor Lindemann – known to the Churchill circle as 'the Prof' – and Jones was impressed by the extent to which Randolph was under Lindemann's influence. It was an influence which many considered unfortunate, if not harmful.

Professor Frederick Lindemann, the future Lord Cherwell, was, like Brendan Bracken, one of Winston Churchill's controversial bachelor friends. Born in Germany – a country he came to hate – of an Alsatian father and an American mother, Lindemann, when Churchill first met him in 1921, was Professor of Experimental Philosophy at Oxford. The two men had quickly become friends and Churchill relied on Lindemann for scientific advice. It was a curious association. Lindemann, an austere non-smoker, teetotaller and vegetarian, was in many ways the direct opposite of the outgoing, self-indulgent Churchill. What bound them together was mutual respect: each admired the other's intelligence, expertise and forceful personality. But Lindemann was far from popular among Churchill's political colleagues. Sharp tongued, spiteful, opinionated, snobbish and appallingly class-conscious – he 'regarded all miners, if not all the working classes, as species of sub-human,' complained Thomas Jones – the Prof's extreme right-wing views could shock even die-hard Tories. For all that, Lindemann was a loyal, humorous, often charming friend and Churchill, while wary of his political views, thoroughly enjoyed his company. Few men were as devoted to Winston Churchill as was Professor Lindemann.

That devotion was savoured by all the Churchills. Like Brendan Bracken, Lindemann was fully alive to the value of cultivating his friend's family and was lavish with his attentions to the Churchill children. Generous gifts, lively tennis matches and outings in his much admired Mercedes Benz were all part of the Prof's regular visits to Chartwell. The children adored him. His parties were always great fun and his periodic descents on Eton invariably delighted Randolph. Whether his snobbish influence was beneficial to a boy already so tiresomely conceited is another matter.

Fully aware of the criticism surrounding Lindemann, Randolph refused to see any harm in his father's friend. He gleefully accepted the Prof's presents, blandishments and motor car holidays and no doubt absorbed the bigoted opinions that went with them. Lindemann, he insisted, was merely a lonely man who was naturally fond of children. His parents apparently thought the same: neither Churchill nor his wife saw any reason to object to the clean-living, scholarly family friend. Indeed the reactionary Professor Lindemann was, somewhat surprisingly, one of her husband's few friends to gain Clementine Churchill's approval. She did nothing to discourage whatever influence the Prof had over her son.

Mrs Churchill was not always so lenient. Some of Randolph's adult acquaintances she viewed with the utmost suspicion. This was certainly the case with Randolph's godfather, Lord Birkenhead.

Worldly, witty, a brilliant orator and a gifted lawyer and politician, the former F. E. Smith was one of the outstanding men of his age. He was one of the few adults whom Randolph regarded with awe. As a young boy he would become strangely flustered at the prospect of a visit from Lord Birkenhead, giving his sisters long lectures on how to behave, on what they could or could not say, and generally setting out to make a favourable impression. This, from the self-confident Randolph, was unusual indeed. And the older he grew the more admiring he grew. Birkenhead became his model of worldly behaviour. As a youth, Randolph tried desperately to ape his dashing godfather's mannerisms, to memorize his famous anecdotes and witticisms and to master his command of language. His failure to do so only increased his admiration. Randolph's hero was always his father, but Lord Birkenhead – who died shortly after he left Eton – was undoubtedly his worldly mentor.

This did not please Randolph's mother. The last person she wanted her son to model himself on was the volatile Lord Birkenhead. 'She thought him [Birkenhead] a vulgarian,' says Sir John Colville, 'which perhaps he was; she disliked his drinking habits, which sometimes made him insolent and overbearing; she was sure he encouraged Winston's inclination to gamble; and she objected to the thoughtless encouragement he gave to his godchild, her already turbulent and outspoken son, Randolph.' But her protests went unheeded. Randolph was captivated and, like his father, he blithely ignored his mother's warnings. He was a frequent guest at Lord Birkenhead's house during his holidays; he ate there, played cards there and later, it is said, started to drink there. According to his friends, it was by trying to match his godfather's drinking habits that Randolph acquired a taste for hard liquor.

Randolph's holiday experiences were by no means limited to social occasions with his father's friends. As the son of the Chancellor of the Exchequer, he was able to enjoy rarer privileges. Among his more memorable experiences was an exciting, but rushed, Mediterranean tour with his father and uncle Jack at the beginning of 1927. Crammed with tantalizing glimpses of European cities and meetings with foreign dignitaries, it was a heady excursion for a sixteen-year-old boy.

The Churchills left London on 4 January 1927, crossed to France, visited Paris, travelled by train to Genoa and then caught a coastal steamer to Naples. After a day's crowded sight-seeing in Naples and Pompeii they boarded a British destroyer which took them to Malta from where, a couple of days later, they sailed in H.M.S. *Warspite* to Athens. Another destroyer took them back to Italy and, after a hurried visit to Rome, they returned overland to France. The holiday ended when, on 27 January, they arrived back in England.

Randolph's recollections of this whirlwind journey are muddled – he dates it two years earlier – but he retained vivid impressions of the highlights. Although he makes no mention of seeing an eruption of Vesuvius, he clearly recalls his annoyance at being left behind when his father and uncle inspected the erotica in the newly discovered ruins of Herculaneum. Travelling in destroyers obviously impressed him and he delighted in the naval exercises they witnessed between Malta and Athens. Equally memorable was a picnic at the Parthenon and the experience of sailing through the Corinth Canal. But it was Rome that provided the greatest thrills. Here Randolph and his father were introduced to Mussolini – then a rising, but not yet formidable figure on the European scene – at a dinner at the British Embassy; and they were granted an audience with Pope Pius XII. Unlike his father, who found Mussolini a charming, mild-mannered opponent of Leninism, Randolph was not particularly impressed by the Fascist dictator. Only later was he to realize the significance of this meeting. Far more to his liking was the pomp and protocol surrounding the Papal audience. He was surprised at how smoothly it all went. The conversation, he admits, was a little sticky at first but once Churchill and the Pope got on to the iniquities of the Bolsheviks there was no stopping them. Randolph's only regret was that his father forbade him to ask for the Pope's blessing on some statuettes he had bought for his Catholic friends. He had instead to persuade himself that the parting benediction he received from the Pope, at his father's request, was somehow transmitted from his head to the objects of piety concealed in his pocket. A blessing, after all, was a blessing.

Churchill welcomed this opportunity to broaden his son's horizons. 'I am having a vy interesting trip,' he wrote to Stanley Baldwin from Malta, '& it is a new pleasure to me to show the world to Randolph.' His pleasure was undoubtedly increased by his son's exceptional behaviour. Throughout the long, often exhausting, journey Randolph appears to have fully lived up to his father's expectations: he was polite, tidy and restrained. Only when Churchill discovered that his son, in mid-winter, wore no vest beneath his shirt did he have cause for concern. 'He is *hardy*,' he acknowledged in a letter to his wife, 'but surely a vest is a necessity to white people. I am going to buy him some.'

Otherwise Churchill had no complaints. So encouraged was he that he began to involve Randolph more and more in his semi-official duties. Later that year when, as a former Minister of War, Churchill attended a demonstration of some new armoured cars and small tanks he took his son with him. Once again Randolph was on his best behaviour. As Churchill briskly inspected the armoured vehicles, Randolph walked solemnly behind him chatting to one of the officers. He 'made some shrewd comments,' recalled the officer, 'and in an unassertive way that would have surprised those who came to know him in later years.' Occasions such as this must have made Churchill think that the complaints of Randolph's schoolmasters were exaggerated, if not entirely misplaced.

But the complaints continued to pour in. In an end of term report, which Churchill received shortly before he and Randolph set off on their Mediterranean tour, Colonel Sheepshanks had again listed Randolph's shortcomings. Churchill dutifully rebuked his son, but it was a rebuke that lacked the force of conviction. Randolph, he chided, must try harder, use his abilities, and take advantage of the opportunities that Eton offered. He could hardly have said less. Judging from his recorded reactions, it is fairly obvious that Churchill was not unduly alarmed by his son's reputation for rebelliousness. He might even have anticipated the complaints. Not having been a model scholar himself, he could have had little faith in the pedantry of school-masters. The Churchills were notoriously ill-disciplined; it was more a sign of individuality than of their wilfullness. An ungovernable temperament had not prevented him, or his father, from making their mark in the world. Randolph was cast in the same mould. Everyone agreed that his son was a bright, high-spirited youngster: better that than a dullard. Churchill had no doubt that Randolph would run true to family tradition.

His faith in his son's destiny became only too apparent on his visits to Eton. He paid little attention to the inevitable complaints about Randolph's behaviour and became positively annoyed if he suspected the criticism to be biased. Robert Birley, Randolph's history tutor, was never to forget one of Churchill's visits. It happened on a day when Birley – then a young master in his early twenties – had been correcting one of Randolph's essays.

The subject set for the essay had been 'unemployment' and, as usual, Randolph's effort reflected more enthusiasm than attention to detail. 'He had obviously not bothered to master the most elementary facts,' said Birley. After reading it, Birley had written across the top of the first page: 'Until you discover the difference between unemployment insurance and the dole, you are not ready to tackle this subject.' He had then placed it on the top of the pile of papers on his desk. Shortly afterwards Churchill arrived. His eye immediately fell on the essay and, recognizing Randolph's handwriting, he picked it up. When he saw Birley's comment he was furious.

'This is most unfair,' he snorted, flicking through the essay. 'The boy's written at great length, done his best, and should be given a word or two of encouragement.' Birley's attempts to explain were brushed aside.

'Randolph has a great future,' muttered Churchill as he left the room. 'He comes from an important political family. There's been two before – Pitt the Elder and Pitt the Younger – but never three. He's going to be a great man.'

＊　　　＊　　　＊

Randolph remained something of a misfit throughout his school-days. He was never really popular with boys of his own age. How much Randolph was to blame for this is debatable. It may have been, as Sir John Colville suggests, that mixing freely with his father's friends and being encouraged to join in their arguments, Randolph 'found his schoolfellows uninteresting companions by comparison.' On the other hand it is extremely doubtful whether Randolph's abrasive personality and smart-alec posturing would ever have endeared him to his classmates: schoolboys always dislike a show-off. Looking back on his years at Eton, Randolph admits that he was unpopular and says that this was because he was lazy, bad at games, and generally at odds with the accepted patterns of behaviour. Whatever the truth, the fact remains that young Randolph Churchill was decidedly out of tune with his contemporaries.

The extent of Randolph's estrangement from his classmates was demonstrated during his last year at Eton, when one of the masters fell ill. To fill the temporary gap the headmaster, Dr Alington, asked a young Oxford don to take over the top form for a couple of weeks. The young don was Frank Pakenham – later Lord Longford – and Randolph was among the boys he was asked to teach. Having little experience of classroom work, Pakenham decided to improvize: for his first lesson he told the boys to select a piece from the *Oxford Book of English Prose* and learn it for the second session. When the time came for them to present their chosen piece, Pakenham was struck by the way in which a particularly handsome youngster declaimed Macaulay's 'Trial of Warren Hastings': assured, eloquent and stylish – an articulate Adonis – the boy seemed to possess all the attributes of a born leader. Pakenham did not then know that the boy was Randolph Churchill. He was soon to find out and to be disillusioned. For his third lesson he staged a mock election, asking the boys to propose and vote for a committee and fully expecting the budding orator to feature prominently. To his astonishment, Randolph, for all his golden good-looks and silver tongue, did not receive a single vote. 'I was completely mystified,' claimed Pakenham.

Frank Pakenham was not alone in his bewilderment. Most of the masters who taught Randolph during his last year complained about his failure to live up to his promise. He seemed, at times, to find a perverse pleasure in undermining any confidence shown in him. 'Is it unkind – it is not meant to be – to suggest that he is too quarrelsome,' asked one despairing teacher, 'that he likes being in a minority, and enjoys, not rubbing people up the wrong way, but the result of having rubbed them up the wrong way?' Many people were to ask the same question as Randolph grew older. It was as if he deliberately cloaked himself in arrogance to disguise his weaknesses; that he assumed a bold front to gain recognition as a rebel and delighted in the results of his pose. He loved to shock, to challenge conventions, to argue for the sake of argument and so prove himself a Churchill. What doubts he may have experienced were invariably expressed cynically; he looked not for answers but for reassurance. This was particularly true of his approach to religion.

Like most youngsters, Randolph went through a phase of

37

religious uncertainty at school. His doubts appear to have surfaced shortly after he was confirmed in the Church of England at the age of sixteen. Unable to reconcile the doctrine of free will with an omnipotent God, he sought the advice of his headmaster, Dr Alington – a distinguished, though worldly, Doctor of Divinity. According to Randolph, the suave Dr Alington – known to the boys as 'Creeping Christ' – was so offhand in answering his questions that his faith was shattered, that he spent the rest of his life trying to regain it. But this is another of Randolph's exaggerations. Dr Alington was certainly not the only person he consulted about his misgivings. With characteristic assertiveness, he continued to air his religious objections and to scoff at orthodox opinion. Once again it was Robert Birley who pin-pointed the problem.

'At the moment,' wrote Birley in July 1928, 'he is going through a mental crisis. I consider it almost inevitable that a boy with a mind as logical as his should experience very real religious difficulties. It is almost a sign of mental honesty. But while it is good that he should be honest in this, and that he should be ambitious, I hope he will not become too self-centred. There *is* a danger of this.'

Earlier that year Churchill had been treated to a display of his son's 'rabid Agnosticism' when Randolph provoked an argument with one of the guests at Chartwell. He 'more than defended his dismal position,' Churchill reported to his wife. 'The logical strength of his mind, the courage of his thought, & the brutal & sometimes repulsive character of his rejoinders impress me vy forcibly. He is far more advanced than I was at his age, & quite out of the common – for good or ill.' In the same letter Churchill speculated on his son's future. Given the boy's rapid development, his lively mind and independent attitudes, there was, he thought, every chance of Randolph making a career for himself 'in politics, at the bar, or in journalism.'

Churchill had good reason to give serious thought to his son's career. Later that year Randolph was due to sit his university entrance examinations and a decision would have to be made about his further education. Randolph, for his part, had no doubts as to what that decision should be: for over a year he had been nagging his father to allow him to go to Oxford. But Churchill had refused to entertain the idea. Until Randolph's progress at Eton improved, he argued, there could be no question of his going to university. That, as far as Churchill was concerned, settled the matter.

But Randolph did not give up so easily. He was accustomed to his father's periodic lectures and was more than capable of defending himself. 'During the time I was at school,' he admitted, a few years later, 'we had many differences of opinion. My father – and reasonably, as I thought – was always urging me to work harder and to reap the benefits of the education which he afforded me. I am afraid I showed myself incapable of taking his good advice.

'I used to have to invent all sorts of excuses, subterfuges, and palliatives to gloss over my scholastic failures ... Sometimes I reinforced my arguments by pointing to his own undistinguished academic career and observing that it did not appear to have materially hampered him. He had, after all, become Chancellor of the Exchequer without knowing more about mathematics than I did. This cogent argument was not, however, usually very well received.'

And so he continued his pleading to be sent to Oxford. He was still pleading as late as Christmas 1928, when he had only one term to complete at Eton. By that time he had passed his university entrance examination and saw no reason why he should be sent back to school for another four months. Professor Lindemann was staying at Chartwell that Christmas and, in the inevitable family rows, he tended to take Randolph's side. Convinced that he could procure a place for Randolph at his own college, Christ Church, he tried to persuade Churchill that – although it was the middle of the academic year – Randolph would be wise to take it. How successful his arguments were is uncertain. Outwardly Churchill seemed determined that Randolph should complete his schooling. Father and son were still bickering when the Prof returned to Oxford.

There is reason to think that Churchill was not as resolute as he appeared. He may even have privately agreed with Lindemann. That at least is the only conclusion to be drawn from Randolph's own account. He makes no mention of the family squabble and claims he was completely taken by surprise when, a week or so later, the Prof telephoned him to say that a place was available at Christ Church for the January term and, if he wanted it, he could be admitted immediately. Churchill, he says, was overjoyed by Lindemann's conniving. Obviously that is an exaggeration – there seems, in fact, to have been further bickering between father and son – but there can be no doubt that Churchill did finally relent. By the end of the month Randolph was snugly installed at Christ Church. 'I am so enjoying being here,' he wrote to his father, 'and I cannot tell you how glad I am that I did not have to return to Eton.'

CHAPTER THREE

A Little Learning

Randolph was no stranger to Oxford. As a schoolboy he had been
entertained at Christ Church by Professor Lindemann, had dined at
the High Table, drunk port in the Senior Common Room and mixed
freely with the dons. His striking good-looks, his friendship with
the Prof, and his standing as the son of the Chancellor of the
Exchequer, had made him a popular guest. Little effort had been
needed to include him in after-dinner conversation; he was always
completely at ease. With his lively intelligence and abounding
self-confidence, few could have doubted that young Randolph
Churchill would make his mark as an undergraduate. Certainly
Randolph had no doubts. His arrival at Christ Church, says
Christopher Hollis, was 'heralded by a great fanfare of trumpets
from the London press announcing that he proposed to attain the
Presidency of the Oxford Union in a shorter time than any other
undergraduate.'

His confidence was not inspired entirely by visits to the Senior
Common Room. He had friends among the undergraduates, many
of whom he had known as older boys at Eton. Others he had met at
Chartwell as sons of his father's political colleagues. Freddie
Furneaux and another friend, Seymour Berry, were at Christ
Church; Basil Ava – the future Marquess of Dufferin and Ava – was
at Balliol; James Lees-Milne was at Magdalen; and, two months
before Randolph's arrival, his cousin, Johnny Churchill, had been
admitted to Pembroke from Harrow. All things considered,
Randolph should have had no difficulty in settling into his new life.

Unfortunately things did not work out as expected. In many
ways, Oxford proved a harder nut for Randolph to crack than Eton.
There was, to start with, the disadvantage of arriving at Christ
Church in the Hilary Term. This, according to one of his tutors, set
him at odds with the other freshmen. 'Almost all undergraduates
arrive in Michaelmas Term (October) . . .' says Sir Roy Harrod,
recalling Randolph's early days at Oxford. 'Together they all have
to do a lot of things for the first time. They inquire of one another
and get to know one another while going through identical

experiences. You make quick friendships with those on your own stair or on neighbouring stairs. But if you come up in an odd term, the others have all settled down into their own friendships and do not pay much attention to a newcomer.'

Professor Lindemann, in his well-intentioned haste to secure Randolph a university place, had not forseen this difficulty. Nor, for that matter, did it seem to worry Randolph unduly. Thinking back on his time at Oxford, Randolph made light of having arrived in a 'by-term' and claimed that he deliberately chose to mix with the older undergraduates. 'I enjoyed picking their brains,' he declared. Sir Roy Harrod took a different view. The mistiming of Randolph's arrival seemed to Harrod, not merely a social drawback, but 'the biggest factor . . . that accounted for [Randolph's] failure to achieve all that he might have achieved in his subsequent life.' This is perhaps too sweeping a statement, but it does contain a grain of truth. There can be little doubt that Randolph's emotional isolation, both at Oxford and at Eton, affected his later attitudes, helped to distort his response to others and reinforced his tactless egotism. For, whether he liked it or not, he was distanced from undergraduates of his own age and consequently missed out on the intimacies, soul-searchings, criticism and confidences that strengthen youthful friendships. Such bonds are valuable to a young man's development and are rarely forged in later life.

But Randolph's disadvantage as a late-comer, was only one of his problems. Not being a sportsman and having no deep interest in the arts, he found it difficult to crash the more popular undergraduate sets. This was not for want of trying. At one time or another, he attempted to gain recognition both as a hearty and as an aesthete, but neither pose was successful.

His hopes as a sportsman rested largely on the golf lessons that he and his sister Diana had been given as children. Neither of them had mastered the game – according to their cousin Johnny, their performances on the local golf course were 'totally incredible' – and Randolph showed no inclination to improve his skills until he went to Oxford. Finding that golf was a fashionable sport at the university, he had no hesitation in accepting the challenges of experts. Bombastic as ever, he tried to impress his opponents but, apart from the odd fluke, failed dismally. He quickly abandoned the game. Even more disastrous was his attempt to prove himself as a rider. This too resulted from his determination to impress. Talking one day to an American undergraduate, Boy Scheftel, he confessed to feeling excluded and wondered what he could do to improve his popularity. Scheftel asked him whether he had any athletic abilities. Foolishly Randolph was tempted into boasting about his riding skills and was so convincing that Scheftel not only encouraged him to take part in a local point-to-point race but offered to pay for the hire of a horse. Randolph had no alternative but to accept. It was a grave mistake. He was thrown at the second fence in the first round and had to be rescued by a group of spectators. As he limped his way back to his rooms, badly bruised and bleeding, he was met by Freddie Furneaux and some other friends. 'Here comes Randolph,' sighed Furneaux. 'Unbowed but bloody as usual.'

Randolph's aesthetic pretensions, if not so disastrous, were equally ineffective. For the most part they consisted of cultivating young poets like John Betjeman, frequenting the rooms of the elegant Edward James, declaiming his favourite passages of prose and strolling about the quadrangle in the middle of the afternoon wearing a dressing-gown and nonchalantly puffing a cigar. None of this was bizarre enough to impress the arty set and merely confirmed the suspicions of those who considered him an exhibitionist.

'Everybody hated Randolph at Oxford – except me,' claims Sir Osbert Lancaster. 'I was always rather pro-Randolph. His nuisance value was unbelievable, the highest nuisance value I've ever come across – the rows he involved one in!'

Where Randolph did eventually find a niche of sorts, was on the fringe of a circle known, for want of a better term, as the 'smart bunch'. This was a group of undergraduates who, in the words of John Betjeman, 'were neither aesthetes nor hearties but above both . . . Most of them seemed to have known one another since nursery days. I would even go so far as to say that these people were above University.' They belonged to no particular college, were mostly older than Randolph, and included many of his boyhood friends and acquaintances. But it was common interests rather than a shared background – or perhaps the one acting on the other – that attracted Randolph to this coterie of rich and privileged young men. 'I can see now,' wrote John Betjeman in 1971, 'that what bound Randolph and this set of people together was politics. They were Ministers of State in embryo. The furious discussions Randolph used to have when voices grew louder and louder and tables were banged were about political personalities of the twenties. I did not know who they were then and am no surer now. I do recall that if ever his father was attacked in these discussions, Randolph spoke in his defence.'

This, for Randolph, was what Oxford was all about. Long before going to university he had decided to make politics his career; he regarded his academic education as a mere formality, a phase through which he was expected to pass before launching into the real world. He had not the slightest doubt about his future. Like his father, he saw himself as the bright new hope of a political dynasty and attached a superstitious significance to the fact that his birthday, the 28 May, was the same as that of William Pitt the Younger. 'If he could be Chancellor of the Exchequer at twenty-three and Prime Minister at twenty-five I saw no reason why I shouldn't do the same,' he argued. And Oxford was where he intended to start.

Making contacts, meeting the right people, mixing with the men who would be his political colleagues and arguing with his future opponents was of far greater importance to Randolph than any academic achievement. He refused to take his studies seriously. Within a matter of weeks after his arrival at Christ Church, he had argued furiously with his history tutor and transferred to Sir Roy Harrod in the hopes of being taught economics for the Final Honours School of Philosophy, Politics and Economics. But his hopes were as vague as his intentions were feeble. One of his proudest boasts at Oxford was that he never attended lectures and rarely opened a textbook. This was not merely an undergraduate pose: Randolph genuinely believed such activities were a waste of time. The labour of attending early morning lectures, he would say, did nothing to prepare one for the battle of life.

Far more instructive, and far more to his taste, were the luncheons he gave or attended three or four times a week. These luncheons, which invariably started with lobster and ended with a variety of ornamental puddings, were given by the 'smart bunch'. Usually beginning at one o'clock, they went on until late in the afternoon. A few carefully selected undergraduates and some of the younger, wittier dons would be invited; the food was provided by the college kitchens and lashings of wine accompanied every course. Eating, drinking, talking non-stop and quarrelling with anyone who was foolish enough to contradict him, Randolph discovered his role at university – and perhaps his role in life.

And there were other, less elevating, diversions. When he was not entertaining or being entertained, Randolph was usually to be found gambling and drinking in the rooms of the more rakish undergraduates. It was probably his love of what he archly called 'indoor sports' that ruined his chances at the Oxford Union. Certainly it contributed to the failure of his debut as a speaker. Having been heralded as an accomplished orator, a future President of the Union, great things were expected of Randolph in his first important Union debate. Paul Gore-Booth, who partnered him, seems to have shared the popular view of Randolph's talents and – having resigned himself to playing a minor role – was surprised when he himself stole the show. 'The Churchill debate was awkward,' says Gore-Booth, 'I consulted Randolph Churchill in his rooms in

Christ Church, but he was interested in a current game of poker; I borrowed a *Hansard* and went off and did some homework. As a consequence I made a better speech than he did and felt embarrassed.' His embarrassment was not shared by Randolph. Never one to accept defeat modestly, he blamed everyone but himself. 'There was an impression,' says Christopher Hollis in his history of the Oxford Union, 'that Mr Churchill thought – it is not very clear why – that he had been unfairly treated. He came back at the presidential debate and asked a number of questions of the President about the Society's heating system, culminating in the inquiry whether it was possible to introduce more hot air into the Chamber.'

Hot air was Randolph's speciality. He seemed to have no control over his tongue. He spoke as he thought, and once he started talking – whether across a dining table or in formal debate – he became so intoxicated with the sound of his own voice that he was oblivious to the response, or lack of response, from his audience. Sometimes amusing, often offensive, his waspish remarks were a constant source of embarrassment to his friends and associates. He was no respecter of persons and cared little what other people thought of him. Once, on meeting the Prince of Wales at a rugby match, he shocked Boy Scheftel by a singularly inept display of *lèse-majesté*. 'I warned Randolph not to be difficult,' says Scheftel, 'but, to my horror, heard him say to the Prince on being introduced, 'It's a bit disappointing to meet my future King by courtesy of an American.'

But if, on occasions, Randolph appeared tactless, inconsiderate and boorish, he was equally capable of giving the opposite impression. Some of the people who first met him at Oxford found him utterly charming. Christopher Sykes was one of them. 'He was remarkably handsome,' Sykes remembered, 'reflecting in a youthful, mannish way the beauty of his mother. He was polite, gay, and gentle. My first impression, a most misleading one I later found out, was of a modest, charming young man.'

This charm was not accidental: it was something that Randolph was learning to cultivate. If nothing else, Oxford taught him the value – if not the importance – of polite behaviour. He became more worldly, more polished and more adept at presenting himself in a good light.

The lessons he learnt had, of course, little or nothing to do with his formal education. For the most part he acquired his social skills on the fringes of the university: at those lengthy luncheons and at the houses of his more sophisticated friends. One of the houses he visited regularly was that of his godfather Lord Birkenhead, at Charlton, some twenty miles from Oxford. At the weekend Freddie

Furneaux would invite a group of undergraduates home for tennis, golf and riding and in the evening Lord Birkenhead would entertain them in the dining room. Conversation was always lively, the atmosphere light-hearted and the young men, braving Lord Birkenhead's caustic comments, would be encouraged to make after-dinner speeches. To the eighteen-year-old Randolph these occasions were sheer enchantment. They brought him in touch with a more relaxed world, broadened his views, sharpened his wits and expanded the life he had known at Chartwell. Unfortunately they also allowed him to indulge his already pronounced drinking habits. This was something of which his parents were soon to become aware.

Loelia, Duchess of Westminster, was to remember a revealing incident, involving Randolph and his father, which took place about this time. She gives no date but says that Randolph was still a youth when she and her husband travelled back to England with the Churchills after spending a few days in the south of France. The party had dinner, accompanied by red wine and champagne, on the train and after the meal Winston Churchill and the Duke of Westminster ordered double brandies. Randolph did the same. When the drinks arrived, however, Churchill put his foot down. He told Randolph he was far too young for brandy and forbade him to touch the drink. 'Nonsense, Father,' replied Randolph. 'Don't be ridiculous.' His defiance, according to the Duchess of Westminster, was followed by an unseemly struggle.

'Randolph picked up his glass,' she says. 'Winston seized his wrist. It was a great trial of strength which looked rather like that game when two people grasp hands with their elbows on the table and try to force each other's arms backwards. For several moments they stayed like that, the glass in the air between them, swaying to and fro, while everybody else in the restaurant-car watched, fascinated. Unfortunately the glass slipped and the double brandy spilled straight down Winston's sleeve.'

The Duchess of Westminster was to remember this as one of the rare occasions on which she saw Churchill try to assert his authority over his son. Like many others, she considered Churchill a little too indulgent, and many years later was to blame herself for having intervened when some guests at her country house threatened to duck Randolph in a lake. 'Had they been allowed to do as they wished,' she says in her memoirs, 'Randolph's whole career might have been different.'

*   *   *

In the ordinary way, physical force played little part in Randolph's squabbles with his father. Much as they might argue, bully one another, storm out of rooms in fits of temper, their clashes never went beyond verbal abuse. This is something of which Randolph was proud.

'One subject on which we have always agreed,' he wrote at the age of twenty, explaining his relationship with his father, 'has been in regard to corporal punishment. Like myself, he approves of it in general principle. But he has never practised this principle on me. I have always been in hearty agreement with him on this point. The fact that he has always agreed with me on this important and fundamental topic has no doubt added to the respect and admiration which I have for him. Owing to his vastly superior dialectical skill he has never really needed to resort to chastisement.'

This was written in a light-hearted newspaper article; but its bantering tone does not disguise Randolph's true feelings towards his father. For all their disagreements, the bond between Churchill and his son was secure. It was a bond which both strengthened and stunted Randolph's natural development. As a member of a proud and distinguished family he was always conscious of his place in the Churchill lineage, never doubted his abilities and was confident of his role in life. But by temperament he was a radical, an iconoclast, and all too often his urge to rebel was thwarted by his allegiance to the established order. Had he been born of humbler parentage, had he been forced to fight for recognition, he might have found an outlet for his rebellious instincts; as it was he was born into a world which his strong sense of family loyalty compelled him to defend. It was this conflict between his instincts and his affections – far more than any lack of physical chastisement – that blighted Randolph's career. Like his grandfather, Lord Randolph Churchill, he was never fully attuned to the political causes he espoused.

Of his passion for politics there could be no doubt. His claim that he was 'practically born on a political platform' was not an exaggeration. From his earliest years politics played an all-important part in his life. He was still at school when he became his father's confidant; Chartwell was a hive of political activity and his parents' friends and associates were all connected with politics in one way or another. Randolph's eagerness to keep abreast of political events – in 1926 he rigged up a secret wireless set in his room at Eton in order to follow the General Strike – amounted almost to an obsession. His views tended to be muddled, his talk was often indiscreet, but there was no mistaking the intensity he brought to political discussions. Douglas Jay, who first met Randolph at Oxford in 1929, was startled by his forthright opinions. He was, says Jay, 'the most physically attractive and mentally incoherent character I had yet encountered. He used to denounce Stanley Baldwin . . . with a ferocity that made me realize for the first time how little love was lost between Baldwin and his then Cabinet colleague, Winston Churchill.'

The early months of 1929 – the months following Randolph's arrival at Oxford – were of particular significance to the Churchill family. On 15 April, Winston Churchill delivered his fifth Budget and, as usual, Randolph was in the House of Commons with his mother and sister to witness the event. Churchill's speech lasted almost three hours and was widely acknowledged to be a witty, rivetting and adroit performance. The Budget itself, however, did little to soothe the misgivings of his political colleagues and opponents. Like his previous Budgets it was unimaginative, too closely aligned to orthodox financial thinking of the day to offer any real hope of overcoming the Government's economic difficulties. Already Stanley Baldwin, the Prime Minister, was under pressure to shift Churchill from the Treasury and replace him with Neville Chamberlain and now, with a general election in the offing, these pressures took on new force. A week or so after the Budget speech Leo Amery, the Colonial Secretary, wrote to Baldwin urging him to make the switch which, he said, would be worth at least twenty or thirty seats. Baldwin, however, decided against reshuffling the Cabinet before the election.

It may well have been a garbled version of this Cabinet hostility towards his father that provoked Randolph's rantings against the Prime Minister. Churchill himself does not appear to have been particularly worried by the rumours. He saw the forthcoming election as a straightforward battle between 'modern Conservatism' and Socialism. In an early campaign speech he prophesied that a victory for the Labour Party would result in widespread subversion and might lead to a second general strike. This was the theme of all his election speeches. His efforts to combat what he saw as the dangers of socialism included a meeting with Lloyd George to explore the possibility of Liberal support for a future Conservative Government. The meeting was inconclusive but word of it reached Churchill's Conservative opponents and increased their hostility towards him. Throughout the election campaign various Cabinet Ministers privately debated the question of what was to be done about Churchill.

In the weeks leading up to the election, Churchill was kept busy with his anti-socialist crusade. Most of his time was spent travelling about the country sounding what he called the 'alarm bells'. His wife, assisted by the children, was left to supervise the campaign in his own constituency. On one of his flying visits to Epping, however, Churchill heard Randolph make his first political speech. Unfortunately no record of this speech appears to have survived – it was made without notes – but Randolph's performance was judged a success. After speaking for twenty minutes to an audience of 2,000 he was publicly congratulated by his father.

'I have not had the pleasure of hearing him before,' Churchill is reported to have told the meeting, 'and from what I have heard I think I can say that after having fought and contested elections now for thirty years – this being my fourteenth – I can see at no great distance a moment when I shall be able to sit at home in comfortable retirement and feel that the torch which falls from my exhausted hands will be carried boldly forward by another.'

Messages of congratulations poured in from Churchill's friends and at a luncheon the following day a group of his political colleagues drank a toast to 'Randolph II'. Churchill, says Thomas Jones who was present, 'was very proud.' Later that same month, a couple of days before his eighteenth birthday, Randolph again took to the platform and addressed a women's meeting, chaired by his mother, at Wanstead.

Polling day was 30 May and that night Churchill joined Stanley Baldwin at 10 Downing Street to await the results. It was a disaster for the Conservatives. 'As Labour gain after Labour gain was announced,' noted the watching Thomas Jones, 'Winston became more and more flushed with anger . . . His ejaculations to the surrounding staff were quite unprintable.' The Epping result was not announced until the following day. Churchill was returned to his safe seat but without a clear majority over his two opponents. Nationally the Conservatives won 28 seats less than Labour, and the Liberals, with 59 seats, held the balance. A few days later Baldwin resigned and Ramsay MacDonald became Prime Minister for the second time.

Once again Churchill was without political office. During the weeks immediately following the election he busied himself researching the book he intended to write on the life of his famous ancestor, John Churchill, 1st Duke of Marlborough. His political activities were less inspiring. A further attempt to arrange a pact between the Conservatives and the Liberals was undermined by Neville Chamberlain's public opposition to Free Trade, and he clashed with the Conservative leadership when it gave tacit support to the Labour Government's decision to recall the British High Commissioner in Cairo and withdraw British troops from Egypt. Romantically dedicated as he was to the concept of Britain's civilizing role, Churchill regarded any threat to the fabric of Empire with the utmost suspicion. When he rose to attack the Labour

Government's actions in the House of Commons he was dismayed to find that he received no encouragement from his own party. Baldwin sat 'silent and disapproving' and a few Conservatives even joined in the protests which came from the Labour benches. The divisions which were to affect both his own and Randolph's political careers were already becoming apparent.

In 1929, however, Randolph's political career had hardly started. He had made an impressive speech at his father's election meeting but his enthusiasm was not matched by his experience. It was to further his son's worldly knowledge that, in August of that year, Churchill decided to take Randolph with him on a tour of Canada and the United States. According to Randolph's cousin Johnny, Churchill and his brother Jack had received an invitation from the Canadian Pacific Railway to tour Canada with their wives but, as neither Clementine Churchill nor Jack's wife was anxious to make the journey, the women's places were taken by Randolph and Johnny – both of whom were on vacation from Oxford.

The four men – or the 'Churchill troupe', as Johnny calls them – sailed from Southampton in the *Empress of Australia* on 3 August 1929.

✳   ✳   ✳

During this tour of north America, Randolph made one of his rare attempts to keep a diary. It is a very sketchy affair and the extracts he later published are obviously selective: they omit more than they admit and often they are at variance with other accounts of the trip. Randolph's concept of the truth was always subject to a little bending when discussing his own affairs, and his so-called diary, although not deliberately dishonest, is decidedly slanted. It would have been far more amusing had he been a little less discreet.

The voyage to Canada was uneventful to the point of boredom. Randolph found the other passengers extremely dreary and within a matter of days was longing for the friends he had left behind. He became restless and defied all his father's attempts to get him to keep regular hours and do some serious reading. Apart from sighting an iceberg at seven o'clock one morning, his only excitement came from a meeting with an attractive Canadian girl. How well this affair progressed he does not say, but it may well have accounted for his mysterious disappearance when the ship docked at Quebec. When the time came for the Churchill party to disembark there was no sign of Randolph; a search was made for him but he could not be found and the others had to leave the ship without him. 'Eventually,' says Johnny Churchill, 'he turned up at our hotel in a taxi with some wonderful excuse about being locked in a bathroom, and was thoroughly ticked off.'

Their short stay in Quebec was taken up with sight-seeing and meeting local dignitaries. The day before they left, they drove out into the country and Churchill was highly amused when Randolph, overcome by the beauty and serenity of the lakes and forests, suddenly expressed a desire to turn his back on society, build a house there and settle down to a rural existence. Indulgently his father advised him to see a little more of north America before making any rash decisions. Fortunately Randolph's whimsy did not last long. When, on the following day, they boarded the train which was to take them to Montreal, Randolph was enchanted by the luxurious accommodation provided by the Canadian Pacific Railway. Their ninety-foot private rail car was palatial – three bedrooms, two bathrooms, four lavatories, a sitting room, a dining room, a kitchen and an observation platform – there were fans in all the rooms, a powerful wireless set in the sitting room and refrigerators in the kitchen. By 1920s standards it was a marvel. Churchill described it to his wife as a 'land yacht' and Randolph, served by the resident cook and waiter, wondered whether it was possible to travel in greater comfort. The car, which could be attached to any passing train, was to be their home for the next three weeks. Randolph quickly forgot his vague yearnings for the primitive life.

In Montreal, Churchill made two speeches and Randolph was delighted to see that he did so without notes. He seems to have been unaware that his father had carefully prepared his speeches before leaving Quebec and took comfort in the thought that public speaking did not necessarily entail tedious rehearsal. 'Papa,' he noted in his diary, 'is gradually coming round to my point of view.' From Montreal they travelled on to Ottawa where they stayed for two nights with the Governor-General, Lord Willingdon, had lunch with Canada's bachelor Prime Minister, Mackenzie King – whom Randolph considered one of the most delightful men he had ever met – and attended a dinner-dance at Government House. Churchill addressed the Ottawa branch of the Canadian Club and was delighted by his enthusiastic reception. Writing to his wife, he was full of praise for Randolph who, he said, was a remarkable and appreciative critic of his speeches and was proving 'an admirable companion'. 'I think,' he added, 'he has made a good impression on everybody.'

That good impression did not last long. When they reached Toronto, on 16 August, Randolph made his first public gaffe. As they stepped off the train at seven o'clock that morning, they were met by a newspaper reporter who, rather inanely, asked Randolph what sound he had first heard on arriving. Understandably, Randolph brushed the man aside, saying he could not be bothered to answer 'silly questions'. That evening a paragraph in the local paper complained about Master Churchill's rudeness. 'Papa very angry with me,' Randolph recorded.

The 'silly questions' taunt pursued Randolph throughout his stay in Toronto. Scenting further indiscretions, reporters followed him about trying to provoke his anger. But Randolph refused to be provoked. He stayed close to his father's side and managed to fend off the reporters until his last day in Toronto. It was more mischance than misjudgement that, shortly after visiting Niagara Falls, he was trapped into an interview with the *Toronto Daily Star*.

The Churchill party were saying goodbye to their hosts, after a farewell luncheon at Government House, when Randolph was cornered by a determined young woman reporter. Having tricked him into thinking that she was a fellow guest, she proceeded to lambaste him with 'silly questions'. What did he think of the Niagara Falls? Would he like to live in Canada? Had he ever thought of taking a Canadian wife? Randolph, nonchalantly smoking a large cigar, proved adept at finding non-commital answers. Niagara Falls, he said, 'was quite up to his expectations.' He would like to live in Canada – if he had time. Unfortunately he had not met enough Canadian girls to say if he would marry one.

Not until the reporter tried a new line did Randolph become agitated. When asked whether he approved of women in politics, his answer was 'most emphatic'.

'No, I do not.'

'In this modern age. Why not?'

'Women in politics might be all right for a young country where historic procedure is not rooted deeply, but an old country like England where seriousness counts in parliament, the presence of women creates a certain lack of dignity. Women have as good minds as we, yes, but they do not fit in parliament.'

'So forty years hence when you are a statesman sitting in parliament, you can't see any women around?'

'Now that's a silly question.'

Realizing he had made a *faux pas*, he hurriedly tried to redeem himself. 'Don't you see how absurd it would sound in a newspaper,' he explained lamely, 'if I was reported as saying that I did not want to sit in parliament with women? Of course I do not mean that absolutely.'

But the reporter had her story and made the most of it. 'To be laughed at,' she observed slyly in her article, published two days after the Churchills left Toronto, 'is not the ambition of a young

Oxford student studying history and hoping to study law "in order to become a statesman." '

This was the first lengthy newspaper interview given by Randolph, but it is doubtful whether either he or his father saw it. By the time it appeared in the *Toronto Daily Star* the Churchills were in Winnipeg. This was probably just as well: Churchill would not have been happy about his son's politically inept remarks. Randolph might also have regretted being caught off-guard but it is unlikely that he would have regretted anything else. The views he expressed, at eighteen, about women in parliament were not to change much over the years. He belonged firmly to the school that considers women more effective as supporters of their husbands than as active politicians. As late as 1964 he was still maintaining that women had made a mistake in agitating for the vote and that Margot Asquith had greater political influence, as a Prime Minister's wife, than did Nancy Astor as the first woman MP to enter the House of Commons. According to his unlikely friend, Michael Foot – who took a very different view – Randolph was a 'raging, rampaging male chauvinist long before the term had ever been considered sexually apposite.'

If Churchill was unaware of some of Randolph's indiscretions, he was becoming more and more aware of his virtues as a companion. This tour of North America was the longest period father and son had spent together and, as they crossed Canada, they became increasingly conscious of their fondness for each other. Randolph's diary was devoted largely to his father's comments and witty observations and Churchill's letters to his wife were full of the support he received from Randolph. Whatever differences they may have had were quickly forgotten. Churchill could never stay angry with his son for long. Even when chiding him for his bad reports from Eton he had been apt to soften his criticism with stories of his own unfortunate experiences at Harrow. Now, with the horrors of school behind them, they met on a more equal footing and revelled in their shared delights. 'I love him very much,' Churchill confessed to his wife.

When not attending official functions, the Churchill 'troupe' – wearing the ten-gallon stetson hats presented to them in Quebec – spent their time exploring the surrounding country. Randolph and Johnny bathed in the lakes or joined Jack Churchill on a fishing expedition while Churchill painted; and the entire party came together for the early morning pony rides. At Calgary they toured the oilfields, at Banff they spent a few days in a lakeside chalet and at Vancouver they visited a lumber camp – where Randolph made a brave attempt to climb a tree with the help of steel spurs, a belt and a rope. 'It was really quite easy,' he noted in his diary, 'but I doubt if I could wield an axe.'

At almost every stop Churchill was obliged to make a speech or two. Occasionally Randolph was called upon to say a few words – or would interject with a few pithy observations of his own – and his father was delighted by his obvious self-confidence. 'He speaks so well,' Churchill told his wife, 'so dextrous, cool and finished.' There were times, however, when Randolph's ease of manner proved disconcerting. More than one pompous local dignitary was deflated by his caustic remarks and, if rumour is to be believed, his flaunting of convention on one occasion produced a particularly embarrassing result.

Anecdotes about Randolph's outrageous behaviour are legion: some are suspect, others exaggerated, and those told about his youthful escapades are often based on hearsay – but a few are worth retelling. For, true or not, they became part of the legend from which Randolph derived his colourful reputation. One such story was told about this Canadian tour.

The Churchills, it is said, were entertained in a large hall at one of the towns they visited. A formal luncheon was arranged and Randolph and his father, as guests of honour, were seated at a table on a raised platform at the far end of the hall. The meal was lengthy and the speeches interminable. As speaker after speaker droned on, Randolph was alarmed to find himself trapped: however urgent his need to leave the table, he could not do so without creating an upheaval. He endured his discomfort as long as he could. Then, having reached bursting point, he gathered all the empty champagne glasses within reach and lined them up. One by one the glasses disappeared beneath the table to be returned brimming with liquid which looked like, but was decidedly not, champagne. Blatantly obvious as was this manoeuvre, it was made even more obvious by the fact that the table-cloth was so short that the legs of those sitting on the platform could be clearly seen by those below. Apparently Randolph's impromptu performance stole the show. Whatever the truth of this story, his friends had no difficulty in believing it.

The Churchills spent their last day in Canada at Victoria, on the west coast. They arrived there from Vancouver on the morning of 6 September. After attending a luncheon at the Canadian Club – where Churchill was given a 'rapturous reception' and Randolph's witty, five minute speech was wildly applauded – they devoted the rest of the day to salmon fishing. Randolph, envious of his uncle Jack who had landed a ten-pounder, was terribly disappointed when the three fish that took his line all managed to break the hook and escape. He was consoled by his father. ' 'Tis better to have hooked,'

Churchill assured him, 'than never hooked at all.'

Their Canadian journey was over. Reflecting on his experiences, Randolph had mixed feelings. The Canadians had been warm, loyal, friendly and generous. He was impressed by their determination to remain independent from the United States. There was, he thought, a lamentable lack of culture and he found some aspects of Canadian life crude, but he admired the vigour and enterprise of the young and rapidly developing nation. With the condescension of an eighteen-year-old, he admitted to sharing his father's optimism about Canada's future.

These thoughts were duly recorded in his diary. 'We are now,' he noted later that evening, 'on the ship bound to Seattle, American soil and Prohibition.'

*   *   *

Prohibition was uppermost in Randolph's mind as the ship carrying the 'Churchill troupe' glided into Puget Sound. Before leaving Vancouver he and his father had consulted the Chief of Police about the prospects of survival in a liquorless America. They had been told not to worry. To Randolph's astonishment, the Chief of Police had personally undertaken to telephone his counterpart in Seattle and arrange for a supply of drinks to be put on the Churchill train when they arrived in America. Even so, Randolph decided to take no chances. Unknown to his father, he filled a large flask with whisky and a smaller one with brandy; to make doubly sure he then poured the remains of the two spirits into medicine bottles. With these reserves hidden in his attaché-case and the knowledge that his father carried a diplomatic visa, signed by the American ambassador in London, he felt well-equipped to brave the parched New World. All the same he remained uneasy.

His fears were only partly realized. When the American Customs officials boarded the ship they brusquely waved aside Churchill's credentials and insisted on a thorough search of the luggage. This infuriated Churchill. Waving his visa, he demanded an explanation. 'We are looking,' said one of the officials, 'for guns and ammunition.' The idea that they were being treated as gangsters stunned the entire party. 'My uncle,' says Johnny, 'got so angry I thought he would explode.' But the Customs men were unmoved. As Churchill strode about muttering 'Monstrous! Absolutely monstrous!' they continued their search until they were satisfied. Luckily they stopped before Randolph's attaché-case was opened.

Actually there had been no reason for Randolph to worry. As far as liquor was concerned, the Customs men were not so much interested in private consumers as they were in profiteering boot-leggers. This was explained to the Churchills by the apologetic official who accompanied them to their hotel where he further astonished them by happily accepting drinks from the hotel manager.

Not so happy was Randolph's first brush with the American press. On leaving the ship he was again confronted by an attractive young woman reporter. 'Do we see you now or on the train?' she asked brightly. 'I'm not sure you see us at all,' snapped Randolph. His politically astute father was more amenable. When the girl followed them to the train, Churchill not only agreed to a ten-minute interview but, to Randolph's annoyance, appeared completely captivated. His example did nothing to soften Randolph's churlish attitude. As the girl was leaving, she tackled him again. Was he, she wanted to know, going to marry an American wife? To this 'silly question' Randolph retorted that he had no intention of revealing his matrimonial plans and walked off in a huff. That evening he noted in his diary that reporters should realize that interviews were a favour, not an obligation. He was never to appreciate the value of polite public relations.

Travelling across America was more arduous than travelling in Canada. The Churchills missed their luxurious private rail-car. From Seattle they journeyed by train to Grant's Pass in Oregon and then transferred to a motor car. The drive to California took them along the celebrated Redwood Highway and both Randolph and his father were enchanted by the size and beauty of the gigantic trees. 'The road is an aisle in a cathedral of trees', observed Churchill. 'Enormous pillars of timber tower up to 200 ft without leaf or twig to a tapering vault of sombre green and purple.' They stopped to picnic under one of the tallest trees. Randolph and Johnny bathed in the nude and after lunch they were joined by a group of naval officers. To test the width of the tree they made an experiment. Several men pressed themselves against the trunk, spread their arms and joined hands. They were amazed to find that it took fourteen of them to complete the circle.

The further they drove, the more sceptical they became about the Prohibition laws. On their second day they stopped for lunch at the house of an expatriate Frenchman who was authorized to supply wine to the churches for sacramental purposes. His cellars were stocked with over a million gallons and he told them that he sold about two hundred thousand gallons a year. In addition to this he supplied the locals with unfermented grape-juice and then sent men to ferment it. 'So Christ,' noted Randolph, 'has come to the aid of Bacchus in a most wonderful way.'

Arriving in San Francisco they discovered that Bacchus reigned supreme. When Randolph and Johnny attended a dinner-dance in one of the largest hotels, they were served cocktails in a private room but champagne was drunk openly at dinner in the ballroom. Prohibition, Randolph decided, was nothing but a farce. Only at official or semi-official functions was the law strictly observed. Even then Randolph and Johnny were able to help their parents through a non-alcoholic meal by lacing their coffee with generous dashes of whisky or brandy from their secret stock.

Most of their time in San Francisco was taken up with sight-seeing. At Churchill's insistence they were taken on a tour of the famous Seal Rocks and later drove out to inspect the Lick Observatory. Randolph has nothing to say about these visits. His attention was far more readily caught by the delightful Mrs Russell, a married daughter of one of their hosts. Unfortunately Mrs Russell's main topic of conversation was stocks and shares and, somewhat characteristically, Randolph found that her talk tended to cloud her charms. Women who engaged in financial speculations were, in his opinion, every bit as outlandish as women politicians. He consoled himself by going for an early morning ride with another married woman whom he picked up at the dinner-dance. Randolph was developing a decided *penchant* for married women.

After leaving San Francisco, the Churchills drove on to San Simeon where they stayed for four days in the fabulous mock-castle of that equally fabulous newspaper mogul, William Randolph Hearst. This visit had been arranged some months earlier with the help of Churchill's American stock-broker friend, Bernard Baruch. Churchill had written to Hearst at Baruch's suggestion and Hearst had replied with a 'pleasant invitation'. But, for all the polite formalities, the meeting between Churchill and Hearst was half-expected to prove explosive. A powerful and rich meglomaniac, Hearst – on whom the film *Citizen Kane* was based – was a notorious critic of Britain and at that time his newspapers were conducting a particularly virulent anti-British campaign. Any encounter between the patriotic British statesman and the hostile American newspaperman was bound, it was thought, to be contentious. Surprisingly, it was not. Hearst was courtesy itself and Churchill found him to be a solemn, almost childlike, eccentric. Both men were on their guard but, by the end of the visit, Randolph was quite certain that Hearst had been won over by his father's charm.

All the Churchills were suitably impressed by the Hearst mansion. This huge, white stone castle, of no known period, stood on a hill some three miles from the sea and had been designed by Hearst himself. Johnny thought the main building was copied from a Spanish church and Randolph likened it to a cathedral – although two Moorish towers were among its more notable features. Inside it was crammed with art treasures brought over from Europe, or copied from originals – pictures, furniture, tapestries and statues amassed with more enthusiasm than taste – and the carefully guarded grounds were a reserve for a weird assortment of wild animals. The total effect, says Johnny, was 'unbelievable'. Randolph was no less impressed by the fact that the contents of the castle were insured for sixteen million dollars and that Hearst's reputed income was twenty million dollars.

Among the other twenty odd guests were a number of pretty girls but it was Hearst's daughter-in-law who first caught Randolph's eye. Her husband he dismissed as a 'fat oaf' and in no time he had involved the exquisite young woman in one of his gambling ventures. Much to his delight they both won eighty dollars. Flirting with the female guests became a matter of rivalry between Randolph and Johnny. Churchill watched their progress indulgently and was highly amused when Johnny managed to steal one of Randolph's more desirable conquests. His amusement, however, did not extend to their nocturnal activities. The guests were housed in bungalows dotted about the grounds and one night Randolph and Johnny decided to invade the sleeping quarters of two of the more amenable girls. They forced the window of one of the bungalows and it was not until Randolph had climbed through that they realized their mistake. In the darkness their geography had become confused and Randolph, as he quickly discovered, had landed in his father's bedroom. 'Blasted by a withering reprimand,' says Johnny, 'we both retired feeling very sheepish and fed up.'

Not all the windows at San Simeon opened into Churchill's bedroom, however. One of Randolph's proudest boasts in later life was that it was at the Hearst mansion that he first slept with a woman. The accommodating lady, he claimed, was not one of the flirtatious younger guests whom he and Johnny pursued but the beautiful and more experienced Viennese dancer, Tilly Losch. The truth of this, however, is uncertain. Edward James, who later married Tilly Losch, maintains that Randolph and Tilly did not start their affair until much later. He claims that it was in the early 1930s that his housekeeper surprised Randolph and Tilly 'having it off on a sofa' in his London house. But he might not have known about San Simeon. Whatever the truth, it seems that Randolph was successful in seducing a young woman at the Hearst mansion: about that he was quite adamant.

The one woman the Churchills did not meet at San Simeon was Hearst's film-star mistress, Marion Davies. For the duration of their visit, Hearst had prudently banished the flamboyant Miss Davies to her beach house at Santa Monica and summoned his estranged wife, Millicent, from New York to act as hostess. This polite deception was quickly abandoned once the formal reception was over. At the end of their four day stay, the Churchills were driven by Hearst to Los Angeles and installed in the 'plush' Biltmore hotel as guests of a well-known banker, James R. Page. But it was Marion Davies's exotic seaside villa, with its huge heated swimming pool and black marble bathrooms, that became the centre for their social activities.

The week Randolph and Johnny spent in Hollywood was the highspot of their American tour. Shortly after they arrived, Hearst told them to draw up a list of all the film-stars they would like to meet so that he could arrange a banquet. It was the first of many similar entertainments. Starting with a crowded celebrity luncheon at the Metro-Goldwyn-Mayer studios – where a twenty-piece orchestra and twenty five chorus girls competed with the star entertainers – they were rushed from public functions to private dinner tables, from hectic parties to camera-popping first nights, and ushered through a bewildering maze of film sets and studios throughout their stay. With the exception of the always elusive Greta Garbo, they met and were entranced by all the reigning Hollywood stars – Joan Crawford, Pola Negri, Bessie Love, Anita Page, Bebe Daniels, Ramon Novaro, Douglas Fairbanks Jnr and Wallace Beery – as well as a host of aspiring actresses of whom they had never heard but whom Randolph found 'infinitely more attractive than the best in London.'

Of all the beautiful women he met, Randolph – always drawn to another man's partner, be she wife or mistress – was most enamoured of Marion Davies. Blonde, blue-eyed and vivacious, the lovely Miss Davies seemed to epitomize all the brittle glamour of Hollywood. Not that this prevented Randolph from joining Johnny in pursuit of the many desirable, often available, young starlets. Deftly shaking off their parents, they had a marvellous time flirting with some of the lesser-known actresses and felt extremely dashing as they greeted chorus girls by kissing their hands 'continental style'. (They were somewhat startled when Churchill gallantly followed their example on parting from Marion Davies.)

Hollywood was then approaching its hey-day: the atmosphere was frenetic, most entertainments decidedly vulgar and the endless round of parties exhausting. Even the resilient Churchill was slightly confused by the dazzle of it all. 'You motor ten miles to luncheon in one direction,' he wrote incredulously, 'and ten miles to dinner in another. The streets by night are ablaze with electric lights and moving signs of every colour. A carnival in fairyland.' To obtain

58

a little breathing space they spent one day relaxing at Santa Barbara and another deep-sea fishing from Hearst's yacht off Santa Catalina Island, but always they returned to Hollywood.

Not everything they saw came up to expectations. Harold Lloyd proved disappointingly ordinary off-screen and they quickly became bored touring the studios. After a while, they found, one film set tended to look very like another. An exception was the visit they paid to Charlie Chaplin on the set of *City Lights*. Both Randolph and his father were captivated by the jaunty little comedian. They had first met him at Marion Davies's house and Churchill, although critical of Chaplin's 'bolshy' political views, had sat talking to him until three in the morning. 'He was too sweet for words,' noted Randolph in a hurried diary entry.

Chaplin was equally impressed. He was to describe Randolph, rather pompously, as 'a handsome stripling of sixteen [*sic*], who was escurient for intellectual argument and had the criticism of intolerant youth. I could see Winston was very proud of him. It was a delightful evening in which father and son bantered about inconsequential things.'

On their return journey across America, the Churchills again enjoyed the luxury of private railcars. After leaving Los Angeles they drove by motor car to the Yosemite National Park where they boarded a train, to which a coach – provided by Charles Schwab, head of the Bethlehem Steel Corporation – was attached. In this coach they travelled to Chicago – stopping on the way at the Grand Canyon, where Randolph and Johnny thoroughly alarmed their fathers by standing on their heads at what appeared to be the edge of the canyon – and then completed the journey to New York in another private coach belonging to Churchill's friend, Bernard Baruch.

They arrived in New York at the beginning of October, after almost two months of continuous travelling. A few days later Churchill and his brother left for Washington, intending to tour the Civil War battlefields. But for Randolph and Johnny the holiday was over. They were both due back at Oxford for the Michaelmas term and after spending a week in New York, sampling various night clubs and a rather tame speak-easy, they sailed for England in the *Berengaria*. Randolph's godfather, Lord Birkenhead, was also on the ship and the homeward voyage was a lively one. According to Johnny, Randolph enjoyed himself stalking a fifteen-year-old Dutch girl throughout the six-day crossing; Randolph, on the other hand, gives the impression that his time was largely devoted to trying to make good his losses at the bridge table. Lord Birkenhead, it seems, cheerfully approved of both activities.

CHAPTER FOUR

The Youthful Ambassador

The American tour did nothing to stabilise Randolph. If anything it made him more restless. It could hardly have done otherwise. Travelling with his father had been a heady experience. For two months he had basked in Churchill's limelight: with very little effort on his part, he had been invited onto public platforms, entertained by the rich and the powerful, pursued by the press, questioned, listened to, applauded and fawned over. Few eighteen-year-old undergraduates achieve recognition so easily; even fewer – and certainly not an ambitious, readily flattered youngster like Randolph – return to the demands of university life without a sense of anti-climax. Oxford must indeed have seemed dreary after two months of high-living. 'Despite the devotion with which he applied himself to making his life at Oxford one of pleasure,' says his friend Boy Scheftel, 'it became plain to me by the end of the spring term [1930] that Randolph was bored.'

To relieve his boredom, he sought out new friends, indulged in extravagant entertainments, gambled heavily and escaped to London whenever he could. His recollections of the period immediately after his return from America are mostly social. He tells of sneaking off to the Derby, in morning coat and top hat, and being caught out there by his father; of driving to Bath with Brendan Bracken to take part in a political campaign and creeping back to Oxford armed with a medical certificate from Bracken's doctor to excuse his over-night absence; of ducking lectures and failing his preliminary examinations; and of entertaining well-known actresses in his rooms.

One of these actresses was the bizarre and beautiful Tallulah Bankhead, who was invited to Oxford by the University Balloon Club to make the first ascent in a newly acquired balloon. The much publicized ascent turned into a fiasco but Randolph afterwards invited Miss Bankhead to his rooms and arranged to see her in London. Surprised at the readiness with which she agreed to his vaguely proposed date, he was disappointed, on arriving at her Farm Street house, to find that she had forgotten all about it and was surrounded by a throng of admirers. But Randolph was nothing if not persistent; eventually he persuaded the husky-voiced actress to allow him to escort her to a bottle party. This posed a problem: by the time he had discovered exactly what was meant by a 'bottle party' it was too late for Randolph to buy a bottle. He had to improvise. At the time he was staying in Seymour Berry's house and there, after much searching, he discovered a decanter of whisky. Deciding he could not take the decanter, he scoured the house for a more suitable container and finally found a huge bottle of hair lotion which he emptied, washed, and refilled with whisky. He then set off, determined to seduce Miss Bankhead. But luck was not with him. No sooner had they arrived at the party than his 'girl for the night' was whisked off by a new pack of admirers and Randolph was left standing alone. Disconsolately he slipped his hair lotion bottle onto a table – hiding it behind a more respectable display of liquor – and went home. Chasing popular actresses in London was obviously a very different sport from being chased by unknown chorus girls in Hollywood.

More rewarding was the meeting he had about this time with Evelyn Waugh. Precisely where, when or even how he was introduced to the young novelist is a matter of contention. In his account of his early years, *Twenty One Years*, Randolph says he was taken to meet Waugh – then writing his second novel, *Vile Bodies*, after the success of *Decline and Fall* two years earlier – by their mutual friend Basil Ava and that the meeting took place outside a small country inn in a Cotswold village. Waugh disagreed. 'I am pretty sure,' he wrote after reading Randolph's book, 'we first met at Diana Guinness's bedside in Buckingham Street.' Diana Guinness was, of course, the former Diana Mitford and when she published her memoirs she gave yet another version of the meeting. She says that when her son Jonathan was born in March 1930, she asked both Randolph and Waugh to act as godfathers and they 'met for the first time at the font.' Whoever is right, there can be no doubt that the eighteen-year-old Randolph and the twenty-six-year old Evelyn Waugh met sometime in the spring of 1930. It was, as Diana Mitford rightly observes, the beginning of a 'stormy friendship.'

Randolph does not feature in Waugh's diary until June of that year. The first mention of him is typical. At a party which Waugh attended in Oxford, Randolph distinguished himself by throwing a cocktail in the face of one of the woment guests and was seen off by 'masses of young men in Bullingdon ties'. A few days later Waugh and Randolph were again guests at a party – in London this time, given by Diana Guinness – and finished up drunk and rowdy, fighting each other in the servants' hall. The spectacle of these two

61

pugnacious egocentrics slogging it out – either physically or verbally – was to become all too familiar to their friends. That their extraordinary love-hate relationship lasted, on and off, until Waugh's death thirty-six years later was almost as astonishing as the relationship itself.

Another gossipy diarist whom Randolph met on his London sprees was Robert Bruce Lockhart. A former diplomat turned journalist, Lockhart had recently taken over as chief diary-writer for the *Evening Standard*'s regular feature 'Londoner's Diary' and was recognized as a shrewd and well-informed observer of the political and social scene. With an eye for political eccentrics, he was quick to recognize young Randolph's potential. 'Met Randolph Churchill – Winston's son,' he noted in his private diary, on 13 April 1930. 'He is a good-looking boy with fair hair and distinguished features rather marred by a spotty complexion. Talks nineteen to the dozen and is a kind of gramophone to his father. Very egocentric and conceited and therefore very unpopular. I rather liked him.' After listening to Randolph's unbridled criticism of the Beaver-brook and Rothermere press, Lockhart liked him even more. 'This is pure Winston,' he purred delightedly.

The combination of 'pure Winston' and far-from-pure Randolph was irresistible: few political commentators were, over the years, to record the fluctuating fortunes of father and son with more relish than Robert Bruce Lockhart.

Randolph's lack of popularity was emphasized when Lockhart met Freddie Furneaux a few months later. Always on the look-out for gossip, Lockhart pressed Furneaux – whom he considered a modest and intelligent young man – for news of his fellow undergraduates. He was rewarded by a tirade against Randolph. 'He is very down on young Randolph Churchill,' runs Lockhart's diary entry for 10 August, 'and thinks he will do no good. Winston was always a worker. Randolph does not know what work means.'

Freddie Furneaux was not the only one prophesying a dismal future for Randolph. Churchill was also becoming increasingly concerned about his son's fecklessness. Whether he realized the full extent of Randolph's gadding about – not to mention his mounting debts, which were estimated to be between £600 and £700 – is not certain, but he knew enough to be disturbed. Churchill was in no mood to countenance his son's frivolity: he was weighed down with his own financial worries.

Before leaving America, Churchill had returned to New York and, while there, had witnessed the results of the disastrous Wall Street crash. He had not escaped unscathed himself. According to his daughter, he had speculated on the American stock-market and lost a 'small fortune' when the market collapsed. He was hoping to restore part of this fortune with the contracts he had signed for a series of articles – articles which were to earn him £40,000 – but, as he told his wife, completing the contracts required hard work. In the early months of 1930, industry and economy were the watchwords at Chartwell. They were words which Churchill found impossible to apply to his son.

There is reason to suppose that Randolph would have liked to follow his father's example. A series of newspaper articles would certainly have relieved his own financial problems and he had long regarded journalism – or some form of writing – as an attractive stop-gap in a political career. The only drawback was his failure to interest editors. His frustration was obvious to all his friends. 'I may not at this stage of my career,' he complained to Frank Pakenham who, having taught him briefly at Eton, came to know him better at Oxford, 'be armed at every point with the equipment of my best contemporaries but I possess to an extent that none of them can begin to equal this overwhelming desire to express myself. And the tragedy of it all is that I have nothing in the whole wide world to express. I am like an explosion that goes off and leaves the house standing.'

That was one way of putting it. Like all exhibitionists Randolph loved to over-dramatize his real or imaginary short-comings. It was an easy way of attracting attention to himself, of hinting at hidden talents. His more sceptical friends must have grown heartily sick of his breast beating. One of his more persistent boasts at this time was that he could write a great book if only he could find the right subject. It was not an unusual boast for an aspiring writer and hardly warrants the significance placed upon it later by some of his friends. Randolph was merely making excuses. What he lacked as an undergraduate was not inspiration but application. The hard grind of writing, the need for sustained effort, entailed too much sacrifice, at this stage of his career, for him to contemplate writing a book. He would have been only too ready to settle for a few lucrative newspaper articles.

Few, and certainly not those subjected to his finger-wagging monologues, could have taken his claim that he had nothing to express seriously. Randolph held strong opinions on most subjects and was only too eager to voice them. His tendency to monopolize conversations, to glory in the sound of his own voice, to argue, pick quarrels, pass judgements and talk other people down was probably his most notable and enduring characteristic. Heads spun, jaws sagged and eyes glazed once Randolph was launched on a subject of his own choosing. 'He possesses,' wrote a bemused contemporary, 'what the Americans call a "wide open talk valve" and should be prosecuted by the R.S.P.C.A. for removing more hind legs from donkeys than anyone else since the Tower of Babel.' Not surprisingly it was his gift of the gab rather than his vague literary aspirations that eventually rescued him from debt and despondency.

*   *   *

'A fair haired handsome youth 18 years of age,' reported a correspondent of the *New York Times* on 21 February 1930, 'electrified the audience at the Oxford Union debate tonight by launching a smashing attack on the proposed Anglo-Egyptian treaty for which he used all the colourful rhetoric and manners of Winston Churchill. He was Randolph Churchill, son of the former Chancellor of the Exchequer.'

The prominence given to this report in a leading New York newspaper was as remarkable as it was fortuitous. It appeared in what Randolph called the 'silly season' – when news is invented, rather than made – and followed a lead given by the British press. A similar report had appeared in the *News Chronicle* under the heading 'Reporting a Parliament of Youth' and several London papers had carried the item as a matter of course. But such are the vagaries of fate that it was these chance reports – particularly that which appeared in the *New York Times* – that were to have a decisive effect on Randolph's career. The 'silly season' had produced what his Oxford tutors considered a silly solution to his problems.

The debate itself had not, in all truth, warranted the publicity. It caused no stir in the annals of the Oxford Union. At the time, however, Randolph regarded it as an opportunity to redeem his earlier failure as an orator. The subject chosen for the debate was one on which he felt well qualified to speak. The Labour Government's Egyptian policy had been well aired in the Churchill household. Not only had his father roundly condemned it in the House of Commons before embarking on his American tour but had repeatedly returned to it during the tour. Soon after the Churchills had arrived in Quebec, they had been informed by telegram of the British Foreign Secretary's decision to include the demands of Egyptian nationalists in a new Anglo-Egyptian treaty. This, as Randolph noted in his diary, had upset Churchill considerably: the treaty, he had predicted, was bound to lead to 'grave trouble' in Egypt. His warnings were echoed by Randolph in the Union debate.

'Egypt's interests,' he growled, in a fair imitation of his father, 'demand as strongly as our own that British forces should not be

64

withdrawn from Egypt. Under British control Egypt has attained a measure of order and well-being greater than it has experienced in the last 2,000 years. What guarantee is there that Egypt will preserve such a condition once our control is withdrawn? Not only is it because of our duty of protecting foreigners, but of protecting the Egyptians themselves that we remain to guard them against the inevitable tyranny of the Pashas.'

This stirring defence of benevolent despotism was, as Robert Bruce Lockhart might have remarked, 'pure Winston.' It went straight to the Imperialist hearts of Randolph's audience. 'Not only the speech,' says the *New York Times* report, 'but the personality of the speaker impressed the Union which is always critical of budding reputations. As the students left for their rooms it was freely predicted that young Mr Churchill should have a brilliant career in the Conservative party and would probably leave his mark on British politics.'

Not all the Tory students were predicting as rosy a future for Randolph. Earlier Quintin Hogg (the future Lord Hailsham), a Baldwin supporter, had tried to have the debate adjourned on the grounds that it was not in the national interest for the Union to criticize such a serious Imperial issue. Thanks to some timely advice from Lord Birkenhead, Randolph had managed to defeat the adjournment motion and Quintin Hogg had angrily left the hall. But this factional hostility was not without significance. In proclaiming his father's unpopular views, Randolph was attracting the wrath of his father's opponents. This was to play a greater part in determining his future in the Conservative party than his isolated triumph in the Oxford Union.

Such considerations did not bother Randolph at the time. It was his immediate prospects that he was concerned with and it was those prospects which were directly affected by the debate. A week or so later he received an exciting, and totally unexpected, offer. It came from the head of a well-known American lecture agency, William B. Feakins Inc., who, having read the report in the *New York Times,* wrote inviting him to make a lecture tour of the United States. Randolph had no hesitation in accepting. The proposed fee was generous, he was free to choose his own subjects and his audiences were guaranteed. What more could he ask? Living as he was on an allowance of £400 a year, weighed down with debts, bored with Oxford and longing to express himself, he saw the lecture tour as the answer to all his problems.

What his father thought of Mr Feakins' proposal is another matter. In his book *Twenty One Years,* Randolph was to claim that Churchill – after warning him to prepare his lectures – encouraged him to embark on the venture. But once again his memory is at fault. Shortly after returning from the tour he gave a very different version. 'My father,' he wrote somewhat more truthfully, 'has always felt, and he has repeatedly told me, that I should equip myself with an adequate body of knowledge before exposing myself to this harsh and competitive world. He would, indeed, have liked me to spend another two years at Oxford, rather than go and tell the Americans all my varied and illuminating views on life. However, I won my way over that, and am still as uneducated as ever.' This corroborates the impression gained by his Oxford tutor, Sir Roy Harrod, who was to recall his own disappointment when Randolph applied for leave of absence. 'I congratulated him, but urged him not to go,' says Sir Roy. 'I very much wanted Randolph to complete his degree. I felt that he had a certain pride that would make him *wish* to get a good class.' Harrod also remembers spending a weekend at Chartwell and listening to Churchill trying to persuade his son to give up the American tour. For the best part of an evening, he says, Churchill, in his most eloquent vein, lectured Randolph on the merits of a university education, pointing out the value of academic training and regretting his own lack of formal scholarship. But it was no use. Throughout his father's discourse, Randolph lounged on a sofa looking bored and sceptical. 'He was obviously unshaken in his resolve to go out to the U.S.A.' Sir Roy remembered.

Certainly Randolph received no encouragement from his mother. Clementine Churchill had no illusions about her feckless son and knew that once he interrupted his studies he would never return to Oxford to take his degree. She was against the 'hair-brained' scheme from the very outset. Time was to prove her objections well founded.

But, whatever his parents might think, Randolph's mind was made up. He prided himself on his independence and, having decided to accept Mr Feakins' offer, considered the matter closed. Churchill does appear to have had second thoughts as the time approached for Randolph to leave. Not only did he provide his son with letters of introduction to influential Americans but wrote to his New York publisher, Charles Scribner, requesting that Randolph be supplied with twenty copies of his recently published memoirs, *My Early Life*, to give to anyone who was kind to him on his travels. The publicity given to the lecture tours, thought Churchill, might help the sales of the book. It could have been this pleasing thought that finally took the edge off paternal disapproval.

Randolph claims he left for America within a few weeks of receiving Mr Feakins' offer: in fact he did not sail until eight months later. Surprisingly he makes no mention of an important event that took place during that waiting period. On 13 July his first full length newspaper article was published in the *Sunday Dispatch.* Written, one suspects, with greater artifice than ardour it was headed 'Youth Challenges the Church' and featured on the leader page.

The views expressed in the article are hardly original. Given Randolph's loudly proclaimed agnosticism, they cannot be taken seriously. He attacked the stodginess of church leaders, pleaded for a new and more vigorous approach to religion and lamented the estrangement of young people from the church. 'The newspapers point to the empty churches,' he argued; 'Bishops assail youth with charges of levity and cynicism. But, in fact, the post-war generation is more genuinely Christian in its ethical standpoint than either the bishops or even themselves would have us imagine.'

A few weeks earlier Randolph had celebrated his nineteenth birthday and the article reflects his age and ambitions rather than his convictions. For all that, it can be said to mark his debut as a journalist and, as journalism played an important part in his life, it deserves a mention.

Apart from this small triumph, Randolph achieved little else between the Oxford Union debate and his departure for America. Preoccupied with his social activities, he had neither the time nor the inclination to prepare for his lecture tour. When warned by his father of the pitfalls of speaking without notes, Randolph fobbed him off with vague promises. The nearest he came to fulfilling those promises was his decision to speak on three subjects – 'Why I am not a Socialist', 'Can Youth be Conservative?' and 'The British Empire and World Progress' – all of which, he felt, could be suitably interchanged and adapted for any occasion. The content of all three lectures he was willing to leave to chance.

He was still prevaricating on the eve of his departure. Answering a last minute enquiry from his father, he solemnly swore that he would compose the lectures on the ship. This was too much even for his indulgent father. 'Ah,' Churchill growled, 'the first day you are on the ship you won't be feeling very well, the second day you will be feeling better, the third day you will meet a pretty girl and then you will be nearly there.'

And Churchill was right. Randolph sailed from Southampton in the White Star liner *Majestic* on 1 October 1930 and arrived in New York a week later. Throughout the crossing his intentions were good but, as his father predicted, the pages of his note-books remained blank.

※　　　※　　　※

While Randolph was in America, his father's career took another dramatic turn. The crisis which Churchill was about to face had been building up for well over a year and was a matter of serious concern when Randolph left England. The issue involved was to become an important factor in Randolph's early political career and was one on which he, like his father, held very strong opinions.

The rapidly developing political storm was, in a way, an extension of the Egyptian controversy. It centred on the demand for a further loosening of Imperial ties, or what Churchill called the diminution of 'the King's Dominions'. This time the country to be 'abandoned' was India and therefore the threat to Imperial prestige was much more serious. It was hardly a new problem. As early as 1917, Lloyd George's government – of which Churchill was a member – had acknowledged that Dominion Status for India was desirable and had promised to work towards that goal. But very little had been done in political terms, despite the campaigns of non-violent civil dis-obedience launched in the early 1920s by Mahatma Gandhi and the Congress Party, who were pledged to obtaining Home Rule for India. The first realistic move had been made in 1928 when Baldwin's Conservative administration had set up a Statutory Commission, under Sir John Simon, to draw up a programme of constitutional advance for India but limited to preparing the country for provincial self-government. As this was a far cry from the promised Dominion Status – let alone Home Rule – the departure of the Simon Commission for India had not unduly alarmed the more rampant Imperialists whose chief spokesman was Lord Birkenhead – the then Secretary of State for India. On the other hand, it did nothing to placate the Indian Congress Party which announced that it would boycott the Commission.

The deliberations of the Simon Commission were long and tedious. Before its report was published the Conservative govern-ment had fallen. Things were further complicated by the interven-tion of the Viceroy of India, Lord Irwin – better known later as Lord Halifax. On 31 October 1929, the Viceroy published a statement in the *Indian Gazette* reaffirming the goal of Dominion Status and, at the same time, it was announced that a 'Round Table Conference' would be held in London at which Indian opinion of the Simon Commission's findings could be aired. Churchill had just returned from America when the Viceroy's declaration was debated in the House of Commons. Although he did not speak in the debate, it was noticed that he cheered loudly when Lloyd George attacked Lord Irwin for making what appeared to be a new commitment – rather than reaffirming an earlier one – and not waiting for the findings of the Simon Commission to be made public.

Churchill's own feelings on the issue were forcibly expressed in a bellicose article he wrote for the *Daily Mail*. He argued that the deliverance of India from 'ages of barbarism, internecine war and tyranny' constituted one of the finest achievements of British history. But that achievement entailed responsibility. 'Dominion status,' he maintained, 'can certainly not be attained while India is prey to fierce racial and religious dissension and when the withdrawal of British protection would mean the immediate resumption of mediaeval wars.'

These – the divisions between Hindu and Muslim, the oppressive caste system and the helplessness of the Indian masses – were arguments which Churchill was to repeat time and again in opposing self-government for India. Had such conditions not existed he would no doubt have found equally convincing arguments to support his case. For, sincere and consistent as was his opposition, it was inspired more by emotion than by reason. So fervently did he believe in the role of the British Empire as a civilizing force, so ready was he to disregard the aspirations of the Indian nationalists, that even his most sympathetic admirers were bewildered by his intransigence. 'Churchill's Indian policy in the between-war years,' confessed Sir Evelyn Wrench, 'has often puzzled me.'

The immediate result of Churchill's opposition was a widening of the gap between himself and the Conservative leadership. Having already lost the confidence of some of his former Cabinet colleagues, and suspicious of his party's drift towards Tariff Reform, Churchill seized upon the issue of Indian constitutional reform – which Baldwin regarded as a matter for bi-partisan agreement between Conservatives and Labour – to reassert his independence. He was not alone. A group of Tory rebels, who were soon to form the Indian Defence Committee, ranged themselves alongside him and he was able to claim public justification when, after further disturbances in India, Gandhi and other Congress Party leaders were arrested. The man on whom he most relied for support, however, was no longer available. Lord Birkenhead, the former Secretary of State for India and Churchill's 'valiant friend', had been taken seriously ill and, on 30 September 1930 – the day before Randolph sailed for America – he died of cirrhosis of the liver due to alcohol poisoning. His death was a personal and political blow to Churchill. More than ever, he realized that it rested with him to lead the opposition to the government's plans for India.

This was the position when the *Majestic* steamed into New York harbour. For the reporters assigned to interview Randolph on his arrival, India was the subject most closely associated with the name of Churchill and it was about India that they questioned him. They were well rewarded. Obviously flattered to be the centre of attention, Randolph was at his bumptious best. The journalists, expecting a shy and gauche nineteen-year-old, were astonished by his lordly, pontifical manner and his sharp-edged responses to their questions. 'He has,' noted one of them, 'his share of the fiery temperament and eloquence of his grandfather, Lord Randolph Churchill, who was the stormy petrel of the Conservative party of his day.'

After a few preliminary questions about Randolph's ambitions – he told them that he was 'looking forward to entering Parliament in 1932, when he became of age' – the reporters turned to India. Had he any opinions on the present unrest there? Randolph most certainly had. The trouble, he claimed, 'had been caused by the lack of a firm hand to suppress anarchy and treason. He said the followers of Gandhi were a very small minority in India. He added he did not believe in Dominion status for India because the people were not capable of handling their own local affairs.' What, he was asked, was the Indian Government going to do about Gandhi? 'There is nothing to be done about Gandhi,' replied Randolph airily. 'He is in jail.'

Having casually dismissed the Indian Congress Party, he went on more decisively to demolish the British Labour Party. Here he felt himself to be on firmer ground. 'The reason for all these troubles and misfortunes,' he declared, 'is that our country is controlled by the silliest and sloppiest of sentimentalists who have ever in all history sat on the Treasury bench. The government of Britain and her Empire has for some peculiar reason been entrusted to the weakest invertebrates in the country.'

'If India is ever separated from the empire,' he added knowingly, 'the blame will not lie in India.'

This intemperate outburst delighted the journalists. Randolph's arrival was given prominent coverage in the New York newspapers the following day. Not everyone, however, approved of his outspoken views. When Randolph called on his father's friend, Bernard Baruch, a few days later, he was given some wise advice. 'I cautioned him,' Baruch wrote to Churchill, 'about being too critical in this country of those to whom he was opposed in England. I tried to impress upon him that as a young man he ought to be restrained in his criticisms . . . I told him to go ahead and talk about any views he may have as strenuously as he wishes, but I would not engage in personalities.'

Baruch might have saved his breath. Randolph would never be restrained in his criticism and certainly not when, as now, he was assured of a wide captive audience. His lectures, for all their lack of preparation – or perhaps because of their lack of preparation – were as lively as they were controversial.

He got off to a somewhat shaky start. Among the people waiting for him when the *Majestic* docked was his lecture agent, Mr Feakins, who gleefully announced that he had managed to arrange an extra lecture that same evening at Princeton University. The lecture, Feakins stressed, was extremely important. Randolph would be addressing a distinguished audience, the press would be out in full force and the success of the entire lecture tour could depend on the reports that appeared the following day. Randolph, having only the headings of his lectures to rely on, noteless and apprehensive, boarded the train for Princeton feeling, he says, 'distinctly queasy'.

But his dismay did not last long. He spent the train journey gaily chatting to a gossip columnist from the Hearst newspapers and was no more prepared for his speech when he stepped on the platform that evening than he had been when he boarded the *Majestic* a week earlier. His chief recollection of that evening's talk was of glancing at his watch after he had exhausted all the relevant facts. To his horror he discovered that he had only spoken for twenty minutes of the hour allotted to him. Breathless, but undaunted, he ploughed on. The next time he looked at his watch he found he still had half-an-hour to fill. He continued to waffle until he finally decided that he could repeat himself no longer and sat down. By that time he was fully convinced that his lecture tour would have to be abandoned.

Only later did he realize that his watch had stopped half way through his talk and he had improvised for well over an hour. He was even more surprised to read the reports of his speech the following day: most were flattering, some were gushing, all predicted success. From then on, he says, he was able to chalk up one triumph after another. He preferred to forget his failures.

But failures there were. The subjects he had chosen were not always geared to the audiences he addressed. America was in the grip of an economic depression and reactionary bombast was not always welcomed. Speaking to the League for Political Education in New York, Randolph was forced to express his disappointment. 'Most of the young men here,' he complained, 'are Socialists and believe in this sob-stuff about international relations, that America should join the League [of Nations] and that sort of thing.' Only the older people seemed to have the 'healthy notions' that he championed.

It was among the older people, particularly the older women, that he was most popular. Handsome, poised and engagingly outspoken, his greatest success was in what one New York commentator

71

described as, 'lightening idle mornings for American women's clubs'. After a while he learned to tailor his talks to his audiences. India was pushed into the background and the glories of Empire were linked with the advantages of Anglo-American co-operation. He liked to describe himself as 'an ambassador, youthful and in truth self-designated, of the greatest empire in the world, the empire of the future, the empire of the English-speaking peoples.' Britain and America, he declared, should pursue a policy of 'enlightened self-interest' because they had 'gotten the best land in the world and intended to keep it, while all the other nations of the world were wanting something.' All that was needed was a great man at the head 'of each of our countries . . . who were agreed that they were going to rule the world, maintain peace, and use their power if necessary.' It was a familiar enough cry in the troubled 'thirties.

One of Randolph's favourite themes was speculating on what he would do if he were Prime Minister of Great Britain. He left his audience in no doubt about the firm guidance he could offer his countrymen. With America's help, he explained, he would place an embargo on Russia until that country stopped its 'foul propaganda' and 'learned to behave'; a naval and military expedition would be sent to China to open up trade and stop the Chinese from 'killing each other'; and India would be kept firmly under Britain's thumb. After that, apparently, everyone would live happily ever after.

It was a pleasing fantasy: far more rousing than listing the sins of Mr Ramsay MacDonald.

∗　　　∗　　　∗

Perhaps Randolph's greatest joy on this second American tour was his freedom. Released from his father's inhibiting presence, no longer forced to watch his words, explain his conduct and behave with a semblance of decorum, he was at liberty to indulge his every whim. For the first time in his life he was accepted as a celebrity, if not in his own right, at least on his own terms. That, in itself, was an exhilarating experience.

He savoured it to the full. Everywhere he went he was courted, reported, feted and flattered. What he lacked as a political heavyweight, he made up for by his pose as an *enfant terrible*. His rudeness, his swagger, his patronizing manner, his heavy-handed jokes and his outrageous behaviour both shocked and delighted his hosts. Whether pontificating in public or posturing in private, young 'Randy Churchill' – as he quickly became known – was always considered good for a laugh.

For the most part, his attempts at humour were sadly lacking in originality. He made great play, for instance, of trying to master the

72

'American language' – 'I went to all the New York theatres,' he quipped, 'at first, of course, with an interpreter.' He was equally sarcastic about his quest to discover a 'real American'. Having, he explained, 'traversed the Continent from Portland (Maine) to Portland (Oregon) and from Augusta (Maine) to Augusta (Georgia)' he had not met a single citizen who did not claim alien origins until he reached Grand Rapids in Michigan where he met a man who boasted that he was truly American because his ancestors had arrived on the Mayflower. 'So now I knew,' smirked the jubilant Randolph. 'To call yourself a hundred per cent American you really have to be English. I felt enormously flattered . . . Why need we worry about the War of Independence?'

Undergraduate humour never fails to draw a response. Randolph's banter was no exception. 'The English habit of laughing at the Americans,' he later confessed, 'is in a sense commendable, but no more commendable than the American habit of laughing at the English . . . I had a great many silent laughs at the expense of the inhabitants (though probably not as many as they had at mine).' He was right. Years later American newspaper correspondents were still chuckling over Randolph's breathtaking impudence.

'I observed him,' recalled the veteran columnist Heywood Broun, 'in drawing-rooms interrupting his elders and telling them where they got off. But it came to be so magnificent that you could hardly call it bad manners. It was Promethean.'

There were times, though, when even the unshockable Mr Broun was floored by Randolph's effrontery. He was never to forget an argument between Randolph and the formidable editor of the New York *World*, Herbert Bayard Swope, which ended with Randolph boldly remarking: 'Herbie, you talk like an utter idiot.' Broun, who worked for the *World* and trembled in the presence of his editor, could hardly believe his ears. He sat gripping the arms of his chair, eyes averted, waiting for the heavens to split. 'Any second,' he thought, 'the lightning would come through the roof and strike Randy dead or Mr Swope would rise quietly and strangle him.' But nothing happened. To Broun's amazement, the chilling silence which followed Randolph's remark was broken by Swope deftly changing the subject. 'And that,' commented Broun, 'was another world's record.'

Embarrassment of a very different sort followed Randolph's encounter with young Ruth McKenney in Columbus, Ohio. Miss McKenney was a student of journalism at Ohio State University and her interest in Randolph was entirely professional. Never having met an Englishman, and intrigued by the secrecy surrounding his engagement to speak at an exclusive men's dinner club – the press were barred from the club and interviews were forbidden – she decided that, as the star-reporter of the student newspaper, the *Ohio State Lantern,* it was her duty to trap Randolph in his hotel. The decision was easier made than achieved. Arriving at the hotel, her nerve deserted her. For almost an hour she dithered in the hotel lobby before plucking up courage to approach 'the forbidding door of Mr Churchill's room.' When at last she did tap on the door, her nerves received a further jolt. Instead of the door being opened as she had envisaged – 'I planned to stick my foot in the crack and ask him a lot of questions very fast' – her knock was answered by a plummy English voice bellowing, 'Come in.' The invitation threw her completely off balance. Dare she march boldly into a strange young man's bedroom? What would her grandmother say? Would this all seem a joke when she became a hardened journalist? She hesitated. Randolph roared again.

'Finally,' remembered a slightly older Ruth McKenney, 'I opened the door very timidly indeed, and beheld Mr Churchill, surely the blondest young man in the world, seated at a desk writing. He wore a smoking jacket over his dinner trousers, black vest, and starched shirt front. His bare feet were stuck in floppy leather slippers. Mr Churchill looked so very public-school English he was faintly incredible . . . [His] eyes were a china blue and his smoking jacket the same, overlaid, however, with old rose and gold.'

Faced with this Noël Coward-like apparition, she became more nervous than ever. As Randolph continued to scratch away at his desk, Miss McKenney felt she was interrupting the labours of a young genius. (Only later did she suspect Randolph of deliberately trying to impress her.) Eventually the young genius put down his pen, rose, and greeted the intruder with a show of graciousness. Drawing up a chair, he invited her to sit beside his desk. He continued to write for a few more minutes and then briskly pushed his papers aside.

'Now,' he beamed, 'what can I do for you?'

Shyly Miss McKenney explained her mission; condescendingly Randolph agreed to be interviewed. She trotted out her carefully prepared questions, he rattled off his answers. At first Miss McKenney had difficulty in understanding his affected Oxford drawl, but she quickly caught the drift of his arguments. Every politician she mentioned, British or American, was peremptorily dismissed as a Socialist.

Having put the politicians in their place, Randolph relaxed. He lost interest in the interview, dropped his pompous man-of-the-world pose and reverted to his normal speaking voice. Pulling a bottle of whisky from his suitcase, he persuaded Miss McKenney to join him in a drink. Miss McKenney felt very daring. Soon they were behaving like nineteen-year-olds – teasing each other about their accents, enthusing over their favourite film-stars, chatting naturally and ordering lamb chops from the hotel kitchen. Then, suddenly, Randolph remembered his lecture. He decided to call it off. Instead, he said, he would take Ruth McKenney to the cinema.

But Miss McKenney took fright. She had lurid visions of the exclusive men's dinner club becoming more and more impatient as they waited for their speaker to arrive. Among the diners would be the publisher of the Columbus *Dispatch,* for whom she acted as campus correspondent, and the mere thought of her employer's wrath made her quake. The speech, she told Randolph firmly, would have to be made. Glumly he agreed and reached for his dinner jacket. Only when he came to put on his patent-leather pumps did he discover he was bare-foot and one of his black socks was missing. They began to search the room. Randolph ducked under one side of the bed and told Ruth to look under the other side. They were both sprawled, groping in the dust under the bed, when there was a knock at the door.

Later Ruth McKenney was unable to remember the names of the three 'well-starched, beautifully tailored citizens who marched in on that sock-hunting expedition.' But she did remember that, after Randolph explained what he was doing under the bed, one of the men walked across to a bureau and returned waving the lost sock. Randolph was delighted.

Miss McKenney was terrified. Slowly she crawled out from under the bed and stood up to face the three visitors. Until then they had not realized there was a young woman in the room. 'Each leading citizen,' she says, 'did a combination gasp and snort.'

There was embarrassment all round. Only Randolph remained unmoved. Calmly pulling on his sock, he insisted that Miss McKenney accompany him to the exclusive all-male dinner. But the three leading citizens would not hear of such sacrilege. Quietly, but firmly, the ace-reporter of the *Ohio State Lantern* was taken aside and told to disappear. She accepted her fate gratefully.

Ruth McKenney was left to console herself with her scoop. Her article on Randolph Churchill was a huge success and, she says, enraged her rivals. But it was a fleeting triumph. Long after her college-fame faded, long after she had exchanged her journalistic studies for hard-nosed reporting, she still blushed at the thought of Randolph's lost sock. 'Life,' she concluded some six years later, 'can hold no further terrors for me.'

It was a thought which haunted many disconcerted females after a chance encounter with Randolph Churchill. 'What lascivious eyes and lecherous lips you have,' Randolph is reported to have remarked to a girl he met in America. 'I hope you live up to what you look.' On that occasion the only red face was Randolph's – smarting from a well-aimed slap.

There were some ladies, however, who welcomed Randolph's bold approach. Disconcerting he might be; precocious, irreverent and overbearingly conceited he undoubtedly was; but his arrogance was often so dazzling that it outshone his impertinence. For those more easily amused than offended, Randolph possessed a magnetic charm. One such young woman was Kay Halle, the daughter of a well-known Ohio business-man, Samuel Halle, who found Randolph's magnetism irresistible. The mutual attraction between Randolph and Kay Halle caused more speculation than anything Randolph said on the lecture platform.

They met at a wedding reception at Cleveland, Ohio, shortly after Randolph arrived in the town to address the local English-Speaking Union. Kay Halle arrived at the reception with an escort and was surprised when she was summoned to Randolph's table. The young Englishman, she was told, had demanded an introduction. Her surprise was even greater when, on being introduced, Randolph announced that she was to accompany him to a racoon hunt that evening. As Miss Halle already had a dinner date, she refused. But Randolph would accept no excuses: if she did not join him, he said, he would offend his host and refuse to go himself. Finally, by way of a compromise, it was agreed that Randolph would accompany Miss Halle on her dinner date and that she would then join him at the racoon hunt.

As it happened, the hunting expedition was a failure. The fault was entirely Randolph's. After joining the hunters at a mountain lodge, Randolph – never the most enthusiastic of sportsmen – took one look at the roaring fire and was overcome by humanitarian feelings. He had no intention, he announced, of spending the night hunting poor defenceless animals. With that said he placed himself in front of the fire and began rehearsing his speech for the following day. Miss Halle provided him with an audience.

Randolph's speech – a variation of his responsibilities of Empire theme – was apparently aimed at putting the Americans in their place. Kay Halle was to remember his ranting against the lynching of Negroes in the southern states and comparing the 'outrageous treatment' of American Red Indians with the benevolent care shown to Indians in the British Empire. Such a confusion of issues and Indians might have puzzled Mr Gandhi, but it deeply impressed Miss Halle. She was captivated by Randolph's noble sentiments. His 'skill with words', she says, his logic and ability to speak on 'the unpinioned wing' dazzled her. Her sneaking fear that he would antagonize Cleveland's English-Speaking Union with his one-sided arguments proved groundless. His speech the following day, she claims, was a *tour de force* and his audience 'found it hard to refute him.'

Kay Halle found it equally hard to resist Randolph's advances. Infatuated and purposeful, Randolph went a-wooing with all the bravado and self-confidence that he brought to politicking. From now on, all his spare time was spent either in New York or in Cleveland. He set the pace of the romance, became a frequent visitor to the Halle home, and adopted a distinctly proprietorial approach to Mr Halle's daughter. Once, finding Kay Halle asleep on the drawing-room sofa, he had no compunction in cutting her hair to shoulder length because, as he later explained, her long hair made her look older than himself. Miss Halle, who was indeed slightly older than Randolph, found this explanation 'touching' and apparently did not question Randolph's right to mould her to his youthful image. In love, as in most things, Randolph was not open to argument.

That Randolph's infatuation with Kay Halle should be talked about is hardly surprising. As a young, handsome, self-promoting celebrity, the son of a distinguished politician and a distinctly eligible bachelor, Randolph was a heaven-sent target for the gossip columnists. His every move was reported, his every word was weighed and his slightest acquaintance was commented upon. It was therefore inevitable that his frequent returns to Cleveland should arouse speculation. His friendship with the Halle family was no secret and his fondness for the Halle daughter soon became apparent. Stories about Randolph's liking for Ohio began to appear in the press. Readers of the social pages were reminded that another Randolph Churchill – the visiting Randolph's grandfather, Lord Randolph Churchill – had chosen the daughter of an American business man for his bride.

Added point was given to the rumours when, at the beginning of 1931, it was learned that Randolph's lecture tour had been extended. Mr. Feakins, delighted at the success of the tour so far, had arranged for a further three months' bookings. Randolph was evidently overjoyed. He appears to have had no hesitation in agreeing to prolong the tour.

His decision, however, could not have been taken lightly. He must have known that by staying in America he was risking his parents' wrath. Neither Churchill nor his wife had been happy about this American tour. Their misgivings had been emphasized in a letter which Randolph received from Brendan Bracken shortly after his arrival in New York. 'When are you coming back to England . . . ' Bracken enquired bluntly. 'A brat of your age ought to be reading hard, and ought not to disregard the great chances given you at Oxford; and so I hope that you will go back to Oxford next term. I know Winston is very keen that you should do so, and his wishes ought to overcome your desire to do almost anything in the world except the hard reading which alone can make you a good politician or a good business man.' As Randolph well knew, Bracken's rumblings were an echo of soundings taken at Chartwell.

Whatever Churchill might have felt about Randolph's decision to extend his tour, there can be little doubt about his wife's feelings. It could hardly have been a coincidence that Clementine Churchill chose this time to join her son in New York. According to Randolph's sister Mary, Mrs Churchill made up her mind to visit America on an impulse. Winston Churchill had given her some money to buy herself a car and she decided instead to spend it on a hurried trip to New York. She wrote and told Randolph of her intention, asking him whether he approved and suggesting that she arrive at the end of January or the beginning of February and stay for a week. Randolph replied immediately. Not only did he approve, he seemed positively enthusiastic.

Randolph's eagerness to see his mother so soon after he had defied his parents' wishes is difficult to understand. He must surely have guessed what had prompted her to visit New York; he must also have been apprehensive about meeting her. One can only suppose that his show of enthusiasm was pure bluff – or what passed with him for diplomacy – and was meant as a peace offering rather than a welcome. Certainly he needed to be diplomatic. His relationship with his mother was not, at the best of times, a happy one.

＊　　　＊　　　＊

In her excellent biography, *Clementine Churchill,* Mary Soames – Randolph's youngest sister – frankly admits that Randolph and his mother were antipathetic. They were too dissimilar in character, personality and outlook, she says, ever to 'establish a close relationship.' The hostility with which mother and son came to regard each other appears to have originated in Randolph's childhood. Rebellious, truculent and resentful of authority, the young Randolph displayed all the disruptive tendencies that Clementine Churchill both despised and feared. He needed a firm masculine hand to control him but, with his father preoccupied with politics and ever mindful of his own tortured childhood, day-to-day discipline was left almost entirely to his mother. Randolph's outrage at being subjected to feminine tyranny – as he saw it – was monumental. Right from the early days, says Lady Soames, Randolph and his mother were 'at loggerheads'.

Randolph was more specific. He too recognized the significance of his childish resentments but he interpreted them somewhat differently. His mother, he would claim, was not so intent on controlling his waywardness as she was in separating him from his father. To justify his often bitter outbursts against his mother he was fond of citing an incident that occurred when he was about ten years of age. One day, he would tell his friends, he was about to go to his father's room when he was stopped by his mother who told him that his father was not to be disturbed. When Randolph, defiant as ever, tried to push past his mother she slapped him so hard that he stumbled and fell backwards down the stairs. Randolph became furious whenever he recounted this incident. In his mind, what was obviously an accident, was magnified into an example of his mother's jealousy of his relationship with his father. Nothing would convince him otherwise. So jealous was his mother, he would say, that she always resented the fact that Churchill never rehearsed his speeches in front of her but always tried them out on his son.

That Clementine Churchill was possessive of her husband there seems little doubt. She made no secret of her hostility towards certain of Churchill's friends and she always gave priority to his needs over those of her children. Jealousy is probably too harsh a word to describe her partiality but her resentments could at times be formidable. Randolph was not alone in feeling excluded from his mother's affections; his sister Diana, it is said, was also alienated by Clementine Churchill's remoteness. There was undoubtedly a lack of maternal warmth in the Churchill household.

For all that, it would be a mistake to accept Randolph's view of his mother at face value. Gossips, it is true, rejoiced in his unfilial sentiments but Randolph liked to shock, and all too often he tended to use his mother as a scapegoat for his own inadequacies. Clementine Churchill might have been a critical, abrasive and somewhat distant mother, but she was not unfeeling, nor was she incapable of sympathizing with her children. When she felt that Randolph genuinely needed and deserved her support she responded wholeheartedly. The trouble was that, while Randolph often needed support, he did not always deserve it.

The differences which separated mother and son were by no means uncommon: they were the differences which inevitably arise between a wilful child and an exacting parent. And, as always in such a relationship, the resulting antagonism lends itself to a trite analysis – had Randolph been open to advice, had his mother been more restrained in her criticism, had they both been more pliable, more ready to make allowances for each other, they might have quarrelled less and been drawn closer together. Unfortunately, Randolph was too intractable and his mother too unyielding for such a simple resolution of their antipathies. As it was, the breach between them was never healed. If anything, it grew wider as the years passed. There were times when no house was big enough to contain Randolph and his mother.

Unending and often bitter as was this domestic feud, there were occasions when both mother and son recognized its futility. A truce would be called and an attempt would be made at reconciliation. One such occasion was Clementine Churchill's visit to America in February 1931. Randolph, having so recently defied his parents' wishes and knowing himself to be on the brink of disclosing yet another controversial decision, no doubt appreciated the importance of gaining his mother's sympathy and consequently was on his best behaviour. When the *Europa* docked at New York, Clementine Churchill was delighted to be met by her smiling, apparently joyful, son. In a letter she wrote to her husband, she admitted to feeling extremely touched by Randolph's welcome.

Firmly gripping his olive-branch, Randolph lost no time in hinting at the peace terms. Within two hours of meeting his mother, he confessed that he was in love with Kay Halle and wanted to marry her. The news startled Clementine Churchill but she wisely refrained from appearing hostile. She listened, she sympathized and, in the long talks she had with Randolph during her stay in America, she offered him motherly advice. Tactfully she pointed out the pitfalls of a youthful marriage and emphasized the importance of his first making a start on a career. Her reasoning was sound, her approach was conciliatory, but her advice was lost on Randolph. He had made up his mind to marry and had every intention of doing so if Kay Halle would have him. Things were not helped when the American press began to publish items claiming that Clementine Churchill's purpose in visiting New York was to put a stop to the romance.

Yet, despite this unpropitious start, the visit was a success. Randolph evidently did not give up easily. Set on winning over his mother, he was at his charming, attentive best. Soon Clementine Churchill was writing ecstatic letters home, singing her son's praises and declaring herself captivated. It was almost, she claimed, like being on a honeymoon. Her original intention of staying a week was quickly abandoned. When Randolph suggested that she accompany him on his next round of lectures, she enthusiastically agreed. The tour lasted for six weeks and was as happy as it was hectic. In the years to come, both mother and son were to look back on this

American excursion as a rare and rewarding interlude in their stormy relationship.

They went to Palm Beach where even the spendthrift Randolph was astonished by the extravagance and vulgarity of the nightly entertainments. 'One of the more bizarre and extraordinary dinners I attended,' he wrote, 'took place in the huge patio of one of the clubs. A thousand people sat and consumed a ten-course dinner round the edges while pugilistic encounters were staged on a raised platform in the middle . . . before long the faces of the combatants were as incarnadine as the lips of the female spectators. In the intervals between the fights the guests danced in the ring upon the canvas floor, adding thereby a pleasing barbaric touch to what might otherwise have been thought a tame method of enjoyment.' They went to Washington and were feted by politicians. And, of course, they went to Cleveland so that Randolph could introduce his mother to Kay Halle and her family. Clementine Churchill was favourably impressed by her son's girl-friend but remained steadfast in her objections to the proposed marriage. Needless to say, her continued opposition in no way lessened Randolph's resolve.

Restrained as was the disagreement between Randolph and his mother, the gossips were quick to sniff it out. By the time Clementine Churchill returned to England, her refusal to consent to her son marrying had become public knowledge. 'Young Randolph Churchill,' Robert Bruce Lockhart noted in his diary on 14 April 1931, 'is determined to marry his American lady in spite of the fact that she has very little money and is a Jewess. She is several years older than he is. Mrs Winston has just come back from America. She went there to try to persuade Randolph to come home but without success.'

In fact Randolph had needed no persuasion to return to England. He had completed his second lecture tour and, once again, was heavily in debt. What money he had earned in America had been dissipated in flying to and from Cleveland, in visiting New York, in reserving suites at the best hotels and in pandering generally to his taste for the high-life. 'I had very grand ideas in those days,' he later admitted. He had indeed. After seven months of tall talk and lordly living, he was as broke as the day he sailed for New York. He had no option but to go home.

He left America a few weeks after his mother's departure. And in leaving America he more or less put an end to his romance. When Kay Halle visited England the following year there was a flutter of speculation but it came to nothing. Years later, writing about Randolph, Kay Halle quoted a remark that was once made about his father. 'The first time you meet Winston,' a friend was reported to have said, 'you see all his faults and the rest of your life you spend discovering his virtues.' This tribute, says Miss Halle, could be applied to her friendship with Randolph. Once the 'tremors from the quake' of their first meeting had subsided, they became close, life-long friends – but the gossips were treated to no more talk about marriage.

Randolph published his impressions of the United States in a series of articles he wrote for the *Daily Mail* shortly after his return to England. They were light-hearted and inconsequential – poking fun at American customs and prejudices and offering tongue-in-cheek advice to prospective travellers – and were obviously written more for effect than for enlightenment.

'The Americans,' he concluded in a final, patronizing, flourish, 'are essentially a serious-minded people. Their lives are conducted on a basis of resolute endeavour and unflagging energy. Repose and relaxation find little part in their existence. They address a golf ball with as much grave resolve as they do a shareholders' meeting . . . In the American continent, which has only been blessed with western civilization for a few centuries, there must of necessity be an aura of crudity. There must be a certain inadequate imitative impulse. But from the cultural standpoint it is the future of America that arrests the attention, not the past or the present.'

With a few minor deletions, the same might have been said of 'the brilliant young son of Mr Winston Churchill' – as he was described in an introductory heading to his articles – over whose future there now hung a tantalising question mark.

CHAPTER FIVE

Coming of Age

For all his solemn promises before going to America, it is doubtful whether Randolph ever seriously contemplated returning to university. As far as he was concerned, his four terms at Oxford had taught him all he needed to know for a career in public life. He had learned to mix confidently with people of all ages and opinions, to conduct a civilized conversation, to entertain urbanely, to hold his drink and to think and speak on his feet in debate. What more was required of an aspiring politician? He had no academic ambitions, he found studying tiresome and saw no advantage in taking a degree. Confident of his own abilities, he was more anxious than ever to put schooling behind him and get to grips with what he termed the 'battle of life'. That he was in no way qualified to embark on a professional career bothered him not at all. He returned from the United States owing some two thousand dollars and determined to make his way in the world.

Once again he found himself in conflict with his parents. Clementine Churchill had always stressed the importance of Randolph returning to Oxford and her husband was no less emphatic in supporting her arguments. But Randolph's mind was made up and nothing his mother or his father said made any difference. He insisted that he was now a grown-up man and capable of making his own decisions: Oxford undergraduates, in his opinion, were nothing more than 'silly boys'. By sticking to his guns, he eventually overcame his father's objections. Churchill, while still arguing that Randolph was ill-equipped for a profession, finally agreed to allow him to leave Oxford on the condition that he first got a job. This apparently posed no problem: Randolph took the first job he was offered.

The offer came from his friend Lord Melchett who, as a director of I.C.I., suggested that Randolph join the firm as assistant editor of the I.C.I. house magazine. It was hardly the job Randolph would have chosen and, as he later admitted, it was not one which he enjoyed but at least it met his father's conditions, provided him with a small income. But he did not take easily to the tedium of office routine. He was quickly bored with the job and deeply resented having to keep regular office hours. 'One of the few principles on which I base my life,' he wrote shortly after starting work, 'is that of never rising till eleven unless I am paid to. Now that I am earning my own living instead of being educated at University I have to be up at eight o'clock six days a week.' It was all very different from the idle mornings he spent lecturing American women's clubs.

But his lecturing days were not yet over. To supplement his meagre office salary he undertook to give a series of lectures for a British lecture agency which had sponsored his father some thirty years earlier. He spoke about his American experiences but it was the magic of the Churchill name that drew the crowds. Billed as 'the son of the former Chancellor of the Exchequer', Randolph – now an accomplished public speaker – was always sure of an enthusiastic reception from a packed audience. So handsome was his fee that some of his friends were convinced that he was 'paying super-tax before he was twenty-one', but this seems highly unlikely. Randolph was never able to earn enough to meet his expensive tastes, was always overdrawn at the bank, and frequently had to turn to his father for assistance. Almost a year later Churchill was still struggling to pay off the debts his son had accumulated in America.

Somewhat less lucrative than his lecture tour, but equally congenial, were the occasional articles Randolph wrote for the Sunday newspapers. Here again he was able to put the sparkle of his father's reputation to good use. 'We get a human peep,' promised a *Sunday Graphic* caption to his article 'When I Differ With My Father', 'into the household with the name that is traditional in Britain.' That was claiming too much. If the peep was human, it was hardly revealing.

'The most constant subject for dispute between my father and myself,' boasted Randolph, 'has always been in regard to the length of my hair. He has a strong aversion to what he calls the "short-haired woman" and the "long-haired man". Consequently he is always urging me to pay a visit to the barber and have my hair cut to what I consider a grotesque shortness.'

After this breathtaking disclosure, he went on to admit there had been some minor skirmishes about his schooling, a sharp encounter over a cocker spaniel puppy, and a divergence of opinion concerning his sluggardly habits, but he was careful not to venture beyond cosy generalities. Most of his other articles were in a similar vein: they earned money but did little to further his literary ambitions.

A more promising opportunity for him to display his talents came shortly after he started work with I.C.I. In July 1931 he went to Berlin to report on the grave economic crisis facing Germany for the

Sunday Graphic. It was, in many ways, an extraordinary assignment for a young, inexperienced, untried reporter to undertake. The situation in Germany was as complex as it was serious. Having been governed during the post-war years by a succession of unstable coalitions which, since 1929, had ruled with the help of emergency powers, Germany-plagued by five million unemployed, a paralyzed Parliament, and a floundering government – appeared once again to be drifting towards economic collapse.

To meet the most recent crisis, the government had used its emergency powers to impose stringent financial restrictions on the banks, and these restrictions had created a tension which was viewed with some alarm throughout Europe. The tension was not eased by the growing threat of political extremism. In the elections of September 1930, not only had the Communists won 77 seats in the *Reichstag* but, more ominously, the National Socialists – led by a relatively obscure, rabble-rousing politician named Adolf Hitler – had secured 107 seats and a sixth of the votes. With an international conference about to convene in London, Europe was faced with issues of profound importance. The outcome of the conference, it was reported, 'may decide between dictatorship and constitutional government in Germany.' It was to make an on-the-spot investigation of the German crisis that the twenty-year-old Randolph went to Berlin.

His report was competent, colourful and surprisingly mature. With his natural flair for the dramatic and shrewd political instincts, he was able to concoct a report which was highly suited to a popular newspaper. Human interest and acute observation was balanced by a judicious spattering of economic detail. He toured the important industrial suburbs, spoke to queues of small householders outside the savings banks, and was impressed by the prevailing mood of optimism. 'Those to whom I talked,' he noted, 'seemed hardly to realize that Germany is standing on the brink.' He was surprised to find cinemas and places of entertainment well attended and was amused to see theatre patrons paying for their seats 'with cheques which at the moment cannot be cashed.' The only outward signs of panic he detected were the excessive demands being made on the department stores. 'Those who are able to draw wages,' he pointed out, 'are spending their money chiefly on food. . . . It is evident that the people are beginning methodically to hoard food in case payments are completely stopped, and the critical moment will come when they have exhausted their savings or when wages cease to be paid.'

A somewhat more sombre view of the situation was apparent in the interviews he had with prominent business men. Many of them were apprehensive about the future and feared that the financial freeze would result in anarchy. Indeed, if there was a weakness in Randolph's report it was the stress he tended to put on these interviews. Unlike his father, who, after the September elections, had expressed concern about the successes of the National Socialists, Randolph scented only the dangers posed by left-wing agitators. 'How can the rest of the world,' asked a German industrialist, 'allow 60,000,000 of the most highly-skilled workers to decline to a state of starvation, bloody rapine and bolshevism?' It was a view which Randolph dutifully echoed. That many German industrialists were already supporting Adolf Hitler appears to have escaped his notice.

But if his report lacked foresight, it undoubtedly won the approval of his editor. The *Sunday Graphic* splashed it across a centre page under the arresting heading 'Germany Stands On The Brink', and related it to the forthcoming international conference. Accompanied by a fetching photograph of 'Our Special Correspondent' it carried more weight than anything Randolph had so far written and can be said to mark his debut as a serious journalist.

That debut was followed, shortly afterwards, by a more substantial achievement. In September 1931, Gandhi arrived in England to attend the second Round-Table Conference. His visit was well-publicized and the newspapers stressed his wish to meet his chief opponent, Winston Churchill. Regrettably, Churchill showed little inclination to meet the Indian leader and Gandhi was forced to resort to other means of contact. 'Gandhi,' reported the *Daily Mail* on 15 September, 'who has not so far had his desire to meet Mr Winston Churchill fulfilled is to meet Mr Randolph Churchill, the latter's undergraduate [*sic*] son, at St James's Palace this afternoon.' The report that Randolph wrote about his encounter with the 'little brown man in a loincloth' was fairly routine and contained no surprises. More significant was the fact that, at twenty years of age, he was considered important enough to act as his father's representative. There could no longer be any doubt about his status as a journalist.

At last, it seemed, the clouds of Randolph's youth were beginning to lift. Within a year of leaving university he had toured the United States, won acclaim, thought seriously of getting married, found a job for himself and achieved at least one of his ambitions. He had also, to all intents and purposes, left home.

✻   ✻   ✻

Randolph made few friends at Oxford but those that he did make he kept. One was John Betjeman. Like Randolph, Betjeman had failed to take his degree – he was unable to pass the examination for Holy Scriptures – and, on coming down from Oxford, he decided to become a prep-school master. 'Randolph kept in touch,' he says, 'and when terms were over for both of us, Edward James [who was then in America] arranged that we should share a house of his in Culross Street, London. This was small, luxurious, with limewood walls and pale carpets.'

Living with Betjeman, Randolph was truly in his element. The elegant Culross Street house appealed to his love of gracious living, the frequent coming and going of guests satisfied his gregarious instincts, and the constant dinner parties allowed him to continue the social life he had delighted in as an undergraduate. Free from the demands of his parents and his tutors, he could live and entertain as he pleased.

He was genuinely fond of John Betjeman whose poetic genius he had been quick to recognize at Oxford. Fully sharing his father's whimsical humour, Randolph responded to Betjeman's satirical gifts with bubbling glee. He never lost an opportunity of prodding the embarrassed young poet into reciting at dinner and luncheon parties. 'He used to ask for special favourites,' says Betjeman, 'and then listen with his eyes wide open, and laughter in his face, and lead applause at the end. It was through him that I gained self-confidence.' It was partly through Randolph also that John Betjeman first appeared in print. Always quick to champion his friends, Randolph helped to persuade the wealthy Edward James – who published his own poetry privately – to include a collection of Betjeman's poems under the imprint of the James Press.

These poems, originally intended for private circulation, were later taken up by a book distributor and marketed commercially. 'But I am sure,' claims the modest Betjeman, 'that if it had not been for Randolph the edition would not have sold out as it did.' Throughout his life, Randolph was an enthusiastic admirer of John Betjeman's poems, many of which he knew by heart and could recite at length.

For all his loyalty, Randolph was not easy to live with. His tendency to monopolize the telephone, quarrel with guests, entertain mysterious strangers and bang about at all hours – doctors would be summoned in the middle of the night to tend his wounds after a fracas – continually threatened the peace at Culross Street. It says much for Randolph's more endearing traits that John Betjeman was to recall their bachelor existence with affection and to remember Randolph 'in terms of noise, light and laughter'. All the same, Betjeman was left with the feeling that Randolph, for all his infectious buoyancy, was essentially a lonely young man.

He was probably right. During these early years in London, there was more than a hint of desperation in Randolph's frenetic pursuit of amusement. His constant search for diversion, his heavy drinking, his womanizing, his determination to assert himself and his soon-to-be-notorious quarrels, all seem to suggest a fragmented personality, a lack of personal fulfillment. So fierce was his desire to become self-reliant, to accentuate his individuality, that – or so it appears – he was incapable of forming close friendships. Acquaintances he had a-plenty: he loved to surround himself with people, sought out audiences to impress and shock and delighted in their reactions to his wild behaviour, he adored gossip and the superficialities of fashionable society, but, despite his many kindnesses to those he liked, he refused to commit himself to a more intimate relationship. Even with the women he so relentlessly pursued his approach was more romantic than binding. In adult life, as at Eton and Oxford, Randolph's egotism was a barrier to shared confidences. Others, besides John Betjeman, were to detect the underlying loneliness of Randolph's crowded existence.

To the less discerning, however, the young Randolph Churchill appeared as carefree as he was privileged. His successful lecture tours, his newspaper articles, his family connections and social contacts completely eclipsed his lack of solid achievement. Handsome, witty, intelligent, brimming with self-confidence, he was soon being hailed by the gossip columnists as one of the promising young men of his generation. In a random survey conducted by the Marquess of Donegal in his widely-read social column 'Almost In Confidence', in February 1932, Randolph was listed – along with Noël Coward, Oliver Messel, Ellen Wilkinson, Cecil Beaton, Harold Acton, Beverley Nichols and Ethel Mannin – as one of the potential geniuses of the age. A couple of months later the same column boldly announced that 'Mr Randolph Churchill is commonly credited with being the most brilliant young man in England.'

It may have been puffery of this sort that encouraged an enterprising publisher to offer Randolph a lavish advance and generous royalties to write a biography of his father. Randolph was only too ready to accept the commission. He immediately wired his father, who was lecturing in America, explaining that the book would be a light-hearted and informal survey of political events of the last thirty years and would cause no embarrassment. His hopes were quickly dashed. Churchill replied the following day, refusing to countenance the idea. His archives, he said, were worth ten times what Randolph had been offered and any attempt at publication would be premature and improvident. For once, Randolph was obliged to heed his father's advice.

He must have done so reluctantly. The offer of a substantial advance for the book, coming at a time when his financial position was even more shaky than usual, had been particularly attractive. For some months he had been trying desperately to keep pace with his mounting debts. The money he received from his lecture agent was invariably spent as soon as he was paid and, at the beginning of October 1931, his long-standing overdraft had led to hints that the banks might close his account. Nor were things helped by his gambling. So disastrously had he burnt his fingers speculating on the outcome of the October general election that he had been forced to call on his father to bail him out. Churchill agreed to settle this debt but had protested vehemently on learning that Randolph had signed a contract to hire a motor car and chauffeur at the cost of something like £700 or £800 a year. Economy for Randolph was always a matter of reducing his liabilities rather than living within his income.

Indeed the possibility of adjusting his needs to his means does not appear to have occurred to him. His only concern was in increasing his earning capacity: he was forever toying with bizarre money-making schemes. The idea of writing his father's biography was merely one of a series of bright notions. A few days before the publishers made their offer, for instance, he had been proclaiming his intention of taking a job as 'speaker at the Trocadero'. Negotiations were under way, he told Robert Bruce Lockhart, and if the Trocadero agreed to pay him £100 a week he would accept the position. A few months later he was equally enthusiastic about a scheme to start a London newspaper which would be published at 6.a.m. and carry later news than the other morning papers. And earlier, when Charlie Chaplin visited the Churchills at Chartwell, he emphatically denied that he had come to discuss the possibility of a 'film career' for Randolph. How serious Randolph was about any of these projects it is impossible to say. Often he talked simply for the sake of talking. Day dreaming aloud was an entertaining pastime and probably reflected his boredom more than his ambitions.

About his eventual career, his destiny, he had not the slightest doubt. Once he became of age, he fully intended to follow in the footsteps of his father and his grandfather and become a politician. The rest – the lecturing and journalism, the job at I.C.I., his get-rich-quick fantasies – were simply means of marking time until he entered the House of Commons. 'If anyone had said to me,' he later admitted, 'that I wouldn't get into the House of Commons by the time I was twenty-one, or immediately afterwards, I would have thought them absolutely too ridiculous for words.' That, after all, was what being a Churchill meant.

* * *

When Randolph had left England for New York in October 1930, the question of constitutional reform for India had been the burning political issue. This torturous problem had continued to dominate British politics throughout his tour of America.

The first Round-Table Conference, attended by Indian politicians and members of the three main British political parties, had opened in London on 12 November 1930 and remained in session until 19 January the following year. Boycotted by the radical Indian Congress Party, it nevertheless produced some concrete results. At the close of the conference, Ramsay MacDonald, the Labour Prime Minister, promised that India would advance towards self-government. First, however, a new Indian constitution would have to be devised so that the divergent interests in the sub-continent could be brought together in a single All-India Federal Parliament. Britain would supervise the safeguards for minorities and retain power over defence and foreign affairs. It was a compromise that pleased neither the Indian nor the British extremists.

Leading the British opposition was, of course, Winston Churchill. From the day the first Round-Table Conference opened he was said to be plunged in the deepest gloom. His despondency, however, did not prevent him from voicing his misgivings. He was convinced that, while it might be possible for Indians to govern individual provinces, only Britain could provide the necessary central control. At a meeting of the Indian Empire Society in December 1930 – when the Round-Table Conference was still in session – he publicly prophesied anarchy if Britain abdicated its responsibilities. 'Gandhi-ism and all it stands for,' he declared, 'will, sooner or later, have to be grappled and finally crushed. It is no use trying to satisfy a tiger by feeding him with cat's-meat.'

He was still prophesying disaster when the House of Commons debated the proceedings of the Round-Table Conference. The proposal to set up an All-India Federal Parliament, Churchill maintained, was doomed from the outset. It would not win the support of the radical elements nor would it command the respect of the 'excitable' Indian masses. The weakness of the proposed constitution was all too obvious: while promising eventual self-government it retained formidable powers for Britain which, if used, would subject the Viceroy to popular hostility. Such a policy, Churchill contended, could only lead to the complete separation of Britain and India.

His arguments were forceful but futile. There was little support for his standpoint from other speakers in the debate and he was answered, not by a Government spokesman, but by the leader of his own party. After defending the Government's plans, Stanley Baldwin, as Leader of the Opposition, went on to pledge Conservative support for the proposed constitution. This, for Churchill, was the last straw. His deepening suspicion of the Tory leadership was confirmed. The following day he formally wrote to Baldwin resigning from his party's Business Committee (the then equivalent of the Shadow Cabinet).

Baldwin, while professing personal friendship, promptly accepted Churchill's resignation. Once again Churchill found himself outside the main stream of British politics. This time his isolation was to last much longer.

Randolph had been kept well informed of these events. While he was frolicking through the United States, his father kept him up to date on affairs in England. Any gaps were filled in by Brendan Bracken. Churchill, Bracken assured Randolph in February 1931, was not alone in the stand he had taken. 'He has untied himself from Baldwin,' wrote the optimistic Bracken, 'rallied all the fighters in the Tory Party, re-established himself as a potential leader and put heart into a great multitude here and in India.' Newspaper reports of Churchill's public speeches seemed to tell much the same story.

Randolph's own support for his father was never in question. His faith in Churchill's political wisdom was unshakeable. 'I loyally embraced, with conviction, all my father's causes,' he boasted. Returning to England he was able to translate his loyalty into action. Delighting in political challenge, he made a point of being in the House of Commons gallery whenever his father made an important speech. Members of Parliament became accustomed to his piercing blue eyes concentrated on their proceedings and soon Sir Samuel Hoare was referring to Randolph and Brendan Bracken as part of Churchill's 'stage army'. Outside parliament, Randolph never lost an opportunity to defend his father's viewpoint and was always at hand to lead the cheering at Churchill's public meetings.

It was all good belligerent fun, but it was also frustrating. Brendan Bracken was now an MP and could take a purposeful part in Churchill's campaign: Randolph, alas, could only wave a banner from the side lines. He was more impatient than ever to enter parliament. Not only was he sure of his own abilities but he saw himself as a spokesman for his own generation. And like many ambitious young men, he was convinced that his generation would change the world. The time was rapidly approaching when the youth of Britain would sweep aside the fumbling old men who were degrading their heritage and he, Randolph Churchill, intended to be at their head. After the next election, he predicted in January 1932, Parliament would be composed entirely of men under forty, his father, and the 'eternally young' Lloyd George. 'If all the young men were to combine together,' he wrote in an article a couple of months later, 'they would prove irresistible . . . Too many young men are satisfied with serving age, too few of them care to risk all on a single chance. We have no right to expect anyone to have confidence in us unless we have confidence in ourselves.'

Randolph's desire for new, younger and more positive political leadership was intense but not unusual. Many youngsters, of all political persuasions, felt the same way. Never, in fact, had Randolph's denunciations of the 'humbug and compromise, the "middle course," "muddling through" incompetence and stagnation which permeate our national life' appeared more justified than in the latter half of 1931.

The autumn of that year had seen a weakening of traditional political loyalties in Britain. First had come a split in the ruling Labour Government. This had been brought about by the serious economic crisis facing the country. In order to meet this crisis – which had followed in the wake of the disastrous Wall Street Crash of 1929 – Ramsay MacDonald had agreed to proposed cuts in public expenditure, including unemployment benefits. Such socialist heresy had, not surprisingly, alienated the Trade Unions and led to the resignation of senior Cabinet Ministers. Faced with this opposition, MacDonald had no alternative but to resign himself. He had been prevented from doing so by King George V who, after consulting leaders of the Conservative and Liberal parties, had urged the Labour Prime Minister to form a National Government of all parties to meet the crisis. This MacDonald agreed to do but, in allying himself with Conservatives and Liberals, he ruined his standing with his own party.

The general election of October 1931 resulted in a victory for the National Government and staggering losses for the Labour party. The Conservatives, nominally supporting the National Government, won 473 seats and Labour was reduced from 288 to 52 seats. However, MacDonald, as leader of the National Government, remained Prime Minister, although no less than eleven of the Cabinet posts were held by Conservatives, with only two by National Liberals and three by National Labour. Stanley Baldwin became Lord President of the Council, Neville Chamberlain became Chancellor of the Exchequer but Churchill, whom some had hoped would be asked to join the Cabinet, was isolated. With all three main parties divided, to a greater or lesser extent, talk was rife about coalitions to form an opposition.

Outside parliament some of the despairing young saw hope in the emergence of a new and vigorous leader. A year or so earlier Sir Oswald Mosley, disillusioned with the economic policies of the Labour Government, had resigned his Cabinet post and launched the auspiciously-named New Party. This party – soon to become the British Union of Fascists – had all the attraction of a fashionable novelty; its appeal to youngsters was inevitable. Randolph, with his sneaking respect for authoritarianism, was not immune to Mosley's magnetism. He even appears to have persuaded his father that the New Party was worth cultivating. That, at any rate, is the most likely explanation of Churchill's only known flirtation with an aspiring Fascist dictator.

In the summer of 1931, Randolph accompanied his parents on a motoring jaunt through France. The political crisis in England was then developing and the family holiday was not entirely carefree. At the beginning of August, Churchill was summoned back to London for a few days and, on his return, Randolph was sent hurrying home across the Channel. According to Harold Nicolson, Randolph arrived in England on a mission for his father. Churchill, he says, had sent his son to investigate the possibility of Mosley joining 'the Tory toughs in opposition'. The idea was not new. Earlier that year Mosley had made similar courting noises but Churchill had appeared distinctly uninterested. One can only suppose that Randolph had helped to change his mind. If this was the case, the change came too late. Mosley was no longer available. He asked Randolph why Churchill did not combine with others to form an opposition. 'Oh,' replied Randolph, 'because without you he will not be able to get hold of the young men.'

So ended all thought of the unlikely partnership. It did not, however, end Randolph's dalliance with the New Party. He continued to take an interest in Mosley's posturing and occasionally lent his support to the New Party's political activities. A few months later Robert Bruce Lockhart was to record a luncheon at the Carlton Grill at which Randolph and Alexander Kerensky – the former Russian Menshevik Prime Minister – argued the merits of dictatorship and democracy in 'execrable French'. Kerensky was firmly on the side of democracy. 'Randolph Churchill,' noted Bruce Lockhart, 'has been speaking in the New Party Club. He said that castration was a modern remedy for ineffectives in the hygienic world of thought. It ought to be applied to political ineffectives. It would, however, be unnecessary in the case of Baldwin and Ramsay, as they were old women already (loud applause).'

Political fringe meetings were the only forums at which Randolph could command an audience. He must indeed have found this frustrating. More than anything he longed for the chance to parade his views before an appreciative public; a public which would not only applaud his denunciations of tired old statesmen but would recognize him as a future leader of a revitalized nation. About his political career he had not the slightest doubts. It was a subject he returned to again and again, sometimes on the most unlikely occasions. His distant cousin, Anita Leslie, remembers him holding forth on his political prospects about this time in circumstances which another young man might have found distinctly embarrassing.

Anita Leslie was on her first visit to Blenheim. She was accompanied by her father and the only other guests were Randolph and a beautiful Australian girl, Patricia Richards, whom Randolph had enticed to Blenheim for the week-end. According to Miss Leslie it was a far from carefree house party. The Duchess of Marlborough spent most of her time sniping at her churlish husband, the meals were uneatable, the staff offhand, the accommodation lacked the basic comforts, and poor Miss Richards – who had been expecting a merry gathering – was obviously dispirited. None of this seems to have worried Randolph. His intentions, as he sat staring lustfully at Miss Richards across the dining table, were abundantly clear; he was waiting for an opportunity to pounce.

But no such opportunity presented itself. Randolph was obliged to employ bolder tactics. That night he ventured along the corridor from the bachelor wing and rapped on the door of Patricia Richards's bedroom. Unfortunately he had misjudged his timing. He arrived while Anita Leslie was saying goodnight to Miss Richards before going to her own room and was extremely disconcerted when his knock was answered by his cousin. Nor was he pleased when his cousin refused the bribe he offered her to disappear. 'I scorned his pound note,' says Anita Leslie, 'turned back and jumped into Patricia's bed beside her. There we sat stolidly, in our nighties and dressing gowns with cold cream on our faces . . . Randolph was stymied. All he could do was ask for a corner of the eiderdown and hold forth about his future as Prime Minister.'

*   *   *

The milestone so eagerly awaited by Randolph was reached in May 1932. That month he celebrated his twenty-first birthday. To mark this momentous occasion his father organized a magnificent birthday dinner for him at Claridges. It was a party that Randolph was never to forget.

Originally it was intended that the dinner – held two weeks after Randolph's actual birthday – would not only be an all-male affair but that each of the distinguished guests would be accompanied by his son. Unfortunately, Churchill's bachelor entourage – men like Brendan Bracken, Professor Lindemann and the ubiquitous Eddy Marsh – made this novel idea impracticable. There were, however, sufficient father and son combinations for the press to play up the 'chip off the old block' theme. Lord Beaverbrook was there with his son Max Aitken, Lord Rothermere with Esmond Harmsworth, Lord Hailsham with Quintin Hogg, Lord Camrose with Seymour Berry, Lord Reading with Lord Erleigh . . . Indeed the only notable exceptions, as one newspaper snidely remarked, were Mr Baldwin and Mr Baldwin's son Oliver.'

'The occasion,' reported the *Sunday Times*, 'was in reality more noteworthy than the celebration of a birthday . . . it afforded a common meeting ground on which those separated by years, outlook, and upbringing might discuss the differences between them.'

Certainly everybody was given an opportunity to air their differences. There could have been few guests who did not speak and most of them took the opportunity to have a dig at Randolph. Freddie Furneaux – now Lord Birkenhead – had great fun in outlining Randolph's graceless career at Eton and Oxford. 'It was not,' commented a reporter, 'the usual speech on such occasions; his respect for Mr Randolph Churchill had to be inferred rather than applauded.' Slightly more flattering, but equally equivocal, was Winston Churchill's reference to his son as 'a fine machine-gun' who it was hoped, 'would accumulate a big dump of ammunition and learn to hit the target.'

A great deal was said about idealism and purpose, about faith in the younger generation, about opportunity and ambition and it was generally acknowledged that Randolph's impromptu reply to the speeches was highly accomplished. Even so he did not entirely escape criticism the following day. 'Not a word of Randolph Churchill's speech was prepared,' noted a gossip columnist, 'but there was ample evidence of fine natural abilities. To him an old codger may say "Work, my boy, work! The way is wide open to you in politics if you do!"'

This appeared in 'Londoner's Diary' of the *Evening Standard*. It was probably written by Robert Bruce Lockhart, to whom Randolph telephoned details of the dinner the following morning. In his private diary, however, Lockhart was more explicit. 'What an amazing thing privilege and position still are in England!' he observed. 'Here is a boy who, born in a less privileged circle, would have had to work hard and make his own way. As it is, he is lazy, lascivious, impudent and, beyond a certain rollicking bumptiousness, untalented, and everything is open to him. One thing his position has given him is good looks and charm.' Precisely how position bestows good looks and charm only the acidulous Lockhart could say.

Lockhart was not Randolph's only Fleet Street critic. Indeed his well-publicized birthday celebration had been heralded by a newspaper attack which set all fashionable London talking. The attack was the beginning of a public vendetta that was to delight the gossips for years. Not only Randolph but other privileged young men came under fire.

'Pity these Great Men's Sons,' ran the heading of an article which appeared in the *Daily Express* at the beginning of June 1932. 'All the young pigeons are aping the habits and fine feathers of peacocks,' claimed the article. 'These pigeons are the sons of eminent fathers, and they are basking in the shade of a parental halo. Wherever I go I am confronted by the son of some magnate on whom the son of some other magnate passes favourable comment . . . These bantams, by their own confession, expect to step straight into their father's shoes. Some of them have put their foot in it quite successfully, considering the restrictions of credit, but otherwise I cannot see signs of blossom in these buds. Who are they?'

The first to be singled out for mild criticism were Lord Borodale, the son of Admiral Lord Beatty and Max Aitken, the son of the *Daily Express*'s proprietor, Lord Beaverbrook. 'Then there is Randolph Churchill,' the writer went on. 'He is a charming youth, but he is late in keeping appointments, and his powers are even more latent, though possibly they may also be there. There are others also. However one and all, they seem to think that fate and fathership have ordained them to immediate importance and command. They forget that there is a buffer-state of middle-aged buffers who stand between them and leadership . . . History proves almost indisputably that major fathers as a rule breed minor sons, so our little London peacocks had better tone down their fine feathers and start trying to make a name of their own.'

This, to all intents and purposes, was little more than a good-humoured tease. Those who knew the background against which it was written might even have thought that Randolph had been let off lightly. For the writer of the article was the waspish Lord Castlerosse who, it is said, bore Randolph a 'lasting and savage grudge'. And, for all its light-hearted banter and cosily mixed metaphores, there can be little doubt that the article was inspired by personal spite. The feud between Randolph and Castlerosse had been simmering for months.

Valentine Castlerosse was the fat, flamboyant, egocentric Irish peer whose weekly column 'The Londoner's Log' was an influential feature of the *Sunday Express*. A former officer in the Irish Guards, Castlerosse had been taken up by Lord Beaverbrook shortly after the First World War and had established himself as a witty newspaper columnist. Since the early 1920s he had entertained readers of the popular press with his reflections on the London social scene; his column, says one of his biographers, 'seemed to be the effortless conversation of an agreeable, if talkative friend.' But if he wrote knowingly about the rich, titled and famous personalities of the day, he was not without claims to notoriety himself. In the clubs, restaurants and casinos of London's West End, few men could rival Valentine Castlerosse's reputation as a wildly extravagant, outrageously boisterous; *bon viveur*. He drank heavily, gambled recklessly, knew everybody and was rarely seen without an attractive woman on his arm. His colourful reputation had been greatly enhanced in 1928 when he married the bewitching and temperamental Doris Delavigne. No two people could have been more unsuited or more unfitted for marriage. The new Lady Castlerosse was every bit as inflammable as her fiery husband. They quarrelled incessantly, often violently, and were forever threatening divorce or rushing to their friends to display their battle scars. In this respect, at least, they were well matched. Doris Castlerosse's mouth was as foul, it is said, as her legs were shapely, and she spat as viciously as she kicked. Bruises were trophies on both sides. The story is told of a woman tackling Noël Coward after the first night of *Private Lives* and complaining about the matrimonial fights and rolling around on the floor in the play. 'No couple,' she protested, 'could possibly quarrel like that in real life.' 'Couldn't they?' replied Coward. 'You obviously don't know the Castlerosses!'

Randolph came to know the Castlerosses only too well. He first met the portly Valentine at a party given by Venetia Montagu shortly after his return from America. Both men were at their brawling best. As the wine flowed tempers became shorter, insults more pointed. Castlerosse made the fatal mistake of attacking Randolph's father: Churchill, he claimed, had murdered 250,000 men at the Dardanelles. Randolph made a stinging reply. 'For two pins, I'd hit you,' roared Castlerosse. 'Don't do that,' warned Randolph. 'I'm *not* your wife.' Like had undoubtedly met like.

How well Randolph knew Castlerosse's wife at this time is uncertain. He was soon to push himself to the front of her train of admirers. So enamoured did he become of the vivacious Doris Castlerosse that he left his bachelor *menage* and moved into an hotel to be near her. When Castlerosse got wind of the liaison he telephoned Randolph. 'I hear you're living with my wife,' he hissed. 'Yes, I am,' Randolph gaily admitted, 'and its more than you have the courtesy to do.' Certainly the affair was no secret. Randolph delighted in boasting about his conquest and made a point of introducing Doris to his father. He was highly amused when Churchill rebuked him for using the word 'bloody' in front of the salty-tongued lady and shared the joke with all his friends. Lady Castlerosse, however, took the hint: from then on she watched her words in the presence of Randolph's father. How intimate the affair was is another matter. Doris always insisted they were just good friends. Her surprising reason for keeping Randolph out of her bed was that – or so she said – 'he smelt of castor oil'. It was an ingenious excuse but it obviously did not convince her husband.

So all things considered, the article Castlerosse wrote for the *Daily Express* was admirably restrained. Randolph thought otherwise. Furious at being made fun of in public, he telephoned Lord Beaverbrook and claimed the right of reply. His request was granted. Beaverbrook invited him to dinner, listened to his complaint, and agreed to give him space in the newspaper. 'You can't attack God in the *Daily Express*,' said Beaverbrook, 'but you may attack Castlerosse.'

Randolph's reply – concocted it is said with the help of Brendan Bracken and Freddie Birkenhead – was published two days after his birthday celebration. Headed 'Poor Castlerosse' it was more of an exercise in venom than an attempt at vindication.

'Whoever it may be that the younger generation fear to compete with,' declared Randolph, 'it is certainly not Lord Castlerosse . . . Lord Castlerosse has principally endeared himself to his friends because he is supposed to be amusing. I have always found him more amusing to look at than to listen to, but what a tragedy it is, as he is supposed to be a wit, to have a wife who is so much more amusing than himself. It is certainly pertinent to inquire: "Why did he write this article? What is the cause of this unprovoked mewing, this pathetic protest of middle age?" I fear the answer is very simple. He is jealous. He is consumed with the ridiculous jealousy of any success that his juniors may gain.'

The precise nature of these youthful successes was left conveniently vague. Randolph's friends might have hazarded a guess; but what, one wonders, did the readers in Bethnal Green make of it all? Even the uninitiated, however, must have smiled at Randolph's pompous conclusion. 'As for his attacks on me,' he trumpeted, 'I refuse to be provoked.'

This outburst did not end the quarrel between Randolph and

Valentine Castlerosse. If anything, the sniping intensified. The two of them could never be in a room together without locking horns. A climax was reached some years later when, at the opening of a London restaurant, Castlerosse hurled a vase at Randolph, missed his target, and almost floored one of the women guests. (Another version of the same incident has it that Randolph aimed a punch at Castlerosse and accidentally struck the unfortunate lady.) It is hardly surprising that Randolph contemplated forming a society to exclude all gossip writers from parties.

*   *   *

'I had expected,' Randolph wrote on Saturday, 30 July 1932, 'that when I arrived in Berlin on Wednesday morning I should find intense excitement and disorder. I found instead a city as calm and orderly as London.'

Once again he had been commissioned by the *Sunday Graphic* to report on a national crisis in Germany. This time he was covering an important election. It was the third national election to be held in Germany in five months. Earlier that year two rounds of presidential elections had taken place and those elections had seen the emergence of the Nazi party as a powerful force in German politics. Adolf Hitler and his followers could no longer be regarded as a band of loud mouthed, but eccentric, political opportunists. The outcome of these July elections could, it was feared, pose a threat not only to German democracy but to European stability.

In the earlier elections, the eighty-four-year-old President Hindenburg had been challenged by Adolf Hitler. Although the challenge had not succeeded, Hitler had spectacularly increased the Nazi vote and come dangerously near to winning the presidency. So near, in fact, that the Nazis had been encouraged to intrigue with the sinister General Kurt von Schleicher to force further elections. First, in a series of astute political moves, they had brought about the downfall of the German Chancellor and replaced him with the slightly ludicrous Franz von Papen. Obligingly Papen had then dissolved the Reichstag and called for new elections at the end of July.

Somewhat more alarmingly, Papen had also lifted and earlier ban on the Nazi stormtroopers and unleashed a wave of political violence and murder. In the early weeks of July several German towns had been convulsed by street fighting and riots. It was news of these clashes that had led Randolph to expect an explosive situation in Berlin. His surprise in finding the city so calm was due entirely to the fact that martial law had been proclaimed a few days before his arrived. All the same, the election promised to be exciting.

From the moment he arrived, Randolph's eyes were fixed on Hitler. Together with the right-wing Nationalists, led by Alfred Hugenburg, the Nazis seemed to hold the key to the election. 'Everything turns on two issues,' Randolph reported. 'First can Hitler obtain a majority by himself? Secondly, if he fails to achieve that, will the Nazis and the Hugenburg party between them obtain a plurality over all the other parties?' Randolph's money was firmly on Adolf Hitler. Like many other British observers in Berlin, he was clearly fascinated by the strutting, upstart Nazi leader. Throughout the campaign he was to watch Hitler with a mixture of suspicion, amusement, condescension, grudging admiration and apprehension.

His arrival in the German capital could not have been more timely. The Nazi election campaign was in full swing and about to reach its theatrical climax. During the earlier presidential elections Hitler had taken full advantage of a relatively new method of political campaigning by crisscrossing Germany in a Junkers passenger plane, addressing frenzied crowds in three or four cities each day, and appearing to be as omnipresent as he was tireless. These tactics were again employed during the July elections. Wednesday, 27 July – the day of Randolph's arrival – saw Hitler at his most effective as an air-borne, rabble-rousing orator. That day he harangued a crowd of 60,000 in Brandenburg, appeared at another massive rally in Potsdam and ended the day as the star-performer at the giant Grünewald Stadium in Berlin, his speech being relayed to an additional 100,000 outside. Randolph accompanied the Nazi cavalcade for most of the day and gave his readers a graphic account of its progress.

'All Wednesday afternoon,' he reported, 'I spent flying round with Hitler from one meeting to another. First of all we lunched at the aerodrome just outside Berlin. Hitler is a teetotaller, a non-smoker and a vegetarian. On this occasion he ate his favourite scrambled eggs and salads. His lieutenants and I fortify ourselves with a more substantial meal. We all climb into Hitler's three-motored ten seater aeroplane. Nazi guards click their heels and raise their hands in the passive salute and we are off.

'In twenty minutes we have landed in a field of clover. A special bodyguard – twelve magnificent looking men in black uniform, all carrying concealed firearms – salute their leader. We drive 12 kilos to the meeting. At every corner of the road, at every cottage door, there is a group of people. All the young boys and girls raise their hand to Hitler. A few older people, with a sour look upon their faces, but they are in the minority.

'We arrive at the stadium. For 300 yards the road is lined with brown uniformed Nazis standing rigidly at attention, and holding hands to keep the crowds off the roads. Hitler mounts the platform; 15,000 arms are raised, 15,000 voices yell "Heil Hitler". The chairman shouts "Achtung", and a pin-drop silence ensues. Hitler speaks – quietly at first, but as he proceeds his voice becomes charged with emotion and enthusiasm rises to a challenging note . . . We drive off as the crowd sings with impressive fervour "Deutschland Uber Alles". Soon we are flying over Berlin . . .

'Hitler is clearly tired, but there is no time for rest. We must start immediately for the last and biggest meeting. By the time we arrive there are certainly no fewer than 120,000 people crammed into the stadium. Fifteen thousand storm troopers are drawn up in the centre. It is dark and most of them hold flaming torches. Massed bands play the marching song of the Nazis as Hitler drives slowly round the stadium in an open car. For ten minutes the crowd shout "Heil Hitler," until they are almost chanting the refrain.

'I can only describe the meeting as a mixture between an American football game and a boy scouts' jamboree, animated with the spirit of a revivalist meeting and conducted with the discipline of the Brigade of Guards.'

Such descriptions were to become all too familiar to newspaper readers. But in 1932, with Hitler poised on the brink of power, it made for startling, chilling, almost unbelievable, reporting. Young Randolph Churchill was one of the first journalists to capture the electrifying atmosphere of Nazi mass meetings, the mob mentality and suppressed hysteria, and to hint at the menace that lay behind it. He was shrewd also in recognizing the threat such skilfully induced fervour posed to the peace of Europe.

'Nothing is more foolish,' he warned, 'than to underestimate the intensely vital spirit that animates the Nazi movement. Hitler has no detailed policy. He has promised all things to all men. Many Germans say that he no longer wants power – that he is frightened of the forces he has called into being. They say he does not want a majority and merely wishes to be part of a Coalition. I do not believe this to be true.

'He is surrounded by a group of resolute, tough and vehement men who would never tolerate any backsliding from their leader. Nothing can long delay their arrival in power. Hitler will not betray them. But let us make no mistake about it

'The success of the Nazi party sooner or later means war. Nearly all of Hitler's principal lieutenants fought in the last war. Most of them have two or three medals on their breasts. They burn for revenge. They are determined once more to have an army. I am sure that once they have achieved it they will not hesitate to use it.

101

'For the moment, however, the danger is postponed. It is virtually impossible for Hitler to win this election. He will have to continue his support of the present Government.

'In the last 12 months there have been four elections, which have cost Germany over £6,000,000. They cannot afford another one yet, but all the time the Nazis will attain strength and impetus, and within three years at the most Europe will be confronted with a deadly situation.

'Nothing except a radical revision of the Treaty of Versailles can quench the fire that burns in German hearts. The removal of the sense of injustice which the German nation feels is the most vital task that confronts European statesmanship today.'

Randolph was later to republish part of this *Sunday Graphic* report and point with pride to his youthful perception. However, with a show of modesty he claimed that his views had been fashioned by his father before he left for Berlin. How true this was is debatable. Certainly Churchill, who made no secret of his suspicions about the rise of National Socialism in Germany, would have warned him about the dangers of 'Hitlerism'. But Randolph's report does not entirely reflect his father's views. Significantly he refrained from republishing the last paragraph which calls for a revision of the Treaty of Versailles. This was not a particularly novel argument – it was strenuously advocated by the Nazis – but it was not supported by Churchill. Indeed a few months later Churchill was to be criticized for siding with Sir John Simon in claiming that the disarmament clauses of the Treaty of Versailles were still binding on Germany. There is certainly reason to think that Randolph, for all his barbed asides, was not completely immune to the spell cast by Adolf Hitler.

He was young and, although he would have hated to admit it, he was impressionable. His apprehensions about the Nazi movement were aroused not so much by Hitler as by the men who surrounded the Nazi Führer. This was to become more apparent later. As he predicted, the Nazis did not win this election (they obtained only 37.1 per cent of the total poll) but they emerged as the largest single party in Germany and this seems to have impressed Randolph. He appears to have left Berlin convinced that, for good or ill, the one German politician his father should meet was Adolf Hitler.

CHAPTER SIX

From the Lido to Fleet Street

Within weeks of leaving Berlin, Randolph was back in Germany. This time he joined his father on a working holiday. Some two years earlier Churchill, taking advantage of his political idleness, had embarked on a mammoth biography of his illustrious ancestor the First Duke of Marlborough. Work on the book had suffered from unavoidable interruptions but, by the summer of 1932, Churchill's researches had reached the stage where he felt it necessary to make a tour of the battlefields connected with Marlborough's campaigns. In August of that year, accompanied by his wife, his daughter Sarah, Professor Lindemann and the military historian Lieutenant-Colonel Pakenham-Walsh, he set off for Holland and Belgium to visit the scenes of Marlborough's early triumphs at Ramilles and Oudenarde before travelling to Munich and Blenheim. Whether Randolph was with the party from the outset is not clear, but he had certainly joined his parents by the time they reached Munich.

The Churchill party was staying at Munich's Hotel Continental and it was from there that Randolph tried to arrange a meeting which, had he succeeded, might well have proved historic. Certainly it would have proved interesting: his aim was to bring his father face to face with Adolf Hitler. Unfortunately his plans misfired.

Randolph was forced to act through a third party. The man he chose as a go-between was the notorious Ernst Hanfstaengel, better known to his friends as 'Putzi'. A graduate of Harvard, Putzi Hanfstaengel, was the son of a Munich art dealer and had been a friend and financial supporter of Hitler since the early 1920s. He was a highly social young man and, as a gifted pianist, was a great favourite with hostesses in London and New York. How and when he and Randolph first met is uncertain but their friendship was undoubtedly strengthened during Randolph's coverage of the recent German elections. It was apparently during the election campaign that the idea of a meeting between Churchill and Hitler was first mooted. 'I had seen quite a lot of . . . Randolph during our election tours,' recalled Hanfstaengel some years later. 'I had even arranged for him to travel once or twice in the plane with us. He had indicated that his father was coming to Germany and that we should arrange a meeting.' Churchill's stopover in Munich seemed to provide an excellent opportunity.

Randolph invited Hanfstaengel to dine with his parents at the Hotel Continental and suggested that he bring Hitler with him. Hitler, however, refused the invitation. He was far too busy, he protested. There seemed no point in his meeting Churchill. 'What on earth would I talk to him about?' he asked. 'My heart sank,' says Hanfstaengel. 'Hitler produced a thousand excuses, as he always did when he was afraid of meeting someone.' At last Hanfstaengel was obliged to leave for the Continental alone. Perhaps, he suggested as a parting shot, Hitler would collect him at the hotel and stay for coffee? But Hitler refused to commit himself. 'In any case,' he growled, 'they say your Mr Churchill is a rabid Francophile.'

The dinner started well enough. About ten people sat down to eat and Hanfstaengel was seated on Clementine Churchill's right. He found her 'serene, intelligent and enchanting.' Churchill was no less fascinated by his guest who, he claimed, appeared to be completely under Hitler's spell. But mutual interest did not prevent a certain degree of embarrassment. 'We talked about this and that,' says Hanfstaengel, 'and then Mr Churchill taxed me about Hitler's anti-Semitic views. I tried to give as mild an account of the subject as I could, saying that the real problem was the influx of eastern European Jews and the excessive representation of their co-religionaries in the professions, to which Churchill listened very carefully, commenting: "Tell your boss from me that anti-Semitism may be a good starter, but it is a bad sticker." '

As the talk grew more political, Hanfstaengel became increasingly edgy. He found himself hoping that Hitler had changed his mind and would arrive to rescue him. But he waited in vain. Finally, after coffee had been served, Hanfstaengel excused himself and went into the hotel lobby to telephone Hitler. His calls were unsuccessful but, on leaving the telephone booth, he was astonished to find the Führer standing on the hotel staircase, saying goodbye to a friend. Once again he pleaded with Hitler to join the Churchills and once again Hitler refused. This time he excused himself because he was unshaven. Resignedly Hanfstaengel returned to the dining room.

The following day Hitler tried to justify his evasion. 'In any case,' he complained to Hanfstaengel, 'what part does Churchill play? He is in opposition and no one pays any attention to him.' This infuriated Hanfstaengel. 'People,' he pointed out, 'say the same thing about you.' All the same, Hitler was careful to keep well clear of the Hotel Continental until the Churchills left two days later. Randolph's disappointment can only be imagined. With his flair for the dramatic, he must – like Putzi Hanfstaengel – have deeply regretted his failure to organize 'one of those confrontations which would have been the delight of historians.'

From Munich the Churchills travelled on to Blenheim. This was the high-spot of Winston Churchill's tour. The letters he later wrote to his friends reflect the excitement he felt at re-peopling the battlefields 'with ghostly but glittering armies.' That excitement was not, alas, so evident in the heart-to-heart talks he had with Randolph about this time. Judging from the account of these talks which Randolph later gave to Robert Bruce Lockhart, it seems that the scenes of Marlborough's great triumphs merely served to emphasize for Churchill the contrast between his family's brilliant past and what appeared to be its dismal future. 'What are you doing?' he asked his son. 'When I was your age, I was reading five hours a day. You spend most of your time in night-clubs, staving off a vast army of debtors by eking out a precarious living as a hack-journalist.'

The spirit of optimism which had enlivened Randolph's birthday *fêtes* a few months earlier was already beginning to look like wishful thinking.

Churchill's tetchiness might, in part, have been the result of illness. Somewhere on the journey he had drunk contaminated water and contracted paratyphoid and this weakened him considerably. So serious was his fever by the time he reached Saltzburg that he cancelled his original plan of travelling across the Alps to Venice and spent the next two weeks in a sanatorium. This effectively ended the family holiday. Randolph was left to continue on to Venice by himself.

*   *   *

Of all the mistakes made by Randolph in his book *Twenty One Years*, none was more misleading than the account he gave of his riotous sojourn in Venice. The events he describes did not occur, as he says, in the summer of 1930, nor was he correct in claiming that he went to Venice as the guest of Brendan Bracken. Evelyn Waugh remarked on both these errors shortly after *Twenty One Years* was published. 'I think,' wrote Waugh, when thanking Randolph for a copy of the book, 'you have misdated by two years the Venetian season when the English were so obstreperous and I don't think you were then staying with Brendan but with Mona Williams.' Waugh's memory, although often shaky, was better than Randolph's. The points he makes were confirmed, quite independently, many years later by Lady Mosley and Lady Diana Cooper – both of whom were involved in the chaos created by Randolph. Lady Mosley says she is sure the year was 1932 and, she adds, 'I am sure Randolph was not

there [Venice] in 1930. I was there both summers.' Lady Diana
Cooper is equally emphatic in claiming that Randolph did not stay
with Brendan Bracken but with Mrs Harrison Williams, with whom
she says he 'was very friendly at that time.' Unfortunately
Randolph's lapse of memory has led at least two of Brendan
Bracken's conscientious biographers astray.

If further confirmation of the year were needed, it is to be found
in contemporary press reports. Gossip writers looking for copy in
the summer of 1932 were kept well supplied by dispatches from
Italy. Most of the excitement tended to revolve around Randolph
who was at his battling best. Fights were liable to break out
wherever he showed his face.

Venice that year was crowded with fashionable English visitors.
Many of them, like Bryan and Diana Guinness (formerly Mitford,
now Lady Mosley), Duff and Diana Cooper, Oswald Mosley,
Robert Boothby, Lady Cunard, Sir Thomas Beecham, Brendan
Bracken and Edward James, were friends of Randolph's and no
doubt familiarity encouraged – if encouragement were needed – his
eagerness to show off. He was very much in evidence from the
moment he arrived.

Not the least of the holiday attractions for Randolph was the
presence of the bewitching Doris Castlerosse. Heavy hints about
their relationship soon began to appear in the press. 'By day the
Lido is equally gay,' reads an early report of the Venetian festivities.
'Mr Duff Cooper strides along the beach – a true outpost of Empire
in his khaki, shorts and vest ... The voice of Mr Randolph
Churchill – whom Lady Castlerosse calls "Fuzzy-Wuzzy" – goes
booming down the canals, presaging at least an audible political
career.' But it was not only down the canals that Randolph's voice
boomed, nor were the names applied to him always so coy.

It would be tedious to detail every slanging match, every scrap
and scuffle in which Randolph was involved. His three weeks in
Venice were among the most riotous of his early career. One
incident, however, deserves mention if only for its sensation. This
was the occasion when, as Evelyn Waugh puts it, 'the English were
so obstreperous' and which Randolph modestly describes as a
'tremendous fracas.' For once, neither of them was exaggerating.

The rumpus started at a party on the island of Murano, given by
the rich, amusing and socially conscious 'Chips' Channon. It was a
lavish affair, held to celebrate the fortieth birthday of Lady Diana
Cooper. The fact that things got out of hand was not the fault of the
discriminating host: Chips Channon's choice of guest was, as
always, impeccable. Most of the fashionable English visitors in
Venice were invited and, socially, the party should have been one of

the highlights of the summer season. What turned this elegant entertainment into a rough-house, was Randolph's penchant for mischief making. By deliberately interfering in a personal, but well publicised, quarrel between two of the other guests, Randolph provoked uproar.

For some days the gossips of Venice had been rivetted by newspaper reports of a tiff between an 'American heiress and a British baronet.' The heiress was the much sought-after, much cossetted Doris Duke. The baronet was Sir Richard Sykes. Apparently Sir Richard, eagerly pursuing Miss Duke, had pounced upon her while travelling in her car through France and had been unceremoniously turfed out of the car by her bodyguard and forced to walk home. Since then Miss Duke had kept well clear of Sir Richard. The two of them had not, in fact, met again until the party on Murano. The meeting was not a happy one. Sir Richard, abject and repentant, tried to patch things up but Miss Duke would have nothing to do with him. When he sat next to her, she flounced off leaving him sulking in a corner.

It was then that Randolph decided to step in. No doubt sensing some fun, he stalked over to the miserable, slightly drunk, Sir Richard, yanked him to his feet and dragged him across to Miss Duke's table. In a loud voice he insisted that they kiss and make up. But Sir Richard was no longer in a conciliatory mood. Perhaps by accident, but more likely on purpose, he responded to Randolph's demand by stubbing out his lighted cigarette on Miss Duke's hand. This was too much for Randolph. Forgetting his role as peacemaker, he thumped Sir Richard and a fight broke out. Within minutes the entire party had joined in.

'They were all terribly drunk,' remembers Lady Diana Cooper, 'it was too frightening, fists were flying, bottles were broken, there was glass everywhere. People were pounding each other for no known reason. I hung on to Duff as he would have loved to have joined in.'

Eventually the fight calmed down. 'The rats,' says Lady Diana, 'decided to leave – Randolph among them – and returned to Venice taking all the boats with them, leaving us stranded.' Shortly afterwards, Lady Cunard arrived. Blissfully unaware of the fracas, she looked round approvingly at the pathetic group that was left. 'What a marvellous party,' she beamed. She spoke too soon. Hardly had she voiced her approval than a bottle broke and the fighting started all over again. All the 'rats' had not departed: Sir Richard Sykes was still on the rampage.

Lady Diana Cooper was never to forget the horror of her ill-fated birthday party. Almost fifty years later she could recall every incident vividly, but with a shudder. 'When the British are carnivalling,' she sighed, after describing the glass bespattered finale, 'they behave disgracefully and become quite impossible.' Her accounts of Randolph's antics, however, were softened by a smile. 'I was very fond of him,' she confessed. 'He was stimulating, irritating, often infuriating but he was marvellous to his friends. I loved him and miss him very much.'

Others were not so indulgent. Accounts of the fracas, and Randolph's part in it, featured on the social pages of several newspapers that weekend. The Italian press professed outrage and made acid comments about the pernicious influence of British nannies. (According to Randolph a special train was needed to convey back to England the army of British nannies and governesses who were hastily dismissed by their Italian employers.) In the *Sunday Dispatch*, that indefatigable gossipmonger, the Marquess of Donegal, treated the incident as a world-shattering event. Relying on a garbled account, he attributed the blame to a chance remark made by Randolph while Sir Richard Sykes was trying to placate Doris Duke. 'What Did Randolph Say?' demanded a banner headline which appeared above the photographs of Randolph and Venetian gondolas on one of the centre pages. If Randolph was not achieving the distinction his father hoped for, he was certainly acquiring notoriety.

None of this seems to have bothered Randolph. He was singularly unperturbed by the sensation he created. Reading *Twenty One Years* one would imagine he was a bystander at the Murano shindy. This might have been intentional – he tended to play down his excesses in the book – or it could be that he genuinely forgot his own contribution to the fighting. Such lapses of memory were not unusual. He had a remarkable knack for putting unpleasant incidents out of his mind. After a night of exchanging insults he would turn up the following morning and look bewildered if anyone tackled him about a wounding remark he had made. 'Oh that was *last night*,' he would laugh. 'Today's another day, you must forget about last night.'

Truculence, particularly truculence when he was drunk, was part of his nature and he expected others to accept it as such. He would no more have thought of excusing his churlishness than he would have apologized for having blue eyes. That this self-deception, this convenient forgetfulness, was mentally dishonest did not occur to him. One of his greatest virtues, he insisted, was his strict adherence to the truth. Nothing pleased him more than catching one of his friends out in a deliberate lie. He was particularly merciless in exposing the fabrications of Brendan Bracken.

Although he does not appear to have stayed with Bracken in Venice, he undoubtedly saw a great deal of him during this holiday. Bracken was living in a palazzo opposite the Grand Hotel and claimed that he had inherited this splendid abode from his mother. Randolph was immediately suspicious. Not only had Bracken produced both the palace and his mother out of the blue but, when Randolph inspected the rooms, he discovered that the furniture and books were distinctly German in origin. He taxed Bracken on his unexpectedly acquired Teutonic tastes. Bracken's response was ingenious. His mother, he explained, had married a German late in life and the palazzo still contained her belongings. Only later, when some mutual friends hired the palazzo for a season, was it confirmed that Bracken had rented his furnished lodgings and had left with the rent still owing. Randolph was delighted. Bracken, he announced at a luncheon at Boulestin's a few weeks later, was 'God's greatest liar because he does not mind being found out.'

Of an equally typical encounter with Bracken in Venice, Randolph makes no mention. Those who witnessed it, however, found the incident extremely embarrassing. There are several versions, but that recounted by Lady Mosley is the most credible. ('I remember it so well,' she says.) At luncheon at the Lido Taverno, Randolph was apparently in a merry mood. He amused himself by teasing Bracken and ended by calling him 'my brother'. This infuriated Bracken. Jumping up from the table, he lunged at Randolph who turned and fled to the beach. 'When Brendan caught up with him,' says Lady Mosley, 'Randolph reached out, snatched off his spectacles and threw them in the water. Brendan, half blind, stood in the shallow sea roaring like a bull and peering short-sightedly at the sand until somebody retrieved the spectacles, broken, for him. An American was heard to say: "Fon is fon, but that Randolph Churchill goes too far." '

The love-hate relationship between Randolph and Brendan Bracken bewildered outsiders. At times they appeared to be loyal companions, at one in their love of politics and their shared devotion to Winston Churchill; often, however, they would quarrel bitterly, express mutual distrust, and sneer behind each other's backs. There was no knowing how things would develop when they met.

Randolph was the more openly antagonistic. He never reconciled himself to Bracken's close friendship with his father and was offended – although he pretended to be amused – at the gossip about Bracken being Churchill's bastard. He was also jealous of Bracken's political influence. All too frequently, these resentments would erupt into a display of petulance which, thinly disguised as banter, left no doubt about his true feelings. Bracken was more circumspect.

Scathing as he could be about Randolph, he was careful to keep his hostility within bounds. Only when deliberately provoked did his control slip: he had no wish to appear an outright enemy of Churchill's only son.

Indeed Bracken did his best to cultivate Randolph's friendship. Few adults were more attentive to Randolph as a child and those attentions continued throughout Randolph's career at Eton and Oxford. In many ways Bracken behaved to Randolph like an indulgent uncle or a watchful elder brother: writing to him when they were separated, offering advice, keeping him up to date with family and political news and generally showing concern for his welfare. Even after the embarrassing Venice incident he strove to further Randolph's interests. It was with Brendan Bracken's help – or so it is said – that Randolph, shortly after his return to England, landed his first important job as a journalist.

* * *

'Each week during the forthcoming Parliamentary session Mr Randolph Churchill, the brilliant son of a famous father, will contribute exclusively for the *Sunday Dispatch* a causerie on political matters of the moment. Mr Randolph Churchill will express his own views, which will be largely representative of the younger men interested in politics.'

So read an announcement which appeared in the *Sunday Dispatch* on 9 October 1932. It marked a new departure for the newspaper. Until then the political column of the *Sunday Dispatch* had been written by an assortment of Tory backbench MPs, who contributed notes on parliamentary affairs under a variety of headings. Randolph's column, 'Searchlight on Politics', was the first to be written by a contributor who was not an MP and whose political experience was minimal. He was also, at twenty-one, the youngest commentator to be entrusted with such an influential column.

But if his appointment was novel, it was a very fashionable novelty. The 1920s and 1930s saw the beginning of a cult of youth which was to transform – some would say distort – the political thinking of generations to come. Starting in the years of disillusionment which followed the First World War and gathering momentum after the Second World War, the belief that the expectations of the young provided the best guide for the future became an article of faith for politicians of all parties. Callow judgement was preferred to received wisdom, experience was discounted, desire replaced knowledge and age was regarded as an infirmity. Although Randolph did not fully share these modish prejudices, he was not above exploiting them. In an article, 'Rejoice

110

In Thy Youth' – written a few months earlier – he had scathingly attacked the obstruction of the elderly.

'Nothing,' he observed disdainfully, 'is more sad than the lack of enthusiasm and capacity for action which seems to descend upon everyone as they grow older. So soon as they have acquired an adequate experience of life they begin to lose the fierce ardour which formerly spurred them on . . . The aged business man and the faded actress spending their retirement pottering around the garden provide a charming spectacle and are often agreeable members of society. They may rightly be treated with deference and respect *even* by the youngest. But the old man gibbering in his office long after his ability has been exhausted is as pathetic and loathsome an object as the disintegrating and gauche old actress who still clings passionately to the frail remnant of her youthful success. They must inevitably be the easy target at which youth can direct its most piercing arrows.'

Now, given the freedom of the *Sunday Dispatch*, he began to sharpen his arrows. His first column, ominously headed 'Ministers Must Work Hard,' was published the following week. It was fairly innocuous, confined for the most part to speculation about the forthcoming parliamentary session. Some time was to pass before those arrows began to hit the target and even then they were aimed with discretion. The column, a *pot-pourri* of political comment, anecdote and gossip presented in short paragraphs, was, on the whole, relatively moderate in tone. It reflected not so much the opinions of the younger generation as the views of the fifty-seven-year-old Winston Churchill – India, the League of Nations, the Geneva Disarmament Conference and the need to strengthen the Royal Air Force, all featured prominently – and it may have been a sense of responsibility towards his father, as well as keeping a wary eye on his own political prospects, that held Randolph in check. He could not, however, resist an occasional thrust. Various minor politicians (mostly Tory, mostly now forgotten) came in for some crudely offensive abuse; and, of course, Ramsay MacDonald and Stanley Baldwin were singled out for criticism. But the martyr, the St Sebastian, of Randolph's more pointed shafts was undoubtedly the recently appointed Under-Secretary for Foreign Affairs – Mr Anthony Eden.

Randolph's vendetta against Anthony Eden was intense and long lasting. So bitter were his attacks against Eden's policies and person that his friends were reluctant to mention Eden's name in front of him for fear of provoking a scene. In later years Randolph liked to claim that his hostility was entirely political and that privately he harboured an affection for Eden, but his jibes were often so personal

111

that it is impossible to take his protestations seriously. His antagonism was certainly politically inspired but, as so frequently happens, the man became indistinguishable from the cause.

A variety of factors could account for Randolph's enmity. Like many ambitious politicians he tended to see a greater threat to his career among men in his own party than in the ranks of his declared opponents. Political differences are a matter of principle, political rivalry involves personalities: Randolph was apt to be suspicious of any promising young Tory. Anthony Eden was some fourteen years older than Randolph but he was young and popular enough to block the advancement of a latter-day 'younger Pitt'. Moreover he had the advantage of being favoured by the Tory leadership while Randolph, staunch in his loyalty to his father, was forced to languish on the side-lines. Eden's rise in the Conservative ranks, while not spectacular, had been rapid enough to arouse the jealousy of younger men. Of more immediate concern was the fact that Eden was a member of the National Government and, as such, was ostensibly opposed to the policies of the 'Churchill camp'. Randolph was later to express resentment of the way in which Eden had been promoted over the head of his friend Duff Cooper whose intimacy with Winston Churchill would have ensured a more robust opposition to the European dictators. The fact that Eden later supported Churchill in no way absolved him from blame in Randolph's eyes.

All these things – suspicion, jealousy, genuine political distrust – could have contributed to Randolph's campaign against Eden. What is more certain is that the campaign started in earnest shortly after Randolph began to write his column for the *Sunday Dispatch*. He depicted the Under-Secretary for Foreign Affairs as weak, indecisive, compromising and ineffectual. At the beginning of 1932, Eden began to attend the Disarmament Conference in Geneva as Head of the British Delegation and his regular departures invariably provoked an acid comment from Randolph. The flavour of his attacks, however, is probably best conveyed in the full-scale article he wrote a couple of years later after Eden had been appointed Lord Privy Seal. The elevation of his rival appears to have reversed Randolph's professed faith in the worthiness of youth.

'The latest political fad,' starts the article, 'is the cult of Mr Anthony Eden. He first leapt into international fame last summer when a French newspaper decided he was the best dressed Englishman. Since then the political prophets and wiseacres have been tipping him as the next leader of the Conservative Party . . . Many powerful individuals and groups are uniting at the moment to puff him. We are told how remarkable it is that such a young man should attain such high office. Considering his limited abilities, it is remarkable. But he is not really young. He is thirty-six . . . In the past most politicians of real merit have got further at that age . . . I have never been one of those who subscribed to the foolish campaign which sought to boost youth at the expense of the old men . . . If youth is any good at all it will make its own chances. Many of the old men are far more virile than the milk-and-water young men who today permeate the Tory Party. The young men who do get advancement only do so by a sedulous aping of the older men. Mr Anthony Eden has none of the qualities of youth. He is sedate, not fiery; respectable, not dashing . . .' And so he went on.

No one could have failed to appreciate the comparison between Anthony Eden and a fiery young man of promise. To emphasize this point, Randolph stressed the achievements of the Churchill family – Lord Randolph Churchill was thirty-five when he entered the Cabinet, Winston Churchill thirty three – and concluded by remarking on the formidable reputation Lord Randolph had established before attaining office. With another Churchill waiting in the wings, Eden had no reason to feel smug.

Randolph was twenty-two when he wrote the article. What is perhaps surprising is that he republished it twenty-five years later and claimed that he saw little reason to alter his harsh judgement. The embarrassments of time, the reversals of fortune, had done nothing to soften his attitude towards his adversary.

Inevitably Churchill was suspected of inspiring many of Randolph's caustic comments. The extent of his influence, however, is uncertain. As was only to be expected, Randolph's political views reflected those of his father and he undoubtedly used his column to promote Churchill's cause. The column also carried heavy hints of information gleaned from the table-talk at Chartwell. But Randolph remained his own man and presented his opinions in his own way. There were times when Churchill was positively embarrassed by his son's tactlessness.

Churchill's inability to control Randolph was no secret. The frank talk they had had in Germany had produced no discernible results and Randolph remained as defiant as ever. Clashes between father and son continued unabatedly. One such clash had occurred, in the presence of Professor Lindemann, shortly after Randolph returned from Venice. Robert Bruce Lockhart heard about it from Harold Nicolson. 'Winston,' noted Lockhart in his diary on 5 October 1932, 'had had a real row with Randolph, who finally had flung out of the room in a furious temper. Winston went to the mantelpiece, turned round an ornament, and then more in sorrow than in anger addressed Lindemann. "Lindemann," he said, "you

113

are a professor of biology and experimental philosophy. Tell me am I as a parent responsible for all the biological and chemical reactions in my son?" '

What sparked off this particular quarrel is not known. It may have been yet another of Churchill's attempts to curb his son's extravagance. Randolph's irresponsible attitude towards money was a constant source of friction: it probably caused more family rows than anything else. He appeared utterly incapable of appreciating the need for economy. While Churchill battled on to pay off debts and meet the expenses of Chartwell, Randolph insisted on living like a lord. Any increase in his income was invariably offset by an expansion of his lifestyle. As far as he was concerned, money earned was money to be overspent. His father fulminated and despaired.

A telling example of Randolph's *folie de grandeur* followed his appointment as a regular columnist on the *Sunday Dispatch*. Having secured a position of influence he decided to live up to it by moving into a suite – three rooms and a bathroom – at the Mayfair Hotel. Few young journalists could have afforded such luxury: only one of Randolph's pretentiousness would have considered it necessary.

*   *   *

On 9 February 1933 the Oxford Union conducted what Christopher Hollis, the historian of the Union, describes as 'the most famous – or, if it be preferred, the most notorious – debate in its history.' This was the debate in which the controversial motion 'that in no circumstances would it [the Union] fight for King and country' was carried by 275 votes to 152.

The debate originated in a chance suggestion by one of the Union members. When the motion was accepted doubts were expressed as to whether anyone would be found to speak in its favour. However the President, Mr Frank Harvie, considered the subject worthy of debate and decided to enliven the proceedings by inviting two guest speakers. The visitor chosen to support the motion was Professor C. E. M. Joad – later to become a popular radio personality – and the opposing speaker was Mr Quintin Hogg, the future Lord Hailsham. The debate was expected to be interesting, but not sensational. Six years earlier the Cambridge Union had passed an almost identical motion without undue fuss and there seemed no reason why the Oxford debate should create a stir. The London newspapers did not even bother to send reporters.

The arguments advanced by both sides were, over the years, to become all too familiar. Quintin Hogg's case centred on the contention that 'the unilateral disarmament of Britain would render

114

us impotent to prevent war in other parts of the world.' Professor Joad, somewhat more colourfully, concentrated on the horrors and futility of armed conflict. 'Within half an hour,' he warned, 'a single bomb from an aeroplane would poison every living thing within an area of three quarters of a mile.' By and large the debating honours were equal. It therefore came as a surprise when the motion was carried by a decisive majority.

'I hope this gets into the press,' Frank Harvie was heard to remark as he left the hall.

But at first it looked as if the press would ignore the debate. The only report the following day appeared in the *Oxford Mail* and dismissed the proceedings as 'not particularly interesting or inspiring.' Other papers merely published the bare result. Not until the weekend, when a letter condemning the vote as the product of 'Communist cells in the Colleges' appeared in the *Daily Telegraph*, was any real indignation aroused. The letter, it is thought, was a deliberate plant by one of the newspaper's senior leader writers, J. B. Firth, and it provided a lead for the national daily press. The Beaverbook dailies were well to the fore and the *Daily Express* was particularly scathing. The vote, it thundered, was the work of 'practical jokers, woozy-minded Communists and sexual indeterminates.'

Even so the clamour might have subsided and been forgotten had Randolph Churchill not decided to keep it alive. He let it be known that he intended to challenge the vote by speaking in a further debate at the Oxford Union. His aim, he said, was to have the perfidious motion expunged from the Union's minute book.

Randolph's anger at the outcome of the debate was genuine and predictable. He could not have reacted otherwise. The vote outraged everything he believed in. He was very much his father's son, very much a Churchill, and held firmly to the robust ideals his family sought to defend. His sense of pride, his patriotism and loyalty to the Crown, his courage, his aspirations, his very birthright had all been brought into question by the actions of his contemporaries. In his *Sunday Dispatch* column he had made no secret of his contempt for the faint-hearted advocates of disarmament; the seekers, as he saw it, of an unrealizable Utopia. That a refusal to serve King and country had been applauded in the Oxford Union – the scene of one of his few public triumphs – simply added personal shame to public ignominy. Randolph's determination to have the resolution rescinded was fervent.

His feelings of outrage were shared to the full by his father. With his flair for invective, Winston Churchill had denounced the Oxford resolution as 'an abject, squalid, shameless avowal.' Randolph did not have far to look for encouragement in his decision to confront the Oxford pacifists.

Not everyone welcomed his intervention, however. Even the opponents of the resolution had doubts as to whether he was the right person to tackle such a controversial issue. His reputation for recklessness did not inspire confidence. The Conservative Association, for instance, wanted the debate to be left in the hands of Oxford men and actively canvassed for an undergraduate to act as spokesman. But Randolph refused to give way. Egged on by, among others, Quintin Hogg and Frank Pakenham, he pressed ahead with his campaign.

Unfortunately the opportunity he sought was not immediately available. Malcolm MacDonald, the Prime Minister's son, had been invited to speak at the next Union debate, on 16 February, and the President insisted that his visit go ahead as planned. Randolph and his supporters had to wait another two weeks.

The delay proved fatal. At Malcolm MacDonald's debate there occurred an ugly incident which put paid to any chance Randolph might have had of swaying the Union. The proceedings had hardly started on 16 February when a gang of undergraduates – some of them claiming to be 'supporters of Sir Oswald Mosley's Fascist party' – invaded the hall, seized the minute book, ripped out the page recording the 'King and Country' resolution and carried it off to be burnt at the Martyrs' Memorial. Even the more moderate members of the Union were outraged by this crude interference in their affairs. Nor were tempers cooled when a black box containing 275 white feathers – one for every vote supporting the motion – was sent to the President of the Union. External bullying, it was felt, should not be allowed to influence the outcome of a Union debate.

Further trouble was expected on 2 March when Randolph arrived to address the Union. Over 1,000 tickets were issued for the debate and police were posted outside the hall to prevent rowdyism and scrutinize all the admission cards. This time, however, it was not outsiders but vouched-for members of the Union – some disguised in false beards – who caused the rumpus.

Things got off to a lively start. The motion calling for the 'King and Country' resolution to be expunged was moved by Lord Stanley of Alderley who, for some mysterious reason, arrived dressed in a grey morning coat. This odd choice of clothing apparently delighted the audience. So loud were the cat-calls which greeted Lord Stanley that he found it almost impossible to make himself heard. 'Many of his sentences,' says Frank Pakenham, who was seated next to Randolph on the the platform, 'got cut short in the middle amid uproarious laughter . . . Finally, hearing a derisive cry of "Hitler" he struck a disarming attitude and proclaimed "I am not Hitler". The laughter could now have been heard a mile away, and not unduly discomfited he sat down.'

Randolph was to be even more discomfited. When he rose to speak the good-natured barracking gave way to a torrent of abuse. 'There were hisses and a general din which can rarely have been experienced in an English assembly of this kind,' claims one observer. 'It was a very hard ordeal for a young man.' Randolph faced the onslaught with steely eyes and Churchillian courage. 'I saw him brace his shoulders,' wrote a newspaper reporter, 'just as his father used to do in the House of Commons, and indeed he becomes daily more like Mr Winston Churchill in appearance.

' "Throw me personally in the river if you like," he said, "but do not let your dislike of our action prompt you to vote against the motion." '

But he was pleading against prejudice. His audience was in no mood to listen to argument. The louder Randolph shouted for a hearing, the more vociferous the heckling. His warning that a further endorsement of pacifism would be misunderstood by the outside world was drowned in a storm of jeering; his attempt to invoke a 'love of country' was answered by cries of 'rot' and 'bunk'. Stinkbombs were hurled from the gallery and before long the debate had become a farce. Eventually Randolph and his supporters decided to end it by asking for permission to withdraw their motion. There was an immediate protest from the floor. Amid shouts of 'cowards' and 'apologize', one of their opponents pointed out that it was not permissible to withdraw a motion once it had been moved and demanded a division. The President had no alternative but to agree to the demand. The result of the division was a massive – 750 votes to 138 – defeat for Randolph's motion.

On leaving the hall, accompanied by Frank Pakenham, Randolph was made to run the gauntlet. As he pushed his way to the door, attempts were made to trip him up with walking sticks and outstretched legs and outside he was confronted by a mob of excited undergraduates. For a moment it looked as if he might be taken at his word and ducked in the river. 'A raucous cry went up, from the crowd,' says Pakenham. ' "To the Cherwell with both of them" . . . But perhaps because by this time I was a Lecturer at Christ Church, perhaps because of the freezing stare to which they were treated by Randolph, perhaps because of the earlier comedy of our morning-coated companion, we were allowed to pass by unscathed.'

Later that evening Randolph was asked why he had tried to have his motion withdrawn. His reply was disarming. 'We realized,' he explained to a reporter from the *Daily Mail*, 'that the president was right when he admitted that the Union is no longer representative of Oxford. We wished to withdraw our motion to avoid any further misunderstanding outside, to save Oxford from doing itself more harm than it had already done.'

Well meant as was this gesture, it had come too late. Far from wiping out the impression made by the 'King and Country' resolution, Randolph's intervention helped to ensure its indelibility. There was hardly a newspaper the following day which did not carry a full report of the rowdy proceedings. Randolph's humiliation was seen as confirmation of the Oxford Union's defeatist attitude. Instead of being dismissed as an undergraduate whim, the 'Oxford resolution' – as it became known – acquired a notoriety far in excess of its importance. Over the years it was to be adopted as a 'symbolic expression of pacifism' by English universities all over the world and as such was debated, passed or rejected, on numerous occasions. At one time it was even thought to have contributed to events leading up to World War II by giving Hitler a false impression of Britain's willingness to fight. There seems to be little, if any, truth in such a claim – Hitler had only recently become Chancellor, Germany was not then seen as a potential foe – but it underlines the debate's subsequent significance.

Randolph, to his credit, freely acknowledged that he had acted unwisely. Interviewed by the *Oxford Magazine* in 1936 he repeated his condemnation of the original motion but admitted that 'the steps taken by himself and his friends to undo the mischief were unhappy in their results, as they only spread the news of the Union's crime still further with the final result of horrible mischief.' This, his willingness to accept blame when he knew he was in the wrong, was one of Randolph's more endearing characteristics.

But if his intervention was ill-timed, it was not entirely ill-advised. Randolph emerged from the debate with his cap well-feathered. The popular press hailed him as a hero, praising his bravery in taking on such an hostile audience and turning his failure into a triumph. Even some of the undergraduates were reported to have had second thoughts about their boorish behaviour. 'That fellow Churchill,' one of them was heard to remark, 'had shown no end of pluck, my word, and had not been treated at all well, all things considered.' No one, however, was prouder of Randolph than his father. Writing to a friend shortly after the debate, Churchill made no secret of his admiration for his son's courage. 'Nothing,' he told Lord Hugh Cecil, 'is so piercing as the hostility of a thousand of your own contemporaries, and he was by no means crushed under it.'

Opportunities for Churchill to applaud his son's activities were rare. Fond as he was of Randolph, constant as were his hopes for the boy's success, he was undoubtedly troubled by the way his son's career was developing. All too often when Randolph's name featured in the gossip columns it caused his parents acute embarrassment. No stranger to notoriety himself, Churchill was probably less perturbed by adverse criticism than was his wife, but as his continual lecturing of Randolph illustrated, he found no reason to rejoice in his son's reputation. He was forever urging Randolph to make the most of his gifts, warning him against exploiting his privileges, emphasizing the need for single-mindedness, tenacity and a fixed sense of purpose. If nothing else, the Oxford debate showed that Randolph was not devoid of ideal-ism. This must have boosted Churchill's sorely tried faith in his son. It may even have encouraged him to guide Randolph's political activities into more conventional channels. In the month following the Oxford debate he arranged for Randolph, then resident in London, to attend a forthcoming Conservative conference as one of the delegates for his own constituency of Epping. Certainly Churchill needed all the support he could muster for the extra-parliamentary battle he was then waging within the Conserva-tive party.

*   *   *

On 17 March 1933 the National Government issued its long-awaited White Paper, outlining its proposals for a new Indian constitution. As expected, these proposals advocated sweeping changes in the status and administration of India. They recom-mended that each Indian province be granted autonomy and that central authority, previously vested in the Viceroy, be transferred to an elected Federal Government in which Indians would participate. Before legislation was drafted, however, the proposals were to be examined by a Joint Select Committee of Lords and Commons.

As a leading opponent of the Government's plans, Winston Churchill played a prominent part in the Commons debate on the White Paper. Unfortunately his elaborately prepared speech was undermined by his failure to substantiate a charge that the promotion of British officials depended more on their sympathy with government policy than on merit. Sir Samuel Hoare, the Secretary of State for India, judged his performance 'a most surprising crash.' For all that, when the time came to appoint members to the Joint Select Committee, Churchill was among those invited to serve. The invitation was tempting – it would have provided him with an excellent platform for his views – but, after five days deliberation, he turned it down. He told Sir Samuel Hoare that, having studied the list of nominees, he considered the Committee too heavily biased in favour of the government and saw no point in joining it merely to be outvoted.

He turned instead to his supporters outside parliament. Backed by two important newspapers – the *Morning Post* and the *Daily Mail* – he launched a campaign which his opponents claimed was designed to 'smash the Government.' This was an exaggeration, but there was no mistaking Churchill's determination to make his voice heard. One of his first moves was to found the Indian Defence League – an extension of the Indian Defence Committee, formed by rebel Conservative MPs – through which he hoped to mobilize the Tory rank and file. If it was not Churchill's intention to 'smash the Government' he appears to have had no qualms about splitting the Conservative party.

Randolph supported his father's campaign wholeheartedly. Not only did he share Churchill's views on India but he found the scent of battle irresistible. Politics to him was more a trial of strength than the art of the possible and the livelier the action the more eagerly he responded to the challenge. In Randolph Churchill the Indian Defence League gained a recruit who was as bellicose as he was committed.

His skirmishing started well. On 6 May 1933, two months after his Oxford defeat, he chalked up a minor, but encouraging, debating success. At the annual conference of the Junior Imperial League, he moved a motion condemning the National Government's Indian policy. His introductory speech is worth quoting as it set out his own paternal approach to recent events.

'The Conservative Party,' he maintained, 'had been misled into accepting the Socialists' policy on India, and that, as embodied in the White Paper, was essentially a defeatist policy. It tried to do too much. It would have been wiser to proceed step by step, and to set up some form of self-government in a few selected places. If this succeeded, then a Government might be set up. All over the world today democracy was coming into increasing disrespect. Wherever Western democracy had been applied in the East it had failed.' (Statements like these were to make Randolph suspect among liberal Conservatives.) He went on to accuse the Tories of being 'misled into adopting the India policy out of loyalty to their leader, Mr Baldwin, who had been misled by his association with Mr Ramsay MacDonald.' The aim of 'patriotic organizations like the league,' he concluded, should be 'to recall their leaders to their own proper path of duty. It was more important to save our Indian Empire than to save the National Government.'

His performance was impressive and won him much praise.

Flushed with this acclaim, Randolph accompanied his father later that month to Manchester where Churchill addressed a large audience in the Free Trade Hall. The meeting was an important one. Lancashire was an area from which Churchill expected strong support. Any change in Britain's relationship with India was bound to affect the Lancashire cotton trade. The Indian Congress Party was known to be hostile to trade with Britain and was already operating a boycott of British goods. This, together with the prevailing economic depression, had, over the past three years, seriously reduced British cotton exports to India. Now, with the promise of central government, the Lancashire cotton trade looked like losing whatever influence it had, through Whitehall, on Indian fiscal policy. The result could spell disaster for the north of England.

Randolph, like his father, was well aware of importance that Lancashire voters attached to the loosening of ties with India. He had hammered home the dangers posed for the cotton industry in a series of articles, recently published in northern newspapers. His name and opinions, if not his person, were familiar to many of those attending his father's meeting.

The meeting was successful, but not quite as successful as Churchill expected. His speech – and that of his friend Lord Lloyd, a former Governor of Bombay – was sympathetically received but failed to spark off real enthusiasm. Any sense of anti-climax Churchill might have felt, however, could not have been shared by his son. For Randolph the excitement of this Manchester visit came, somewhat surprisingly, from outside the Free Trade Hall. Either before or after the meeting, he was approached by a group of Manchester businessmen and asked whether he was prepared to contest a forthcoming by-election. The election was to take place in Altrincham and the businessmen were unhappy with the National Conservative candidate, Sir Edward Grigg, whose views on certain aspects of the government's India policy they found 'not sufficiently forthright'. They intended, they said, to question Grigg closely at his adoption meeting and if they were not satisfied with his replies they wanted an independent Conservative to oppose him. Randolph seemed to be the ideal man to champion their cause.

Randolph appears to have had no hesitation in accepting the invitation. He may, though, have done so with some misgivings. Sir Edward Grigg, a one-time Liberal MP and Private Secretary to Lloyd George, was a former colleague and long-standing friend of his father's (he and Churchill had shared a frontline dugout during the First World War) and by opposing him Randolph was bound to cause his family embarrassment. Any doubts he may have had, however, were completely eclipsed by the tantalizing prospect of

121

making his political mark. He left Manchester promising to return if his services were required.

Required they certainly were. At his adoption meeting, on 29 May, Sir Edward Grigg was called upon to answer a list of specific questions concerning India and his answers were found by his opponents to be disturbingly inadequate. Two days later, amid a flurry of political excitement, Randolph arrived in Manchester. 'The Conservative Association here,' reported the local correspondent of *The Times*, 'was taken by surprise today by the announcement that Mr Randolph Churchill had been invited to Manchester to discuss with the cotton trade interests averse to the India White Paper proposals the suggestion that he should become an independent candidate for the Altrincham by-election . . . Any chance for Mr Randolph Churchill, should he decide to become a candidate, must lie not among the industrial workers [the Labour party was expected to poll 9000 votes, the Liberals considerably more] but in successfully splitting the normal Conservative vote of between 26,000 and 29,000.'

With the prospect of a lively internecine fight in the offing, Randolph became the centre of nation-wide interest. On his arrival in Manchester he was besieged by journalists. Did he, they wanted to know, seriously intend to become a candidate? Would he receive sufficient backing? 'Yes, certainly,' Randolph replied firmly, before being swept off by his cheering supporters. But wiser heads – perhaps his father's among them – prevailed. The following evening, after a day of intensive discussion and a telephone call to Sir Edward Grigg, Randolph cried off. Considering his youth, and the age and distinction of his would-be opponent, his withdrawal statement was, to say the least, highly patronizing.

'I have decided,' he announced in lordly fashion, 'not to intervene in the Altrincham by-election. Although Sir Edward Grigg's attitude upon India has in the main been studiously vague, he has assured me that he is opposed to the handing over of the police to the Indian administration in the Provinces. Believing, as I do, that the Conservative Party is opposed to the White Paper policy, and that they may yet save the situation, I am not prepared at this point to split the Conservative vote and run the risk of losing Altrincham to a Liberal. I must express my thanks to the numerous and ardent supporters of all parties who, even at the eleventh hour, were so anxious to strike a blow in the interests of Lancashire trade and of our Indian Empire.'

Not surprisingly Sir Edward Grigg found Randolph's attitude insufferable. 'Any suggestion that I gave Mr Churchill . . . [any] assurance for the purpose of securing his withdrawal is false,' he protested in an angry statement repudiating Randolph's claims. He was backed by the chairman of the Conservative Association who had been present during the telephone conversation and confirmed Sir Edward's version of it. Grigg was still fuming the following day. 'I wish,' he told reporters who rushed to his Committee Rooms, 'to make it clear that there is no breach, however small, in the unity of the Conservative Party in this division. Neither I nor my supporters saw any reason for anxiety in the threat of Mr Randolph Churchill's candidature.'

Sir Edward's outburst left Randolph unmoved. Having made what he considered to be a noble renunciation, he refused to be drawn into such petty wrangling. The threat he had momentarily posed, was sufficient warning to the Tory compromisers. He had hinted that he might not be so lenient if a similar opportunity presented itself and that, for the time being, was how he was prepared to leave things. Everyone was now aware that the youngest Pitt was waiting in the wings.

In the meantime he was content to seek more amusing diversions. Two months later he was featuring in the news columns in an all-too-familiar role. At the beginning of August 1933, he and Lady Inverclyde – better known as June, the popular musical-comedy star – were sailing off Devon when their small dinghy overturned and they were thrown headlong into the sea. 'Lady Inverclyde, who is a poor swimmer,' it was reported, 'and Mr Churchill were eventually rescued by a passing yachtsman.' Once again, Randolph had proved himself unsinkable.

CHAPTER SEVEN

Randolph Hope and Glory

Randolph's political sights were now fixed firmly on Lancashire. Although he had failed to realize his ambition to enter parliament as soon as he became of age, that ambition had by no means diminished. His trial run in challenging Sir Edward Grigg at Altrincham had merely intensified his desire to find a suitable seat and he saw Lancashire as the most promising area in which to make a second, more determined, attempt. Even so, opportunities for him to do so were strictly limited. The chances of his receiving official backing were, of course, extremely slight. Very few, if any, Conservative constituencies were prepared to adopt him as a candidate for a safe seat. Not only did his stalwart support of his father's controversial views place him squarely in the camp of the Conservative rebels but by openly threatening to split the Conservative vote to further his father's cause he had deepened suspicion of his reliability. His only real hope now was to stick to his guns, concentrate on the grievances of the Lancashire cotton trade and look for a vulnerable opening. That he was genuinely convinced of the rightness of his father's stand added virtue to opportunism.

Throughout the early months of 1934 he continued to attack the Government's Indian policy in his *Sunday Dispatch* column. His accusations were often intemperate and were sometimes broadened to include members of the Joint Select Committee which was then examining the White Paper proposals. On at least one occasion Churchill felt obliged to step in and disclaim personal animosity towards one of the Tory appointees whose credentials Randolph had questioned. Somewhat more serious, perhaps, was Randolph's renewal of his father's taunt that Indian officials were appointed to support Government policy rather than for their merit. He singled out a new Governor of an Indian province who, he claimed, lacked 'distinction and political experience' and was immediately pounced upon by Churchill's critics. Explaining himself in a letter to *The Times* he claimed his attack had been misinterpreted: his accusations of Government favouritism had not been directed at a particular appointment but at Indian appointments in general. Such appointments, he suggested, were made 'in order to justify Mr Baldwin's statement that all the men on the spot were in favour of the White Paper.' His only criticism of the new Governor was that he did not possess the necessary qualifications. It was a fine distinction and not one calculated to endear him to the Tory hierarchy.

Needless to say, this did not bother Randolph in the slightest. Loyalty to his father made him regard it as a point of honour to distance himself from the Conservative leadership: the wider the gap the more righteous he felt. Never was this more apparent than in his enthusiasm for his father's attempt to expose the backstairs machinations of the Secretary of State for India, Sir Samuel Hoare. The battle was Churchill's but no one, least of all Sir Samuel, was left in any doubt about Randolph's eagerness to see his father's sword bloodied.

It was a lengthy and complicated affair and has been fully explored by Churchill's biographer, Martin Gilbert. As far as Randolph was concerned, a broad outline will suffice. In June 1933 the Manchester Chamber of Commerce drew up a document embodying its objections to the proposals of the Government's White Paper on India. One hundred copies of this document were printed and sent to London for the consideration of the Joint Select Committee. The document, however, was never circulated. Six days after it was dispatched the leaders of the Manchester Chamber of Commerce were invited to London by Lord Derby – a member of the Joint Select Committee who exercised a powerful influence in Lancashire – to dine with Sir Samuel Hoare. After that dinner the Manchester Chamber of Commerce withdrew its evidence and changed its character.

Churchill learned of this dinner and other suspicious incidents from a private informant five months later. He was naturally incensed. On 16 April 1934 he raised the matter in the House of Commons on the grounds that it was a breach of parliamentary privilege. With his charges levelled at two distinguished members of the Joint Select Committee, Churchill's move created a considerable stir. However, the Speaker found that there was sufficient *prima facie* evidence for the matter to be referred to the Committee of Privileges.

The ensuing inquiry lasted two months. Churchill appeared before the Committee of Privileges but his evidence was restricted: documents from the India Office which he wanted to submit were never produced and he was not allowed to question other witnesses. Consequently his case appeared somewhat weak. So weak, in fact, that when the report of the inquiry was published at the beginning of June 1934, he suffered a public humiliation. It was found that, although Churchill's facts were substantially correct, there had been no breach of privilege because the Joint Select Committee was not a judicial body and there was nothing to prevent anybody from trying to persuade witnesses to change their evidence. Persuasion or advice, it was argued, could not in this case be described as 'wrongful pressure'. Certain written evidence submitted by Churchill was not allowed to be published on the grounds that it would be harmful to the public interest.

No one was more angered by this crushing rebuff than Randolph. Throughout the affair he had ranged himself alongside his father, urging Churchill on and helping him collect and collate evidence. To have their crusading efforts so peremptorily dismissed was, in his eyes, not merely unjust but insulting. The day after the Committee of Privileges published its report, Randolph launched a furious attack on its verdict in his *Sunday Dispatch* column. What, he asked, was now to be made of earlier assertions that the Joint Select Committee was sitting in 'a judicial capacity'? Would not this verdict hold the door wide open for all sorts of influence to be exerted on witnesses summoned before Parliamentary Committees? 'I wonder what,' he added sardonically, 'would have been the attitude of the Committee of Privileges if persons who had an interest in the outcome of its report had spoken with its witnesses in the same fashion as their report finds that Sir Samuel Hoare and Lord Derby spoke with the witnesses before the Joint Select Committee?'

In taking on his father's opponents, Randolph moved into the range of the heavy artillery. Sir Samuel Hoare, deeply offended by Churchill's accusations, was fully aware of the role Randolph had played in the affair. His bitterness did not discriminate between father and son. 'I do not know,' he wrote to a friend, 'which is the more offensive or more mischievous, Winston or his son. Rumour, however, goes that they fight like cats with each other and chiefly agree in the prodigious amount of champagne that each of them drinks each night.'

The louder Randolph banged Churchill's Indian drum, the greater suspicion he tended to create. On 2 July he set off on a tour of northern towns, making speeches on behalf of the 'Save Lancashire' campaign. Churchill followed his son's progress with interest and was soon boasting about Randolph's talent for winning hearts and making converts; his manly, forthright manner, claimed Churchill, made a splendid impression on the crowds who flocked to his meetings. Others were somewhat less ecstatic. 'It would seem,' commented one local newspaper, 'to be a political and newspaper stunt, however, and in no way directed to the economic welfare of our cotton operatives.' Randolph took this sniping in his stride. When he deigned to acknowledge it, he did so with contempt. 'There were some newspapers,' he told Lancashire supporters of the India Defence League, 'in the country which seemed to think that Liberalism was more important than the welfare of the country. The people of Lancashire had been let down by their leaders. They sent seventy Members of Parliament to Westminster to stand up for their interests. Their only function was to stand up for Lancashire. It was not their duty to please the Government Whips or to avoid being cut by Mr Baldwin.'

Instinctively a rebel, Randolph had at last found a cause which enabled him to thumb his nose with one hand and wave a patriotic flag with the other.

*   *   *

Involved as Randolph was in politics, he still found time for journalism. The day after his attack on the Committee of Privileges' report appeared in the *Sunday Dispatch* a more sensational article by him was published in a daily newspaper. 'The ex-Kaiser Wilhelm of Germany,' announced the *Daily Mail* on 11 June 1934, 'has received at Doorn Mr Randolph Churchill . . . the brilliant son of a brilliant father – and discussed international affairs with him . . . From Mr Winston Churchill . . . the Kaiser has received the sharpest criticism; to Mr Churchill's son he was a gracious and outspoken host.'

By wangling an interview with the Kaiser, Randolph had pulled off a journalistic scoop. Since 1920 the exiled Kaiser Wilhelm II had lived in semi-seclusion at Doorn in Holland. Now seventy-five years of age, he was no longer the flamboyant, bombastic, highly conceited figure who had once strutted so confidently across the European stage. If the defeat of the Second Reich in the First World War had not mellowed him entirely, it had at least sobered him. His manner was more subdued, his posturing less arrogant: his famous spiked moustaches had been replaced by a snowy-white beard, his showy uniforms by country tweeds; his interests centred not in military aggrandisement but in his dogs, his gardening and his wood-chopping. Married to his second wife, Princess Hermine of Schönaich-Carolath, he had become decidedly more domesticated, more a rural squire than an Emperor. 'I look at the world today,' he told Randolph, 'entirely from the standpoint of a private gentleman.' He had by no means forgotten the past – he had published three volumes of memoirs in exile – but he seemed wary of courting publicity for his lost cause. Journalists, it was said, frightened him. He gave few interviews and none to representatives of the British press. The only English-speaking journalist to overcome his reluctance to speak had been George Sylvester Viereck, an American of German-Jewish origin whose account of life at Doorn had appeared in the American press some years earlier. In 1929, Robert Bruce Lockhart had visited Doorn where, in return for a favour, he had been permitted to submit a list of written questions which the Kaiser had answered and altered in his own hand. A watered-down version of Lockhart's visit was featured on the front page of the *Evening Standard* on 15 December 1929, headed 'first allied journalist who has obtained an interview' but, as most readers must have realized, the claim was shaky. Randolph was the first British reporter to publish a face-to-face interrogation of the former German monarch.

The interview was remarkable more as an historic first than as a piece of investigative journalism. The Kaiser's opinions were forthright but not particularly startling. Randolph was invited to luncheon at Doorn on two consecutive days. On each occasion he was accompanied by an unnamed Dutch friend. He found the Kaiser charming, dignified, courteous, remarkably alert and looking a good fifteen years younger than his age. He was equally impressed by Princess Hermine whose loving companionship, he claimed, had turned her husband's old age 'from what might have been tragedy into one of tranquillity and contentment.'

Tranquillity and contentment were reflected in the Kaiser's conversation. There were few jarring notes. According to Randolph, the ex-Emperor's hopes for the return of his dynasty were benign, not fervent. The German people, he said, had turned him out and if they wanted him back they would have to come and fetch him. About recent developments in Germany he was wistfully optimistic. 'Hitler', he told Randolph, 'has done marvellous work in putting new life and soul into the German nation. If ever they felt it right that his endeavours should be crowned by a return to constitutional monarchy I am sure that my family would not fail in their duty.'

For the rest, the Kaiser's views coincided, conveniently or selectively, with Randolph's own. He was pessimistic about Western democracy, saw the need for a strong hand, was scathing about the League of Nations ('the talking circus at Geneva') and laughed at talk of disarmament when every nation was busy rearming.

Never one to miss a political opportunity, Randolph questioned his host about India. He was well rewarded. 'The Kaiser', he wrote in a calculated aside, 'also showed much interest and, indeed, perplexity as to British policy in India. "If the British leave India you will be bound to get a cleavage between the Mohammedans and the Hindus . . . India is incapable of governing herself; all the great Moguls were foreigners." ' It did not require a discerning reader to detect a familiar ring to the Kaiser's words.

Certainly Churchill's opponents needed no guidance. 'Have you seen Monday's *Daily Mail*? . . .' Thomas Jones, the former Deputy Secretary to the Cabinet, wrote to his daughter the day after Randolph's article was published, 'an interview by Randolph Churchill with the ex-Kaiser on the Indian White Paper. What a fool Rothermere [proprietor of the *Daily Mail*] must be to think that such evidence was going to help the Die Hards.'

Whether Lord Rothermere was responsible for the interview is uncertain. He may or may not have pulled strings on Randolph's behalf. But, whoever was responsible, there is reason to think that the interview was obtained more by stealth than by enterprise. The Kaiser – a regular reader of the *Daily Mail* – was furious when he read what Randolph had written. His grandson, Prince Friedrich of Prussia, was to claim that the Emperor had not agreed to an interview but had invited Randolph as a private guest. How true this was is another matter. The Kaiser must surely have known that Randolph was a journalist and should have made his position clear. Most newspaper men will do almost anything for a scoop: Randolph was no exception.

Throughout 1934 Churchill pens were extremely active. While Randolph concentrated mainly on British domestic policy, his father was no less busy writing newspaper articles on the same subject as well as attacking the Government's White Paper on disarmament – which advocated a continuation of arms limitation in Europe – and pointing to the dangers posed by the rise of Nazism in Germany. In September that year, after spending a holiday together in France, both father and son were caught up in another, more agreeable, project. King George V was due to celebrate his Silver Jubilee in May 1935 and, with this in mind, Alexander Korda asked Churchill to write a full-length film script on the King's reign. Churchill agreed and Randolph was roped in to help with the planning and research. Apparently Randolph's task was not an onerous one. His Oxford friend, John Sutro, was to remember him sitting idly in the offices of London Films in Grosvenor Street complaining that he was underpaid. When Sutro asked him why he thought his salary should be raised, Randolph's reply was shameless. 'For working in the same building as X,' he snapped, naming another of Korda's employees who did even less work than he did.

Unfortunately Churchill's script, although completed by the

following January, was never used. Alexander Korda got tangled in red-tape which prevented him from releasing his film before November 1935 and consequently abandoned the project. Churchill was to use the material which he and Randolph had accumulated for a series of Silver Jubilee articles in the *Daily Mail*. Randolph, by then, had other things on his mind.

His work as a journalist, however, continued to play an important part in his life. In May 1935 he extended his activities by going to South America for the *Daily Mail* to cover the closing stages of the long-running conflict between Paraguay and Bolivia known as the 'Chaco War'. This war over the disputed territory of Chaco on the borders of the two republics was notable more for its length – hostilities began in earnest in 1932 but there had been several earlier incidents – than for its outcome and Randolph experienced little excitement. But at least it enabled him to add 'War Correspondent' to his credentials and to boast of experience as a journalist beyond the whispering galleries of Europe.

But military campaigns in South America were of secondary importance to Randolph. The year 1935 was to find him more deeply involved in hard-fought campaigns of his own.

*   *   *

In January 1935 Randolph embarked on one of the most lively, certainly the most sensational, fights of his political career. As Randolph told it, his decision to enter the lists at Wavertree in Liverpool was completely unpremeditated. There seems little reason to doubt him. Certainly his decision was rushed, risky and highly controversial. The events leading up to it were, on the surface, fairly straightforward.

On 18 January Randolph arrived at Wavertree to report a forthcoming by-election. Three candidates were contesting the seat – Conservative, Labour and Liberal – but the outcome was not in doubt. Wavertree, a respectable residential division of Liverpool, at the time consisted of rows of neat terraced houses stretching to semi-rural areas and was solidly Conservative. At the general election in 1931, in a straight fight between Labour and Conservative, the Conservative candidate had held the seat with a massive 29,973 majority. There was no reason why the present Tory contender, Mr John Platt – admittedly a novice at the hustings – should not chalk up a similar triumph. No reason, that is, until Randolph appeared on the scene.

Mr Platt's disadvantage, in Randolph's eyes, was that he was a staunch supporter of the National Government. His views on India and the cotton industry echoed those of Stanley Baldwin, Ramsay

MacDonald and Sir Samuel Hoare. If Randolph was unaware of this before his arrival, which seems unlikely, he had no doubts after attending one of Mr Platt's meetings.

'The public pronouncements of Mr Platt,' he later declared, 'have led me to the conclusion that he is not prepared, if he is elected to Westminster, to fight for the vital requirements of Lancashire trade.' For that reason, he added, 'I have decided to contest Wavertree in the Conservative cause.'

This statement was issued after a long discussion in Liverpool's Adelphi Hotel. On leaving Platt's meeting Randolph and some friends had returned to the hotel and had debated the possibility of successfully splitting the Tory vote. Their hopes were not high. Polling day was less than three weeks away, Randolph knew no one in Liverpool, he could count on few supporters, lacked any sort of organization and was without funds. What chance would he have against Liverpool's powerful Conservative Association? The talking went on throughout the night. One of Randolph's friends, James Watt – Agatha Christie's nephew and a loyal follower of Churchill – offered to contribute £200 to the campaign fund. Randolph felt he could whip up further support. The decision to go ahead was finally taken at four o'clock in the morning. Randolph immediately ordered a car and, with two drivers taking turns at the wheel, drove at breakneck speed to London to consult Lord Rothermere. He quickly obtained his employer's support and was guaranteed the full backing of the Rothermere press. His candidature was then announced in the *Evening News*.

That afternoon Randolph caught the 2.45 train back to Liverpool. He was met at the station by a crowd of reporters. 'Would he', one of them asked, 'call himself the Independent Conservative candidate?' No, Randolph replied sharply, 'he was the Conservative candidate and he did not find it necessary to attach any labels to himself or adopt any other camouflage to try and capture a few Liberal votes. He was a supporter of the Government in most things.'

Before leaving London, Randolph had given a short interview to his own newspaper. The following day the *Sunday Dispatch* came out firmly in his support. In Randolph's candidature the newspaper saw not merely a challenge to the National Government but a rallying point for true-blue Tories. 'Many Conservatives', it declared, 'think Mr Churchill may prove to be the leader long awaited'. That he was acting entirely on his own initiative was made clear in the account Randolph gave of his decision to intervene in the election. 'I did not want my father, Mr Winston Churchill, to have the responsibility of advising me,' he told the *Sunday Dispatch*.

Randolph was wise not to consult his father. He would have received no encouragement. Indeed, when Churchill read the announcement of his son's intention in the *Evening News* he was very put out. Clementine Churchill was on holiday at the time, cruising in the Far East, and the following day Churchill wrote to her sending cuttings from the *Evening News* and the *Sunday Dispatch*. He told his wife that he was worried and annoyed by Randolph's rash behaviour. Not only, he said, did Randolph lack support in Liverpool but he had no electioneering experience. There was a very real danger that, by taking votes from the Conservatives, he would let the Labour candidate in. 'My son', he observed cautiously, in a statement to the Press Association, 'has taken this step upon his own responsibility and without consulting me. He is of age; he is eligible; he is deeply interested in Lancashire affairs and imperial politics.'

This announcement was followed by another disquietening press report. On Monday, 21 January, it was learnt that Sir Thomas White, leader of the Conservative Party in Liverpool, had issued a writ of libel against Randolph and the *Sunday Dispatch*. The libel was contained in an article which Randolph had published in the Manchester edition of the *Sunday Dispatch* the day before. In this article he had alleged that, a year earlier, Tories had voted for a Socialist Lord Mayor of Liverpool in return for Labour support of their proposal that the freedom of the city be conferred on 'the all-powerful Sir Thomas White.' This was intended as the first salvo in Randolph's campaign. Throughout the election he was to do his utmost to divide the Tory vote by accusing Liverpool's Conservative caucus of bribery and corruption. Always contemptuous of bumbledom, he cited the 'municipal honours deal' as an example of small-minded officials placing private gain above public integrity. But, as Churchill could have told him, Randolph was playing a dangerous game. To a contest which was bound to be bitter, he had introduced the weapons of a private vendetta.

For all his misgivings, Churchill was unable to remain aloof from the contest for long. His love of his son, family pride, the conviction that Randolph was upholding a worthy cause – his own cause – the irresistible lure of the hustings, all combined to rouse his fighting instincts. His next letter to his wife was somewhat more optimistic. He had decided, he told her, to contribute £200 to Randolph's campaign fund and thought that the rest – £1,200 was allowed for election expenses – would be provided by Lord Rothermere. A lot, of course, would depend on Randolph's first meeting but he had no doubt that his son possessed the looks and personality to make a good impression. With luck there might even be a chance of

Randolph winning; or, at least, of coming a creditable second. Churchill was already toying with the idea of going to Liverpool himself nearer polling day.

Churchill was not the only member of his family to become involved in the election. One of Randolph's first moves was to send peremptory telegrams to his sisters, Diana and Sarah, demanding their assistance. Sarah, a little put out at having to interrupt her dancing classes, arrived by train on Monday night. She was met at the station by Randolph, hatless and swathed in a huge muffler, and his decidedly unimpressive election team: her twenty-one-year-old cousin, Peregrine Churchill, Randolph's secretary, Miss Buck, a few anonymous young men and a photographer. Sarah posed as the camera flashed and was then bundled into Peregrine's car and driven to the Adelphi Hotel.

She arrived an hour before Randolph's first meeting was due to start. Everyone was tense. The Wavertree Town Hall, which seated between 400 and 500 people, had been booked and Randolph was to be the sole speaker. Without even a chairman to introduce him he would face the audience alone – if there was an audience to face. At seven-thirty Randolph could bear the suspense no longer and, trying to look unconcerned, he asked Sarah to telephone the Town Hall to find out how things were going. Sarah, having contacted a grumpy caretaker, returned with the news that not a soul had turned up.

Distinctly worried, and cursing himself for not putting up posters outside the hall, Randolph ushered his party into a taxi and drove to Wavertree. There was still almost half-an-hour to go. Sarah tried to console herself with the thought that the taxi's passengers would at least provide a semblance of an audience. But they need not have worried. On arriving at the Town Hall they were amazed to find the place packed and a crowd milling about outside. Randolph had difficulty in finding room on the platform. While he was speaking a group of stewards arranged an overflow meeting at the Women's Institute down the road. Winding up his second speech, Randolph appealed for volunteers to help at his committee rooms. About one hundred people joined him on the mile-and-a-half march back to his headquarters.

A newspaper man from the *Daily Express* dubbed him 'Randolph, Hope and Glory.' This was immediately taken up by his supporters. For the next two-and-a-half weeks a hymn to one who was about to be made 'mightier yet' greeted Randolph wherever he went. Whatever his campaign may have lacked it was not enthusiasm.

*　　　*　　　*

The 1935 Wavertree election was Randolph's finest political hour. He was, as his father remarked, in his 'seventh heaven'. Addressing on an average five crowded meetings a day, lambasting party 'bosses' in general and Liverpool's Conservative hierarchy in particular, he appeared to be as ubiquitous as he was tireless. His sister Sarah marvelled at his energy, his repartee, his detailed knowledge and his ability to fire his supporters with enthusiasm. More experienced, but no less proud, Churchill advised his son to make sure he was in bed by eleven and to watch his larynx.

Churchill's optimism increased with every report from Liverpool. By 23 January he was hearing, and half believing, that Randolph was bound to beat the hapless John Platt and had only the Labour candidate to fear. Gleefully Churchill rubbed his hands in anticipation of Baldwin's and MacDonald's embarrassment. But he did not confine himself to cheering from the sidelines. As the campaign progressed, he became ever more active. Not only did he make a firm promise to speak at two of Randolph's eve-of-poll meetings, on 5 February, but he helped to draft his son's policy statements. Churchill's hand lay heavily on Randolph's election address.

The main target, of course, was the Government's India policy. As it happened, the India Home Rule Bill – based on the findings of the Joint Select Committee – was published shortly after Randolph's campaign was launched. Realizing the hopelessness of trying to forestall legislation, Randolph changed his tactics and advocated amendments to the Bill. His most important, if somewhat short-term, demand was for a reduction of the tariff on British cotton exports to India. Since the first tariff of $3\frac{1}{2}$ per cent was placed on Lancashire piece goods in 1917, he argued, it had steadily increased and now stood at 'the present penal figure of 25 per cent'. If Indian politicians wanted to show their good will towards Lancashire they should, in exchange for sovereign rights, agree to an unbreakable clause in the new Constitution reducing the tariff to 15 per cent or even lower. This was an argument he hammered home at all his meetings. A distinct Churchillian note was sounded in his second election plea. This was for a vigorous slum clearance policy, a freer use of national credit on public works and a 'live Conservative Party free from the taint of Socialism and independent of caucus influence'. True to the tradition of all political manifestos, he seemed to be offering something to everybody.

Promises were one thing, acceptance another. Not everybody was prepared to take him at his word. Some of his meetings were extremely rowdy; he was heckled unmercifully and, on one occasion, became so angry that he leapt from the platform and stalked out of the hall. One of these lively meetings was attended by his future colleague and friend, Michael Foot. Then a newcomer to Liverpool and a recent Liberal convert to socialism, Foot delighted in an interjection made shortly after Liverpool had suffered a devastating defeat in a football match. 'And who is responsible for putting Liverpool where she is today?' demanded Randolph in a rhetorical flourish. 'Blackburn Rovers!' came an instant reply from the back of the hall.

Not every interjection was so telling. On another occasion, when a group of bright sparks blew 'raspberrries' through a stage door while Randolph was speaking, they were neatly put in their place. Promptly turning to the audience, Randolph asked whether there was a doctor in the house 'as there were evidently gentlemen in severe distress behind the stage.'

There were less amusing incidents. Touring dockland, Randolph had a narrow escape when a brick was hurled at his car. Another, less violent, blow was delivered outside the Adelphi Hotel. Greeted by a group of photographers and a man he mistook for a potential voter, Randolph graciously extended his hand. To his horror he found himself grasping Sir Thomas White's writ for libel. There was an explosion of flashbulbs as the Independent Conservative candidate for Wavertree registered his dismay. Politics in Liverpool could take some unexpected turns.

More predictable was the abuse flung at him by his political opponents. He was attacked on every front, not least for his looks and his lifestyle. No longer the slim gilt youth of his Oxford days – he was much fuller in the face and sufficiently paunchy for a newspaper to describe him as the 'Fat Boy' of Wavertree – Randolph was still a handsome, impressive looking young man. With his sleek blonde hair, penetrating eyes, resolute jaw and padded shoulders he had the air of a slightly dissipated matinee-idol. And it was as a matinee-idol, dissipated or otherwise, that he was pilloried.

Sir Samuel Hoare, fuming in the background, complained that sightseers went to Randolph's meetings as if they were attending a new film show. Sir Thomas White, raging around Liverpool, was more explicit. 'I understand', he told a meeting of John Platt's supporters, 'that he [Randolph] is in receipt of £2,000 a year as a consequence of his own efforts. That is more than you get on the dole. I have not discovered that any of you who draw the dole live in the Adelphi Hotel . . . We in Liverpool have a grievance with the Government which we want to see rectified, but we are not going to have a revolution or send any half-baked film star to do the song-and-dance business that we see being exhibited in Liverpool'. Later Randolph was to accuse White of describing him as 'a

135

Casanova'. Younger Tories were dismissive of Randolph's flamboyance for other reasons. For them, his strident right-wing campaign reawakened the suspicions about his flirtation with Oswald Mosley's fascist organization. So strong were these suspicions that the Junior Imperial League were moved to pass a resolution 'warning the nation that Mr Churchill is setting himself up as a dictator.'

Conservative criticism, whatever its nature, did not bother Randolph. He seemed, in fact, to welcome it. Nothing pleased him more than to lump all his Tory opponents together as crypto-socialists and he took heart from the loyal support he was attracting. 'I am tremendously pleased with my prospects . . .' he announced on nomination day. 'The numbers of people at my meetings have increased beyond my greatest dream. Really the enthusiasm has been tremendous.' And it was not only in Liverpool that he was able to claim success. The Wavertree election had become a national issue and politicians were raising their voices all over the country. Perhaps the greatest boost to Randolph's campaign came when, after some hesitation – because they had not been consulted – the India Defence League decided to back him. This meant that he was able to call on at least two MPs to speak on his behalf every night. Soon he was able to boast an impressive list of parliamentary supporters: Sir Roger Keyes, Lord Lloyd, Sir Henry Page Croft, Viscount Wolmer, the Duke of Westminster, Sir Alfred Knox and lesser luminaries such as Oliver Locker Lampson, Sir Robert Horne and, inevitably, Brendan Bracken.

Winston Churchill was delighted by the response of what he called his 'circus' and lost no time in writing to his wealthier friends urging them to contribute extra money and transport to the campaign. Randolph, as he told his wife, now had all the speakers he could want.

But these rebel MPs were taking a risk. They were roundly denounced by their colleagues and a rumour spread that the Government intended to withdraw the Whip from any MP supporting Randolph. Lord Stonehaven, the Chairman of the Conservative Party Organization, issued a public warning to this effect. Randolph was quick to reply. 'It would be odd,' he snapped, 'if Sir Henry Page Croft and Lord Wolmer were hounded out of the Tory Party in order to make room for Sir John Simon and Mr Ramsay MacDonald.' Within half-an-hour Lord Stonehaven had denied making such a threat. To counteract the accusation that he had split the Conservative Party was one of Randolph's main concerns. If the party was split, he insisted, the person responsible was Stanley Baldwin for 'forcing his Socialist policy upon his

136

unwilling followers.' Only the faithful believed him.

The venom with which Randolph attacked Government leaders offended even his long standing friends. At his first meeting he was reported to have described Baldwin and Ramsay MacDonald as 'sitting like fat toads on the nostrils of the Tory lion'. Among those to object publicly to this description was Duff Cooper. Churchill immediately sprang to Randolph's defence. In a telegram to Duff Cooper he explained that the description had been applied to caucus bosses and not to Baldwin and MacDonald. Duff Cooper privately accepted this explanation but continued to express doubts in public. In a letter to *The Times* he said he had no idea of what was meant by 'the caucus, nor who its bosses may be'; but, he added, 'I assume that one of those bosses must be the gentleman who has led the party for a dozen or more years.' Randolph's fashionable friends were equally indignant. 'Everyone is wild with Randolph,' Chips Channon noted in his diary, 'for he may easily put the Socialist in by splitting the Conservative vote; I think he has finally cooked his goose, and I hope so. I have never known so much social and public indignation.'

Randolph welcomed the cheers and ignored the hisses. He had no doubts about the outcome of the election, he was confident that he would win. The closer polling day drew, the more cocksure he became. His sister Sarah was torn between hoping her brother would win and dreading what victory would do to his insufferable conceit.

On 5 February, Churchill arrived to make his eve-of-poll speeches. Almost as excited as Randolph, he was every bit as belligerent. 'We are told by Mr Baldwin', he observed at his evening meeting, 'that these are not the days to go back to party dog fights. In what fool's paradise does he live if he believes that a party dog fight is not going on all over the country? ... The great Conservative Party to which the country would so gladly have given their confidence in 1931 is paralysed. There is a Socialist at the head of the Government, a Socialist at the head of his Majesty's official Opposition, and a Socialist – one of the same old gang – representing Great Britain at the Disarmament Conference at Geneva ... Meanwhile the Conservative Party lies tame and dumb while its leaders and party managers mouth slogans and incantations which have no relation to the realities of the time.'

He went on to say that if the voters of Wavertree returned Randolph as the Conservative candidate they would not only create a sensation but would have participated in a decisive political event.

Randolph remained brashly confident throughout the following day. Not until that evening, when he arrived at the Town Hall for

137

the count, did his bravado falter. On being told by two of his helpers that he did not stand a chance of winning, he blanched for a moment and then, in a flash, recovered himself. No one, said Sarah Churchill, would have suspected his true feelings.

A little earlier, in London, his father experienced similar emotions before hearing the result. Surrounded by guests at Lady Cunard's dinner party, Churchill was seen to be 'bowed with anxiety over Randolph . . . his hand shook.' Before leaving for the House of Commons, however, Churchill likewise regained his composure. He offered to bet anyone that Randolph would come either first or second. Luckily he found no takers.

Randolph came third. The Labour candidate, Joseph Cleary, won with 15,611 votes; John Platt came second with 13,771 votes; Randolph obtained 10,575 votes, and the Liberal trailed behind with 4,208 votes. In the eyes of Conservatives the unspeakable had happened: Labour had a 1,840 majority and a safe Tory seat had been lost. Wavertree marked the ninth Labour win since the general election.

Disappointing as was the result, Randolph claimed it as a triumph. Entering the contest at the last minute, unsponsored, relatively unknown and appallingly disorganized, he had run the official Tory candidate a close race: only 3,000 votes had separated them at the final count. He had also been launched as a national political figure. There seemed good reason for him to congratulate himself. His farewell to his supporters carried distinct messianic overtones. 'Do not be downhearted,' he exhorted them. 'Great is the machine and White [Sir Thomas] is its name. But this is only the first round. I shall be back among you very soon to organize a Conservative Association which I believe will sweep the Socialists from power.'

He was still glowing when he arrived back in London the following day. That evening he bounced into a supper party at Mrs Somerset Maugham's, bright-eyed and expectant. The other guests were singularly unimpressed. 'There was no ovation, not even a slight sensation,' noted Chips Channon. 'I got up without speaking to him, and walked away, and his dramatic entrance was a fiasco. London is seething with indignation about Wavertree.'

* * *

If Mayfair was unappreciative, the same could not be said of Fleet Street. Announcing the election result, the Rothermere and Beaverbrook newspapers showered Randolph with praise. The *Daily Express* sent a reporter to Churchill to ask for his reaction. 'I am delighted,' smiled Randolph's father. 'It just shows what a power the Conservative Party would be if it had the courage of its convictions.' William Barkley, the newspaper's political commentator, had no doubts as to who was the real victor. 'It is a remarkable debut for Mr Randolph Churchill,' he wrote, 'a young man of brilliant gifts and attractive personality ... Even in the irritated mood which the result may create among National Government supporters, Mr Churchill's achievement must candidly be admitted as a great personal triumph. For a young man to put himself over and secure one-sixth of the possible votes in such a short time is something quite unusual in Parliamentary fights, and particularly significant in Liverpool where the official machine is so strongly organized.'

There were also, of course, a number of dissenting voices. *The Times* was particularly acid, blaming both Churchills – 'The Young Chevalier backed by the Old Pretender' – for the Labour victory. 'The Wavertree election,' it warned, 'shows nothing more clearly than the fact that those who, in obedience to short-sighted or personal views seek to destroy the system of National Government, may indeed achieve success, but only the success of suicide.'

Needless to say, Randolph saw nothing suicidal in his defeat. For him the Wavertree election represented not an end but a beginning: having now embarked on his active political career, he was determined to keep up the momentum. His first move was to write an article for the *Sunday Dispatch* entitled 'My Fight' – a heading which could be interpreted in the past or future tense – in which he analysed the Wavertree campaign and announced his intentions. The election had taught him many lessons. Not the least of these was the significance he saw in the increased Labour vote. In the general election, less than four years earlier, the Socialist candidate had obtained 9,000 votes in a straight fight with the Conservatives; in the four-cornered by-election, Mr Cleary had boosted the Labour vote to over 15,000. Randolph was wise enough not to draw attention to this increase, but he obviously had it firmly in mind. His article, while strongly flavoured by his father's imperialism, was seasoned with a pinch of the Tory Democracy advocated by his grandfather, Lord Randolph Churchill.

'I am afraid,' he wrote, 'the Conservative Party is becoming suspect as consisting largely of people whose main desire is merely to avoid higher taxation. If the Conservative Party is to be an association of people huddling together to preserve their own personal possessions and wealth, and if it cares nothing for the integrity of the Empire or defence of the country, its life will be very short.' In an attempt to bring about much needed reforms, he explained, he intended returning to Liverpool to organize a new

139

Conservative Association. 'This Conservative Association,' he went on, 'will be independent of the rule of Sir Thomas White, and it will have affiliations throughout the City of Liverpool which will enable us to build up an effective organization to instil true Conservative principles in all the eleven divisions of the city.'

Here he was imitating his grandfather's tactics as well as his grandfather's 'idealism'. In the 1880s, Lord Randolph Churchill, recognizing the importance of party organization, had made a bid to capture the faltering National Union of Conservative Associations, in order to challenge the aristocratic leadership of the Tory party. His grandson's plan, if not so ambitious, was similarly inspired. Indeed, a few weeks later, Randolph announced that his new organization would be known as the Conservative Union and, if successful in Liverpool, would be extended to the 'country in general'. Traces of his grandfather's, as well as his father's, philosophy are easy to detect in all Randolph's political thinking.

Before embarking on his new venture, Randolph had a more immediate task to perform. Within days of the Wavertree election it was announced that, as a result of the Conservative MP for Norwood, Sir Walter Greaves, being appointed High Court judge, another by-election was to be held. Randolph, with his sights set squarely on Liverpool, had no wish to contest this election and decided instead to sponsor a candidate of his own choosing to stand as an Independent Conservative. The man he chose was an R.A.F. officer named Richard J. Findlay, a former member of the British Union of Fascists (he was to be interned during the Second World War) and an extreme right-winger. It was not, as Randolph quickly discovered, the most judicious of choices.

When Churchill heard of Randolph's plan he was furious. Not only did he disapprove of the ex-Fascist candidate but he was alarmed at the thought of what another intervention at a by-election by Randolph might do to his own reputation. Already smarting from taunts that he had helped to secure a Labour victory at Wavertree, he had no desire to add to his opponents' ammunition. He adamantly refused to have anything to do with this second campaign. There was a stormy scene over the breakfast table at Chartwell. Churchill accused his son of behaving in a totally irresponsible and insanely selfish manner. Randolph, he insisted, thought only of himself, was blind to reason, refused to take advice and seemed bent on acquiring a reputation for subversion. No less angry than his father, Randolph brought the slanging match to an end by jumping up from the table and slamming out of the house. His father did not see him again until after the election.

Churchill's attitude was echoed by that of Randolph's former supporters. The India Defence League refused to back his candidate and even Lord Rothermere, after promising the support of the *Evening News*, cried off once the campaign started. Lord Beaverbrook made a vain attempt to talk Randolph out of his foolishness, but gave up in despair. None of the rebel Tory MPs was willing to risk his neck a second time. As was only to be expected, the widespread opposition merely strengthened Randolph's resolve. Once started there was no going back. Win or lose, Randolph – as his father remarked – was determined to brazen the election out.

He needed all the resolution he could muster. The official Conservative candidate this time was Duncan Sandys – then embarking on his political career after leaving the Foreign Office – who was firmly tipped as the favourite to win. Labour was represented by a crusading pacifist, Mrs Ayrton Gould, who, like her main opponent, had the full backing of her party. 'While Mr Sandys and Mrs Ayrton Gould have the help of numerous party speakers,' observed a political commentator, 'Mr Findlay and Mr Randolph Churchill have to battle on their own.' Battle Randolph certainly did. He was as tireless in this campaign as he had been at Wavertree: speaking at meetings, writing Findlay's election address, giving interviews to the press and supervising the organisation. When Stanley Baldwin sent a letter of encouragement to Duncan Sandys, Randolph, failing to find an influential champion for Findlay, fired off a blast of his own. 'What shall we say,' he thundered, 'of a man who, having been entrusted by a great party with the duty of carrying its banner, takes it over into the enemy lines, where it is trampled in the mire?' His attempt to depict Richard Findlay as a more worthy standard bearer was not, however, very convincing.

Impoverished as was his campaign, Randolph was not completely lacking in financial or family support. Lady Houston, a rich, elderly patron of aeronautics and an admirer of Mussolini, made a healthy donation to Richard Findlay's fighting fund and Randolph's sisters were again dragooned into service. But neither purse strings nor blood ties were able to match the organization of Norwood's Conservative Association. Once again the party gallows triumphed over Randolph's hastily rigged gibbet and on election day it was Richard Findlay who was left dangling. Duncan Sandys was a clear winner with a 3,348 vote majority over his Labour opponent. Findlay, with a meagre 2,698 votes came bottom of the poll and lost his deposit.

Churchill greeted the result with mixed feelings. His fatherly pride was hurt – despite his own opposition – but his political acumen was vindicated. He could only hope that Randolph had been taught a lesson.

The election produced a flurry of hostile comment, there were more murmurings against the 'Churchill cabal', but this time the bitterness was sweetened by events. Less than eight months later, Duncan Sandys, the victor of Norwood, was not only to speak on a political platform in support of Randolph but to do so as Randolph's brother-in-law. He and Diana Churchill were married in September, shortly before the 1935 general election.

CHAPTER EIGHT

More Elections and Alarums

On 14 April 1935 a bizarre photograph of Randolph Churchill was published in the *Sunday Dispatch*. It appeared as an illustration to the Marquess of Donegal's regular column 'Almost In Confidence' and treated readers to the sight of Randolph sporting a heavily pencilled-in beard. In his main story that week the gossipy Marquess explained the reason for the crudely attempted disguise.

'Fleet Street and not Chelsea,' he wrote, is the birthplace of young beards. Whether it is the influence of Fleet Street, a penance, or just a whim, I do not know, but young Randolph Churchill is growing a beard. It began as he lay in bed with the attack of jaundice which now, I am glad to hear, is almost gone. He threatens to keep the beard. My artist has therefore reconstructed his photograph to show what he will look like when his beard has become a replica of the one sported by his grandfather, Lord Randolph Churchill.'

Randolph had suffered his jaundice attack shortly after his two months of intensive electioneering at the beginning of the year. Jaundice is a symptom of many diseases, including infectious diseases such as yellow fever, malaria and, in some cases, syphilis. When the Marquess of Donegal made his light-hearted reference to Randolph's grandfather, he was probably unaware that Lord Randolph Churchill had died – as Randolph was later to reveal – of General Paralysis, which is the medical description of the ultimate stages of syphilis. The connection, however, may not have escaped Winston Churchill. Lord Randolph had grown his beard during the last years of his life, when his illness was well advanced, and Churchill retained sad memories of his bearded father. Visiting his sick son, he was thoroughly alarmed by Randolph's haggard appearance and noted his uncanny likeness to Lord Randolph. There was a pensive note to the letter Churchill wrote to his wife, on 13 April, reporting on Randolph's progress and recalling Lord Randolph's last illness. He took comfort from the fact that his son was in high spirits and did not lack visitors. Randolph, he said, thought that his beard made him look Christ-like.

Severe as was his jaundice attack, Randolph was quickly on his

…in. His illness appears to have been nothing more than a
…tion of exhaustion and, perhaps, excessive drinking. It
…did not prevent him from doing that two-month-long stint
…ing on the Chaco War for the *Daily Mail*, nor, on his return
…late July, from throwing himself into the affairs of his
newly-formed Conservative Union.

The initial meetings of this Liverpool ginger group had been held
before Randolph fell ill; as early as March he had boasted of a
'nucleus of some hundreds of workers ready to begin work at
Wavertree.' Whether his recruits could be numbered in hundreds is
questionable, but there can be no doubt that a reasonably effective
organization had been formed. The Conservative Union, with
Randolph as its president, had begun to make its voice heard. After
Randolph's return from South America that voice was slightly less
defiant. No longer did it concentrate on denouncing local Tory
politicians, but called instead for a return to Conservative unity.
Responding to recent political developments, Randolph had been
obliged to shift his ground.

While he had been in South America, events in Europe had taken
an ominous turn. Not only had concern about German rearmament
intensified – in March Hitler had occupied the Rhineland,
introduced compulsory military service and, in defiance of the
Treaty of Versailles, increased the strength of German forces – but a
new menace seemed imminent. Noises from Italy had made it
obvious that Mussolini was stepping up his demands on Abyssinia
and was intent on war. These threats of foreign aggrandizement
appear to have put Randolph on the alert. Whatever muddled
sympathy he might once have had for Fascism was stifled and he
became more vocal in supporting his father's warnings about the
martial ambitions of the European dictators.

His stance, if more resolute, was hardly new. Ever faithful to his
father, Randolph had long been an advocate of a stronger defence
force, particularly a stronger air force. But, while he championed
such causes in his column, his political activities had of necessity
tended to centre on the Government's policy in India. From now on
his priorities were to be reversed: Indian affairs faded into the
background and those of Europe became more prominent. A new
note of urgency became apparent in his column.

Like his father, he was critical of the new Anglo-German Naval
Agreement signed on 18 June, which appeared to condone Hitler's
breaking of the Treaty of Versailles. ('This extraordinary act of
appeasement, indeed of abasement,' Randolph later called it.) He
was also dismayed by the negotiations which Anthony Eden, as
Minister for League of Nations Affairs, was then conducting in

Rome. As these negotiations included concessions to Mussolini's demands in Africa they could not fail to meet with Randolph's contempt. For him diplomacy was a matter of academic interest rather than policy. He despised compromise and preferred to see political issues in terms of heroes and villains. 'The gaucherie of Mr Eden's visit to Rome,' he sniped in the first column he wrote on his return, 'is inexplicable.'

Evidence of the influences undermining British resolve seemed all too apparent. To combat these influences now became Randolph's primary concern. Compared with the possibility of a European war, his differences with the Tory hierarchy were of minor importance. Unity now became his watchword.

He was no doubt encouraged by developments on the domestic front. On 7 June, Ramsay MacDonald had retired as Prime Minister and his place was taken by Stanley Baldwin. This slight shift of emphasis, for all its mutual backslapping, seemed a move in the right direction. With the National Government's term of office running out and a general election in the offing, who could tell what might happen? There was just a chance that the Tories would emerge as an unimpeded force in the next administration. With the last remnants of socialist influence eliminated, the Conservative party might yet return to its traditional loyalties. Randolph, for all his distrust of Baldwin, had sound reasons for rallying to the party banner.

The first indication of his change of tactics came when, shortly after his return, a by-election was called in the West Toxteth division of Liverpool. This time there was no question of Randolph contesting the seat. Instead he called a meeting of the Conservative Union and sent a promise of support to the official Conservative candidate. To this pledge of 'common action against our common enemy' Randolph added his personal *imprimatur*.

'The increasing menace of war,' he wired grandly to the Tory candidate, Mr J. W. Cremlyn, 'coupled with the weakness of our defences, compels all who love their country to rally round and start a blow against the sinister and insidious forces of Socialism which, if allowed to grow unchecked, would plunge the nation into bankruptcy and involve us in bloody war . . . In the Conservative Union I am sure you will find a band of devoted true blue Conservatives who will do all in their power to aid your fight.'

A few days later, with less of a flourish, he retired from another party feud. On 15 July 1935, Sir Thomas White's libel action against Randolph and the *Sunday Dispatch* came up for hearing at the Manchester Assizes. A formidable array of lawyers were engaged to fight the case but, before the hearing began, it was announced that, after consultation, the action had been withdrawn and a settlement of £1,000 agreed to in favour of the plaintiff. Randolph, said Sir Thomas White's counsel, 'was a young man, and Sir Thomas was quite ready and willing to accept the view that the defendant in his youthful enthusiasm, had rather run away with himself.'

For the next couple of months, Randolph's political attention – after returning from a short holiday in Europe – was divided between Liverpool and Fleet Street. With the help of the Conservative Union he continued to nurse Wavertree and in the *Sunday Dispatch* he continued to argue the case against Mussolini. No less than his father, he considered it was Britain's duty to lead other members of the League of Nations in making a stand against the Italian dictator. At the end of July, Parliament adjourned and political attention was diverted to Geneva. Sir Samuel Hoare was now Foreign Secretary and, for once, Randolph found words of approval for his old antagonist. In a stirring address to the Assembly of the League of Nations in September, Hoare pledged Britain's support for 'collective resistance to all acts of unprovoked aggression.' This speech, Randolph later recalled, 'thrilled the Assembly and electrified the world.'

But words were not enough. A few days later Robert Bruce Lockhart met Randolph at Lord Beaverbrook's country house and found him spoiling for a fight. 'Much talk about Abyssinia,' Lockhart noted in his diary. 'Winston and Randolph want strong action and are convinced that really strong action would make Mussolini climb down. Randolph says his father is fully satisfied that our fleet is completely capable of dealing with the situation and that the Italians would be faced with the greatest surrender in history.' It was an exciting thought, never to be realized. The strong action, when it came, was taken by Mussolini. On 3 October Italian troops invaded Abyssinia and the League of Nations resorted, not to arms, but to futile sanctions.

✳ ✳ ✳

Stanley Baldwin's decision to call a general election at the end of 1935 caused little surprise. The election was expected: the only question was whether it would be held in the winter or in the spring. Baldwin favoured the winter, dissolved parliament on 25 October, and named 14 November as polling day. Many friends of Winston Churchill, whose recent speeches had been even more conciliatory than Randolph's, fully expected that he would be asked to serve in Baldwin's reformed Cabinet after the election, and rumours to this effect were constantly heard throughout the election campaign. Substance was given to such talk by the apparent eagerness with which Churchill offered to support the Government at the hustings.

Randolph's allies were equally hopeful. At last, it seemed, the moment had come for him to realize his loudly proclaimed ambition to enter parliament. At first, however, it looked as if the unpredictable Randolph would ruin his chances by opposing the Conservative party machine and repeating his wrecking tactics. He had declared as much long before the election was called. At a meeting of Liverpool businessmen, on 21 August, he had announced his firm intention to oppose the prospective Tory candidate for Wavertree – a cousin of the former MP – and stand again as an Independent Conservative. To add substance to his challenge, he had gone on to renew his attack on Sir Thomas White and Liverpool's Conservative Association. His brief exercise in peace making seemed, for the moment, to be over. 'Apparently,' sighed *The Times* the following day, 'there is no prospect of avoiding a three-cornered fight in the Wavertree Division of Liverpool.' Efforts to talk Randolph out of his foolishness had no immediate effect. He had pledged himself to Wavertree, he repeated on 16 October, and he was determined to honour that pledge. It was not until he was promised official Conservative backing in another of Liverpool's divisions, that Randolph – probably aware of the harm he was doing to his father's chances of a Cabinet post – finally relented. When the general election campaign opened, Mr Randolph Churchill was listed, for the first time in his life, as the Conservative party candidate for West Toxteth.

West Toxteth was a very different proposition from Wavertree. Although not then the depressed and dilapidated area it later became, it was a predominantly working-class district, much rougher and tougher than most of its neighbours. Electorally it was unpredictable. In 1929 the Labour party had held the seat with a 3,679 vote majority. At the general election three years later, however, the Tories had overturned this majority and emerged as the victors by 5,635 votes. Their triumph had been short lived. In the recent by-election, the unlucky Tory candidate – with Randolph's blessing and the assistance of the Conservative Union – had been heavily defeated and the Labour majority had been restored to a healthy 5,343 votes.

Tackling West Toxteth so soon after this crushing Conservative defeat, Randolph's chances of regaining the seat were extremely slim. He had no illusions about the difficulties. 'It is hard to predict how the fight will go here,' he admitted shortly after the campaign opened, 'but there is no doubt the Tories will make a vigorous and determined onslaught.' In other words, he did not rate his chances high.

Just how vigorous and determined an onslaught was needed soon became apparent. West Toxteth's voters were nothing if not lively. Election meetings in the area tended to explode into fist fights; chairs would be broken, windows smashed and unpopular candidates felt themselves lucky if they survived a campaign unwounded. Randolph entered this electoral jungle primed for a fight. He did not have long to wait: his initiation was as swift as it was violent.

The trouble started when, accompanied by his sister Diana and her new husband, Duncan Sandys, he launched his campaign by touring the constituency in a loud-speaker van. The attention he attracted could hardly be described as vote-catching. On entering one of the main streets, the van was attacked by a fist-shaking mob, Diana's hat was torn from her head and an unfortunate Tory official was knocked unconscious. Before they could escape a frantic attempt was made to slash the tyres of the van. Later that evening, at a meeting in a local school hall, there was another rowdy demonstration. Churchill's old friend Lord Lloyd, speaking in support of Randolph, was howled down and forced to flee to another meeting and, when the stewards tried to remove the hecklers, there were even louder shouts to Randolph to remove the stewards. Randolph obliged. Ordering the stewards to leave the hall, he stepped forward and, with the same courage he had displayed at the Oxford Union, faced his jeering audience alone. It was a bold but successful move. Once he had obtained silence, Randolph continued talking for nearly an hour 'with very little interruption.'

All Randolph's early meetings were plagued by hooliganism. A climax was reached when, on 5 November, Clementine Churchill arrived in Liverpool to speak on her son's behalf. She and Lord Melchett spoke at the Wellington Road School and Randolph, detained at another meeting, arrived only after his mother had sat down. Until then the audience had behaved reasonably well. Once Randolph took over, however, all hell broke loose. He braved the cat-calling for as long as he could and then, after giving several warnings, ordered the stewards to throw out the hecklers. His challenge was immediately taken up. A group of rowdies sprang to their feet, scuffles broke out all over the hall, chairs were smashed, belts wielded and 'women with children in their arms ran screaming to the doors.' Not until the police were called in was some sort of order restored. 'Mr Churchill then addressed the meeting,' it was reported, 'but several interrupters were ejected before it ended.'

Randolph left the hall that evening in a very subdued mood. Most of his stewards had had their clothes ripped, four were seriously injured and one had been taken to hospital suffering from concussion. Obviously stronger measures, or at least stronger stewards, were needed if he was to get a fair hearing. Always at his best when the going was tough, Randolph lost no time in reinforcing his bodyguard. At his next meeting a band of bruisers patrolled the hall and the following week he was able to claim success.

'In West Toxteth,' he wrote in his *Sunday Dispatch* column on 10 November, 'we have won our battle and free speech has been restored. The formation of a strong corps of stewards and the general resentment of all fair minded people, irrespective of party, have combined to make the rowdies lose their nerve. If you surrender to the rowdies and let them get the upper hand you not only lose the right of free speech but you will lose the Election . . . A week ago I was very doubtful of my chances of success in West Toxteth. Today I am confident I shall win.'

His optimism was transmitted to his helpers. Tory canvassers knocked at doors with greater confidence and once again the streets of Liverpool echoed to cries of 'Randolph, Hope and Glory.' Randolph's most successful slogan, though, was based not on a patriotic song but on a popular Guinness advertisement of the day. It appeared on his posters and read:

> *If you agree as we do*
> *Churchills are good for you*
> *Just give your vote for Randolph*
> *And see what two can do.*

Randolph considered this, although he did not think it up himself, the height of wit.

By the time Winston Churchill arrived in Liverpool, on 11 November, to wind up the Conservative campaign, Randolph had his own organization well under control. Buoyed up by what he described as 'a mountain tide of enthusiasm' and protected by his strong-arm brigade, he felt he had the opposition on the run. 'West Toxteth,' he was later to boast, somewhat equivocally, 'was the only Liverpool division in which complete free speech was maintained . . . In the end we could hold meetings in any part of the division and maintain absolute silence.'

Churchill addressed a mass eve-of-poll rally for the eleven divisions of Liverpool in the city centre and made two speeches in West Toxteth in support of Randolph. This time there were no direct attacks on Baldwin but both Churchills, in contrast to Government speakers, hammered home the need for rearmament. 'Terrible preparations are being made on all sides for war . . . ' warned Churchill in an article published in the *Daily Mail* the day after his arrival in Liverpool. 'I do not feel that people realize at all how grave are the dangers of a world explosion.'

But more than dire warnings and fiery speeches were needed to ensure victory for Randolph. Even with the backing of the Tory machine, he was unable to defeat his Labour opponent, J. Gibbins – a former MP for West Toxteth, sponsored by the Boilermakers' Society. He did, however, reduce the Labour majority from 5,343 to 2,004 votes. This, in the circumstances, was no mean achievement. Randolph had no reason to be ashamed of the result; nor was he. He had enjoyed the election enormously.

'We had a great fight in West Toxteth,' he bragged on his departure from Liverpool, 'but I was short-headed on the post. Talk of apathy in other parts of the country leaves us cold in Liverpool. We had the rowdiest election for years.'

A few days later he was called to face another, if minor, challenge. On 25 November, Randolph Frederick Edward Spencer Churchill of Chartwell Manor, Westerham, Kent was charged with 'exceeding the speed limit in a built up area at Beckenham.' He had no defence and was fined £1.10s for speeding and an additional £1 for failing to produce his driver's licence and insurance certificate. Trivial as this incident might appear, it was not without significance. Throughout his life Randolph's reckless driving was to land him in trouble. His vices, though conventional for a young man of his time and class – wine, women and fast cars – were invariably taken to excess. He could no more discipline his emotions than he could effectively control his appetites; his contempt for petty restrictions – as he saw them – was as much a symptom of self-indulgence as it was of an inflated ego.

Randolph took his fine, and the endorsement of his driving licence, in his stride. Of more pressing concern were the all-over results of the general election. While not spectacular, these were a disappointment to others besides the defeated candidate for West Toxteth. The Labour party, now headed – outside the National Government – by its former deputy leader, Major C. R. Attlee, had gained 108 seats. Compared with its poor showing in the 1931 general election – when it had been reduced to a pathetic 46 Members of Parliament – it had made a healthy advance. All the same, Baldwin and the National Government still retained a comfortable majority. With no less than 432 seats, the new Prime Minister was free to ignore the rebels in his own party. Winston Churchill's hope of obtaining a Cabinet post – preferably as First Lord of the Admiralty – seemed unlikely to be realized.

Even less fortunate were the fortunes of Ramsay MacDonald's family. Both the former Prime Minister and his son, Malcolm MacDonald – the recently appointed Secretary of State for the Colonies and Dominions – had stood as National Labour candidates in the election and both had been defeated by their Labour party opponents. The question of what was to happen to the MacDonalds was now a matter for speculation among political commentators.

Randolph was particularly fascinated by the prospects of Malcolm MacDonald. Different as were their politics, the younger Churchill and the younger MacDonald, as sons of prominent politicians, occupied similar positions. Both were relatively young – MacDonald was the elder by ten years – both were politically ambitious, both were in the public eye, and both were obviously intent on following in their fathers' footsteps. So far Malcolm MacDonald's progress had been more impressive, though less flamboyant, than Randolph's. While they could hardly be described as rivals (they were following different paths) Randolph undoubtedly resented the advancement of his Labour counterpart. He hinted as much in his *Sunday Dispatch* column.

'Mr Malcolm MacDonald's search for a seat,' he wrote, 'will prove even more difficult than that of his father. A Conservative seat can give an opening for Ramsay MacDonald on the grounds that he has been three times Prime Minister, but the needs of the son are not so clamant as those of the father. If he were to get in he would merely be occupying a Cabinet seat which could far more appropriately be given to a Conservative.'

His readers did not need to be told which deprived Conservative Randolph had in mind. What they could not have guessed, what Randolph himself did not know, was precisely how the MacDonald dilemma was to be solved. As it happened, the younger Churchill was to play an active part in helping to decide the immediate fate of the younger MacDonald.

* * *

The opening months of 1936 were trying for Randolph. He was making one of his rare attempts to forswear liquor. This valiant decision, taken on New Year's Eve, was not an effort to reform and had nothing to do with his health or his conscience. He was merely trying to win a £500 bet he had made with Lord Rothermere. Partly to encourage him, his less resolute father had joined in the bet by agreeing – for £600 – not to touch a drop of brandy or undiluted spirits during Randolph's term of abstinence. The strain on both Churchills must have been taxing. They would have been well advised to keep apart until the bet was won. Instead they chose to embark on the experiment while holidaying together in North Africa.

Winston Churchill had decided to take a winter holiday, of at least six weeks, long before the general election was called. Sticking to his plan, he spent a week on Majorca with his wife and then continued on alone to North Africa. At Tangier he met Lord Rothermere who accompanied him to Marrakesh where their friend Lloyd George was holidaying. Here, at the end of December, the party was joined by Randolph and here Randolph and his father took up Lord Rothermere's bet.

It was a curious time for self-denial. As both Churchills must have known, the next few weeks promised to be extremely demanding. Winston Churchill, despite recent setbacks, still nursed a hope that he would be offered a Cabinet post. Throughout his holiday he had been preoccupied with political events in Britain. Randolph had kept him up-to-date in a string of tub-thumping letters.

A full-scale political crisis was threatening when Churchill left London. Early in December details of the notorious Hoare-Laval Pact had been leaked to the press and produced an uproar. The terms of this pact – signed in Paris by Sir Samuel Hoare and the French Foreign Minister, Pierre Laval, on 6 December – were designed to produce a compromise solution to the Abyssinian crisis. The representatives of France and Britain proposed that Mussolini should be bought off by Abyssinia surrendering some 20 per cent of her territory. This cynical attempt to placate an aggressor undermined League of Nations sanctions and shocked the British public. Such was the outcry that Baldwin, who first backed the proposals, was forced to abandon the pact. Sir Samuel Hoare resigned and was replaced by Anthony Eden.

Following these dramatic events from North Africa, Churchill had been tempted to return to England. He then decided to play a more cautious game and wrote to Randolph warning him not to write any articles attacking Baldwin or Eden. He appears to have hoped that Baldwin, in a weakened state, might yet turn to him in order to strengthen the Cabinet. With this in view, he was anxious not to rock the boat. But he was reckoning without his impetuous son. The alarm signals were sounded, not by Randolph's articles, but by a seemingly unrelated development.

On 29 December 1935, an emergency committee of the Ross and Cromarty Liberal Association had met to decide on a candidate for a forthcoming by-election. The vacancy in this remote and scattered constituency in the north of Scotland had been caused by the resignation of the sitting National Liberal MP, Sir Ian Macpherson. After discussing possible successors, the Liberals faithful to the National Government decided to offer the nomination to Malcolm MacDonald. A few days later a delegation was sent to interview MacDonald who agreed to appear before their executive committee.

These moves were fully approved by Stanley Baldwin. He had good reasons for wanting Malcolm MacDonald to accept. With only six National Labour candidates having been elected in the general election, the new Government looked distinctly less 'national' than its predecessor and Baldwin, eager to retain a show of unity, was anxious to boost the National Labour representation in his administration. A promising seat had already been found for Ramsay MacDonald as a representative for the Combined Scottish Universities; now, if the National Liberals of Ross and Cromarty accepted Malcolm MacDonald, he would gain another National Labour MP. He urged the local Conservative Association to fall into line and support Malcolm MacDonald.

Unfortunately Ross and Cromarty's Conservatives were not as pliable as their National Liberal partners. Many of them recognized the MacDonald candidature for what it was: blatant political juggling. Within a matter of days a group of Conservative farmers met and decided to sponsor an independent candidate of their own. As the term 'Independent Conservative' was now synonymous with the name of Randolph Churchill, they had no difficulty in deciding upon a nominee. Shortly after his arrival in North Africa, Randolph received a cable asking him to contest Ross and Cromarty. He immediately wired back indicating his willingness to stand.

Apparently Randolph had not then consulted his father. When he did there was another unholy row – this time involving the entire party at Marrakesh. Lloyd George was caught in the thick of it. According to his secretary (and future wife) Frances Stevenson, the little Welshman 'intervened more than once to allay the quarrel between Winston and Randolph, on the subject of the Ross candidature.' Churchill, she went on, was 'very anxious to appear favourably in the eyes of this Gov. as long as there is a possibility of his securing a job, & he was very wrath with Randolph for queering his pitch.'

If his father's anger failed to convince Randolph, it at least made him pause. A few days later he announced that he was postponing his decision until he had made further enquiries. The issue, he said, affected the Conservative organization and he wanted to discover precisely what the 'attitude of the party' was. To do this he despatched an agent to Ross and Cromarty to act on his behalf.

Churchill was left to fume. Writing to his wife, at the beginning of January, he despaired at the prospect of a Churchill versus MacDonald fight. He could understand why the Tories in Ross and Cromarty were angry with Baldwin and had turned to Randolph, but he had no intention of becoming involved in yet another party vendetta. But, angry as he was, Churchill felt a sneaking sympathy for his son. He no doubt saw reflections of his own youthful ambitions in Randolph and recognized the symptoms of frustration in a young man barred from the political arena. He seemed even to have been secretly pleased by the support Randolph was receiving from the Rothermere and Beaverbrook press as well as from Lloyd George. Whether he approved of the nature of Lord Rothermere's support is another matter.

Not satisfied with the spectacle of two sons of famous fathers battling out an election, Rothermere had decided to call in a third contender. Stanley Baldwin's elder son, Oliver, was a member of the Labour party (he had been a Labour MP from 1929 to 1931) and Lord Rothermere now proposed that Oliver Baldwin should cover the Ross and Cromarty election for his newspapers. As an opponent of all National Labour candidates, the younger Baldwin could be depended upon to attack the younger MacDonald and in so doing boost the chances of the younger Churchill. Should anyone fail to appreciate this heavy-handed newspaper ploy, Rothermere then suggested that Oliver Baldwin write an article on the relationship between politicians and their sons. Altogether the contest in Scotland looked like becoming a bull-fight, with the matadors replaced by the *banderilleros*. Churchill, unwilling to denounce Randolph publicly, took comfort from the thought that modern fathers could not be held responsible for the actions of their sons. He could only hope that Baldwin shared this sentiment.

With or without his father's blessing, Randolph was determined to go ahead. The lure of a well-publicized fight with Ramsay MacDonald's son proved irresistible. His show of hesitation did not last long. A further telegram from the Ross and Cromarty Conservative Association, asking him to appear before their executive committee, settled the matter. Convinced that he could rely on more than a band of rebels, Randolph wired back on 8 January accepting the invitation. At the same time, the chairman of the Conservative Association, Sir William Martineau, announced his resignation. 'I intend,' declared Martineau, 'to give full support to Mr Malcolm MacDonald, the National Government candidate.' Once again an ominous crack had appeared in the Tory ranks.

Randolph arrived in London the following day. Before leaving for Scotland from Kings Cross station, he sounded his battlecry for the forthcoming campaign. 'I gather,' he told reporters, 'the people of Ross and Cromarty very much resent their constituency being used as a dumping ground for Ministers who have been defeated and want to get back. That is presumably the reason why I have been sent for.' This, a defence of the right to democratic choice, was to form the basis of his election platform. Whatever policy differences

154

Randolph had with the National Government were pushed to the background so that he could shine as a champion of the people. That he might not be accepted as a candidate seems never to have occurred to him.

His confidence was justified. At a full meeting of the Ross and Cromarty Conservative Association, on 12 January, Randolph's nomination was approved by 160 votes to 47 votes. Having scored his first victory, Randolph then magnanimously offered to retire if a suitable National Liberal candidate could be found. If no such candidate appeared, he warned, 'we shall take off the gloves and have such a fight as has never been seen at any election in England or Scotland.' His challenge was immediately taken up by the recently resigned chairman of the Conservative Association. The following day Sir William Martineau accused his former colleagues of packing the meeting with sixty ploughmen 'brought in by their masters' to vote for Randolph. 'But for these farm labourers' votes,' claimed Martineau, 'it would have been *exit* Randolph Churchill.' Precisely what would have happened to the other 100 votes in Randolph's favour he did not explain.

There was, in any case, no time for explanations. War had been declared, the troops had been mobilized and, with only a couple of weeks to polling day, all efforts were concentrated on organization. Randolph was confronted by the same problems he had met at Wavertree. With the Tories again divided, he was short of workers, short of speakers, short of accommodation and short of money. Things were made even more difficult by the fact that it was mid-winter and many of the out-lying districts were snow-bound. For the first few days of the campaign Randolph battled with the elements as well as the electoral rolls.

Once he had established his committee rooms in Dingwall, he set to work. Halls were booked, posters printed, transport mustered and canvassing begun. Randolph, tireless when meeting a challenge, seemed to be everywhere at once. He was soon addressing two or three meetings a day and touring whatever parts of the constituency the weather allowed him to reach. As Malcolm MacDonald was standing as a National Government candidate – Randolph had great fun in pointing out that he had avoided the National Labour tag – the problem of nomenclature was simplified. Randolph, discarding the qualification 'Independent', was able to stand squarely as a Conservative. There were two other contenders: Hector McNeil – later to become Secretary of State for Scotland – stood for the Labour party and Russell Thomas represented the Liberal party. But, for Randolph, the four-cornered contest was incidental; his chief concern was in opposing Malcolm MacDonald. Revelling in

155

his true-blue colours, he had nothing but contempt for those Tories who disowned him. 'These people,' he assured a Dingwall audience, 'are merely a handful of country snobs who can be got at from London.' It was rather like a re-run of his Wavertree campaign.

For all that, the election lacked the excitement of Wavertree. The Ross and Cromarty meetings were not so rowdy as those in Liverpool; there were no fist-fights, little heckling and scarcely any need for bodyguards. The only person to be seriously injured was Malcolm MacDonald who received a nasty blow in the eye from a snow-ball. Randolph, for all his energy and enthusiasm, was given little chance of fulfilling his promise to turn the election into an epic-making contest. What faint hope he had of grabbing the headlines was sadly diminished when, on 20 January, King George V died. All electioneering came to a halt and the rest of the campaign was overshadowed by the period of national mourning. The run-up to polling day was something of an anti-climax.

So, for that matter, was the result. The only real surprise was the smallness of Randolph's vote. As expected, Malcolm MacDonald was a clear winner. His total of 8,949 votes was less than that obtained by the National Government candidate in the general election but he was almost 3,000 votes ahead of the Labour party candidate. Randolph came a poor third with 2,427 votes, and the Liberal party candidate lost his deposit.

When news of the National Government's victory reached Westminster, congratulations were showered on Ramsay Mac-Donald from all parts of the House of Commons. Winston Churchill, who had returned to England after the King's death, received a few messages of sympathy from his friends. Most Tories, however, were delighted by Randolph's defeat and his father's embarrassment. Many of them suspected Churchill of urging his son on – he seems, in fact, to have toyed with the idea of making a last minute speech in support of Randolph – and at least one newspaper saw the election result as a final blow to Churchill's hopes of a Cabinet post. The Ross and Cromarty election, claimed the Edinburgh *Evening News*, emphasized 'the unpopularity of the Churchillians.'

Randolph's own lack of popularity was emphasized the following month. Once again a lost election was capped by court proceedings. On 30 March, Randolph was summoned to a Liverpool Police Court for not paying the rates on offices he had hired for an earlier campaign. 'Was this the young man,' enquired the presiding magistrate, 'who came to Liverpool in a hurry and dashed in to tell people how to run the city?' On being told that Randolph was indeed that young man, the magistrate glowered. 'A nice example he is showing,' he snorted.

*   *   *

One familiar face missing from Randolph's Dingwall committee rooms had been that of his sister Sarah. Usually a valiant supporter of her brother's political crusades, the twenty-one-year-old Sarah, was far too occupied with her own concerns to spend three or more weeks in Scotland. In that year – 1936 – she had finally put her dancing classes behind her to embark on a full-time theatrical career. Somewhat to her own surprise, and with her father's approval, she had been engaged as one of C. B. Cochran's celebrated Young Ladies in a new revue called *Follow The Sun.* Heady as was this experience, it had become headier still when she and the star of the show, Vic Oliver – an Austrian-born comedian from America – fell in love. Unfortunately her enchantment was not shared by her parents.

Sarah's announcement that she intended marrying the forty-seven-year-old, twice married and divorced Vic Oliver shocked Churchill and his wife. They tried desperately to make her change her mind. When their pleas failed, they urged her to wait at least a year before committing herself. Churchill was particularly worried by the fact that Vic Oliver, although he had lived in America for several years, was still an Austrian citizen. According to Sarah, this – in her father's eyes – weighed heavily against Vic Oliver's suitability as a husband. He told her as much during one of his long parental harangues. Dramatically producing his British passport, he warned Sarah that she would lose the protection such a passport gave her if she married Vic Oliver before he changed his nationality. As the wife of an Austrian citizen, he said, she would find herself in three years' time married to the enemy. This prophecy, made in 1936, was never forgotten by Sarah.

At the time, though, her thoughts were on love rather than war and she remained unmoved by her father's warnings. Known in the family as 'Mule', Sarah was a very determined young lady. She promised her father that she would wait until Vic Oliver became an American citizen before marrying him but that, in effect, was the only concession she was prepared to make. She had no wish to hurt her parents and was distressed at the thought of clouding her happy relationship with them. On the other hand, she recognized the force of their arguments and the hopelessness of trying to win them over. This appears to have prompted her to open defiance. When Vic Oliver returned to America for business reasons – he was part-owner of a theatrical agency – Sarah decided to take matters

157

into her own hands. After writing a letter to her parents, which she gave to a friend to deliver, she boarded a German ship, s.s. *Bremen*, and sailed for New York.

Her sudden departure was immediately seized upon by the press. Newspapers on both sides of the Atlantic bristled with rumour and speculation. In London, the *Evening News* suggested that Miss Churchill was about to announce her engagement to Vic Oliver. In New York reporters rushed to Vic Oliver's apartment in the Hotel Dorset in the hopes of having this confirmed. They were unlucky. 'I haven't the least intention of becoming Miss Churchill's husband . . .' declared Vic Oliver. 'I met her in London about a year ago in C. B. Cochran's show . . . She told me she wanted to come to America. She's a good dancer and she's coming here contemplating a dancing career in this country.' Nobody, of course, believed him.

The headlines became even more lurid when it was learned that, two days after Sarah's departure, her brother Randolph was sailing for New York in the *Queen Mary*.

Actually Randolph's decision to visit America was not entirely unexpected. He had already been commissioned to cover the forthcoming Presidential election – Franklin D. Roosevelt's bid for a second term of office was being challenged by Alfred M. Landon, the Republican Governor of Kansas – and Sarah's flight had merely meant that, at his father's request, he had brought the date of his departure forward. His parents were hoping that brotherly persuasion might succeed where parental advice had failed. Randolph, with his love of drama, rose to the occasion admirably. As the *Queen Mary* chased after the *Bremen*, urgent messages flashed from ship to ship. Randolph begged his sister not to do a thing until he arrived.

A mob of reporters swarmed aboard the *Queen Mary* when she docked at the Cunard White Star pier in New York on Tuesday 21 September 1936. Randolph tried to dodge them but was eventually cornered in one of the lounges. 'I have nothing to say,' he told the reporters. 'If I had anything to say I would be glad to give it to you.' Asked about Sarah's engagement, Randolph looked astonished. 'I didn't know anything about this until now,' he protested. His performance, as more than one newsman noted, was not very convincing.

Far more to the point was the meeting between Randolph and Sarah on the pier. As brother and sister embraced, the reporters crowded round trying to overhear their conversation. 'Efforts to get a definite statement,' one of them complained, 'were unavailing.' After a hurried consultation, Randolph and Sarah left for the Waldorf Astoria where Randolph had booked a tower apartment.

All attempts to play down Sarah's escapade were doomed from the outset. Once the story leaked out, the newspapers milked it for more than it was worth. Later, Winston Churchill was to receive sympathy from friends and foes alike – even Stanley Baldwin commiserated – concerning the scandalous conduct of the press. During his first few days in New York, Randolph was hounded by reporters. They followed him wherever he went and besieged the offices of the lawyers he consulted on Broadway. Sarah, much as she hated the publicity, remained resolute. Finally, Randolph gave up. No doubt recognizing a reflection of his own obstinacy, he left his sister to her chosen fate and turned his attention to the impending Presidential election. A few days later, Sarah joined Vic Oliver in his new show *Follow The Stars*, which opened in Boston. They were married in New York on Christmas Eve.

Randolph extended his American visit to cover more than Roosevelt's impressive victory – he carried every state except Maine and Vermont – and went on to enjoy himself in Hollywood. He was even able to combine pleasure with business. The scoop he pulled off was hardly world-shattering, but it did make the headlines. After being entertained to tea by Charlie Chaplin and his 'protégée' Paulette Goddard, Randolph was able to scotch rumours that his host and hostess were engaged. Mr Chaplin and Miss Goddard, he announced, 'have been married for more than a year and both have certain definite reasons for maintaining secrecy.' Chaplin refused to comment.

Slightly more amusing was Randolph's venture into the film world. While he was in Hollywood he fulfilled two predictions for his career by becoming a Member of Parliament and a film actor in a single day. It happened when he visited one of the studios for his newspaper and became fascinated by a set of the House of Commons, constructed for the film *Parnell*. His interest was seized upon by the director who invited him to become an extra, as an MP, in the film. Randolph accepted and – presumably in costume – took his place on the green benches of the House of Commons for that day's shooting. The irony of performing in a charade, a mere ten months after being denied the same role in real life, did not bother Randolph. Nor did it escape his newspaper colleagues. 'Defeated Three Times For British House, Gets Chance As Extra,' read a headline in the *New York Times*. Randolph's own comment was more matter-of-fact. On being handed a cheque for $7.50 for his day's work he looked surprised. 'That's more than a real Member of the House receives,' he announced wonderingly.

159

CHAPTER NINE

'Londoner's Diary'

To the astonishment of his friends, Randolph won his bet with Lord Rothermere. Throughout 1936 he did not touch a drop of alcohol. What is more, he appeared to survive the ordeal without undue suffering. At the parties he attended in Hollywood, he was as rumbustious, as assertive and as argumentative as ever. Meeting him at Harpo Marx's house, two days after the Presidential elections, Oscar Levant, the flamboyant popular pianist, was highly amused at the spirited way in which Randolph defended the defeated Republican candidate, despite their host's well-known partiality for Franklin Roosevelt. Randolph, says Levant, arrived at the party 'with the reputation of being more than a London equivalent of me – the most bumptious, loud-mouthed impertinent person that English society has produced in our generation. At dinner he succeeded in insulting everybody at the table before the main course had arrived.'

Nor, it seems, did a lack of alcohol impair Randolph's other appetites. At another party, the following evening, Levant watched in wonder as Randolph munched his way through a gigantic meal of mushrooms, shrimps, double pork chops, salad, a large dessert and cheese and coffee, ordering an extra helping of each course. 'Americans,' he told Levant, 'just pick at food. I like to eat heartily.' He went on to explain – to a table of Hollywood celebrities – that he never attended a play because 'you can't smoke in the theatre.' Dry Randolph might have been; restrained he never was.

Not the least remarkable thing about the bet with Lord Rothermere was Randolph's apparent willingness to renew his pledge. Having remained teetotal for a year, and having pocketed £500, he agreed the following January to continue the experiment for a further year: this time for double the money. According to one of his friends, the wager was made more attractive when Lord Beaverbrook decided to join in the fun by matching Rothermere's offer and raising the stakes to £2,000. Randolph, ready to take on all comers, rose to the challenge magnificently. As far as is known, he faltered on only one occasion.

During 1936 Randolph's resolution had surmounted, among other things, a lost election, a domestic crisis and the temptations of Hollywood; in 1937 he faced a more agonizing test. He was in France when, in May of that year, Stanley Baldwin resigned as Prime Minister. The event was not unexpected – Baldwin had announced his intention to retire a month earlier – but the news that his *bête noire* had finally stepped down was almost more than Randolph could bear. He was beside himself with excitement. Such a heady occasion, he told his friends, demanded a special celebration. But how did a teetotaller celebrate? He rang his father for advice. In these exceptional circumstances, he pleaded, would it not be possible for him to be released from his pledge for a single day? Did Churchill think that Lords Rothermere and Beaverbrook would grant him a day's dispensation? Churchill, no less delighted than his son, thought that they might. And they did. When Randolph telephoned his challengers they recognized his need, rejoiced in the occasion, and gave him their blessing.

Even so Randolph approached the celebration with caution. Such a delicate operation called for careful planning. He invited two or three journalists to join him for dinner and took great pains with the menu. They were to eat well and drink wisely: not more than two whiskies, to be sipped slowly, beforehand and then some judiciously chosen wines. But it did not work out like that. Glass in hand, Randolph weakened. 'There were several whiskies before it was time for dinner,' admits one of the journalists. 'There followed a fine selection of vintage château wines with the meal, especially his favourite clarets, then champagne, then port, then cognac, then some final whiskies. Then oblivion. [Randolph] was back on the wagon the next day.'

Perhaps nothing better illustrates Randolph's reserves of will-power than his determination to win his bets with the press barons. Given the incentive, forced – as in this case – to defend his concept of honour, he could reflect all the sterling qualities of his family: tenacity, pride and an unswerving loyalty to a cause. Unfortunately, the incentives were often more challenging than worthy; they reveal a strength of will rather than a strength of character. What, in his father, was seen as bulldog courage was all too often dismissed in Randolph as misguided obstinacy, a perverse desire to have his own way at any cost. He seemed more intent on proving himself than he did in upholding an ideal. Rarely did he display his hidden strengths to noble effect. His motives, for the most part, were too self-interested, his aims too transitory.

*　　*　　*

The dispensation granted by Lords Rothermere and Beaverbrook, on Baldwin's retirement, was not the only respite allowed to Randolph that year. There had been a partial lifting of the embargo on alcohol when, a couple of months earlier, he had gone to Spain to report on the civil war for the *Daily Mail*. On that occasion, Lord Rothermere, the owner of the *Daily Mail*, had agreed to Randolph sampling the local beers and wines but had insisted that he refrain from drinking spirits. This concession, however, lasted only a few weeks. On his return from Spain, Rothermere again demanded total abstinence.

The Spanish venture was Randolph's own idea. His father, knowing of his son's recklessness, was very much against his going and even Lord Rothermere was guarded in approving the assignment. But once Randolph's mind was made up, nothing could keep him from the battle front. He left England at the beginning of February 1937 and joined the Nationalist forces outside Madrid. Here he earned his war correspondent's spurs by coming directly under fire for the first time. It was an exhilarating experience and Churchill's worst fears might well have been realized had the army authorities not prevented Randolph from becoming more deeply involved in the fighting.

But it was an interview with General Franco that provided Randolph with his greatest scoop. He was obviously impressed by the future Spanish dictator and, in a report published in the *Daily Mail* on 1 March, he presented Franco as a magnanimous war leader. 'The mere fact that a man has borne arms against our forces,' the General told him, 'is not regarded by us as a crime. We prefer to think it a folly or misfortune.' Churchill was pleased with this report and Lord Rothermere regarded it as evidence of Franco's humanity.

It was shortly after leaving Spain that Randolph went to France. He was again on an assignment for the *Daily Mail*: this time to report on the aftermath of King Edward VIII's abdication. Having been in America during the more intense period of the constitutional crisis created by the King's decision to marry the twice divorced Mrs Ernest Simpson, Randolph had missed much of the excitement leading up to the abdication. He could not, however, have been taken by surprise by the so-called 'King's Affair'. Like many well-informed Englishmen, Randolph had been well aware of the royal romance for months and was, in fact, a personal friend of the King and Mrs Simpson. Although the events leading up to the abdication had been tactfully ignored by the British press, Randolph would have been kept well-informed of the impending crisis by the blow-by-blow accounts published almost daily in American newspapers. His father, who was deeply involved in the last minute attempts to prevent the King from abdicating, could have filled him in on the less public aspects of the affair. There can be little doubt that, by the time Randolph arrived back in England, he was fully briefed for his assignment in France.

The former King, now Duke of Windsor, had joined Mrs Simpson at the Château de Candé, near Tours, at the beginning of May. They were to be married in this rebuilt Renaissance castle the following month. The timing of the wedding had been arranged to follow the crowning in London of King George VI, on 12 May, and it was on the new King's Coronation Day that Randolph arrived at the Château de Candé. That afternoon he joined the mob of reporters at the main gates of the château. Kenneth T. Downs, chief of the International News Service's Paris bureau, who met him there for the first time, was to remember Randolph for a 'shock of golden hair, blue eyes, an engaging smile, and a determination to shake up Britain and arouse it to an appreciation of Baldwin's folly in letting a great king go.'

That was Randolph's chief concern. Like his father – and unlike his mother – Randolph's sympathies were entirely with the former King. An ardent monarchist, an incurable romantic and a faithful friend, he considered the abdication a disaster and fully upheld the Duke of Windsor's right to choose his own wife. His partisanship was not unappreciated. The Duchess of Windsor was later to include Randolph among her husband's 'old friends whose hearts and loyalty had remained steadfast in his time of trouble'. True as this was, there was also a political slant to Randolph's defence of his sovereign. The abdication crisis emphasized the gulf which separated the Churchills from the Tory leadership. With Baldwin insisting that the King must choose between the throne and Mrs Simpson and Churchill arguing in the King's favour, old political divisions had widened and old animosities had surfaced. The opposing factions, for and against Edward VIII, carried the scars of earlier battles.

Obvious as were these scars, they were not healed by Lord Beaverbrook's intervention. Never a slavish admirer of royalty, Beaverbrook's emergence as one of the 'King's men' was somewhat surprising. He is said to have supported the King out of sympathy for 'a human being in distress'; Randolph told another story. Indeed, one of Randolph's favourite abdication stories was gleaned from a conversation he had with Lord Beaverbrook. Why, he asked Beaverbrook, had he so vigorously opposed the abdication? 'To bugger Baldwin,' grinned the cynical old press baron. Randolph was to dine out on that reply for years.

In France he dined mostly with other journalists, occasionally at the Château de Candé. The journalists he favoured were usually Americans. Fresh from the States, Randolph was eager to discuss American politics, about which he held his customarily strong opinions. So strong were they, in fact, that his press colleagues sometimes found them difficult to swallow. Kenneth T. Downs was frankly astonished at the ferocity with which Randolph denounced President Roosevelt as a hypocrite, and the New Deal as a sham. But Randolph was not always so provocative. For the most part the Americans found him an engaging companion. They delighted in his wit, intelligence and generosity and marvelled at his ability to quote, from memory, long passages from the classics. It was with these same journalists that Randolph celebrated Baldwin's resignation, thus adding hilarity to exuberance. Downs never forgot the three weeks he spent with Randolph between King George VI's Coronation and the Duke of Windsor's wedding. It was, he says, one of the most delightful periods of his life.

Randolph's visits to the Château de Candé were more subdued. The atmosphere at the château was tense, the mood of the inhabitants apprehensive. Preparations for the wedding were overshadowed by the drama of the preceding months and the only person who appeared genuinely relaxed and happy was the Duke of Windsor himself. Randolph, as a personal friend, was invited to dine at the château on a number of occasions. He was present at dinner on the eve of the wedding – a meal made gloomy by the news that Mrs Simpson had been refused the title of Her Royal Highness – and, the following day, attended the marriage service in the small, pale-panelled salon. Randolph was one of the seven English guests to witness their former King's tears of joy after the ceremony and to pose with the bridal pair for photographs. Obviously conscious of his historic role, Randolph stood beaming at the bridegroom's side as the cameras clicked. Not everybody was impressed. 'Randolph only frock-coat present,' crowed Robert Bruce Lockhart when the photographs were published.

More impressive was the caution with which Randolph guarded his privileged position. Regarding his visits to the Château de Candé as those of a friend, he refused to exploit them as a journalist. While other newsmen clamoured for 'inside stories', Randolph maintained a dignified silence. He was not, in any case, expected to cover day-to-day events. As the Daily Mail's special correspondent he was free to leave the routine reporting to other members of the Mail's staff and to provide his own stories when and how he saw fit. Occasionally he would provide his colleagues with some background 'colour' but that was all. Any gossip he kept to himself.

The only story Randolph planned to write, based on his private observations was a carefully balanced appreciation of the Duke of Windsor's position. He did this after the wedding and, according to Kenneth T. Downs, read it over the phone to his father before posting it to London. Apparently Churchill's only objection was to the repeated mentions of 'the woman he loves.' This phrase, said Churchill, had become so hackneyed that it was used by every tradesman to excuse his shortcomings. Lord Rothermere was more critical. On receiving Randolph's story, he refused to publish it because it 'lacked balance.' Randolph, proud of his reputation, was highly indignant. He immediately telephoned Lord Beaverbrook and offered him the story for the *Daily Express*. The offer was accepted. Beaverbrook is said to have liked 'the light flavour of malice in young Churchill's regret for the Government's mishandling of the Abdication' and to have welcomed yet another opportunity of hammering Baldwin.

Whether this single story accounts for Randolph's sudden switch from the Rothermere to the Beaverbrook press is another matter. He could have been contemplating the move for some time. Certainly the speed with which he transferred his allegiance seems to indicate some earlier negotiations. Within days of his return to England Randolph was engaged as a regular contributor to the 'Londoner's Diary' in Beaverbrook's *Evening Standard*.

*   *   *

The 'Londoner's Diary' was one of the most widely read gossip columns of the day. A regular feature of the *Evening Standard*, this lively mixture of social, political, literary and theatrical snippets was concocted by a team of talented journalists under the guidance of Robert Bruce Lockhart. Since the late 1920s Lockhart had been the chief contributor to the Diary and it was largely his intimate knowledge of the London scene that had assured the column's success. By June 1937, however, Lockhart had become weary of journalism and a combination of boredom and ill-health had decided him to leave Fleet Street for a more peaceful career as a country-based writer. It may well have been news of Lockhart's impending retirement that encouraged Randolph to join the 'Londoner's Diary' team. This, at any rate, was the impression Lockhart was given on his farewell visit to the *Evening Standard*. 'My last day at the office . . . ' he noted in his private diary on 11 June. 'Went to see Randolph who has also been engaged for the Diary and hopes to succeed me as chief Diary writer.' Unfortunately Randolph's ambition was not to be realized. He shared Lockhart's love of gossip, knew as many people and was assiduous in unearthing secrets, but he lacked the older man's discipline and

165

flair for organization. His role on the Diary team was to be simply that of an assistant contributor.

The *Evening Standard* office was in a bleak, ramshackle building in Shoe Lane, off Fleet Street. The entire newspaper was produced in one large room, of which the Londoner's Diary team occupied a small disorderly corner. Working conditions were chaotic, the noise appalling, and the constant pressure to meet deadlines punishing. It was the sort of frenetic atmosphere – not unlike that of a political campaign – in which Randolph showed himself at his best. The excitement, the constant comings and goings, the race against time and the challenge of competition suited his combative nature and roused his zeal for one-upmanship. The very demands which some journalists found debilitating merely spurred Randolph to greater effort.

Opinions differ about his journalistic skills. Kenneth T. Downs was convinced that, had he not been distracted by his political ambitions, had he made journalism his chief interest, Randolph could have been 'one of the greatest newspaper men who ever lived.' This is a fond, but obvious, exaggeration. Not all Randolph's colleagues held him in such high esteem. Many of them were scathing about his slap-dash approach to reporting, his lack of objectivity and tendency to allow personal or political animus to colour his writing. He was difficult to work with, had little sense of *camaraderie*, and was jealous of younger reporters. His loudly voiced contempt for his profession and its practitioners earned him many enemies. 'Journalists,' it was later said, 'as a group, are hostile to Randolph Churchill. They are made uneasy by the ambiguity of his position in the profession. Is he a news commentator or a news creator? Is he an opponent or a pet of the newspaper proprietors? They complain that he is not a real pro.' The chances of Randolph becoming a successful editor, let alone a Fleet Street legend, were extremely slight.

Yet he was not without talent. He undoubtedly had a good nose for a story and the grit to follow it through; he wrote competently and apparently effortlessly and shared his father's love – if not mastery – of the English language; his privileged position provided him with valuable contacts and, at his best, he could be as amusing as he was provocative. Not the least of his assets was his ability to slant, sometimes twist, a story to suit a particular purpose. So pronounced was this knack that Christopher Hollis was once inspired to write a ballad in which every verse ended with: 'But have you seen what Randolph wrote today?' It might not have been the most enviable of journalistic traits, but it was certainly effective. A newspaper article by Randolph Churchill rarely failed to claim attention.

A later colleague, James Cameron, judged Randolph to be a good but not outstanding journalist. 'His strong point,' says Cameron, 'was his intense interest in and knowledge of British politics. He was essentially a retailer of anecdotes and he could be beguilingly bitchy about British politicians; he adored being malicious and that, after all, is what attracts readers to gossip writers.' Cameron – one of the few journalists whom Randolph came to respect – was referring to the post-war period but what he says applies to most of Randolph's career as a journalist. Certainly it was his detailed knowledge of politics and caustic tongue that won him the admiration of his associates on the 'Londoner's Diary.'

Work on the Diary was shared by various members of the team, each member being responsible for a particular aspect. Bruce Lockhart, for instance, had, as a former diplomat, handled such things as ambassadorial postings, visiting dignitaries and Foreign Office gossip; cultural happenings were dealt with by Patrick Balfour (later Lord Kinross) and literary paragraphs were supplied by the *Standard*'s book critic, Howard Spring. Randolph's 'portfolio' was, of course, political. His suitability for this post was vouched for by Malcolm Muggeridge who had recently returned to the *Standard*, after a year's absence, and was the Diary's random reporter. 'Politics,' says Muggeridge, 'rested largely in the hands of Randolph Churchill, who, to the considerable awe of the rest of us, could telephone almost anyone without fear of rebuff. That you Bobbity? Fruity? Bob? Rab? There was also, of course, his father to whom he could always turn . . . Randolph still had about him some of the glow of his youthful promise, when he was called – alas, only by the first Lord Rothermere – England's young man of destiny.'

If, at the age of twenty-six, Randolph's youthful promise was beginning to fade, the same could not be said of his personality. He was as bumptious, boisterous, arrogant and alarming as he had ever been. Not for a moment did he give the impression of failure; never – even at times of frustration – would he admit to disillusionment or despair. Lost elections, missed opportunities and repeated disappointments he took in his stride; his self-confidence seemed unshakeable. He lived for the moment, had faith in the future, and demanded acceptance on his own terms. Working for Lord Beaverbrook suited him admirably. It kept him at the centre of things and provided a reasonable salary. The *Evening Standard* might not have been the most influential of newspapers, but as a stop-gap in his political career – and he never regarded journalism as anything else – Randolph could have found no happier haven than the 'Londoner's Diary.'

Work on the Diary was highly informal. Contributors were

167

expected to report to the office at about ten o'clock in the morning and to remain until the newspaper went to press at twelve-thirty; after that they were free to hunt 'paragraph fodder' where and how they pleased. Randolph never had to look far. His own circle abounded with political gossips, he had contacts on both sides of the House of Commons and, like other fashionable members of the Diary team, he was eagerly pursued by publicity-hungry hostesses. Life could hardly have been easier or, come to that, more pleasant. He was invited everywhere, courted by politicians, flattered, listened to and feared; he was free to say what he liked, be as rude as he liked, offend those he disliked and, for the most part, behave in a manner to which his friends had become accustomed. The only person to whom he was accountable was his employer, Lord Beaverbrook, and – at least at this stage of his career – Beaverbrook was remarkably indulgent towards Randolph.

After joining the *Evening Standard*, Randolph became an accepted member of Lord Beaverbrook's inner circle. He had, of course, known the despotic press baron since childhood and from time to time had been entertained at Beaverbrook's country house, Cherkley, in Surrey, but their relationship had depended more on family ties than on mutual interests. Now, as a member of Beaverbrook's staff, Randolph joined the gatherings of bright young men with whom Beaverbrook liked to surround himself. For the first time in his adult life, he found himself one among equals and was expected to shine accordingly. It was a test which Randolph was well equipped to meet.

Beaverbrook's gatherings were nothing if not lively. Guests were invited to Cherkley for their merits as individuals rather than as a harmonious social mixture. The success of Beaverbrook's week-end parties was always problematical. Politicians of every hue, journalists, diplomats, well-known writers and obscure adventurers, aristocrats and upstarts, were thrown together indiscriminately and left to fare as best they could. Few escaped without battle scars. Clashes of temperament, heated arguments, impassioned harangues and wounding debates were all considered part of the entertainment. Michael Foot, whom Randolph met for the first time as a colleague on the *Evening Standard*, has testified to the cut and thrust of a typical Cherkley weekend.

'Beaverbrook's household,' he says, 'bore little enough resemblance to what the outside world thought of as West End society; it was rather a private Hyde Park Corner, with many of the best debators and arguers in the land proclaiming their contradictory creeds from well-upholstered soapboxes. Few holds were barred; no one was ever expected to speak anything but his mind; that was the only law.'

Randolph was in his element. Pitted against such convinced and articulate left-wingers as Michael Foot and Aneurin Bevan, egged on by the mischief-making Beaverbrook and allowed full scope for his rhetoric, he quickly made his mark. If he did not win every argument, he never failed to put on a show. Visitors to Cherkley were astonished by his table-thumping arrogance. No respecter of age or rank, he could reduce the most eminent and experienced of his opponents to silence.

But if he shocked strangers, he delighted Beaverbrook's regular guests. For once Randolph was able to trade insults with opponents who welcomed the rough and tumble of political debate. Abiding by the rules of the house, they spoke their minds freely, gave no quarter and expected no mercy; but once the argument was over they buried their differences. Nothing could have suited Randolph better. As thick-skinned as he was hot tempered, he could never understand why a political row should disrupt social intercourse. In his mind, the two things had no connection. Once he had had his say he was ready, if not to forget and forgive, at least to change the subject and start afresh. He expected his barbs to be wounding but not fatal and was mystified by people who paraded their scars. At Cherkley he discovered some kindred spirits and made some unexpected friends.

One of those friends was Michael Foot. It was a curious friendship. In politics Randolph and Michael Foot were poles apart; their ideals and values were imbibed from different sources, their sympathies and their goals were as irreconcilable as their interpretations of society and its needs were antipathic. There were unalike in temperament, they had few interests – apart from politics and journalism – in common, and they moved, for the most part, in widely different circles. Yet a mutual attraction surmounted all these hostile influences. Each recognized qualities in the other which, if not always endearing, were worthy of respect. For Randolph, it was Foot's basic integrity that shone the brightest: Michael Foot, he vowed, was a man with whom he could 'go tiger-shooting.' Foot, on the other hand, admired Randolph's forthrightness, his 'streaks of kindness' and his ability to rise above defeat with 'super-Churchillian courage.' From the moment they met, it is said, they got on 'like a house on fire.' Their friendship, sorely tried as it sometimes was, lasted until Randolph's death. 'He was a friend and enemy worth having,' said Foot when the break finally came.

Randolph's relationship with Lord Beaverbrook was less heartfelt. He clearly did not trust his father's volatile friend. Indeed, Beaverbrook was one of the few people whom Randolph treated with caution. Although – unlike his old rival Lord Castlerosse and his friend Robert Bruce Lockhart – he was never regarded as a 'Beaverbrook toady', Randolph appears to have recognized the limits set by his employer. There are fewer stories of Randolph criticizing Beaverbrook to his face than there are of his mocking Beaverbrook behind his back. Of his irreverent attitude towards the formidable little press baron, however, there can be no doubt. He took a fiendish delight in mimicking Beaverbrook's Canadian twang and one of his most often quoted witticisms was at his employer's expense. Telephoning Beaverbrook's house one day, Randolph was informed by an obsequious valet that 'The Lord' was walking in St James's Park.

'On the water, I presume?' quipped Randolph.

✻   ✻   ✻

The freedom Randolph enjoyed at Cherkley was exceptional. Not all his hosts were amused by his outrageous behaviour. His influential connections and his position on the *Evening Standard* ensured his inclusion on fashionable guest lists – invitations continued to pour in – but all too often his presence at a dinner party was something to be endured rather than enjoyed. He had always been a difficult guest. His tendency to monopolize the table-talk, his open contempt for other people's opinions, his determination to carry every argument and his obvious delight in embarrassing his opponents, had earned him a fearsome reputation as a diner-out. In the past, however, excuses had been made for his youth. He had been seen as a gauche but ambitious and intelligent young man whose natural desire to assert himself was, to a certain extent, understandable. Judging from later assessments of his character, the more discerning appear to have recognized his basic insecurity, his need to establish himself as a Churchill and to reflect his father's braggadocio. Now, in his mid-twenties and considerably more experienced, such excuses carried less weight. Considered old enough to know better, he had fewer allowances made for his temperamental outbursts. The older Randolph grew the more criticism he attracted and, of course, the more violent became his response. 'It was as if,' observed a later acquaintance, 'he welcomed being unpopular. He tended to dramatise his ability to make enemies. "People regard me as a bastard," he seemed to think, "so I'll be an even bigger bastard and surprise them."'

Indeed it seemed, at times, that to be a 'bigger bastard' was Randolph's sole aim in life. He not only surprised but often shocked people by his offensive behaviour. This was particularly true of his dealings with those who could not answer him back. Even his more indulgent friends were disgusted by his treatment of servants: his bullying of waiters and club stewards, his rudeness to tradesmen, clerks and shop assistants. Demanding, touchy, fault finding and impatient, he would rant and storm at any unfortunate employee who displeased him. 'You could overlook many of Randolph's faults,' claimed a fellow journalist, 'but the way he humiliated servants was quite unforgivable.'

He was at his most objectionable when he was drinking. During his two years of abstinence he had enlivened many a gathering with his natural exuberance – he did not need stimulants to start an argument – but once his bets were won, once his glass was refilled, his liveliness turned to rowdiness and once again Mayfair trembled. To attend a dinner party with Randolph could be a frightening experience. One of his companions at the time was the American journalist Virginia Cowles, who had first met Randolph in New York and now worked with him on the *Evening Standard*. She found his party antics more than a little alarming.

'I greatly admired the courage with which he launched his views,' she recalled: 'nevertheless, going out with him was like going out with a time bomb. Wherever he went an explosion seemed to follow. With a natural and brilliant gift of oratory, and a disregard for the opinions of his elders, he often held dinner parties pinned in a helpless and angry silence. I never knew a young man who had the ability to antagonize more easily. When I once told him he ought to be less tactless, he replied: "Nonsense! my father used to be even ruder than I am."'

That was all the justification Randolph needed. The Churchills were a law unto themselves; an example to each other. What matter it if they offend lesser mortals?

But Randolph was not content with offending lesser mortals. When the mood took him, when he was annoyed, frustrated or feeling skittish, he was more than capable of wounding his father. The Churchill family rows had long been a subject of gossip. Usually they were sparked off by Randolph's political transgressions, but they could just as easily be provoked by domestic disagreements. Little attempt was made to confine these squabbles to the family circle, and private wrangling quickly led to public whispering. 'Randolph rather rude at the moment,' Victor Cazalet noted in his diary after an embarrassing weekend at Blenheim with the Churchills. 'Clemmie and Winston are furious with him.' Such was the bond between father and son, however, that the rupture rarely lasted long. A timely apology, or even a change of mood, could effectively heal wounds and restore harmony. There were occasions, though, when Randolph went too far. Carried away by

171

his talent for invective, he could – often unintentionally – hurl insults which even his father found difficult to forgive. One such occasion occurred, in the early months of 1938, at Chartwell.

The row was caused by a seemingly trivial incident. In January 1938, Leslie Hore-Belisha – then Secretary of State for War – visited the Churchills at Chartwell and shortly afterwards Churchill sent him a small gift. Randolph was reminded of this gift a few days later when, at dinner, his father began sharply to criticize Hore-Belisha. Probably as a tease, Randolph countered Churchill's criticism by mentioning the gift, hinting that in sending it his father had been looking for favours. Churchill was outraged at the suggestion: so much so that he finished his meal in silence. The following day, realizing that he had overstepped the mark, Randolph sent his father a grudging apology. But Churchill refused to be placated. He had been deeply hurt by his son's accusation, considered it unworthy, and told Randolph as much when he replied to his letter. It would be best, he concluded, if they did not see each other for a while.

Further letters followed. Churchill stubbornly refused to accept an apology or Randolph's explanation that the offence had been committed in jest. Randolph, he complained, was too fond of insulting people and then passing off his insults as a joke. His taunts appear to have hit home; Randolph's replies became less apologetic, more defensive. He dug up secret grievances and opened old wounds. Churchill was reminded of occasions when he had questioned Randolph's judgement in front of 'hacks' like Brendan Bracken. Why, Randolph wanted to know, could he not enjoy the same degree of confidence that his father placed in Bracken? The acrimonious correspondence continued for weeks: it marked the most serious breach that had so far occurred between father and son. More, perhaps, than his social tantrums it revealed an essential flaw in Randolph's nature.

Yet, for all his disruptive tendencies, it would be misleading to picture Randolph as a high-handed, insensitive braggart. Provocative he certainly was, insolent he could be, but there was a more endearing side to his character. It was a side which he was careful to disguise, a side which he seems to have regarded as a weakness, a side known only to his more perceptive friends and colleagues. Those who detected vulnerability behind Randolph's bluster did so with good reason. As an unproven Churchill he was forced to keep his armour buckled. One of his proudest boasts was that he had never experienced the feeling of shyness. This, in a sense was true; but shyness can take different forms and in Randolph it manifested itself in his reluctance to admit to gentler virtues.

Strangely enough, it was as he matured that those virtues came to be appreciated. If age had made his social behaviour less acceptable, adulthood placed his personal relationships on a firmer footing. To those he trusted and considered 'sound', those with whom he did not have to prove himself, friends who saw through his posturing and with whom he could relax, he was a warm, amusing, thoughtful and sincere companion. He may not have been the easiest person to get on with – even his closest associates found Randolph intolerable at times – but his unpleasant traits were balanced by his loyalty towards his friends. Randolph never really grew up: if his tantrums were often childlike, so were his affections. His devotion to anyone who earned his admiration, for whatever reason, was unquestioning. Friendship, for Randolph, was an unassailable bond. His attachments were not always intimate but they were never less than staunch. With those he called his friends, he was at his affable best: kindly, considerate, generous, jovial, ready to make allowances and – if occasionally quarrelsome – always forgiving.

Randolph's more amiable traits were apparent to some of his colleagues on the *Evening Standard*. His embarrassing behaviour at dinner parties was offset for Virginia Cowles by the charm he displayed at luncheons with Sir Robert Vansittart and his teasing relationship with Lloyd George. Michael Foot was as much attracted by Randolph's acts of kindness, his wit and his honesty, as he was by his unflinching courage. Malcolm Muggeridge, while acknowledging his faults, was equally aware of his redeeming features. 'However irritating, or, in certain circumstances, despicable he might appear,' Muggeridge was to write, 'his intimates knew that underneath he was a sensitive, perceptive person, easily wounded, very unsure of himself, and, ultimately, loveable and affectionate.' Other friends, at other times, were to say much the same thing. There were even those who were prepared to excuse his bullying of servants on the grounds that he 'also upbraids millionaires, browbeats press lords, contradicts Cabinet Ministers.'

Nowhere, however, were Randolph's sensibilities more exposed than in his relationship with women. Women were, and remained, essential to Randolph's happiness. There was always one or more in the background of his life and occasionally a particular love became an all-consuming passion. He wanted to marry and more than once had proposed only to be rejected. Not monogamous by nature, he appears to have considered marriage as an important ingredient to his career and an essential part of his destiny. He was always conscious, as his father's son, of his duty to produce an heir; the chain of Churchills, so binding to English history, could not be broken; three Pitts were not enough, a link was needed to the future. But finding the right wife – a suitable mother, an attractive

173

helpmate, a socially acceptable partner – was not easy. So far neither his own preferences nor those of his parents had provided an answer. The women to whom he was attracted all too often failed to meet his requirements; they were either slightly disreputable, married, divorced or, for some reason or other, they spurned him. His controversial reputation did not help matters; his emotional instability, his explosive temper and his notoriety as a philanderer made him suspect as a husband; nor was his possessive, all-demanding approach to marriage encouraging.

Randolph's attitude towards women was romantic, sentimental and, even for the 1930s, distinctly old-fashioned. Modern feminism, or any suggestion of true sexual equality, would either have bewildered him completely or aroused his contempt. He never reconciled himself to women politicians. For him women were there to be courted, cherished and cosseted, to advise and influence, but never to usurp the male prerogative. The male and female roles were, in his opinion, complementary not competitive; a wife should support her husband, mother his children, entertain his friends and be sparing with her opinions. 'I think,' he would say, 'a woman must learn to be a good listener.' It was not an unfamiliar nor, given Randolph's basic insecurity, an unexpected attitude. But it made the selection of a suitable wife extremely difficult.

For, conventional prejudices aside, the women who most attracted Randolph were neither docile nor servile. In love, as in most things, he respected intelligence, admired a show of independence and despised the *hausfrau* mentality. His ideal politician's wife was the witty, sharp-tongued Margot Asquith; a woman, he claimed, who wielded tremendous influence 'behind the scenes.' Unfortunately Margot Asquith belonged to an earlier generation and, equally to the point, was decidedly plain. Randolph's female contemporaries were the marcel-waved, eye-brow-plucked younger sisters of the 'Bright Young Things' who, a decade earlier, had revolutionized social thinking. Cigarette smoking, cocktail drinking and jazz-strutting, they had little in common with the world of Margot Asquith. That Randolph, in his search for a wife who matched up to his ideals, should have suffered several rebuffs is hardly surprising. He was not seeking the impossible but he moved in the wrong circles, gave out the wrong signals, and was far too easily distracted for his quest to be anything but protracted.

Rebuffs or no rebuffs, Randolph went on looking. Girls came and went, some stayed longer than others; the precise duration of any affair is difficult to calculate and impossible to ascertain; his friends remember the frequency of his changes of heart rather than the

174

identity and staying-power of his partners. For the most part he appears to have survived his disappointments in love stoically. If he suffered, he suffered in silence; his recovery was usually swift, philosophic and complete. There was, however, one important exception. While working on the 'Londoner's Diary' – 1937 or 1938, the exact date is not certain – Randolph met and fell deeply in love with a young married woman. He was to remain in love with her for years. It is probably no exaggeration to say that the romantic attachment Randolph formed in the years immediately preceding the Second World War was the most important emotional experience of his life.

*   *   *

By the late 1930s Laura Charteris, the second daughter of the Hon Guy Charteris – one of the younger sons of the 11th Earl of Wemyss – had been separated from her husband for some years. The marriage had been a mistake from the start. Laura had only just turned eighteen when, in 1933, she married the twenty-one-year-old Viscount Long. They had known each other for less than a year and for the most of that year David Long, an officer in the Coldstream Guards, had been stationed with his regiment in Germany. The separation, partly enforced by their families, had been meant to test them but, in effect, it simply increased their determination to marry. High-spirited and adventurous, the dark-eyed, piquant-faced Laura saw marriage as an entry into the adult world; she wanted, she says, to 'have a home of my own', and to gain this she suppressed any doubts she may have had about her love for David Long. Only later did she appreciate how misguided her decision to marry had been.

Laura's hopes of having a home of her own were not realized. Immediately after their marriage the young couple left for New Zealand where David Long, having resigned from the army, was appointed A.D.C. to the Governor, Lord Bledisloe. It was not the happiest of postings. Laura felt exiled in New Zealand and her fear of isolation became more intense when, on arriving in Wellington, a doctor confirmed that she was pregnant. Desperately she wrote to her grandfather, Lord Wemyss, to rescue her from 'this sheep-ridden country.' Her pleas were answered. Lord Wemyss arrived and, with his help, it was arranged for David Long to be sent back to England. Laura's daughter, Sara, was born shortly after her arrival back in London.

Motherhood did nothing to assuage Laura's yearning for freedom. Delighted as she was with her child, she hated being trapped in the role of a conventional young married woman. At last she had a permanent London house – in Gloucester Place, north of Hyde Park – but, with her husband's cronies constantly drifting in and out, it seemed to her more of a club than a home. All her life she had been used to mixing with older people and, by comparison, she found David Long's friends immature and uninteresting. So she began to look for companions of her own. 'In that first year of marriage,' she says, 'I began to "feel my wings" a bit . . . I was constantly out at parties or having them at home – all this with people much older than myself.' Young, vivacious and extremely attractive, she had, she admits, 'many beaux'. It was all highly enjoyable, mostly harmless, but disastrous for her marriage. With different tastes, friends and interests there was little hope of Laura and David Long settling down. Eventually she could take the strain no longer. After a trivial quarrel with her husband, she slammed out taking her baby, her baby's nanny and her pets – she had a monkey and a Pekinese – with her. Her marriage, to all intents and purposes, was over.

Laura moved into her father's house in Oxford Square, converting the top floor into a nursery. Her family was shocked by her behaviour. 'For about six months I was treated rather like a leper,' she says. But this was a price she was willing to pay for her freedom. Her separation from David Long was made official and she had every hope that, after living apart for three years, they would be granted a divorce. In the meantime she set about making a life for herself. To help meet the expenses of her nursery staff she took a job with a Mayfair dressmaker. This not only ensured that she was always fashionably dressed – she got her clothes for nothing – but introduced her to the world of 'couture', a world she was later to make her own when she worked for Christian Dior and then opened her own dress shops. Of more immediate importance, however, was her new-found independence. She was now at liberty to see whom she liked, go where she wanted and enjoy the youthful pleasures denied to her by her ill-timed, ill-matched marriage.

In her autobiography, *Laughter From A Cloud*, Laura has described the joys of this breathing space in her life. 'I was out every evening,' she writes, 'and luncheons too . . . Life rolled along and I never thought what would happen next. London was very gay.' Dinners at Ciro's, luncheons at Quaglino's, dancing at the Embassy Club, fashionable nightclubs, weekend parties and a constant stream of admirers were all part of the gaiety. Her days were divided between her work, the hours she devoted to her child, and an endless round of amusement. 'A rather fruitless and pointless way of life, one might say,' she later confessed, 'but I was young, gay and thoughtless, and felt I had already had enough of the harsh realities of life.'

That Randolph should have been attracted to Laura is hardly surprising. In looks, personality, background and temperament she possessed all the qualities he admired in a woman. She was stylish, provocative, fun-loving and undemanding. Outspoken but not assertive, her strong independent streak in no way eclipsed her femininity: she was a good listener. The fact that Laura was married only added to her attractions: Randolph always had a poacher's eye. Precisely how, when and where they met is uncertain – Laura was much sought after and kept no tally of her admirers – but there can be no doubt that Randolph quickly made his presence felt. He became a regular, persistent and attentive suitor. What started as a casual flirtation developed, for Randolph, into an ardent pursuit. There were, and would continue to be, other girls in his life but his love for Laura remained constant. She was the one to whom he repeatedly returned, the only woman he genuinely wanted to marry.

For her part, Laura was extremely fond of Randolph. She admired his courage, his self-confidence, his ebullience and his irrepressible enthusiasm for life. He became and remained a dear and valued friend, a person whose faults she recognized and forgave, whose confidences she welcomed and returned, but she did not love him in the way that he loved her. This was something that Randolph never fully understood nor accepted. So well-matched did he and Laura appear to be, so exceptional was their relationship – she was one person with whom he never quarrelled – that he seems never to have doubted that they would one day marry. There was nothing she could say or do to convince him otherwise. Any explanation she offered, any obstacle she presented, he either dismissed as irrelevant or ignored completely.

But obstacles there were. One in particular was formidable. A year or so before Randolph appeared on the scene, Laura had met the widowed 3rd Earl of Dudley and, as she admits, fallen hopelessly in love with him. The attraction, despite a twenty year age difference, was mutual. Their love affair, although protracted and somewhat unconventional, was sufficiently intense to over-shadow Laura's feelings for Randolph. She knew that, if she were to marry again, she would marry Lord Dudley.

Randolph was fully aware of all this – Laura made no secret of her attachment to Lord Dudley and fended off Randolph as tactfully as she could – but he refused to be disheartened. He had, says Laura, 'that very strong Churchill quality of determination, so whatever I said or did made not the slightest difference to his attitude and determination to marry me.' Nor were his hopes entirely groundless. The circles in which he moved were notorious as romantic roundabouts: affairs crumbled, passions cooled, partners changed and affections faded. Emotional involvements were often short-lived, their outcome could never be taken for granted.

In any case, Randolph had no immediate cause for despair. Time appeared to be on his side. Legally Laura was still married and, as things stood, looked like being married for some years to come. Divorce in the 1930s was not as automatic as she had been led to expect; her battle to obtain her freedom was both complicated and protracted: not until some five years after she first met Randolph was her divorce finalised. Frustrating as this was, it did give Randolph a reprieve. As Laura could reach no decision about her future until she was free, he was encouraged to go on hoping. Who could tell what might happen while the lawyers quibbled? Never one to admit defeat until the last votes were counted, Randolph continued with his campaign. No date had yet been set for polling day.

*   *   *

As a member of Beaverbrook's staff, Randolph's reporting was not confined to the 'Londoner's Diary.' He was given every opportunity to spread himself by contributing news stories as well as snippets of gossip. One of his first notable successes was a scoop he obtained through his friendship with the Duke of Windsor. In October 1937 he was able to inform the readers of the *Evening Standard* that the Duke and Duchess of Windsor had no intention of settling in England. After visiting the Windsors in Paris, he reported that the former King – who was about to visit Germany and the United States – would eventually return to Europe but had 'abandoned all idea of ever returning to England.' The story was featured on the front page of the *Standard* and picked up by newspapers all over the world. If Randolph was not Lord Beaverbrook's favourite journalist, he was undoubtedly an asset to the Beaverbrook press.

Not everything he wrote, however, met with approval. On a number of political issues both Randolph and his father – who contributed fortnightly articles to the *Evening Standard* – were openly at odds with the Beaverbrook press. Never was this more obvious than in their combined opposition to the 'appeasement' policies of the Chamberlain Government.

When, in May 1937, Neville Chamberlain had succeeded Stanley Baldwin as Prime Minister there had again been hopes that Churchill would be appointed to the Cabinet. These hopes proved false but Churchill appeared to accept his disappointment philosophically. As the senior Tory Privy Councillor in the House of Commons, it fell to him to second Chamberlain's nomination as leader of the Conservative party and he did so with a show of good will. 'There is no rivalry,' he announced. 'There are no competing claims. Mr. Chamberlain stands forth alone.' Only in private, to friends, did Churchill show signs of resentment. In his public speeches he was more conciliatory; his criticism of Government policy, if occasionally tinged with bitterness, was less stringent. But this outward semblance of accord was too brittle to last. The dramatic events of 1938, and Chamberlain's response to them, destroyed what little hope there might have been of Churchill returning to the Tory fold.

The menace of Nazism, the unmistakable ambitions of the European dictators, Hitler's territorial demands, the build-up of Germany's military might – everything that Churchill had warned against for years – now plainly threatened world peace. It was a threat that Churchill hoped would be squarely faced by the new Prime Minister. That hope, of course, was not realized. By the beginning of 1938, others besides Churchill had grave doubts about Chamberlain's resolution. Not least among these doubters was Anthony Eden, the Foreign Secretary, whose inability to work with Chamberlain quickly became apparent. In February 1938, after refusing to treat with Mussolini on Chamberlain's compromising terms, Eden resigned. Unlike Randolph, Churchill had come to respect Anthony Eden and saw his departure from the Government as further evidence of Chamberlain's defeatist attitude. On the night of Eden's resignation, Churchill lay awake until dawn, plagued, as he put it, by 'the vision of Death.' A couple of weeks later, when Germany invaded and annexed the independent state of Austria, that vision loomed larger. Expected as was the German invasion, its implications were ominous: few doubted that Czechoslovakia – now surrounded by the Nazis on three sides – would be the next country to fall into Hitler's net. Even so Chamberlain stuck firmly to his policy of appeasement. Steadfastly he ignored calls for national unity and the need to make common cause with France and Russia. He was convinced that the only way to meet the threat was to negotiate with the dictators and, where possible, to accommodate their demands. Once again Churchill found himself in open opposition to the Government and isolated from the bulk of the Conservative party.

This time he was not entirely alone. Although Anthony Eden was careful not to identify himself too closely with Churchill, he and a small group of worried Tories were clearly in sympathy with Churchill's aims. Outside parliament also Churchill's public meetings attracted large, attentive audiences and there was evidence of growing support for his views among people of all parties. All the

179

same, compared with the widespread encouragement given to Neville Chamberlain's policies, his following remained insignificant. Few newspapers were prepared to back him. Indeed, after Eden's resignation, Beaverbrook's *Daily Express* openly accused Churchill of promoting a 'violent, foolish and dangerous' campaign designed to propel Britain into war and, a few weeks later, the *Evening Standard* abruptly terminated the contract for his fortnightly articles.

Randolph's support for his father was, of course, wholehearted. Through his influential contacts – including, surprisingly, M. Maisky the Russian Ambassador to London – he was able to keep Churchill informed of political gossip and to alert him to any backstairs manoeuvering. Never happier than when sniffing out intrigue, Randolph was as ready to suspect Chamberlain's supporters of treachery as he was to accuse them of cowardice. Most of his outbursts at London dinner parties were occasioned by clashes with the appeasement brigade. 'These pusillanimous Chamberlainites,' he told Virginia Cowles, 'they need someone to give it to them.'

Giving it to them became an obsession with Randolph. As concern over the plight of Czechoslovakia mounted, so did his sense of frustration. The apparent ineptitude of Britain's leaders appalled him; he seemed unable to think or talk of anything else. Neither social nor professional considerations deterred him from speaking his mind. He hit out his opponents indiscriminately; when lost for argument he resorted to personal abuse. The story is told of a vicious attack he launched against the appeasement slant of the *Daily Express* while dining at Cherkley. His unfortunate victim on this occasion was Beverley Baxter, an *Express* editor favoured by Beaverbrook. Drunk, and having exhausted his considerable vocabulary, Randolph rounded on Baxter himself. 'You wretched little Canadian piano-tuner,' he jeered. He went on repeating the taunt until, finally, Baxter's outraged wife forced her husband to leave. 'We didn't come here to be insulted,' she snapped as she swept out. Her indignation would have made no impression on Randolph. Years later he was still tabulating the names of Chamberlain's supporters and insisting that they be made to account for their actions.

Randolph's dinner-table tantrums were merely a sideshow. His main concern in the early months of 1938 was to further his father's cause. For years he had listened to Churchill being derided as a war-monger, had seen his pleas for a stronger defence force brushed aside, his warnings of the Nazi menace belittled; now things looked very different. An opportunity for him to do something construc-

7   (a) and (b).   With Laura at her house in Buckinghamshire in the early
1960s.

8   On his way to his father's ninetieth birthday party, 30 November 1964.

tive came in April 1938 when he was asked by his father to prepare for publication in book form a collection of speeches, on defence and foreign affairs, that Churchill had made over the past ten years. It was a task well suited to Randolph's talents and he set to work immediately.

The speed with which he worked was matched only by his enthusiasm. A year earlier, in February 1937, he had moved into a flat in Westminster Gardens and he now closeted himself in the flat until his book was finished. Friends visiting him were amazed at his industry. 'His flat,' says Virginia Cowles, 'was cluttered with *Hansards* and he worked feverishly, prefacing each speech with appropriate dates, and quotations giving the background.' So absorbed was he with his work that he scarcely had time to notice his visitors: his sole topic of conversation was Churchill's prophetic genius. 'His adoration for his father,' noted Harold Nicolson after an evening call, 'is really touching.'

The book, *Arms and the Covenant*, was published by George Harrap in July 1938 and delighted Churchill's friends. It was the first of a series of books, devoted to his father's speeches, that Randolph was to edit over the years.

Stimulating as was this literary activity, it failed to appease Randolph's sense of urgency. With crisis following crisis and the war bells sounding, he felt the need for a more positive response. The times, in Randolph's opinion, demanded a show of military preparedness and he was among the first to answer the call to arms. He consulted his father about the possibility of enlisting in the supplementary reserve of the regular army. Churchill considered the matter and then wrote to the Colonel of his old regiment, the Fourth Hussars, to ask whether a place could be found for Randolph. His request was successful. In September 1938, after a few weeks' holiday in Greece, Randolph reported to Aldershot to begin his military training.

No more appropriate regiment could have been chosen. Some forty years earlier, Churchill had obtained a commission in the Fourth Hussars and had served as a cavalry officer in India before leaving the army to become a war-correspondent. Randolph, in reverse order, was following his father's footsteps. And this undoubtedly pleased his father. Not only did Churchill provide encouragement but, during Randolph's training period, he agreed to safeguard his son's job on the *Evening Standard* by contributing paragraphs to the 'Londoner's Diary.' He insisted, however, that the salary for these paragraphs should continue to be paid to Randolph.

Further evidence of Churchill's pride in his son's enlistment came when, at the beginning of October, he was interviewed by a young BBC producer. The producer was the then outwardly respectable Guy Burgess – later to become notorious as a Communist agent – who visited Churchill at Chartwell. Among the things they discussed was an appeal for 'advice and assistance' which Churchill had recently received from Eduard Beneš (or Herr Beans, as Churchill called him) the beleaguered President of Czechoslovakia. What help, Churchill wanted to know, could he offer? 'I am,' he protested, 'an old man, without power and without party.' Burgess suggested that he could stump the country making speeches of protest. Churchill agreed, but remained despondent. 'What else can I offer Herr Beans?' he asked. 'Only one thing: my only son, Randolph. And Randolph, who is already I trust, a gentleman, is training to be an officer.'

CHAPTER TEN

War and Marriage

As a Territorial officer, Randolph was not overburdened with military duties. Once his initial training was over, he returned to London. He kept on his Westminster flat, continued to hunt up stories for the *Evening Standard* and was as active as ever in opposing the 'pusillanimous Chamberlainites.' The events of the latter half of 1938 – Hitler's claim to the Sudetenland, Chamberlain's compromises at Godesberg and Munich, the belated rearmament drive in Britain – had, if anything intensified his contempt for the Prime Minister and his supporters. Now he was able to add 'the men of Munich' to his terms of abuse for the appeasers. As trenches were dug in London parks, as gas masks were distributed and air raid sirens were tested, Randolph's anti-Government rantings took on a new urgency.

One of his main preoccupations in January 1939 was with a movement called 'The Hundred Thousand'. This somewhat grandiose title had been suggested by his brother-in-law Duncan Sandys and was inspired by the name given to the men who, in 1914, had answered Lord Kitchener's call for volunteers to reinforce the regular army. The intentions of the movement's organizers were never clearly stated but the general idea was to mobilize a group of men and women from all political parties who would oppose the purely negative attitude of the Chamberlain Government. Unfortunately this aim was never realized and, according to Captain Basil Liddell Hart – one of the founding members – it was Randolph's participation that was partly responsible for the failure. His presence at an early meeting of the movement was apparently resented by members of the group who suspected him of trying to utilize the movement to further his father's opposition to Chamberlain. If this was indeed Randolph's intention, he received no encouragement from his father. From the very outset Churchill had expressed doubts about starting such a movement which, he considered, was bound to do him harm.

Undeterred by the controversy, Randolph continued to attend meetings and was soon being reported as one of the principal organisers. This merely deepened suspicion of his motives and some of his opponents withdrew their support. There were further resignations after a muddled meeting at Caxton Hall. Intended as a private discussion group this meeting developed into a public farce. Once again it was Randolph who was held responsible. There appears to have been little doubt that it was he who inspired a front page story in the *Evening Standard*, a day before the meeting, which not only gave details of the points to be discussed but was headed: 'Hundred Thousand Against Premier is New Group's Aim.' Annoyed as most members of the group were by this unwelcome publicity, they were shocked by its result. 'When we went along to Caxton Hall,' says Liddell Hart, '[we] found the streets swarming with onlookers and newspaper boys with flaring posters "100,000 against Chamberlain". On entering the hall we found a milling crowd of several hundred people trying to get into a committee room that could only accommodate a fraction of that number. A number of them said they had come on Randolph's invitation.' A larger room was found and the meeting went ahead, only to reveal further divisions among the organisers.

The new movement, in fact, seemed doomed from the outset. Arguments, personality clashes and a vagueness about aims and policy made it impossible for the group to achieve a united front. Over the next few weeks the so-called 'Hundred Thousand' dwindled to a mere two or three hundred and finally both Randolph and Duncan Sandys resigned. By May of that year the movement had, to all intents and purposes, collapsed.

Not all Randolph's efforts proved so futile. His most widely publicised public appearance in the early months of 1939 was an undoubted success. It followed the introduction, in April, of a form of compulsory military service and again involved Basil Liddell Hart. This time, however, Randolph and Liddell Hart were fighting in opposite corners.

The new Military Training Bill could hardly be described as draconian. It applied only to future age groups who, as they reached the age of twenty, were to be conscripted for six months. All the same, coming as it did in peacetime, it met with fierce opposition. The Government was accused of aping Nazism and of surrendering to militarism. 'We have lost,' thundered Aneurin Bevan, 'and Hitler has won.' Inevitably such protests were echoed in universities throughout the country. On 25 April the question of compulsory military training was formally debated in the Cambridge Union and a similar debate was tabled for the Oxford Union two days later. At Cambridge Basil Liddell Hart – who considered the Military Training Bill to be a hasty and empty 'political gesture' – led the opponents of conscription and defeated his chief antagonist, Leo Amery. He was asked to perform the same role at the Oxford Union debate, but was warned that he could expect a more determined fight. The leading pro-conscriptionists at Oxford were to be Stephen King-Hall and Randolph Churchill.

That Randolph should have been chosen to defend conscription was, perhaps, only to be expected. His intervention in the notorious 'King and Country' debate six years earlier had not been forgotten and his status as an army officer provided him with a semblance of authority. In many ways the conscript debate staged by the Oxford Union was like a re-run of the 'King and Country' controversy: the same conflicting loyalties, the same arguments and the same passions were involved and on both sides there were suspicions of outside interference. Once again the police were stationed outside the debating chamber to keep order, once again the hall was packed. 'There were over 1,000 people present,' reported the *Oxford Mail*. 'Every available bit of space on the floor, on the window sills and even on the President's dais was occupied. Scores of people were turned away.'

The motion to be debated read: 'That in view of this country's new commitments and of the gravity of the general situation in Europe, this House welcomes conscription.' It was proposed by Leo Amery's son, Julian, who was then an undergraduate at Balliol. 'Captain Liddell Hart,' claimed Julian Amery in his opening speech, 'has come hot foot from his triumph at the Cambridge Union, and his hands still reek of my father's blood ... I welcome him especially warmly since his visit gives me the chance to carry out a filial vengeance.' This was stirring stuff but, spirited and effective as was Amery's introduction, the real vengeance was taken by Randolph; his performance that evening more than made up for the humiliation he had suffered in the 'King and Country' debate.

Even Liddell Hart was forced to admit that Randolph outshone the other speakers. 'I had expected,' he says, 'that Stephen King Hall would be my more formidable opponent, but ... he obviously jarred on the audience in some respects, whereas Randolph Churchill made a clever debating speech, sparkling with the witticisms that the Oxford Union particularly enjoys. Describing the Government as a lot of "inferior third-raters" he took the line that the way to make the best of a bad job was to support their Conscript Bill. As Chamberlain was the only man who could induce the "propertied classes" to stand up to Hitler, it was necessary for those who opposed Hitler to rally behind Chamberlain like "seconds did round a reluctant pugilist".'

Randolph's most amusing sally was saved for the end. Concluding his speech he quoted an old parody: 'Onward conscript soldiers, marching as to war, you would not have been conscripts had you gone before'. He sat down to roars of laughter. The debate, which continued until late that night, was later described as 'one of the most outstanding' in the history of the Union. It ended in a clear victory for Randolph and his supporters: 423 votes in favour of the motion and 326 against. After a wait of six years, Randolph had settled old scores and reversed the 'King and Country' decision. Oxford, it seemed, was now ready to fight.

His success was followed by further invitations to speak. One came from the Gray's Inn Union in London where his opponent was that dedicated pacifist Fenner Brockway who readily admits he was outflanked. 'Randolph,' says Brockway in his memoirs *Towards Tomorrow*, 'outdid his father in denunciation of Neville Chamberlain's appeasement of Hitler. Of course in such company I was defeated, the KC chairman expressing surprise that "Good King Charles" and "Good Queen Bess" had not descended from their portraits on the wall in protest against my views.'

By that time the situation in Europe had worsened considerably. In March Hitler had annexed the whole of Czechoslovakia, making it abundantly clear that the Sudetenland was not, as he had claimed, his 'last territorial demand in Europe'. Nor was there any doubt as to where he intended to strike next. On the day after Randolph spoke at the Oxford Union, Germany had repudiated its non-aggression pact with Poland as well as the 1935 Anglo-German naval agreement. Chamberlain's earlier assurance to the Poles that, if their country's independence was threatened, 'His Majesty's Government and the French Government would at once lend them all the support in their power' was, it seemed, soon to be put to the test.

As summer advanced, so tension in Britain increased. There were renewed – and, in some cases, belated – calls for Churchill to be included in the Cabinet. He was, declared the *Daily Telegraph* on 3 July, 'a statesman not only schooled in responsibility by long and intimate contact with affairs of State, but possessing an un-rivalled practical knowledge of the crucial problems which war presents.' Influential politicians of all parties wrote to the *Telegraph* expressing agreement and other newspapers – including the *Daily Mail* and the *Evening Standard* – added their voices to the demand. Placards with the slogan 'Churchill Must Come Back' began to appear in London. But the Prime Minister refused to be swayed. Convinced that, with Churchill in the Cabinet, war with Germany would become inevitable, he continued to vacillate. Neville Chamberlain was not alone in holding Randolph partly responsible for the pro-Churchill press campaign.

With or without Churchill in the Cabinet, war was already inevitable. This was something about which Randolph, like many others, had not the slightest doubt. He never hesitated to make his feelings known. Both in public and in private he was confident in his predictions. During the debate with Fenner Brockway, he had boldy prophesied that Britain would be at war within three months. And, of course, he was right.

Randolph was in his Westminster flat on the day war was declared. His sister Sarah and her husband, Vic Oliver, were living in a flat immediately below but he did not join them to listen to Chamberlain's gloomy broadcast at eleven fifteen that morning. However, shortly after the Prime Minister had finished speaking, the air raid sirens sounded and Randolph rushed to the window. Looking down – he was on the ninth floor – he saw Sarah and Vic Oliver hurrying across the court yard. 'What are you people doing down there?' he yelled. 'We're going into the air raid shelter,' Vic Oliver shouted back. 'Aren't you coming?' Randolph gave an indignant roar. 'Like hell I am!' he bellowed and banged the window down. Unlike his parents who had left their London flat and retired to a basement shelter 'armed with a bottle of brandy and other appropriate medical comforts,' Randolph was entering the war with a brandished fist.

He was still in a fighting mood when he joined the rest of his family for luncheon at the Olivers' flat that day. His father and mother were there and so were his sister Diana and her husband Duncan Sandys. Churchill was sombre and resolute. He had spent the morning at the House of Commons where he had made a short speech expressing satisfaction at the way in which the country was now united against Hitler's aggression and emphasizing the gravity of the task which lay ahead. Afterwards he had been sent for by Neville Chamberlain who had ended his exile by offering him office as First Lord of the Admiralty with a seat in the Cabinet. His appointment was probably uppermost in his mind when, at the end of the meal, he raised his champagne glass and proposed a toast to 'Victory.' The family had then discussed what they would do in the war. Randolph, in his best table thumping manner, declared that his place was with his regiment. As always his response to a challenge was bellicose and determined.

There can be little doubt that Randolph welcomed the war. For him it marked the end of the years of muddled thinking, indecision, compromise and humiliation which had driven his father into isolation, betrayed British values and traditions and undermined national confidence. An outright confrontation with Nazi Germany had been inescapable, its delay had in no way invalidated its purpose. On a personal level, also, the war heralded new beginnings for Randolph. His political career was by no means over – he was not yet thirty – but it could hardly be counted a success: he had made several splashes but had failed to make a worthwhile impression. What reputation he had was derived more from his name and notoriety than from political achievement. He would have been foolish not to recognize the opportunities that the war offered him to make a fresh start. Had not his father won his first election after returning as a hero from the Boer War? If politicians made war, war could also make politicians.

But, for all his eagerness, Randolph did not immediately join his regiment. His first war-time duty was performed at the command of his father. Shortly after the declaration of war, he was instructed by Churchill to join a naval destroyer which had been detailed to bring the Duke and Duchess of Windsor back from France (the couple were to spend only a short time in England.) The request for a ferry across the Channel had come from the Duke himself; it was Churchill, as First Lord of the Admiralty, who decided to send a destroyer. Alive to its historical significance, Churchill had planned the naval mission with an eye to posterity. The destroyer he chose was H.M.S. *Kelly* whose captain was the Duke of Windsor's cousin, Lord Louis Mountbatten; Randolph was included in the party as a personal gesture. Preparations were completed by 11 September and the *Kelly* sailed from Portland soon after sunrise the following morning.

Randolph had joined the ship wearing battledress but during the crossing he changed into dress uniform, complete with spurs and a somewhat overlong sword. He seemed, however, to have swapped uniforms with more eagerness than care. With his uncanny talent for turning the sublime into the ridiculous, Randolph was to add a touch of farce to an otherwise solemn occasion.

The *Kelly* arrived at Cherbourg shortly before noon. The Windsors, who had arrived at the coastal town the previous afternoon, were guests of the port commandant and were gathering up parcels on the lawn when the naval party arrived. They greeted Mountbatten and then turned to the beaming Randolph. Unfortunately what should have been a touching reunion was spoiled by a loud chortle from the Duke.

'Randolph,' he spluttered, 'your spurs are not only inside out, but upside down! Haven't you ever been on a horse?'

Fully aware of Randolph's gaffe, Lord Mountbatten considered the incident a huge joke. He was still smiling when, out of the Duke's hearing, he was tackled by Randolph. 'Damn it, why didn't you tell me?' Randolph exploded. Mountbatten chuckled. 'I wanted the Duke to have the pleasure,' he explained. 'Don't take it to heart! It broke the ice.'

* * *

'You will be amused to hear that Randolph Churchill met Pamela Digby in a blackout,' Marie Belloc Lowndes wrote to her daughter on 7 October 1939. 'She was with a lot of people and they were in the street together. He and she made friends, and he did not *see* her for an hour! This was only three weeks ago! They were actually engaged *one week*. All this is true, told to me by Eddie.'

'Eddie' was Winston Churchill's former private secretary, Sir Edward Marsh, who, as a practised raconteur, probably added a touch or two to the story. But what is certain is that Randolph's first meeting with the nineteen-year-old Pamela Digby was accidental. According to the account which he gave to his friends, Randolph (after his return from France) had telephoned an acquaintance; finding him out, he had made a date with the girl who answered the phone. They met, were attracted to each other, and shortly afterwards became engaged. A week later they were married. Their courtship, from blind date to the altar, had lasted less than a month.

The speed with which Randolph rushed into marriage astonished his friends. Not that Pamela Digby was not an eminently suitable bride – auburn haired, freckle-faced, lively and pretty, she was the elder daughter of Lord and Lady Digby whose family had been established in Dorset for centuries – but she was very different from the wordly, often married women whom Randolph usually pursued. At nineteen she was relatively inexperienced – after leaving Downham College, she had completed her education in Germany and France and then worked briefly at the Foreign Office – and she appeared to share few of Randolph's interests. Why the haste? According to Pamela, it was Winston Churchill who urged them to marry immediately. Her own family and Clementine Churchill, she says, 'thought we ought to wait'. Randolph's explanation, at the time, was different and somewhat ungallant. He gave it to, among others, his friend John Gunther the American writer. Like many of his countrymen, Gunther had decided to return home when war was declared and Randolph took Pamela to see him off at Southampton. Their engagement had not then been announced and Gunther had never before met Pamela. After introducing them, Randolph explained that 'he was about to marry Pamela, and that he must have a son and heir as soon as possible. Since he was convinced that he would soon be killed.'

Gunther was not the only one to hear this explanation. That Randolph Churchill was marrying to beget an heir was soon common gossip in London. Convinced that he would be posted overseas, Randolph was leaving nothing to chance. The Churchill line, it seems, weighed as heavily with Randolph as did Pamela's undoubted charms.

One of the few people he consulted before his marriage – outside his family – was, of course, Laura. He was still in love with her, still waiting for her final decision, but the war had made it impossible for him to wait any longer. This was something that Randolph had been forced to recognize. At no stage had Laura promised to marry him and, even if she were to change her mind, she was still not free to do so: the complicated divorce proceedings were still dragging on. There was not the remotest chance of her providing him with an heir before he was sent abroad. All the same, he sought her advice. Wisely she refused either to encourage or dissuade him. Any decision he reached, she insisted, would have to be his own.

Randolph and Pamela Digby were married, on 4 October 1939, at St John's Church in Smith Square. The newspapers described it as 'a real war wedding.' Pamela was dressed in a deep blue coat, trimmed with dyed fox fur, and a beret-shaped blue velvet hat; Randolph, looking plump and proud, wore his army uniform. They left the church under an archway of raised swords held by the bridegroom's fellow officers. For the waiting crowd, however, the main attraction was the newly appointed First Lord of the Admiralty. When Churchill and his wife appeared, they were cheered 'again and again'. At the reception afterwards the state rooms at Admiralty House – specially opened for the occasion – were packed with Randolph's friends and relations.

Contrary to his expectations, Randolph was not immediately sent abroad. The first few months of his marriage were spent at Beverley, in east Yorkshire, where his regiment was stationed. These were the months of the 'phoney war', the months when the expected air attacks failed to materialize, when tension relaxed, emergency plans were modified and – apart from the alarm caused by heavy losses at sea – Britain was lulled into a false sense of security. For soldiers stationed in England it was a time of boredom and frustration. Randolph was luckier than most. With a new wife, a new career, and his father in the War Cabinet he did not have far to look for distractions.

His social life in Yorkshire was less active than it had been in London, but he was not without friends. One of those friends was Christopher Sykes, whom he had first met at Oxford. Sykes, who was in the army and stationed at nearby Bridlington, often visited the newly married Churchills and on one occasion his wife stayed with them. Randolph appears to have been happy enough, although he was still given to temperamental outbursts. And they were still as terrifying as ever. Christopher Sykes recalls a disastrous luncheon party at a local country house where 'Randolph did everything he knew, and he knew a lot, to distress, anger, exasperate and make miserable his host and everyone of his fellow guests!' Randolph, he says, 'was a man of many moods.'

He was indeed. But he could, on occasions, still be a charming companion. He was probably at his best when coping with his duties as an officer. However 'phoney' some might have thought the war, Randolph took it, and his army career, very seriously. Certainly his dedication impressed Christopher Sykes. 'He was thrust as an officer,' observes Sykes, 'into a new milieu and he was determined to learn the ropes. Again, I saw the modest, interesting, delightful young Oxonian of ten years before.'

Randolph's preoccupation with the army did not prevent him from taking an active interest in his father's career. Politically these were stirring times. From the Queen Anne mansion, Ickleford House, which he had rented near Hitchin in Hertfordshire – some thirty-five miles from London – Randolph was able to keep in touch with events. Early in 1940 he accompanied his father to a mass meeting in Manchester, where Churchill appealed for the recruitment of a million women into industry, and he was in close contact with Admiralty House during the crisis which followed Hitler's invasion of Denmark and Norway in April.

The success of the German army, and the failure of British operations in central Norway, added to the growing unrest about Chamberlain's leadership. Speculation was rife as to who would, or could, replace him. Winston Churchill was not everyone's first choice. His popularity had increased considerably but the past had not been completely forgotten. In a Gallup poll, at the beginning of April, he had been placed second to Anthony Eden as a possible Prime Minister. Among politicians, Lord Halifax – the Foreign Secretary – was a more obvious choice. Things came to a head on 7 May when the House of Commons debated the Norwegian campaign. So fiercely was the Prime Minister criticized, and so dramatically did the Government's majority drop when a vote was taken, that Chamberlain was forced to bow to the inevitable.

Churchill seems to have sensed what was about to happen. When Randolph telephoned him on 9 May, he was full of confidence. 'I may be in a big position tonight' he said.

He was right, of course. That afternoon Chamberlain sent for Churchill and Halifax and told them of his intention to resign. When the question of his successor arose, Churchill said nothing. Halifax – realizing that with Churchill in the Cabinet he would be

191

overshadowed – declined the post on the grounds that, as a peer, it would be awkward for him to become Prime Minister. A decision had, to all intents and purposes, been reached. Churchill left the room conscious of his impending responsibilities.

Just how heavy those responsibilities were to be became apparent the following morning when Hitler launched his long-delayed attack on Holland and Belgium. So caught up with this crisis was Churchill that he appeared to lose interest in the Premiership. When Randolph tackled him about the 'big position', he was dismissive. 'Oh that's off,' he snorted. But it was not off. That evening, when Chamberlain went to the Palace to resign, he had no alternative but to advise the King to send for Winston Churchill. Neither his own last minute hesitations, nor the efforts that were made to get Halifax to change his mind, were of any avail. At last the years of exile were truly over and 10 Downing Street was to be occupied by a Churchill.

In the event, it was occupied by two Churchills. When the new Prime Minister arrived at Downing Street on the morning of 11 May 1940, he was accompanied by Brendan Bracken – his Parliamentary Private Secretary – and the triumphant Randolph. Churchill's first concern was to clear the decks. He was anxious to remove Neville Chamberlain's followers and particularly wanted to see the last of Chamberlain's enigmatic Civil Service adviser, Sir Horace Wilson, who was reputedly the *eminence grise* of the protracted appeasement policy. He therefore sent a polite message to Wilson asking him to vacate his Downing Street office, which opened on the Cabinet Room, by two o'clock that afternoon. Apparently Sir Horace failed to appreciate the extent of his disgrace and replied, with equal politeness, asking if he could be given until six that evening to clear his papers. This infuriated Churchill. Turning to Bracken, he growled: 'Tell that man if his room is not cleared by 2 p.m. I will make him Minister to Iceland.' Bracken needed no further prompting. Sending for Randolph, he discharged the word with the deed. When Wilson came back from lunch that day he discovered, as Hugh Dalton put it, 'the paratroopers had arrived before him.' Seated on a couch in his office were the tight-lipped, bespectacled Bracken and the uniformed, equally grim-looking, Randolph. Not a word was said, not a smile exchanged. Wilson simply 'withdrew, never to return to that seat most proximate to power.'

*　　*　　*

Within four months of his father becoming Prime Minister, Randolph also achieved a life-long ambition. At the beginning of September 1940, he was invited by an emergency committee of the

Preston Conservative Association to stand as a candidate for the parliamentary vacancy created by the death of Mr A. C. Moreing. He accepted and his nomination was unanimously endorsed a few days later. This, in effect, meant that his election to parliament was guaranteed. With Churchill now heading a coalition Government, an electoral truce was being observed and opposition from either the Labour or the Liberal parties was ruled out. There were rumours of a 'Britain's Pensions Movement candidate' being nominated but this came to nothing and, to all intents and purposes, Randolph stood unopposed.

There was, however, one serious objection to his candidacy. It came not from an opposition party but from a fellow Tory. Preston was then represented by two Members of Parliament, both Conservatives, and it was the town's 'senior' member, Captain E. C. Cobb, who displayed a distinct reluctance to embrace Randolph as a colleague. Remembering the disaster of Wavertree, four years earlier, he predicted trouble for the future. So strongly did Captain Cobb feel that he wrote to the chairman of the Preston Conservative Association, Sir Norman Seddon Brown, threatening to resign at the next general election if Randolph was adopted as a candidate. He was supported by a few local Tories who agreed that Randolph would be 'difficult to work with.' The bickering was kept out of the press and, as the dissidents were in a minority, the Selection Committee was able to announce their choice as 'unanimous'. Second thoughts were to come later.

That Randolph was elected on his father's name there can be no doubt. One of the reasons privately given for his selection was that 'the Churchill name would guarantee his election after the war.' On a broader front, accusations of nepotism now began to be levelled at Churchill and were to continue over the years. (Later, when his son-in-law, Duncan Sandys, was given office there was a cry of 'What about Vic Oliver?' in the House of Commons.) But none of this worried Randolph. As far as his critics in Preston were concerned, he confined himself to a few pointed remarks when, on 25 September, his unopposed election was announced. In a press statement he emphasized that he 'hoped that at Preston he had found a political home for all time' and went on to add: 'He was particularly glad that at a time like this he had been returned without a contest. As a result of the intensification of the war [these were post-Dunkirk days] and under the leadership of the Prime Minister, Britain had attained a unity of purpose never equalled before in our history. That was our most valuable national effort, and all of us must play our part in promoting it.' Set against such momentous events the quibbling of Captain Cobb seemed irrelevant.

Randolph took his seat in the House of Commons on 8 October 1940, two weeks after his formal election. He was almost thirty, considerably older than he had envisaged when starting his political career, and his chances of rivalling the younger Pitt had long since disappeared. Nor did he enter parliament as he had hoped, after a spectacular election victory; his path had been smoothed and his only claim to recognition was as the Prime Minister's favoured son. For all that it was a proud day for the Churchill family. Before leaving for the House, Randolph – looking mature and self-confident in his lieutenant's uniform – was photographed outside 10 Downing Street, standing between his smiling, obviously delighted, mother and father. The smiles continued when he was introduced at the Bar of the House by his father and Captain David Margesson, the Chief Government Whip. As Churchill left his seat on the Treasury Bench to perform this duty, there were cheers from all sides of the chamber. It may not have been a triumphant ceremony but it was impressive.

Two days later the Churchill family had further cause for rejoicing. On 10 October, Randolph's first child was born at Chequers. The son he had hoped for was named, true to what was now family tradition – Winston Spencer Churchill. If nothing else, Adolf Hitler had secured the Churchill line.

Family events were inextricably linked with public occasions. They featured prominently in Randolph's maiden speech as a Member of Parliament. When he rose to address the House, on 26 November, his opening words produced a roar of laughter.

'Twenty years ago,' he observed, 'a young Member, concluding his maiden speech to this House, thanked the House for the kindness and patience with which it had listened to him, not on his own account but because of the splendid memory which many Members still preserved. I hope that the House will pardon me for striking this personal note, but I today have the personal privilege and satisfaction of having my father here. Therefore, I would like to ask an extra measure of indulgence, on account of the added embarrassment occasioned by paternal propinquity.'

This typical Churchillian flourish set the tone of the rest of his speech. Spiced with an occasional historical allusion and a quote from Gibbon, it was obviously carefully prepared. His main concern was to defend the present Government. In doing so he asked the House to 'overlook any relationship which I may perhaps have with a prominent member of the Administration.' He spoke as a serving soldier – he was again dressed in uniform – and was at pains to reflect the opinions of the army. Turning at one point to look round the chamber, he could not resist a dig at his father's old opponents. 'One can see,' he remarked, 'a number of hon. and right hon. Gentlemen who in a greater or lesser degree bear some measure of responsibility for the state of our Forces and for any shortage of equipment which might perhaps handicap those who plan our strategy. I have no wish to recriminate about the past. We have often been advised from different quarters against this evil tendency, but what about all this recriminating about the present from people whose conduct in the past has largely led up to the not altogether satisfactory position in which we find ourselves today?' He was also scornful of those who talked vaguely about 'war aims' and prophesied a brave new world. 'In one way,' he declared, 'I myself think that this is already a better world in a spiritual sense, than two years ago. Then we were giving in to evil, and today we are resisting it.'

'I believe,' he concluded magniloquently, 'that the ordinary men and women of this country feel they have been misled by the caucuses of all three political parties . . . When victory is won they will not be concerned with the easy shibboleths of reconstruction but will wish to breast the hills of the future without the burden of futile commitments and to be inspired instead by the enduring hope of their own genius and sacrifices.'

He sat down to loud cheers. His debut, if long-delayed, was an undoubted success. The speaker who followed him, Major-General Sir Alfred Knox, congratulated him on carrying off the trial of a maiden speech with brilliant colours. 'He has come to this House,' enthused Sir Alfred, 'as the inheritor of a terrifyingly great tradition, and the sample he has given us today of his powers shows that he is going to act up to the traditions of the greatest of all his forebears.'

These sentiments were shared by Randolph's family. Throughout his speech, he had been listened to by his mother, his wife and his sister Mary in the gallery and his father on the front bench. To lessen his son's embarrassment, Churchill had sat with his back studiously turned but, it was noted, once Randolph had finished 'the Prime Minister made no attempt to hide his satisfaction.' 'This,' declared one newspaper, 'was Churchill day in the House of Commons.'

But it was a day that could not be prolonged. Britain was at war, south-east England was under constant attack from German bombers and a full-scale invasion was daily expected. The nation had rallied to Churchill's call for them to brace themselves and so make this 'their finest hour', but the tension remained and reminders of the ever-present threat tended to cloud even the most joyous of occasions. The sounds of war were not entirely absent when, on 1 December, Randolph's baby son was christened at the Ellesborough parish church, near Chequers. Both the Churchill and

195

the Digby grandparents were present at the simple ceremony, which was held after Sunday matins, and Lord Beaverbrook, Lord Brownlow, Brendan Bracken and Virginia Cowles acted as god-parents. Afterwards friends attended a luncheon at Chequers where a proud Winston Churchill proposed a toast to his grandson. One of the guests, Lady Diana Cooper, was to remember the occasion for its 'champagne and tenantry on the lawns, the nannies and cousins, and healths drunk, all to the deafening accompaniment of aeroplanes skirmishing, diving, looping and spinning in the clear air, teaching children to be pilots'. More specifically she recalls there were no 'alarums or excursions' that evening 'although Randolph's wife, straight from Chequers, told me that invasion was fully expected now.'

Randolph was fully alive to the urgency of the hour. He had every reason for being so. In his maiden speech to the Commons he had regretted not being present at an earlier debate which, he said, he had been obliged to follow 'from a distance.' Secrecy prevented him from being more explicit. He was, in fact, under intensive training with a commando unit in Scotland.

*   *   *

The idea of organising 'striking companies' to match the highly efficient German storm troops was first mooted by Winston Churchill in June 1940, shortly after the evacuation of Dunkirk. Faced with the possibility of an enemy invasion, his thoughts had turned to retaliation. Why, he asked his military advisers, should Britain sit back and wait to be attacked? 'It is of the highest consequence,' he said, 'to keep the largest numbers of German forces all along the coasts of the countries they have conquered, and we should set to work to organise raiding forces on these coasts.' What he had in mind were self-contained units of highly trained men who could land secretly on the coasts of occupied Europe and take the enemy by surprise. 'How wonderful it would be,' he enthused, 'if the Germans could be made to wonder where they were going to be struck next, instead of forcing us to try to wall in the Island and roof it over!' He suggested that these raiding parties, trained to spring at the enemy's throat, be called 'Leopards.'

His proposal, although not entirely original – similar tactics had been used during the unsuccessful Norwegian campaign – was adopted. Under a plan suggested by Lieutenant-Colonel Dudley Clarke, the name 'Leopards' was changed to 'Commandos' and the training of a selected striking force went ahead. By August the scheme had been extended to allow for commando operations in the Middle East.

The commandos were formed of volunteers from existing army units. One of the earliest volunteers was Lt. Randolph Churchill of the 4th Hussars. Fired by his father's enthusiasm and his own eagerness for action, Randolph leapt at this chance to prove himself. The idea of secret night landings, surprise attacks and hand-to-hand fighting was too tempting for him to resist; from such cloak and dagger operations heroes were bound to emerge. He joined No 8 Commando which, under the command of Lieutenant-Colonel Robert Laycock, has been raised at Burnham-on-Crouch and then transferred to Scotland. By the beginning of November, Randolph was in training at the sea-side town of Largs, near Glasgow.

No 8 Commando, at that time, consisted of ten troops, each of fifty men. Training, which had started zealously, had become somewhat lax and discipline bordered on the farcical. To avoid undue administrative costs both officers and men were paid a special lodging allowance and lived in billets of their own choice. Most of the officers, including Randolph, took up residence in the Marine Hotel. As regulations concerning dress were never strictly observed, uniforms were rarely worn; leave was easily obtained – particularly by officers – and life at Largs was, on the whole, free and easy. The holiday atmosphere became more pronounced when some of the officers' wives turned up at the Marine Hotel – Pamela Churchill joined Randolph there three weeks after little Winston was born – and, despite the odd female intrigue, a distinctly social note was struck.

Meeting old friends was probably Randolph's greatest joy. No 8 Commando was divided between a 'smart set' and a group of more serious soldiers; and in the smart set – or 'dandies' as they were sometimes called – Randolph discovered some familiar faces. Mostly the sons or brothers of peers, ex-Etonians and men from established county families, they had either been at school or university with him or were related to political friends and associates: it was Bobbity, Bones, Toby and Fruity all over again. Not the least welcome of these old cronies was Evelyn Waugh, who joined No 8 Commando shortly after it arrived at Largs. From their very first meeting in the early thirties, Randolph and Waugh had kept up an intermittent, often belligerent, friendship but it was to be their shared army experiences that drew them closer together. Over the next few years they were frequently to cross paths, and cross swords, in strange places and in outlandish circumstances.

For all its informality, camaraderie and relaxed family atmos-phere, life at Largs was extremely boring. The smart set of No 8 Commando fought off the tedium by drinking heavily, gambling recklessly, dining nightly in Glasgow and running up huge bills at their hotel. Living up to their reputation as dandies, they rivalled each other in affectation. 'All the officers,' noted Waugh shortly after his arrival, 'have very long hair & lap dogs & cigars & they wear whatever uniform they like.' Their bizarre extravagance shocked some of the more fastidious soldiers, one of whom openly denounced them as 'scum'.

Randolph, a born exhibitionist, was among the more outrageous. Never able to curb his spending, or his drinking, he found it impossible to live on his lodging allowance of 13s 4d a day. His hotel expenses were always enormous and, when payment was demanded, he invariably flew into a rage. One of his more spectacular rows occurred when the hotel proprietress charged him an extra £1 a week for his pekinese dog. 'Do you realize, my good woman,' he exploded, 'that that is the interest on £2000?' The good woman was unmoved. 'What's a pound a week to you?' she retorted. 'Ha!' shrieked the triumphant Randolph, 'so your prices are based on what you can get, and not on the service you give.' The row, which was heard all over the hotel, went on for some time. In the end Randolph paid the bill to a waiter, shouting to him to make sure he got the ten per cent service charge. 'These seem to me,' he thundered, 'the kind of people who would try and cheat you.' Randolph was not the most popular guest at the Marine Hotel.

Nor, for that matter, was he the most popular officer in No 8 Commando. During his first bout of intensive training in the north of Scotland he had been expelled from a field course for heckling the instructors and his subsequent behaviour did nothing to commend him to his superiors or to the men under his command. Group loyalty was never Randolph's strong point. For all that, the training sessions were not entirely a waste of time. Before joining the commandos, Randolph – as his wedding photographs show – was fat, flabby and decidedly overweight. The extent to which he benefited from the physical exercise involved in the field courses can be gathered from the fact that, by the beginning of November 1941, he was boldly taking on bets which challenged him to swim to an island off the coast of Largs. As a far from robust sportsman, Randolph must indeed have been feeling in trim. Unfortunately this sudden burst of athletic self-confidence was not to last for long.

At the beginning of December, No 8 Commando was sent on a further course of training in the isles of Scotland. They sailed northwards on troopships from which they were to practise sea-to-shore landings. On arrival, part of the force was stationed on the isle of Arran, where they were exercised in attack marches and climbs, while the rest remained aboard the troopships for boat training. Every two weeks the land and sea contingents changed places. The operation was not an immediate success. Inexperience and muddled orders resulted in the landing craft running repeatedly aground, accommodation in the ships and on shore was totally inadequate, and things were not helped by the hostility which developed between the lordly commandos and the junior naval officers. To the dismay of the men separated from their wives, the training continued well into January.

Randolph was given a short reprieve. On Christmas Day he and Pamela arrived at Chequers to spend the holiday with his family. His three sisters were also there – Diana and Sarah with their husbands – and the eighteen-year-old Mary Churchill described it as one of the happiest Christmasses she could remember. There was an unexpected lull in the fighting on all fronts, no urgent calls came through from Whitehall, and the day was spent free from the thought of war. It was the last Christmas the Churchill family was to spend together for four years.

Shortly after Randolph returned to Scotland, No 8 Commando was given two weeks leave. There was a rumour that they were about to be sent abroad, but no one took it seriously. Such rumours were common enough in wartime to be dismissed as yet another false alarm. This time, however, the rumour proved correct. When the men of No 8 Commando reported back for duty they discovered that they were now part of the newly formed 'Z' force which, commanded by Lieutenant-Colonel Robert Laycock, was under orders to sail for the Middle East. Three troopships – the *Glenroy*, the *Glengyle* and the *Glenearn* – were waiting to receive them and, at the beginning of February 1941, they set sail in convoy for Egypt. Randolph was on board the overcrowded *Glenroy*. The long voyage round the coast of Africa was to last for over a month.

CHAPTER ELEVEN

The Middle East

Plans for the defence of Britain against a German invasion had been considerably complicated when, on 10 June 1940, following the Dunkirk retreat, Italy not unexpectedly entered the war. Attention was immediately diverted to the Middle East. An estimated 215,000 Italian troops were spread along the coast of north Africa – their garrisons and supply depots linked, or about to be linked, by a magnificent road which stretched from their main supply port at Tripoli to the Egyptian frontier – and it was here that the Fascist threat loomed most alarmingly. Far outnumbering the scattered British forces in Egypt, the Italian army was splendidly placed to invade the strategically important Nile Delta. No one was more aware of this danger than Winston Churchill. As early as July he raised the question of troop landings along the African coast to cut the motor road and disrupt the Italian advance. In the event, this did not prove necessary: British action, when it was taken, was far more purposeful.

At the beginning of December, after a period of suspense, criticism and mounting impatience, a period when Cairo was dubbed 'Headquarters Muddle East', the British surprised the world by going on the offensive. What was announced as a tentative raid on the Italian outposts, turned into a full-scale invasion. After a cunning inland sweep, the reinforced British troops swiftly captured Sidi Barrani and pushed on into Libya to Bardia and then Tobruk. By the beginning of February they had occupied the vital Italian base at Benghazi. The lightning campaign was a triumph for the enigmatic British Commander-in-Chief in the Middle East, General Sir Archibald Wavell, and brought a ray of hope to the otherwise gloomy military situation. News of the great desert victories was still coming in when the convoy taking Randolph to Egypt left Britain.

The voyage southwards was uneventful. Confined to their cramped quarters, the officers on board the *Glenroy* moped about, bored and irritable, seeking distraction where they could find it. The younger men filled their days with makeshift training exercises; the older, more blasé, hands occupied themselves as best they could. Officially there was nothing for them to do and, apart from the daily P.T. sessions and an occasional written exercise, they were left to their own devices. Randolph, more restless than most, took comfort in reading *War and Peace* for the first time, but he only really came to life in the evenings when the gambling began. There were endless games of poker, chemin-de-fer and roulette. The stakes were high – rarely less than a £50 bank for chemin-de-fer – and Randolph's losses were correspondingly heavy. For him to end the night £400 down was not unusual and, although he won some of the money back, he was in debt for £800 by the time the *Glenroy* reached Suez. Evelyn Waugh had visions of Pamela Churchill being sent out to work to pay off her husband's debts. It was a vision which the unhappy Pamela appears to have shared. Shortly after arriving in Egypt, Randolph received a very tart letter from his wife deploring his gambling extravagances.

The one bright spot of the voyage came when the convoy called at Cape Town. Here the troops were allowed ashore and lavishly entertained by a crowd of well-wishers who whisked them off in cars, fed them on peaches and grapes, plied them with drinks and returned them to their ships drunk and happy. Randolph and Evelyn Waugh were snatched by a 'sugar daddy' who not only crammed them with rich food but sat by contentedly while Randolph pontificated on the political situation. Even more impressively Randolph was invited to luncheon at the House of Assembly by his father's old friend General Smuts. The invitation, however, was not without its embarrassments. With troop movements being conducted in secret, it came as a surprise to newspaper readers in London when, the following day, it was reported that the Prime Minister's son was in Cape Town. Rumour had it that Randolph had flown to South Africa on a special mission for his father. Why else, it was asked, would he be entertained by General Smuts? Some weeks were to pass before Pamela Churchill announced publicly that her husband was taking part 'in the Western Desert campaign.'

Two weeks after leaving Cape Town the convoy arrived at Suez and then proceeded along the Canal – rumoured to be mined – to Kabrit where the troops disembarked. They left the ships with few regrets. The strain of living in close confinement for over a month had proved an unnerving experience for both officers and men. Their collective feelings were wittily summed up by an inscription scrawled on the troopdecks of the *Glengyle*. 'Never,' it read, parodying Winston Churchill's famous tribute to the R.A.F., 'in the history of human endeavour have so few been buggered about by so many.' Nor was this the only written evidence of the soldiers' rancour. Later a two volume diary kept by a disgruntled commando sergeant on board the *Glenroy,* came to light and was found to contain a running commentary on the outrageous behaviour of various officers. His most spiteful comments were levelled at Lieutenant Randolph Churchill. And there was even an ugly rumour that Randolph's name had been included among the officers who were likely to be knifed by their own men once the commandos went into action.

Once ashore the commandos went into camp and resumed training. Their presence in Egypt was only incidentally connected with the fighting in north Africa. Before leaving Britain they had been instructed to prepare themselves for an assault on the island of Rhodes where, it was thought, the Germans intended to set up an air base. Whether this assault would be possible was, however, already in doubt. While they were at sea, German activity in the Balkans had made it obvious that the long-threatened invasion of Greece was imminent and this posed a serious threat to a landing on Rhodes. All the same, while the politicians and military commanders argued, the commando training went ahead. A line was marked out in the desert, objectives were designated and attack routes planned; Robert Laycock was promoted to Colonel, the name 'Z' force was changed to 'Layforce' and No 8 Commando became 'B Battalion'. If Rhodes was to be attacked, the newly arrived assault force intended to be ready.

It was probably to find out exactly what was happening that, shortly after his arrival, Randolph visited Cairo. Anthony Eden, now Foreign Secretary, had just flown in from Athens and Randolph met him at the British Embassy. They spent 'several agreeable hours' together. It is unlikely that their casual meeting had any influence on events, but it did produce an amusing result. So impressed was Eden by Randolph's enthusiasm, that he concluded one of his telegrams to Churchill with a personal message. 'Have just seen Randolph, who has just arrived,' he wired. 'He sends his love. He is looking fit and well and has the light of battle in his eye.' Unfortunately, or perhaps mischievously, the wording of this telegram was muddled in transmission. By the time it arrived in London – or so it is claimed – the word 'battle' read 'bottle'. Randolph's friends were highly amused. 'All too true,' was Waugh's comment.

One of the results of Eden's Middle East tour was the decision to despatch five army divisions – some sixty thousand men – to assist in the defence of Greece. This proved a grave mistake. German reinforcements had already arrived in north Africa to bolster the retreating Italians and now, taking advantage of the depleted state of the British force, they launched a counter offensive. In a startlingly swift campaign, under the command of the then little known General Erwin Rommel, they swept along the African coast and regained most of the ground the Italians had lost. All the coastal towns, with the exception of Tobruk, were recaptured and the Egyptian frontier was again threatened. Rommel, as Churchill put it, had 'torn the new-won laurels from Wavell's brow and thrown them in the sand.'

Cairo was thrown into confusion. Earlier plans were scrapped and new ones hastily devised. 'Layforce', as part of the 6th Division, was put on reserve. 'This,' Wavell reported to London, 'will involve the postponement of the attack on Rhodes.' With their fate now decided, Randolph's battalion were rushed into camp at Sidi Bish near Alexandria where they awaited further orders. The mood of the camp was one of unrelieved gloom. Having volunteered for special service, having left their regiments in the hope of immediate action, the erstwhile commandos now found themselves part of the general defence force in the Middle East. The older officers, says Waugh, 'were homesick and the younger impatient to get into action. All spent every available hour in Alexandria leaving their troops in an uncomfortable camp.'

In an attempt to maintain the morale of 'B Battalion' – the former No 8 Commando – Colonel Laycock arranged for them to be exempted from the reserve force. Instead they were sent on sorties along the coast with the intention of harassing the enemy. Most of their operations were either cancelled at the last minute or produced farcical results. One of their more spectacular failures occurred when they were ordered to raid the harbour at Bardia. Having been informed that the town was held by 2,000 enemy troops they set off in the *Glengyle* in the dead of night and, amid some confusion, made a beach landing. To their astonishment they discovered Bardia was deserted; the only enemy they sighted was a solitary motor-cycle patrol. Three hours later they returned to their ship with two casualties: an officer accidentally shot by his own men and a soldier injured by his own grenade.

Further raids, which Randolph tried to organize from a gunboat, were equally unsuccessful. Two or three trips were made but each time it proved impossible to effect a landing. Undaunted, Randolph then began planning a combined air and sea attack on the coast. This time he was frustrated by the refusal of the R.A.F. to sanction the operation. Not for nothing was it suggested that the name 'Layforce' be changed to 'Delayforce.'

Randolph, of course, put every disaster down to military

incompetence. His denunciation of the British High Command in the Middle East knew no bounds. He did not hesitate to make his views known and attacked everyone regardless of rank or circumstances. And the more he raged the more he appeared to be justified by events. This was particularly true of the disaster which befell the ill-fated British expedition in Greece. After putting up a gallant fight against the German invaders, the combined British force in Greece found themselves hopelessly outmatched by superior Nazi air power and were driven into retreat. By the end of April the exhausted Greek army was sueing for a separate armistice and the British troops, aided by the remarkable skill of the Royal Navy, were being hastily evacuated from the Greek mainland. All hope of gaining a much needed foothold in Europe appeared to have been lost.

Randolph's fury over this *débâcle* was monumental. He gave voice to it when, on 5 May, he was entertained by the British ambassador to Egypt, Sir Miles Lampson, in Cairo. Among the other guests at the Embassy were a distinguished admiral and Major-General Louis Spears, the Head of the British Mission to Syria and the Lebanon, and it was on the heads of these two officers that Randolph's wrath fell. Throughout dinner that evening he raved and ranted, contrasting the performance of the British army with that of the British navy, and singling out General Spears for particularly scathing criticism. He would not let the subject alone and after the meal he continued his hammering until his audience was reduced to a state of bemused exhaustion. 'Spears bore the brunt of the attack . . .' noted the weary Sir Miles Lampson in his diary. 'It was not till 2 a.m. before I crawled up to bed having I fear been somewhat indiscreet in some of my conversation, drawn from me during Randolph's extravaganza.'

But, for all his fuming and fault finding, Randolph refused to give into despair. Once his Churchillian spirit was roused, no set-back, however bad, could dampen it. Not for one moment did he doubt that the tide would turn and that Britain, in the end, would emerge victorious. He was even tempted to seek comfort where it did not not exist. In the middle of May, for instance, when waves of German parachutists invaded Crete, he was somehow able to convince himself that their attack had failed. So sure of this was he that for days he went around in a state of high exhilaration. But he was wrong, of course. Two days after their first landings on Crete, the Germans succeeded in gaining a foothold at the Maleme airstrip – enabling aircraft to bring in more troops – and ten days later, after some extraordinary fighting and heavy casualties, they were more or less in control of the island. Randolph was forced to swallow his cheers.

The invasion of Crete had one important effect on Randolph's career: it ended his commando activities. Before the battle for the island was over, part of 'Layforce' was sent to Crete to reinforce the garrison commanded by General Freyberg. They left Alexandria towards the end of May and arrived in time to take part in the doomed rear-guard action. Although many of his friends were included in this force, Randolph did not go with them. He remained behind in Cairo where, in one capacity or another, he was to serve for almost two years.

*   *   *

Cairo, in the summer of 1941, has been aptly described as 'the Clapham Junction of the war.' With the Mediterranean blocked to passenger shipping, it was impossible to travel to the Middle East from Britain without passing through Cairo. There was, it is true, the long boring route round the coast of Africa – the route by which Randolph had reached Suez – but this took weeks, sometimes months, and was avoided by anyone in a hurry. Most visiting military men, politicians, diplomats, foreign dignitaries and journalists preferred to fly in and out of Cairo on their way to India, Russia, Australia and the Far East. They came and went with such bustling frequency that Cairo's hotels, clubs and embassies were often more active than the military command posts and certainly more lively than their London counterparts. Throughout the early years of the war this hot, noisy, brightly-lit and overcrowded city served not merely as the cross roads of the Middle East but as a rallying point for the British Empire.

Although officially neutral, Egypt was the centre of British operations in the Mediterranean. The nominal independence of the country, established in the 1930s, had, despite Churchill's fears, done little to lessen British influence in Egypt. Since the outbreak of war, the small British army force in Egypt had been massively strengthened; the British Middle East Command was headquartered at Garden City in Cairo – close to the British Embassy – and from there the North African campaigns and those in Greece and Crete had been planned and directed; and the inadequate port at nearby Alexandria had become the Royal Navy's Mediterranean base. Outside Europe no place was more important in the war against Hitler than this largely barren north African kingdom. Anyone who was anyone in the 1940s – high ranking military officers, colonial dignitaries, exiled monarchs, diplomats, social celebrities, well known explorers, entertainers, newspaper proprietors and statesmen of every nationality – seem, at one time or another to have passed through war-time Cairo.

And on the heels of the famous and the feted came the obscure, the secretive and the devious. As a supposedly neutral seat of power, Cairo attracted friends and foes alike. Undercover agents, spies, paid informers and men of doubtful allegiance mixed freely in the bars, the bazaars and the brothels, and haunted the clubs and the embassies. The streets of Cairo hummed with rumour and intrigue. Randolph, with his taste for cloak and dagger politics, his love of gossip and conspiracy, could have found no better outlet for his talents than that offered by Cairo at this stage of the war. He was to make the most of his Egyptian sojourn.

As a staff officer at General Headquarters in Cairo, Randolph was attached to the Intelligence Division. Promoted in one jump from Lieutenant to Major he became the press relations officer in the army's far from effective propaganda branch. He was assisted by one of his fellow commandos, Captain Robin Campbell, a gifted writer, who was the son of the British ambassador to Portugal. They made a formidable team. Randolph brought to the job not only his experience as a journalist but the energy and gusto with which he had embarked on his political campaigns. The writer Alan Moorehead, then a war-correspondent for the *Daily Express,* gives a delightful picture of Randolph's irruption on the Cairo scene.

Randolph, says Moorehead, arrived at G.H.Q. 'like a hot gusty wind. He was an unabashed reflection of his father, whom he always referred to as Winston. He was aggressive, headstrong, opinionated, full of rushing energy and he went around G.H.Q. mortally offending one brass hat after another. He was a notable figure with his heavy leonine head, his thick greying hair, his husky voice and big shoulders.

'His politics, to me, were deplorable, and he had a habit of riding rough-shod over everyone he could. He disliked advice. Inevitably he made many enemies and many mistakes. But that limp, lifeless and pathetic thing we called British propaganda in the Middle East suddenly revived under his impulsion. He got things done. He broadened the censorship and let in criticism. He revived the local press which at that time consisted of Reuters Foreign News Service and not much else . . . Randolph brought in a new service of foreign cables, articles and cartoons.

'He brightened the press conferences and he dared to publish for the army a weekly digest of the best magazine and newspaper articles appearing in America and England. Some of these articles were frankly critical of army methods. They were packed with well-written information and some contained left and liberal opinions (not that Randolph was left-wing – far from it) . . . Other reactionary minds of the type that was blocking all originality in the British Army wrote bitter and abusive letters to the editor. One officer I remember protested that the troops in the desert did not need this kind of subversive literature. What they really wanted, he said, were magazines like *Country Life*. Certainly Randolph was shaking things up.'

He was undoubtedly helped by his pre-war contacts and his knowledge of the newspaper world. With many of the journalists he was surprisingly popular. Some of them were old colleagues from his days with the Rothermere and Beaverbrook press and he never failed to support them when he could. In most clashes between the press and the military, Randolph was firmly on the side of the journalists. His efforts to reform the rigid, often fatuous, rules of the British and Egyptian censorship won him the heart of many a harassed reporter. Kenneth T. Downs, his old American acquaintance, was unstinting in his praise. 'With almost ferocious energy,' he says, 'and great skill, [Randolph] began to transform the inept information section into the most efficient operation of its sort that I saw throughout the war.'

But perhaps those who most appreciated Randolph's efforts were the news starved troops in the desert. In a sturdy Ford station wagon he would tour the isolated outposts to sound out opinions and acquaint himself with the soldiers' needs. Once he knew what was wanted he did his best to supply it, even if it meant offending the authorities. More than one former 'desert rat' has paid tribute to Randolph's entertaining news sheets. Not only did he start the *World's Press Review* (referred to by Alan Moorehead) but he was instrumental in launching the equally popular *Eighth Army News*. Unfortunately the joy these newspapers brought to the men was not always shared by their senior officers. Indeed one copy of the *World's Press Review* so enraged a diehard brigadier that he had it publicly burnt at his desert camp. Randolph was no doubt delighted. Nor was it only army officers who were affronted. Winston Churchill was later to protest about an article attacking Gracie Fields which appeared in the *Eighth Army News*. He was answered by the author of the attack, Hannen Swaffer – no friend of Randolph's – who took great delight in reminding him that the newspaper was the brain-child of his son.

Had Randolph confined himself to his press liaison duties, he would no doubt have continued to annoy the military brasshats and to make himself unpopular with his immediate superiors, but he would have avoided the deep suspicion roused by his meddling in high politics. This suspicion came mainly from the fact that he was known to be in direct and constant contact with his father. He made no secret of the fact that he used the confidential diplomatic 'bag' to send home personal letters to his family and friends. So well known was this that, on the voyage to Suez, Evelyn Waugh advised his wife to consult Pamela Churchill for information about the movements of 'Layforce'. Pamela, he said, 'in the nature of things' had 'great superiority' in such matters. Randolph was to avail himself of the 'bag' for his correspondence throughout the war. All too often, however, his letters to Churchill contained more than family chit-chat and details about his movements.

This is particularly true of the letters he wrote from Egypt. In Cairo he communicated with his father through General Wavell's office and Major Peter Coats, Wavell's personal A.D.C., was put in the embarrassing position of according him this privilege. It was not a duty which Coats relished. 'I never liked Randolph much,' he says, 'though we had known each other always, and I had a vague suspicion he was anti-, or at least, critical of, Wavell . . . Several times he had asked me to put letters to his father in the Commander-in-Chief's bag. I suppose I should not have done so; I have often regretted it, but it was difficult to suggest censoring his letters or to refuse to accept them when they were addressed to the Prime Minister.' His vague suspicions were soon to become more substantial.

There can be little doubt about Randolph's influence on his father. Evidence of his meddling was later published by Churchill himself and further intrigue has been strongly implied. The published evidence relates to a telegram which Randolph sent to his father shortly after he arrived in Cairo. In this telegram he complained of the lack of all-over political direction in the Middle East and suggested that a member of the War Cabinet be sent out to remedy this. 'Most thoughtful people here,' he argued, 'realize need for radical reform along these lines. No mere shunting of personnel will suffice, and the present time seems particularly ripe and favourable for a change of system.' Churchill, as he admits, was impressed. He was aware of Randolph's 'considerable contacts' and claims that the suggestion had the backing of the British ambassador, Sir Miles Lampson. After thinking the matter over for a fortnight, he decided to take action. Captain Oliver Lyttleton, then President of the Board of Trade, suddenly found himself included in the War Cabinet as Minister of State resident in the Middle East. He left immediately for Cairo. Randolph - not to everyone's approval – was also rewarded. 'We hear,' noted Anthony Eden's disapproving Private Secretary, Oliver Harvey, on 4 August 1941, 'P.M. has made Randolph liaison officer between War Cabinet and Lyttleton in Cairo – another bad appointment.'

Far more controversial was Churchill's decision to replace General Wavell as Commander-in-Chief in the Middle East. Rumour had it that Randolph played a decisive part in effecting Wavell's transfer to India. As his criticism of the military set-up in Cairo was so outspoken, few doubted that this criticism was included in his uncensored letters to his father. No doubt it was. Whether Churchill, as some claim, was unduly influenced by Randolph's rantings is another matter. There was more to the removal of General Wavell than that.

Churchill had never really trusted Wavell. His dislike of the General had become apparent when they met in London in August 1941. On that occasion Churchill had astonished his colleagues by referring to Wavell as a 'good average colonel' who had the makings of a 'good chairman of a Tory Association.' Since then little had happened to make him change his mind. The early successes in north Africa had been followed by losses to Rommel, the reversals in Greece and Crete and, more recently, the failure of operation 'Battleaxe' in which an assault launched in the Western Desert at the beginning of June, met with fierce opposition and was called off by Wavell. Although Wavell could not be held entirely responsible for these setbacks, they undoubtedly strengthened Churchill's resolve to replace him. Whatever Randolph might have said to his father, he was obviously preaching to the converted.

So Randolph could not have been sorry to see General Wavell go. By an odd coincidence he was present when the Commander-in-Chief undertook his last mission. On 25 June – three days after Germany attacked Russia – Wavell flew to Ethiopia to receive the thanks of the Emperor, Haile Selassie, for the part the British forces had played in restoring him to his throne. Randolph, at the invitation of Peter Coats, travelled part of the way with Wavell's party. He had wanted to accompany the Commander-in-Chief's party to the Ethiopian capital but this was not considered advisable and he was dropped at Asmara, in Eritrea, to await Wavell's return. Frustrated in one direction, he reaped his reward in another. On the way back from Addis-Ababa Wavell's plane got lost, ran out of petrol, and was forced to land in the wilds. A Blenheim was despatched from Asmara to rescue the stranded party. Randolph was delighted by the mishap. When Peter Coats eventually arrived back in Asmara, he was treated to some heavy sarcasm from Randolph who crowed openly over the fact that the Commander-in-Chief's plane had been allowed to run out of petrol. 'Once more,' says Coats, 'I felt he was critical of the Wavell set-up . . . And I wondered again what he had been writing in the letters I had sent home for him to his father.'

For some, the answer to that question came when Wavell returned to Cairo. While he had been in Ethiopia the newly appointed Commander-in-Chief, General Auchinleck, had arrived in Egypt to replace him. This came as no surprise to Wavell. Shortly before he left, he had received Churchill's telegram telling him of his transfer to India but, not wanting to spoil the Ethiopian trip, had said nothing to his staff. Now, with the arrival of Auchinleck, the secret could be kept no longer. 'For the moment,' confessed Peter Coats, 'I felt my world had collapsed.' He was not alone in his dismay. There were many others who thought that Wavell had been treated shabbily. His sudden removal to India, it is said, 'was not liked in Cairo, or the desert.' Randolph, it seems, was once again in a minority.

❄   ❄   ❄

Cairo's climate is not invigorating. In mid-summer an oppressive, steamy heat engulfs the city and leaves even the most robust of men limp, listless and dejected. At this time of the year new arrivals, unacclimatized and caught off-guard, suffer innumerable minor complaints – stomach disorders, diarrhoea, heat rash, boils, swollen feet and eye strain – which drain them of all energy. The smallest task becomes a burden and, at times, work becomes impossible. Most offices close from one until late in the afternoon or early evening. So it was in the summer of 1941 when even the military establishments ground to a halt at midday. 'Few people,' claims Alan Moorehead, 'who had tried both G.H.Q. and the desert would have chosen a permanent job in Cairo.'

But for those who had no choice and had the right connections there were compensations. In a country where all the wealth was in the hands of less than five per cent of the population, the more fashionable British officers were rarely at a loss for amusement. The face of Cairo was one of poverty, disease and abject misery but behind certain doors life was lived on a grand scale. In the city's rich houses, smart hotels, exclusive clubs and elegant restaurants, the austerities of wartime Britain were easily forgotten; food and drink – French wines and grouse in season – was plentiful, tarbooshed servants waited at table and the nights were filled with noise, light and laughter as the bands played, the dice rattled and glasses clinked. The Cairo-based officers may often have felt tired and queasy, but they certainly knew how to enjoy themselves. Their lot was cynically summed up in a verse which ended:

'We fought the war in Shepheard's and the Continental Bar,
We reserved our punch for the Turf Club lunch
And they gave us the Africa Star.'

Needless to say, Randolph made the most of his time in Cairo. Nothing could have suited him better than the city's hedonistic atmosphere. He felt at home there. Cut off, for the time being, from the more immediate excitements of the war, he at least found himself in a *milieu* which appealed to him; and where his social contacts still counted for something. Away from Cairo's sleazy, beggar-infested streets, Mayfair and Belgravia still held sway and Eton and Oxford continued to provide the passport to privilege and influence.

He was plunged into Cairo's hectic social life soon after he arrived there. One of his first calls was to Peter Coats's Office in Grey Pillars Building, where Wavell's staff was then quartered. As it happened, Coats was that day booked for luncheon with Mrs Maud Marriott, the wife of Colonel (later Major-General Sir John) Marriott of the Scots Guards, and he took Randolph along with him. 'That,' says Coats, 'is how friendship with the Marriotts began.' It was a friendship which was to brighten Randolph's social life considerably.

Known to her friends as 'Momo', Mrs Marriott was the daughter of the well-known American financier, Otto Kahn, and probably the most influential English-speaking hostess in Cairo. Small, dark and vivacious, she prided herself on her long red finger-nails, her girlish figure, her dress sense – her clothes might change in colour, but never in style – and her reluctance to rise before midday. She was a strong-minded, intelligent, well-informed woman who knew everyone, entertained generously, pulled strings for her protégés and kept a merry open house for her friends. Rich, feminine and married, Momo Marriott possessed all the attributes that Randolph looked for in a woman. She became his greatest female friend in Cairo.

Randolph's close friendship with Momo Marriott did not, however, interfere with his more casual liaisons. Like many British officers in Cairo, he was rarely seen without a 'pretty little Egyptian girl' at his side. He made no attempt to disguise these relationships. The girls, often of questionable character, went everywhere with him – except, of course, to Momo Marriott's soirées. He would sit openly in Shepheard's Hotel whispering to one or more of these girls and it was obvious that they were not chosen for their conversational powers. 'They were not,' as one of his Egyptian friends put it, 'platonic friendships. I sometimes saw him in bed with the girls.'

But it was outside the bedroom that Randolph's antics caused the most embarrassment. His insistence on taking his questionable girl friends to the exclusive Mohammed Ali Club created a minor scandal.

The Mohammed Ali Club was the most luxurious of all Cairo's private clubs. It was also the most select. A great many army officers belonged to the Turf Club and some joined the Automobile Club, but only the privileged became members of the Mohammed Ali Club. Few junior officers claimed this privilege and Randolph was probably admitted only because of his father's position. Membership of the Mohammed Ali Club was greatly prized. For, not only was it one of the few places in Cairo where entertainment was provided on the roof, but it was the only club where military men could mix socially with wealthy Egyptians. (As the loyalty of some of these Egyptians was doubtful, the Mohammed Ali Club was also considered dangerous by the British authorities.)

The rarefied atmosphere of the club made little impression on Randolph. It was no novelty for him to mix with the elite and he behaved there much as he behaved everywhere. Not the least of his impudent gestures was his habit of entertaining his girl friends in a room where women were not allowed. This so incensed the other members that a staff member eventually plucked up sufficient courage to tell Randolph that he was infringing the rules. It was a brave, but unwise move. Randolph's response was terrifying. The scene he created far surpassed his usual tantrums and was talked about in Cairo for days. As a result of this incident the Mohammed Ali Club was forced to change its rules. From then on all members bringing women to the club were asked to sign them in so that 'undesirable ladies could be kept out.'

Randolph's ability to offend, to infuriate, to reduce even the most placid of men to jabbering incoherence, never ceased to amaze. There were few who knew him in Cairo who did not have a story to tell about his incredible rudeness. Even his more indulgent friends confessed themselves shocked on occasion. It was impossible to predict how he would act at any given moment. When, for instance, Freya Stark – the distinguished travel writer – arrived in Cairo in June 1941, there seemed every reason for Randolph to cultivate her friendship. Miss Stark was on a propaganda tour of the Middle East and her knowledge of Arabic was invaluable to the British war effort. Randolph must have known this when he was invited to meet her for luncheon at Shepheard's Hotel. But if he knew it, he certainly did not show it. On being introduced to Miss Stark, he pointedly turned his back on her and walked over to speak to some friends. The luncheon was not a success. Once again the Cairo gossips were kept busy.

Miss Stark was certainly not amused. 'Yesterday,' she wrote to a friend, 'I lunched at Shepheard's and met Randolph Churchill whom I thought a quite insufferable young man with appalling manners. I was told afterwards that he is doing more harm than any two Germans, just by being himself. He is extraordinarily like his father to look at except that his father is *solid* where he is *fat*. Perhaps he may yet emerge from all this chrysalis: but he is over thirty and should have done something by now.'

Randolph's behaviour did not escape the notice of the authorities. All too often his outbursts were not only offensive but alarmingly indiscreet and this became a cause for concern. So much so that, at the end of July, Sir Miles Lampson decided to give him a friendly word of advice: he particularly stressed the need to keep a guarded tongue in the Mohammed Ali Club. Well meant as was this warning, it came too late. The following morning another complaint landed on the ambassador's desk; this time it concerned Randolph's indiscretions at a dinner in Alexandria.

'I felt,' Lampson noted in his diary on 29 July, 'justified in sending for him this evening when I showed him the report. He denied it in toto and said he was sure he knew the source, namely Edward Stanley (Lord Stanley of Alderley) who had already been making mischief for him. I said that his denial was good enough for me, but it did very aptly point the moral of what I had said to him last night as to the vital necessity of keeping a curb on his tongue especially amongst Egyptians.'

Lampson was a forceful, giant of a man – he was 6 foot 5 inches tall – and one of the few officials able to intimidate opinionated young officers. No doubt recognizing that he had met his match, Randolph promptly apologized and promised to behave in a more responsible manner in future. 'All in all,' concluded Lampson, 'I think this conversation was probably a very good thing. Our young friend has got very good stuff in him but is his own worst enemy, and if he is not careful will one of these days get himself into a serious scrape. Let us hope that this will help him to help himself.'

It was a forlorn hope. Only when confronted by a formidable personality like Sir Miles Lampson did Randolph display a semblance of contrition. Such personalities were few and far between. The only other person to whom he appears to have shown some respect at this time was another towering six-footer – the newly arrived General Auchinleck. Randolph's attitude towards Auchinleck became apparent when – somewhat to the annoyance of Freya Stark – he conducted a woman journalist on an unauthorized tour of the desert outposts. The journalist was Eve Curie, daughter of the famous French scientists, Marie and Pierre Curie, and the tour was undertaken when a crucial battle was in progress. Auchinleck had just launched his long-delayed counter offensive against Rommel and when Randolph and Eve Curie reached him in the desert the news from the front was confused and not at all encouraging. Amazingly Randolph had no advice or criticism to offer the Commander-in-Chief. So resolute did the sunburned, blue-eyed Auchinleck appear that, says Eve Curie, his presence 'rendered Randolph Churchill for once absolutely mute and motionless.'

Auchinleck's confidence was justified. A few days later, Randolph and a group of journalists joined Brigadier Gatehouse's column and witnessed the clash of tanks and guns which was to lead to victory at Sidi Rezegh and open up Cyrenaica to the British forces. Throughout the month of December, Auchinleck's army was to push along the coastal area, relieve beleaguered Tobruk, recapture Benghazi and advance as far as Agedabia. 'Enemy is apparently in full retreat towards the west,' Auchinleck wired to Churchill.

Randolph did not accompany the troops. After the battle at Sidi Rezegh he returned to Cairo. He was in the Egyptian capital when, on Sunday 7 December, the Japanese attacked Pearl Harbour. The news that America had entered the war created a tremendous sensation. Randolph greeted it with a typical mixture of bombast and tactlessness. That evening he arrived at a party given by an American woman, rubbing his hands and shouting: 'Hurrah, Hurrah, they're in it at last.' This, for his hostess, was the last straw. Already sickened by the snide remarks of the 'Bright Young British', she promptly packed her bags and left Cairo. Randolph could never guard his words for long.

As it happened, Randolph was also about to leave Cairo. The following month he returned to Britain for a couple of month's leave. His arrival in London could not have been more opportune. The opening weeks of 1942 saw yet another turn about in the Western Desert. By the middle of January it had become obvious that Rommel had no intention of retreating indefinitely. He was in fact mustering his forces to strike back at his pursuers. His counter attack was launched on 21 January and by the end of the month he had reoccupied Benghazi and driven the British army back to a line running south from Gazala. This reverse – together with setbacks in the Far East, where the Japanese had sunk the *Prince of Wales* and the *Repulse* – decided Churchill to have a Commons debate on a vote of confidence. There was never much doubt that he would win the vote, but the debate – opened by Churchill on 27 January – allowed critics of the Government to air their views. It also allowed Randolph to make a contribution as a serving soldier.

His opportunity came on 28 January, the day after Churchill had addressed the House. ('We are now having an answer to a Debate,'

214

protested an angry MP, 'given, not by the father, but by the son.')
He was listened to attentively, but his speech made little impression.
The facts and figures he produced reflected a knowledge of earlier
debates but his oratory fell flat. He appeared more intent on settling
old scores than in exploring new ground. What criticism he had to
offer was levelled at 'the Parliament of Munich . . . the Parliament
which failed to rearm the country.' Not until he came to the reverses
in the Western Desert did his arguments carry any force. He made a
spirited defence of Auchinleck's decision to attack Rommel and was
able, from personal knowledge, to contrast the strength of the
opposing armies. The situation had worsened, he explained, because
Rommel had now brought in reinforcements and new equipment
and the British army was deprived of its railhead. 'No one,' he
declared, 'should be surprised that the battle should now go through
a difficult phase.'

Throughout the speech, Randolph was careful to avoid references
to his own experiences. Others were not so reticent. There were
constant interjections and at one stage an opponent shouted:
'Before the hon. and gallant Member leaves that point – he speaks
with such authority as a soldier – will he tell me on what occasion he
has been, as a soldier, in a battle where he has been shot at by the
enemy at 1,500 yards?' Randolph brushed the taunt aside, but its
implications were obvious.

The sad fact was that, through no fault of his own, Randolph was
speaking as a staff officer from Cairo, not as a fighting soldier. There
was, as he well knew, no glory attached to an army propagandist. It
was a sore point and one which he was determined to rectify.

*   *   *

In April 1942, shortly after his return to Egypt, Randolph cabled his
wife to say he had volunteered to join a parachute unit. The news
came as a shock to his family. His mother made no attempt to
conceal her dismay. She considered that Randolph was behaving
irresponsibly. Her concern, however, was not so much for her son
as for her husband. As she saw it, Randolph, by deliberately
courting danger, would be placing an extra burden on Churchill's
already overloaded shoulders. Why, she argued, could he not have
quietly rejoined his regiment if he were tired of Cairo? Why did he
always have to seek the sensational? So agitated did she become that
she toyed with the idea of sending a cable to Randolph, begging him
to change his mind for his father's sake. She even wrote to Churchill
suggesting this but then appears to have had second thoughts. No
doubt realizing that a show of opposition – particularly from his
mother – would simply spur Randolph on, she finally decided not to

interfere.

It was just as well. Randolph had probably resigned his post before informing his family. Any interference on his mother's part would have come too late. His desire for adventure was such that he had no time to waste on arguments.

The parachute unit for which Randolph had volunteered was no ordinary army unit. It had been formed only a matter of months before he arrived back in Egypt and its activities were highly unconventional. In effect it was an extension and refinement of the early commando units and included among its officers were some of Randolph's friends from 'Layforce'. One of those officers, David Stirling, was responsible for the formation of the unit.

When 'Layforce' had been dispersed, David Stirling – a quietly-spoken, unassuming young officer who had arrived in north Africa with Randolph on the *Glenroy* – had been among those left behind at Alexandria. Like most of the disbanded force he was sadly disappointed with the performance of the commandos. The situation seemed to cry out for commando tactics and the failure to disrupt the German supply line appeared inexcusable. One of the troubles, of course, had been the inability of the raiding parties to make successful sea-to-shore landings. As Stirling saw it, the commandos had relied too heavily on the navy in what was essentially a desert campaign. There must, he thought, be other ways of penetrating the enemy's lines. One such way was demonstrated by the German parachute tactics in Crete. Partly inspired by this German success, Stirling came up with the idea of dropping small groups of trained men into enemy territory by parachute. Their object would be to raid air bases, destroy planes, blow up ammunition dumps and storage depots, and generally cause chaos. Stirling presented his plan to the High Command in Cairo and, more by luck than anything else, it was approved. He was raised to the rank of captain, given permission to start recruiting, and allocated an area in the Suez Canal Zone in which to set up camp.

Officially the new unit was known as 'L' Division of the then non-existent Special Air Service. (The name had been invented to make the enemy think that the British had parachute troops in the Middle East.) In time, however, they were to adopt the initials that brought them lasting fame – S.A.S. Training started immediately. Although most of the men were former commandos, Stirling and his second-in-command, Jock Lewes, decided they should be toughened up by a more exacting training course. With little equipment – most of it had to be begged, borrowed or stolen – the new recruits were drilled in assault tactics, in the handling of captured weapons, in rifle practice, map reading and desert navigation. They were also subjected to gruelling route marches and expected to make at least six parachute jumps. By the beginning of November – just before Auchinleck launched his winter campaign – they were ready for action.

The first raiding parties met with mixed success. Their initial attempt at a parachute landing was ruined by bad weather and muddled planning. Only a handful of men returned from the unsuccessful operation. There was a hasty change of tactics. Stirling decided that, for the time being, he would scrap the parachute drops and confine himself to land activities. He sought the assistance of the Long Range Desert Group – a recently formed motorized unit, then operating from the Siwa oasis – and on their second attempt the raiders were conveyed to a spot close to their targets by L.R.D.G. trucks. This proved far more effective. In two weeks, it is estimated, the unit destroyed some ninety aircraft.

Other successes followed. In the middle of January, for instance, a raiding party led by David Stirling (now promoted to Major) managed to sneak into the small coastal town of Buerat and create havoc among the storage depots and workshops at the harbour as well as destroying several petrol carriers parked at the outskirts of the town. Encouraged by this triumph, Stirling then – in March – made an attempt on the more closely guarded harbour at Benghazi. The Germans had recently reoccupied Benghazi and were using it as their principal supply port, but most of the harbour guards were Italian. Stirling's plan was to enter the town, make his way to the water front, launch a small collapsible canoe and then approach the ships in the harbour. If all went well, he hoped to festoon these ships with 'limpet' time bombs and then make a quick get-away. Unfortunately all did not go well. Rough weather and technical difficulties made the canoe unseaworthy and the raid had to be called off at the last minute. Stirling did, however, manage to have a quick look round at the harbour before leaving the town. He was determined to return to Benghazi.

News of these swashbuckling activities leaked out. Randolph had heard of them shortly after his return to Cairo. That he was immediately attracted to the S.A.S. is hardly surprising. This, after all, was the type of cloak-and-dagger warfare he had envisaged when he joined the commandos. He must also have been aware of the dangers involved. In the course of the raids, several men had been killed, some had been captured and others had disappeared without a trace. Clementine Churchill was right in thinking that Randolph's new venture would cause his father anxiety.

Like all new recruits, Randolph had to undergo a course of

training. It was not a pleasing prospect. As Freya Stark observed, the fleshpots of Egypt had completely undermined his earlier training and he was now shamefully overweight. But David Stirling was not one to make exceptions. Physical, as well as mental, fitness was essential in the S.A.S. and Randolph was accepted only on condition that he take the course.

He started with a practice parachute jump. Surprisingly, the thought of leaping from an aeroplane does not appear, at first, to have worried him. 'I have no imagination,' he later explained to a friend, 'so action doesn't bother me in advance.' All the same, once he was on the plane a more natural reaction set in. Strapped into his parachute and standing in line, he suddenly became afraid that he would freeze when the doors opened. He decided not to leave this to chance. Turning to the sergeant behind him, he produced a five pound note and told the man to give him a shove if he appeared to hesitate. For once Randolph was underrating himself. When the time came to jump, he jumped. He followed David Stirling and then passed him on the way down. 'Thank God the bloody thing opened,' he yelled when they were level. 'Yes,' Stirling shouted back, 'but look how fast you're travelling.' Until then Randolph had taken the speed of his descent for granted: now he became uneasy. He was indeed falling too fast. It may have been that the parachute was faulty, or, more likely, that his weight was too much for it but, whatever the cause, he hit the ground with a crash. Luckily no bones were broken and, after picking himself up, he was able to hobble back to the camp, badly bruised and severely shaken.

Randolph was never to forget this landing. In time he became more adept at handling a parachute, but his confidence was sadly impaired. The worst moments of any parachute jump, he would say, 'were just before you jumped and then about twenty feet from the ground, when it suddenly seemed to leap at you.' His misgivings were shared by others. Very few of the recruits enjoyed their parachute training, particularly after their first jump.

As things turned out, Randolph did not need a parachute on his first mission with the Special Air Service. Indeed, on this mission, there was really no need for Randolph himself. He was included in the party partly because he insisted on being included. This insistence came when he learned that David Stirling was planning another attempt on the harbour at Benghazi. Preparations for the raid were conducted in secret and only those involved knew of Stirling's intentions. However, Randolph had his own way of finding out such things and once he had latched on to the plan there was no shaking him off. He begged to be taken along. Stirling was not at all keen. The operation would, as he knew, be an extremely risky one and the men chosen for it had been selected for their skills and experience. As Randolph had not, at that stage, even begun his ground training, the only operational skill he had demonstrated was his parachute jump. It was hardly a recommendation.

Randolph had to use all his persuasive powers to get Stirling to relent. He insisted that he could get fit in three days and 'immediately started on a frantic series of setting-up exercises and early morning runs.' Finally Stirling agreed to a compromise. Randolph could join the party, but purely as an observer. He would have to stay behind with the Long Range Desert Group when the time came to enter Benghazi. Randolph had no option but to accept this arrangement.

The party left the training base on a mid-May morning in David Stirling's 'blitz-wagon'. This was a converted Ford Utility, painted dark grey to resemble a German staff car and fitted with special mountings for four machine-guns. Besides Randolph and Stirling there were five other S.A.S. men in the party: three N.C.Os – Corporals Seekings, Cooper and Rose – all seasoned raiders, and two officers. One of the officers was Lieutenant Gordon Alston, who had accompanied Stirling on the earlier Benghazi raid, and the other was Captain Fitzroy Maclean. Like Randolph, Maclean was a new recruit to the S.A.S. but, unlike Randolph, he had completed his training. His help in preparing for the raid had been invaluable. Determined not to repeat his earlier mistake, Stirling had entrusted Maclean with the task of finding and testing suitable boats for the harbour launch. This had proved something of a problem but Maclean had finally found the answer in two inflatable rubber boats which he obtained from the Royal Engineers. Each of these boats could accommodate two men and their equipment, they were black in colour, easily transportable, and seemed ideal for the raiders' purpose. Together with guns and explosives, they were stowed away in the car.

In another, less obvious, way Fitzroy Maclean's inclusion in the party was to prove invaluable. The graphic account he gives of this raid in his fascinating book, *Eastern Approaches*, is unique in the early annals of the S.A.S. Rarely has the cool courage, the audacity and quick-thinking, the nonchalance and wit of David Stirling's remarkable band of volunteers been more vividly captured than in Maclean's eye-witness account.

After calling in at Alexandria to study maps, photographs and a wooden model of Benghazi at the Naval Intelligence Office, the party drove along the coast road to Mersa Matruh and then branched off into the desert. Two days later they arrived at the Siwa oasis. Here they picked up their L.R.D.G. escort which was to

219

accompany them to the Jebel mountain range, some forty miles south-east of Benghazi. For the next couple of days they travelled across the heat-hazed sands, stripped to their shorts and wearing Arab head-dresses, stopping only for a hurried midday lunch of tinned fish and fruit. At night they made camp. A desert fire would be lit in a sand-filled tin sprinkled with petrol, supper would be served and then, huddled in their sleeping-bags, they would snatch what sleep they could. Once they were parallel with Gazala – where, in the north, the opposing armies faced each other – their routine changed. Entering enemy occupied territory they were forced to drive by night and sleep – buzzing flies and blazing sun permitting – during the day. It was an exhausting and, for the most part, uneventful journey.

They arrived at the hilly, scrub-covered Jebel area on 20 May. That evening they parked at the edge of an escarpment and looked across the coastal plain to the shimmering blue Mediterranean. In the distance they could make out the white walls of Benghazi. Their raid had been timed for the following night, when there would be no moon, and they now had twenty-four hours in which to prepare themselves. After camouflaging the trucks they settled down for the night. Intermittent flashes in the sky told them that the R.A.F. were carrying out a prearranged bombing raid on Benghazi. But, fanned by a moist coastal breeze, they slept well that night. Everything seemed to be going according to plan.

The first hitch came the following morning. As they busied themselves testing their equipment – inflating and deflating the rubber boats, checking their guns and priming the explosives – an accident happened. Corporal Seekings, one of the more experienced men, injured his hand with a detonator. He was not seriously hurt but it was obvious that he could not join the raiding party. Randolph immediately seized his opportunity. 'The crack of the detonator had hardly died away,' says Fitzroy Maclean, 'when Randolph appeared . . . Already he was oiling his tommy-gun and polishing his pistol in preparation for the night's work.' Stirling did not have the heart to disappoint him. Dismissing the extra N.C.O. who had been brought along as a possible replacement, he allowed Randolph to take Corporal Seeking's place.

They set off for Benghazi late that afternoon. Stirling, Maclean and Gordon Alston sat in the front seat of the 'blitz-wagon'; Randolph was seated in the back between Corporal Cooper and Corporal Rose. The L.R.D.G. patrol escorted them as far as the road and then turned back. It was by now dark. The fourteen mile drive to the road had taken them five hours; it had also severely jolted the car. Just how badly the car had fared became apparent once they reached the tarred road leading to Benghazi. Speeding along the smooth surface, they were suddenly deafened by a high-pitched screech. They stopped, drew off the road, examined the car's wheels and found they had been forced out of alignment. One of the corporals, lying on his back, did what he could to remedy the fault but his tinkering only made things worse. When they started off again the screech was louder than before. 'We could hardly have made more noise,' declares Maclean, 'if we had been in a fire engine with its bell clanging.' They had no alternative but to press on. Working to a tight schedule, they could not afford a further delay. Luckily the road was deserted and the noise did not affect the speed of the car.

Further shocks awaited them. As they approached Benghazi, they were startled to see a red light swinging in the middle of the road. Jamming on the brakes, Stirling brought the car to a halt. In front of them was a heavy wooden bar, from which a red lantern was suspended. An Italian sentry, armed with a tommy-gun, stepped out of the darkness and approached the car. He asked who they were. 'Staff officers,' replied Maclean, who spoke fluent Italian, 'in a hurry.' For a moment the man looked puzzled. Then, just as the tension was becoming unbearable, his manner changed. Giving a limp salute, he advised them to have their headlights dimmed, raised the barrier and waved them on.

But their troubles were by no means over. When they reached the outskirts of Benghazi, they realized that they were being followed. A car that they had passed earlier had turned around and was keeping pace behind them.* Once he was sure of this Stirling took the only action open to him. Pressing down on the accelerator, he drove into the city at top speed – with the car screeching louder than ever. At the first corner, he turned into a side street, stopped, switched off the headlights and waited. Seconds later the other car flashed past and disappeared into the darkness.

They were still recovering from the chase when another alarm sounded. Suddenly rockets began to explode in the sky and the air was split by the wailing of sirens. Had they not arranged for the R.A.F. to keep clear that night, they might have thought another air raid had started. As it was they thought it more likely that their arrival in Benghazi had been detected and a search was about to begin. They had to act quickly. The first thing they had to abandon was the noisy 'blitz-wagon'. Stirling decided not merely to abandon it but to blow it up. A detonator fitted with a thirty minute fuse was placed among the explosives at the back of the car and then, in single

* It is said that Randolph had deliberately provoked pursuit by taking pot-shots at the car. This would explain an otherwise puzzling car chase.

file, the six men started off into the night.

They did not go far. The Arab quarter, in which they found themselves, was a maze of narrow streets and bombed buildings; many of the houses were deserted, some were in ruins or had gaping holes in their walls. Filing through a breach in one wall, the party ran into an Italian carabiniere. Maclean decided to be bold. He promptly tackled the man about the sirens and rockets. What, he asked, was all the noise about? 'Oh just another of those damned English air-raids,' replied the Italian gloomily. When Maclean suggested it might mean a raid by English ground forces, the man thought he was joking. There was no need to be worried about that, he laughed, now that the British had been pushed back to the Egyptian frontier. Highly relieved, Maclean wished the man goodnight and the party walked on.

The encounter caused Stirling to change his mind about the situation. He now saw no reason why they should not go ahead with their original plan. They would raid the harbour and, if possible, rescue the 'blitz-wagon'. Hurrying back to the car, they found they had five minutes in which to remove the detonator. Nervously they defused the explosive and threw the detonator over the nearest wall. A few minutes later, it went off with a loud crack. The party then prepared for action.

The harbour was about a mile away, but they decided it would be unwise to approach it in the screeching car. So Stirling announced that he would lead the raid on foot. He chose Maclean, Alston and Cooper to accompany him and instructed Randolph to remain behind with Corporal Rose. Their job, he said, would be to hide the car. A kitbag was filled with explosives and, carrying this and one of the rubber boats the raiding party set off for the harbour.

Randolph could not have been happy with his role. Having wangled his way into Benghazi, the least he could have expected was to be present when the action started. Instead he found himself, a mile away, looking for a makeshift garage. But if his task was tame, it was not without its problems. There were no obvious hiding places in the street. Eventually he decided to back the car into a hole in the wall of a bombed-out building. Even this was easier said than done. Randolph and Corporal Rose were still entertaining Arab passers-by with their efforts to manoeuvre the vehicle into the hole when Fitzroy Maclean and Corporal Cooper returned.

Maclean had a sorry tale to tell. The raiding party had met with difficulties. First, on reaching the wire fence surrounding the harbour, they had been stopped by a sentry. Maclean had managed to bluff the man into allowing them to pass and, once out of sight, they had slipped through a hole in the fence. Dodging between the cranes and railway trucks, they arrived at the water-front. Then they split up. Stirling and Alston left Maclean and Cooper to inflate the rubber boat while they made a quick tour of the docks. Crouching beneath a low sea wall, Maclean set to work. He produced a pair of bellows and began to pump. Nothing happened. The bellows wheezed alarmingly but the boat stayed flat. Suddenly, a sentry on one of the boats in the harbour called out and asked what was going on. Maclean told him to mind his own business and went on pumping. Still nothing happened. The boat was obviously punctured. Cursing his luck, Maclean had had no option but to return to the car for the second boat.

Having collected the boat, Maclean went back to the harbour with Corporal Cooper. Randolph and Corporal Rose busied themselves with the car. Finally they succeeded in easing it into the building. Then there was another, much longer, wait. This time all four of the raiders staggered back together. They arrived shortly before dawn to report that the raid had failed. Another run of bad luck – the second boat was also punctured – had forced them to admit defeat.

Throughout the following day, the raiders remained hidden in the house where Randolph had concealed the car. They had some tins of bully beef with them as well as a bottle of rum. After they had eaten, five of them dozed while one kept guard. They were in an upstairs room and only once were they disturbed. This happened during Randolph's watch, late in the afternoon. Footsteps were heard on the stairs and everyone sprang to life. Randolph was the first through the door, the first to catch a glimpse of an Italian sailor approaching the room. The panic was short lived. One glance at Randolph standing majestically on the landing – his six-day beard bristling, his tommy-gun at the ready – was sufficient to send the sailor scurrying from the building.

That evening Stirling began to get restless. As soon as it got dark, he suggested they go for a stroll through the town. He was already thinking of a return to Benghazi and wanted to get his bearings. Convinced by now that boldness was the best disguise, the six men made no attempt to hide their presence. They walked down the main street, arm in arm, whistling and laughing, until they reached the harbour. Here they spotted two motor torpedo boats tied up at the quayside. The idea of blowing them up before they left the town was too tempting to be ignored. They hurried back to their hide-out, hauled the car through the hole in the wall and drove back to the harbour. But they were too late. In their absence a sentry had been posted and he looked far too vigilant for them to take any risks. Reluctantly, they decided the time had come for them to leave

Benghazi.

Turning the car round, Stirling drove out of the town. On the outskirts they got caught up in an enemy convoy of trucks and at the road block Maclean again had to bluff in Italian to get them through, but by now this sort of hazard had become routine. Their main concern was to reach the Jebel before daybreak. They arrived, in fact, at six o'clock the following morning and found the Long Range Desert Group waiting for them. Twenty-four hours late, they had at least arrived in time for breakfast. 'Hungrily,' says Fitzroy Maclean, 'we threw ourselves upon mugs of tea and steaming mess tins of porridge.'

CHAPTER TWELVE

An Unhappy Leave

After the excitement of Benghazi, the journey back to the Siwa oasis was relatively uneventful. It was not until they had left Siwa and were on their way back to Cairo that the party met serious trouble. It came, not from the enemy, but from an accidental brush with British army vehicles.

On 27 May, five days after leaving Benghazi, the 'blitz-wagon' fell in behind a convoy of lorries some forty miles outside Alexandria. Speeding to overtake the convoy, Stirling collided with the last lorry and the car went spinning off the road and landed upside-down in a ditch. The accident was serious and, for one of the passengers, fatal. At Siwa, Stirling had given a lift to the elderly and distinguished war-correspondent of the *Daily Telegraph*, Arthur Merton, who, on being dragged from the wreckage, was discovered to be unconscious and bleeding badly. He was rushed to the military hospital at Alexandria where he died a few hours later. Fitzroy Maclean was also knocked out by the crash and did not regain consciousness until three or four days later. He was to remain in hospital for over a month with a fractured collar bone, a broken arm and head injuries. The other occupants of the car were only slightly more fortunate: Corporal Rose fractured his arm and David Stirling – although quickly released from hospital – later discovered that he had cracked a bone in his wrist. Randolph's injuries appeared, at first, to be minimal. On arrival at the hospital he cabled his family to say that he had been 'severely bruised' and expected to be laid-up for 'about ten days.' But he was wrong. He had in fact dislocated a vertebra and, like Fitzroy Maclean, was detained in hospital for almost a month.

Throughout his convalescence, Randolph displayed remarkable stoicism. Encased in plaster and subjected to excruciating pain, he seldom spoke about his injury and surprised even his most jaundiced critics with his unquenchable optimism. His attitude was not only brave but, at that stage of the desert war, extremely rare. The news from the front could not have been more depressing. On 26 May – the day before Randolph's accident – Rommel had launched a new offensive and by the beginning of June his troops had broken through the strongly defended Gazala line. Then, reinforced from Germany, he had pushed along the coast, recaptured Tobruk, and before the month was out the German army had reached El Alamein – a mere fifty odd miles west of Alexandria. The long-feared offensive against Egypt seemed imminent. Randolph, however, refused to give in to despair. Out of touch with events, relying mostly on gossip and often wildly misinformed, he remained as confident as ever that the tide would eventually turn.

On his discharge from hospital, he returned to Cairo to continue his convalescence. One of his first visitors was his friend Cecil Beaton. Randolph had long been an admirer of Beaton and was, in fact, partly responsible for the photographer being in Egypt. Earlier that year, while on leave in England, he had been instrumental in persuading Brendan Bracken – now Minister of Information – to authorize Beaton's visit to the Middle East as an official war-photographer. Beaton had arrived in Cairo in March and was staying at Shepheard's Hotel. He called on Randolph intending to cheer him up; to his surprise he found their roles reversed.

'I had dinner off a tray by his bed,' Beaton noted in his diary, after his visit. 'He was at his most enthusiastic for four hours on end, shouting with relish, "The situation's splendid!" He'd like to see the Germans come within fifty miles of Cairo, then, with their long transport lines, be cut off. He said he was glad I was going home soon so that I could tell "them" what had happened at Tobruk; but when I asked him what did happen at Tobruk he was unable to answer. Randolph's stout heart makes me feel ashamed of my anxieties. Just to hear such exuberance is encouraging'.

But Randolph did not have to rely on Cecil Beaton to carry his glad tidings to England. His injury was considered sufficiently serious for him to be invalided home himself. He left Cairo in the middle of July and flew to London by way of America. In New York he received a hero's welcome. Newspaper men flocked to interview him and at a special press conference, on 22 July, he was peppered with questions about the Middle East situation. His optimism was undimmed. Dressed in an open-necked sports shirt, cigarette in hand, he positively bubbled with enthusiasm.

The English, he explained, were amateurs when it came to warfare. Germany's professional soldiers had been preparing for the present conflict for fifteen years. 'We were caught unawares,' he went on, 'and lost a great deal of equipment at Dunkirk. However, I can't see any reason for discouragement. Taking a long-range view, we must expect things to go wrong – but it is in the bag . . . If we're lucky we might win the war by next year and if we're unlucky it will last until the year after.' He had reached this conclusion, he said, while convalescing in hospital and saw no reason to change his mind.

Before leaving America, two days later, Randolph was flown in an army bomber to Detroit where he conferred with Henry Ford and inspected various war plants in the area. He was greatly impressed by what he saw and heard. 'I don't believe,' he told reporters, 'the British are cognizant of the tremendous work Americans are doing in the production field.' Then, smiling, he added: 'I don't see how the Americans can be cognizant of it either.' This regrettable ignorance was something Randolph was determined to rectify. The stirling efforts of the American war-workers added substance to the message of hope he was taking to Britain.

✳   ✳   ✳

'Randolph returned in a straight waistcoat,' Evelyn Waugh noted in his diary at the beginning of August, 'full of exuberant confidence in American production.'

Waugh himself had returned to England several months earlier, after taking part in the unsuccessful commando operation in Crete, and he had seen little or nothing of Randolph until they met at a London party. For once they had both been in high spirits and Randolph's stories of the S.A.S. and the cheeky assault on Benghazi had delighted Waugh. David Stirling's 'prodigies of courage', he observed, 'become more legendary every day.' Other than that, Waugh had not been particularly impressed by Randolph's bombast. When he came to write up his diary, he devoted more space to what had not been said at the party than to Randolph's 'exuberant confidence.' Like many others at this time, Waugh was fully aware of the despair that lay behind this exuberant facade. For despair there was. However confident Randolph might have appeared about the outcome of the war, he could not disguise his misgivings about his own future. His private life was a mess. Not only was his marriage breaking up but his stormy relationship with his wife had become public knowledge. While he tried to fool his friends by assuming indifference, the more disastrous the situation was becoming.

'It is a bitter thing,' wrote Waugh, 'for Pamela to have him speaking of three months' leave of absence to devote himself to politics. She hates him so much she can't bear to be in a room with him.'

The sizeable cracks in Randolph's marriage had become apparent during his leave in England earlier that year. Looking back on this period many years later, Pamela Churchill was to blame their long

227

enforced separation for the predicament in which they found themselves. 'When he came back from the mid-East,' she explained, 'we both realized we'd made a mistake . . . it was difficult being married and not being married. If we'd been together it might have worked. But it didn't have a chance.' There is some truth in this, but it is not the whole story. The separation helped to drive them apart but there were other factors involved in the break up of their marriage. It seems fairly obvious that, together or apart, they were bound to run into serious trouble sooner or later.

For one thing, Randolph was temperamentally ill-equipped to sustain a lasting union. He was far too self-centred, far too domineering and far too insensitive to accommodate the demands of another person in his life. Intolerant and unimaginative, he could not hope to negotiate the pit-falls of marriage. Like his father, Randolph had no real insight into people; he chose his friends instinctively and had little appreciation of the complexities of human nature. His approach to companionship, whatever its nature, was hopelessly immature. Addicted as he was to romantic clichés, he tended to mistake the tinsel for the truth of a relationship; for him, love was a sentimental attachment rather than a deeply felt emotion. Whatever his reasons for rushing into marriage, he undoubtedly thought he was in love at the time – at least he would have persuaded himself that he was – but it was an adolescent's love, more possessive than sharing. He prized his wife, not as an equal partner but as a reflection of his own personality.

This had become clear during that earlier leave. Within weeks of Randolph's arriving home in January, Pamela had complained to a friend that he treated her 'like a pasha.' 'I want you,' he told her, 'to be with my son.' And when Pamela, not unreasonably, pointed out that the child was also *her* son, he exploded. 'No,' he snapped, 'my son. I'm a Churchill.'

'I think he needed,' Pamela was to say, 'someone like his own mother, who lived entirely for her husband.' Given Randolph's strained relationship with his mother this was not, perhaps, the happiest of suggestions. A strong-minded woman like Clementine Churchill would have clashed with Randolph at every turn and Randolph, lacking his father's respect for fidelity, would quickly have sought comfort elsewhere. On the other hand, a wife who was prepared to devote herself to furthering his career might well have avoided the dilemma which Pamela now faced.

That dilemma appears to have been rooted in the changes that had taken place in Pamela's life over the past couple of years. Pamela, as she herself admits, was somewhat naive and inexperienced when she married Randolph. The war, and the Churchill family, changed all that. Her worldly education started a few months after her marriage. Even before her baby was born Pamela was persuaded by her parents-in-law to move to 10 Downing Street. For the next two years the Prime Minister's house was her London home. When Randolph was posted to the Middle East, she left their Hertfordshire house – it was later converted into a residential nursery under the Ministry of Health's evacuation scheme – and spent more and more time in London. Inevitably, she was plunged into the world of big events, important decisions and influential people. Her own family had always been politically involved but, for the most part, their involvement had been that of landed gentry. Living at the centre of things was a new and heady experience for Pamela. She was young, she was pretty and she was greatly admired. Few visitors to Downing Street left without commenting on the charms of the Prime Minister's daughter-in-law. The 'auburn alluring Pam Churchill,' Chips Channon called her.

Flattered, privileged and much sought after, Pamela began to assert her independence. She took a job with the Ministry of Supply until, as she puts it, 'Brendan Bracken had this wonderful idea.' Bracken's wonderful idea was that Pamela should run a club in London where American army officers could meet British professional men and discuss mutual interests. Called the 'Churchill Club', it was intended to fulfil a sadly neglected need. Nothing could have pleased Pamela more. She had her own reasons for wanting to work with and for Americans. Among her new admirers was President Roosevelt's special envoy, Averell Harriman – 'he was mightily smitten by Randolph Churchill's glamorous wife,' recalls Lord Drogheda – and friendship with the Harriman family had made Pamela enthusiastic for all things American. So pro-American was she, in fact, that her English friends were already accusing her of affecting the American accent that she was later to perfect.

How far plans for the Churchill Club had advanced by the time Randolph returned from Cairo at the beginning of 1942 is not clear. What is more certain is that he greatly resented Pamela's independence. Outraged, probably suspicious, he lost no time in making his views known to his wife and family. The scenes he created greatly distressed his mother. As always, Clementine Churchill's chief concern was for her husband. With the war at a critical stage, she had no wish for Churchill to be burdened with their son's marital troubles. But there was little she or anyone else could do about it. By the time Randolph returned from Egypt, things – as James Lees-Milne noted in his diary on 18 March – had passed the point of reconciliation. 'Met Clarissa Churchill [Randolph's cousin] ... ' wrote Lees-Milne. 'She told me that

229

Randolph's wife had no intention of sticking to him; and that Mr Churchill would be very sad if their marriage broke up.'

The quarrelling continued for the next couple of months. Throughout Randolph's brief training for the S.A.S. and, it seems, throughout his convalescence, husband and wife had bombarded each other with angry, unforgiving letters. Inevitably, Clementine Churchill was caught in the crossfire. 'She did her best,' says her daughter Mary, 'but any intervention in such situations nearly always results in bitter reproaches being levelled, and this case was no exception to the rule.' Later Randolph was to apologize to his mother for the trouble he had caused her but by then it was too late. There can be little doubt that, coupled with the anxiety she felt about his joining the S.A.S., this period of marital tension destroyed what little faith Clementine Churchill had in her son's sense of loyalty. It was to lead to the undisguised hostility which characterized Randolph's relationship with his mother.

'One of his troubles,' Sir Osbert Lancaster was to say of Randolph, 'was that his mother hated him, absolutely loathed his guts.' This might well be an exaggeration, spread by Randolph himself, but it was an exaggeration which his friends found all to easy to accept.

Clementine Churchill's worst fears were realized when Randolph arrived home in August 1942. Then it was that all hopes of a reconciliation between her son and daughter-in-law were finally shattered. Scarcely had Randolph stepped off the plane from New York than the fighting began. This time no attempt was made to disguise the situation: he and Pamela quarrelled openly in front of their friends. Evelyn Waugh was one of the first to recognize the hopelessness of the situation. He and Cecil Beaton and another friend called on Randolph, shortly after his return and walked straight into a full-scale family row.

'It was very interesting,' Waugh told his wife the following day. 'At first Lord Digby [Pamela's father] was there & he and Panto [Pamela] went into the bedroom for a long conference. Was he attempting to adjust a difference between the young couple, I asked myself. Randolph was exuberant & vociferous. Panto hates him so much that she can't sit in a room with him but paced up & down the minute hall outside the the door after her father had gone. When we . . . obliged her to come in she could not look at him & simply said over her shoulder in acid tones "Ought you not to be resting?" whenever he became particularly jolly. She was looking very pretty & full of mischief.'

Pamela was not the only one who was full of mischief. Several of Randolph's fair-weather friends were enjoying themselves enormously. Nothing delighted them more than the news that young Mrs Churchill now found her husband physically repulsive. 'Pamela,' noted that incorrigible gossip, Robert Bruce Lockhart, 'can no longer bear the sight of Randolph who . . . repelled her with his spotted face and gross figure . . . Winston loves Randolph; Mrs Churchill is not so proud of him.'

The only person who tried to console Randolph was, of course, his old flame, Laura. Hurt, rejected and not a little humiliated, Randolph turned inevitably to the one woman he felt he could trust. Laura's long-drawn out divorce proceedings were on the point of being finalized and this gave Randolph hope. It was, admittedly, a vague hope. Nothing had happened to make him assume that Laura would change her mind about marrying him. His own life had become more complicated and Laura, as she told him, was still very much in love with Lord Dudley. But Randolph was in no mood for realism. For the time being he was ready to interpret sympathy as a promise for the future. Who could tell what might happen? Later he was to say that it was only with Laura's understanding and advice that he had managed to survive this difficult period in his life.

There was, as he well knew, nothing he could do to save his marriage. He and Pamela met only to quarrel. Occasionally, very occasionally, they went to parties together but, for the most part, Randolph's leave was spent either with Laura or with his drinking cronies. Finally he could stand the pretence no longer. According to Pamela, their life together came to an end when Randolph announced that he was 'fed up' and walked out on her. Shortly afterwards she moved to a flat in Grosvenor Square to be near the American Embassy and her own friends. Her husband, she said, 'seemed to prefer a bachelor's existence.'

* * *

'Randolph Forsees a New Party,' announced a headline in the *Daily Mail* on 3 September 1942.

'Mr Randolph Churchill,' the report went on, 'speaking at Preston last night, forshadowed the rise of a Centre Party in Britain after the war.

'During the period of the two-party system – first Whig and Tory, later Liberal and Conservative – the country, he said, on the whole was well and wisely governed. But the rise of the Labour Party resulted in the Liberal Party being devoured by Labour and Tories.

'The fact that the Labour Party avowedly claimed the support of only a single class, the wage earners, progressively induced the Conservative Party, greatly to their own and the national disadvantage, to become more and more identified with the interests of the propertied classes. Mr Churchill declared: "Many evils thus came upon our country."

'Though the Conservative Party still retained many of its traditions and principles, those who controlled and dominated the party increasingly tended in pre-war years to serve the interest of the purse-proud, acquisitive and selfish minority who, for the most part, were more alarmed at the spread of Socialism than by the rise of Hitlerism. As a result they allowed themselves to be seduced from the national and Imperial traditions which had so long been their watchword.

'If, after the war, he went on, neither Labour nor Conservative should be found worthy of their responsibilities, a party of the centre based around all the best political elements of the Labour, Tory and Liberal parties would, no doubt, arise. It would attract all those progressive men of sanity and good will who believe that the country must come before any class.

'Mr Churchill ended: "I earnestly hope that the Conservative Party will regain its soul and show itself worthy, as in time gone by, to serve the true interests of the British people and the British Empire.'

Most of the other popular newspapers carried similar reports. Few, if any, commented editorially. In war time Randolph's outbursts were not taken seriously enough to warrant considered political attention and the surprise caused by this Preston speech was confined to his friends and constituents. All the same, his seemingly outspoken attack on the Conservative Party was to produce some unexpected repercussions.

Among other things the speech gave rise to a legend. Years later, those wishing to defend Randolph from his right-wing bias, would proudly point to his advocacy of a centre party which 'in the spirit of his grandfather Lord Randolph Churchill's Tory Democrats, might replace the Labour or Tory Party.' It is an interesting thesis but, as a study of contemporary reports of his speech show, not entirely accurate. The sentiments expressed by Randolph do indeed reflect the Tory Democracy of his grandfather, but at no stage did he propose the formation of a centre party. All he was doing was warning his fellow Tories of the danger they faced in ignoring the demands of a wider electorate. He was not the first, nor the last, Conservative politician to do this and, as so often happens, his social conscience was conditioned by political considerations. His aim was to gain votes rather than to ensure social justice. He had used similar tactics during his election campaigns in the mid-30s but, although he made the right noises, he was conveniently vague about the methods he would employ to correct the injustices he claimed to deplore. When set against his strongly felt Imperial ambitions, his arguments in favour of genuine democracy are suspect.

Those closer to Randolph's political thinking gave a slightly different interpretation of his 'democratic' outbursts. 'Politically,' it was said of him later, 'Randolph Churchill is a Tory, because he believes that the Tories are more intelligent, mature, efficient and gentlemanly than the Socialists . . . By the Tories, he means top Tories. He passionately believes that it is the duty of the undeserving rich to support the deserving poor – of whom he will often elect himself the articulate representative. The central tenet of his political philosophy is that the class with power should be kept in power, but only so long as it proves itself morally superior to any alternative.' Randolph, in other words, was a paternalist rather than a true democrat.

A more intriguing question mark hangs over his reasons for making this Preston speech when he did. Several answers suggest themselves. It could, for instance, have resulted from his unhappy state of mind. The break-up of his marriage and the opposition within his own family might have made him want to hit back. A display of political defiance would have released his emotions at this time. He was undoubtedly nursing a feeling of political neglect. Shortly after his election as an MP he had told his friends that he expected to obtain a ministerial appointment. Churchill's weakness for nepotism was, after all, well known. (A popular joke at the time of Duncan Sandys' appointment as Financial Secretary at the War Office was that Vic Oliver had opened his act at a variety theatre by saying: 'Sorry I'm late, I've been expecting a call from Downing Street.') But, so far, nothing had come Randolph's way. He may well have thought that, by attacking his father's party, he would draw attention to his need to be pacified. There is a possibility, also, that Randolph's contacts with the soldiers in the desert had alerted him to the growing resentment against the old governing class in England. This, as the post-war elections were to show, was a political consideration which could no longer be ignored: Randolph might have sensed it earlier than most. On the other hand, it could simply be that he was up to his old tricks. He could never resist taking a swipe at the more complacent members of his own party.

Whatever his reasons, his speech was given a mixed reception. One of the first to react to it was his fellow MP for Preston, Captain E. C. Cobb. Having protested to no avail when Randolph was nominated for the Preston seat, Cobb now felt that his objections had been justified by Randolph's attack on the Conservative Party. As it happened, he was booked to address a Conservative Women's

Association meeting a week after Randolph delivered his attack and he used this occasion to air his views. Not only did he strongly object to Randolph's denunciation of the Tories – 'he had never imagined,' he said, 'he would have to defend the record of the party from his own colleague' – but he revealed that he had protested to the Selection Committee when Randolph was nominated. He then went on to make it clear that he had no intention of running in harness with a disloyal Tory at the next election.

Captain Cobb's attack took Randolph by surprise. Until then he had been oblivious of his colleague's resentment and considered it a personal insult to have been rounded upon in public. 'The gravamen of my complaint against yourself,' he was to tell Cobb, 'is that you should have made such an attack upon me without giving me prior notice.' However, having recovered from his surprise he was quick to rise to the challenge. After consulting the chairman of the Preston Conservative Association, Sir Norman Seddon Brown, Randolph requested that a meeting of the General Council be called so that he could state his case. Captain Cobb was not invited to attend.

The meeting, held on the 16 October, lasted two and a half hours. Two resolutions were debated. The first, a motion of confidence in Randolph, was passed by 44 votes to eight. The second proved more controversial. It requested that 'in view of his statement that he does not wish to stand at the next General Election,' Captain Cobb should be asked to vacate his seat so that a new candidate could be selected. This time the voting was 32 for the motion and 11 against. Those in favour were probably encouraged by the chairman who later pointed out that, long before Randolph appeared on the scene, Captain Cobb had agreed to resign his seat because he lived too far from the constituency 'to give it the attention it deserves.' All the same, the meeting caused a good deal of ill-feeling. During the debate on the second motion one angry Conservative, Thomas Flintoff, reminded Randolph that Captain Cobb had actually won an election 'whereas he had not faced the electors.' So strongly did Flintoff feel on this point that he rallied some of the members of the executive and demanded another meeting of the General Council. By the time this meeting was held, on 3 November, Randolph was again in Africa. But Captain Cobb was present and was able to persuade the General Council to rescind the resolution asking for his resignation. Randolph was furious.

'If Preston,' he wrote in an open letter to Cobb from Africa, 'were wise enough to choose a man who, unlike yourself, bears no responsibility for the vacillating unworthy foreign policy and the disgraceful lack of armaments which brought this war upon us, he might well be a help instead of an electoral liability.'

234

The rumpus at Preston attracted far more press attention than Randolph's original speech. Here was something that everyone could understand. Once again the younger Churchill was on the rampage. If he had not succeeded in splitting his constituency down the middle, he had certainly frayed the edges of the local Tory party. The prospect of some internecine warfare at the next election looked promising.

*   *   *

While Randolph had been on leave in England, important decisions had been reached concerning North Africa. Within days of his arrival in London, his father had flown to Moscow to confer with Josef Stalin. On his way to Russia, Churchill had stopped at Cairo where he held talks with General Auchinleck and other military advisers. He had also visited the front at Alamein and inspected several large army camps outside Cairo. As a result of this first-hand investigation, Churchill had decided to make radical changes in the Middle East command. General Auchinleck was dismissed and General Alexander appointed Commander-in-Chief in his place. Churchill also proposed to place Lieutenant-General Gott – a popular Eighth Army Commander – in charge of the army, but his proposal was defeated by events. Two days after Churchill decided to make the appointment, Gott's plane – flying to Cairo – was shot down by the Germans and Gott was killed. His place was taken by General Bernard Montgomery who immediately flew out from England to assume the post of Commander of the Eighth Army.

These decisions taken, Churchill continued on his journey to Russia. His talks with Stalin began on the evening of his arrival in Moscow. Among the issues they discussed was a recent change in Allied strategy. After consultation with the Americans, Churchill told the Russian leader, it had been decided to postpone the launching of a Second Front in Europe and to concentrate instead on the north African campaign. The plan – which President Roosevelt claimed as his brain-child – was to make a two-fronted assault on Rommel's army. At the end of October, the Eighth Army was to launch an offensive at Alamein and a few days later Allied troops were to land in French North Africa and attack the German force from the rear. The Allied landings had been codenamed *Torch* and would be under the command of General Dwight D. Eisenhower, who had already arrived in London to plan the operation. It took Churchill three days to win Stalin's acceptance of this change of course – the Russians were strongly in favour of a Second Front in Europe – but by the time he left Moscow he was fairly confident that he had succeeded. He arrived back in England, after spending a few

235

more days in Cairo, on 24 August. His wife and Randolph were at the Lyneham air-base in Wiltshire to welcome him home.

With Churchill's return the detailed planning of *Torch* went ahead. Nominally the Americans were in charge of the operation, but not all their plans met with Churchill's approval. He was particularly put out by their proposal to confine the landings to Casablanca and Oran. In his opinion the further east the Allies could gain a foothold on the African coast the better chance they would stand of controlling future events. For this reason he insisted that an attempt should be made to seize Algiers and the ports of Bône and Philippeville. Eventually he got his way. It was agreed that *Torch* become a three-pronged assault, with the Americans landing at Casablanca and Oran while a joint British and American force attacked Algiers. The British First Army was already in Scotland training for the campaign.

Every precaution was taken to keep the planning of *Torch* a secret. Leaks there inevitably were, but few people – other than those directly involved in the operation – were officially informed about the impending invasion of French North Africa. One of those to be unofficially informed was Randolph. He not only knew about *Torch* but, in the midst of his marital and political upheavals, was planning to return to Africa with the invading force. The promise of new excitements was, as he later admitted, too good to be missed. All the same, he kept his plans to himself. Even to his closest friends, he insisted that he intended returning to the Middle East as soon as he was fit enough to do so.

This is what he told Laura when, in the middle of October, he met her to say goodbye. Laura by that time had left London and was living at Himley Hall – Lord Dudley's family estate in the Midlands – and training as a nurse at a hospital in Birmingham. The fact that she was carefully chaperoned could hardly have disguised her intention – once her divorce was finalized – of making Himley Hall her home. She made no pretence about this to Randolph, although she did assure him that she still had not finally committed herself to Lord Dudley. This, apparently, was enough for Randolph. His only regret seems to have been that he was no longer in a position to propose marriage. He parted from her with a lover's sigh. She gave him a writing case; he gave her a cigarette case (which she discovered later to be too small for her brand of cigarettes). A few days later he wrote her a farewell letter from Glasgow in which he begged her not to take an irrevocable step without first consulting him. He still insisted that he was sailing to the Middle East.

Not until he had been at sea for three days did he confess to Laura that he had deceived her. In a 'diary' letter which he then started, he admitted that he was embarked on a more adventurous enterprise. He felt it safe to say this as, by the time his letter reached England, he was sure that his destination would have become apparent from reports in the newspapers. (In fact, *The Times* merely announced that he had 'returned to his unit'.) Writing to Laura was one of the few distractions Randolph enjoyed during this slow, if unnerving, voyage. The mood aboard the ship was very different from that on board the s.s. *Glenroy* a year or so earlier. Everyone was just as bored but there were fewer wild spirits, no chemin-de-fer and roulette, and the only gambling was a modest evening game of bridge for modest stakes. Randolph shared a cabin with an amiable R.A.F. Squadron Leader and spent most of the day lying on his bunk, to avoid sea sickness, reading Shakespeare and Damon Runyon.

Some 650 ships were engaged in the operation and Randolph was greatly impressed by the effectiveness of the convoy. Tension mounted as they approached Gibraltar. Here General Eisenhower had established his headquarters and, with so many ships and aircraft converging on the Rock, it was feared that Spain might feel threatened by the possibility of invasion. A number of Axis agents in the vicinity of Gibraltar were known to be active during the period leading up to the North African landings. Fortunately all attempts at intervention failed. The convoy arrived safely and the landings went ahead as planned.

Randolph's ship anchored off Algiers on 8 November and, after scribbling a hurried note to Laura, he went ashore that afternoon. Algiers was seized with relative ease. Unlike Oran, where there was some fierce fighting, the Vichy French in Algiers put up little resistance. By the end of the first day the Allies were more or less in possession of the town. Two days later, Admiral Darlan – the Vichy Second-in-Command, who was visiting Algiers when the landings took place – ordered all Frenchmen in North Africa to lay down their arms.

The success of *Torch* followed soon after the Eighth Army's breakthrough at Alamein. News of these victories was greeted in England by the ringing of long-silent church bells. When the cease-fire was ordered in North Africa, Churchill spoke at a luncheon in the Mansion House. 'The bright gleam has caught the helmets of our soldiers,' he declared, 'and warmed and cheered all our hearts.' It might not, he went on, be the 'beginning of the end, but it is, perhaps, the end of the beginning.'

*   *   *

After the North African landings, Allied troops advanced eastwards along the mountainous coastal region. They met with little opposition until they entered Tunisia. Here they came up against a strong German force – hastily rushed by air, sea and land to defend North Africa – and were brought to a dispiriting halt. Matters were made worse when the rains set in and the roads and airfields became unusable. By that time the British and American troops were within twelve miles of Tunis, but they had no hope of advancing further before the end of the brief winter.

During this period Randolph was attached to a Tank Regiment – the North Irish Horse – and his time was divided between the war front and Algiers. He appears to have had little time to write letters and when he did write he was deliberately vague about his movements. Not until the middle of January did he surface long enough to be plainly seen and heard. Then it was that he took a short break to be reunited with his father.

They met in the Moroccan city of Casablanca. Churchill had flown to North Africa to discuss future strategy with President Roosevelt – Stalin had also been invited but had cried off – and, as always, the Prime Minister's departure from England had been kept secret. Randolph was at the airport to welcome him. 'Well,' exclaimed Churchill when they met on the tarmac, 'this is a surprise for you, Randolph.' 'Not at all,' quipped Randolph, 'a woman in Algiers told me a week ago.'

The Churchill-Roosevelt conference was held not in Casablanca but at Anfa, a holiday resort to the south of the city. The Churchill party was housed in the Villa Mirador and the President occupied a film star's nearby villa. During the next ten days there were constant comings and goings between the two headquarters. Harold Macmillan, who had joined the Prime Minister's entourage, was to describe this high-level meeting as 'a mixture between a cruise, a summer school, and a conference' with Field Marshals and Admirals sneaking off at the end of the day 'to play with the pebbles and make sand castles' on the beach. Churchill was in a merry mood. According to Macmillan, he 'ate and drank enormously all the time, settled huge problems, played bagatelle and bezique by the hour, and generally enjoyed himself'. His son was no less merry. Never happier than when caught up in a combination of high politics and high living, Randolph was to claim that he felt very close to his father during this African interlude.

Important decisions were reached at the Conference. The talks were detailed and wide ranging. Not the least exciting outcome of the meeting, for Randolph – who was handling the Conference publicity – was the decision to launch an early assault on Sicily. Here again was the promise of an adventurous campaign in which

238

Randolph could play a part. His commando training had not, it seemed, been entirely a waste of time.

The Conference over, President Roosevelt prepared to return home. He had arranged to fly from Marrakesh, some 150 miles south of Casablanca, and Churchill decided to accompany him to the airfield. The desert crossing was accomplished in a fleet of cars with Randolph, at one stage, joining the President to read him 'an extract from Machiavelli which he thought appropriate.' Roosevelt's reaction to this seemingly strange choice of literary enlightenment is, unfortunately, not recorded. Nor, for that matter, is his reaction to Randolph who, six years earlier, had strongly disapproved of his re-election. Nothing, however, was allowed to dampen the collective high spirits. At a farewell dinner for the President in Marrakesh that evening, the toasts and speeches were followed by a sing-song which continued late into the night. Next morning Churchill got up so late that he was still wearing his slippers and a brightly embroidered dressing gown when he saw Roosevelt off at the airport.

Two days later, Randolph and his father flew on to Cairo. Churchill had decided to extend his tour in order to visit Turkey where he was hoping to persuade President Inönü to abandon his neutrality. Randolph's leave was, apparently, open-ended. They arrived in the Egyptian capital on 26 January and were welcomed at the British Embassy by Sir Miles Lampson. Churchill, now in his sixty-ninth year, showed no signs of strain after the lengthy conference and days of travelling. At dinner that evening he kept everyone entertained with his streams of jokes. 'Randolph,' observed Lampson, 'who has quite recovered from his accident, also seems in good fettle . . . On going up to bed I discovered that Winston was now going to play bezique for a quarter of an hour with Randolph before going to sleep.'

Not everyone was so impressed with Randolph's filial devotion. Some members of Churchill's party regarded him as an uninvited nuisance, an intruder who demanded too much of his father's time. Even Churchill found him too assertive at times. Sir Alexander Cadogan, Churchill's Foreign Office adviser, was witness to one embarrassing brush between father and son. The occasion was a dinner in Cairo. 'Sat between Winston and Randolph,' Cadogan noted in his diary on 2 February. 'The latter a dreadful young man. He has been an incubus on our party ever since Casablanca . . . Very silly of Winston to take him about. Father and son snapped at each other across me which was disconcerting.' The scene is not difficult to imagine. But Randolph had good reason to feel ill-tempered. A couple of days earlier he had received some extremely disturbing news from Laura.

The news was not entirely unexpected. Shortly before leaving Algiers Randolph had met his journalist friend, Virginia Cowles, who had just arrived from London. She had recently seen Laura and was able to bring Randolph up-to-date with her romantic entanglements. Not only, she said, was Lord Dudley still firmly in the picture but Laura was planning an early wedding. This had so alarmed Randolph that he had immediately written to Laura pleading with her not to complicate matters by throwing away her freedom. Enclosed with his letter was a pencilled note of support from Virginia Cowles. Life, she assured Laura, would be far more stimulating with the now slim and handsome Randolph than with 'the Earl'.

Randolph had received Laura's reply shortly after arriving in Cairo. It confirmed all that Virginia Cowles had told him. Laura's mind was more or less made up. She now intended marrying Lord Dudley.

Randolph was crushed but stoical. His answer to Laura was full of forgiveness. He said he was grateful for her frankness and had no right to question her decision. He hoped that she would be happy and assured her that he would always love her. To him, she would remain an angel and he would never cease to be grateful for the joy she had brought to his life. Whatever the future might hold, the memory of their happiness together would endure forever. Then, abruptly – as if to put the matter from his mind – he changed the subject and reeled off the latest Cairo gossip. Somewhat touchingly he concluded by telling her that he was sending her some silk stockings, although he was not sure of her size. Nowhere did he mention Lord Dudley by name.

This letter was to set the pattern of Randolph's future correspondence with Laura. He would go on writing to her, go on sending her presents and repeating that he loved her, but he was careful to avoid all reference to her husband, his wife and the things that separated them. As far as he was concerned, nothing ugly had happened. He created a fantasy world in which he and Laura were devoted lovers, kept apart not by events but by space. Randolph's capacity for self-deception was undoubtedly one of his sustaining strengths.

In the meantime, he busied himself in Cairo. The vivacious Momo Marriott had left Egypt but he discovered plenty of old friends, as well as a few new ones, to fill the gap. He was suitably impressed by General Montgomery and expressed great admiration for General Alexander. Although his criticism of the Middle East Command would remain as acid as ever, his confidence in the outcome of the war seemed less like whistling in the dark.

After leaving Cairo, the Churchill party travelled on to Turkey. Here, at Adana – under the shadow of the Taurus mountains – Churchill met President Inönü in a closed train at a deserted railway siding. All attempts to lure Turkey into the war were unsuccessful but, by the end of the conference, Churchill felt he had at least made some headway with the President. The only real excitement came when Randolph, suspecting there were enemy agents in the vicinity, suggested to one of his father's aides that they institute a night patrol. Only the bitterly cold weather and the sight of some evil looking Turkish guards induced him to return to the train and entrust Churchill's safety to some additional British sentries.

From Turkey they flew first to Cyprus – where Churchill and Randolph visited their old regiment, the Fourth Hussars – and then returned to Cairo before ending the tour at Tripoli in North Africa. By this time Randolph and his father appear to have resumed their earlier, more harmonious relationship. Apart from an incident on the flight between Cairo and Tripoli – when Churchill, alarmed by Randolph's early morning coughing, found it necessary to lecture his son on his incessant cigarette smoking – no more clashes between them were recorded. The visit to Tripoli was, for Randolph, the most memorable event of the tour. The city, a little more than a week before, had been in enemy hands, and the Churchills arrived in time to witness the ceremonial entry of the Eighth Army. Churchill, accompanied by General Montgomery, was cheered everywhere he went and was seen to be in tears as he inspected the troops.

At the last moment, Churchill decided to visit Algiers before returning to England. Randolph went with him. Here, on 7 February, they said goodbye. Randolph had now to seek other diversions.

＊   ＊   ＊

He did not have far to look. One of the first Frenchmen he had met on stepping ashore in Algiers in November had been Pierre Etienne Flandin, an old friend of his father's. For a brief period in the mid-thirties, Flandin had been Prime Minister of France and had later become Foreign Minister. Randolph had first met him in 1936 when Flandin, as Foreign Minister, had visited London during the Abyssinian crisis. At that time Flandin had been at loggerheads with Anthony Eden and this had probably helped to warm Randolph to the Frenchman. Their friendship had continued, sporadically, for the next couple of years. Since then, however, Flandin's reputation had become sullied. Not only had he sent a telegram of congratulations to Hitler after Munich but he had served, for a spell, as Foreign Minister in the Vichy administration. Among the Allied troops in North Africa he was widely regarded as a collaborator.

Randolph, admirably loyal to his old friends, refused to join in the denunciation of Flandin. He was to maintain that the former Foreign Minister had supported the Vichy regime solely to ensure stability in France and was at heart a convinced anti-Nazi. When they met in Algiers, claimed Randolph, Flandin had been eager to give what help he could and had supplied him with 'useful information' about the political and military situation in France. So strongly did Randolph feel on this score that, on 28 December 1942, he wrote a long letter to his father defending Flandin's position. Churchill, for his part, had accepted Randolph's word and, to the surprise of some of his colleagues, became an equally fervent champion of Flandin.

Now, on his return to Algiers, Randolph went several steps further. Flandin and his wife were then living on a wine farm near the coastal town of Philippeville some three hundred miles east of Algiers. Randolph spent whatever spare time he had at the farm and seems to have gone out of his way to drum up support for Flandin. He was always ready to take any stray journalist on a visit to the farm in the hopes, presumably, of obtaining a favourable mention for his friend in the British or American press. One such journalist was the American gourmet writer, A. J. Liebling, who was to retain vivid memories of a hair-raising drive, with Randolph at the wheel, along the winding *corniche* road. The journey lasted two days and during the course of it Randolph managed to force a two-and-a-half ton truck into a cliffside and to land his own lorry in a ditch. When they eventually arrived at the low white farmhouse, they found the Flandins waiting for them. Liebling was immediately impressed by his distinguished looking hosts – Flandin was six-foot five and his wife only a little shorter – but mystified as to the purpose of his visit. 'There was nothing to do but talk,' he says, 'except for a bit of drinking, and it was soon clear that M. Flandin had no political plans that he wanted to impart to me.' In fact, the only political talk came from Randolph who, in his cups that evening, argued loudly in favour of Oswald Mosley being released from internment in England. Liebling left the farm the following morning still uncertain about the role he had been expected to play. He never did discover whether Randolph had taken him along for propaganda purposes or simply as a companion on the road.

But the impulsive Randolph was not always prepared to leave his efforts on behalf of Flandin to chance. In February 1943, shortly after his return to Algiers, he decided to speak out himself. Having recently received a batch of British and American newspapers he was incensed by what was being said about the Vichy French in North Africa. He promptly wrote a letter to the *Evening Standard*.

'There seems to be a widespread tendency,' he thundered, 'to assume that any Frenchman who has occupied any official position under the Government of Vichy, whether at home or abroad, must necessarily be a traitor, or possessed of a Fascist mentality . . . Such an intransigent outlook can only serve to perpetuate disunity among the comparatively few Frenchmen who are lucky enough to be outside the power of the enemy . . . This Pharisaical attitude, which is, I fear, fostered by certain French elements in London, is devoid of any real moral justification . . . Surely it is time a truce was called in this campaign of recrimination. In the last analysis it is Frenchmen who must settle such differences among themselves.'

His letter was not published until 2 March. When it did appear there was an outcry. One of the first to rise to the bait was Aneurin Bevan who tabled a question to the Prime Minister in the House of Commons. He wanted to know if Churchill was aware 'that a letter appeared in the *Evening Standard* . . . written by a serving officer attached to an intelligence unit in North Africa; whether he could inform the House if that letter was passed by a senior officer; and whether he had any comment?'

Churchill turned an embarrassment into a joke. He seized upon the fact that Bevan had not mentioned Randolph by name. 'This question,' he replied, 'should normally have been addressed to the Secretary of State for War but since Mr Bevan, no doubt from those motives of delicacy in personal matters which are characteristic of him, has preferred to put it to me, I will answer it myself.' When the laughter had died down, he went on to say that he had indeed read the letter and had been advised that it did not fall under 'the restrictions of paragraph 547(a) of the King's Regulations as it dealt with political and not military matters.' It had not been passed by a senior officer because the base censorship only dealt with security matters, not matters of opinion. In his view the letter expressed 'a perfectly arguable point of view and one which is shared by many responsible people, American, British and French, in this theatre of war.' For the benefit of those Members who had not seen the letter, Churchill arranged for it to be published in the House of Commons Official Report.

Not everyone agreed with the Prime Minister's interpretation of the King's Regulations. Some of Randolph's old Tory opponents joined in the argument and objected to a serving officer writing to the press. To make matters worse, Randolph heightened Tory anger by dragging his Preston constituency squabble into the open. On 1 April, *The Times* published an open letter which he had addressed to Captain Cobb from North Africa. In it he not only repeated his demand for Captain Cobb's resignation but, by implication, attacked the pre-war Conservative Government. Even at a distance Randolph was still able to provoke political controversy and embarrass his father.

His attempts to defend Flandin were doomed to failure. Later that year, the former French Foreign Minister was arrested and imprisoned by the Allies in North Africa. Churchill protested vigorously against this display of vindictiveness – 'Weakness', he argued, 'is not treason, though it may be equally disastrous' – but his protests did not help matters much. After the war, Flandin was brought to trial by the French on a charge of collaboration with the Germans. Randolph attended the trial at Versailles and, on behalf of his father, spoke in defence of his friend. Flandin was acquitted of the main charge but was declared ineligible for parliament.

*　　　*　　　*

When, in February 1943, Randolph returned to Algiers with his father, the stage was set for the final dramatic clash between the opposing armies in North Africa. Rommel had poured reinforcements into Tunisia from southern Italy and, with an estimated 150,000 men, had established a strong defensive position at what was known as the Mareth Line. Powerfully entrenched as was the German force, however, it now faced a double attack: from the combined Allied army in the west and the Eighth Army advancing from Libya in the east. What followed was perhaps inevitable. Late in March the Eighth Army broke the Mareth Line in southern Tunisia and, on 7 April, joined hands with the Allied force from Algeria. The Germans were now confined to the northern corner of Tunisia, deprived of supplies and reinforcements by heavy air and naval bombardment. They capitulated after a final assault by the Allies at the beginning of May.

The conclusion of the North African campaign opened the way for the next Allied move. This, at the time, was a matter of controversy. Churchill favoured the invasion of Italy – 'the soft under-belly' of the Axis, he called it – but he ran into opposition from the American Chiefs of Staff. In North Africa, General Eisenhower refused to make an attempt on Italy until he was assured of the success of the proposed invasion of Sicily. This much at least was decided: whatever else happened, the Sicilian invasion – codenamed *Husky* – was to go ahead.

Preparations for the launching of an invasion force was soon under way. It was with these preparations that Randolph was to be mainly concerned. His activities centred on the training of an S.A.S.

unit. The unit – the 2nd S.A.S. Regiment – was under the command of David Stirling's brother, Lieutenant-Colonel W. S. (Bill) Stirling and had been operating with the Allied army in Algeria. Unfortunately the rugged terrain of North Africa and the static position of the enemy had, until now, hampered its usual hit and run tactics. The prospect of invading Sicily was far more enticing. Officially it was part of 62 Commando, a raiding unit which had recently arrived from England, and was headquartered at Philippeville. Randolph was to claim that he had selected the site for the camp – a headland close to the Flandins' farm – himself. A. J. Liebling, when he visited the Flandins, considered it an inspired choice.

'I could see,' says Liebling, 'that the place offered advantages for small-scale amphibious manoeuvers – not only concealment and a shelving beach but rocks to be scaled, which are the *sine qua non* of all Commando operations.'

Randolph was less ecstatic. 'Splendid place for landing exercises,' he admitted. 'Hidden. Pity the chaps haven't a boat.' This was probably meant as a joke. Major Roy Farran, who was also at the camp, says that the exercises included training 'to land by sea in fast surf using West African dories.' In any case, the camp had other attractions for Randolph. With a base at Philippeville, he was able to combine his army duties with frequent visits to the Flandins.

Administration was never one of Randolph's strong points. He was too continually on the move: even, on one occasion, travelling as far as the Congo on a special assignment. Even so, he became a familiar figure at the camp, bustling about in his commando outfit – which, it is said, 'fitted like a greengrocer's bag around a single onion' – but he paid little attention to the day-to-day routine. 'That,' an instructor once told a group of trainees as Randolph roared past, 'is *not* how an officer should behave.' As always, Randolph was more concerned with action than with theory.

Action eventually materialized. On the night of 9 July, operation *Husky* was launched. A firm foothold was secured on the southern coast of Sicily and from there the invasion force, fighting off a determined German counter-attack, pushed inland. The fate of the island was decided in a matter of thirty-eight days. On 22 July, Palermo fell to General Patton's Seventh Army and, after the capture of Messina on 16 August, the entire island was claimed by the Allies.

Randolph's role in the landings was incidental but not without its risks. About a fortnight before the attack, Bill Stirling called a group of S.A.S. men together for instruction. They were to land, he said, just ahead of the Highland Division and seize a lighthouse which

245

was thought to house a number of machine guns. These guns had to be put out of action to prevent them being used against the landing force. Randolph was to act as liaison officer between the S.A.S. and the Highland Division.

The raiding party ran into trouble before they left North Africa. At a camp to which they were moved before embarking for Sicily, several of the men fell ill. It was discovered that they had been bitten by the malarial mosquitos that flourished in the lush Philippeville area and, at the new camp, the effects of these bites had become apparent. The casualties mounted until no less than thirty-two of the forty-five men in the party were laid up. Even the survivors felt groggy. But the raid went ahead.

They landed on the tip of Cape Passero, in the south-east of Sicily, and were unopposed. The depleted S.A.S. group rushed ahead, seized the lighthouse, then filled in the time picking off machine-gunners further inshore. They were still sniping away when Randolph suddenly appeared. Strolling nonchalantly through a stream of bullets, he informed the S.A.S. that they had been ordered back to North Africa. The coolness with which he delivered the message was astonishing.

The early successes in Sicily encouraged Churchill to renew his plea for an attack on central Italy. Why, he argued, concentrate on the toe of the Italian boot when it was possible to strike at the knee? His view was now shared by the Combined Chief of Staff. Had any further encouragement been needed, it came with the announce-ment, on 26 July, that Mussolini had been deposed and a new Italian government, headed by Marshal Badoglio, had been formed. Rumour had it that Badoglio intended to sue for a separate peace.

Ten days after Mussolini's downfall, Churchill left England to confer with President Roosevelt at the hastily arranged Quebec Conference. At this conference agreement was reached about the terms of surrender to be offered to the Italians. The terms were signed on 3 September – the fourth anniversary of Britain's entry into the war – but were not publicly announced until five days later. The following morning, 9 September, an Allied force, commanded by General Mark Clark, landed at the Gulf of Salerno to the south of Naples. It met with fierce German resistance. Soon the situation in Italy was reported to be grave.

Churchill was in America when news of the Salerno landings was received. He was visiting Washington to say goodbye to President Roosevelt. As reports of the fighting poured in he became so concerned that he seriously contemplated flying back to England instead of returning by sea. But he changed his mind and, in a somewhat calmer mood, sailed home in H.M.S. *Renown*. His voyage, as he later admitted, would have been less pleasant had he known that Randolph was among the troops who had landed at Salerno.

Randolph had not had time to let anyone know about his Italian venture. It was not an S.A.S. operation; his presence at Salerno had come about almost by accident. At the beginning of September he had gone to Malta on a recruiting mission. Here he had bumped into his old friend Brigadier Bob Laycock, commander of No 8 Commando. Laycock had told him that there was going to be 'a show for the Commandos' and asked whether he would like to join in. The invitation was too tempting to refuse. A few days later Randolph was in the thick of the battle at Salerno.

The fighting at Salerno lasted for six days before the Germans were forced to retreat. General Mark Clark's troops were joined by the Eighth Army, moving up from the south of Italy, and the combined armies pushed the enemy back beyond the Volturno River. After that, with the Germans occupying Rome and the north of Italy, the Italian campaign settled into a phase of stalemate. But Randolph did not have to endure this stalemate long; within a few weeks he returned to England.

CHAPTER THIRTEEN

Further Afield

Randolph arrived back in London at the beginning of October. To his friends he appeared to be in a buoyant mood; optimistic and high spirited. He was soon caught up in the social round – dining out, renewing his old contacts and arguing and drinking as riotously as ever. Evelyn Waugh, who met him shortly after his return, was struck by his 'antiquated sort of competitive national patriotism' and thought that his loudly proclaimed views would harm him at the next election. Other friends were surprised by his continuing support for social reform. During this leave he startled some of his more conventional acquaintances by – unlike his father – welcoming Sir William Beveridge's epoch-making report, *Social Insurance and Allied Services*, which, published the previous December, was to pave the way for the post-war Welfare State. This, again, threatened his relationship with certain sections of the Conservative party.

Behind the scenes, at home with his family, his high spirits were not quite so evident. He was moody, petulant and quarrelsome. Pamela was now living in Grosvenor Square and seems to have seen little of Randolph. This surprised no one. James Lees-Milne, told of the break-up of the marriage by a friend, could note in his diary that 'Randolph only married to have a son. And the young Winston is now born.' Clementine Churchill was not nearly so resigned to the prospect of a divorce. She was still fond of Pamela and, during Randolph's absence, had done what she could to smooth over the differences between husband and wife. Her efforts had been in vain. They may well, in fact, have been partly responsible for her son's moodiness. There were further outbursts from Randolph and further chilly silences from his mother.

Churchill was no less concerned about his son's political tantrums. This concern sprang from Randolph's behaviour on his previous leave. At that time, Churchill had tried to smooth things over by asking his Parliamentary Private Secretary, George Harvie-Watt, to organize a meeting between his son and the Chairman of the Conservative party. His hopes of restoring peace were short lived. A dinner at the Carlton Grill was arranged but

Randolph showed no sign of repentance. In one of his noisy harangues he had offended his hosts by announcing that he did not like the Conservative party 'but was prepared to make use of it.' Harvie-Watt thought his attitude 'pretty poor'. So, for that matter, did Churchill. All the same, he persisted in peace making efforts. When Randolph returned on leave this time, his father again asked Harvie-Watt to take his son under his wing. 'I could never imagine,' says the disillusioned Harvie-Watt, 'my being able to do that.' But he agreed to do what he could.

Again a table was booked at the Carlton Grill and again the Chairman and Deputy Chairman of the Conservative party were invited to meet Randolph. This time they had a long wait for their meal. The party had arranged to meet at 7 p.m. and everyone but Randolph arrived on time. After an hour had passed and there was still no sign of Randolph, Harvie-Watt decided to start dinner without him. However, in the middle of the first course, the head-waiter arrived to say that 10 Downing Street was on the phone. Harvie-Watt went to take the call. 'When I picked up the receiver,' he says, 'it was Mrs Churchill's voice. She sounded upset and apologized for Randolph's being late. He had just left No 10. She was afraid he was very late but there had been a bit of a family row and she hoped my friends would not be too put out by his delay.' Hardly had Harvie-Watt returned to the table when Randolph stormed in. He was obviously drunk and in a filthy temper. Throughout the meal he railed against the Conservative party and its bosses. 'It was a most uncomfortable evening,' admits Harvie-Watt, 'and I had to bring it to an early close as the other customers were all agog.'

Randolph's temper, even when sober, was not helped by the strains of his private life; particularly his unsatisfactory relationship with Laura. As the Countess of Dudley, Laura was now a married woman and Randolph could not pretend otherwise. When they met their relationship was on a different footing: the shadow of Lord Dudley could not be ignored. According to Laura, her husband liked Randolph but the feeling was not reciprocated. Both were touchy, temperamental men and encounters between them were abrasive. Sometimes they quarrelled openly. Randolph, having to hide a broken marriage and to brave a shattered romance, can be forgiven the occasional outburst.

But his leave was not all gloom. Surrounded by his friends, buoyed up by a sense of wartime camaraderie, he could still put on a show of merry-making. His high spirits were very much in evidence at a dinner which he organized at the Savoy, on 3 November, for his friend Robin Campbell. A former member of No 8 Commando,

Robin Campbell had worked with Randolph in Cairo. Since then he had seen active service, lost a leg, and been captured. The dinner was a welcome-home celebration which Randolph had devised himself. He went to great pains to ensure its success by rounding up all available members of No 8 Commando – including Bob Laycock and Evelyn Waugh – and organizing a lavish meal. Oysters, turkey and champagne, followed by brandy and 'Churchillian cigars' were served in a private room at the Savoy and afterwards some of the guests went on to a night club. The next morning, Evelyn Waugh rang to congratulate Randolph but was unable to locate him. 'So I think,' Waugh wrote to his wife, 'it must be either the cells or a house of ill fame.'

Whatever the after effects, Randolph quickly recovered. The following evening he accompanied his father and cousin Johnny to a concert at Harrow. Again he was on the top of his form, joining in the singing of the old school songs which Churchill knew by heart. This was to be the last celebration he would attend in England for some time. Ten days later, after a farewell dinner with Laura, he was on his way back to North Africa.

This time he travelled in style. Together with his father and his sister Sarah, he sailed from Plymouth in H.M.S. *Renown*. Churchill was on his way to Cairo where he was to meet President Roosevelt and, after their conference, the two leaders were to continue on to Teheran for talks with Stalin. For the first part of the voyage, Churchill, suffering from a heavy cold, was in a depressed mood. His doctor, Lord Moran, was hoping he would benefit from the sea air and was dismayed when he insisted on spending half the day and most of the night sitting in his stuffy cabin playing cards with Randolph. His cold got no better and was to plague him for the rest of the trip. Moran was probably relieved when, on reaching Malta, Randolph left the party and travelled on alone to Philippeville.

He was not to remain at Philippeville long. Hardly had he arrived than he received word from his father that he was to proceed to Cairo. He left immediately but did not arrive at the Egyptian capital until after Churchill and Roosevelt had left for Teheran. This was a disappointment for Randolph: he had been hoping to meet the formidable Madame Chiang Kai-shek who, at her husband's side, was said to have dominated the Cairo talks. Randolph eventually caught up with his father at Teheran.

He arrived at Teheran in time to attend the great social event of the Conference. This was the much-written-about banquet at the British Legation, on 30 November, hosted by Churchill to celebrate his sixty-ninth birthday. It was a splendid occasion. There were endless toasts, flowery speeches and a good deal of fraternal mixing among the British, American and Russian delegates. After dinner, Stalin walked round talking to each of the guests in turn. When he encountered Randolph the conversation became positively boisterous; they stood talking for a long time, exchanging jokes through an interpreter and generally behaving like old friends. 'England is becoming a shade pinker,' remarked Churchill when he joined them. 'That,' replied Stalin deftly, 'is a sign of good health.'

Like his sister Sarah, Randolph was greatly impressed by Stalin – or Uncle Joe as he always referred to him. He did not, however, share Sarah's high opinion of the Russian dictator's sense of humour. The banter, he complained, was heavy going. Randolph was to tell many stories about this meeting with Stalin. How true they were is another matter. He was to assure Laura that, by the time they met, he was too fuzzy with drink to remember what was said. He was simply left with the impression that Uncle Joe was a pretty determined customer.

Randolph's behaviour at Teheran was, for once, remarkably restrained. At the banquet his sister was surprised by his apparently subdued manner. 'He is trying you know – ', Sarah wrote to her mother, 'there is a big change in him.' His good behaviour was still in evidence after the conference. When Churchill and Roosevelt returned to Egypt, Randolph was entrusted with a special mission. He flew to Adana in his father's personal aircraft to collect President Inönü and a Turkish delegation and escort them to Cairo for talks with the two leaders. But by that time another, far more exciting mission had been arranged for him.

*   *   *

Among the policy decisions taken at the Teheran Conference, one was to be of particular importance to Randolph. This was the agreement to provide aid to the partisans fighting in Yugoslavia. The effect of this decision was to resolve the quandary in which the Allies had floundered for the past two-and-a-half years.

When, on 6 April 1941, the Germans had invaded Yugoslavia they had hoped for a swift and decisive victory. Hitler's contempt for the nations of Eastern Europe had encouraged him to act with ruthless determination. He expected to meet with little resistance. Not only was the country a hotchpot of rival peoples – Serbs, Croats, Slovenes, Montenegrins and Macedonians – but only a month before the invasion the Regent of Yugoslavia had agreed to form an alliance with Germany. What Hitler did not forsee was the response of a large section of Yugoslavian patriots. As soon as Prince Paul's deal with Germany became known, there was a spontaneous uprising. The Regent was deposed, the pact with Germany denounced, and a new Government was formed in the name of the eighteen-year-old King Peter. But this show of defiance was not enough to deter the German invaders. After a token resistance, the poorly trained and equipped Government forces capitulated and young King Peter and his Prime Minister fled abroad. They eventually settled in London and established a Royal Yugoslavian Government in exile.

Resistance in Yugoslavia appeared to have ended. The country was divided into separate entities, ruled by Nazi puppets. However, after a couple of months of confusion, groups of guerrillas began to emerge to harry the occupying forces. The news received by the Allies about these guerrilla bands was at first muddled, indecisive and misleading. What, in time, did become clear was that the resistance movement was seriously divided. There were two distinct and fiercely opposed groups of fighters. One of these groups, known as Četniks, had evolved from a nucleus of Royalist officers and men and was commanded by Colonel Draza Mihailović who was recognised as the agent of the Yugoslavian Government in exile. The other group were Communists and were called partisans. Little was known of the partisan leader, except that he operated under the name of Tito. Faced with a choice between the two groups, the British decided to back the Četniks who, if nothing else, were nominally loyal to their Government in exile. In September 1941 a British mission of twelve men was landed by submarine on the Montenigrin coast with orders to contact Colonel Mihailović. Other agents followed.

Not until May 1943 was a serious attempt made to contact Tito. This attempt followed disturbing reports from British agents about the loyalty of Mihailović. The Četnik leader, it was said, was more intent on destroying the partisans than he was in opposing the occupying power; some of his officers were known to be collaborating with the Germans and their puppets. Once Tito had been contacted the truth of these reports became apparent. The British, realizing they were backing the wrong horse, then decided to establish firmer links with the partisans. This they did by sending a military mission to Tito's headquarters. The man chosen to head this mission was Randolph's old friend Fitzroy Maclean who, since his days in North Africa, had been operating as a free-lance S.A.S. agent.

Maclean's lively experiences with the partisans quickly convinced him of the need to assist Tito's sorely pressed, extraordinarily daring, guerrillas. His reports on the situation in Yugoslavia contributed, in no small measure, to the decisions reached at the Teheran Conference. Not content with sending reports – which, in any case, was becoming increasingly difficult in an occupied country – Maclean decided to return to Cairo and drum up support himself. As luck would have it, he was in the Egyptian capital shortly after Churchill returned from Teheran.

Churchill listened to all Maclean had to tell him and responded enthusiastically. They discussed the recent Teheran Conference and the political issues involved in assisting Tito. It was Churchill's firm opinion that, Communists or not, the partisans should be encouraged: above all else, it was important that aid be given to the force that was inflicting most harm on the Germans. Later Maclean attended a meeting of the combined service chiefs in Alexandria. He was promised the assistance he asked for and it was agreed to increase the air support and supplies to the partisans. A base would be established at Bari in southern Italy and from there supplies and officers under Maclean's command would be flown across the Adriatic and dropped by parachute to the principal partisan formations in Yugoslavia. The recruiting of the necessary officers was left to Maclean.

What made Maclean choose Randolph as one of his recruits is not entirely clear. He claims the idea 'occurred' to him, but one suspects that Randolph exerted more than a little pressure. Certainly he would not have wanted to miss out on such an exciting venture. In listing Randolph's qualifications for the job, Maclean is disarmingly frank. He would not, he admits, have chosen Randolph for a purely diplomatic post. 'But,' he goes on, 'for my present purposes he seemed just the man. On operations I knew him to be thoroughly dependable, possessing both endurance and determination. He was also gifted with an acute intelligence and a very considerable background in general politics . . . I felt, too – rightly, as it turned out – that he would get on well with the Jugoslavs, for his enthusiastic and at times explosive approach to life was not unlike their own. Lastly I knew him to be a stimulating companion, an important consideration in the circumstances under which we lived.'

However it came about, Randolph was thrilled at the prospect of setting out on a new adventure. His position with the mission was somewhat vague but, in essence, his job was to act as a public relations officer between the Allied force and Tito and to take charge of propaganda. For this he was duly promoted. When he had left his staff post in Cairo and joined the S.A.S. he had been demoted to the rank of Captain; now – to the confusion of many newspapers – he regained his former status and became one again Major Randolph Churchill. He was to retain this rank for the rest of his military career.

Before the mission could leave there were a number of delays.

Maclean was kept busy rounding up recruits; Randolph had personal worries. His father, after leaving Cairo, had travelled on to Tunis. He was still suffering from his bad cold and, on arriving at Tunis, was forced to take to his bed. His doctor became alarmed, ordered an X-ray, and diagnosed pneumonia. This, at the age of sixty-nine, was a grave illness and his family were immediately informed. Randolph flew to Tunis to be with his father and a day or so later they were joined by Clementine Churchill. The crisis lasted for almost a week. Mercifully, Churchill had begun to recover by the time his wife arrived and a few days later he was sitting up in bed playing bezique with Randolph. By Christmas Day the worst was over and the following day Randolph returned to his new base at Bari in Italy.

He was not separated from his family long. Shortly after his return to Bari, he introduced Fitzroy Maclean to the commander of a Commando unit who was eager to involve his men in the Yugoslavian operation. To obtain permission for the unit to join him, Maclean had to fly to Marrakesh where Churchill was then recuperating. He was offered a lift in General Alexander's aeroplane and Randolph seized the opportunity to join them. They arrived in Marrakesh to find Churchill, perky in a bright blue boiler suit, surrounded by army officers. His illness already seemed a thing of the past.

This time the visit was far more businesslike. Among other things, Churchill dictated a memorandum to Anthony Eden in England based on the discussions he had had with Randolph about the situation in Yugoslavia. In it he advised that positive action be taken against Mihailović by both the British Government and the exiled King Peter. He included the arguments that Randolph had put to him concerning the harm that would be done to the young King's reputation if Mihailović were not repudiated. He agreed with them wholeheartedly. 'Let me know . . .' his letter to Eden concluded, 'the form in which you will repudiate Mihailović, and invite the King to do so. It is, in my opinion, Peter's only chance.' Randolph's propaganda activities had, it seems, already started.

By the time they left Marrakesh, on 10 January 1944, Randolph and Maclean had had disturbing news. They had learned that the partisans' headquarters in Bosnia had been attacked and captured by the Germans and that Tito was again on the move. This, however, appears only to have added to the excitement. According to Clementine Churchill they were both in good spirits when they boarded their plane. For once Randolph's mother seems to have fully approved of her son's risky venture. The work, she told her daughter Mary, would suit him.

Churchill's understated pride in Randolph was reflected in a letter which Maclean was taking to Tito. 'It is my earnest desire,' wrote Churchill to the partisan leader, 'to give you all the aid in human power by sea supplies, by air support, and by Commandos helping you . . . Brigadier Maclean is also a friend of mine, and a colleague in the House of Commons [Maclean was MP for Lancaster]. With him at your headquarters will be serving my son, Major Randolph Churchill, who is also a Member of Parliament . . . '

*   *   *

They flew from Bari in a Dakota aircraft, escorted by a dozen Thunderbolts. It was a clear, fine January morning and it was not until they had left the sparkling Adriatic behind that they became aware of patches of cloud over the mountains of the Yugoslavian mainland. Luckily no enemy planes appeared and the anti-aircraft batteries were silent. They were headed for the highlands of West Bosnia. As they approached their destination the plane began to lose height, the exit doors were opened, and orders were given to prepare for the jump. Fitzroy Maclean was to go first; followed by Randolph, an officer of the United States Engineer Corps – Major Linn Farish – two British sergeants and a corporal. Below them was a small village close to an open patch of grass and, looking down they could see the signal fires being lit. Through the billowing smoke they could make out several figures scurrying about. The sight was not altogether reassuring. Fitzroy Maclean became decidedly uneasy: to him the figures seemed a little too distinct, the fires too close, for comfort. He felt they were flying too low for a parachute jump.

And he was right. Hardly had his parachute opened than he landed with, as he put it, 'considerably more force than was comfortable.' Looking up, he saw Randolph hurtling towards him with a look of disgust on his face as he realized he was about to hit the ground. He narrowly missed a telegraph pole and crashed into a puddle of melting snow. The only fortunate thing about the jump was that the entire group landed within a few yards of each other. Bruised and shaken, they had no time to feel sorry for themselves. A British airforce officer, looking more like a brigand than a Wing-Commander, was there to meet them and with him was one of the partisan leaders. The rest of the reception party – a row of weather-beaten, oddly uniformed and heavily armed guerrillas, formed a guard of honour in the background. Maclean went through the motion of inspecting these formidable warriors before riding into the village where, in the upper room of a wood and plaster cottage, a meal was waiting for his party.

After they had eaten and sampled the local *slivovic* – the only available alchohol – it was decided that Maclean should visit Tito to discuss further plans. At that time Tito was living in the woods, waiting to move to his new headquarters, and the partisan leader agreed to take Maclean to his hideout. Randolph and the others were lodged in a peasant's cottage and told not to move until they received instructions to do so.

Those instructions did not come for several days. Then a partisan escort arrived to conduct them to Tito's headquarters. He was now established in a broad valley close to the war-battered village of Drvar. Here, in a cluster of wooden houses on a hillside, the British party settled in. But Tito and his senior staff kept themselves apart. The partisan chief was firmly entrenched in a cave 'half way up the rock face on the far side of the valley.'

Word of Randolph's arrival in Bosnia soon spread. Not all the partisans welcomed him. Some, once they knew who he was, regarded him with suspicion; others doubted whether he had the nerve for guerrilla warfare. An early test of his courage came when, on the way to Tito's headquarters, a German plane flew overhead. The escort watched to see how Randolph would react; they expected him to duck. They were disappointed. 'Randolph,' says Vladimir Dedijer, 'remained standing, as still as the Rock of Gibraltar, and that was that! The partisans realized he was brave, which was the first quality they looked for in a man.' From then on Randolph was accepted by most of Tito's staff. Indeed his presence among them was seen as a token of Churchill's good faith. If the British Prime Minister was prepared to send his only son to Tito, it was argued, then surely he must have repudiated the Četniks.

A few, however, remained unconvinced. As good Communists they questioned Churchill's motives in sending a military mission to Yugoslavia. Suspicions voiced in these early days were still to be heard after the war. Tito was repeatedly depicted as a victim of capitalist plots. 'Western liaison officers,' declared Lazar Brankov in 1949, 'were highly experienced secret service men whose real aim was to carry out a plan of Mr Churchill's for turning Yugoslavia into a bourgeois capitalist State, as a nucleus round which other European countries were to be grouped . . . They were headed by Brigadier Fitzroy Maclean, Major Randolph Churchill . . . the American officer Colonel Hamilton and two named Firo and Farts.' Precisely who the last two quaintly-named gentlemen were is not clear.

There were others who were equally convinced that the mission had been sent by exiled Royalists. Randolph, it was said, was intent on restoring King Peter to his throne after the war. No doubt Randolph encouraged such rumours by giving Tito the impression that he was in a position to influence the young King. Some of the hostility must also have resulted from Randolph's loudly voiced views on the evils of Communism. Even with the most friendly of partisans he would cause offence by vehemently denouncing Marxist doctrine. Communism, he was fond of saying, 'is like a man talking on a cold day, it looks like he's breathing fire when he's really breathing ice.' This type of remark would no doubt have gone down well in the Oxford Union; it was not so well received by the revolutionary partisans.

Not that everyone took Randolph seriously. There were some, like Milovan Djilas – one of Tito's close advisers – who first doubted his role with the mission and then came to doubt their own doubts. 'He himself,' Djilas was to write, 'convinced us by his behaviour that he was a secondary figure . . . Randolph soon enchanted our commanders and commissars with his wit and unconventional behaviour but revealed through his drinking and lack of interest that he had inherited neither political imagination nor dynamism with his surname.' Churchill, Djilas decided, had sent Randolph to Yugoslavia 'out of his sense of aristocratic sacrifice and to lend his son stature.'

* * *

For his first few weeks in Bosnia, Randolph was more or less housebound. He did attempt a couple of pony rides in the district but the snow was too deep and the weather too bad for him to venture far. Most of his days were spent in pottering about the makeshift camp, reading, writing letters and performing trivial domestic chores. Conditions were depressingly primitive. When he wanted to wash his treasured silk pillow case, his handkerchiefs, his hair or even his person – baths were out of the question – Randolph sometimes had to scrape snow from the roof and melt it on a stove. Like the others, he got used to feeling unwashed and comforted himself with the legend that one did not get dirtier after the first thirty days.

There was little he could do to relieve the boredom. Apart from card playing and listening to the wireless there were few amusements. He quickly exhausted the reading matter in the camp which, for the most part, seems to have consisted of translated Russian novels. *Anna Karenina* moved him, but he greatly preferred *War and Peace* when he now read it for the second time. For want of other occupation he started to grow a beard. He aimed at cultivating an Imperial and spent hours examining its progress: somewhat to his surprise it sprouted in four colours – ginger and black, shading to grey and white. Equally distressing was his discovery that the hair on his head was now turning white. Another cause for concern was the fact that his cigarette supply was dwindling rapidly. On his recent visit to Turkey, President Inönü had rewarded him with a gift of a thousand gold-tipped cigarettes but these were now running low and he had to ration his smoking severely. Self-denial did nothing to improve his frayed nerves. In his letters to Laura and his faithful secretary, Miss Buck, he was forever begging them to send him cigars and cigarettes. Not until some weeks later was the shortage relieved by a further, unexpected, present from the Turkish President.

What most bothered Randolph, however, was the loss of contact with the outside world. Mail was occasionally dropped by parachute, but the letters were usually out of date and rarely what he expected. He was obliged to rely on the B.B.C. to keep him in touch with events. Unfortunately the broadcasts were often more infuriating than informative. What Randolph longed for was political gossip rather than day to day facts; he hated being relegated to the role of an outsider and missed the confidences of his political associates. He continually urged Laura to send him newspaper cuttings or whatever snippets of London chit-chat happened to come her way.

He wrote endless letters, even when there was little hope of getting them out of the country. One of his greatest joys was when his own typewriter, complete with a new ribbon, was dropped along with the mail. Not only did he write to Laura, Miss Buck and his family, but he kept in constant touch with Brendan Bracken who, as Minister of Information, was his link with the Political Warfare Executive in England. Inevitably misunderstandings arose. Officials in the Political Warfare Department resented the fact that Randolph had been sent to Yugoslavia by his father without their having been consulted and they particularly objected to his being passed off as one of their representatives. Soon angry telegrams were flying between London, Cairo and Yugoslavia. This inter-departmental wrangling infuriated Randolph. He wrote to Bracken complaining that his work was being sabotaged and assuring him that he had 'no desire to sport the P.W.E. "old tie".' Randolph was not so cut off from the world that he could not manage to raise a few hackles in Whitehall.

To raise anything in Bosnia – apart from his companions' blood-pressure – proved more difficult. The snows lasted well into March and made communications inside Yugoslavia almost impossible. Nor were things helped by Randolph's uncertain health. He was still suffering from the back injuries he had received in the car crash with David Stirling and the jolt he experienced on his parachute drop had done nothing to speed his slow recovery. At times he found it troublesome to sit up straight, let alone walk and travel. That he found camp life dull and frustrating is not to be wondered at.

Excitement of a sort was created, on 23 February, by the arrival of a full-scale Soviet military mission. Headed by General Korneyev of the Red Army, they landed at Tito's headquarters not by parachute but, to the disgust of the partisans, in two Horsa gliders. The entire camp turned out to watch as the gliders detached themselves from their Dakota escorts and swam gracefully to the ground. Excusing their comfortable choice of transport, the Russians claimed it had been forced upon them because their leader had wounded his foot. The partisans remained suspicious.

So, for that matter, did the British. Not until it was discovered that the gliders were loaded with vodka, caviare and other luxuries was a more cordial relationship established. 'After one or two encounters,' says Maclean, 'we decided unanimously that [the newcomers] were a great social asset.' The sociability of the Russians soon became evident. A few days after their arrival, they entertained the entire camp to a sumptuous meal of caviare, sardines, steak and eggs, chocolate cake and lashings of highly perfumed vodka. Randolph ate and drank his fill and enjoyed himself enormously. The only thing that appears to have displeased him was the obvious bias which crept into some of the toasts. This was particularly true of the speech made by Tito in which he 'thanked all the Allies but . . . underscored the extraordinary role of the Red Army.' The British were markedly restrained in their response.

Randolph, as a patriot and a propagandist, decided that it was his duty to correct the balance. During the next couple of weeks he busied himself preparing a counterblast. Somehow or other he managed to obtain a copy of the film *Desert Victory* and invited Tito and the Russians to view this and some British newsreels. Arranging a return meal proved more difficult. Most of the supplies dropped to him were army rations – bully beef and biscuits – and only by bartering parachute silk for some local *slivovic* was he able to provide alchohol. For all that, Randolph managed to chalk up a success. The film show made the impression he had hoped for and what the meal lacked in quality it made up for in quantity. To round things off, Tito was presented with a jeep that had been smuggled in for the occasion.

Towards the end of March, the weather began to improve. Snow still covered the mountain tops but on the plains a springlike greeness transformed the bleak countryside. The sun shone for days at a time and with the sun came a longed-for increase in air supplies. Mail was received by the British Mission on a more frequent and regular basis. Randolph had reason to rejoice. Among the first parcels to reach him was an additional supply of gold-tipped cigarettes from President Inönü and a batch of novels from Laura. However, even the sun had its drawbacks. The clearer weather encouraged enemy aircraft and the parachute supplies became targets for attack as they drifted to the ground. On more than one occasion Randolph's mail arrived riddled with bullet holes (one of the worst casualties being a letter from Rab Butler outlining the 1944 Education Act). Every bit as welcome as the mail, was the sense of freedom that accompanied the disappearance of the snow. After weeks of confinement Randolph was at last at liberty to explore his surroundings.

He made the most of his opportunities. Setting out alone, often on foot, he spent days roaming the mountainous countryside. The fact that he could speak little Serbo-Croat, bothered him not at all. When he was lost he would produce a pencil and paper from his pocket and draw diagrams to explain his predicament. Vladimir Dedijer was to treasure for years the crude drawing of a horse which Randolph once presented to some peasants when he needed guidance home. 'Half an hour later,' says Dedijer, 'he was riding back to Tito's headquarters at Drvar on a Bosnian pony.' As an exercise in public relations, Randolph's roamings were highly successful. Some twenty five years later, a visitor to Yugoslavia was to report meeting peasants who remembered Randolph with affection and admiration.

At the beginning of May he was engaged on a more purposeful mission. This was his attendance at the clandestine Youth Congress of Yugoslavia in Drvar. Randolph was asked to address the congress on behalf of the younger generation of Great Britain and in his speech he expressed his regret that more representative delegates from England were unable to attend. Having to speak for youth to a gathering of earnest young communists was indeed a bizarre undertaking for Randolph, but the conspiritorial tone of the congress would undoubtedly have appealed to his sense of drama. Among the 850 young people present were some who had walked for months across the mountains, often crossing German lines to get to Drvar; others were emissaries from German-occupied towns and cities. To escape the attentions of enemy bombers they met at night in a wood-processing factory and between sessions Randolph spent hours chatting to the delegates about their way of life and their sex and drinking problems. It was all a far cry from his drunken sprees at Whites and the Mohammed Ali Club.

About this time he also paid a lightning visit to Italy. He spent a week there, mostly in Naples, and met a surprising number of his old friends – including his brother-in-law, Duncan Sandys, and his cousin, Tom Mitford. He returned refreshed and full of gossip. His elation, however, did not last long. Within days of his return to Drvar, he was on his way back to Italy. This time under very different circumstances.

On 25 May the Germans arrived at Drvar. They landed by parachute and, having taken a leaf out of the Russian's book, were supported by glider-borne infantry. Their intention was to capture the partisan leadership and they almost succeeded. The British Mission had been alerted to the attack when, a couple of days earlier, they had become suspicious of a lone enemy plane circling over the valley. Fitzroy Maclean was away at the time, visiting London, but his deputy, Vivian Street, had taken the precaution of moving his men and wireless equipment to a little house a mile or two away. Tito had been warned but had refused to move. Now, when the Germans began to land – after first bombing Drvar – the British gathered their equipment together and made contact with the partisans.

In the village the partisans had driven back the German invaders but others had landed on the slopes of the nearby hills. They advanced on Tito's hideout and reached a position from which they commanded the mouth of the cave in which he was living. Soon the cave was under heavy bombardment. Luckily Tito was able to escape. With the help of a rope he managed to scale a cleft in the rock-face and reach the high ground above. From there he was able to join the retreating partisans.

Retreat was inevitable. The Germans had returned to the attack in Drvar and, with the help of strong reinforcements, had captured the village. The partisans, hopelessly outnumbered, had suffered heavy losses. They retreated to some huts in a mountain forest some miles away. Here they were joined, after a gruelling ten-hour march, by Randolph and the rest of the Allied contingent. The wireless was still working and an urgent message was sent to Bari for air support.

They were not able to enjoy their respite. Soon the sound of gunfire heralded the German approach. Tito decided that they must all make a dash for it. In the dead of night, with fierce fighting raging all round them, they broke out and made for a railway siding in the woods. Here they boarded a waiting train. As they steamed off, enemy bullets whizzed through the surrounding trees.

On leaving their train, at the end of the five mile track, the force made their way through the woods. Even though they moved at night and slept during the day, they were not able to escape the German patrols completely. The trouble was that a force of a few hundred partisans – accompanied by the Allied missions – was too small to counter attack and too large to hide. Time and again they came close to being captured. Air support was sent from Italy and, on one occasion, managed to drop supplies, but the situation became increasingly precarious. Finally Tito, who had remained amazingly calm throughout, was forced to recognize the hopelessness of trying to conduct a campaign under such adverse conditions. Near to despair, he asked for arrangements to be made to air lift him and his staff to Italy.

A message was dispatched to Bari and the R.A.F. agreed to send a plane. In the event the plane which arrived was a Dakota manned by Russians. The communist crew was operating under British control as part of a lease lend arrangement but this did not prevent them from boasting that they had rescued Tito. They were to magnify this boast out of all proportion. Among the many false stories spread about Tito's escape was one that claimed that Randolph had tried to turn it into a British *coup*. He is said to have urged the partisans to leave Yugoslavia on a British warship but that 'Soviet intervention had foiled this plan.' If there were any truth in this, it certainly was not apparent at the time. There was simply no opportunity for making political distinctions. As soon as the plane arrived, Tito, his staff and members of the Russian and British missions – including Randolph – were bundled aboard and flown straight to Bari.

Of one thing there can be no doubt. Throughout the retreat, throughout the skirmishes, and throughout the hectic days in the forest, Randolph displayed remarkable courage. He fought side by side with the partisans every step of the way. He seemed to go out of his way to court danger. According to one Yugoslav, he became known as 'the incredible Englishman'. At no stage, claimed Stoyan Pribichevich, did he fuss 'about the cold, hunger, thirst, sore feet, or German bullets, and only raised hell when the Partisan barber wanted to give him a shave without hot water.' That, at least, sounds like the true Randolph. Certainly his fellow officers were impressed by his bravery. For his deeds in this action, Randolph was recommended for the Military Cross and was, in fact, awarded the M.B.E. the following September.

* * *

At Bari arrangements were made for Tito to return to Yugoslavia: not to the mainland but to the island of Vis, some thirty miles off the Dalmatian coast. Most of the offshore islands were, at this time, occupied by the Germans but Vis was sufficiently distant to withstand an invasion. Fitzroy Maclean had earlier recognized this and, through his insistence, Vis had been garrisoned by a Commando Brigade and an Allied air base had been established there. For the next few months the island was to serve as Tito's headquarters.

Randolph did not accompany the partisan leader. He had other concerns. For one thing, the war in Europe had just entered an exciting phase. Tito's flight from Yugoslavia coincided with two momentous events. First, on 2 June, the German defence of Rome crumbled and two days later American troops entered the city. Immediately following this victory had come an even greater turn in Allied fortunes. The 6 June 1944, the day known to history as 'D-day', saw the crossing of the English Channel by a joint Allied force and the beginning of the invasion of Normandy. 'Nothing,' Churchill told the House of Commons, 'that equipment, science, or forethought could do has been neglected, and the whole process of opening this great new front will be pursued with the utmost resolution.' For Randolph to have returned to the isolation of Yugoslavia at such a time would have been unthinkable.

He had other reasons for delaying his return. In his travels through the wilds of Yugoslavia, he had become aware of the fact that many of the peasants – particularly the Croatians – were devout Catholics. He knew little about Catholicism but was not blind to the advantages to be gained by exploiting religious loyalties. And, with Communism now becoming the driving force of the resistance movements in Yugoslavia, he realized that a pro-Western counter balance was essential. What more effective balance could there be than the Catholic Church? This must have been what he had in mind when he decided to seek the help of Evelyn Waugh. Not only was Waugh one of his few Catholic friends but, as a former member of No 8 Commando, he was well qualified to join the Military Mission. Randolph's decision to visit England, before returning to Yugoslavia, was both timely and purposeful.

On his way to London he stopped over in Rome. Here he was able to combine curiosity with a diplomatic *coup*. On 13 June, he was granted a private audience with the Pope. Reporting this unusual event, *The Times* claimed that the audience had been arranged at the Pope's request. His Holiness, said the paper, 'was anxious to discuss conditions in Yugoslavia, especially the attitude of Marshal Tito and General Mihailović towards the Roman Catholic Church.' It seems more likely that Randolph, with his new enthusiasm for Catholicism, had pulled a few strings. Precisely what was discussed at the audience is not clear. The Pope was undoubtedly concerned about Allied support for Tito and his fears, it is said, were not allayed by Randolph's explanations. For the most part, it seems, he and Randolph were at cross-purposes. This is certainly borne out in the comic incident which brought the audience to a close.

Many stories were to be told about Randolph's farewell to the Pope. Most of them are wildly exaggerated. The version which Randolph later gave to Christopher Sykes appears to be nearest to the truth. Apparently, as he was about to leave, Randolph told the Pope that he was hoping to recruit Evelyn Waugh to his staff. The Pope looked mystified: he had never heard of Evelyn Waugh. Randolph was equally mystified. Had his Holiness not, he asked, read Captain Waugh's book? The Pope had not. 'Unperturbed,' says Sykes, 'Randolph explained his enquiry: "I thought Captain Waugh's reputation might be known to your Holiness, because *he's* a Catholic too."' Randolph could never quite understand why other people thought this funny.

Recruitment was uppermost in Randolph's mind when he arrived in London. Bursting into White's Club one morning, shortly after his return, he demanded to know whether anyone had seen Evelyn Waugh. 'I've got to get hold of him,' he yelled. 'Where the devil is he?' As it happened, Waugh was then training in Scotland. He had just completed his novel *Brideshead Revisited* and was hoping to join the 2nd S.A.S. Regiment. Christopher Sykes, who was in White's, told Randolph this and offered to send a message to Waugh. But why, he asked, did Randolph want him? 'Because,' announced Randolph at the top of his voice, 'my father has agreed to me taking charge of a mission to Croatia under Fitzroy Maclean, and Fitzroy and I have been hunting for Evelyn everywhere, because I need him. I can't go to Croatia unless I have someone to talk to.' Discretion, as Sykes says, was never one of Randolph's virtues.

Christopher Sykes telephoned Waugh and so, it seems, did several other people. The message came as something of a relief. Waugh's enthusiasm for the S.A.S. had not impressed his superior officers and, realizing this, Waugh was beginning to have doubts about his future. Randolph had caught him at an opportune moment. He returned to London and met Randolph at the Dorchester to discuss the project. Waugh was given the impression that his role with the mission would be 'to heal the Great Schism between the Catholic and Orthodox churches' but he did not allow this grandiose project to daunt him. It was agreed that they would leave for Yugoslavia in five days time.

His success in recruiting Evelyn Waugh was one of the few happy incidents of Randolph's brief leave. His behaviour, during the three weeks he was in London, was even more outrageous than usual. Almost every member of his family appears to have been attacked by him at one time or another. His temper was quite uncontrollable. Even his long-suffering father was driven to despair. A formal dinner at 10 Downing Street, with some Chiefs of Staff present, was completely ruined by Randolph's drunken rantings. His old friend Lord Birkenhead gave a graphic account of this dinner to Robert Bruce Lockhart. According to Lockhart, Randolph's bark was so loud that 'the Marines on duty outside the door could hear every word. Sarah had tried to rebuke Randolph, telling him not to worry his father who had so much to do. Randolph had lost his temper and struck her. In the end Winston had to threaten to have him removed by the Marines. He had even said at last that he did not wish to see Randolph again. Freddie [Birkenhead] said there was only one thing to do with Randolph when he was tight: to hit him hard and knock him out.'

CHAPTER FOURTEEN

Return to Yugoslavia

'Randy rang up from the hotel,' wrote Lady Diana Cooper from Algiers on 6 July 1944, 'to say could he bring Evelyn Waugh? So he's swallowed something; it must have been his pride. Randy is thin and grey, keen and sweet. Evelyn is thin and silent. I had to put them both on improvised beds in the unused dining-room.'

Diana Cooper had been living in Algiers for the past six months. In January of that year her husband had been appointed British Representative to the French Committee of Liberation in North Africa – which was, in effect, the French Government in exile – and the Coopers had taken up residence in a large, ugly, decidedly dilapidated, villa in Algiers. Randolph had visited them there, shortly after their arrival, when he and Fitzroy Maclean were on their way to Marrakesh to see Churchill before leaving for Bosnia. He had sympathized with Diana Cooper's distress over her squalid accomodation and had promised to do what he could to help. With a little persuasion, he thought, Churchill might arrange for them to move to the luxurious house which General Eisenhower had recently vacated. His efforts, unfortunately, were only partly successful. The Coopers were still living in their highly inconvenient – though gaily refurbished – house when Randolph and Waugh arrived in Algiers on their way to Yugoslavia.

No amount of inconvenience could deter Randolph from landing himself on his friends. Diana Cooper had by now overcome her original distaste for Algiers and, accomplished hostess that she was, was attracting everyone worth knowing in North Africa. Harold Macmillan lived nearby and was a frequent visitor, as were Victor Rothschild, 'Bloggs' Baldwin – Stanley Baldwin's son – and a never-ending stream of French diplomats and politicians. With so much social activity on hand, Randolph far preferred a makeshift bed in the Cooper's dining-room to a drab hotel room. He and Waugh were given an ecstatic welcome and spent three amusing, gossipy days in Algiers. Before they flew off to Catania in Sicily, Waugh – who had appeared deceptively glum – assured Diana

Cooper that he was thrilled at the thought of the active life awaiting him in Jugoslavia 'with his beloved Randolph.'

They were to have flown direct from Catania to Yugoslavia, but were prevented from doing so by bad weather. Instead they travelled first to Bari and then to Tito's headquarters on the island of Vis. Here they met Fitzroy Maclean and here also Waugh was introduced to Marshal Tito. He was singularly unimpressed. 'Tito,' he noted in his diary, 'like a Lesbian. Randolph preposterous and lovable.' The two remarks were not unrelated. There can be little doubt that Waugh's first impression of Tito was influenced by Randolph. It appears that in the early years there had been conflicting rumours about Tito's identity. These rumours had started when the partisan leader – whose real name was Josip Broz – was still a shadowy figure on the European scene. At that time speculation about him had been rife. Some refused to believe that such a person existed; others claimed that Tito was simply a code-name for various guerrilla leaders; but the most popular theory was that Tito was not a man at all, but a bold and beautiful young woman. It was an intriguing thought and one which neither Randolph nor Waugh was prepared to dismiss. To them Tito was, and would always be, a woman. In their conversation and, later, in their letters they invariably referred to Tito as 'her', 'she' or 'Auntie T.' Waugh's Lesbian taunt was a variation on a familiar theme.

So gleefully did Randolph and Waugh pursue this joke on Vis, that – in true Balkan fashion – Tito got to hear about it. An embarrassing moment came when the partisan leader one day joined the British party on the beach. He was wearing nothing but a pair of tight-fitting swimming trunks when Fitzroy Maclean introduced him to Waugh. Extending his hand, Tito was all smiles. 'Ask Captain Waugh,' he said to Maclean, 'why he thinks I am a woman.' For once, the quick-witted Waugh was speechless.

The main purpose of the visit to Vis, appears to have been to arrange a meeting between Tito and the Commander-in-Chief in the Middle East, General Wilson. Randolph and Maclean busied themselves with this but were unsuccessful. In the end, Randolph gave up and returned to Italy to report his failure. Waugh went with him. At Bari they were inoculated in preparation for their flight to mainland Yugoslavia. This time they were not to drop by parachute but to fly direct to Croatia in a Dakota transport plane. With them was going a war-correspondent, Philip Jordan of the *News Chronicle*, an Air Commodore, and a group of partisans. By Sunday 16 July they were ready to leave.

Randolph boarded the plane in a bad temper. At the last moment it had been decided to include three Russian officers and a political commissar in the party and, in order to accommodate them, some valuable stores had to be offloaded. It was this that had caused Randolph to fly into a rage. Night had fallen before the Dakota took off and, to add to the gloom, all the lights were switched off once they were over the Adriatic. For the next few hours they sat dozing in the eerie darkness. 'The stars went out,' reported Philip Jordan, 'the new moon had not risen. Even our wings were not visible except when the summer lightning gave them substance. The only lights were sparks from exhausts which flew past like tracers. Once we flew over a road convoy, a row of moving lights which went out as we approached.' Eventually they became aware, from the noise of the engines, that they were descending. Far below them they could see safety flares being lit as they headed towards the landing strip. Then, suddenly, and unaccountably, they shot upwards before crashing to the ground.

'It was dark when we hit the ground,' says Jordan, 'but when those of us who were lucky enough to regain consciousness, perhaps two minutes later, opened our eyes the aircraft was illuminated by what seemed thousands of little candles, for the flames were burning from one end to the other, flicking in through every split in the flands. There had been darkness and cold but now there was infinite light . . . It was enchanting until I realized that my own hair was one of the candles and that the fallen jack was across my body . . . When we "put ourselves out" and went to the door, it was buckled and would not open, but they say we squeezed between it and the aircraft's body. Later when we had forced the door, others walked or were carried out, but they could not get them all out.'

Jordan's was the most detailed description of the crash. Most of the other passengers were too dazed to remember what had happened. Evelyn Waugh remembered nothing between the plane's sudden upward lurch and his arrival in a cornfield, walking 'by the light of the burning aeroplane talking to a strange British officer about the progress of the war in a detached fashion.' Wisely the officer advised him to sit down. Later, though, it was said that Randolph was largely responsible for his party's escape. It was he who led them to the exit and then forced open the buckled door so that others could be rescued. Throughout the emergency his courage, as always, was extraordinary.

The British officers were lucky to be in the tail of the plane. The crew and some of the partisans were not so fortunate. Out of the nineteen people who had flown from Bari, ten – including a girl partisan – were killed. Randolph burst into tears when he discovered that his batman was among the dead. What caused the crash is not clear. From an account given later by Randolph, it seems the pilot had misjudged the length of the landing strip and when he tried to rise the plane lost speed, stalled, and then crashed. 'Our failure,' said Philip Jordan, 'was a double tragedy, for there was no return journey for the wounded partisans who were waiting so patiently for us in the fields.'

Randolph did not escape without injury. Both his legs were lamed and the jolt had put his back out again. Unable to walk, he had to be carried to the hut in which the injured were being tended. Lack of mobility, however, did not affect his voice. Once the emergency was over, he reverted to his old belligerent self. Soon he was lashing out at his rescuers and shouting for morphine. Nor were things helped when the survivors were transferred to houses in the nearby village. Separated from Waugh and Jordan, Randolph protested furiously at being moved from the air-strip. He claimed he had signalled for a rescue plane and wanted to be on hand when it arrived. In the end he got his way and he, Waugh and Jordan were taken back to the airfield and bedded down for the night on straw. Somehow or other Randolph managed to get hold of some brandy the following day and this helped to ease his pain. It also seems to have oiled his vocal chords. He was still bellowing out orders when a Dakota arrived to take the injured back to Bari. On arrival there, he and Waugh – who was suffering from burns – were rushed to the General Hospital.

∗   ∗   ∗

Mercifully Randolph's sojourn in hospital was short. After a course of treatment – he was suffering from water on the knee – he was discharged and ordered to convalesce. He decided to spend a few days in Algiers with the Coopers. His arrival there, on 25 July, seems to have taken Diana Cooper by surprise. 'On this day of all days,' she wrote to her son, 'Randolph staggered in looking like the man that was – grey-haired, ashen-faced, black pits harbouring dead blue eyes, emaciated, with perished thighs and bandaged knees. I was really alarmed . . . He lies in a hot cupboard upstairs and is carried down to the sitting-room by four Wop gorillas.'

Nursing Randolph was a thankless task. A couple of days later Diana Cooper was complaining about his habit of invading her bedroom first thing in the morning, quarrelling with her other guests, sprawling on her bed with dirt-encrusted feet and covering her sheets with cigarette ash. His invalid habits obviously left a great deal to be desired. 'Randolph,' noted his sorely-tried hostess, 'chain-drinks from noon on. It's quite alarming. He does not get any tighter. I should think he must go through two bottles of gin a day . . . His coughing is like some huge dredger that brings up dreadful sea-changed things. He spews them out into his hand or into the *vague* – as soon as I get up he takes my place in my bed . . . He is cruelly bored and leaves his mouth open to yawn.' Even so Diana Cooper was always ready to make allowance for her impossible visitor. 'Of course,' she would say, 'Randolph was uneducated and completely unhouse-trained, but you could never be annoyed with him for long. When he wished to be, he was totally disarming. That is what you must remember.' All the same she was relieved when her doctor advised electric treatment for Randolph's legs. 'He is not to put them on the ground for a week . . .' she told her son, 'so now we have him where we want him.'

The electric treatment may have helped Randolph to walk more easily. His legs still pained him but at least he was able to move about by himself and within a matter of days was thinking of returning to Italy. Indeed he was on the point of leaving when he heard that his father was on his way to Algiers and this decided him to stay a little longer. Churchill, in fact, was himself flying to Italy to see Marshal Tito and appears to have taken in Algiers *en route* in order to see his son. He had undoubtedly been shocked by the news of Randolph's air crash and his anxiety had alarmed his colleagues. 'Randolph's got immense courage,' General Ismay told Sir Robert Birley about this time. 'He welcomes danger and loves getting into dangerous corners. One of these days he will get himself killed and that will finish Winston. What is going to happen to this country then?' The bond between father and son, despite their frequent quarrels, was as firm as ever.

Churchill was in Algiers for only a few hours. He arrived on the morning of 11 August and drove straight to the Coopers' house. Having apparently satisfied himself about Randolph's health he flew on to Naples. Throughout his father's visit, Randolph was in the highest of spirits. He welcomed Churchill at the airport and from the moment they met he never stopped talking. If nothing else, Algiers had reawakened his interest in politics as well as his animosity towards Anthony Eden; abuse of the Foreign Minister seems to have been his pet theme. With Rome occupied and Europe invaded Randolph was beginning to think of developments after the war and did not relish the thought of Eden succeeding his father. If he could not become the next Prime Minister himself – and he had by no means abandoned the idea that he might achieve that office one day – he was determined to lessen his rival's chances. His own candidate for the Premiership, he told Diana Cooper, was Harold Macmillan. 'Anything,' he explained, 'is better than Anthony. You must think so darling.' He seems, at this stage, to have taken it for granted that his father would retire once the war was won.

By the 20 August, father and son were in Italy, visiting the Italian front. According to General Lemnitzer – the American Deputy Chief of Staff to General Alexander – their relationship was nothing if not lively. Churchill had recently met Tito and it was the situation in Yugoslavia that was now Randolph's main concern. He launched into an argument with his father, advocating greater material aid for the partisans. Lemnitzer was impressed by the way in which Randolph hammered home his points. Discussing this with some of his British colleagues later, he was assured that such arguments were not unusual. 'They told me,' he says, 'they thought that Randolph was playing a most useful role in discussing face-to-face with his father with courageous candour and directness certain sensitive issues that government officials and members of the Prime Minister's staff were frequently loath to raise with him.' Such compliments did not often come Randolph's way.

Arguments or no arguments, Randolph enjoyed this short interlude. Writing to Laura, he claimed he was very happy to be friends with his father again. He returned to Naples in a buoyant mood, met Evelyn Waugh, and the two of them went to Corsica to complete their recuperation. Randolph was hoping to strengthen his legs by a few days swimming on the island but, if Waugh is to be believed, spent most of his time in a drunken rage searching for accommodation. The leave granted for convalescence was drawing to a close. At the beginning of September they returned to Italy and from there they were flown to Yugoslavia in an R.A.F. transport plane. This time they landed safely.

*   *   *

For the next three months, they were based in a farmhouse on the outskirts of the Croatian town of Topusko, some forty miles south from Zagreb. Randolph's role was similar to that he had played in Bosnia. He was essentially a liaison officer between the partisans and the British Mission to Tito and his activities were free-ranging. Waugh, on the other hand, was entrusted with the task of contacting the leaders of the Catholic community in Croatia. Just how he was meant to influence these leaders has never been fully explained. Indeed the choice of two such tactless, intolerant, quick-tempered and heavy-handed men for what was obviously a delicate diplomatic mission is incomprehensible. Neither of them had the slightest sympathy with Communism and they never attempted to pretend otherwise. Two more unlikely ambassadors to a peasant people is difficult to imagine. That their posting to Croatia proved – as far as one can judge – unproductive is hardly astonishing.

Nor is it surprising that they found life at Topusko excessively boring. The town itself was larger than Drvar and before the war it had been a popular spa – the baths were still in good repair – but it had fallen into neglect and was now partly deserted. It offered little in the way of entertainment and, outside the taverns, was distinctly unexciting. The few young women to be seen were, for the most part, hefty, rifle-carrying partisans whom even the lecherous Randolph found unappealing. With endless time on their hands, Waugh and Randolph spent most of their days mooning about the farmhouse. Even here they found little to comfort them. The farmhouse was little more than a rat-infested four-roomed cottage; its only distinction being that it was the one house in Topusko that could boast an indoor lavatory. Randolph and Waugh each had a room to himself and they were looked after by their batmen and by Croatian servants who lived in tents pitched in the yard. The first thing that visitors noticed about the place was that it reeked of animals, manure and woodsmoke.

Time, as Waugh noted in his diary, passed slowly. Occasionally they would be invited to an entertainment or a meal by the partisans and from time to time a visiting priest or some political emissaries would call on them. They made one or two excursions into the surrounding district and, at the beginning of October, they drove out to watch a skirmish between the partisans and the enemy – taking a picnic lunch with them. At his earlier posting in Bosnia, Randolph had complained bitterly to Fitzroy Maclean about the other officers in the Military Mission. The trouble was, he had said, that so few of them were his social or intellectual equals. He had hoped that Waugh would fulfil these requirements. What he had not allowed for was their similarity of temperament: they were both ill-suited to the conditions under which they were living. They bickered, they quarrelled, they sulked in their rooms.

Inevitably Randolph began to drink heavily. For all his repeated avowals that he hated the taste of *slivovic* he appears to have taken to it with gusto. Waugh's diary is full of references to his drunken outbursts and blatant indiscretions.

Nor was Randolph the only one to suffer the ill effects of too much drink. When, for instance, he and Waugh returned from one of their outings in early October, they stumbled on their telegraphist wandering about without his trousers, in a stupor from which he eventually collapsed. Shortly after this Randolph's batman – who was first driven to distraction and then to drink – had to be ordered back to base because of his drunken antics. Considering that the farmhouse was under surveillance from the local secret police, this Bacchanalian behaviour was highly irresponsible.

There were occasional clashes with the secret police. Some of Randolph's political visitors were members of the non-Communist opposition parties and they were eyed with suspicion by the partisans. At times this suspicion led to friction. On one occasion a leader of the Peasant Party arrived from Zagreb to discuss an alliance with the Communists and was entertained to luncheon at the farmhouse. As he left, the secret police arrested him. 'Randolph,' wrote Waugh, 'half drunk, rushed off to see Hebrang, the Communist boss, and has been typing signals ever since.' Incidents like this did nothing to ease the nervous tension under which Randolph and Waugh were living.

Their only ray of hope was the expected arrival of their mutual friend, Lord Birkenhead (the former Freddie Furneaux). Precisely why Birkenhead was chosen for the mission – or what role he played – is a matter for speculation. Birkenhead himself claimed that it was not until he arrived at Bari that he was told he was to be second-in-command to Randolph in Croatia. Fitzroy Maclean, on the other hand, implies that the appointment was decided much earlier. It is also said that Randolph had recruited Birkenhead in London at the same time as he had recruited Waugh. To confuse matter still further, Robert Bruce Lockhart, who saw Birkenhead shortly before he left England, gained the impression that Brendan Bracken was sending him to Croatia for the sole purpose of looking after Randolph. Whatever the truth, it confirms the theory that the Croatian mission was assembled casually and for an indeterminate purpose.

Every bit as uncertain was the timing of Birkenhead's arrival. Randolph and Waugh had almost given up hope of his coming when, on 13 October, they received a message to say he was at the airfield. This news sent Randolph into ecstasies. He pranced about 'chuckling and slapping himself', says Waugh, 'making it plain to me that he had found the restraints of my company irksome.' To make sure that his message hit home, Randolph behaved even more ecstatically when Birkenhead arrived. Standing at the door of the farmhouse, he welcomed his childhood friend with open arms and whoops of joy. Birkenhead knew Randolph too well to be impressed. 'I had,' he says, 'the perhaps unworthy suspicion that the warmth of his greeting owed much to the rigours of his enforced confinement with Evelyn.' That suspicion was reinforced when Waugh appeared, dressed in a brown woollen dressing gown. 'There he is!' bellowed Randolph, 'there's the little fellow in his camel-hair dressing gown! Look at him standing there!' Waugh merely remarked that Randolph was more drunk than usual and turned away. Birkenhead was hardly surprised when Randolph and Waugh later confessed to him that their relationship had almost reached breaking point.

With Birkenhead came Major Stephen Clissold, a former lecturer at Zagreb University and a fluent Serbo-Croat speaker. Tall, charming and reserved, he was the only member of the party really qualified to deal with the partisans and Birkenhead valued his company. Unfortunately they were quickly parted. Randolph insisted on Birkenhead sharing his room and pushed Clissold in with Waugh. It was a sleeping arrangement that Birkenhead had cause to regret.

'I came to regard with dread the approach of night,' he admits, 'for Randolph proved an unnerving bedfellow, and his thunderous snores and other even less pleasing eructations precluded sleep.' And when he was not asleep, Randolph was even more unnerving. His habit of tuning into the B.B.C. Balkan service throughout the night – turning the volume to full blast – made life almost unbearable for the others. A climax came when Birkenhead, unable to stand the disturbance any longer, rose one dawn and pitched into Randolph. Their quarrelling woke everyone in the house and was clearly heard by the servants in the yard.

But, if nothing else, Randolph's passion for news kept the mission in touch with outside events. A week after Birkenhead's arrival they learned of the combined partisan and Red Army advance on Belgrade. This news excited Randolph but appears to have left Waugh unmoved. So contemptuous was he of the partisans that he did not even mention the fall of Belgrade in his diary.

The Germans had suffered a reverse, but they were by no means defeated. In Croatia and Bosnia they retained a firm foothold and, with their lines of communication intact, were still able to strike back. A couple of days after the Communists entered Belgrade, the Germans attacked Topusko. Precisely what decided them to bomb the little town is not certain. Randolph produced his own explanation. He was quite sure that the enemy was aware of his presence and were determined to kill or capture him. He could have been right.

As the only son of the British Prime Minister, Randolph was undoubtedly a prize worth seeking. If, as seems likely, the Germans knew he was at Topusko they might well have considered it worth their while to attack the town. Randolph had certainly made no secret of who he was. Indeed, it is thought that the only reason he was sent to Yugoslavia was to advertise Churchill's solidarity with the partisans. This, in itself, would have attracted enemy attention. As it happened, the raid was a failure. The only noticeable effect of the bombing on the British Mission was that it deepened the rift between Randolph and Evelyn Waugh.

Randolph had sprung into action as soon as the alert sounded.

Beside himself with excitement, he roused the household and ordered everyone to take refuge in a ditch in the fields. There was an immediate stampede. With the exception of Waugh, the entire mission – officers and servants – rushed to the ditch and took cover. For some reason, perhaps to annoy Randolph, Waugh hung back. He was the last to leave the house and the only one to refuse to get into the ditch. Standing alone in the field, he watched the German planes approach and drop their bombs. He was still standing there when they returned for a machine-gun attack. Foolhardy as was his behaviour, it was made even worse by the fact that he was wearing a gleaming white sheepskin coat which, says Birkenhead, 'might have been designed to attract fire.' Certainly it attracted Randolph. Purple with rage, he yelled at Waugh to take the coat off. 'You bloody little swine,' he screamed, ' . . . its an order! Its a military order!' Waugh remained unperturbed. According to Birkenhead, Waugh blithely ignored the command and, still wearing the coat, coolly lowered himself into the ditch. Randolph, however, was to claim that Waugh took the coat off, threw it on the ground – where it lay as a conspicuous target – and then climbed into the ditch. Whoever was right, the incident made no difference to the raid. The German planes bombed some houses in Topusko, killed a number of people, and then flew off, leaving the British Mission and the farmhouse unharmed. The bombardment had lasted only a matter of minutes.

The quarrel between Randolph and Waugh lasted much longer. 'The facts are,' Waugh noted in his diary on 27 October, 'that he is a bore – with no intellectual invention or agility. He has a childlike retentive memory and repetition takes the place of thought. He has set himself very low aims and has not the self-control to pursue them steadfastly. He has no independence of character and his engaging affection comes from this. He is not a good companion for a long period, but the conclusion is always the same – that no one else would have chosen me, nor would anyone else have accepted him. We are both at the end of our tether as far as work is concerned and must make what we can of it.'

Randolph also appears to have realized the inevitability of the situation. Although lacking Waugh's sensitivity and insight, he was shrewd enough to recognize that, thrown together as they were, a truce of some sort would have to be called. Gradually their outward displays of hostility were abandoned and, although their attitude towards each other remained critical and suspicious, each softened sufficiently for a *modus vivendi* to be reached. But not until the beginning of November was there any real attempt at reconciliation. They then made an effort to resume a normal adult relationship.

According to Birkenhead, Randolph's relief at having patched up the quarrel was excessive. His incessant babbling – often stimulated by bouts of drunkeness – strained everyone's nerves. Even the patient Major Clissold found him impossible and eventually refused to act as his interpreter. The telegraphist was completely bewildered by his insistence on sending constant, often meaningless, signals to the base in Italy. Bored and restless, cut off from the world of events, Randolph had no intellectual resources with which to combat the drudgery of isolation. Like everyone else he lived for the mail-drops but as these were not more frequent than they had been in Bosnia, they provided only temporary relief.

In desperation, Waugh and Birkenhead devised a form of mental occupation. Trading on Randolph's inability to resist a gamble, they each bet him £10 that he could not read the Bible from cover to cover in a fortnight. Randolph rose to the challenge. Sprawled out in the living-room and fortified with *slivovic*, he started at Genesis and worked his way through. The longed-for silence descended. But was not for long: the Bible produced unexpected revelations. Soon his companions were startled by loud chuckles as Randolph came across familiar quotations. 'I say,' he exclaimed repeatedly, 'I didn't know this came in the Bible!' This was often followed by an explosive snort: 'God,' he would growl, 'isn't God a shit.'

Randolph kept up his Bible reading for ten days, but failed to win his bet. On 20 November, four American officers arrived at Topusko and, after entertaining them to midday drinks, Randolph capitulated. Pushing the Bible aside, he wrote out cheques for Waugh and Birkenhead, and gave his undivided attention to the newcomers. Nothing, not even the word of God, was allowed to distract Randolph from pontificating to a captive audience.

Once the Americans left, boredom returned. Waugh was kept busy correcting the recently arrived proofs of *Brideshead Revisited* and Randolph had to amuse himself as best he could. He made a half-hearted attempt to compose verse – grunting and counting the syllables on his fingers – but the end result was one, painfully contrived, line. There was, it seems, nothing else for him to do. Indeed he appears to have had very little to do throughout his stay in Topusko. Apart from assisting some escaped prisoners of war, who arrived at the farmhouse in early November, it is difficult to see what useful purpose was served by the British Mission in Croatia.

Certainly Randolph and Waugh had done nothing to improve Anglo-Yugoslav relations. Their continual taunting of the partisans had, if anything, caused more ill-feeling than rapport. Although Randolph made an effort from time to time, he never disguised his true feelings. Waugh's hostility was open and unashamed. Birkenhead, for instance, became positively alarmed by Waugh's unguarded references to Tito as a woman. He once told him to stop talking such nonsense. 'Everyone,' he protested, 'knows that he's a man and a good looking one at that.' But Waugh was unrepentant. 'Her face is pretty,' he joked, 'but her legs are *very* thick.'

It may well have been the superfluousness of the mission which led to the recall of Birkenhead and Clissold. Precisely when they left Topusko is another of those uncertainties. Waugh claims they left the day before the Americans arrived; Birkenhead implies their departure was much later. What is more certain is that they were back in Bari before the end of November. Waugh followed them soon afterwards. He was then posted to Dubrovnik, on the Dalmatian coast. Randolph remained in Yugoslavia longer but, in effect, the British Mission at Topusko was wound up at the beginning of December 1944.

* * *

Randolph's legs were still troubling him. At times he found it difficult to walk and any undue exertion tended to cripple him. This is apparently what happened when he attended a ball in Belgrade before he finally left Yugoslavia. It was obvious that he would have to receive further treatment.

However, as long as he could walk, he remained active. In December he paid a quick visit to Athens. Greece was then very much in the news. Following the German evacuation of Athens in October, the threat of a Communist take-over had plunged the country into a state of civil war. There was street fighting in the capital and Churchill had instructed the commander of the British force there to act as if he were 'in a conquered city where a local rebellion is in progress.' To outsiders this had seemed unwarranted intervention in a civil dispute and had earned the Prime Minister widespread criticism in England and America. Randolph, with his knack of smelling out trouble spots, arrived in Athens when the controversy – and the fighting – was at its height.

A British journalist, Stephen Barber, was to remember Randolph arguing his father's case in the beleaguered Grand Bretagne Hotel. The setting was eerie – shooting could be heard outside, the electricity had been cut off and the freezing cold bar was lit by candles – but there was a generous supply of brandy and Randolph was obviously spoiling for a fight. He was not disappointed. His opportunity came when a Brigadier-General was foolish enough to criticise British intervention. Rounding on him, Randolph put up a spirited defence of his father's actions. 'He spoke with a certain passion,' says Barber. 'He crushed the brigadier.' But the encounter did not end there. A young captain at the bar was incensed by Randolph's rudeness to a superior officer. He told him as much. 'You'd never get away with it if you were not your father's son,' he snapped. 'Randolph,' says Barber, 'put down his glass deliberately. There was a hush. Then he said, quite gently: "I don't see why you have to bring M Y father into this discussion. I would never bring up *your* father, even if I knew him, which I don't. I assume you do . . . As a matter of fact, I am bloody sure he's an utterly dreary, middle class bore . . ."'

The incident, trivial in itself, is not without significance. For all his attempts to present himself as a radical – his attacks on the 'propertied classes' and his advocacy of Tory democracy – Randolph was, and remained, an incurable snob. His private behaviour never matched up to his platform rhetoric; a mere pin-prick could reveal his prejudices. This was a fatal flaw in his career as a politician. He was far too easily rattled to inspire confidence, too emotionally unstable to evolve a consistent political philosophy.

The truth is, Randolph found the minutiae of politics boring. He might toy with a fashionable political theory but he could never follow it through. Much as he enjoyed a rip-roaring election campaign, his interest tended to wane once it was over. Committee work was irksome to him as was the day-to-day business of nursing a constituency. He preferred the bravura of politics: the meetings of heads of state; the occasions when might was challenged by might; the coming together of important men to discuss matters of world importance.

He had the opportunity of attending one such occasion when, a couple of months later, he joined his father and sister Sarah in Cairo. Churchill had just returned from the Yalta Conference and was visiting Egypt for talks with various Arab leaders.

Hurried as were the few days Churchill spent in Cairo, they were not without sparkle. Besides the talks he had with King Farouk of Egypt, he also met the Emperor of Ethiopia and President Shukri of Syria. The most exciting event, however, came on the second day of his stay when he drove to the Fayoum Oasis – some fifty miles from Cairo – for luncheon with the King of Saudi Arabia. It was an exotic, somewhat bizarre occasion.

King Ibn Saud and his entourage – which included three Royal Princes and forty four of his subjects – travelled to Egypt in a British cruiser. With them they brought a flock of sheep which, to the astonishment of the naval commander, they proceeded to slaughter on the ship's deck at regular intervals. Even greater astonishment was caused when, on their arrival at the Fayoum Oasis, smoke was seen issuing from a window of their hotel and it was discovered that the King's bodyguard had killed one of the remaining sheep and were roasting it on a bedroom floor. These minor embarrassments aside, the Churchill luncheon was a huge success. Randolph was formally presented to the splendidly robed King who, flanked by his heavily armed bodyguard, his official food-taster and two ceremonial coffee servers, looked, it is said, every bit the 'master of the Arab world'. After the meal the British visitors were showered with magnificent gifts. Churchill was given a jewel-encrusted sword and dagger, his aides received gold wristwatches or gold daggers, and Sarah Churchill was presented with an 'enormous trunk filled with silks, Arab robes, jars of rare perfumes, and diamonds and pearls' to share with her mother. Unfortunately all these costly presents were later commandeered by the British Treasury to pay for the bullet-proof Rolls Royce which Churchill promised to send the King.

Nothing, however, could dim the splendour of the occasion. And this was undoubtedly the world to which Randolph felt he belonged.

He responded accordingly. Throughout his father's visit Randolph was on his best behaviour. He was as argumentative as ever but, for once, his arguments seem not to have caused offence. Sir Miles Lampson, who met him at dinner, was pleasantly surprised. 'I thought that he had improved a lot since we last saw him,' he noted after driving Randolph home, '– much mellower and more restrained.' An indulgent headmaster could hardly have said more. Randolph was then in his early thirties, but people still tended to speak of him as a wayward child, still continued to hope he would mature.

How much Randolph's apparent transformation was the result of trying to please his father is, however, open to question. There could have been another explanation. His legs were still giving him pain and this may well have dampened his spirits. The Cairo jaunt was to be his last fling for some months. Shortly after his father returned to England, Randolph went to Italy and was admitted to a military hospital in Rome where he underwent a minor leg operation.

Randolph was a demanding, unmanageable patient. The staff at the hospital in Alexandria had discovered this when they nursed him after his car crash in North Africa. Fitzroy Maclean says the nurses were glad to see the back of him. The same was true of the VADs who looked after him in Rome. He created more trouble than all the other patients put together. Refusing to remain in bed, he littered his room with papers which he would not allow anyone to touch. The routine inspections became a nightmare for the hospital staff. Such was his contempt for officialdom, that he did not even bother to look up from his incessant typing when the Colonel in charge made his rounds. This so enraged the hospital superintendent that, on one occasion, he stormed back into Randolph's room after the Colonel had left. 'Major Churchill,' he spluttered, 'did you realize that your visitor was the *Colonel*?' Randolph was unperturbed. 'Oh, yes,' he grunted, 'but my work is more important than his.' Exactly what this work was, nobody ever discovered.

It was the nurses who feared him most. They were kept constantly on guard when visiting his room. Crippled as he was, Randolph could equal any Italian in his bottom-pinching attacks. So outrageous was his behaviour that the prettier VADs refused to be alone with him. He seemed to take a fiendish delight in embarrassing the more blush-prone nurses. One of them, for instance, found herself cornered in his room and ordered to sit down. 'Now,' leered Randolph, 'let us have a talk. In my opinion there are only three subjects suitable for serious conversation: religion, politics and sex. But, as I am not interested in religion and you, being a woman, can know nothing about politics, it leaves us only one topic . . . ' He got not further: the girl fled.

Every bit as embarrassing were his occasional successes. One day – although still hobbling about on two walking sticks – Randolph disappeared from the hospital, taking one of the more amenable nurses with him. He left no explanation and the hospital staff became concerned. They need not have worried. That evening Randolph returned in a merry mood. He made no attempt to excuse his absence but threw a tremendous tantrum when he discovered his bed had not been made.

One thing on his mind while he was in hospital was the likely ending of the war. Randolph had no intention of making the army his career and his thoughts were turning to his political prospects. Churchill had already announced his intention of calling a general election as soon as Nazi Germany was defeated and Randolph must have realized that he would have a fight on his hands. Preston was by no means a safe seat and, after his quarrel with Captain Cobb, he was no longer an unassailable candidate. His political ambitions remained as strong as they had ever been. To reach the highest office was still his aim. Much would depend on his clearing the first post-war hurdle.

As it happened, he had not long to wait. By the middle of April the Allied forces in Europe were relentlessly advancing on all fronts. In Italy the British crossed the river Po and pushed on to the cities in the north, taking thousands of prisoners; the Americans and Russians linked up in Germany and the Red Army surrounded

Berlin; on the last day of the month came the news that Hitler had committed suicide in his Berlin bunker. On 2 May came the end of the fighting in Italy and five days later General Jodl signed the act of total surrender at General Eisenhower's headquarters at Rheims. The war in Europe was over. Officially hostilities ceased at one minute past midnight on Tuesday 8 May, VE-Day. On that day, Randolph – who had returned briefly to Yugoslavia – boarded a plane in Belgrade and flew to Naples on his way back to England.

Although the war with Japan did not end until August, a semblance of peace returned to Europe. On 23 May 1945, Churchill formally resigned as Prime Minister and was immediately invited by the King to form a new government. It was announced that 5 July had been fixed as the date for a general election. This gave the political parties six weeks in which to conduct their campaigns.

✻   ✻   ✻

Very few doubted that the Conservatives would win the election. That Churchill, having so resolutely guided the country to victory in Europe, would be dismissed seemed to most observers – both in England and abroad – unthinkable. But to the more discerning, Randolph perhaps among them, there were signs to the contrary. Since 1942, in fact, public opinion polls had shown Labour leading in popularity and at some recent by-elections victory had gone to opponents of the Coalition Government. Memories of the pre-war Conservative administrations, of the crippling Depression and the hesitancy to arm the country effectively, were still keen. Moreover the war had kindled a new spirit in electorate. Men fighting for a 'brave new world' were more than ever conscious of the appalling inequalities that needed to be rectified, of the need to make the defence of democracy a reality rather than a political slogan. Divisions which had been based largely on considerations of class, tradition and loyalty had now become divisions of ideology.

Electioneering began immediately. In Woodford Churchill was, by common agreement, unopposed by the main opposition parties and had to face only a middle-aged, somewhat eccentric farmer, named Alexander Hancock, who stood as an Independent. This allowed him to devote most of his time to the national campaign. Randolph, in Preston, was not so fortunate. Industrial Preston was still a 'double-barrelled' seat – where electors had two votes and returned two members – and, in this post-war election, it was contested by no less than six candidates. Besides the two Conservatives, there were two Labour candidates, Squadron Leader S. Segal, a medical officer in the R.A.F., and Councillor J. W.

Sunderland, an official of the Textile Workers Union; a Liberal candidate, Flight Lieutenant J. M. Toulmin, and a Communist, P. J. Devine. The outcome of such a contest could not, even with the name of Churchill, be taken for granted.

Randolph could, however, draw comfort from the fact that he was not forced to campaign in harness with Captain Cobb. After the public dispute in 1943, Captain Cobb had finally agreed to stand down at the next election and so allowed the Preston Conservative Association to find another candidate. In fact it was Randolph himself who had chosen his running mate. He was in Cairo when, in 1943, he received news of Captain Cobb's withdrawal and he immediately set out to fill the expected vacancy. He did not have far to look. In the Mohammed Ali Club he had run into Julian Amery, by now a young aspiring Tory politician, and had promptly offered to suggest him for the Preston seat. Amery had accepted the offer and, after a protracted selection process – protracted because Amery was on active service – he was eventually nominated to stand for Preston in the general election.

From Randolph's point of view, a more suitable partnership could hardly have been arranged. Julian Amery, like himself, was the son of a strong-minded former Tory Minister and both their names were well-known to the public. Moreover, Amery, unlike Captain Cobb, shared many of Randolph's political views – they had first met when Amery, as an undergraduate, had proposed the motion welcoming conscription which Randolph had carried at the Oxford Union in 1939 – and had served in the Balkans during the war. Some years younger than Randolph, Amery was inexperienced at electioneering and this made him, if not exactly pliable, at least receptive to Randolph's ideas. There was every reason to think that they would work well together. Amery, on the other hand, had reason to feel apprehensive. He was warned by his friends to expect trouble from Randolph. 'They told me,' he says, 'that I would find him quarrelsome, overbearing and selfish. They begged me to stand almost anywhere but Preston.' But Amery shrugged off the warnings and later claimed he was glad he did so. Campaigning with Randolph, he discovered, was an exhilarating experience.

Their assault on Preston did not start in earnest until parliament was dissolved on 15 June. Until then Randolph seems to have occupied himself in warming-up operations. Among other things, he was one of the few people to read his father's first election broadcast before it was delivered. This was the soon-to-be notorious speech in which Churchill told voters that a Labour Government, if elected, 'would have to fall back on some kind of Gestapo, no doubt very humanely directed in the first instance.' It was a wild, ill-considered and uncalled for thrust at men who, until recently, had been his trusted colleagues and is said to have cost the Conservative party thousands of votes. When Clementine Churchill saw the 'odious and invidious reference to the Gestapo' she begged her husband to delete it from the speech. Randolph, not surprisingly, appears to have had no qualms about his father's inept scaremongering.

The Conservative candidates for Preston started their campaign in style. They drove to the constituency in a large open car, lent to Randolph by King Peter of Yugoslavia, and were accommodated in a house belonging to a friend just outside the town. To help them on their way, Randolph brought with him several cases of champagne. He was, as always, full of self-confidence. He was also surprisingly co-operative. Even when it came to the tricky business of agreeing to a joint election address, he raised no serious objection to the points Julian Amery wished to make. His main concern was for the way in which the campaign was to be conducted. Here he had very definite ideas. Spontaneity was the key-note of Randolph's electioneering and this was something he was determined to teach his less-experienced colleague. When, at their second meeting, Amery arrived with a carefully prepared speech, Randolph was unimpressed. After glancing at the text, he coolly tore it up. Platform speeches, he announced, were always more effective when they were made without notes. Amery was furious – this, he says, was the nearest they came to a quarrel – but afterwards he was forced to admit that Randolph was right and from then on he ceased to rely on his notes.

Randolph's other innovations were more colourful. One of the first was that the Conservative candidates should have a campaign song. He had the fixed idea that 'Lily of Laguna' was a Lancashire tune and this decided him to have it adapted as a battle hymn. Some rather uninspired lyrics – which put more stress on 'Winston for Premier' than on advertising the candidates – were written and the tune was recorded and played whenever Randolph or Amery appeared. They played it in the streets and on the doorsteps as well as at meetings. If for some reason the tune was not broadcast at a Conservative rally the candidates, according to one of their supporters, 'went into quite a frenzy'. But it was good publicity. Amery, on one occasion, was delighted to hear a crowd of children singing it in the streets.

The trouble with most of Randolph's publicity gimmicks was that they tended to shock the good, solid committee men upon whom he was forced to rely. Some of his helpers, for instance, considered the campaign song vulgar and accepted it reluctantly. They were even more outraged by another of his bright ideas. Convinced that the campaign was flagging, Randolph decided to liven things up. To do this he suggested that two elephants should be hired from Manchester Zoo and that, after they had been draped in Tory colours, he and Julian Amery should ride on them through the main streets of Preston. What better way, he argued, to attract attention than by calling for votes from the back of an elephant? So keen was he on this idea that he went as far as booking the elephants for three days. This time he ran into determined opposition. His committee, for the most part, were frankly appalled at the thought of introducing elephants to Preston. Julian Amery was one of the few who supported him. Randolph was furious. The committee's attitude – even after he had offered to cut expenses by employing only one elephant – was incomprehensible to him. He became so angry, says Amery, that he 'told the committee that they were narrow-minded, middle-class provincials with no imagination or guts. They never forgave him.'

But it was not all side-shows and circuses with Randolph. Indeed he refused to take advantage of the more obvious vote-catching tricks. Both he and Amery, for instance, were advised by Churchill to wear their uniforms during the campaign and to display whatever medals they have won but neither of them did this. Afterwards they agreed that their civilian status had made no difference to the result of the election. Randolph was sufficiently experienced to know that, in the end, it was chiefly hard work that counted in an election and there can be no doubt that he worked hard. Every morning he was out canvassing. He would spend at least two hours pounding the pavements, knocking at doors, waylaying voters in the street, shaking hands and listening to complaints. Julian Amery was greatly impressed by the tact, courtesy and skill which Randolph displayed when answering questions. This was particularly apparent when they met deputations from local organizations in the afternoons. Faced by implacable opponents, says Amery, Randolph had a knack of 'luring them into quarrelling among themselves' and telling them to sort themselves out before bothering 'busy candidates'.

But Randolph was at his best at the evening meetings. These were often noisy affairs which sometimes ended in uproar. Randolph's forthright, strongly expressed views are said to have done little to win over floating voters but he invariably won cheers from his supporters. His method of dealing with hecklers may not always have proved effective but it was guaranteed to raise a laugh: when he was booed, he simply booed back. His meetings were never less than lively and there were times when he had to battle his way out of a hall. Once, when he and Amery were speaking in different parts of the town, they met half-way before changing places. When Randolph asked how things had gone at Amery's meeting, he was told the hall had been very quiet. 'You could hear a pin drop,' Amery assured him. 'Oh,' said Randolph. 'Well you wouldn't hear an elephant drop in the one you're going to.'

Between them the two candidates attracted an impressive array of speakers – including Amery's father and Randolph's old commander, Bob Laycock. But the highspot of their campaign was a visit from Winston Churchill. Preston was the last stop in Churchill's lightning tour of the North West. For the past couple of days he had been travelling and talking non-stop and was clearly exhausted. Randolph and Julian Amery met him at Blackburn and drove into Preston sitting proudly on the folded hood of his open car. Churchill insisted on standing with his arm raised, giving the V sign. The streets were packed and all along the way there were cheers and shouts of 'Good old Winnie.' A crowd of over twenty thousand people had gathered in the Town Hall square; tired as he was, Churchill spoke for twenty minutes from the balcony of the Public Library. There were more shouts and cheers as he drove away. It was a rally that none of the other candidates could hope to rival. Randolph had every reason to believe the confident predictions that he and Amery would romp home with a majority of at least five thousand.

Similar predictions, backed by canvass figures, were still being made on polling day. As far as anyone could see, the Tory candidates had been the only ones to whip up any enthusiasm. They were popularly known at the 'lively lads' or 'terrible twins'. A crowd of almost three thousand attended their eve of poll meeting at a local theatre. Randolph and Julian Amery marched onto the stage to the strains of 'Land of Hope and Glory' and their speeches were loudly cheered. Afterwards they were carried shoulder-high, down the main street to the Conservative Club. On polling day itself they toured the town in a cavalcade of open cars, their campaign song heralding their approach, and were given a 'lyrical' reception wherever they went. 'People cheered and waved their handkerchiefs,' says Amery. 'Even our opponents smiled. In the centre of the town, barmaids came out into the streets proffering trays of drinks. At almost every polling station the policemen on duty wished us good luck. I was sure we had won.'

They had a long wait before learning the truth. With so many men still serving abroad, the election result could not be declared until the 'soldier vote' was collected and counted, and this took three weeks. Randolph went home to sit out the delay. His father was abroad most of the waiting period – first in France for a week's holiday and then in Germany for the Potsdam Conference – and did not return to England until 25 July, the day before the Declaration of the Poll. That evening Randolph dined with his parents before returning to Preston on the night train. According to his sister Mary, he was full of confidence.

But more than confidence was needed to match the mood of the nation. When the Preston result was announced, neither of the 'lively lads' was among the victors. They had been decisively beaten by the two Labour candidates. Squadron Leader Segal headed the poll with 33,053 votes, next came Councillor Sunderland with 32,889 votes, Randolph obtained 29,129 votes and Julian Amery 27,885 votes. The expected five thousand majority for the Conservatives had been turned into a combined majority of almost nine thousand for Labour.

Randolph and Amery were both deeply depressed. Only when news of other Conservative defeats began to come in did they lose their sense of shame at letting their party down. The election was a landslide victory for Labour. Churchill easily won his Woodford seat – although his eccentric opponent, who advocated a one-day working week, polled a surprising 10,488 votes – but Randolph's brother-in-law, Duncan Sandys, was defeated, as were his friends Brendan Bracken and Harold Macmillan. The final count gave Labour a majority of 146 seats over all other parties in the new 393 member House of Commons. When they compared their showing with some of the other results, Randolph and Julian Amery had reason to think that they had not done too badly. But it was a comparison of failure which brought little consolation.

Nor could Randolph look for consolation from his election helpers. On entering parliament some five years earlier, he had proudly announced that he hoped to make Preston his permanent political home. There now seemed little chance of his realizing that hope. Not only had he lost his seat but he had lost the confidence of his supporters. His quarrel with Captain Cobb, his clashes with the committee during the election, his high-handed manner and his contempt for local officials had seriously undermined his chances of acceptance by the Preston Conservative Association. He was made aware of this when he and Julian Amery made a round of the constituency to thank workers who had helped them in their campaign. At most meetings they were politely received and complimented on the fight they had waged. The chairman of one Conservative Club, however, was a supporter of Captain Cobb and made no secret of his dislike of Randolph. In his speech he expressed regret for the party's defeat and deplored the ingratitude shown to Churchill but he studiously avoided mentioning the exceptional efforts made by the two candidates. Randolph's reply was scathing. Pretending to be flattered, he sarcastically thanked the chairman for his heart-warming concern and then listed the work which he and Amery had put in to deserve such sympathy. To the chairman's intense embarrassment, the audience found this highly amusing. Whether, as Julian Amery claims, their laughter helped to sweeten 'the bitterness of defeat' is debatable. It certainly highlighted the divisions created by Randolph.

Defeat at Preston depressed but did not dishearten Randolph. Always at his best in adversity, he was quick to bounce back. An opportunity for him to contest another seat came shortly after the general election. In August the MP for Bromley in Kent, Sir Edward Campbell, died and – together with several other hopeful applicants – Randolph put his name forward for the seat. What chances he had of securing the nomination will never be known. One of the later applicants was Harold Macmillan and Randolph withdrew from the contest as soon as he heard that Macmillan's name was being considered. 'He is a great friend of mine,' he wrote to the President of the Bromley Conservative Association, 'and I think no-one has a greater claim.' Loyalty to his friends was always paramount with Randolph. Anxious as he was to return to the House of Commons, he was prepared to wait a little longer.

CHAPTER FIFTEEN

The Roving Reporter

Randolph's prospects on his return to civilian life were anything but promising. The excitements of war were over and, as he admitted, he had failed to achieve 'any particular merit or glory.' He had no reason to be ashamed of his military record – he had proved himself a courageous soldier, had never shirked danger, and had been awarded the MBE for his services with the partisans – but he was merely one of thousands and could lay no special claim to heroism. Nor, for that matter, could he any longer claim the privileges to which he had become accustomed. His father was no longer Prime Minister, he had lost his seat in parliament and his army rank now counted for nothing. To all intents and purposes, Randolph was no further advanced in a career than he had been before the war.

Every bit as gloomy were his hopes of fulfilment in his personal life. His marriage was beyond repair and, as he well knew, it would only be a matter of time before Pamela started divorce proceedings. Laura was still married to Lord Dudley and, although her marriage was proving far from idyllic and she and Randolph were again seeing each other, he had no reason to think their relationship would progress beyond that of a close and sympathetic friendship. He had kept on his house in Hertfordshire but his life there merely reflected the loneliness of his unsettled and apparently pointless existence. Evelyn Waugh, with whom he was now reconciled, went to stay with him for a few weeks while waiting to reoccupy his own house in Gloucestershire, and found the experience chastening. 'Randolph's house . . .' Waugh told his wife, 'has only the furniture which Pam chose not to take. My heart sank. We have a lame cook but no other servants so far. It is presumed that the Melchetts will feed us whenever we are hungry.' Even allowing for Waugh's exaggerations, it is obvious that Randolph's domestic arrangements were as bleak as his post-war prospects.

Yet, to all outward appearances, he was as buoyant and carefree as ever. He was quickly caught up in the London social round: visiting his old haunts, playing billiards at Whites for £50 a game, dining at Claridges and the Carlton Grill, meeting old friends and causing his usual disruptions at private parties. And he quickly found employment. Shortly after withdrawing from the Bromley nomination contest, he signed a two year contract with an American newspaper syndicate. The syndicate was United Features – a subsidiary of United Press – and the terms of Randolph's contract were demanding. In his first year he was expected to write six articles a week and in the second year his contributions were to be reduced to three articles a week. His column was to reflect his observations on events in post-war Europe and was syndicated to various countries throughout the world. It was an appointment well suited to his talents and enthusiasms.

Unlike many of his pompous English friends, Randolph was always openly and expansively pro-American. His early experiences in the United States – his lecture tour and his subsequent visits – had made a lasting impression and he was proud of his family's American connections. He never allowed anyone to forget that his grandmother, the beautiful Jennie Jerome, was thought to have descended from an American-Indian princess. His admiration for the United States did not prevent him criticizing American institutions, politicians and attitudes, but his criticism, if vehement, was that of a friend, often more teasing than hostile. For Randolph, America was part of the wider English-speaking world, a place where he immediately felt at home, a place where the name of Churchill was honoured, a place where his own claims to recognition were acknowledged. He had many American friends, delighted in using American expressions, and went out of his way to cultivate American journalists. The brash, flamboyant reporting of the popular American press appealed to his sense of humour (he loved to quote a headline, said to have appeared in *Variety*, about a lunatic rapist who had escaped – 'Nut Screws and Bolts') and the ruthlessness of American editors appealed to his aggressive instincts. All in all, he could not have found a better temporary home than in the American newspaper world.

Not the least of the advantages of this new appointment was that he was free to travel where he liked to gather material. He set off on his first important assignment in October 1945, visiting Russia and the Scandinavian countries. With his flair for creating as much news as he reported he succeeded in attracting attention in Moscow by first making an anti-Communist speech and then posing for photographs in Red Square, smoking a big cigar in imitation of his father. In Finland he interviewed the Prime Minister and in Stockholm he amazed a fellow journalist by recommending a local tailor who could run up a suit in twenty-four hours. He returned to England laden with gifts of caviare and cigars for his friends.

The year ended on a more subdued note. On 18 December, Pamela was granted a decree *nisi* of divorce on the grounds that her husband had deserted her 'for upwards of three years.' Randolph did not defend the suit and Pamela was given custody of their five-year-old son, Winston. Two days later the well-known American journalist, C. L. Sulzberger, dined with Randolph and found him 'quite meek'. He was brooding about his future and his career. He assured Sulzberger that he still intended to enter politics and said he was continuing with his newspaper work only 'because he needs money'. In what was obviously a rare moment of weakness – he seldom confided in his male friends – he went on to admit that there were times when he found it difficult 'to reconcile his "dignity" as an Englishman and a Churchill with his reporting.'

But if Randolph was down he was by no means out. 'He hopes to be Prime Minister some day,' noted Sulzberger after they had parted.

Randolph's determination to become Prime Minister was neither as wild nor as misplaced as it appears. Given his family background, he had every reason for thinking he could overcome the setbacks of recent months. True he had not realized his youthful ambition to enter parliament in his early twenties and become the 'youngest Pitt', but he had sufficient confidence to ignore his failures. Nor can his assertion that journalism was beneath the dignity of a Churchill be taken seriously. Both his father and his grandfather had been happy enough to work as journalists while out of office and had taken full advantage of newspaper reporting and comment to further their political careers.

Where Randolph failed to live up to family traditions was in his lack of a sound political base. He had no seat in parliament, had never won an election, was without a following and did not speak with a distinctive voice. The causes he championed, the opinions he held, the fights he fought were all, to a greater or lesser extent, the causes, opinions and fights of his father. He was an observer rather than an instigator, a crusading politician without convictions of his own. More and more he had taken refuge in the thought that as long as his father continued as an active politician he would be overshadowed. It was not a new idea. Even before the war he had complained to a friend that his growth was bound to be stunted. 'Under a great tree,' he claimed, 'nothing can grow.' But it was a claim which belied his earlier ambitions. Other sons – including the younger Pitt – had equalled and even outshone their father's achievements. Churchill himself had slipped from under Lord Randolph's shadow and had given Randolph every encouragement to follow his example. Randolph's inability to make the most of his abundant opportunities could not be blamed entirely on the shadow cast by his father.

All the same, in these post-war years, Randolph tended to stress his disadvantages as a great man's son. He never resorted to self-pity – whining was not in his nature – and he never dwelt on his past mistakes but his predictions of success were now often tinged with misgivings. However confidently he proclaimed his determination to become Prime Minister, however much he believed he would achieve his goal, he was careful to guard himself against comparisons with his father. 'I think,' he once told the millionaire, Paul Getty, 'Enrico Caruso had a son who was a tenor. Everyone agreed that Caruso had been the greatest tenor in history. And so everyone measured the son's talents against those of his father. Naturally no matter how well he sang, it wasn't good enough. I've always been in the same boat.'

＊   ＊   ＊

During 1946 Randolph was constantly on the move. He spent the early months of the year touring Europe – collecting material and making contacts for his newspaper articles – and then extended the tour to cover North Africa, Egypt and the Middle East. As always he managed to keep himself in the limelight. Most of the stories told about his outrageous behaviour – his drinking, his rudeness and his political indiscretions – have such a familiar ring that they do not warrant repetition. There were times, however, when his irresponsible remarks aroused more serious criticism. One such occasion was his visit to Spain, where he not only published an article that was considered to be hostile to Franco but was reported to have informed the British ambassador 'that his self-imposed mission abroad was to discredit as much as possible the Socialist Government in England.' This, not surprisingly, produced uproar in the House of Commons. Angry Labour MPs had to be silenced by Harold Wilson, the Parliamentary Secretary to the Minister of Works, who assured them that Major Randolph Churchill was working for an American newsagency and had been granted only 'routine assistance'. 'He is not, of course,' explained Harold Wilson, 'on any official mission.' The Tories found it all highly amusing.

More amusement followed Randolph's appearance at the trial of his friend M. Flandin in Versailles. Here he was representing his father and was welcomed to the hearing by the President of the High Court. So flippant were his answers to some of the questions that the court repeatedly rocked with laughter. He refused, for instance, to be shocked when tackled about the congratulatory telegram that Flandin had sent to Hitler after Munich. 'I myself,' he explained, 'was almost kicked out of my club for daring to criticize Mr Chamberlain.' Stanley Baldwin, he told the court, had been very irritated by one of Flandin's visits to England because 'he wanted to go to see the cherry trees in bloom at his Worcestershire home.' But, for all his quips and wry observations, Randolph was intent on clearing his friend's name. He had brought with him a letter from his father and testified that Churchill had been 'very sad and very cross when he received the news that M. Flandin had been arrested in Algiers.' His evidence undoubtedly helped to secure Flandin's acquittal on the main charge of collaboration with the Nazis.

It was not, however, until the end of the year that Randolph was truly into his peace-time stride. Then it was that he embarked on a lecture tour of the United States. His subject was 'Europe Today' but his widely publicized antics made it appear more like America Yesterday. Now in his mid-thirties, his high-handed, totally irresponsible behaviour was similar to that of the capricious nineteen-year-old who had toured America some fifteen years earlier. Randolph's reluctance to grow up had never been more apparent.

Before setting off for America, Randolph told friends that he intended to hire a car for the tour. He wanted, he said, to avoid the tedium of relying on local committees and groups for his travelling arrangements. This decision was to involve him in endless trouble. Nowhere was Randolph more at risk than at the wheel of a car.

The trouble started shortly after his arrival in the States. One of his first speaking engagements was at a women's club in the small town of Derby in Connecticut. Apparently the speech was a success but the meeting was overlong and, on returning to his car, he found that he had been served with a parking ticket. Refusing to pay the fine – the ticket was later quashed – he set off at breakneck speed along the Merritt Parkway to New York. He had not gone far before he was stopped by a patrolman and was warned that he was dangerously exceeding the speed limit. The warning had no effect. Some miles further on he was again stopped and this time he was booked for reckless driving. (It could be that this was the occasion which gave rise to a typical Randolph story. 'You wouldn't want me to dawdle, and obstruct traffic,' he is said to have protested to a traffic officer. 'Young man,' replied the policeman, 'that's one thing you're NOT going to be charged with.') He was, in fact, charged with driving at over 80 miles an hour and ordered to appear in court at New Canaan three weeks later.

At the hearing, on 9 December 1946, Randolph conducted his own defence. He claimed to be bewildered by the charge, explaining that he had been driving for eighteen to twenty years and considered the Merritt Parkway to be 'one of the safest in the world.' The judge was not impressed. Randolph, protesting that he intended to appeal, was fined $50. He left the court in a huff and ran into his agent who had come to warn him that his car had been parked for ninety minutes. 'Oh my God,' yelled Randolph, as he dashed to the parking lot. 'I forgot all about it.' Luckily, he escaped without another fine.

He was not so lucky ten days later. Completely oblivious of speed limits, he was again arrested for reckless driving between New York and Florida. This time he was charged with travelling at between seventy-five and eighty miles an hour. The case was heard at Petersburg in Virginia but Randolph did not bother to attend. His fine of $55 was paid, after the hearing had been postponed three times, from a cash bond he had posted at the time of his arrest.

Trivial as were these incidents, they set the tone for Randolph's American tour. The war was over and from now on Randolph would have to create his own excitements. Everywhere he went the gossip columnists were kept busy. Much of what they wrote was obviously contrived to attract public attention to his lectures, but they did not have to rely entirely on publicity handouts. Randolph could always inspire a lively news item simply by being himself. His rudeness to waiters, his complaints about hotel service, his impatient outbursts in public places and his quips at the expense of his hosts were all faithfully reported. Even an altercation with a plumber in his Denver hotel – the plumber complained about Winston Churchill 'putting all those kings back' in Europe – was given headline treatment in the *New York Times*.

In addition to his 'Europe Today' lectures, Randolph occasionally spoke on 'The British Empire in the Modern World' but little of what he said on either subject appeared in the newspapers. What Randolph thought was never as interesting as what Randolph did. The strange thing is that, for all the rows he sparked off, for all the offence he gave, Randolph endeared himself to a surprising number of people. He was looked upon as a travelling showman and his rudeness was either applauded, excused or forgiven. 'Randolph,' says his sister Sarah, 'was very popular in the United States, as I would discover from taxi-drivers and doormen and the people I met in my own professional life. He was popular because of his real understanding of many of America's problems and because of his utter directness and outspokenness in interviews.'

Randolph's closer, more critical friends were not so impressed. At the beginning of March he arrived at Beverley Hills in California and spent a few days with Evelyn Waugh. This meeting had been arranged some weeks before and Waugh – who was visiting

Hollywood for discussions with film makers – had claimed to be looking forward to it. His pleasure was short lived. No sooner had they met than he was once again complaining about Randolph's 'abominable' behaviour. 'I thought,' Waugh told his agent, 'he could never shock me any more but he did. Britishly drunk all the time, soliciting respectable women at luncheon parties etc.' But even the jaundiced Waugh was forced to recognize Randolph's powers as a public speaker. He attended a lecture given by Randolph at Pasadena and confessed that it was 'surprisingly good considering the grave condition he was in.'

A couple of weeks later, Randolph returned to England on the *Queen Elizabeth*. His homecoming was as trouble-fraught as his tour had been. The southern coast of England was shrouded in fog and the *Queen Elizabeth*, on entering Southampton Water ran aground on a sandbank. She was eventually towed off by tugs but remained fog bound in the Cowes Road for an entire day. Infuriating as was this sixty-hour delay, it was made worse by the action taken by the ship's captain. To prevent garbled reports of the incident reaching shore, the captain suspended all telephone calls and censored all telegrams. To add to the passengers' frustration – particularly Randolph's – the ship's bars were closed throughout the waiting period. Cut off from his two main-stays – drink and the means of communication – Randolph worked himself into a towering rage. He gave vent to his feelings by detailing the trials of the 2,446 passengers in a long and outspoken article which was published by the *Daily Telegraph* the following day. It was a fitting end to a hectic six months.

By now, Randolph seemed settled in his peacetime role. His activities in 1946 had set the pattern of his life for the next few years. His determination to re-enter politics would continue to be expressed, in one way or another, but in the meantime, he had to content himself with journalism and with making the most of his talent for self-advertisement. Travelling the world in search of news and excitement, he remained restless and discontented. He sought solace in drink and either courted or created trouble wherever he went. But he adamantly refused to acknowledge defeat. The impression he gave remained one of unbounded confidence: Randolph was as audacious, as arrogant, as courageous and as witty as he had ever been. 'Dear Randolph,' as Noël Coward once quipped during these post-war years, 'utterly unspoiled by failure.'

What was lacking now was the promise of his youth. He was no longer regarded as the golden boy, the inevitable successor to his father; his career had climaxed during the war years and he had failed to take advantage of his opportunities. Never again would he enjoy the same reflected glory, the same privileges or the same chances to prove himself. From now on he would have to battle from the sidelines and it was a battle for which he was ill-prepared.

* * *

Randolph's inability to live within his means was apparently incurable. Before the war he had repeatedly to turn to his parents for financial assistance and he showed no signs of reforming as he grew older. After the war Churchill set up a Trust for his children and grandchildren and, somewhat surprisingly, appointed Randolph as Chairman. But according to his sister Mary, Randolph was constantly in financial difficulties and having to turn to his mother for advice and help. None of this prevented him from living in great style. The war had made no difference to his extravagance and the advantages he enjoyed must have bewildered other working journalists.

In 1946, after his appointment with the American syndicate, Randolph rented a house in Hobart Place, Belgravia. Robert Bruce Lockhart, who visited him there, was impressed both by the house and Randolph's working methods. 'Most attractive,' he wrote of the house, 'and, I imagine, most expensive with a lovely garden which from the outside no one would suspect ... Found Randolph drinking champagne from a large tankard and dictating letters to two secretaries – one male and one female.' The secretaries were essential to Randolph's life. He needed them both for his work and as domestic companions. His male secretary, Dennis Rhodes, accompanied him on his tour of America and, from now on, Randolph was rarely without an assistant of some kind at his side.

From Hobart Place he moved to Cliveden Place – an equally expensive address – but he was more frequently to be found at his clubs. Randolph was a member of both Whites and Brooks and, more recently, Evelyn Waugh had succeeded in getting him elected to the Beefsteak Club. This he regarded as a triumph. On an earlier occasion, when he had been nominated by the Duke of Devonshire, he had been blackballed and the success of his second attempt had astonished some of the other members. 'No one else in England,' one of them observed, 'could have dreamed of even going near the place again after being turned down.' Randolph, it was thought, must either have possessed a thick skin or exceptional courage.

The answer was probably a good deal simpler. There can be little doubt that, in these years, Randolph was a very lonely man. Friends he had, but they were mostly social friends and his home life was depressingly bleak. This no doubt accounted for his incessant travelling. In 1947 he embarked on a lecture tour of Australia and

New Zealand – visiting India on the way and interviewing Gandhi in Calcutta – and later that year he returned to America for a second lecture tour. But this travelling was as much a means of escape as it was a professional requirement. He could have obtained a post on any number of English newspapers but he hated the thought of a staff job and preferred a wandering life: a life which matched his restlessness and allowed him little time to brood. Club life, when he was in England, helped to fill a void and satisfied his gregarious nature.

What he needed, of course, was a wife. Women were essential to Randolph, not only as sexual partners but as companions and confidantes. His relationship with his male friends was warm, honest and often affectionate but it was based entirely upon common interests and lacked the intimacy of shared emotions. This he sought in his liaisons with women. The only man with whom he established a really close bond was his father but there were times when they found each other's company a strain. Never was this more apparent than during these post-war years.

Churchill, now in his seventies and exhausted by the war, had lost his relish for private political debate and needed time to relax. According to his daughter Mary, he grew increasingly impatient with Randolph's interminable rantings and 'insatiable appetite for controversy' and was now reluctant to confide in him. This, in turn, both 'grieved and embittered' Randolph. There was no open rift – a mutual sense of loyalty prevented that – but the coolness which developed between father and son was, at times, unmistakable. Churchill's loss of confidence in Randolph was obvious to his political associates. Sir John Colville, his private secretary, is one of those who have remarked on it. After the war, says Colville, it was Christopher Soames who 'without malice or intrigue or indeed intention on his own part, stepped into the shoes so long destined for Randolph.'

Politically distanced from his father, Randolph was unable to turn to his mother for sympathy. Nor would he have considered doing so. The family rows which had accompanied the break-up of his marriage had widened the gulf between them. To his many other grievances, Randolph now added resentment of his mother's open sympathy for Pamela. That this sympathy emphasized Clementine Churchill's concern for both parties in the marital dispute does not appear to have occurred to Randolph. In his personal affairs, as in so much else, he expected blind loyalty to his cause and regarded anything else as a betrayal. Grateful as he was, from time to time, for his mother's practical advice, he could never draw near to her emotionally.

His emotional life was, in fact, sadly wanting in stimulus. After his divorce he had made yet another attempt to win back Laura but it was more a token show than anything else. He had also, as Evelyn Waugh noted in America, continued to pursue other women with little success. How serious he was about any of these affairs is impossible to say, but, whatever his intentions, he had failed to find a permanent companion, let alone a wife. At thirty-seven – bloated, overweight and noticeably greying at the temples – he was as footloose and questing as he had been in his twenties.

Not until his friend Alastair Forbes introduced him to June Osborne did Randolph's hopes of remarrying revive. June Osborne, the attractive daughter of Colonel Rex Osborne of Malmesbury in Wiltshire, was a wide-eyed, elfin-faced and much sought-after young woman. Then in her mid-twenties, she was some twelve years younger than Randolph but, to all outward appearances, seemed to possess all the qualities he looked for in a woman. Vivacious, witty, elegant and articulate, she not only knew her own mind but was well-informed, socially accomplished and assuredly feminine. That Randolph fell in love with her is not surprising.

But, inevitably, his love was that of an infatuated schoolboy rather than that of a mature man seeking a lasting partnership. The mistake he had made in rushing into his first marriage had taught him nothing. In his courtship of June, Randolph appears to have been unaware – or chose to ignore – the danger signals. For, as he was to discover, June Osborne's assured manner was deceptive. Behind her apparent worldliness lay a mass of uncertainties. Her personality was anything but resolved. She was highly-strung, tense and given to a fretfulness that called for subtle handling and deep understanding. Randolph, with his bluff, unimaginative and essentially selfish approach to life, was hardly the person to cope with such contradictions. There were bound to be clashes of temperament.

The clashes started during courtship. Both in private and in public they would snap at each other and sometimes launch into full scale rows. On the day that their engagement was announced, Evelyn Waugh wrote to congratulate Randolph. He said that he did 'not know the young lady but she must be possessed of magnificent courage.' His joke misfired. When, shortly afterwards, he was introduced to June he found that courage was needed on both sides. The account he gives of a quarrel in which he became involved is revealing. For once Randolph was not entirely to blame.

The trouble started at a party given by Lady Milbanke. June was running a temperature when she and Randolph arrived and

Randolph, presumably to brighten her up, had dosed her with benzedrine tablets. This was a grave mistake. After a few drinks, June became so whoozy that Randolph decided to take her back to his sister Diana's house. On reaching the door of the house, however, June became frantic. Shouting that she had lost her keys and that she intended to commit suicide, she ran down the street towards the river. Randolph ran after her. When he caught up with her, on the embankment, there was a struggle. By this time June had become hysterical. Hitting out at Randolph with her fists, she shouted for the police. A squad car eventually arrived and, if Waugh is to be believed, June charged Randolph with indecent assault. While Randolph was arguing with the policemen another car drew up. Seizing her opportunity, June leapt into the car and ordered the driver – a complete stranger – to drive her away. Later that evening, Waugh was called in to help sort things out. He had a long talk with June, brought about a reconciliation, and then he and Randolph went off to 'get a bit drunk at Bucks, Pratts, Whites.'

Not every squabble was so easily settled. All the same, Randolph remained convinced that, given a chance, the marriage would work. He made this quite clear when he discussed his emotional problems with Laura. His idea of what made for wedded bliss was, to say the least, extraordinary. 'Ah well,' he sighed, after detailing his battles with June, 'you always quarrel before you are married, not afterwards.'

Neither his friends' warnings nor his own past experience could shake Randolph's resolve to go ahead with the marriage. At least he could congratulate himself on having his parents' approval. Apparently neither his mother nor his father knew about his stormy courtship and, being concerned only with Randolph's happiness, they welcomed June into the family circle. Only later were they to discover that their son had made yet another grave mistake.

Randolph and June were married at Caxton Hall on 2 November 1948. The entire Churchill family attended the ceremony. Afterwards, the wedding party was entertained at a luncheon, given by June's parents, at the Savoy Hotel. Conspicuous among the adults was Randolph's eight-year-old son, Winston.

Randolph's second child, a daughter, was born the following year. The baby was christened Arabella at St Peter's Church, Eaton Square, on 8 December 1949. Her godparents were Randolph's old friend Seymour Berry, Laura's sister Ann – then the Viscountess Rothermere, later Mrs Ian Fleming – and Mrs Howard Dietz. By that time Randolph and June were settled in their London house, 12 Catherine Place, Westminster and, with the birth of their daughter, appeared to have weathered the first twelve months of their ill-omened marriage. Only their close friends and their families knew otherwise.

Marriage had not, of course, put an end to their bickering. It had continued and, if anything, their quarrelling had become more intense. Clementine Churchill was made only too aware of this when, a few months after Arabella's birth, she received a long, sad letter from June complaining of Randolph's behaviour. The brief, but sympathetic, reply she wrote to this letter appears to exist only in draft form. Whether it was ever sent is not clear. There was, in any case, little chance of it doing any good. Once again Clementine Churchill was faced with the daunting prospect of becoming involved in her son's matrimonial troubles.

*   *   *

By the end of 1949 the post-war Labour Government's term of office had almost run its course and politicians, of all hues and conditions, were eagerly awaiting a general election. The hopes of both the main parties were high but guarded. The Labour party, which had effected a quiet but major social revolution, was confident that – having implemented its declared programme and not having lost a by-election – it could face the electorate with reasonable confidence. The Conservatives, on the other hand, felt that voters, sated with nationalisation and tired of austerity, no longer had faith in their opponents' ability to achieve national econmic recovery and would opt for a change. Both sides were anxious to put their arguments to the test.

Few were more eager to enter the contest than Randolph. For over four years he had waited for a chance to re-enter parliament; now it seemed the day for him to do so was drawing near. His position as an aspiring MP was clarified when, on 21 December 1949, he was officially adopted as the prospective Conservative and National Liberal candidate for Devonport. The seat held peculiar attractions for him. Until 1945, it had been held by Leslie Hore-Belisha, a former Cabinet Minister in the pre-war Baldwin administration, first as a Liberal and then as a National Liberal with Conservative backing. Randolph had never approved of Hore-Belisha and the thought of occupying the seat of a one-time opponent was an enticing one. Even more enticing was the thought of waging a campaign against the sitting MP for Devonport. For Hore-Belisha had been defeated by Randolph's old friend and sparring partner from his Cherkley days – Michael Foot

There was nothing vindictive or petty about Randolph's wish to challenge Foot. He regarded himself as a professional politician and saw any opponent, friend or otherwise, as fair game. Personal considerations, when a clash of policies and principles were involved, did not enter into his reckoning. Prepared as he was to make way for an admired fellow Conservative such as Harold Macmillan, he would not yield to a declared socialist, whoever that socialist might be. Indeed, in a straight fight with Labour, he preferred an opponent he could meet on equal terms. Pitted against, say, a manual worker or a trade unionist who concentrated entirely on bread-and-butter issues, Randolph would have been out of his depth. This could have accounted, in part, for the interminable war he waged against those members of his own party who differed from him on matters of internal organisation and national aims rather than on down-to-earth economic policies. Randolph's passion was for high politics, and a member of the intellectual left, like Michael Foot, provided him with the target he was seeking.

As it happened, Randolph did not have to contain himself for long. On 11 January 1950 – a mere three weeks after his adoption at Devonport – the Prime Minister, Clement Attlee, announced the dissolution of parliament and named 23 February as polling day for the general election. Churchill was on holiday in Madeira at the time and returned to England immediately. Politicians in all parties sprang into action. As the Conservatives intended to fight the election in co-operation with the National Liberals, Randolph's candidature was not only timely but apt. Even so, and allowing for the equivocal stance of the National Liberals, it was a strange banner – Conservative and National Liberal – for him to wave.

Devonport, a division of Plymouth, was considered a marginal seat but Michael Foot, as the sitting MP and a local boy, had a distinct advantage. He regarded Randolph's arrival with amusement. 'He bustled in,' said Foot, 'like something not merely from another world, but another country, talking as if the place belonged to him.' There can be little doubt that both candidates enjoyed themselves enormously. Every morning they would wake up, as Michael Foot puts it, 'polishing the thunderbolts which each hoped to unloose on the unbowed head of the other before the night was done.' The unfortunate third candidate, A. C. Cann, had to struggle for a hearing. To add to the fun, both the main contenders received powerful support. On 7 February, Winston Churchill arrived to speak on Randolph's behalf and one of the most successful meetings of the campaign was staged by another stalwart of the Cherkley days, Aneurin Bevan, who effectively promoted Michael Foot.

Unfortunately not all Randolph's supporters were as powerful as his father. Some of his London friends, who lent a hand with the canvassing, proved more of an embarrassment than a help. The story is told of one bibulous peer who staggered from Whites to

300

Plymouth under the impression that he could whip up Tory support. On the way, however, he seems to have lost his bearings. Arriving in one of the poorer quarters of Devonport, he startled fishwives by knocking on doors and declaring: 'Surely you don't want to go on paying taxes at 19s 6d in the pound for the rest of your lives!'

Randolph needed all the support he could muster. Past experience had taught him nothing and his handling of the local Tories was every bit as unfortunate as had been his dealings with constituency workers in Preston. Rumours of defections from the Tory camp gladdened the hearts of his opponents. 'The brilliant cascade of abuse,' says Michael Foot, 'poured forth in all directions, sometimes drenching his own supporters. They say that the joists and beams of Conservative clubs in Devonport still quiver at the name of Randolph.' This is a pardonable exaggeration. All the same, over thirty years later, veterans of this campaign either could not or would not speak of Randolph's descent on the constituency. So outcast did he feel that he sometimes sought consolation in the most unexpected quarters. Occasionally, after a meeting, Michael Foot and his wife would find Randolph waiting for them and, no doubt to the surprise of the locals, went off with him for a drink.

Politics might separate Randolph from his friends, but they provided a common language: it was the 'committee men' – the men so vital to his interests – to whom Randolph could not respond. His was a common Churchill fault. The family had never warmed to the British middle-class. 'It is remarkable,' Lord Randolph Churchill had once observed, 'how often we find mediocrity dowered with a double-barrelled name.' And he was scathing about the 'lords of suburban villas, owners of vineries and pineries.' These were sentiments which Randolph shared; but it was extremely unwise for a Tory politician to voice such sentiments in the course of an election.

Battling on two fronts, Randolph still managed to put up an impressive fight. With June at his side, he worked hard, displayed his usual bravado, and appeared confident of victory. It was a worthy effort but it was not enough. On polling day he had again to face defeat. The results, announced on 24 February, showed that Michael Foot had obtained 30,812 votes to Randolph's 27,329 votes. This meant that in Devonport the Labour candidate had a majority of 3,483: a majority which contrasted sharply with the national trend. Elsewhere Conservative gains had reduced the Government's overall majority to a shaky six seats.

Randolph accepted defeat gracefully. So calm did he appear when the result was announced that Michael Foot could not resist complimenting him.

'I thought you took that marvellously,' said Foot.

'Yes,' sighed Randolph, 'I've had plenty of practice.'

*   *   *

Not all the stories told about Randolph's quarrels with his party workers in Devonport can be taken at face value. Many of them were told in fun and inevitably Randolph – always good for a laugh – was made to appear more unpopular than he was. Clashes there undoubtedly were but they were clashes with individuals; by and large the Devonport Tories remained loyal to their defeated candidate. So loyal, in fact, that they were prepared to ignore reports of Randolph's gaffe at the end of the campaign. Apparently – or so the story goes – after the polling stations had closed, he set off in a loudspeaker van to thank those voters who had supported him. All went well until, having toured the town, he asked to be taken to a pub. Then, still driving through the streets, he launched into 'a long, offensive tirade against the incompetence of the petit-bourgeois local Tories.' Only later did he discover he had forgotten to switch off the microphone.

The story might or might not be true. Randolph was capable of the most extraordinary indiscretions. In any case, it did him no serious harm. A couple of weeks later he was chosen by the local Conservatives to stand as their candidate at the next election. It was a rare and soothing honour. The prospect of another election loomed large in everyone's mind. With Labour having so narrowly escaped national defeat, it was unlikely that the new Government would run its full course: there were some who measured its life in months rather than years. As a candidate in waiting at Devonport, Randolph had firm political ground to build upon. He would be no stranger to the constituency and, with the tide running strongly in favour of the Tories, his chances of success in a marginal seat were bound to increase. So quickly did he recover from his defeat that he was soon able to turn it into a joke. 'I tell you what the trouble at Devonport was, old boy,' he said to Evelyn Waugh. 'There just weren't enough Conservatives.'

Now he had to await events. As it happened there were plenty of other events in 1950 to keep him occupied. In June of that year, after months of mounting tension, North Korean forces invaded South Korea. President Harry Truman responded to the invasion by announcing American support for South Korea and sending United States troops to that country's aid. The following month, in accordance with a resolution of the United Nations Security Council, a U.N. force – mainly American, commanded by General

MacArthur – was ordered to South Korea. So started a war which was to last three years.

The early fighting was covered by an army of journalists from all countries. Randolph was among them. He went to Korea as a correspondent for the *Daily Telegraph*. Love of action, a thirst for adventure and excitement, probably made it impossible for him to resist volunteering for this potentially dangerous assignment. Some of his more cynical friends, however, saw his hurried departure in another light. They were convinced that he jumped at the chance to go to Korea simply to escape the miseries of his married life. Whatever the truth, to Korea he went.

Like most newsmen, Randolph flew first to Japan. He arrived in Tokyo early in August and quickly made his presence felt. Ansel E. Talbot, an American journalist, was among the crowd of reporters who gathered round him when, with the concentration of a born gambler, he played a slot-machine in the Tokyo Press Club. The machine took only $1 coins and Randolph changed several £5 notes during his game, which lasted from late one afternoon until the early hours of the following morning. According to Talbot he must have spent the $100 jackpot he was trying to win many times over. But, fortified by a chain of drinks and an occasional snooze in a leather chair, he kept at it and finally won. As a shower of silver coins poured from the machine, Randolph rejoiced. 'Champagne was ordered for all,' says Talbot, 'including those he didn't know, as long as the $100 lasted. After that, the party continued, with Randolph still insisting on playing the host. To all offers of buying the next round, he would counter with: "It's my victory celebration".' That night Randolph left for Korea.

He was soon in the thick of the fighting. The North Korean troops were advancing eastwards, across the Naktong River, and meeting with strong resistance from a combined American and South Korean force. In the three-day battle which followed, the tide was turned and the South Korean town of Taegu was saved. Randolph's reports of the action were full of praise for the American troops. He emerged unscathed from the fighting but not without regrets. Like the rest of the press contingent, he mourned the deaths of two British journalists – Christopher Buckley of the *Daily Telegraph* and Ian Morrison of *The Times* – whose jeep was blown up by a land mine at the tail end of the three day battle.

As there were no means of wiring a report from Korea, Randolph had to return to Tokyo, in an American cargo plane, to file his story to the *Daily Telegraph*. He arrived back in Japan at the same time as the news of the British reporters' deaths reached Tokyo. So shattering was this news that no one could be found to break it to

Christopher Buckley's wife, who was also in Tokyo. 'Even the British Minister,' says Ansel Talbot, 'and members of the British diplomatic mission ducked the unpleasant task.' On an impulse, Randolph – as Buckley's colleague on the *Daily Telegraph* – offered to perform the task himself. He did so with such tact, sympathy and sincerity that his more hardened associates were astonished. This was the endearing side of Randolph, a side he guarded as a weakness, a side that was rarely glimpsed and seldom appreciated.

He returned to Korea a day or two later. By that time the main Northern force had retreated and patrol groups were hunting out stragglers. Randolph and an American journalist, Frank Emery of the International News Service, decided to join them. They set out on the night of 23 August, with a reconnaissance party, and waded across the shallow Naktong river. The bank on the other side appeared deserted and the only sounds to be heard were Randolph's penetrating whispers. Whether, as was later claimed, his continual hissing of advice alerted the hidden enemy is not certain, but alerted the enemy was. This became apparent as the patrol made its way back along the bank and a mortar shell exploded close to them, spraying shrapnel in all directions. Both Randolph and Frank Emery were wounded, as well as two soldiers in the patrol. Randolph's right leg was pierced by shell splinters and Frank Emery's left thigh, side and leg was peppered by shrapnel. One of the soldiers was more seriously wounded.

The two journalists were helped back across the river and handed over to the American army medical staff. Typically, before Randolph would allow the doctors to attend to his wounds, he insisted on writing his newspaper report and arranging for it to be flown to Tokyo for despatch. His wounds were not considered serious but he was advised to return to Japan for a few days rest. Once again he found himself crippled and put out of action. His chagrin became obvious when, as he lay on a stretcher waiting to be flown out, a G.I. asked him if he was really Winston Churchill's son. 'Well,' he snapped, 'I'm certainly not one of Clem Attlee's offspring.'

There was, of course, no chance of Randolph taking things easy. Back in Tokyo he was soon hobbling about, haunting the Press Club, and making a pest of himself. James Cameron, who was then representing *Picture Post*, first met Randolph in Korea and remembers how he terrified his fellow journalists. 'He was a bar-bully,' says Cameron, 'and the younger reporters tended to steer clear of him. They would peep into a bar to make sure Randolph was well surrounded before they entered. Things could become extremely embarrassing for anyone trapped alone with him.' Randolph, in fact, caused so much embarrassment that he was barred from the Press Club and had to make the Maronouchi Hotel his headquarters. Here he would entertain those journalists who were prepared to risk, or ignore, his blistering tongue for the sake of an evening's entertainment.

One of his admirers was Michael Davidson. Randolph, says Davidson, was 'the most agreeably boorish man I've ever met . . . that brilliantly flashing mind, fraught with epigram and repartee, loaded with the perfect barbed phrase, used to keep me – over a well-wined luncheon, or through an evening of flowing drink – in agog delight.' A perfect example of Randolph's barbed wit came during an evening's drinking at the Maronouchi Hotel. Davidson was there with two other journalists, Louis Heren and Frank Owen, and Randolph was in a merry mood. So, it seems, was Frank Owen who spent part of the evening recounting how he had benefitted financially from his quarrels with various newspapers. 'My dear Frank,' Randolph sighed when he had finished, 'you were born with a silver dagger in your back.'

Limping but restless, Randolph flew from Tokyo to Hong Kong to witness the arrival of the first sizeable British reinforcements to the United Nations force in Korea. He then – shortly before the Inchon landings – returned to Korea himself where he was able to cover the retaking of Seoul and the reverse crossing of the 38th parallel. After that the Communist onslaught appeared to have been halted, and Randolph – like many exhausted British correspondents – returned to England

*   *   *

As had happened before, Randolph was trying to run before he could walk. He should have taken the doctors' advice and rested. On his return to England his leg began to trouble him again and, in February 1951, he was admitted to the London Clinic for further treatment. The healing process was slow; on and off, he was under surveillance for a couple of months. Matters were not helped by his inability to relax. Malcolm Muggeridge, who visited him in the London Clinic at the beginning of April, found him 'propped up in bed, drinking and smoking, writing letters to newspapers, telephoning etc: a sort of parody of a man of action; of his father indeed.' They talked about politics and this did nothing to calm Randolph down. 'Poor Randolph,' concluded Muggeridge, 'who looks almost as old as Winston, still trying to be a wild young man of destiny.'

Another visitor about this time was Evelyn Waugh. To him Randolph confessed that he was in legal and financial trouble. Nor was this his only worry. There was, as Waugh later told Nancy

305

Mitford, no sign 'of June at his bedside.' He also left the clinic muttering 'poor Randolph'.

But not everyone regarded Randolph as a tragic figure. Once he was up and about again he displayed all his old confidence, his old ability to startle and amaze. At a dinner party, a couple of months later, he thoroughly shocked his American friend Cyrus Sulzberger with his extreme views on world politics. 'Randolph Churchill,' noted Sulzberger, 'kept saying the only thing to do to end the cold war would be to send the Prime Minister of Britain and the President of the United States to Moscow immediately and advise the Russians that if they did not pull back to their 1939 frontiers within seventy-two hours, we would blow up all their main cities with the atom bomb; that instructions had been left behind with the commands of the United States and British forces to proceed to do just this, regardless of what happened, unless the Russians accepted this proposal "carte blanche".'

One can only hope that Randolph was drunk at the time. He might not have been. Dropping atom bombs on the Russians was a favourite theme of the 'wild young man of destiny' at this time. That some people considered him to be politically unstable is under-standable.

Another opportunity for him to air his opinions came in October 1951. It was then that Clement Attlee decided to call another general election. He did so on the advice of the King, who was about to undergo an operation and wanted to ensure a degree of political stability during his proposed tour of Australia and New Zealand the following year, but the decision caused little surprise. The election had long been regarded as inevitable. Parliament was dissolved at the beginning of October and the 25 October was fixed as polling day.

Once again Randolph faced Michael Foot at Devonport. This time he had reason for slightly higher hopes. For some time the opinion polls had been showing a marked lead for the Conservatives and it was probably only the outbreak of the Korean war that had prevented an earlier election. Even so, throughout the campaign – which was more or less a repeat of that of the previous year – Randolph was plagued by private doubts. When the time came for the votes to be counted, he became so nervous that he could not remain in the room. Returning shortly before the result was announced, he asked the Town Clerk how he had done. To his amazement he was told that he had won. So overjoyed was he that he rushed out and embraced members of his committee. But, alas, the rejoicing was short lived. A couple of minutes later the Town Clerk plodded out to explain that he had made a mistake: he had muddled Randolph's figures with those of Michael Foot. Labour had held

Devonport with a reduced majority of 2,390 votes.

Randolph's disappointment can only be imagined. Again he was called upon to accept defeat gracefully. This time it was harder. For this time the Conservatives had won the election with a small, but workable, majority of 17 seats in the House of Commons. Churchill was again Prime Minister and had Randolph won Devonport he would have served under his father, not as a suspected placeman, but as a clearly elected Member of Parliament. His hopes of achieving that long-held ambition, if not entirely crushed, were now too time-worn to be asserted with confidence.

But, bitter as was his disappointment, it was not entirely unexpected. Earlier that year, in one of his more temperate talks with Cyrus Sulzberger, he had admitted to doubts about the future. 'He told me,' wrote Sulzberger, after meeting Randolph in Paris, 'his ambition is still to be Prime Minister of England but he thinks now he has rather less chance in the long run than he optimistically felt last time he proclaimed this desire to me two or three years ago.' His failure to win Devonport must have confirmed Randolph's doubts.

Less than a month after the election, Randolph informed the Devonport Conservative Association that he did not wish to be readopted as a candidate. He may have been hoping for a more promising seat or, as seems more likely, his decision may simply have reflected his disillusionment. For disillusionment there certainly was. Far from drawing encouragement from the fact that his father was again Prime Minister, Randolph seems to have regarded Churchill's return to Downing Street as an obstacle to his own success. 'I could do nothing,' he was to say later, 'while he is alive.'

CHAPTER SIXTEEN

Odd Man Out

By the time he reached the age of forty, Randolph had become so paunchy, so overweight, so grey-haired and balding, that he looked like a man in his mid-fifties – or even older. At his best he could be described as distinguished, at his worst he looked fleshy to the point of grossness. He took no exercise – he hated all forms of sport – he drank to excess, he chained-smoked and his appetite was enormous. People sitting opposite him at dinner would notice the way his eyes lit up with the arrival of each new dish and would stare in amazement as he cleared plate after plate of food. His idea of moderation was extraordinary. Discussing his father's drinking habits with a friend, for instance, he was at great pains to point out that Churchill knew little about food, nothing about wines, and drank 'less than a bottle of spirits a day.' This, it seems, was Randolph's testimony to frugal living. He never made such claims for himself. As he well knew, it was almost impossible for him to curtail his drinking.

Yet there were times when he tried. On selected occasions, and for limited periods, he would make a determined effort to lose weight, to remain sober and to get himself in trim. Concern for his health was only incidental to these efforts: often they were made in response to a bet. Challenged to demonstrate his will-power he could, as he had proved before the war, submit to a most rigorous regime of abstinence and self-discipline. His 'banting' bouts – as Evelyn Waugh called them – followed no definite pattern and were sometimes taken with outside help. Given the right incentive, he would retire to a health spa for a 'cure' and reappear a few weeks later looking fitter, slimmer and a year or two younger. Unfortunately the benefits of these cures were quickly dissipated. Having won a bet or met a challenge, Randolph would invariably reward himself with an alcoholic spree. The result was that, within a matter of days, he put on more weight than he had lost. Life for Randolph hovered between the swings and the roundabouts.

He embarked on one of his periodic diets at the time of the second Devonport election. So successful was it that, a few months later, he was able to boast that he had won his bet and lost thirty-four pounds. But, not surprisingly, he quickly slipped back into his old ways. In February 1952, he went to Lisbon to cover a NATO Council meeting for the *Daily Telegraph* and was seen to be drinking heavily and expanding visibly.

The year was not, however, without some surprises. One of these came in the form of a new journalistic enterprise. Since the ending of his contract with United Features, in 1948, Randolph had worked as a free lance. He liked to boast that, during the next few years, he wrote for a wide variety of newspapers and magazines – including the *Manchester Guardian*, the *New York Times*, *Punch* and *Women's Illustrated*. In May 1952, however, he went to Paris as a representative of a television company. He was working, together with his sister Sarah and her second husband – Anthony Beauchamp, the photographer – on a series of interviews with well-known statesmen and world leaders. Several of these leaders, including his old war-time associate, Marshal Tito, had agreed to appear, and it was Randolph's task to present them. Paris was one of the first European capitals he visited.

The role of television interviewer was, in some ways, one for which Randolph was well suited. His knowledge of politics, his love of controversy and his ability to ask probing questions were undoubted assets; so was his name and his familiarity with most European statesmen. Less of an asset was his reputation as an iconoclast. His unpredictability could, and did, put any interview at risk. He could never resist a sly aside or a wicked dig. This was never more true than when he interviewed Signor Togliatti, the leader of the Italian Communist party. The fact that Togliatti could neither speak nor understand English gave Randolph a marvellous opportunity for mischief. He made the most of it. As the lights dimmed and the signal was given for the interview to start, he turned to the camera and smiled. 'Here,' he announced sweetly, 'is the most dangerous Communist outside the Iron Curtain. Know Your Enemy – Signor Togliatti.' The interpreter, presumably, did not translate.

So at home on television or the radio, Randolph was frequently invited to speak on BBC programmes which dealt with current affairs. In 1951 he was, to the dismay of some of his colleagues, one of the Tory spokesmen in a radio series called 'Argument' and later he was engaged both as a political commentator and as an interviewer. His arrival at Broadcasting House was an event few producers easily forgot. Not only would they be kept on edge throughout his broadcast but, all too often, they would have to cope with the chaos he created both before and after he went on the air.

Jack Ashley, who worked for the BBC in the 1950s, has described the panic that preceded Randolph's interview with Aristotle Onassis. On the way up to a fourth floor studio for a voice test, Randolph, in a 'merry' mood, stepped out of the lift at the wrong floor and got lost. Ashley, left without an interviewer, dashed frantically from floor to floor shouting his name. He finally found him in the hospitality suite where Randolph was bellowing at a producer who had decided to cancel the interview. 'Churchill,' recalls Ashley, 'was angry, yet I found his flamboyant fight against the decision engaging.' Even in his cups, Randolph was capable of winning an argument. The interview went ahead and was a great success.

'It was interesting,' admits Ashley, 'to see Churchill dominating the powerful Onassis; his intimate references to 'Arey' evoked deferential responses from the tycoon.'

Similar stories are told of Randolph's behaviour at television studios. Here things became even livelier after visiting personalities had been refreshed at a running buffet. More than one well-known politician appeared before the cameras in a befuddled state. But, claims Robert Dougall, the 'ultimate terror of talks producers was Randolph Churchill, especially when he had dined too well.' Randolph's most notorious television appearance, however, was in America. Here he was interviewed on a current affairs programme shortly after his sister Sarah had been arrested in California for drunken behaviour. John Wingate, the interviewer, made the mistake of referring to Sarah's arrest. Randolph, to the delight of American television viewers, exploded.

'I never discuss matters affecting members of my family with total strangers,' he snapped. 'I wouldn't think of asking you about your sisters . . . I didn't bother to look up what your sisters had done or who your father was. I don't even know if you had a father or if you know who your father was.'

For all that, Randolph still managed to charm some of his unfortunate victims. If at times he tended to hit below the belt he did so in self-justification and not out of petty spite. Those who were resilient enough to withstand his attacks often came close to admiring him. 'The more I saw of him later,' says Jack Ashley, 'the more I liked him.'

*   *   *

Randolph was busy but adrift. Temporarily cut off from active party politics he could find no other occupation to satisfy his still fervent, but by now ill-defined ambitions. More than ever he regarded journalism as a stop-gap; a necessary evil, a means of earning a living but not, in his opinion, a profession for an 'English gentleman.' More than ever he needed an independent base from which to work.

But how to establish such a base? He had no academic qualifications, no flair for business and, other than journalism, no practical experience. Now that he had drawn back from active politics, his options were severely limited. His only natural assets were a ready, if barbed, tongue, a lively wit, and an ability to write with ease. So far, only his writing talent had been put to profitable use. This gift he took for granted. The speed with which he could dash off an article required little effort; often he wrote without thinking and as a result he rarely did justice to his craft as a journalist. With Randolph, as Julian Amery has observed, it was often a case of 'the good being the enemy of the best.'

For all that, Randolph was not entirely oblivious to the outlet offered by writing. He must have realized that only with his pen could he hope to achieve a new status. This thought appears to have contributed to his decision to write at greater length and to publish his writings in book form. The idea was not altogether new. He already had books to his credit. These were the collections of his father's speeches which he had begun to edit before the war. Since then he had edited further volumes. But, worthy as were these volumes, they could hardly be described as products of Randolph's pen. He had yet to produce a book he could claim as his own.

A chance for him to do so came with the death, in February 1952, of King George VI and the accession of Queen Elizabeth II. With the prospect of a Coronation in the offing, Randolph – always an ardent royalist – decided, or agreed to, publish two books. These books – *The Story of the Coronation* and *They Serve the Queen* (a collection of his newspaper articles) – were no better and no worse than the many other pot-boilers churned out at that time. They set out to explain the pomp, traditions and trappings of the royal occasion and consisted of a mass of hastily assembled facts, presented with little imagination. Any competent journalist could have researched and written them. They can hardly, in all truth, be said to mark the beginning of Randolph's literary career.

The encouragement he needed did not come until the following year. It was provided, not surprisingly, by his father. In August 1953, Churchill informed his solicitor that he had decided to make Randolph his biographer. The decision was not unexpected. As early as February 1932, Churchill had hinted that Randolph would one day 'make thousands' out of his archives and had nursed the idea over the years. Randolph must always have known of his father's intention and, as he later confessed, had 'long aspired to write a filial and objective biography.' That the work to which he was now legally entrusted could not be published until after his father's death was of minor importance. What mattered was that he again had an objective. His task, as he realized, would not be an easy one. To do justice to his father's dramatic, varied and distinguished career, he would need time and patience. The biography could not be completed in a single volume; the work would have to match the man.

To test himself for this mammoth undertaking, Randolph decided to write the life of one of his father's contemporaries. The man he selected for this trial run was the 17th Earl of Derby. An aristocrat, a great hereditary landowner, a Tory who had served as Secretary of State for War under Lloyd George and a man of strong patriotic principles, Derby – who had died in 1948 – possessed many of the qualities which Randolph most admired. Although Derby and Churchill had often clashed politically and were never intimate, they shared a common background, had lived through the same period, knew the same people and had weathered the same political crises. Derby may not have been the obvious subject, but in studying his career Randolph certainly extended his own knowledge of his father's trials and times.

Randolph's new dignity as a 'gentleman of letters' demanded an appropriate setting. This may have influenced his decision to detach himself from London and establish himself as a country squire. The house to which he moved, in the summer of 1953, was Oving House, near Aylesbury in Buckinghamshire. It belonged to Lord Camrose, the newspaper proprietor and father of his old friend Seymour Berry. But if, by moving to the country, Randolph hoped to escape the distractions of urban life and settle down to work, he quickly discovered that solitude left a great deal to be desired. Hardly had he moved in than he was seeking the company of friends. John Sutro was one friend who spent weekends at Oving House. 'On one occasion,' says Sutro, 'we stayed talking until four in the morning and he told me from the heart many intimate thoughts . . . he suffered deeply from the inevitable change in his relationship with his father after the outbreak of the war.'

Randolph, as many of his friends observed, was essentially a very lonely man. Neither a change of occupation nor a change in his surroundings could stifle his craving for companionship.

*   *   *

By distancing himself from Fleet Street, Randolph had by no means divorced himself from journalism. His interest in the conduct of newspaper men remained as intense as it had ever been and he continued to work free-lance. Now, however, he felt free to express himself with less restraint. He never missed an opportunity, both in private and in public, of denouncing what he regarded as the cheap sensationalism of the popular press. This was a subject upon which he held very strong opinions and one which he stressed in his columns for various newspapers and periodicals. There was hardly a newspaper which he had not, at one time or another, openly accused of lowering literary standards, of pandering to depraved tastes and, in some cases, of publishing pornography. He had mounted a one-man crusade to make newspaper proprietors – his friends among them – accountable for the more irresponsible items in their columns. In a letter to *The Times*, in July 1952, for instance, he suggested that the editor should abandon the practice of allowing rival, offending newspapers to be criticized by implication rather than by name. 'The pillory of your correspondence column,' he pointed out, 'must surely prove largely ineffective unless the offender placed in it be plainly identified, so that he may become the just target of public execration.'

The role of moral crusader was a strange and unexpected one for Randolph. Nevertheless there can be no doubt about his sincerity or the vigour with which he waged his Holy War. In biting the hands that fed him, he might well have been seeking an outlet for his frustrations but this did not detract from his conviction that public decency needed to be upheld. Unfortunately he received little public support. His demand that *The Times* identify specific culprits was ignored and he was left to fume alone. In the relative isolation of Oving House, he brooded upon what he saw as a conspiracy of silence and decided to step up his campaign.

An opportunity for him to do so came, in September 1953, when he was invited to chair a Foyle's literary luncheon. The luncheon was held at the Dorchester Hotel in honour of Hugh Cudlipp's book. *Publish And Be Damned* – a history of the *Daily Mirror* – and was attended by distinguished representatives of the press. When he accepted the invitation, Randolph had not read *Published And Be Damned* but this in no way deterred him. He intended to use the occasion for his own purposes. And use it he did. Instead of observing the customary procedure of politely commenting on the book, its author and its subject, he launched a vicious attack on the press in general. He accused Fleet Street of churning out a 'lush and fast flowing' river of pornography and crime and suggested that it would be appropriate, in Coronation Year, for a Pornographer Royal and Criminologist Extraordinary to be appointed.

'By far and away the strongest candidate for the new office,' he went on, 'indeed the People's Choice, was, in the early spring, Lord Rothermere's editor of the *Sunday Dispatch*, Mr Charles Eade . . .[but] a Mr Clapp, the editor of the *Daily Sketch*, entering new into the race, has set so fast a pace that old hacks like Mr Eade have now seriously to look to their laurels.' He made a point of singling out Lord Rothermere by name. One of the reasons why the London press was so bad, he claimed, was because Fleet Street acted on the principle of Dog Don't Eat Dog. 'This handful of wealthy men have formed a cartel to immunise themselves from anything said against them,' he declared.

Emanuel Shinwell, the veteran Labour politician, who had to follow Randolph as a speaker, has described this outburst as 'a bitter performance which produced an air of embarrassment and annoyance.' Many of the other guests agreed with him. Randolph, on the other hand, was to claim that Miss Christina Foyle was delighted with his performance and thanked him warmly afterwards.

The greatest disappointment came the following day. Expecting an explosion in the press, Randolph was furious to find that most of the popular papers carried only brief reports of his speech and avoided mention of the editors and press lords he had attacked. Only the *Manchester Guardian* gave him full coverage. *The Times* did not report his speech at all.

Determined not to let things rest there, Randolph persuaded Michael Foot to publish the speech verbatim in the left-wing *Tribune*. The following month he returned to the attack in another outspoken speech to the Manchester Publicity Association. This time he concentrated, first on *The Times,* and then on Odhams Press and its Sunday paper *The People.* During the previous week, he observed, the 'four nastiest and most caddish stories were all published in the same paper, one that goes by the name of *The People* . . . I think we just ought to put on record the name of the editor, Mr H. Ainsworth.'

But still Randolph was unable to draw blood. There was a flurry of criticism in various newspapers, but it came nowhere near the explosion for which he had been hoping. In desperation he decided to publish his two speeches in a pamplet entitled, *What I Said About the Press*, and offer them for sale at one shilling a copy. Even here he was somewhat frustrated when W. H. Smith refused to sell the pamphlet on their bookstalls for fear of a libel action.

The opposition, silent though it might have been, merely spurred Randolph on. In November 1953, he made yet another fighting speech to the Fleet Street Forum – a journalists gathering – and, in the articles he wrote free-lance, he continued to snipe at *The People* and its editor. Not until over a year later was he rewarded by a show of open hostility.

*   *   *

Randolph's second marriage had, by now, crumbled beyond repair. He and June quarelled incessantly, bitterly and sometimes hysterically. They made little effort to disguise their incompatibility and thought nothing of involving their friends in their rows. Laura, who at one time lived round the corner from Randolph, was repeatedly being called upon to restore peace. Angry and distraught, Randolph would arrive at her door to beg her to come and calm June down. On one occasion he reported that he had left June screaming on the balcony of their flat. Laura hurried round but June refused to let her in. After pleading with her through the door, Laura gave up. 'Anyway,' she later admitted, 'there was nothing an outsider could do.'

The fault, of course, was not all on one side. Randolph was every bit as capable of creating a public scene as was June. Christopher Sykes recalls an unseemly incident which took place, in the early 1950s, when he and John Sutro had arranged to meet Randolph and June at a restaurant near Sloane Square. They arrived to find June and another guest, but not Randolph. After waiting five minutes, they sat down at a table. Then it was that Randolph stormed in. He was drunk and in a towering rage. 'It was a rainy night,' says Christopher Sykes, 'and Randolph was dripping. After curt greetings he turned to his wife and in a voice like a trumpet asked why he had been kept waiting in the rain on his own doorstep for so long a time before anyone could be found to open the door to him. To her quiet reply that since he came back so late she had assumed he would come straight to the restaurant, he responded in yet louder tones.' By this time the entire restaurant was agog. A hush had fallen on the room and all eyes were turned on Randolph. Eventually Christopher Sykes felt obliged to intervene. 'Randolph,' he said, 'you should not talk to your wife like that in a restaurant.' This well-meant rebuke was not so well-received. Randolph's anger was instantly diverted from his wife to his friend. 'What the hell!' he bellowed, 'what the HELL do you mean by butting in on this purely private conversation?' Sykes knew Randolph too well to be intimidated. 'I am sorry to have made a mistake,' he replied, 'but I had the impression that it was a public one.' With that John Sutro burst out laughing and the tensions lessened. But there were very few more laughs that evening.

Laughter, in fact, was hardly a feature of Randolph's second marriage. According to her friends, June was not lacking in a sense

315

of fun. When she was not accompanied by Randolph she was merry enough and could on occasion, be quite amusing; but once Randolph appeared her smiles faded and she became withdrawn, even morose. Those, like Evelyn Waugh, who did not know her well and only met her with Randolph, were inclined to consider her dull and humourless. So rarely did she appear to be enjoying herself that once, when she made a joke, Waugh thought it such an exceptional event that he noted it in capital letters when writing to a friend. The poor girl, he observed, felt quite 'poorly' once she had exhausted her stock of wit.

For the most part Randolph's relationship with June was one of simmering hostility. Domestic peace was unknown to them; there were merely lulls between periods of open conflict. They 'soldiered on' together, says Randolph's sister Mary, simply for the sake of their daughter.

Randolph may have been hoping that the move to the country would make for a happier family life. If so he was mistaken. The constant stream of visitors to Oving House and Randolph's frequent visits to London and Paris reflect the same restlessness and discontent that had marked his life as a bachelor. In many repects he had changed very little over the years. His social behaviour as a married man in his forties was no more mature than it had been when, as a bachelor in his early twenties, he had created havoc at London dinner parties. He still insisted on laying down the law, still resented any show of opposition, still bullied his audience into submission and was still incapable of controlling his temper. Few of those who were forced to endure his political harrangues wished to repeat the experience. 'His conversation,' says Sir Rupert Hart-Davis, 'deteriorated into a very loud monologue. If anyone attempted to speak he would bawl "DON'T INTERRUPT ME!" and carry on with the monologue.' Arranging a dinner to which Randolph was invited was a trial which even the most adventurous hostess was reluctant to undergo.

If he can be said to have changed at all in his observance of social niceties then that change only became apparent after he had given offence. He no longer gloried – at least not so openly – in his reputation as a trouble-maker. There were even times when he displayed genuine regret at having behaved outrageously. One such occasion was when he dined with some visiting Americans. A fellow guest, the ever-attentive Cyrus Sulzberger, recorded what happened. Randolph, he says, was 'at his worst. He got completely tanked and then proceeded to insult everybody successively . . . At the end he was tottering. Finally his best friend made the cruelest remark I have ever heard: He said: "Randolph, it is perfectly plain why your father despises and hates you; he despises and hates drunkards." ' This caustic remark appears to have had its effect. The following day Randolph sent flowers to all the women who had attended the dinner, together with a note of apology. 'I should never,' read the note, 'be allowed out in private.'

This act of contrition was by no means unusual. 'I should never be allowed out in private,' was one of Randolph's wittier and, significantly, most often quoted sayings. There were few of his friends who could not remember him excuse his bad behaviour with this quip at one time or another. Indeed so often was he obliged to repeat it that, at times, he appeared more pert than penitent.

Living in the country did produce one unexpected result. Before assuming the role of biographer, Randolph embarked on another literary venture. He decided to write a book on English country houses. The idea for this book seems to have come to him while he was looking for a suitable house outside London and he had already written several chapters by the time he moved to Oving House. Knowing little of the field he was entering, he considered his idea to be not only novel but one which could be financially rewarding. He was quickly put to rights by Evelyn Waugh to whom he sent his early chapters for criticism. Could Waugh, he asked, advise him on style and architectural comment? Waugh did more than that: he told Randolph he was wasting his time.

'I do not think,' he wrote, 'that you have chosen a subject well suited to your genius. You have no appreciation of architectural beauty or of the paintings & decorations & treasures which enhance it . . . I do not know what reader you seek to interest. Certainly not the specialist or the amateur. Forgive my bluntness. This is not your proper work. You need hot, whisky-laden, contemporary breath, the telephone, the latest gossip, the tang of the New World, to bring out what is lively in you. History & Culture are for gentler creatures.'

These are wise words. Randolph would have been wise to heed them. Unfortunately they came too late. Having started on the book – he had completed chapters on Blenheim, Wilton, Chatsworth, Althorp and Hatfield – he was determined to complete it. Waugh's criticism made him more determined to do so. He intended, he said, to make the book a popular work and, in any case, he needed the money. That a good idea requires more than enthusiasm for it to be translated into a 'popular' book – let alone for the book to sell in large numbers – does not appear to have occurred to him. Faced with a challenge from his friend, and to his fortune, he pressed on with the book which was eventually published under the title of *Fifteen Famous English Homes*. Waugh's disapproval of the subject did not prevent Randolph from dedicating the book to him (Waugh had earlier dedicated *Put Out More Flags* to Randolph) and Waugh dutifully congratulated him on the 'depth of research and the elegance of presentation.' There was little more he could, in all honesty, say about this ill-advised venture. *Fifteen Famous English Homes* was not the happiest of Randolph's literary efforts.

Had he really been intent on making money, Randolph should have taken Waugh's earlier advice. He was far more qualified to write a gossipy book on a contemporary subject than he was to undertake academic or aesthetic work. With his name and reputation he would have attracted more readers with a political 'exposé' than he could hope to do with a study of English country houses. That he refused to exploit his natural talent is an indication of his newly-acquired ambitions. To have written a quick money-spinner would have meant a return to the sort of journalism from which he was trying to escape. His aim was to become a distinguished biographer, to produce works which would enhance his standing as a Churchill and an 'English gentleman'. A worthy flop was therefore of greater value to him than a sensational splash; better the homes of the great than the secrets of the second-rate. Against all odds, Randolph was determined to strive for dignity.

The pamphlet he had published privately, attacking the press barons, came much nearer to fulfilling Waugh's hopes. Dashed off in anger, it carried the stamp of sincerity. Waugh, to whom he sent it for criticism, found parts of it amusing but even he – no lover of cheap journalism – considered some of Randolph's accusations unwarranted. Others, particularly some of his former colleagues, were more incensed; they lumped him among those journalists who seek notoriety under the guise of conducting a moral crusade. Randolph's persistent sniping at the men who ran Fleet Street was courageous but it added nothing to his professional reputation. 'When he is attacking anyone,' said Robert Bruce Lockhart, 'he hits about him with a flail.'

Perhaps it was unwise of Randolph to attack the press when he was living in a house belonging to a newspaper proprietor. It may have been coincidence, but a few months after *What I Said About The Press* began circulating, he was, as Evelyn Waugh put it, 'peremptorily evicted' from Oving House. Waugh was probably exaggerating. Randolph's landlord, Lord Camrose, was an old and sick man and, a month or so before he died, he decided to give Oving House to his younger son, Michael Berry – the future Lord Hartwell. As Berry and his wife wanted to move in immediately, Randolph had to find somewhere else to live. His search for a suitable property – this time he intended to buy the house – lasted several months.

About one thing he was certain: the house, when he found it, would have to be in the country. The year he had spent in Oving House, with its delightful view over the vale of Aylesbury, had cured him of any desire to return to London. 'I found,' he was to say, 'that I liked the country life and I found I could get on with my work much better and London became less and less attractive to me.' All the same, he did not wish to live too far from London – apart from anything else, his reckless driving had recently resulted in the temporary loss of his licence and he had to do most of his house-hunting in a taxi – so he began his search by concentrating on the fashionable Home Counties. One of the first houses he looked at was a small decaying 'palace' near Bath which, until he discovered the cost of restoring the huge reception rooms, he was tempted to buy. Similar problems arose with the forty or fifty other houses he inspected in Kent, Wiltshire and Sussex; they were either too large, too small or too expensive. Not until he 'stumbled' upon a handsome, three-storied, pink-painted and many shuttered mansion on the borders of Suffolk and Essex did he find what he was looking for.

Stour, East Bergholt, stands on the crest of a hill and from its broad terraces one looks across sloping lawns to the square tower of Dedham Church, the church so often painted by Constable, and the whole scene so typical of the serene, East Anglican countryside. Randolph was immediately captivated by the view which, although not as extensive as that at Oving, had a rural charm which he found irresistible. Until then he had not seriously considered living in East Anglia; one short visit was sufficient to convince him that his earlier prejudices against the region were unfounded. 'Within five minutes of coming into the house,' he later claimed, '[we] decided this was it . . . And here I am. And here I mean to stay.'

Stay he did. Stour was to be his home, and his delight, for the rest of his life.

*   *   *

On 5 April 1955 Churchill resigned as Prime Minister and was succeeded by the recently knighted Sir Anthony Eden. The hand-over of office caused no surprise. Rumours of Churchill's impending resignation had been circulating for some time and Eden's supporters had been conducting what Randolph called a 'loud-mouthed' campaign to hasten his departure. It was a campaign which, it is said, Randolph had done his best to frustrate. Certainly Randolph's liking for Eden had not increased over the years. The ill-natured criticism he had levelled against his rival in the 1930s had continued after the war and he rarely mentioned Eden't name without a sneer. That Randolph bitterly resented the prospect of Anthony Eden assuming the role he had once coveted there can be no doubt. But, resentful as he was, he was no longer in a position to interfere in the political process. His father now kept him at arm's length as far as politics were concerned and, although Randolph continued to argue against Churchill's resignation, his word carried no weight in Conservative circles. Eden had been Deputy Prime Minister for the past three and a half years and, as Churchill did not feel fit enough to fight another election, his decision to hand over to his obvious successor could not be postponed indefinitely. All Randolph could do was bite his lip and accept the inevitable.

In public he adopted a neutral stance. On the day Churchill resigned a newspaper strike prevented the event from being fully reported in London. The provincial papers, however, carried accounts of the Prime Minister's formal visit to Buckingham Palace to take leave of the Queen and Randolph wrote an explanatory article for the *Manchester Guardian*. The articles was confined, for the most part to an outline of the constitutional obligations of an out-going Prime Minister and his successor. In it Randolph predicted that the Queen would send for Eden and ask him to take over the following day. 'Sir Anthony Eden,' he admitted, 'stands out as the obvious choice, acceptable to the overwhelming body of Conservative opinion alike in the House of Commons and the country.' Only in his concluding paragraph did he hint at his true feelings. In 1952 Anthony Eden had married Clarrissa Churchill – the daughter of Winston Churchill's brother Jack – and Randolph, who attended the wedding, had professed himself delighted at the match. He made a great show of welcoming Eden into the family. There were many who doubted his sincerity and few of his friends could have failed to recognize the implications of his reference to this family link in his article. 'Some,' he wrote in his summing up, 'who were saddened by Sir Winston's departure consoled them-selves with the fact that Lady Eden is a Churchill and were saying, happily or ironically: "There will always be a Churchill in Downing Street."' For Randolph the irony of the Churchill succession was double-edged.

His private comments on the new Prime Minister were less restrained. Never having made a secret of his doubts about Eden's abilities – or what he called 'the fundamental defects in his character' – he did not hesitate to voice them now. An incident which occurred on the day Churchill resigned reflects both Randolph's wit and his scepticism. He is said to have spent part of the day at Whites and, on leaving, he was astonished to see a policeman ticketing a car parked outside the club. This, in Randolph's eyes, was little short of sacrilege. 'The Eden terror has begun,' he gasped.

In the general election which followed Eden's assumption of office, Randolph played only a subsidiary role. He wanted to stand as a candidate but, as he ruefully explained, 'no one asked him.' Apart from being photographed with his head on a table while his father was addressing a meeting at Chigwell in Essex, his electioneering activities attracted little attention. What did bring him into prominence were his writings as a political commentator.

Earlier that year, Randolph had signed a contract to write an article a week for the *Evening Standard*. With the general election expected he had also agreed – of his own free will and without being paid extra – to write two additional articles a week during the election campaign. As Charles Wintour, the Deputy Editor of the *Evening Standard* later explained, Randolph was 'very anxious to write about the election.' Of particular interest to Randolph was the campaign that was waged in twelve marginal seats in Lancashire. He was still deeply interested in Lancastrian affairs – Lord Derby, whose biography he was writing, was popularly known as the 'King of Lancaster' – and he naturally paid particular attention to the election struggle in that county. So much so that, shortly after the campaign opened, he decided to combine a research trip to Lord Derby's Lancashire house, Knowsley Hall, with a tour of the twelve marginal seats. It was this combination of interests – literary and political – that involved Randolph in his first widely publicised legal action.

The article he wrote for the *Evening Standard* on 12 May 1955 was, to say the least, outspoken. He had just attended a meeting in Lancashire at which Mr Cyril Lord, the well-known carpet and textile tycoon, had predicted that the Conservatives would lose every seat in the area. Randolph was incensed. He dismissed Cyril Lord's prediction as 'nonsense' and described his anti-Government campaign as 'loud-mouthed vapourings'. This, not surprisingly, provoked a counter-attack. It came, not out of the blue, but from a long-standing antagonist. The following Sunday the Labour-supporting *People* published a column headed 'Voters Beware' which purported to answer Randolph's article about Cyril Lord. Political as the column was in content, the writer obviously intended to pay off some old scores. 'Most of all,' he warned, 'beware of party propagandists – those who haven't seen fit to fight openly for a seat but prefer to be paid hacks, paid to write biased accounts of the campaign. Chief among these – as usual – is Randolph Churchill, that slightly comic son of our greatest statesman, who poses as a political expert, but whose offer to serve as an MP was rejected time and again . . .'

To be labelled a paid hack and, by implication, a coward, in the space of a few lines was more than Randolph was prepared to take. However, angry as he was, he decided to react with caution. He immediately wrote a letter of protest to *The People* in which, in his final paragraph, he suggested that they should publish his letter in full together with a retraction. If this were done, he said, he would be prepared to let the matter drop. His letter was duly published in *The People* but the concluding paragraph was cut and his request for a retraction ignored. Randolph had no alternative but to sue for libel.

His decision to resort to legal action was not taken lightly. Recognizing the need to present a convincing case, he went into training. He briefed himself on points of law, rehearsed his evidence, and sought expert advice. Among the people he consulted was his friend John Sutro who had earlier been called to the Bar and, for a short period, had practised as a barrister. Sutro was summoned to Stour for a week-end to assist in the rehearsal. Not the least of Randolph's fears was that, under cross-examination, he might be provoked into losing his temper; he was determined to test himself before entering the witness box and persuaded Sutro to act as devil's advocate. Sutro, already impressed by Randolph's grasp of the case, was astonished at his confidence as a witness. 'Each day,' he says, 'I would cross-examine Randolph in detail; I could not, try as I might, shake his conviction and veracity.' Only in the use of court language did Randolph prove less than perfect. When addressing the imaginary judge his remarks tended to be over-emphatic. 'My Lord,' he would protest, 'must I go on listening to this insufferable nonsense?' 'No Randolph,' explained Sutro, 'you must say, "My Lord, may I have guidance".'

By the time the case came up for hearing in the High Court, on 9 October 1956, Randolph was ready for battle. He acquitted himself magnificently. Not only did he remain calm, but he responded to questioning with wit and shrewdness. Asked why he objected to being described as a 'paid hack' when, at the long-remembered Foyles literary luncheon, he had called the editor of the *Sunday Dispatch* an 'old hack', his answer was disarming. At the literary luncheon, he explained, he had been talking about a race and in that context the term 'hack' – as used for horses – was not abusive. When the defending counsel went on to suggest that anyone who described another person's opinions as 'loud-mouthed vapourings' must be expected to be answered 'in somewhat appropriate terms', Randolph's reply was equally effective. 'I don't think,' he snapped, 'lies are ever appropriate.' This, in fact, was the ground upon which his case was based. He repeatedly insisted that he was not objecting to the language used by *The People* but to the lies printed in the newspaper.

He was helped by the fact that the defence called no witnesses and relied on what his lawyer described as 'Yo, ho, ho! and a bottle of rum tactics.' In his own support, on the other hand, Randolph was able to produce some convincing evidence. Not every journalist was prepared to back Fleet Street. Charles Wintour, of the *Evening Standard*, testified to Randolph's integrity. He referred to an article, written in 1954, in which Randolph had attacked the Conservative Government led by his own father. 'That,' said Wintour, 'marked him out at once as a journalist of very marked courage and independence.' Tom Hopkinson, as a free-lance journalist, told how Randolph had supported him in a fight against editorial inter- ference. He would never, he said, describe Mr Churchill as a 'hack'. A more surprising witness was Michael Foot, who had lost his Devonport seat in the 1955 election. He supported Randolph both as a journalist and as a politician. Was Mr Churchill, he was asked, the kind of person who preferred not to fight openly? His reply was emphatic. Mr Churchill, he said, had given no 'indication of not wanting to fight when he came to Devonport.'

The jury took three-quarters of an hour to decide on a verdict. They found in favour of the plaintiff. Randolph was awarded £5,000 with costs. The preparation he had put into fighting the case had been justified. So, to a lesser extent, had his crusade against the press barons. To add substance to his victory, he revised his pamphlet *What I Said About The Press*, included a verbatim account of the trial, and published it in book form the following year.

*　　　*　　　*

During the trial mention had been made of Randolph's attacks on the new Prime Minister. In one of his articles in the *Evening Standard* he had accused Anthony Eden of 'whining', and the defence counsel had claimed that the same could have been said of Randolph. A more diligent search through those articles would have produced many similar examples of Randolph's invective. Over the past year his criticism of Eden, always biting, had become positively virulent. He rarely wrote about the Prime Minister without employing a string of derogatory adjectives. As Eden's biographer has put it, Randolph's *Evening Standard* column bristled with 'personal venom'.

Added spice was given to these attacks by the fact that they appeared in the Beaverbrook press. If nothing else, they proved beyond doubt that Randolph was not a 'paid hack' who wrote to please his masters. Malcolm Muggeridge, who sympathized with Randolph's views, pointed this out in an article which he had written for the *New Statesman* several months before the trial. 'Mr Churchill,' he observed, 'has used the platform Lord Beaverbrook has provided to assail Lord Beaverbrook's current favourite, Sir Anthony Eden. This must be counted to him for virtue. He might perfectly well have swelled the Beaverbrookian chorus of praise of his father's chosen successor. To judge from past experience, it is also probably true that, by employing Mr Churchill, Lord Beaverbrook is preparing a rod for his own back. Other newspaper proprietors have likewise employed him, and look what has happened to them! For myself, I would not have him otherwise.'

Other journalists admired Randolph's courage but deplored his tactics. One of these was Robert Bruce Lockhart, who was both a friend and an admirer of Anthony Eden. Randolph, claimed Lockhart, was 'not perturbed by "The Establishment" . . . Doubtless, he regards all politicians as fair game. But there are limits, and more than once his attacks on Anthony Eden provided fodder for the Moscow *Pravda*.'

Such reservations were not shared by Randolph's friends at Whites. Here an anti-Eden faction revelled in referring to the Prime Minister as 'the Jerk'. The nickname appealed to Randolph; he seldom spoke of Anthony Eden without using it. Not everyone, however, found this brand of schoolboy humour amusing. Randolph's father considered it highly offensive. This was made dramatically clear shortly after Eden had become Prime Minister. Randolph and June were visiting Chartwell at the time and Randolph's taunts about 'Jerk Eden' made Churchill so angry that it was feared that he would have a heart attack. No less angry, Randolph stormed out of the room, declaring that he would leave the house and never see his father again. June, who had already gone to bed, was woken up and told to dress and pack. Their departure was prevented by Churchill who, at one o'clock that morning, arrived at their bedroom in his pyjamas. 'I am going to die soon,' he announced. 'I cannot go to bed without composing a quarrel.' With that he kissed them both. Peace, of a sort, was restored.

But nothing could reconcile Randolph to Anthony Eden. He continued to attack the Prime Minister both in the *Evening Standard* and in private. His well-publicised hostility produced an unexpected result. In June 1956, he was approached by a publisher to write a life of Anthony Eden. The publisher was a millionaire named Howard Samuel who, having made his fortune by buying up cheap properties during the war, had recently acquired the publishing firm of MacGibbon and Kee. Randolph appears not to have been aware of Samuel's reputation and found his suggestion enticing. They met to discuss the project over a boozy luncheon at the Savoy Grill. The more Samuel talked, the more interested Randolph became. Eventually he decided to summon his literary agent, Graham Watson of Curtis Brown, to discuss terms. Watson, who had never before met Samuel, was immediately on his guard. He arrived at the Savoy to find a half-empty bottle of brandy on the table and Randolph in an expansive mood. 'It did not,' he says, 'seem to me a propitious moment for doing business.' Nor was he encouraged by Samuel's aggressive attitude. But his reservations – which included a protest that Randolph was already under option to another publisher – were brushed aside and the negotiations went ahead.

Randolph set to work with his usual enthusiasm. The year before, when he had been toying with the idea of writing a lengthy article on Eden, he had frantically telephoned his friends for gossip; he now realized that his research needed to be more detailed and political. Things were further complicated when, a week after signing the contract, Colonel Nasser nationalised the Suez Canal. In the crisis which followed, Randolph was torn between his bellicose patriotism and his reluctance to support any move made by Anthony Eden. At first patriotism triumphed but by the time that the sorry affair had ended – and brought about Eden's resignation – Randolph had changed his mind. Not surprisingly, he came to the conclusion that 'the Suez adventure had been a mistake'. His book, which had started out as a straight biography, ended up as *The Rise and Fall of Sir Anthony Eden*.

Seen in the perspective of history, it was not a good book. To call it a study of the Prime Minister would be a misnomer; it was a badly balanced, obviously biased account of Anthony Eden's career, reflecting more spite than scholarship. Inevitably a disproportionate amount of space was devoted to speculation about the Suez fiasco. One woman, to whom Randolph sent his Suez chapters for criticism, considered his approach so 'brutal' that she objected to the book being published during Eden's lifetime. Randolph brushed her protests aside. Eden, he told her, might live for 'many more years. Is it your view that in that event total silence should be observed on these grave matters?' Other critics agreed with him. At the time, the book was considered to be well-informed and its value was enhanced by revelations of 'collusion' which were then regarded as startling and controversial. That erstwhile champion of Eden, Lord Beaverbrook, was so taken with the book that he decided to serialize it in the *Daily Express*. The newspaper extracts appeared between 1 and 10 December 1958. They created a stir; a stir which was once more to prompt Randolph into legal action.

This time there was no question of party political bias; for Randolph's attacker was a fellow Conservative. The attack came from the flamboyant Tory MP for Kidderminster, Gerald Nabarro. An admirer of Anthony Eden, Nabarro considered that the Suez campaign should have been a 'national crusade' and was incensed by the *Daily Express*'s extracts from Randolph's book. He particularly objected to a passage in which Randolph apparently disclosed details of a Cabinet meeting which, being secret, could not be openly refuted by Anthony Eden. It was this passage which decided Nabarro 'to have a go at Randolph Churchill'. An opportunity for him to do so came when, on 6 December 1958, Nabarro addressed a Conservative Club at Halesowen in Worcestershire. Without waiting for the *Daily Express* serialization to be completed, he singled out the offending passage for stinging criticism. For Randolph to have included it in his book, declared Nabarro, 'was a pernicious, cowardly and uncalled-for action in the present circumstances.'

'Mr Churchill,' he went on, 'made his attack in the newspapers, knowing full well that Sir Anthony Eden could not reply. That is the action of a coward. I grieve that these things should have been done when Sir Anthony, like other Ministers of that time, cannot reveal Cabinet secrets in his lifetime, and has to remain silent.'

Again Randolph had been called a coward. He reacted as might have been foreseen. A reporter from the *Sunday Express* telephoned him that evening to tell him about Nabarro's speech and Randolph immediately sent telegrams to Nabarro's home, office and the House of Commons. 'You are reported,' he wired, 'by the Press Association to have said at a public meeting in your constituency that my writings were "cowardly". You are further reported to have called me a "coward". I call upon you to retract these words immediately or face the consequences of an action for slander.' At the same time he contacted the Press Association and warned them what he would do if the speech was reported in the press.

No report of the speech was published and Nabarro, through his solicitors, denied having made the accusation. But Randolph had no intention of allowing the matter to end there. He gave Nabarro ten weeks to retract and then, having received no reply, went ahead with the prosecution.

The hearing in the High Court, in October 1960, lasted three days. Randolph's main concern, of course, was to clear himself of the charge of cowardice. His counsel cited his war record and the fearless crusade he had waged against the press barons. The suggestion that he had attacked a defenceless politician was strongly contested. Anthony Eden, it was pointed out, was engaged with writing his own biography for a fee of £100,000 and could have answered Randolph had he wished. Great play was made, by the defence, of the provisions of the Official Secrets Act. Asked when he had first heard of this act, Randolph's reply was succinct. 'I suppose in the cradle,' he quipped. But he adamantly denied that he had divulged state secrets. 'I do have quite a lot of inside information,' he admitted, 'but I rather make a point of not trying to parade it. I could tell you a great deal more of this than I put in the articles . . . If what I was told I thought injurious to the interests of the state I would not think of publishing it.'

On the question of his animosity towards Anthony Eden he was equally emphatic. He admitted that he had described Eden as 'a man of exceptional vanity' but claimed that his criticism was not inspired by personal dislike. On the contrary, he said, 'I like him very much personally and he is married to a dearly loved cousin; but I have never admired him as a statesman . . . I have always taken the view that Sir Anthony would not be a successful Prime Minister. That has been my view over the last 25 years and I think my views have been vindicated by the results.'

In his summing up the judge told the jury that, among other things, they had to decide whether Nabarro had spoken in malice. 'It is not malicious,' he explained, 'to refuse to apologise. But if you know that you were wrong, and you still refuse to apologise, that might show malice.' The verdict was in Randolph's favour. This time he was awarded £1,500 damages, plus costs.

*　　　*　　　*

Much as Randolph longed to distinguish himself as a biographer, he was unable to cut himself off from Fleet Street. The rough and tumble of the newspaper world appealed to his combative nature and, as he was always saying, he needed the money he could earn as a journalist. He liked to boast that, with the exception of the *Daily Worker*, he had worked at one time or another on every national newspaper. And not only was he a political commentator but he wrote about the press – in weeklies like the *Spectator* – and even reported on social events. He was always to be seen at international press conferences, baiting official spokesmen with his loud, often crudely expressed, questions which even the hardened Press corps found offensive. 'On occasion,' it is said, 'they had to shout him down.'

One of his regular commissions was his weekly column for the *News of the World*. This dealt with topical, mainly political, events and often involved him in overseas travel. When he was not at Stour, he was to be found wandering the globe on behalf of the *News of the World* or the *Evening Standard*. But, active as he remained, he was no longer an enthusiastic seeker of news and scandal. A combination of heavy drinking and disillusionment had made him cynical and he undertook most of his assignments with reluctance. His journalism had, for the most part, become half-hearted and slip-shod.

This was apparent when, in 1956, he went to Cyprus shortly before the deportation of Archbishop Makarios. He stayed in the same hotel as James Cameron – and most of the other newsmen – but held himself aloof. Cameron, whom he liked, was one of the few journalists he saw regularly. 'I was his exact contemporary,' says Cameron. 'He disliked younger reporters and anyone he thought was a "Red" – which, by his assessment meant most other journalists.' Randolph's lack of sociability, however, did not prevent him drinking. Nor did it improve his concentration. He was unable to give his full attention to the Cyprus crisis and was inclined to blame the British Foreign Office for allowing the situation to get out of hand. So pronounced was his apathy that, on one occasion, he was completely at a loss about what to write and stormed about the hotel complaining that he had left it too late to file his story. Then he had a brain-wave – or so he thought. Sending for James Cameron, he announced triumphantly that he had hit upon a splendid opening for his article. It consisted of two lines from an Edward Lear nonsense verse, starting 'There was an old man with a beard . . .' But, having thus introduced Makarios, he was unable to proceed any further. After begging Cameron to help him, Randolph continued drinking until he flaked out unconscious. Cameron looked at him despairingly and then ground out 1,000 words, signed them in Randolph's name, and sent them to the *News of the World*. 'No one,' says Cameron, 'ever knew that Randolph had not written the piece.'

Only on his visits to the United States did Randolph seem to regain his journalistic zest. American politics fascinated him and he was never happier than when he was in Washington. He was there in late 1956 to cover the American election in which General Eisenhower, who was seeking re-election, was challenged by Adlai Stevenson. Randolph was no admirer of Eisenhower's political abilities and the war-time partnership between Churchill and President Roosevelt had turned him into a Democratic Party supporter. (So impressed was Randolph with Roosevelt that he once told Cyrus Sulzberger that he considered the President 'was in many ways a greater man than his own father and that, above all, he was the greatest politician who ever lived, one who really *knew* public opinion.') During this 1956 election Randolph's Democratic sympathies were very much in evidence. Not until he met Eisenhower's running-mate, Richard Nixon, did he have a slight change of mind. He interviewed Nixon in a car, on the way to Washington airport, and admitted that he had been won-over by the prospective vice-President. Nixon, he declared, was 'a very fine fellow. Quite grown up.' That, in Randolph's phraseology, was praise indeed. 'I am the only man in the world,' he joked later, 'who supports a Stevenson-Nixon ticket.'

Doors opened more easily in America now than they did in England. He was by no means isolated from British politics, but he was no longer trusted by the men who had once supplied him with information. Even that most stalwart of Churchill's disciples, his old childhood ally, Brendan Bracken, had at last deserted him. 'I couldn't be on worse terms with R.S.C.,' Bracken wrote to a friend, shortly before his death. 'He is a raucous bore and, what is worse, never says a good word about anyone. The combination of a noisy mind and a sharp tongue is too much to bear.' The relationship between Randolph and Bracken had, it is true, never been harmonious. Randolph was plainly jealous of Bracken's intimacy with his father and that jealousy had often erupted into outright hostility. Bracken, on the other hand, had tolerated Randolph for Churchill's sake; it was only when Randolph appeared to be tormenting his father that Bracken hit back. All the same, it is to Randolph's credit that when, in August 1956, Bracken died, he paid his strange, enigmatic rival a gracious tribute. Writing in the *Evening Standard*, the day Bracken died, he showed a willingness to forget past differences.

'Despite the ups and downs I have had with him over 35 years,' Randolph's obituary notice concluded, 'I have no hesitation or lack of breath in this valedictory fanfare: "You were always on the good side: you loved truth and honour; you hated cruelty and injustice: fare thee well, my gifted, true and many sided friend."'

Randolph's one political solace during these years was in seeing Harold Macmillan succeed Anthony Eden. Macmillan was one of the few contemporary British politicians whom Randolph truly admired. As far back as 1944 he had announced his intention of backing Macmillan for the Premiership and now, after Eden's unwelcomed term of office, he was delighted to see his candidate installed in 10 Downing Street. He even gained some kudos from the event himself. During the period when speculation was rife as to whether Macmillan or R. A. Butler would step into Eden's shoes, Randolph – acting, it is said, on a tip he received from Lord Beaverbrook – confidently predicted Macmillan's success in the *Evening Standard*. His scoop was made doubly pleasing by the fact

329

that he not only favoured the winner in this contest but was strongly opposed to the loser. If R. A. Butler was denied the post vacated by Eden, he could at least claim to have inherited the contempt which Randolph had once reserved for Eden. From now on the unlucky Mr Butler was to be the prime target for Randolph's political barbs.

With Harold Macmillan as Prime Minister, Randolph's enthusiasm for British politics revived. His keen interest in the new administration was reflected in his activities as a journalist. When, in February 1959, Macmillan visited the Soviet Union – the first such visit since the war – Randolph eagerly accepted Lord Beaverbrook's commission to cover the event for the *Evening Standard*. So eager was he, in fact, that he tried to wangle a flight on the Prime Minister's plane. Arriving at Downing Street, he offered to pay his own way and claimed that, as a passenger, he would be saving money for the British tax-payer. Macmillan gave 'an unamused no.' Denied his lift, Randolph was obliged to join the huge party of British journalists who left England two days in advance of the Prime Minister. When Macmillan arrived at Moscow airport, one of the first sights he saw was Randolph, standing in the snow wearing a bright yellow pullover but with neither hat nor coat to protect him from the biting winds.

Randolph's visit to Moscow was nothing if not lively. Robin Day, who was among the party of journalists, recalls how he 'heckled Foreign Office spokesmen mercilessly, and stormed at the Intourist about his hotel accommodation.' But his most sensational achievement was in obtaining an interview with the notorious Guy Burgess who, together with Donald Maclean, had defected to Russia eight years earlier. Although Burgess had been at Eton at the same time as Randolph, they did not know each other well but this did not prevent Randolph from recognizing his old school fellow when Burgess arrived at his hotel. 'I knew it was Burgess,' he was to say, 'because he was wearing an Old Etonian tie. The only other people in Moscow entitled to wear one were myself and the Prime Minister.' Apparently he thought that not even a Communist would dare to usurp this privilege.

The Burgess interview which Randolph despatched – to the chagrin of the other journalists – from Moscow must be counted among his scoops. It also prompted him to an act of kindness. Burgess was worried about his elderly mother who lived in London and whom he was anxious to visit but he feared that if he set foot in England he would be detained. He asked Randolph to help him to obtain safe conduct for the visit. Never one to turn his back on a past acquaintance in need, Randolph promised to do what he could. He had no sympathy for Burgess's treachery but felt that this particular request called for magnanimity on the part of the British authorities. So, shortly after Harold Macmillan arrived in Moscow, Randolph telephoned Harold Evans, the civil servant who was the Prime Minister's public relations adviser, and invited him to lunch.

When Evans arrived at Randolph's hotel, he discovered him living amid scenes of faded splendour. Randolph's rantings at the Intourist had resulted in him acquiring a royal suite which, according to Evans, exuded 'a musty elegance compounded of red velvet and a profusion of gilt mirrors.' Apparently Randolph had insisted on being given this suite on the grounds that it had once been occupied by his father. There was, however, nothing royal about Randolph's appearance. 'He was still in pyjamas and dressing gown,' says Evans, 'both flung carelessly open to reveal a manly chest. At a table in the middle of this long salon sat a dumpy Intourist girl attempting to take dictation – "attempting" because Randolph was striding majestically round and round the table, catching many-angled glimpses of himself in the long mirrors, and punctuating his dictation with diatribes against the Soviet political system.' The dictation lasted almost an hour.

Then over a makeshift luncheon of omelettes and whisky, Randolph explained Burgess's predicament to Evans. He asked for the matter to be brought to Macmillan's attention, claiming that an act of clemency would work wonders for public relations. Evans agreed to speak to the Prime Minister but warned that it would take time. Macmillan, he said, was extremely busy and Burgess's request would have to take its place at the end of the queue. But patience was not one of Randolph's virtues. At two o'clock the following morning, Evans was startled out of his sleep by a telephone call. Randolph was on the line demanding to know what was being done about Burgess. He threatened that if something was not done soon he would write a piece for his newspaper accusing the Prime Minister of inhumanity and 'there'll be a goddam awful public row.' Evans, he thundered, had better get moving or else . . .

This was too much for Evans. Every bit as angry as Randolph, he answered him in kind. Macmillan, he shouted, was 'not in Moscow to dish out favours for defectors. The British public didn't give a damn about Burgess.' He was not in the least worried about Randolph's threats to denounce the Prime Minister. Randolph, in short, could go to hell.

And there the matter ended. Burgess later approached other journalists and asked them to help him but their efforts were no more successful than Randolph's had been. As George Hutchinson – who accompanied Randolph to Russia – says, 'Macmillan was too old a hand to allow himself to become directly involved in Burgess's affairs, least of all in the capital of the Soviet Union.' But Randolph's attempt at intervention is not without significance. It illustrates, once again, the value he attached to even the most remote of friendships.

Randolph's visit to the Soviet Union was cut short soon after he arrived in Kiev. Here he received some news for which he had been waiting and which demanded his immediate attention. It concerned a bid he was then making to return to active politics.

*   *   *

The controversy surrounding the sitting member for Bournemouth East and Christchurch, Nigel Nicolson, had been raging for some months. During the Suez crisis, Nicolson had angered right-wing Tories in the constituency by his open opposition to Anthony Eden. So angry had they become that they threatened to nominate a new candidate for the seat at the forthcoming general election. This threat had not only divided the local Conservative Association but had received nation-wide publicity. Bournemouth East was a safe Conservative seat and the prospect of it becoming vacant had excited many would-be Tory candidates. Not least among these hopefuls was Randolph who, on 16 January 1959, had informed the Press Association that he wished to fight Bournemouth East 'in the interests of the Conservative Party.'

The fact that Randolph had not been invited to stand worried him not at all. Nor did a critical report from Bournemouth which appeared in *The Times* the following day. 'Few people here,' claimed the report, 'are greatly impressed by Mr Churchill's offer . . . If Mr Churchill's name comes before the adoption committee it will be considered, but unless there is a change of heart on the part of the executive he is unlikely to be chosen.' The objection to Randolph was, of course, similar to the objection to Nigel Nicolson. Both men were anti-Suez. A couple of weeks earlier, the extracts from Randolph's book, *The Rise and Fall of Sir Anthony Eden*, had appeared in the *Daily Express* and those extracts had left no doubt in anyone's mind about his attitude to the Suez war. Nonetheless, Randolph remained hopeful.

He replied to the reported criticism from Bournemouth in a television interview with Robin Day. The interview did nothing to improve his chances. He intended to stand, he said, with or without official support. Back in his old 1930s stride, he was full of confidence and answered Robin Day's questioning with assumed geniality. Among other things, he claimed to know 'a great deal more about politics than at least half the Conservative MPs' and went on to say: 'I don't think they know much about politics, these

332

people at Bournemouth.' As far as Suez was concerned, he admitted that he had changed his mind about the affair because he now knew 'a great deal more than I knew at the time.' In any case, he added, Suez was a 'dead duck.' He had not offered himself as an official candidate, he said, because he did not fancy 'standing in a queue' and answering questions about whether he would live in the constituency. But his greatest gaffe came at the end of the interview when he told Robin Day that he thought Nigel Nicolson was 'an able man and a good MP' and that he would not have dreamed of challenging Nicolson had he been the official candidate.

Revelling in the controversy, Randolph visited Bournemouth. He set himself up in a hotel and grandly invited local Tories to visit him. The response was hardly overwhelming. Only four constituents turned up, two of whom arrived under the misapprehension that Randolph had come to support Nigel Nicolson. However, he did receive an invitation to visit the local Conservative Association. Afterwards the chairman told reporters that he was 'very pleased to have a chat with Mr Churchill. Although he has not applied through the normal channels we shall none the less consider him along with other applicants.' The following day Randolph announced that he had applied to be put on the official list of candidates.

His decision to join 'the queue' was greeted with much merriment. In the *Evening Standard* the cartoonist, Vicky, depicted him bursting into the Committee Room at Bournemouth East saying: 'I hear you are looking for a nice, solid, dependable candidate.' Comic it must all have seemed, but there was no mistaking the fact that Randolph was again in the running for a seat in the House of Commons.

Whether he would be adopted depended, in the first place, on the decision of the Bournemouth East Conservative Association concerning Nigel Nicolson. On the advice of Lord Hailsham, the matter was put to a postal ballot. The result of that ballot was still pending when Randolph left for Russia. It was announced on 27 February: by a narrow margin of 91 votes the Bournemouth Tories rejected Nicolson as their candidate in the next general election, but agreed that he should continue as their MP until the date of the election was decided.

On being informed that Nicolson had been defeated, Randolph announced that he would leave Kiev immediately and return to England. Five days later he was back in Bournemouth. He had come, he told reporters, to 'carry out my reconnaissance'. Exactly what that reconnaissance entailed he would not say, but, whatever it was, it proved unsuccessful. The Bournemouth Tories spurned Randolph as decisively as they had spurned Nigel Nicolson.

Randolph accepted defeat with his usual blend of cynicism and defiance. 'I do not,' he declared, 'wish to represent a lot of stuffy old ladies from Bournemouth. I want to fight for really hard-pressed people.'

But his chances of fighting for anyone, hard-pressed or not, were now little more than dreams. In the general election of 1959, he was again obliged to follow events from the sidelines. His only notable intervention in the campaign came, on 10 September, when he tried to get an interim injunction to restrain the Labour party from using extracts from *The Rise and Fall of Sir Anthony Eden* in their pamphlet *The Tory Swindle 1951-1959*. Despite his determined efforts – he summoned his lawyer to Stour for an all-night meeting to prepare his case – he did not succeed. During the hearing, however, it was emphasised that Randolph was not acting as a party politician but as an author defending his copyright.

For politics had finally given way to literature. Although Randolph may not have realised it at the time, his involvement in the Bournemouth East nomination contest was to be his last serious attempt to re-enter parliament.

CHAPTER SEVENTEEN

The End at Stour

On 18 November 1959, *The Times* announced that Mr Randolph Churchill was seeking an injunction to restrain William Heinemann Ltd from publishing his book, *Lord Derby: King of Lancashire*, 'in a form other than that written by him.' Once again Randolph's talent for turning a trivial incident into a full-scale controversy was being demonstrated. This time it was threatening his career as a biographer.

The dispute between Randolph and his publisher was, on the face of it, a trifling one. It arose from Randolph's love of gossip. Not content with causing offence with his indiscreet table-talk, he had decided to include some embarrassing disclosures in his book. Not surprisingly, his publisher had objected and asked for certain cuts to be made. Randolph's refusal to make these cuts had resulted in him applying for a legal injunction. That a court case might prevent the book from being published at all was, to him, of secondary importance. He was apparently willing to sacrifice five years work for little more than a footnote.

For sacrifice it would undoubtedly have been. Randolph's research for this, his first major biography, was nothing if not thorough. No less than six research assistants had been employed to help him comb Lord Derby's extensive archives and – surprisingly, for an untried biographer – he had been given access to the carefully guarded Royal Archives at Windsor. Three secretaries assisted with the shorthand and typing and the book was read by 'numerous friends', including Harold Nicolson and Robert Blake, before it was submitted to the publisher. Such was Randolph's attention to detail that the final version of *Lord Derby: King of Lancashire* ran to 618 pages and approximately 300,000 words.

Yet, swamped as he was by original material, Randolph – as several reviewers were to remark – still found room for the occasional diversion. One of these concerned General E. L. Spears, a wartime commander of whom Randolph had long been critical; strictly speaking there was no need for Randolph to dwell on General Spears's career. So slight was Spears's association with Lord

Derby that his background was irrelevant to the theme of the book. That Randolph devoted almost a page to a discussion of the General's character and early years in the army is an indication of his weakness for gossip. What fascinated him was the mystery that was thought to surround Spears's origins: no one was quite sure where the General had been born, who his parents were, or where he had been educated.

In his efforts to probe this mystery, Randolph had put his researchers to work. They had unearthed some interesting, but inconclusive, evidence. Spears, it seems, had been born in Paris and his family had lived in France for three generations. More to Randolph's point was the fact that the family name was originally Speirs, which the General had anglicized to Spears in August 1918. This discovery merely whetted Randolph's appetite; he began to make enquiries of his own. Sir Rupert Hart-Davis, who was then married to Spears's stepdaughter, remembers receiving an urgent midnight telephone call from Randolph. 'Can you, my dear Rupert,' he was asked, 'confirm the fact that Spears is an Alsatian Jew?' Sir Rupert was unable to help. Nor, apparently, could anyone else. The only result of Randolph's enquiries was that General Spears got to hear about them and, aware of Randolph's hostility, immediately became suspicious. His suspicions alerted Randolph's publishers who wisely suggested the cuts which Randolph refused to make.

Both sides, as things turned out, were making a fuss about nothing. The squabble between Randolph and Heinemann was settled and when the book was eventually published, in April 1960, Randolph's bombshell failed to explode. Not only had he safeguarded himself by making several complimentary remarks about General Spears but his mention of the General's change of name proved to be of little interest. Roy Jenkins, reviewing the book for the *Spectator*, was almost alone in referring to Randolph's injunction. And even he dismissed it as nonsensical.

'After reading the book,' he wrote, 'which took me two months of intermittent application, one's first thought is that no one need have worried. General Spears (who thought he was libelled) could have shown a thicker skin, Messrs Heinemann a stronger nerve, and Mr Churchill a less frenzied attachment to every detail of his own work. They could all have safely depended upon the protective covering of the mountain of words in which Mr Churchill has chosen to bury Lord Derby. Passages from the inmost recesses of this book are likely to remain as firmly hidden from the public gaze as the contents of a long lost (and little sought after) tomb.'

Roy Jenkins thought that *Lord Derby: King of Lancashire* was

336

overlong, far too detailed and that it exaggerated the importance of Derby's political career and influence. 'My view is,' he wrote, 'that Mr Churchill conceived of his task as being the next best thing to writing a royal biography.' His opinion was shared by several other reviewers. Derby, commented a reviewer in *The Times*, was 'now no more than a name, if that, to many people, although he lived until 1948. His is one of those tricky cases for a biographer of a man who rose high in the service of the state, but not quite high enough to allow for uncomplex treatment as a man of action.'

Inevitably the book was reviewed by a number of critics who knew Randolph as a controversial political journalist and, aware of his inability to resist a gossipy aside or a derogatory comment, they were quick to pounce on any evidence of what one of them called 'tiresome personal interjections.' *The Times Literary Supplement*, for instance, claimed that the main themes of the book were 'interspersed with comments on current politics and anecdotes about the great which vary from the mildly irrelevant to the frankly offensive. They tend to give a misleading impression of journalistic dogginess to what is in fact a serious and valuable work.' Such criticism was not entirely fair. Randolph's occasional lapses were so minor as to pass unnoticed by the general reader. If anything, the book suffered more from the rather pompous prose style Randolph adopted than it did from any suggestion of 'journalistic dogginess'. This was remarked upon in an article about Randolph which appeared in the *Observer* later that year. 'As a writer,' it commented, 'except when moved to passion or fury, his prose can be dull and ponderous in an empty Augustan manner, though it often has subtleties which are easily overlooked and the structure of the argument is strong and formidable.' True as this was, Randolph's standing as a biographer continued to be overshadowed by his reputation as a trouble-maker.

But *Lord Derby: King of Lancashire* was not without its admirers. Paul Johnson, writing in the *New Statesman*, even welcomed Randolph's wordiness. Taken together with the recently published two-volume life of Ernest Bevin, he said, the book marked a return to the 'proper tradition' of comprehensive political biography which presented the 'raw material of a man on which future historians can work at leisure.' Even the most severe of critics had to admit that Randolph's biography was well-informed, thoroughly researched and made a useful contribution to contemporary history. Harold Macmillan was later to claim that the 'life of Lord Derby is the best picture of the politics of that period that I have read.'

*   *   *

In Britain, 1960 was known as 'Africa Year'. It opened with Harold Macmillan's six week tour of the African Commonwealth countries, starting in Ghana and ending in Cape Town – where the Prime Minister made his famous 'winds of change' speech to the South African parliament. From then on hardly a month passed without one or other of the countries in the Dark Continent featuring prominently in the news. Randolph followed these events with more than usual interest.

Both as a political journalist and as a private individual, he felt unable to take sides in the arguments raging over the struggle towards African independence. His attitude towards that struggle was both muddled and typical. It has been summed up, in part, by one of his press colleagues, Stephen Barber. 'Randolph,' says Barber, 'tended, most of his days, to line up on the side of the underdogs of the world. While he was not notably sentimental about Africa's downtrodden blacks, for example, he was none the less contemptuous of those who thought themselves superior by virtue of the colour of their skins.' But his contempt was not strong enough to smother his authoritarian instincts or his desire to preserve the last remnants of the former British Empire. In the same way that his father had opposed Indian independence in the 1930s, Randolph opposed the ending of British responsibility in Africa.

He made no attempt to disguise his sympathies. His views were succinctly expressed in a brief exchange of letter to *The Times* in February 1960. It followed the announcement that the British Labour party intended to support a boycott of South African goods. Randolph immediately wrote to *The Times* condemning the boycott. His attack was directed at the leaders of the Labour party and he gave no reasoned explanation for his opposition. He was answered by an African who accused him of being 'worried about his sherry.' This prompted Randolph to a characteristic reply. 'Though the matter seems scarcely worth mentioning,' he protested, 'I very seldom drink sherry; but as my contribution to Africa Year I am making South African sherry available to my cook and guests during 1960 and particularly during March the month of the boycott.' Randolph was storming the barricades with a bottle in his hand.

As it happened he was unable to supply South African sherry during the month of March. He was far too busy touring the African continent on behalf of the *News of the World*. At the beginning of March he flew to Salisbury in Rhodesia (now Harare in Zimbawe) together with a team of journalists who were accompanying Iain Macleod, the Secretary of State for Colonies; Macleod, an old friend of Randolph's, was embarked on a delicate mission. His purpose in flying to Rhodesia was to secure the release of Dr Hastings Banda – the future President of Malawi – who was then imprisoned at Gwelo, some ninety miles from Salisbury. By doing this he hoped to end the existing state of emergency. Knowing how fierce right-wing opposition to his proposal was, Macleod was anxious to avoid unnecessary publicity, particularly as he hoped to persuade Dr Banda to broadcast an appeal for peace before the news of his release broke. On hearing that Randolph intended accompanying him, Macleod had become doubly apprehensive. 'The last thing I wanted,' he confessed, 'was to have Randolph's genius for uncovering secrets added to my worries.' At first he thought he had succeeded in avoiding Randolph. There was no sign of him when Macleod arrived at London airport. Nor was Randolph to be seen on the plane. Congratulating himself, Macleod fastened his seat-belt and waited for the take-off. 'Then,' he says, 'nothing happened, and we waited and waited. Finally after a small commotion Randolph appeared through the pilot's cabin. Brushing aside my papers and my civil servants Randolph seated himself beside me. "Ho!" he said. "I supposed you thought I'd missed it?" "No," I said, "I just hoped."'

What Macleod did not allow for was Randolph's impatience. The negotiations for Dr Banda's release took time and Randolph soon became tired of waiting. Africa Year was living up to expectations, with events elsewhere on the continent demanding his attention. Those events concerned South Africa. On 21 March 1960 a huge crowd of Africans gathered in protest outside a police station at Sharpeville in the Transvaal and the police opened fire: sixty-nine of the protesters were killed and eighty wounded. The uproar caused by this event completely eclipsed the delicate manoeuverings in Salisbury. Randolph was among the journalists who rushed to Johannesburg.

His arrival in South Africa provided further evidence of his contrariness. Having earlier rounded on the opponents of apartheid, he now proceeded to defy its upholders. Stephen Barber, who accompanied Randolph to Johannesburg, was highly amused by the way he completed the immigration form. Outraged at being asked about his means of financial support in South Africa, Randolph dismissed the question as an impertinence. He was equally incensed at being asked to declare his race. 'Human,' he wrote in reply and then filled the margin of the form with details about his proud descent from a Red Indian princess. This, needless to say, did not please the immigration officials. Randolph's passport was promptly impounded and it was only with the help of a South African friend that he was granted a temporary permit.

He did not, in any case, intend to stay long. The sole object of his visit was to interview South Africa's formidable Prime Minister, Dr Hendrik Verwoerd. This, at a time of extreme tension – a state of emergency had been declared after the Sharpeville shootings – was no simple undertaking. Verwoerd was notoriously anti-British and highly suspicious of foreign newsmen; the chances of him granting an interview to a journalist named Churchill at a time of crisis were, to say the least, remote. But this did not bother Randolph. Hearing that Verwoerd was addressing a meeting at a nearby mining town, he decided to risk a face-to-face confrontation. He drove to the town in a taxi, taking Stepher Barber with him. By the time they arrived the meeting was over and Verwoerd, flanked by dour-faced bodyguards, was driving slowly through the crowded streets in an open car. Randolph saw his opportunity. Dressed in an open-necked shirt and grey flannels and sweating profusely after his hot drive, he looked anything but respectable; but he did not allow this to deter him. He pushed through the crowd, rushed up to the Prime Minister's car and shouted his request for an interview. 'Verwoerd,' says Barber, 'looked stunned, as well he might. But he quickly realized who Randolph was, which probably saved us both from being locked up, if not actually shot on the spot.'

Reports of the incident featured prominently in the South African press. This coverage helped to make up for the fact that Randolph failed to get his interview with Verwoerd: he had at least displayed his journalistic enterprise. Satisfaction of a grimmer sort followed a week later. On 9 April – by which time Randolph had flown to Kenya – a deranged white man fired two shots at Verwoerd while he was attending the Rand Easter Show, wounding the Prime Minister in the face. That weekend Randolph was able to wire a lively article to the *News of the World*. In it he told of his own experiences in South Africa: of how he had heard important people in Johannesburg saying that Verwoerd should be shot; of his astonishment at the Prime Minister's security arrangements; and of how his own impetuous action should have alerted the South African authorities to the possibility of an assassination attempt. It was not the scoop he had hoped for, but it was the next best thing.

Such excitements, unfortunately, were not very frequent. About his routine duties as a columnist, Randolph was less enthusiastic. In fact, as far as his political reporting was concerned, he was rapidly gaining a reputation for laziness. There were times when he had great difficulty in producing his Sunday column for the *News of the World*. Lord Home tells of an incident that graphically illustrates Randolph's slap-dash approach. It happened a couple of months after his return from Africa.

In the summer of 1960, Harold Macmillan reshuffled his Cabinet after the resignation of Derek Heathcoat-Amery as Chancellor of the Exchequer. In this reshuffle Selwyn Lloyd, the Foreign Secretary, replaced Heathcoat-Amery as Chancellor, and Lord Home (then the Commonwealth Relations Secretary) took over as Foreign Secretary. The announcement of Lord Home's appointment angered the Opposition who objected to the Foreign Secretary being in the House of Lords. Randolph decided to join in the protest and wrote to Lord Home saying that he intended to denounce the appointment in the *News of the World*. He suggested that they meet for luncheon at the Ritz that Friday – the deadline for Randolph's column was 5 o'clock on Friday afternoon – so that he could 'confirm his impressions and improve his copy.' Lord Home agreed. However, knowing that Randolph was unlikely to have written anything by the time they met, and would be in no state to do so after a few drinks, Home decided to provide some practical help. He sketched out an appreciation of himself and his approach to British Foreign policy in question and answer form. The meal, as Home had foreseen, lasted until three-thirty. As they rose to leave, Lord Home handed Randolph his notes which, he suggested, might come in useful as an *aide-mémoire*. They proved to be more than that. 'The result,' says Lord Home, 'was better than I hoped, for the document come out virtually verbatim, and until [Randolph's] untimely death I had a committed ally.'

Randolph's lassitude, his boredom with journalism and the affairs of government, resulted in part from the fact that he had cut himself off from the rough and tumble of day-to-day politics. He no longer felt at home in London. He now saw himself as a country squire and preferred to make his professional contacts by telephone. His father's retirement had, in effect, severed Randolph's links with the world of affairs; while his own electoral failures had turned him into a political outcast. Occasionally a particular event – an election, a parliamentary crisis, Suez or Africa Year – would galvanize him into action but for the most part he was happier pursuing his literary interests, entertaining visitors or pottering about his garden at Stour.

When he was not at Stour, it was out of Britain that he looked for excitement. The lure of travel was the one temptation he was unable to resist. The early spring of 1961 found him back in Africa. This time it was north Africa – a return to the scenes of his wartime adventures.

In March 1961, Randolph and his twenty-year-old son, Winston, were part of an expedition which set off from Benghazi to explore the Sahara Desert. The purpose of the safari was vague. 'We travel for adventure,' wrote one member of the group, 'for pleasure and to satisfy our insatiable curiosity about a little known part of the world . . . There is nothing to be gained and every chance that we shall all be lost.' There were fourteen people in the group – mainly Americans, accompanied by some British soldiers – and only one of them had a specific aim. This was Dr Henry W. Setzer, of the Smithsonian Institute, who was studying mammals and intended to trap desert mice. It was his presence in the group which led to the expedition being dubbed the 'Great Saharan Mouse-Hunt'. Randolph had first heard about the venture a year earlier and had insisted on becoming a 'charter member'. His inclusion in the party, with his son, puzzled some of the other members. 'The old war-horse,' noted one of the young women, Miggs Pomeroy, 'has come back to the desert, perhaps to see whether he can still stand up to it, perhaps for sentimental reasons, or to show it to his son Winston; but more than anything, I think, he has come back to taste the tranquillity and quiet strength of this, his "vast desaart" . . . He says that he prefers his flower garden in Suffolk to any of these outlandish places, and yet the mere mention of a distant horizon is enough to set him packing his bags.'

Whatever Randolph's reasons for joining the expedition, he had certainly packed his bags. His preparations for the journey were both elaborate and stylish. Not only did he, like the rest of the party, arrive with his own truck, tent and sleeping bags but included in his equipment were camp beds and an ice cooler which he called his 'Magic Box'. Even more impressive were the food supplies provided by Fortnum and Mason. His companions watched with awe and envy as he unpacked his hampers at various stages of the desert crossing. Every conceivable delicacy had been packed: caviare, pâté de foie gras, lobster bisque, turtle soup and genuine French petit pois, as well as a liberal supply of alcohol. Much as Randolph enjoyed sleeping in the open and cooking over a camp fire, he had no intention of roughing it. Nor did he intend to allow his interpretation of social conventions to be breached. From the very outset he insisted on remaining snobbishly aloof from the soldiers who escorted the expedition.

The party travelled from Benghazi to Agedabia and then branched out towards the wilder mountain ranges of the Tibesti. While the others busied themselves with their explorations, Randolph organized the overnight stops. He assumed the role of a military commander and appears to have paid little attention to the demands of the officer in charge of the soldiers. Towards the younger women of the party he adopted a protective attitude which, at times, became somewhat overbearing. But, for all his bullying ways, his concern for the welfare and safety of the party was both endearing and touching. Miggs Pomeroy compared him to 'some allegorical beast.' He combined, she says, 'the dragon and the teddy bear, unable to turn his back on a challenge, he is brave and heedless as the first when confronted, or sweet as the second when he thinks no one is looking.' Randolph's contradictory nature and qualities have rarely been better described.

What did worry Randolph's companions, was his refusal to eat. He was generous in sharing his Fortnum and Mason hampers with the others – and with strangers they met on the way – but he scarcely touched the food himself. Instead, he would start drinking at breakfast time and make unconvincing excuses for avoiding a more substantial meal. Repeatedly attempts were made to persuade him to take vitamin pills (in order to ward off scurvy) but he waved all such suggestions aside. Pills, Randolph insisted, were an 'impossible American idea'. 'I never take pills,' he said. His obstinacy was not only alarming but symptomatic. The illness that was to shorten his life had, it seems, already begun to manifest itself.

Ill-health may well have decided him to abandon the expedition. After a week's travelling he announced that he intended returning home. He made a number of excuses – the caviare and pâté were finished, the tulips would be coming up at Stour and his little spaniel was in whelp – but it could be that the safari had tired him. They had reached an oil-rig in the desert, a supply plane was expected from Benghazi and Randolph decided to take advantage of its return flight. Winston was left to look after the Churchill Land Rover.

Among the excuses Randolph made for returning home, he had not been able to include his wife. His second marriage had ended shortly after his move to East Anglia. In 1956, June, tired of the endless bickering, clashes of temperament, public rows and humiliations, had walked out on her husband. Divorce became inevitable and, shortly after his return from north Africa, Randolph started legal proceedings to secure his freedom. The case was heard, undefended, on 28 July 1961. Randolph was granted a decree *nisi* on the ground of his wife's desertion and June was given custody of the eleven-year-old Arabella 'on condition that the father has reasonable access.' On the question of Randolph's admitted adultery the judge exercised 'the court's discretion'.

*   *   *

'I read,' Evelyn Waugh wrote to Randolph on 18 July 1961, 'that you have made a highly remunerative contract for your magnum opus. My congratulations.'

The magnum opus was, of course, Randolph's long-contemplated biography of his father. For over eight years he had been preparing himself for this monumental task, but not until *Lord Derby: King of Lancashire* was published did he give it his full attention. He had, in fact, already embarked on the planning stages of the biography by the time Waugh wrote to him.

Randolph's intention was for the biography to consist of five volumes. However, as it would not be possible to accommodate all the documentation at his disposal in those volumes, he planned to publish additional 'Companion Volumes' – containing the bulk of Churchill's correspondence and other relevant material – to accompany the narrative. The complete work was expected to run to fifteen or more volumes. His aim was to produce a biography which would not only be worthy of his father's achievements but would stand the test of time and serve as an essential source book for future historians. It was an extremely ambitious scheme. Not since the publication of Moneypenny and Buckle's six volume *Life of Benjamin Disraeli* had a biography of a British Prime Minister been attempted on such a scale. It was to be Randolph's answer to those who had written him off as a failure.

An incredible amount of organization was required. So extensive were the Churchill archives that, at first, Randolph was all but overwhelmed by his task. 'It is a tremendous undertaking,' he admitted, during the early stages of his research. 'The quantity of papers is vast. For instance we have all his school letters, all his school reports and his medical reports at school . . . We have 380 letters to his mother written as a subaltern.' To tame this wealth of material was, in itself, a daunting challenge. But Randolph refused to be daunted. His response to the challenge was typical; it owed more to his military training than to his academic competence. He saw himself as the commander of an operation which called for detailed planning and discipline, and he acted accordingly.

A large upstairs room at Stour – Arabella's old nursery – was cleared and converted into a 'Book Office'. Divided into three sections, this office became the operational centre. Next came the appointment of the personnel. Directives were issued, duties allocated and spheres of responsibility defined. As his chief lieutenant, Randolph selected Michael Wolff. His job was to direct the research. Wolff's second-in-command was a research assistant – a post held at first by Ian Coulton – who, together with an archivist, Eileen Harryman, collated the material sent to the Book Office. Between them these three were responsible for the upstairs work; Randolph's command post was downstairs. Here he was assisted by his personal aides. At Stour he relied heavily on his private secretary – first a Miss Gibson and later the loyal and long-serving Barbara

Twigg – but when he travelled abroad he was often accompanied by the indispensable Andrew Kerr, who acted both as a research assistant and as a secretary-companion.

The headquarters staff was supplemented by a more mobile force. This was the haphazardly assembled team of young men whom Randolph employed as research workers. Known as Randolph's 'Young Gentlemen' they were attached to Stour on a temporary or, in some cases, semi-permanent basis. A few of them had worked with Randolph on the Derby biography, some came to him through his Fleet Street contacts and others were enlisted during the writing of the Great Work. It was a lively, talented, often well-qualified, research unit. Among the later recruits were men like Frank Gannon, an American postgraduate student from Jesus College, Oxford; Tom Hartman, who was lured to Stour from a publishers' office; and Martin Gilbert, a young Oxford don who was introduced to Randolph by Lady Diana Cooper and who, after Randolph's death, was appointed as Churchill's official biographer for the remaining volumes of the Prime Minister's life.

The duties of the Young Gentlemen varied according to Randolph's needs, and their attendance at Stour was subject to Randolph's moods. At times of 'panic' there could be as many as eight people working at Stour, but on off-days the team could be reduced to one or two (on one memorable occasion the entire staff was summarily dismissed for the day). For the most part, however, Randolph's relationship with his helpers was friendly and affectionate; a surprising number of his staff weathered his tantrums and remained faithful to him. One of Randolph's more endearing idiosyncrasies was his habit of calling his friends 'dear', regardless of age or sex. 'Take a drink dear,' was his usual greeting to a newcomer on the team. This established the informal atmosphere in which Randolph liked to work. Once he had employed an assistant, however, Randolph expected – and, more often than not, got – total loyalty. Dedication to the Great Work was the one requirement demanded from everyone working at Stour.

Such things as hours of work and terms of service were of minor importance. A Young Gentleman contracting to work for three days a week would quickly discover, as one of them put it, that 'Randolph usually decided what constituted three days and the three days appeared at times more like four or five.' But, demanding as Randolph was, he could also be a generous and, in his own way, a thoughtful employer. Indeed he was far more than an employer. He regarded his staff as his friends and, as his friends, they commanded his unswerving allegiance. He interested himself in their lives, their families and their problems. He was aware of their likes and dislikes, their tastes, their strengths and their weaknesses. He shared their private worries. When, for instance, one of Michael Wolff's children was recovering from a serious illness, Randolph displayed undisguised concern. He asked for a daily progress report and went out of his way to choose a suitable gift for the child. Rejecting the conventional sweets and chocolates, he found a 'perfect peach' which he wrapped in cotton wool and gave to Michael Wolff. The gesture was slight but typical. Randolph's gifts, remembered Wolff's wife, Rosemary, 'were not always costly but they invariably reflected his thoughtfulness.'

That thoughtfulness helped to offset Randolph's less pleasant characteristics. In his dealings with his staff and his friends, says Rosemary Wolff, he was like the child in the nursery rhyme: 'When he was good, he was very, very, good; but when he was bad he was horrid.'

Once work on the Churchill biography began, Randolph could think of nothing else. He continued to write his newspaper articles, his letters to the press and his privately printed pamphlets – the so-called 'Country Bumpkins' publications – but the Great Work remained his chief concern. Most of his writing was done at night, after his visitors had left, and he often insisted on one of his staff staying up with him. The Young Gentleman chosen for this vigil, which sometimes lasted until the early hours of the morning, would be asked to read aloud what Randolph had written. As the chapter on which he was working was read, Randolph would check and recheck his facts. 'We must do our prep,' he would bellow, when sending for yet another reference book. He delighted in schoolboy expressions. 'Box on,' was a great favourite. 'Box on,' he would say when he was ready for the reading to continue. According to Michael Wolff, 'Box on' became the motto of Stour.

Randolph could never keep his activities secret. News of his operational centre at Stour quickly leaked out. The idea of a book being written from the end of an assembly line amused both his friends and his critics. Evelyn Waugh teased Randolph unmercifully about his Young Gentlemen, whom he called 'ghosts'. He saw their influence everywhere and even accused them of writing to the newspapers in Randolph's name. This type of ragging Randolph enjoyed. He was distinctly less amused when the satirical magazine, *Private Eye*, decided to join in the fun.

On 31 January 1963, Randolph was interviewed about his work on television. The following week *Private Eye* published a wicked cartoon poking fun at him. In the cartoon, the portly Randolph was depicted slumped in an armchair with a dog across his lap and a whisky and soda at his elbow. Facing him were a group of subservient flunkies, one of whom was reading from the Great Work. 'It's not me that's the hack,' read a balloon above Randolph's head, 'it's the people who write my books.' The pictures which followed illustrated various controversial episodes in Winston Churchill's life – the Tonypandy coal strike of 1911, Churchill confronting Gandhi in the 1930s and the Dieppe Raid of 1942. Captions accompanying these pictures made it clear that Randolph was expected to gloss over such embarrassments and 'concentrate instead on the one short period of [Churchill's] life from which he can be painted as the Great Patriot who did more for his countrymen than anyone else in the 20th Century.'

Nothing could have been more certain to rouse Randolph's anger. On a single page all the old taunts about him were revived. His integrity was questioned, he was accused of employing hacks, his drinking was emphasized and, above all, his father was maligned. *Private Eye* had earlier published a cartoon of the bleary-eyed Randolph appearing on the television programme 'Panorama' with a glass in his hand. That he had ignored. But there was no chance of his ignoring this second lampoon. That night he telephoned his lawyers and instructed them to issue writs against the entire staff of *Private Eye*, including the office girls.

The serving of the writs caused much hilarity in the *Private Eye* office. Merrily the staff responded by filling a downstairs display window with all the material they had published on Randolph. The centre-piece was a William Rushton cartoon, headed The Great Boar of Suffolk, which depicted Randolph as a defecating pig. They should have known better. Randolph already had his spies at work and the display window was quickly spotted. Within a matter of hours an injunction demanding that the exhibits be removed was applied for, challenged, and finally granted. The jokers were forced to obey. They promptly cleared the window and replaced the display with a poster proclaiming that KILLJOY WAS HERE.

But *Private Eye* had met its match. Randolph's skill as a litigant was too formidable to laugh off. The editors of the magazine realized this and sprang into action. One of them decided to contact Martin Gilbert, who had joined Randolph's team a year earlier, to ask him to act as a mediator. A meeting in Oxford was arranged and the *Private Eye* emissary returned from it encouraged by Martin Gilbert's hospitality. Unfortunately, his optimism was short lived. On arriving home he discovered that he had lost his file containing papers related to the dispute and concluded that he must have left them at Oxford. Some days later, the file was returned with a note: 'Yours, I think. R. C.'

Stymied once again, the magazine editors decided to seek out

Randolph at Stour. Two of them, Nicholas Luard and William Rushton, arrived at East Bergholt with a peace offering. Knowing Randolph's political prejudices, they presented him with a framed copy of a recently published, extremely irreverent, cartoon of R. A. Butler. But Randolph was not so easily won over. There was no 'Take a drink, dear' greeting for these visitors. Indeed he declared that no drinks would be served until the matter was settled. The prohibition was severe and Randolph suffered more from it than the *Private Eye* men. He became increasingly short tempered as the negotiations dragged on. Finally terms were arranged. Luard and Rushton agreed to insert a full page withdrawal (without apologies – Randolph believed an apology given under threat of legal action was worthless) in the *Evening Standard*. Randolph accepted their capitulation, poured out drinks, introduced them to his 'hacks' and then took them on a torchlight tour of the garden. He, no less than his father, believed in magnanimity in victory.

Later it was estimated that had *Private Eye* refused to withdraw, they would have faced legal costs in the region of £40,000. As it was the *Evening Standard* advertisement cost them 'a bare £3,000 – and their pride.' Even so, they quickly recouped their losses. Such was the publicity which accompanied the issuing of the writs and the injunction that it 'transformed the status' of *Private Eye*. In the months which followed, the sales of the magazine rose from 35,000 to 80,000. Only later did the *Private Eye* team admit to genuine regret about their brush with Randolph. 'Had it not been for the animosity it created,' acknowledged Richard Ingrams, 'Randolph, I am sure, would have ended up as a regular contributor to *Private Eye*, which is more than can be said of many subsequent litigants.'

*   *   *

Absorbed as he was in the Great Work, Randolph still found time to visit America. He leapt at any excuse to cross the Atlantic and when an excuse was not forthcoming he invented one. One glorious, indeed inescapable, excuse presented itself in April 1963. That month President Kennedy conferred Honorary Citizenship of the United States on Winston Churchill, and Randolph was asked to represent his father at the proclamation ceremony. He was accompanied by his own son, Winston, and supported by the British Ambassador in Washington, Sir David Ormsby Gore.

The ceremony was simple but impressive. First the Congressional resolution, authorising citizenship, was signed in the Presidential office and then President Kennedy addressed a large gathering of guests and officials in the Rose Garden of the White House. Afterwards Randolph read out a letter – 'in a voice reminiscent of his father's' – which Churchill had written for the occasion. It was a memorable performance. Jacqueline Kennedy, who was standing behind Randolph, was so overcome by emotion that she hardly heard what was said. She was never to forget that day. Nor was Randolph. One of his proudest possessions was the quill pen – inscribed 'The President – White House' – which was used in the signing ceremony and presented to him by President Kennedy.

For Randolph the pen was symbolic. Not only was it a memento of a proud day, but it served as a permanent reminder of his friendship with the Kennedy family. His admiration of the Kennedys was enormous. They were, like himself, members of a great political family and he felt a natural kinship with them. He admired the Kennedys' vitality, glamour, and swashbuckling approach to high office. President Kennedy's administration, he claimed, had brought a 'much more free and easy atmosphere' to Washington, an atmosphere which contrasted sharply to that of previous administrations. On the night of the White House ceremony, he met Bobby Kennedy at a British Embassy dinner and came away dazzled. '[We] had,' he wrote, 'a most amusing and high-spirited conversation. He has a wonderful gift of quick repartee, a delightful smile and a most engaging personality.' Few British politicians could have won such compliments from Randolph. 'He was in love with the Kennedys,' says Frank Gannon.

That Randolph, with his right-wing views, should be captivated by the liberal Kennedys is somewhat surprising. Admittedly his politics were never predictable and his sympathy for the underdog often put him at odds with the more die-hard Tories, but his infatuation with the Kennedys seems totally out of character. One can only assume that it was inspired more by his sense of personal loyalty than by his political philosophy. The fact that he was inclined to discard his more pompous prejudices in America may also have something to do with it. Certainly his behaviour in the United States was, at times, very different from his behaviour in Britain.

Outrageous as were his appearances on British television, for instance, it is doubtful whether he would ever have agreed to take part in a popular British quiz show. This he once did in America. Not only did he agree to enter the famous $64,000 Question show but he regarded the contest as a serious challenge. For six months he went into training in order to brush up his general knowledge. But, to everyone's amazement – not least his own – he was stumped by the first question. Locked in a soundproof glass box, he became confused and was unable to explain the origin of the word 'boycott'. Afterwards his sister Sarah tried to console him by saying that he had at least proved himself a popular loser. But her kind words only made Randolph more depressed. 'I don't want to be a popular loser,' he protested. 'I want to be a popular *winner*.'

Randolph's reply reflects more than his disappointment at the outcome of a quiz show. The fact that he later took to naming his pug dogs 'Boycott' is, perhaps, an indication of his unwillingness to acknowledge failure in any sphere. He invariably met adversity with a show of defiance.

His frequent visits to America were not prompted entirely by politics and journalism. He had many acquaintances in the United States and always enjoyed seeing Kay Halle and other friends from former days. In the early sixties his circle was extended to include some of his British friends then living in New York and Washington. Among them was his former wife, Pamela, who had remarried and was the wife of Leland Hayward, the well-known film agent and stage producer. By this time the scars of their turbulent life together had healed and – bound by their son, Winston – Randolph and Pamela had become friends. 'Randolph,' said Pamela, remembering those American visits, 'was a wonderful person . . . if you didn't have to see him every day of the week. There was nobody I would have more enjoyed having lunch with once a week, but a little of him went a long way.'

Randolph was again in America in October 1963. On this occasion his visit was cut short by a political crisis. At the beginning of that month, Harold Macmillan, who had been preparing to address the Conservative party conference in Blackpool, was taken ill with prostate trouble and his doctors advised immediate surgery. His earlier plans were cancelled and he was ordered into hospital. The Conservative party was thrown into confusion. Few doubted that Macmillan would be forced to retire and at Blackpool all other business was overshadowed by speculation about who would succeed him as Prime Minister. There was no shortage of candidates. Canvassing for support among the delegates became urgent and the party conference was turned into a circus.

Randolph heard about the crisis accidentally. He was in Washington at the time and, a few days earlier, he had telephoned Iain Macleod in England on some routine business. Macleod, aware that the crisis was about to break, had been anxious to keep Randolph away from Blackpool and had ended the telephone conversation abruptly. This had aroused Randolph's suspicions. Smelling a political intrigue, he had put through two more calls to London and had discovered what was afoot. Once he knew there was no holding him. The mere suggestion of a political battle was sufficient to rekindle his journalistic enthusiasm. Stopping only to

inform President Kennedy of Macmillan's illness, Randolph had
boarded a plane. Within a matter of hours he was waving a banner in
Blackpool.

The banner declared his support for Lord Hailsham. This was
perhaps inevitable. Among the contenders for the Premiership, only
two candidates appeared – to Randolph – to stand a reasonable
chance of succeeding. They were R. A. Butler, the Deputy Prime
Minister, and Lord Hailsham, the Minister of Science and
Technology. As far as Randolph was concerned, this was not a
choice but a challenge. His dislike of Rab Butler was such that he
had no alternative but to give Lord Hailsham his wholehearted
support. He had made his position clear shortly after he arrived in
Blackpool. Interviewed on television by Robin Day, he announced
that Hailsham would become Prime Minister with the full approval
of Randolph Churchill. When Robin Day suggested that a third
candidate, Lord Home, might be in the running, Randolph
disagreed. 'That's a lot of rot,' he declared.

Having displayed his colours, Randolph proceeded to parade
them. This was the last political campaign in which he was actively
engaged and he fought it with characteristic vigour. His advocacy of
Lord Hailsham was loud, unrestrained and colourful. (One of his
more outrageous pranks was the pinning of a Hailsham campaign
button on Rab Butler's lapel.) But once again he found himself on
the losing side. These were the days in which a Tory leader was said
to 'emerge' – a euphemism for backstairs manoeuvring – and the
man who eventually emerged was the man at whom Randolph had
scoffed – Lord Home. Randolph's only consolation was that,
although Hailsham had lost, Butler had not won.

Once the battle was over, embarrassment set in. The unedifying
struggle to produce the new Prime Minister was something most
Tories preferred to forget. According to Iain Macleod, there was an
'unspoken agreement' among the Conservative leaders to play
down the infighting that had divided their party. But if they
expected Randolph to observe this agreement they were mistaken.
A couple of months later he published his own account of the tussle,
entitled *The Fight For the Tory Leadership*. This 'Contemporary
Chronicle', as he called it, was presented as an impartial 'quest for
the truth.' In fact it was a hurriedly assembled, factory-produced
book which owed more to the efficiency of Randolph's research
team than to his own insight. His claim that he had consulted several
of the 'principal actors in this drama' was weakened by the fact that
he was forced to rely heavily on newspaper cuttings for most of his
information. 'Four-fifths of Churchill's book,' observed Iain
Macleod in his review of *The Fight for the Tory Leadership* in the

Spectator, 'could have been compiled by anyone with a pair of scissors and a pot of paste, and a built-in prejudice against Mr Butler.' That view was shared by other critics. Indeed, Iain Macleod's three-page *Spectator* review – with its hint at an old Etonian conspiracy – caused more of a stir in political circles than did Randolph's book. For Macleod had been one of the contenders for the Premiership and his informed assessment of the fight was considered to be far more illuminating than Randolph's second hand 'disclosures.'

The party squabble which resulted from Harold Macmillan's retirement as Prime Minister was incidental to Randolph's career. More important was the effect of Macmillan's departure on his political aspirations. Apparently Randolph had half-expected that his name would be included in Macmillan's resignation honours list and had confided to Martin Gilbert that he hoped to be made a Peer and sit in the House of Lords. He was disappointed. Macmillan's honours list was short and confined to the members of his personal staff. 'Born to succeed: doomed to failure,' it was once said of Randolph. The truth of this quip was now becoming increasingly apparent.

* * *

The final stages of the Tory leadership struggle were overshadowed for Randolph by family grief. On Sunday, 20 October 1963, his elder sister, Diana, was discovered dead on the floor of the bathroom of her house in Chester Row, Belgravia. At an inquest held five days later it was found that she had taken her own life by swallowing a 'single massive dose' of sleeping tablets. Her doctor testified that he had been attending Diana since 1957 and that before coming under his care she had been treated for a nervous condition in a Scottish nursing home. The nature of her death had surprised him because, he said, she appeared to have 'made an excellent recovery.'

Diana was the first victim of the jinx which plagued Winston Churchill's three eldest children. Both Randolph and Sarah suffered the same curse. Diana's problems were, for the most part, contained within the family circle and her suicide came as a shock. Randolph and Sarah, on the other hand, were notorious for their temperamental outbursts, their unruly behaviour, their belligerence and their excessive drinking. All three of them displayed unmistakable symptoms of nervous instability. Was this a coincidence? Could three members of the same family suffer a common affliction without a common cause? It seems unlikely. Precisely what produced the psychological problems of the eldest Churchill children is, however, a problem in itself. The generally accepted explanation is that Diana, Randolph and Sarah were overshadowed by their father. A great man's reputation, it is thought, must place his children under strain. But how valid is this? When Diana, Randolph and Sarah were growing up their father was a controversial figure but his reputation was no greater than that of other prominent politicians. Indeed, for most of his children's formative years, Churchill was a political outcast. If tension is generated by an illustrious father then surely that tension would have been felt much later – at a time when his family would have been old enough to cope with it. In any case, not all the children of political leaders exhibit nervous disorders.

So was it Churchill's shadow that clouded the childhood of Randolph and his sisters? Or was it – as some of Randolph's friends claim – Clementine Churchill who, in her efforts to protect her husband, placed an unbearable burden on her three eldest children? Certainly Diana and Randolph's relationship with their mother was more tempestuous than their relationship with their father. Both of them are said to have bitterly resented Clementine Churchill's interference in their lives. Whatever the explanation, it requires no profound knowledge of psychology to recognize the effect of early environmental influences on Diana, Randolph and Sarah.

Randolph was fortunate in being an extrovert. He appears to have escaped the danger of a mental breakdown. His nervousness manifested itself in self-indulgence – in heavy drinking, chain-smoking and over-eating – and it was this that undermined his health. Despite his attempts to reform, he suffered from periodic attacks of illness in one form or another. One such attack resulted in his being admitted to the King Edward VII hospital in London three months after Diana's death. He was reported to be suffering from bronchial pneumonia but his condition was more serious than that. Further medical examinations followed and, in March 1964, he underwent a lung operation.

As always Randolph astonished everyone by his courage throughout his illness. 'Randolph is Randolph is Randolph . . .' Iain Macleod informed readers of the *Spectator* on 13 March. 'It was an unforgettable sight to see him in hospital early this week on the eve of a major operation, dictating his column . . . dispensing Pol Roger 1955, and instructing his surgeons on the conduct of the operation.' Michael Foot's wife, Jill Craigie – visiting Randolph after the operation – was amused to find him 'sitting up, smoking, drinking and protesting to one of the most eminent physicians in the land, "Stop treating me like an invalid."' It was left to Evelyn Waugh to offer a more cynical observation. On learning of Randolph's recovery, he told a friend that it was 'a typical triumph of modern science to find the only part of Randolph that was not malignant and remove it.'

On leaving hospital Randolph was kept busy with his literary activities. These were now as varied as they were demanding. His main concern was still, of course, the Great Work but this did not prevent him contributing regular articles to newspapers and magazines. In the *Spectator* he wrote a weekly column entitled The Press and, in August 1964, he accepted an offer from *Queen* magazine to write a column of general interest under the heading 'Randolph Writes.' (Both these columns were later abandoned after rows with the editors.) Of more importance was his decision to publish a slim autobiographical volume, *Twenty-One Years*, which outlined his experiences as a young man. Hurriedly written and poorly constructed, this book must be rated among Randolph's failures. Had he exercised the same discipline that he brought to the writing of his father's biography, he could have produced an interesting account of his early years, but he relied too heavily on his faulty memory and wrote a muddled and misleading book. Few reviewers were impressed by *Twenty-One Years*; it added little to Randolph's literary reputation.

Twenty-One Years was first serialized in the *Sunday Times* at the end of 1964. That same year was also marked for Randolph by two important family events. First came the marriage of his son Winston to Minnie d'Erlanger and then, in November 1964, the Churchill family gathered to celebrate the ninetieth birthday of Sir Winston Churchill. For some years Churchill's health had been a cause for concern. He was extremely shaky on his feet, afflicted by deafness and suffering from lapses of memory which, at times, reduced him to morbid silence. In 1960 and again in 1962 he had injured himself in falls which, as he put it, 'greatly decreased' his mobility. He needed constant attention and spent much of his time in bed. On the eve of his birthday he managed to appear at an open window of his house in Hyde Park Gate to wave to the little crowd gathered outside but on the birthday itself he was again confined to his bedroom. At lunchtime that day his family assembled at his bedside to drink his health in champagne and in the evening he felt sufficiently well to attend a family dinner. He insisted on descending the stairs by himself and gently waved aside Randolph's attempt to help him. At the end of the meal, however, when he tried to rise from his chair to make a speech of thanks, the effort proved too much, and it was left to Randolph to propose a toast on his behalf. It was a memorable, if sad, occasion. The family members were painfully conscious of the probability that this would be the last time they would meet together for a celebratory dinner.

Their fears were realized a few weeks later. Early in January 1965, there was a noticeable change in Churchill's health. He became drowsy and confused and his doctor realized that he had suffered another stroke. His left arm was paralysed and hopes that he would again recover began to fade. At first, news of Churchill's deterioration was kept from the public but on Friday, 15 January, his doctor, Lord Moran, issued the first ominous bulletin. 'After a cold,' it read, 'Sir Winston has developed a circulatory weakness and there has been a cerebral thrombosis.' There was no mistaking the significance of this bulletin. For the next few days the cul de sac at Hyde Park Gate was crowded with newsmen and photographers.

Randolph, like the rest of the family, was in constant attendance. His grief was unmistakable and touching. On one occasion he arrived at Churchill's bedside as Lord Moran was about to leave. 'I got up,' wrote Moran, 'and as I closed the door I saw him lift his father's hand to his lips.' Both Randolph and his son Winston were present when, on Sunday, 24 January 1965, Churchill died. They were summoned to Hyde Park Gate by an early morning telephone call and joined the rest of the family at Churchill's bedside. When it became clear that the end was near, Sarah, Mary and Diana's daughter, Celia Sandys, knelt at the foot of the bed while Randolph, his mother and his son, stood close to Churchill's pillow. They waited in silence. Churchill's breathing, says Lord Moran, 'became shallow and laboured, and at eight o'clock in the morning it ceased . . . I got up and bent over the bed, but he had gone.'

Later that morning Randolph joined his mother and sisters in Clementine Churchill's sitting room. He was carrying a book – a life of Lord Randolph Churchill – in which he had discovered that Sir Winston had died on the same day, almost at the same hour, as his father. Randolph, with his respect for tradition, might also have pondered on another quirk of history. Two days earlier his own son, Winston, had become a father. The newly born child, a boy, was christened Randolph Leonard Spencer Churchill.

* * *

'The word I would use to describe Randolph,' said one of his friends, 'is lonely: he was a very lonely man.'

The friend was remembering life at Stour. Other people, at other times, have said much the same thing about Randolph. Throughout his life Randolph gave the impression of being a man apart. There was an emptiness at the core of his life, a spiritual void, which kept him one stage removed from even his closest companions. It was not aloofness: he was, by nature, gregarious, outgoing and almost childlike in his affections. Incurably sentimental – he would weep openly at mawkish films on television – he was capable of strong emotional attachments but, for the most part, they were instinctive attachments, lacking in real depth. He was too self-centred, too self-assertive, too proudly independent to make the concessions necessary to mutual understanding. Probably the nearest he came to intellectual intimacy was in his relationship with his father but, strong as was the bond between father and son, even that relationship was marred by Randolph's rebelliousness, his obstinate refusal to accept advice or guidance. After Churchill's death there was nobody in whom Randolph could confide openly and honestly. Towards his mother he was dutiful and attentive – he organized an impressive family luncheon at the Café Royal to celebrate her eightieth birthday in April 1965 – but the scars of earlier quarrels remained. Clementine Churchill would occasionally visit Stour for the day and claim to enjoy herself but Randolph was noticeably on edge on these occasions. There was never any suggestion of intimacy and warmth, of shared confidences, between Randolph and his mother.

But if Randolph was lonely it was not because he lacked friends. Female company, in particular, was important to him. At no stage in his life had he been able to exist without a close woman companion and at Stour that role was filled by Mrs Natalie Bevan.

Natalie Bevan was a neighbour. Married first to the author and radio personality, Lance Sieveking and then to the director of an advertising agency, Robert Bevan, Natalie Bevan was a woman of exceptional qualities. Fair-haired, attractive, talented, with strong artistic interests and a strikingly original style of dressing, she was known chiefly for her remarkable vivacity. She was, says one of her close friends, 'a real life enricher'; a woman 'whose main gift is for living and for infecting others with her own vitality.' As such, Natalie Bevan brightened Randolph's days at Stour considerably. She provided, not only a zest that matched his own, but a sympathetic ear. Often she acted as his hostess and, through her contacts with artists, was able to introduce him to people outside the political sphere. Not all her efforts to broaden his interests, however, were successful. Tom Hartman, one of Randolph's Young Gentlemen, remembers a disastrous occasion when Natalie Bevan arrived at Stour with two young aesthetes from Essex. Randolph received them glumly and refused to speak. Undeterred, Natalie Bevan left them alone and returned a little later to hear Randolph breaking the silence with a hearty observation. 'They tell me,' he boomed, 'that Essex is full of buggers.'

By this time Randolph had abandoned his matrimonial pursuit of

Laura. He had settled instead for an affectionate friendship. Laura's marriage to Lord Dudley had finally ended in divorce and, in 1959, she had become the wife of Michael Canfield, a handsome American who was rumoured to be the illegitimate son of the former Duke of Kent. Significantly, Randolph did not appear to resent Laura's third husband and he and Michael Canfield became good friends. For the first three years that Laura and her husband lived at Hertfordshire House in Buckinghamshire, Randolph spent every Christmas with them. He did so, however, with some misgivings. Laura tells of one Christmas when she discovered Randolph alone in her sitting room making a telephone call. He was complaining 'about the food, the people, the cold and a whole mass of other rubbish.' Later he told Laura he had been speaking to Natalie Bevan. 'She was devoted to him,' says Laura, 'and looked after him most wonderfully during his last ailing years. I am sure this talk was quite unnecessary. She knew that Randolph was an old friend and that I was blissfully and happily married. Much as I always loved Randolph, he had a great talent for "trouble bubble" where possible.'

Surrounded by his loyal staff, cared for by Natalie Bevan, Randolph should have been content. His disillusionment with politics was compensated by his new career as a biographer and by the immense pleasure he derived from his house and garden. From the time that he moved into Stour, gardening became a passion. 'I've taken to gardening in my middle age,' he told a journalist friend in 1964. 'When you get the gardening bug in middle age you get it very badly.' From the late 1950s until the end of his life he spent whatever time he could in the garden: reshaping paths, making herbaceous borders, training wisteria, honeysuckle and clematis over the terrace, planting beds of roses, tulips, dahlias and peonies and, his greatest triumph, designing the 'blue polyanthus river' which flowed through the surrounding trees. He consulted experts such as Xenia Field, the gardening editor of the *Daily Mirror*, and spent huge sums on plants, seeds and fertilizers. When he started work the lawns were overgrown and weed-infested and to clear them he organised a competition among the local schoolchildren. Posters advertising 'Operation Plantain' were distributed and the children were invited to enter a contest in which £5 was awarded to anyone pulling the longest plantain root from the lawn. Lady Astor was roped in to present the prize and other friends were invited to watch the operation. One of them – his literary agent, Graham Watson – claims that it would have cost Randolph 'one hundred pounds to clear the lawn by more orthodox methods.'

Once the garden was in shape, Randolph was never happier than when chatting to a guest while playing a hose over the flower beds.

'He really *loved* his garden,' remembers Rosemary Wolff. 'He said he would have liked to be buried in his garden with his dogs.'

But the loneliness remained. He was restless, moody, rarely at ease, always seeking new faces and new friends. Seated in the large green armchair in his study, he would spend hours telephoning acquaintances, colleagues and newspaper editors. The telephone had always been his favourite means of communication; he would ring anyone, on any pretext, at any hour of the day or night. This life-long habit developed, at Stour, into a positive obsession. Randolph's friends came to dread being wakened by his late-night calls: after apologizing half-heartedly for disturbing them he would launch into a long diatribe, or insist on reading out his latest piece of writing, without giving them a chance to protest or even reply. For Randolph the telephone became his life-line to the outside world and he developed the use of it into a fine art. 'The local operators,' it is said, 'were hardened to nocturnal demands for immediate connection with this number in Washington, with that number in Paris . . . Randolph's calls to the United States went through a good thirty minutes faster than any other.' His house had two telephone lines and nine extensions and at one time he was credited with being the largest private subscriber in Britain.

Equally desperate were his efforts to entice visitors to Stour. Old friends like Iain Macleod, John Profumo, Lord Longford, Michael Foot and John Grigg sometimes came for the weekend, and country neighbours were invited regularly for meals. On one occasion, with all else failing, Randolph picked up two foreign hitch-hikers and brought them back to Stour for the night. But there were rarely enough visitors to satisfy his craving for company. In London he would scour the clubs in hopes of finding a friend whom he could bully in to making the journey to East Bergholt. James Lees-Milne, whom he had known at Eton, was once trapped this way. After meeting Randolph at his club, Lees-Milne rashly agreed to spend a night at Stour when he next toured East Anglia for the National Trust. The visit proved more exhausting than he had bargained for. On arriving at East Bergholt, he was given a hearty welcome and a splendid dinner but, over drinks afterwards, Randolph embarked on one of his interminable monologues. Feeling drowsy after a busy day and a hearty meal, Lees-Milne found it difficult to stay awake ten o'clock came, then eleven, then midnight and Randolph was still in full flood. At last, when Randolph abruptly left the room to go to the lavatory, Lees-Milne felt he could endure it no longer and decided to slip away to bed. Hardly had he started to undress than Randolph burst into the room in a furious temper. What, he demanded, did Lees-Milne mean by leaving without saying goodnight? No gentleman would do such a thing. Was this his reward for supplying his guest with an excellent dinner and the best of his cellar? 'Put on your clothes again,' he shouted, 'and come down. I have not finished yet.' Wearily, Lees-Milne put on his dressing gown and went downstairs. Another hour passed before he finally got to bed.

When he was forced to spend an evening alone, Randolph, as a last resort, would argue with the television. He would insist on one of the Young Gentlemen joining him and would then keep up a running commentary throughout the evening's viewing. If anyone he knew appeared on the screen he would cheer everything they said and write to congratulate them the following day. The more banal the show, the more critical he became. Current slang and working-class jargon appeared to baffle him. 'What does *that* mean, dear?' he would ask, digging his companion in the ribs. It was all part of his pretence of divorcing himself from what he called 'the century of the common man and commoner woman.' He was far happier harking back to his schooldays. The older he grew the more his world became populated by 'silly billies', by 'flibbertigibbets', by people who had not done their 'prep'. It was his way of seeking a refuge in old age, of turning his back on the challenge he could no longer meet.

For Randolph would never admit that he was a failure. He preferred to give the impression that he had deliberately chosen his country retirement. 'I've formed a deep aversion to London,' he told Clive Irving in a *Sunday Times* interview. 'And, of course, if one was in the House of Commons one would have to go to that dreadful place. Quite often, I suppose. And then one would have to go to one's constituency, too – even more odious, although that would depend on the constituency. But, anyway, there's no rush of people asking me to go into Parliament, and it really suits me very well. I've found out it's not a question of sour grapes . . . I frankly don't think the House of Commons is what it used to be.'

After Churchill's death, Randolph became even more convinced that his political days were over. But he could not escape an awareness that his life lacked purpose. He hinted as much one day when discussing Lady Mountbatten's tireless works of charity. 'I do envy her,' he confessed to Tom Hartman. 'It must be marvellous to care so deeply about other people. I don't give a bugger what happens to anyone.'

*   *   *

Randolph's last hope of claiming at least one worthwhile achievement rested in the Great Work. He had spent over five years researching and writing his father's biography before he was ready to publish the first volume. That volume dealt with the early years of Churchill's life, from his birth in November 1874 until his election as the twenty-five-year old Member of Parliament for Oldham in October 1900. They were active, adventure-packed years – covering his schooldays, his army career in India and his experiences as a war-correspondent in Africa – and as such did not lend themselves to the detailed, carefully documented approach that Randolph had decided to adopt. His aim, as he explained in his preface, was to allow his father to tell his own story, to publish Churchill's letters and other relevant material and to link them together with narrative passages of his own. He was hampered, of course, by the fact that Churchill had written a classic account of this period in his well-known autobiography *My Early Life*. That book captured all the excitement of his youth and was written with a verve which Randolph could not hope to match. But there was a great deal that had not been said and much that needed to be explained. Randolph had every reason to hope that his first volume – 546 pages in length – would make up for in authenticity what it lacked in immediacy.

There was no mistaking the importance that Randolph attached to the launching of his opus. From the time that the proof pages of the first volume were corrected until its publication in October 1966, he was a mass of nerves. He could think of little else. Speculation about the book's reception dominated his every conversation. Who would review it? Would they be competent and impartial? How many of his enemies would seize the opportunity to pay off old scores? Would he, as had happened with the Derby book, be accused of employing journalistic tricks? The questions were endless and the answers, when they came, were mixed.

On the whole, the book, entitled *Winston S. Churchill: Youth 1874-1900*, was favourably received. Randolph was congratulated on the skill with which he handled his material, his meticulous preparation, his organization, his frankness and the simplicity of his presentation. There were a few quibbles over minor points, his personal comments and asides, but most reviewers were impressed by what *The Times Literary Supplement* described as 'his studied self-effacement.' But Randolph did not escape criticism entirely. A particularly vicious review was published, unsigned, in *The Times*. Almost half a column of this review was devoted to a personal attack on Randolph as a biographer. Had there been a competition for the writing of the book, claimed the anonymous critic, 'Mr Randolph Churchill might not have come in first. He is his father's biographer by inheritance, rather than on the record of his past work. The life of Derby was a solid achievement and he can point to several other books. But they do not add up between them to showing him to be of the stature of the writer of a "definitive", as the publishers call it, biography of his father.' Randolph, who had conducted a vendetta against *The Times* since the days of its notorious 'appeasement' bias in the 1930s, could not have been unduly surprised by this attack. His friends, however, were shocked. Natalie Bevan's husband, Robert Bevan, sprang to Randolph's defence and wrote to the newspaper deploring the 'petty innuendo designed to belittle the biographer.'

Cyrus Sulzberger, reviewing the book for the *New York Times Book Review* was more balanced in his judgement but cautious in his conclusions. 'Randolph Churchill,' he wrote, 'judging by Volume I is well on the road to success in his arduous task. One may hope that his health and energy permit him to complete it.'

Sulzberger was expressing a concern shared by many of Randolph's friends. By October 1966, when the book was published, Randolph's health had deteriorated considerably. He had never fully recovered from his lung operation two years earlier and was now aware that he was seriously ill. His doctors had warned him to stop drinking and to alter his eating habits if he wanted to prolong his life. With characteristic courage, he had accepted this advice without a murmur. He no longer drank spirits and confined himself to lager; he rarely touched solid foods – other than fruit cake – and lived almost entirely on glasses of Complan. Only when he had guests would he, for politeness sake, nibble at a piece of meat or sip a glass of wine. But his reforms had come too late: there was little he or his doctors could do to improve his health. He looked haggard and stark-eyed, he lacked energy and, although he seldom complained, it was obvious that his powers of recovery were failing. Those who knew him best were conscious of the fact that he had not long to live.

Yet, ill as he was, he continued to work. He refused to speak about his illness or to indulge in self-pity. Not only did he busy himself with the second volume of his father's biography – then well under way – but he began to plan other books. In this he was encouraged by an invitation to write the biography of John F. Kennedy. The assassination of President Kennedy, in November 1963, had so angered and saddened Randolph that he could not mention it without tears. When Robert Kennedy suggested that he write a life of the President, Randolph considered it to be the greatest compliment he had ever been paid. How firm the offer was is uncertain. Later, Robert Kennedy's press secretary was to say that 'there had been informal discussions between Mr Kennedy and Mr Churchill about a biography of President Kennedy but that this idea

361

had been abandoned.' At the time, however, Randolph was full of enthusiasm. He told Martin Gilbert that he planned to write a two volume biography and would start work on it, probably in 1969, as soon as he had completed the life of his father.

The book was never attempted. The only additional literary work undertaken by Randolph during this period was of a very different nature. In the summer of 1967, he and his son Winston wrote an account of the six day Arab-Israeli war which erupted in June that year. Randolph, always a champion of the Israeli cause, took an intense interest in the war. His son was in Israel – as a correspondent for the *News of the World* – when the fighting began and was able to send home first-hand accounts of the campaign. A telex machine was installed at Stour to receive Winston's reports and Randolph was able to sketch in the political background. The book, *The Six Day War* – dedicated to Clementine Churchill – was hastily written, speedily published and a huge success. It was translated into several languages (there was even an enquiry about translating it into Icelandic) and Randolph was paid a £50,000 advance.

The Six Day War was published shortly before the second volume of the Churchill biography. This volume, *Winston S. Churchill: Young Statesman 1900–1914*, appeared in October 1967. Dealing as it did with his father's early political career, it held a special significance for Randolph. In writing this volume he was more deeply involved, more directly interested in the events he was recording. Obsessed as he was with the disastrous mistakes made by political leaders in the 1930s, Randolph was anxious to reach the period in his father's life in which those leaders played a part. He was determined to expose the Men of Munich, many of whom he considered had got off lightly, and, as some reviewers noted, could not resist hinting at things to come. The book, in fact, was intended to serve as an introduction to Randolph's central theme.

Once again he met with a mixed reception. He was praised for his industry and chided for a more discernible bias. Some of the praise was fulsome. Nigel Nicolson, for instance, writing in the *Spectator*, could not more accurately have reflected Randolph's hopes and intentions. 'The evidence,' enthused Nicolson, 'has been marshalled beautifully . . . All is so clear and so full that no future book about Winston can hope to be anything but a commentary on Randolph's.' His only reservation was that the book lacked personal insight. Others were less kind. Strangely enough, one of the more perceptive reviews appeared in *The Times*. This time the book had been given to Robert Rhodes James who not only signed the review but was outspoken in his comments. Severe as was his judgement, much of what he says could be applied to all of Randolph's writings.

He fully acknowledged the book's strengths. 'Certainly,' he admitted, 'the merits of this volume are substantial. It is heavily documented, meticulously prepared, and has a high standard of factual accuracy.' He was less impressed by Randolph's abilities as an author. 'The structure of the book,' he went on, 'and some of the chapters, is clumsy and often confusing . . . The author's digressions are rarely illuminating, and his own prejudices and antipathies are depressingly evident. There is a total absence of anything that could be adorned by the description of a literary style. Above all, there is a sad lack of penetration. With all the immense resources at Mr Churchill's disposal – including the companion volumes – we might have expected a more interpretative and stimulating approach.' For all that, his thoughts on Randolph were guarded. 'No judgement,' he pointed out, 'can yet be a final one. It is very difficult indeed to assess his work properly until it is completed.'

*   *   *

No full assessment of Randolph's Great Work was ever made. After the publication of this second volume, his health declined rapidly. There were times when he was unable to write at all. He remained in bed, brooding, scattering the sheets with chocolate crumbs, too weak or too depressed to talk to his staff. He received very few visitors and, for once in his life, seemed to dread 'seeing people who were not close to him.' Those whom he did see found him oddly introspective. One day, talking to Michael Wolff's wife, he turned the conversation to the supernatural. Rosemary Wolff asked him whether he believed in God. Randolph thought for a while and then said: 'No, I don't think I do. But I believe that when you die all the goodness in you comes together as a *force*.'

That force came together for Randolph on the night of 6 June 1968. Many years earlier he had told his second wife, June, that the one person he wanted at his deathbed was Laura. Much had happened since then, and when he died, it was not possible to summon Laura or indeed any of his friends. For death came to him in his sleep and it was not until his secretary, Andrew Kerr, went to call him the following morning that his household realized what had happened.

Later that morning his son Winston issued a short press statement to the effect that his father had 'died peacefully after a short illness.' Randolph had survived his fifty-seventh birthday by nine days.

The jinx that had plagued him throughout his life followed Randolph to the grave. Fated to live in the shadow of his father, he died in the shadow of a friend. There was little room for reports of his death on the front pages of the newspapers. For public attention was focused on a far more dramatic event. On 7 June banner headlines were proclaiming the assassination, in San Franscisco a few hours earlier, of Robert Kennedy.

The irony of this coincidence was apparent to at least one of Randolph's friends. 'Poor Randolph Churchill died today,' noted Cyrus Sulzberger in his diary, 'as always, a footnote.'

Bibliography

Amery, Julian *Approach March* Hutchinson London 1973

Amory, Mark (ed) *The Letters of Evelyn Waugh* Weidenfeld & Nicolson London 1980

Ashley, Jack *Journey Into Silence* Bodley Head London 1973

Asquith, Lady Cynthia *Diaries 1915–1918* Hutchinson London 1968

Ayer, A. J. *Part of My Life* Collins London 1977

Beaton, Cecil *Self Portrait With Friends* (ed. Richard Buckle) Weidenfeld & Nicolson London 1979

Birkenhead, Lord *Walter Monckton* Weidenfeld & Nicolson London 1969

Bolitho, Hector *My Restless Years* Max Parrish London 1962

Boyle, Andrew *Poor Dear Brendan* Hutchinson London 1974

Brockway, Fenner *Towards Tomorrow* Hart-Davis London 1977

Bryan, J. and Murphy, C. *The Windsor Story* Granada London 1979

Carlton, David *Anthony Eden* Allen Lane London 1981

Chaplin, Charles *My Autobiogaphy* Bodley Head London 1964

Churchill, John S. *Crowded Canvass* Odhams London 1961

Churchill, Randolph S. *They Serve the Queen* Hutchinson London 1953

   The Story of the Coronation Derek Verschoyle London 1953

   Churchill: His Life in Photographs (with H. Gernscheim) Derek Verschoyle London 1954

   What I Said About the Press Weidenfeld & Nicolson London 1957

   Portraits and Appreciations Privately Printed 1958

   The Rise and Fall of Sir Anthony Eden MacGibbon & Kee London 1959

   Lord Derby: 'King of Lancashire' Heinemann London 1959

   The Fight for the Tory Leadership Heinemann London 1964

   Twenty-One Years Weidenfeld & Nicolson London 1965

   Winston S. Churchill Vol I & Vol II (and Companion Volumes) Heinemann London 1966–1967

   Six Day War (with Winston Churchill) Heinemann London 1967

Churchill, Sarah *A Thread in the Tapestry* Andre Deutsch London 1967
  Keep on Dancing Weidenfeld & Nicolson London 1981
Churchill, Winston S. *My Early Life* Odhams London 1930
The Second World War (6 vols) Cassell London 1948–1954
Coats, Peter *Of Gardens and Generals* Weidenfeld & Nicolson London 1976
Colville, John *The Churchillians* Weidenfeld & Nicolson London 1981
Cooper, Lady Diana *The Light of Common Day* Hart-Davis London 1959
  Trumpets From the Steep Hart-Davis London 1960
Coward, Noël *Middle East Diary* Heinemann London 1944
Cowles, Virginia *Looking For Trouble* Hamish Hamilton London 1941
  The Phantom Major Collins London 1958
Curie, Eve *Journey Among Warriors* Heinemann London 1943
Dalton, Hugh *The Fateful Years* Muller London 1957
Davidson, Michael *The World, the Flesh and Myself* Arthur Barker London 1962
Davie, Michael (ed.) *The Diaries of Evelyn Waugh* Weidenfeld & Nicolson London 1976
Day, Robin *Day By Day* William Kimber London 1975
Dilkes, David (ed.) *The Diaries of Sir Alexander Cadogan 1938–1946* Cassell London 1971
Djilas, Milovan *Wartime* Secker & Warburg London 1977
Dougall, Douglas *In and Out of the Box* Collins London 1973
Driberg, Tom *'Swaff': The Life and Times of Hannen Swaffer* Macdonald London 1974
Drogheda, Lord *Double Harness* Weidenfeld & Nicolson London 1978
Eade, Charles (ed.) *Churchill and His Contemporaries* Hutchinson London 1953
Evans, Harold *Downing Street Diary* Hodder & Stoughton London 1981
Evans, Trefor (ed.) *The Killearn Diaries 1934–1946* Sidwick & Jackson London 1972
Farran, Roy *Winged Dagger* Collins London 1948
Fisher, Nigel *Iain Macleod* Andre Deutsch London 1973
Fishman, Jack *My Darling Clementine* W. H. Allen London 1963
Flintoff, Thomas *Preston and Parliament* Privately Printed (n.d.)
Foot, Michael *Aneurin Bevan* MacGibbon & Kee London 1962
  Debts of Honour Davis Poynter London 1980
Getty, Paul *As I See It* W. H. Allen London 1976

Gilbert, Martin *Winston S. Churchill Vols III–V* Heinemann London 1971–1983

  Winston Churchill: The Wilderness Years Macmillan London 1981

Gore-Booth, Paul *With Great Truth and Respect* Constable London 1974

Halle, Kay (ed.) *Randolph S. Churchill: The Young Unpretender* Heinemann London 1971

Hanfstaegel, Ernst *Hilter: The Missing Years* Eyre & Spottiswoode London 1957

Harvey, John (ed.) *The War Diaries of Oliver Harvey* Collins London 1978

Harvie-Watt, G. S. *Most of My Life* Springwood Books London 1980

Hoggart, S. and Leigh, D. *Michael Foot: A Portrait* Hodder & Stoughton London 1981

Hollis, Christopher *Eton* Hollis & Carter London 1960

  History of the Oxford Union Evans Bros. London 1965

Home, Lord *The Way the Wind Blows* Collins London 1976

Hutchinson, George *The Last Edwardian at No. 10* Quartet London 1980

Ingrams, Richard (ed.) *The Life and Times of Private Eye* Allen Lane London 1971

Ivanovic, Vane *L.X. Memoirs of a Jugoslav* Weidenfeld & Nicolson London 1977

James, Edward *Swans Reflecting Elephants* (ed. by George Melly) Weidenfeld & Nicolson London 1982

James, Robert Rhodes *Lord Randolph Churchill* Weidenfeld & Nicolson London 1959

  Chips Weidenfeld & Nicolson London 1967

  Churchill: A Study in Failure Weidenfeld & Nicolson London 1970

  Victor Cazalet Hamish Hamilton London 1976

Jay, Douglas *Change and Fortune* Hutchinson London 1980

Jones, Thomas *Whitehall Diary* (ed. by Keith Middlemas) Oxford University Press 1969

Lee, Raymond *The London Observer* (ed. by James Lentze) Hutchinson London 1972

Lees-Milne, James *Ancestral Voices* Chatto & Windus London 1975

Leslie, Anita *The Gilt and the Gingerbread* Hutchinson London 1981

Liddell Hart, Basil *Memoirs* Cassell London 1965

Llewellyn, Harry *Passports to Life* Hutchinson London 1980

Lockhart, Robert Bruce *Friends, Foes and Foreigners* Putnam London 1957

    Diaries 1915–1938 (ed. by Kenneth Young) Macmillan London 1973

    Diaries 1939–1965 Macmillan London 1980

Lowndes, Susan (ed.) *Diaries and Letters of Marie Belloc Lowndes 1911–1947* Chatto & Windus London 1971

Lysaght, Charles E. *Brendan Bracken* Allen Lane London 1979

Maclean, Fitzroy *Eastern Approaches* Cape London 1949

Macmillan, Harold *The Blast of War* Macmillan London 1967

Marlborough, Laura Duchess of *Laughter From A Cloud* Weidenfeld & Nicolson London 1980

Marnham, Patrick *The Private Eye Story* Andre Deutsch London 1982

Moran, Lord *Churchill: The Struggle For Survival 1940–1965* Constable London 1966

Moorehead, Alan *African Trilogy* Hamish Hamilton London 1944

Morris, James *Farewell The Trumpets* Faber London 1978

Mosley, Diana *A Life of Contrasts* Hamish Hamilton London 1977

Mosley, Leonard *Castlerosse* Arthur Barker London 1956

Muggeridge, Malcolm *Chronicles of Wasted Times Vol III* Collins London 1973

    Like It Was (Diaries ed. by John Bright-Holmes) Collins London 1981

Nicolson, Harold *Diaries and Letters* (ed. by Nigel Nicolson) Collins London 1954

Oliver, Vic *Mr Showbusiness* Harrap London 1954

Pakenham, Frank *Born to Believe* Cape London 1953

    Five Lives Hutchinson London 1964

Pawle, Gerald *The War and Colonel Warden* Harrap London 1963

Pearson, John *The Life of Ian Fleming* Cape London 1966

Pelling, Henry *Winston Churchill* Macmillan London 1974

Pilpel, Robert H. *Churchill in America 1895–1961* New English Library London 1976

Pomeroy, M. and Collins, C. *The Great Saharan Mouse Hunt* Hutchinson London 1962

Pryce-Jones, David (ed.) *Evelyn Waugh and His World* Weidenfeld & Nicolson London 1973

Shinwell, Emanuel *Conflict Without Malice* Odhams London 1955

Soames, Mary *Clementine Churchill* Cassell London 1979

Stark, Freya *Letters Vol V* (ed. by Lucy Moorehead) Michael Russell London 1977

Stevenson, Frances *Lloyd George: A Diary* (ed. by A. J. P. Taylor) Hutchinson London 1971

Sulzberger, C. H. *A Long Row of Candles* Macdonald London 1969
The Last of the Giants Weidenfeld & Nicolson London 1972
An Age of Mediocrity Macmillan New York 1973
Sykes, Christopher *Evelyn Waugh* Collins London 1975
Thompson R. W. *Churchill and Morton* Hodder & Stoughton London 1976
Thompson, George M. *Lord Castlerosse* Weidenfeld & Nicolson London 1973
Tree, Ronald *When The Moon Was High* Michael Joseph London 1956
Warner, Philip *The Special Air Service* William Kimber London 1971
Watson, Graham *Book Society* Andre Deutsch London 1980
Westminster, Loelia Duchess of *Grace and Favour* Weidenfeld & Nicolson London 1961
Windsor, Duchess of *The Heart Has Its Reasons* Michael Joseph London 1956
Ziegler, Philip *Diana Cooper* Hamish Hamilton London 1981

References

Chapter One

p. 1   A. P. Herbert on Churchill's humour. *Churchill by his Contemporaries* pp. 429–37

p. 2   'I am counting the days . . .' R. Churchill, *Winston S. Churchill* Vol. III p. 350

p. 3   'At his age . . .' *Ibid* p. 352
'I took (politics) in . . .' *Sunday Times*, 1964.
'She shone for me . . .' W. Churchill: *My Early Life* p. 5

p. 4   'I would far rather . . .' *Ibid* p. 38

p. 6   'full of false . . .' Quoted in R. Churchill: *Winston S. Churchill* Vol. II p. 326

p. 8   'Diana was more . . .' R. Churchill: *Twenty-one Years* p. 12

p. 9   'My cousin Randolph . . .' J. Churchill: *Crowded Canvas* p. 14
'I have appointed you . . .' Gilbert: *Companion Vol. to Winston S. Churchill* Vol. III p. 1098

p. 10   'It is the vy thing . . .' *Ibid*
'Clemmie's eldest child . . .' Asquith: *Diaries 1915–1918* p. 275

p. 11   'Nurses, parents and relations . . .' J. Churchill: *Crowded Canvas* p. 37

p. 12   'was a boss man . . .' R. Churchill: *Twenty-one Years* p. 17
'Randolph and I . . .' J. Churchill: *Crowded Canvas* p. 29

p. 13   'Everyone agreed . . .' *Ibid*
'Randolph promises much . . .' Gilbert: *Companion Vol. (Part II) to Winston S. Churchill* Vol. III

p. 15   'my old private school friend . . .' *Spectator* 3/7/64
'his one disagreeable . . .' and 'caused me to . . .' R. Churchill: *Twenty-one Years* p. 23

p. 16   'His thoughts appear . . .' Quoted *Ibid* p. 25
'We did a complete . . .' S. Churchill: *A Thread in the Tapestry* p. 22

p. 17   'red-haired freak . . .' Lysaght: *Brendan Bracken* p. 58

p. 18   'Being impish as well as . . .' Boyle: *Poor Dear Brendan* p. 117

p. 19   'keeping her guessing . . .' *Ibid* p. 104
'Brendan would shower . . .' S. Churchill: *A Thread in the Tapestry* p. 88
'Diana said: "There's . . ."' Mosley: *A Life of Contrasts* p. 40

pp. 19–20   'But one simply had . . .' Lady Mosley to author 12/9/81

Chapter Two

p. 21   'fewer rules . . .' R. Churchill: *Twenty-one Years* p. 28
'most people prefer . . .' *Daily Express* 6/12/58

p. 22   'some difference . . .' Quoted in Hollis: *Eton* p. 301
'great lashings . . .' S. Churchill: *A Thread in the Tapestry* p. 45

p. 23 'I can do that . . .' Conv. with James Lees-Milne 12/10/81
First year reports. Quoted in R. Churchill: *Twenty-one Years* pp. 44–5
p. 24 'Randolph was very fond . . .' Conv. with Lord Longford 11/11/81
'Anyway you have . . .' R. Churchill: *Twenty-one Years* p. 35
'He will never . . .' Quoted in Gilbert: *Winston S. Churchill* Vol. V p. 222
p. 25 'very attractive . . .' *Ibid* p. 310
'shy facetious and snobbish . . .' Conv. with James Lees-Milne 12/10/81
'At first . . .' Quoted in R. Churchill: *Twenty-one Years* p. 43
'Let it be said . . .' Quoted *Ibid* pp. 46–7
p. 26 'I have never been . . .' *Spectator* 31/7/64
p. 27 'He had a Greuze face . . .' Bolitho: *My Restless Years* p. 131
'an affectionate boy . . .' Conv with James Lees-Milne 12/10/81
'Randolph Churchill did not . . .' Ayer: *Part of my Life* p. 51
'I never wholly . . .' *Ibid* p. 52
p. 28 'He would always defend . . .' Conv with Sir Robert Birley 8/11/81
'I never had any more rot . . .' R. Churchill: *Twenty-one Years* p. 37
'He seems to find . . .' Quoted *Ibid* p. 47
p. 29 'We were both . . .' Conv. with James Lees-Milne
p. 30 'What is the use . . .' Mosley: *Life of Contrasts* p. 40
p. 31 'old-fashioned radical . . .' Soames: *Clementine Churchill* p. 210
'I was born a Liberal . . .' *Sunday Times* 1964
'I realize the truth . . .' Quoted in Rhodes-James: *Churchill: A Study in failure* p. 155
p. 32 'The boy was . . .' Jones: *Whitehall Diary* Vol. II pp. 67–8
p. 33 'She thought him . . .' Colville: *The Churchillians* p. 9
'I am having a vy interesting . . .' Quoted in Gilbert: *Winston S. Churchill* Vol V p. 324
p. 35 'He is hardy . . .' *Ibid*
'made some shrewd . . .' Liddle-Hart: *Memoirs* Vol. I p. 128
p. 36 Churchill and Birley. Conv. with Sir Robert Birley 6/11/81
'found his schoolfellows . . .' Colville: *The Churchillians* p. 22
p. 37 Pakenham and Randolph. Conv. with Lord Longford 11/11/81
'Is it unkind . . .' quoted in R. Churchill: *Twenty-one Years* p. 46
p. 38 'At the moment . . .' Quoted *Ibid* pp. 47–8
'more than defended . . .' Quoted in Gilbert: *Winston S Churchill* Vol. V p. 278
'During the time I was at school . . .' *Sunday Graphic* 26/7/31
p. 39 'I am so enjoying . . .' Quoted in Gilbert: *Winston S. Churchill* Vol. V p. 310

Chapter Three
p. 40 'heralded by a great . . .' Hollis: *The Oxford Union* pp. 181–2
'Almost all undergraduates . . .' Harrod in Halle: *Randolph S. Churchill* p. 30
p. 41 'I enjoyed picking . . .' R. Churchill: *Twenty-one Years* p. 64
'the biggest factor . . .' Harrod in Halle: *Randolph S. Churchill* p. 30
'totally incredible . . .' J. Churchill: *Crowded Canvas* p. 56
p. 42 'Everybody hated Randolph at Oxford . . .' *The Times* 11/10/82
'were neither aesthetes . . .' Betjeman in Halle: *Randolph S. Churchill* p. 40
'I can see now . . .' *Ibid* pp. 40–1
p. 43 'If he could be . . .' *Sunday Times*
'The Churchill debate . . .' Gore-Booth: *With Great Truth and Respect* p. 36

p. 44   'There was an impression . . .' Hollis: *The Oxford Union* pp. 181–2
        'I warned Randolph . . .' Scheftel in Halle: *Randolph S. Churchill* p. 57
        'He was remarkably . . .' *Ibid* p. 43
p. 45   'Nonsense, Father . . .' Westminster: *Grace and Favour* pp. 230–1
p. 46   'One subject on which . . .' *Sunday Graphic* 26/7/31
        'the most physically attractive . . .' Jay: *Change and Fortune* pp. 30–1
p. 48   'I have not had . . .' Quoted in Fishman: *My Darling Clementine* p. 307
        'Randolph II . . .' and 'was very proud . . .' Quoted in Gilbert: *Winston S. Churchill* Vol. V p. 327
        'As Labour gain . . .' Jones: *Whitehall Diary* Vol. II p. 191
p. 49   'Eventually he turned up . . .' J. Churchill: *Crowded Canvas* p. 64
p. 50   'Papa is gradually . . .' R. Churchill: *Twenty-one Years* p. 73
        'an admirable companion . . .' Gilbert: *Winston S. Churchill* Vol. V p. 342
p. 51   'Papa very angry . . .' R. Churchill: *Twenty-one Years* p. 74
        Newspaper interview. *Toronto Daily Star* 19/8/29
p. 52   'raging, rampaging . . .' Foot: *Debts of Honour* p. 186
        'I love him . . .' Gilbert: *The Wilderness Years* p. 23
p. 53   'It was really quite easy . . .' R. Churchill: *Twenty-one Years* p. 76
        'He speaks so well . . .' Gilbert: *The Wilderness Years* p. 23
        ''Tis better . . .' R. Churchill: *Twenty-one Years* p. 76
p. 54   'We are now . . .' *Ibid* p. 77
        Search by customs. J. Churchill: *Crowded Canvas* pp. 68–9
p. 55   'Do we see . . .' R. Churchill: *Twenty-one Years* p. 78
        'So Christ . . .' *Ibid* p. 79
p. 57   'Blasted by a withering . . .' J. Churchill: *Crowded Canvas* p. 72
        'Having it off on a sofa . . .' James: *Swans Reflecting Elephants* p. 55
p. 58   'infinitely more attractive . . .' R. Churchill: *Twenty-one Years* p. 81
        'you motor ten miles . . .' Quoted in Pilpel: *Churchill in America* p. 88
p. 59   'He was too sweet . . .' R. Churchill: *Twenty-one Years* p. 83
        'a handsome stripling . . .' Chaplin: *My Autobiography* p. 364

Chapter Four
p. 60   'Despite the devotion . . .' Scheftel in Halle: *Randolph S. Churchill* p. 57
p. 61   'I am pretty sure . . .' *Encounter* July 1968
        'not for the first . . .' Mosley: *Life of Contrasts* p. 78
        'masses of young men . . .' Davis: *Diaries of Evelyn Waugh* p. 315
p. 62   'Met Randolph Churchill . . .' Young: *Diaries of Bruce Lockhart 1915–1938* pp. 117–18
        'He is very down . . .' *Ibid* p. 125
p. 63   'I may not at this stage . . .' Pakenham: *Five Lives* p. 167
        'He possesses . . .' *Sunday Graphic* 7/5/32
p. 64   'A fair haired . . .' *New York Times* 21/2/30
        'Egypt's interests . . .' *Ibid*
p. 65   'not only the speech . . .' *Ibid*
p. 66   'My father has always . . .' *Sunday Graphic* 26/7/31
        'I congratulated him . . .' Harrod in Halle: *Randolph S. Churchill* p. 31
        'He was obviously . . .' *Ibid* p. 33
p. 67   'The newspapers paint . . .' *Sunday Dispatch* 13/7/30
        'Ah, the first day . . .' R. Churchill: *Twenty-one Years* p. 103
p. 69   'Dominion status can certainly . . .' *Daily Mail* 16/11/29
        'Churchill's Indian policy . . .' Eade: *Churchill by his Contemporaries* p. 292
p. 70   New York press interview. *New York Times* 8/10/30

p. 70   'I cautioned him . . .' Quoted in Gilbert: *Companion Vol (Part II) to Winston S. Churchill* Vol. V p. 209

          'distinctly queasy . . .' R. Churchill: *Twenty-one Years* p. 105

          'Most of the young men . . .' *New York Times* 9/11/30

p. 72   Lightening idle mornings . . .' *Ibid* 14/6/31

          'enlightened self-interest . . .' *Ibid* 9/11/30

p. 73   'I went to all the New York . . .' *Daily Mail* 26/5/31

          'traversed the Continent . . .' and 'So now I knew . . .' *Daily Mail* 1/6/31

          'The English habit . . .' *Daily Mail* 6/6/31

          'I observed him . . .' *New York World Telegram* 15/12/36

          Randolph and H. B. Swope. *Ibid*

pp. 73–75   Randolph and Ruth Mckenney. *The New Yorker* 16/1/37

p. 75   'What lascivious eyes . . .' Young: *Diaries of Bruce Lockhart 1915–1938* p. 172

p. 76   'outrageous treatment . . .' and 'skill with words . . .' Halle: *Randolph S. Churchill* p. 2

p. 78   'When are you . . .' Quoted in Gilbert: *Companion Vol (Part II) to Winston S. Churchill* Vol. V p. 221

          'establish a close . . .' Soames: *Clementine Churchill* p. 239

p. 79   'were at loggerheads . . .' *Ibid* p. 240

p. 81   'One of the more . . .' *Daily Mail* 6/6/31

          'Young Randolph Churchill . . .' Young: *Diaries of Bruce Lockhart 1915–1938* p. 163

          'The first time . . .' Halle: *Randolph S. Churchill* p. 1

p. 82   'The Americans . . .' *Daily Mail* 6/6/31

Chapter Five

p. 83   'silly boys . . .' R. Churchill: *Twenty-one Years* p. 107

p. 84   'One of the few principles . . .' *Sunday Graphic* 26/7/31

          'Paying supertax . . .' Pakenham: *Five Lives* p. 167

          'Subject for dispute between . . .' *Sunday Graphic* 19/7/31

pp. 84–6   Report on Germany. *Ibid.*

p. 87   'Randolph kept in touch . . .' Betjeman in Halle: *Randolph S. Churchill* p. 41

          'He used to ask . . .' *Ibid*

          'in terms of noise, light . . .' *Ibid* p. 140

p. 88   'Mr Randolph Churchill . . .' Marquess of Donegal's column in *Sunday Graphic* 8/4/32

p. 89   'speaker at the Trocadero . . .' Young: *Diaries of Bruce Lockhart 1915–1938* p. 203

          'film career . . .' *Evening Standard* 18/9/31

          'If anyone had said . . .' *Sunday Times* 15/4/64

p. 91   'He has untied himself . . .' Gilbert: *Winston S. Churchill* Vol. V p. 389

          'I loyally embraced . . .' *Sunday Times* 15/4/64

          'stage army . . .' Quoted in Gilbert: *Winston S. Churchill* Vol. V p. 434

p. 92   'If all the young men . . .' *Sunday Graphic* 29/5/32

          'the humbug and compromise . . .' *Sunday Graphic* 29/5/32

p. 93   Churchill and Mosley. Nicolson: *Diaries and letters 1930–39* p. 89

          'Randolph Churchill has been speaking . . .' Young: *Diaries of Bruce Lockhart 1915–1938* pp. 205–6

p. 94   'I scorned his pound note . . .' Leslie: *The Gilt and the Gingerbread* p. 135

p. 95   'Mr Baldwin and Mr Baldwin's son . . .' *Evening Standard* 17/6/32

          'the occasion was . . .' *Sunday Times* 19/6/32

p. 95 'It was not . . .' *Ibid*
      'a fine machine-gun . . .' *Evening Standard* 17/6/32
      'Not a word . . .' *Ibid*
      'What an amazing. . .' Young: *Diaries of Bruce Lockhart* 1915–1938 p. 219
p. 96 'Pity these great . . .' Quoted in Mosley: *Castlerosse* p. 109
      'a lasting and savage . . .' Thomson: *Lord Castlerosse* p. 108
p. 97 'seemed to be the . . .' *Ibid* p. 76
      Coward story. Mosley: *Castlerosse* pp. 95–6
      'for two pins . . .' Young: *Diaries of Bruce Lockhart* 1915–1938 p. 219
p. 98 'I hear you're . . .' *Ibid* p. 203
      'he smelt of castor oil . . .' Thomson: *Lord Castlerosse* p. 162
      Randolph's reply. *Daily Express* June 1932
pp. 99–101 Randolph's German report. *Sunday Graphic* 31/7/32

Chapter Six
p. 103 'I had seen . . .' Hanfstaegel: *Hitler: The Missing Years* p. 184
p. 104 'What on earth . . .' and 'produced a thousand . . .' *Ibid* p. 185
      Dinner at Continental. *Ibid*
      'In any case what part . . .' *Ibid* p. 187
p. 105 'one of those confrontations . . .' *Ibid* p. 184
      'with ghostly but . . .' Quoted in Gilbert: *Winston S. Churchill* Vol. V
        p. 437
      'What are you doing . . .' Young: *Diaries of Bruce Lockhart* 1915–1938
        p. 224
      'I think you have . . .' *Encounter* July 1968 p. 19
      'I am sure Randolph . . .' Lady Mosley to author 12/9/81
p. 106 'was very friendly . . .' Conv. with Lady Diana Cooper 15/11/81
      'By day the lido . . .' Mosley: *Castlerosse* p. 113
pp. 106–8 Party at Lido. Conv. with Lady Diana Cooper 15/11/81
p. 108 'Oh that was *last night* . . .' Conv. with Rosemary Woolf 29/4/82
p. 109 'God's greatest liar . . .' Young: *Diaries of Bruce Lockhart* 1915–1938
        p. 229
      'I remember it . . .' Lady Mosley to author 12/9/81
      'When Brendan caught up . . .' Mosley: *A Life of Contrasts* p. 92
p. 110 'Each week . . .' *Sunday Dispatch* 9/10/32
p. 111 'Nothing is more sad . . .' *Sunday Graphic* 29/5/32
p. 112 'The latest political fad . . .' Quoted in R. Churchill: *The Rise and Fall of
      Sir Anthony Eden* pp. 72–73
p. 113 'Winston had had. . .' Young: *Diaries of Bruce Lockhart* 1915–1938 p. 229
p. 114 'the most famous . . .' Hollis: *The Oxford Union* p. 185
      First Union debate. Quoted *Ibid* pp. 186–7
p. 115 'an abject, squalid. . .' Rhodes-James: *Churchill: A Study in Failure* p. 227
p. 116 'supporters of Sir . . .' Quoted in Hollis: *The Oxford Union* p. 187
pp. 116–18 Oxford Union Debate. Hollis: *The Oxford Union* p. 188. Also *The
      Times, Daily Mail, Daily Express* 3/3/33
      'Many of his sentences . . .' Pakenham: *Born to Believe* p. 70
      'There were kisses . . .' *Daily Mail* 3/3/33
      'I saw him brace . . .' *Ibid*
      'A racous cry . . .' Pakenham: *Born to Believe* p. 70
      'We realised . . .' *Daily Mail* 3/3/33
p. 118 'the steps taken by himself . . .' Quoted in Hollis: *The Oxford Union*
        p. 189
      'That fellow Churchill . . .' *Daily Mail* 3/3/33

p. 118   'nothing is so piercing...' Quoted in Gilbert: *Winston S. Churchill* Vol. V
       p. 456
p. 119   'a most surprising...' Quoted in Pelling: *Winston Churchill* p. 357
p. 120   'The Conservative Party...' *The Times* 8/5/32
p. 121   'not sufficiently forthright...' *Daily Mail* 2/6/32
p. 122   'The Conservative Association...' *The Times* 1/6/32
       'Yes certainly...' *Ibid*
       'I have decided...' *The Times* 2/6/32
       'Any suggestion...' *The Times* 2/6/32
p. 123   'I wish to make it...' *Ibid*
       'Lady Inverclyde...' *New York Times* 14/8/33

Chapter Seven
p. 125   'in order to justify...' *The Times* 2/6/34
p. 126   'I wonder what...' *Sunday Dispatch* 18/6/34
       'I do not know...' Quoted in Gilbert: *Winston S. Churchill* Vol. V p. 536
       'It would seem...' *Cotton Factory Times* 13/7/34
p. 127   'There were some newspapers...' *Manchester Guardian* 14/7/34
pp. 127–9   Interview with Kaiser. *Daily Mail* 11/6/34
p. 129   'Have you seen...' Jones: *A Diary with Letters* 1931–1950 p. 130
       'For working in the...' Sutro in Halle: *Randolph S. Churchill* p. 51
p. 131   'The public pronouncements...' *Sunday Dispatch* 20/1/34
       'Would he call...' *The Times* 21/1/34
       'Many Conservatives...' *Sunday Dispatch* 20/1/35
       'I did not want...' *Ibid*
p. 132   'My son has taken...' *New York Times* 20/1/35
p. 133   'Randolph, Hope and Glory' *Daily Express* 1/2/35
p. 134   Election address. *Daily Express* 30/1/35 and *Sunday Dispatch* 10/2/35
p. 135   'And who is responsible...' Foot in *Evening Standard* 7/6/68
       'as there were evidently...' Llewellyn: *Passports to Life* p. 73
       'I understood that he...' *Daily Express* 22/1/35
p. 136   'I am tremendously...' *Sunday Dispatch* 27/1/35
       'It would be odd...' *Daily Express* 22/1/35
p. 137   'Sitting like fat toads...' *Ibid*
       'the caucus, nor...' *The Times* 26/1/35
       'Everyone is wild...' James: *Chips* p. 23
       'We are told...' *Daily Express* 6/2/35
p. 138   'bowed over...' James: *Chips* p. 25
       'Do not be...' *Daily Express* 7/2/35
       'There was no...' James: *Chips* p. 26
       'I am delighted...' *Daily Express* 7/2/35
p. 139   'It is a remarkable...' *Ibid*
       'The Young Chevalier...' *The Times* 8/2/35
       'I am afraid...' *Sunday Dispatch* 10/2/35
p. 141   'While Mr Sandys...' *Sunday Dispatch* 3/3/35
       'What shall we say...' *Sunday Dispatch* 12/3/35

Chapter Eight
p. 143   'Fleet Street and...' *Sunday Dispatch* 14/3/35
p. 144   'a nucleus of some...' *The Times* 19/3/35
       'This extraordinary act...' R. Churchill: *The Rise and Fall of Sir Anthony
         Eden* p. 81
p. 145   'The gaucherie of...' *Sunday Dispatch* 7/7/35

p. 145 'common action . . .' *The Times* 10/7/35
p. 146 'was a young man . . .' *Ibid* 16/7/35
'thrilled the Assembly . . .' R. Churchill: *The Rise and Fall of Sir Anthony Eden* p. 93
'Much talk about . . .' Young: *Diaries of Bruce Lockhart* 1915–1938 p. 330
p. 147 'Apparently there is . . .' *The Times* 22/8/35
'It is hard to . . .' *Sunday Dispatch* 3/11/35
p. 148 'with very little . . .' *The Times* 4/11/35
'Women with children . . .' *Ibid* 6/11/35
p. 149 'In West Toxteth we . . .' *Sunday Dispatch* 10/11/35
'If you agree . . .' *Ibid*
'a mountain tide . . .' *Ibid*
'West Toxteth was the . . .' *Ibid* 17/11/35
p. 150 'We had a great . . .' *Sunday Dispatch* 17/11/35
'exceeding the speed . . .' *The Times* 26/11/35
p. 151 'Mr Malcolm MacDonald's search' *Sunday Dispatch* 24/11/35
p. 153 'intervened more than once . . .' Stevenson: *Lloyd-George: A Diary* p. 322
'attitude of the party . . .' *The Times* 3/1/36
p. 154 'I intend to give . . .' *The Times* 8/1/36
p. 155 'We shall take off . . .' *Ibid* 13/1/36
p. 156 'These people are merely . . .' *The Times* 30/1/36
'the unpopularity of . . .' *Edinburgh Evening News* 13/2/36
'Was this the young man . . .' *The Times* 31/3/36
p. 158 'I haven't the least . . .' *New York Times* 17/9/36
'I have nothing to say . . .' *Ibid* 22/9/36
'Efforts to get . . .' *Ibid*
p. 159 'have been married . . .' Ibid 11/11/36
'That's more than . . .' *Ibid* 22/11/36

Chapter Nine
p. 160 'with the reputation . . .' Levat: *A Smattering of Ignorance*
'Americans just . . .' *Ibid*
p. 161 'There were several . . .' Downs in Halle: *Randolph S. Churchill* p. 110
p. 162 'The mere fact . . .' *Daily Mail* 1/3/37
p. 163 'shock of golden . . .' Bryan and Murphy: *The Windsor Story* pp. 335–6
'old friends whose hearts . . .' Windsor: *The Heart has its Reasons* p. 294
'To bugger Baldwin . . .' *Sunday Times* 24/4/66
p. 164 'Randolph only frock-coat . . .' Young: *Diaries of Bruce Lockhart* 1915–1938 p. 375
p. 165 'the light flavour . . .' Bryan and Murphy: *The Windsor Story* p. 336
'My last day . . .' Young: *Diaries of Bruce Lockhart* 1915–1938 p. 375
p. 166 'one of the greatest . . .' Downs in Halle: *Randolph S. Churchill* p. 111
'Journalists as a group . . .' *Observer* 30/10/60
p. 167 'His strong point . . .' Conv. with James Cameron 6/7/82
'Politics rested largely . . .' Muggeridge: *Chronicles of Wasted Time* Vol. II p. 53
p. 168 'Beaverbrook's household . . .' Foot: *Aneurin Bevan* Vol. I p. 183
p. 169 'go tiger-shooting . . .' Hoggart and Leigh: *Michael Foot* p. 72
Foot's opinion of Randolph. Foot: *Debts of Honour* p. 165
p. 170 'On the water . . .' *Ibid*
'It was as if he . . .' Conv. with James Cameron 6/7/82
p. 171 You could overlook . . .' Conv. with James Cameron 6/7/82
'I greatly admired . . .' Cowles: *Looking for Trouble* p. 113

p. 171   'Randolph rather rude . . .' James: *Victor Cazalet* p. 184
p. 173   'However irritating . . . *The Times* 7/7/68
       'also upbraids millionaires . . .' *Observer* 30/10/60
p. 174   'I think a woman . . .' *Sunday Times* 1963
p. 175   'having a home of her own' . . . Marlborough: *Laughter from a Cloud* p. 21
p. 176   'In that first year . . .' *Ibid* p. 30
       'For about six months . . .' *Ibid* p. 31
       'I was out . . .' *Ibid* p. 33
       'A rather fruitless . . .' *Ibid* p. 33
p. 177   'very strong Churchill . . .' *Ibid* p. 66
p. 178   'abandoned all idea . . .' *Evening Standard* 8/10/37
p. 179   'There is no rivalry . . .' *The Times* 1/6/37
       'the vision of Death . . .' W. S. Churchill: *Second World War* Vol. I p. 231
p. 180   'These pusillanimous . . .' Cowles: *Looking for Trouble* p. 113
       Randolph and Baxter. Hoggart and Leigh: *Michael Foot* p. 72
p. 181   'His flat was . . .' Cowles: *Looking for Trouble* p. 114
       'His adoration . . .' Nicolson: *Diaries and Letters* 1930–1939 p. 339

Chapter Ten
p. 184   'When we went . . .' Liddell Hart: *Memoirs* p. 209
p. 185   'There were over . . .' *Oxford Mail* 28/4/39
       'Captain Liddell Hart has . . .' Quoted in Amery: *Approach March* p. 115
       'I had expected . . .' Liddell Hart: *Memoirs* p. 234
p. 186   'Onward conscript soldiers . . .' *Oxford Mail* 28/4/39
       'one of the most outstanding . . .' *Ibid*
       'Randolph outdid his . . .' Brockway: *Towards Tomorrow* p. 134
p. 187   'What are you people . . .' Oliver: *Mr Showbusiness* p. 124
pp. 188–9   Meeting with Duke of Windsor. Bryan and Murphy: *The Windsor Story* p. 401
p. 189   'You will be amused . . .' Lowndes: *Diaries and Letters* p. 182
       'thought we ought to wait . . .' *Sunday Times* 31/10/82
       'he was about to marry . . .' Tree: *When the Moon was High* p. 94
       Wedding. *Daily Mail, Daily Express* and *The Times* 5/10/39
p. 191   'Randolph did everything . . .' Sykes in Halle: *Randolph S. Churchill* p. 45
       'He was thrust . . .' *Ibid*
       'I may be in . . .' Young: *Diaries of Bruce Lockhart* 1930–1945 p. 564
p. 192   'Oh, that's off . . .' *Ibid*
       'Tell that man . . .' *Ibid* p. 532
       'the paratroopers . . .' and 'withdrew, never to return . . .' Dolton: *The Fateful Years* p. 321
p. 193   'difficult to work with . . .' Thomas R. Flintoff to the author 26/11/81 (see also *Daily Telegraph* 28/10/42)
       'the Churchill name . . .' Flintoff to the author 26/11/81
       'What about Vic Oliver . . .' Colville: *The Churchillians* p. 28
       'hoped that Preston . . .' *The Times* 26/9/40
pp. 194–5   Maiden speech. *Hansard* 26/11/40
p. 195   'He has come . . .' *Ibid*
       'the Prime Minister . . .' *New York Times* 27/11/40
       'This was . . .' *Ibid*
p. 196   'champagne and tenantry . . .' Cooper: *Trumpets from the Steep* p. 62
       'It is of the highest . . .' W. S. Churchill: *Second World War* Vol. II p. 214
       'How wonderful . . .' *Ibid*

p. 198   'All the officers . . .' Amery: *Letters of Evelyn Waugh* p. 146
         Row in hotel. *Ibid*

Chapter Eleven
p. 201   'in the Western Desert . . .' *The Times* 16/5/41
         'Never in the history . . .' Dovie: *Diaires of Evelyn Waugh* p. 495
p. 202   'several agreeable . . .' and 'Have just seen . . .' R. Churchill: *Rise and Fall of Sir Anthony Eden* p. 179
         'All too true . . .' Amery: *Letters of Evelyn Waugh* p. 153
p. 203   Rommel 'had torn the . . .' W. S. Churchill: *Second World War* Vol. III, p. 309
         'This will involve . . .' *Ibid* p. 181
         'were homesick . . .' Dovie: *Diaries of Evelyn Waugh* p. 494
p. 204   'Spears bore the brunt . . .' Evans: *The Killearn Diaries* p. 169
p. 205   'the Clapham Junction . . .' Amery: *Approah March* p. 285
p. 206   'like a hot gusty wind . . .' Moorehead: *African Trilogy* pp. 192–3
p. 207   'With almost ferocious . . .' Downs in Halle; *Randolph S. Churchill* p. 113
p. 208   'in the nature of things . . .' Amery: *Letters of Evelyn Waugh* p. 149
         'I never liked Randolph . . .' Coats; *Of Generals and Gardens* p. 114
         'Most thoughtful people . . .' Quoted Churchill: *Second World War* Vol. III
         'We hear P.M. . .' Harvey: *War Diaries of Oliver Harvey* p. 27
p. 209   'Once more I felt . . .' Coats: *Of Generals and Gardens* pp. 116–17
p. 210   'was not liked in . . .' Moorehead: *African Trilogy* p. 210
         'Few people who had . . .' *Ibid* p. 189
         'We fought the war . . .' Quoted in Morris: *Farewell the Trumpets* p. 438
p. 211   'That is how . . .' Conv. with Peter Coats 12/11/81
         'pretty little Egyptian . . .' *Ibid*
         'They were not . . .' Conv. with Gertrude Wissa 14/11/81
p. 212   'undesirable ladies . . .' *Ibid*
         'Yesterday I lunched . . .' Moorehead: *Letters of Freya Stark* Vol. V p. 136
p. 213   'I felt justified . . .' Evans: *The Killearn Diaries* p. 187
p. 214   'rendered Randolph Churchill . . .' Curie: *Journey among the Warriors* p. 52
         'Hurrah, hurrah . . .' Moorehead: *Letters of Freya Stark* Vol. V pp. 32–3
         'We are now having . . .' *Hansard* 28/1/42 p. 805
p. 215   'the Parliament of Munich . . .' *Ibid* p. 800
         'No one should . . .' *Ibid* p. 804
         'Before the hon . . .' *Ibid*
p. 218   'I have no imagination . . .' Downs in Halle: *Randolph S. Churchill* p. 113
         'Thank God, the bloody thing . . .' Cowles: *The Phantom Major* p. 124
         'were just before you jumped . . .' Harvie-Watt: *Most of my Life* pp. 99–100
p. 219   'immediately started on a frantic . . .' Maclean in Halle: *Randolph S. Churchill* p. 189
p. 220   'The crack of the . . .' Maclean: *Eastern Approaches* p. 213
p. 221   'We could hardly . . .' *Ibid* p. 214
p. 222   'oh, just another . . . *Ibid* p. 218
p. 224   'Hungrily we threw . . .' *Ibid* p. 225

Chapter Twelve
p. 225   'severely bruised . . .' *Daily Telegraph* 1/6/42
p. 226   'I had dinner off . . .' Buckle: *Self Portrait with Friends* p. 101

p. 226 'We were caught unawares . . .' *New York Times* 23/6/42
p. 227 'I don't believe . . .' *Ibid* 25/6/42
'Randolph returned . . .' Davie: *Diaries of Evelyn Waugh* pp. 524–5
p. 228 'When he came back . . .' *Sunday Times Magazine* 31/10/82
'like a pasha . . .' Young: *Diaries of Bruce Lockhart 1939–1945* p. 159
'No, my son . . .' *Ibid*
'I think he needed . . .' *Sunday Times Magazine* 31/10/82
p. 229 'auburn, alluring Pam Churchill . . .' James: *Chips* p. 314
'Brendan Bracken had this . . .' *Sunday Times Magazine* 31/10/82
'he was mightily smitton . . .' Drogheda: *Double Harness* p. 98
'Met Clarissa Churchill . . .' Lees-Milne: *Ancestral Voices* p. 36
p. 230 'She did her best . . .' Soames: *Clementine Churchill* p. 331
'One of his troubles . . .' *The Times* 11/10/82
'It was very interesting . . .' Amery: *Letters of Evelyn Waugh* p. 160
p. 231 'Pamela can no longer . . .' Young: *Diaries of Bruce Lockhart 1938–1965*
    p. 227
'fed up' and 'seemed to prefer . . .' *New York Times* 19/12/45
'Randolph Forsees . . .' *Daily Mail* 4/9/42
p. 232 'the spirit of Lord Randolph' in Halle: *Randolph S. Churchill* p. 6
p. 233 'Politically Randolph Churchill . . .' *Observer* 30/10/60
p. 234 'he had never imagined . . .' Flintoff to the author 26/11/81
'The gravaman of my . . .' *The Times* 1/4/43
'in view of his . . .' *Ibid* 17/10/42
'whereas he had not . . .' Flintoff to the author 26/11/81
'If Preston were wise . . .' *The Times* 1/4/43
p. 237 'The bright gleam . . .' W. S. Churchill: *War Speeches* Vol. IV p. 343
p. 238 'Well, this is a surprise . . .' Lees-Milne: *Ancestral Voices* p. 162
'a mixture between . . .' Macmillan: *Blast of War* p. 243
p. 239 'an extract from Machiavelli . . .' Moran: *Churchill: The Struggle for
    Survival* p. 82
'Randolph who has quite . . .' Evans: *The Killearn Diaries* pp. 242–3
'Sat between Winston . . .' Dilks: *Diaries of Sir A. Cadogan* p. 511
p. 242 'useful information . . .' *The Times* 26/7/46
'There was nothing . . .' *New Yorker* 13/9/58
p. 243 'There seems to be . . .' *Evening Standard* 10/3/43
Bevan's question in House of Commons. *The Times* 17/3/43
p. 244 'Weakness is not treason . . .' W. S. Churchill: *Second World War*
    Vol. I p. 154
p. 245 'I could see . . .' *New Yorker* 13/9/58
'to land by sea . . .' Farran: *Winged Dagger* p. 165
'That is *not* . . .' Conv. with J. K. Killby
p. 247 'a show for the Commandos . . .' W. S. Churchill: *Second World War* Vol.
    V p. 152

Chapter Thirteen
p. 248 'antiquated sort of . . .' Davie: *Diaries of Evelyn Waugh* p. 554
'Randolph only . . .' Lees-Milne: *Ancestral Voices* p. 141
p. 249 'but was prepared . . .' Harvie-Watt: *Most of my Life* p. 108
'I could never imagine . . .' *Ibid* p. 133
'When I picked up . . .' *Ibid* p. 135
p. 250 'So I think . . .' Amory: *Letters of Evelyn Waugh* p. 173
p. 251 'England is becoming . . .' Moran: *Churchill: The Struggle for Survival*
    p. 143

p. 251   'He is trying . . .' S. Churchill: *Keep on Dancing* p. 71
p. 253   'but for my present . . .' Maclean: *Eastern Approaches* p. 407
p. 254   'Let me know . . .' W. S. Churchill: *Second World War* Vol. V p. 416
p. 255   It is my earnest . . .' *Ibid*
p. 256   'Half way up the rock face . . .' Maclean: *Eastern Approaches* p. 422
        'Randolph remained . . .' Dedijer in Halle: *Randolph S. Churchill* p. 84
        'Western liaison officer . . .' *The Times* 19/9/49
p. 257   'He himself convinced us . . .' Djilas: *Wartime* p. 369
p. 258   'no desire to . . .' Young: *Diaries of Bruce Lockhart* 1939–1965 p. 292
p. 259   'After one or two . . .' Maclean: *Eastern Approaches* p. 434
        'thanked all the Allies . . .' Djilas: *Wartime* p. 374
p. 260   'Half an hour later . . .' Dedijer in Halle: *Randolph S. Churchill* p. 85
p. 262   'the incredible . . .' and 'about the cold . . .' *Ibid* p. 96
p. 263   'Nothing that equipment . . .' W. S. Churchill: *Second World War* Vol. VI p. 6
        'was anxious to discuss . . .' *The Times* 14/6/44
p. 264   'Unperturbed, Randolph . . .' Sykes: *Evelyn Waugh* pp. 261–2
        'I've got to get . . .' Waugh in Halle: *Randolph S. Churchill* p. 46
        'to heal the Great Schism . . .' Davie: *Diaries of Evelyn Waugh* p. 546
p. 265   'the Marines on duty . . .' Young: *Diaries of Bruce Lockhart* 1939–1965
        p. 352

Chapter Fourteen
p. 266   'Randy rang up . . .' Cooper: *Trumpets from the Steep* p. 203
p. 267   'with his beloved . . .' *Ibid*
        Tito like a Lesbian. Davie: *Diaries of Evelyn Waugh* p. 572
        'Ask Captain Waugh . . .' Pryce-Jones: *Evelyn Waugh and His World*
        p. 135
p. 268   'the stars went out . . .' *News Chronicle* 24/7/44
        'It was dark . . .' *Ibid*
        'by the light of . . .' Davie: *Diaries of Evelyn Waugh* p. 573
p. 269   'Our failure . . .' *News Chronicle* 24/7/44
        'Randolph staggered . . .' Cooper: *Trumpets from the Steep* p. 205
        'Randolph chain-drinks . . .' Ziegler: *Diana Cooper* pp. 221–2
p. 270   'Of course Randolph . . .' Conv. with Lady Diana Cooper 15/11/81
        'He is not to . . .' Cooper: *Trumpets from the Steep* p. 206
        'Randolph's got immense . . .' Conv. with Sir Robert Birley 6/11/81
        'Anything is better . . .' Ziegler: *Diana Cooper* p. 218
p. 271   'They told me . . .' Lemnitzer in Halle: *Randolph S. Churchill* p. 137
p. 273   'Randolph, half drunk . . .' Davie: *Diaries of Evelyn Waugh* p. 582
        'chuckling and slapping . . .' *Ibid*
        'I had the perhaps . . .' Pryce-Jones: *Evelyn Waugh and His World* p. 143
p. 274   'I came to regard . . .' *Ibid*
p. 275   'You bloody little swine . . .' *Ibid* p. 151
        'The facts are . . .' Davie: *Diaries of Evelyn Waugh* p. 587
p. 276   'I say . . .' and 'God . . .' *Ibid*
p. 277   'Everyone knows . . .' Pryce-Jones: *Evelyn Waugh and His World* p.151
        'as a conquered city . . .' W. S. Churchill: *Second World War* Vol. VI p. 252
        'He spoke was a certain . . .' Barber in Halle: *Randolph S. Churchill* p. 122
p. 279   'master of the Arab World . . .' Moran: *Churchill: The Struggle for Survival* p. 240
        'enormous trunk . . .' Pawle: *The War and Colonel Warden* p. 361
        'I thought that . . .' Evans: *The Killearn Diaries* p. 325

p. 280   'Major Churchill . . .' and Randolph in hospital. Conv. with Angela
        Colingwood 12/6/81
p. 282   'They told me that I would . . .' Amery: *Approach March* p. 441
p. 283   'odious and invidious . . .' Soames: *Clementine Churchill* p. 382
      'went into quite . . .' Flintoff to the author 23/1/82
p. 284   'told the committee . . .' Amery: *Approach March* p. 443
        'luring them into . . .' *Ibid* p. 442
p. 285   'You could hear . . .' *Ibid* p. 438
        'People cheered and waved . . .' *Ibid* p. 444
p. 287   'He is a great friend . . .' *The Times* 25/8/45

Chapter Fifteen
p. 288   'any particular merit . . .' R. Churchill: *Winston S. Churchill* Vol. I p. 361
        'Randolph's house . . .' Amory: *Letters of Evelyn Waugh* p. 209
p. 289   Variety headline/Gannon in Halle: *Randolph S. Churchill* p. 248
p. 290   'for upwards of . . .' *The Times* 19/12/45
        'quite meek etc . . .' Sulzberger: *A Long Row of Candles* p. 268
        'Under a great tree . . .' *Ibid* p. 648
p. 291   'I think Enrico Caruso . . .' Getty: *As I see it.* p. 118
        'that his self-imposed . . .' *The Times* 12/2/46
        'He is not . . .' *Ibid*
pp. 291–2   Flandin's trial. *Ibid* 26/7/46
p. 292   'You wouldn't want me . . .' Quoted from New York Post in Halle:
        Randolph S. Churchill p. 163
p. 293   'one of the safest . . .' *New York Times* 10/12/46
        'putting all those Kings . . .' *Ibid* 3/2/47
        'Randolph was very popular . . .' S. Churchill: *Keep on Dancing* p. 23
p. 294   'I thought he could . . .' Amory: *Letters of Evelyn Waugh* p. 248
        'surprisingly good . . .' *Ibid*
p. 295   'Most attractive . . .' Young: *Diaries of Bruce Lockhart* 1939–65 p. 563
        'No one else in England . . .' *Ibid* p. 574
p. 246   'insatiable appetite for controversy . . .' and 'grieved and embittered . . .'
        Soames: *Clementine Churchill* p. 413
        'without malice or intrigue . . .' Colville: *The Churchillians* p. 29
p. 297   'not know the young lady . . .' *Encounter* July 1968
p. 298   'get a bit drunk . . .' Amory: *Letters of Evelyn Waugh* p. 287
        'Ah well, you always . . .' Conv. with Laura, Duchess of Marlborough
        2/3/82
p. 300   'He bustled in . . .' Foot: *Debts of Honour.* p. 162
        'polishing thunderbolts . . .' *Ibid*
p. 301   'Surely you don't want . . .' Pearson: *Life of Fleming* p. 167
        'The brilliant cascade . . .' Foot: *Debts of Honour* p. 162
p. 302   'I thought you took . . .' Foot: *Debts of Honour* p. 162
        'a long, offensive . . .' Hoggart and Keigh: *Michael Foot* p. 102
        'I tell you what . . .' Amory: *Letters of Evelyn Waugh* p. 320
p. 303   'Champagne was ordered . . .' Talbert in Halle: *Randolph S. Churchill*
        p. 130
p. 304   'Even the British minister . . .' *Ibid* p. 131
        'Well, I'm certainly not . . .' *Ibid* p. 133
        'He was a bar-bully . . .' Conv. with James Cameron 6/7/82
p. 305   'the most agreeably boorish . . .' Davidson: *The World, the Flesh and
        Myself* p. 257
        'My dear Frank . . .' *Ibid*

p. 305 'propped up in bed . . .' Bright-Holmes: *Like it Was* p. 436
p. 306 'sign of June at the bedside . . .' Amory: *Letters of Evelyn Waugh* p. 348
'Randolph Churchill kept saying . . .' Sulzberger: *A Long Row of Candles* p. 572
p. 307 'He told me . . .' *Ibid* p. 524
'I could do nothing . . .' Sulzberger: *The Last of the Giants* p. 115

Chapter Sixteen
p. 308 'less than a bottle . . .' Sulzberger: *A Long Row of Candles* p. 525
p. 309 'Here is the most . . .' Lyons in Halle: *Randolph S. Churchill* p. 165
p. 310 'Churchill was angry . . .' Ashley: *Journey into Silence* p. 102
'Ultimate terror of . . .' Dougall: *In and Out of the Box* p. 214
'I never discuss' *New York Times* 7/6/68
'the more I saw . . .' Ashley: *Journey into Silence* p. 102
pp. 311–12 'make thousands . . .' and 'long aspired to . . .' R. Churchill: *Winston S. Churchill* Vol. I p. xix
p. 312 'On one occasion . . .' Sutro in Halle: *Randolph S. Churchill* p. 52
p. 313 'The pillory . . .' *The Times* 23/7/52
'By far and away . . .' Quoted in R. Churchill: *What I said about the Press* p. 10
'a bitter performance . . .' Shinwell: *Conflict Without Malice*
'four nastiest . . .' Quoted in R. Churchill: *What I said about the Press* p. 10
p. 315 'It was a rainy . . .' Sykes in Halle: *Randolph S. Churchill* pp. 47–8
p. 316 'soldiered on . . .' Soames: *Clementine Churchill* p. 414
'His conversation . . .' Hart-Davis to the author 23/9/81
'at his worst . . .' Sulzberger: *The Last of the Giants* p. 115
p. 317 'I do not think . . .' *Encounter* July 1968
p. 318 'When he is attacking . . .' Lockhart: *Friends, Foes and Foreigners* p. 210
p. 319 'I found that I liked . . .' *Sunday Times* 1964
'Within five minutes . . .' *Ibid*
p. 320 'Sir Anthony Eden stands out . . .' *Manchester Guardian* 6/4/55
'the fundamental defects . . .' R. Churchill: *The Rise and Fall of Sir Anthony Eden* p. 198
'The Eden terror . . .' Lyons in Halle: *Randolph S. Churchill* p. 166
p. 321 'no one asked him . . .' *The Times* 10/10/56
'Most of all . . .' *The People* 15/5/55
p. 322 'Each day I would . . .' Sutro in Halle: *Randolph S. Churchill* p. 54
p. 323 Libel Case against *People. The Times* 10/10/56
p. 324 'Mr Churchill has used . . .' *New Statesman* 28/4/56
'Not perturbed by . . .' Lockhart: *Friends, Foes and Foreigners* p. 210
'I am going to die soon . . .' Davie: *Diaries of Evelyn Waugh* p. 732
p. 325 'It did not seem . . .' Watson: *Book Society* p. 104
'many more years . . .' *Daily Express* 6/12/58
pp. 326–7 Nabarro case. *The Times* 26–9/10/60
p. 327 'On occasion they shouted . . .' Evans: *Downing Street Diary* p. 59
p. 328 'I was his exact . . .' Conv. with James Cameron 5/7/82
p. 328 'No one ever knew . . .' *Ibid*
'was in many ways . . .' Sulzberger: *Long Row of Candles* pp. 524–5
p. 329 'I couldn't be . . .' Quoted in Lysaght: *Brendan Bracken* p. 310
'Despite the ups and downs . . .' *Evening Standard* 8/8/56
p. 330 'gave an unamused . . .' Sulzberger: *The Last of the Giants* p. 541
'heckled Foreign Office spokesmen . . .' Day: *Day by Day* p. 201

p. 330 'I know it was Burgess . . .' Hutchinson: *The Last Edwardian at No. 10* p. 98

p. 331 'a musty elegance . . .' Evans: *Downing Street Diary* p. 59
'He was still in . . .' *Ibid* pp. 59–60

p. 331 'not in Moscow . . .' *Ibid*
'Macmillan was too old . . .' Hutchinson: *The Last Edwardian at No. 10* p. 98

p. 332 'in the interests . . .' *The Times* 16/1/59

pp. 332–3 Interview with Robin Day. *Ibid* 19/1/59

p. 333 'very pleased to have . . .' *Ibid* 21/1/59
'carry out my reconnaisance . . .' *Ibid* 4/3/59

Chapter Seventeen

p. 335 'in a form other than . . .' *The Times* 18/11/59

p. 336 'Can you, my dear Rupert . . .' Sir Rupert Hart-Davis to the author 23/9/81
'After reading the book . . .' *Spectator* 15/4/60

p. 337 'Now no more than a . . .' *The Times* 14/4/60
'As a writer . . .' *Observer* 30/10/60
'proper tradition . . .' *New Statesman* 16/4/60
'life of Lord Derby . . .' *Sunday Times* 9/6/68

p. 338 'Randolph tended . . .' Barber in Halle: *Randolph S. Churchill* p. 122
'Though the matter . . .' *The Times* 25/2/60

p. 339 'the last thing . . .' Macleod in Halle: *Randolph S. Churchill* p. 204
'Then nothing happened . . .' *Ibid* pp. 204–5

p. 340 'Verwoerd looked stunned . . .' Barber in Halle: *Randolph S. Churchill* p. 124

p. 341 'confirm his impressions . . .' Home: *The Way the Wind Blows* pp. 143–4
'The result was better . . .' *Ibid*

p. 342 'We travel for adventure . . .' Pomeroy: *The Great Saharan Mousehunt* p. 17
'The old war-horse . . .' *Ibid*

p. 343 'some allegorical beast . . .' *Ibid*
'on condition that . . .' *Daily Express* 29/7/61
'I read that you . . .' *Encounter* July 1968

p. 344 'T is a tremendous undertaking . . .' *The Times* 2/5/63

p. 345 'Randolph usually decided . . .' Martin Gilbert, BBC interview 15/1/82

p. 346 'were not always costly . . .' Conv. with Rosemary Wolff 29/4/82

p. 347 'It's not me . . .' *Private Eye* 8/2/63

pp. 347–48 *Private Eye* dispute. Ingrams: *The Life and Times of Private Eye* pp. 9–11 and Marnham: *The Private Eye Story*

p. 349 'much more free . . .' *News of the World* 14/4/63
'We had a most amusing . . .' *Ibid*
'He was in love . . .' Gannon in Halle: *Randolph S. Churchill* p. 247

p. 350 'I don't want to be . . .' S. Churchill: *Keep on Dancing* p. 26
'Randolph was a wonderful . . .' *Sunday Times Magazine* 31/10/82

p. 351 'quest for the truth . . .' R. Churchill: *The Fight for the Tory Leadership* p. vi
'Four-fifths of Churchill's books . . .' *Spectator* 17/1/64

p. 352 'single massive dose . . .' and Inquest *Telegraph* 25/10/63

p. 353 'Randolph is Randolph . . .' *Spectator* 13/3/64
'sitting up smoking . . .' *Evening Standard* 7/6/68

p. 354 'a typical triumph . . .' Davie: *Diaries of Evelyn Waugh* p. 792

p. 355 'After a cold ...' *The Times* 16/1/65
'became shallow ...' Moran: *Churchill: The Struggle for Survival* p. 790
'The world I would use ...' Conv. with Rosemary Wolff. 29/4/82

p. 356 'a real life-encircher ...' Brocas Harris to the author 12/2/83
'They tell me ...' Conv. with Tom Hartman 2/3/82

p. 357 'about the food ...' Laura, Duchess of Marlborough: *Laughter from a Cloud* pp. 163–4
'I've taken to gardening ...' *Sunday Times* 1964
'blue polyanthus river ...' Xenia Field in Halle: *Randolph S. Churchill* p. 276
'one hundred pounds ...' Wilson: *Book Society* p. 145

p. 358 'He really loved ...' Conv. with Rosemary Wolff 29/4/82
'The local operators ...' Irving in Halle: *Randolph S. Churchill* p. 171

p. 359 'Put on your clothes ...' Conv. with James Lees-Milne 12/10/81
'I've formed a deep aversion ...' *Sunday Times* 1964
'It must be marvellous ...' Conv. with Tom Hartman 2/3/82

p. 360 'his studied self-effacement ...' *Times Literary Supplement* 27/10/66
'Mr Randolph Churchill ...' *The Times* 24/10/66

p. 361 'petty innuendo ...' *Ibid* 27/10/66
'there had been informal ...' *New York Times* 12/6/68

p. 362 'The evidence has been ...' *Spectator* 27/10/67

p. 363 'Certainly the merits ...' *The Times* 23/10/67
'No, I don't think I do ...' Conv. with Rosemary Wolff 29/4/82
'died peacefully ...' *The Times* 7/6/68

p. 364 'Poor Randolph Churchill ...' Sulzberger: *An Age of Mediocrity* p. 436

Index

Abingdon, Earl of, 9
Acton, Sir Harold, 88
Ainsworth, H., 314
Airlie, 10th Earl of, 4
Aitken, Max, 14, 95, 96
Alexander, Field Marshal (1st Earl Alexander of Tunis), 235, 240, 254, 270
Alington, Dr C. A., 37, 38
Alston, Lt Gordon, 219, 220, 222
Altrincham (1933 election), 121–3
Amery, Julian, 185, 282–7, 311
Amery, L. S. ('Leo'), 47, 185, 285
Ashley, Jack 310
Asquith, Lady Cynthia, 10
Asquith, H. H. (Earl of Oxford and Asquith), 5, 6, 7, 30
Asquith, Margot, 52, 174
Asquith, Violet, 10
Astor, Viscountess (Nancy), 52, 357
Attlee, Clement (1st Earl Attlee), 150, 300, 304, 306
Auchinleck, Field Marshal Sir Claude, 210, 213–14, 215, 217, 235
Ava, Basil (Marquess of Dufferin and Ava), 40, 61
Ayer, Sir Alfred, 27

Badoglio, Marshal, 246
Baldwin, A. Windham ('Bloggs'), 266
Baldwin, Oliver, 95, 154
Baldwin, Stanley (later Earl), 30, 31, 35, 47, 48, 49, 65, 68, 69, 91, 92, 93, 95, 111, 115, 120, 125, 127, 130, 134, 136, 137, 141, 145, 146, 149, 150, 152, 153, 154, 159, 161, 162, 163, 164, 165, 266, 292, 299
Balfour, Patrick (Lord Kinross), 167
Banda, Dr Hastings, 339
Bankhead, Tallulah, 60–1
Barber, Stephen, 277–8, 338, 339–40
Barkley, William, 139

Baruch, Bernard, 56, 59, 70
Baxter, Sir Beverly, 180
Beaton, Sir Cecil, 88, 226, 230
Beatty, Admiral Lord, 96
Beauchamp, Anthony, 309
Beaverbrook, 1st Baron, 14, 62, 95, 96, 97, 98, 138, 141, 146, 160, 162, 163, 165, 167, 168–70, 178, 180, 196, 207, 323–4, 325, 329, 330
Beecham, Sir Thomas, 106
Beery, Wallace, 58
Beneš, President Eduard, 182
Berry, Michael (Lord Hartwell), 318
Berry, Seymour (2nd Viscount Camrose), 40, 61, 95, 298, 312
Bertie, Lady Gwendoline see Churchill, Lady Gwendoline.
Betjeman, Sir John, 42, 86–8
Bevan, Aneurin, 169, 184, 243, 300
Bevan, Natalie, 356, 357, 361
Bevan, Robert, 356, 361
Bevin, Ernest, 337
Beveridge, Sir William, 248
Birkenhead, 1st Earl of, 3, 6, 12, 21, 24, 33–4, 44–5, 59, 65, 68, 69
Birkenhead, 2nd Earl of, 13, 23–4, 28, 40, 42, 44, 62, 95, 98, 265, 273–7
Birley, Sir Robert, 25–6, 28, 36, 38, 270
Blake, Robert, 335
Blandford, Lord (later 8th Duke of Marlborough), 22
Bledisloe, Lord, 175
Bolitho, Hector, 27
Bonham-Carter, Maurice, 10
Boothby, Robert (Lord Boothby), 106
Borodale, Lord, 96
Bracken, Brendan (later Viscount), 17–19, 60, 77–8, 91, 95, 98, 105, 108–10, 136, 172, 192, 196, 226, 229, 258, 273, 286, 329
Brankov, Lazar, 256

385